Pandemic

Pandemic

Scott Sigler

HODDER

First published in Great Britain in 2014 by Hodder & Stoughton
An Hachette UK company

First published in paperback in 2014

2

Copyright © Scott Sigler 2014

A CIP catalogue record for this title is
available from the British Library.

ISBN 978 1 444 79169 3

Printed and bound by Clays Ltd, St Ives plc

Hodder & Stoughton policy is to use papers that are natural, renewable
and recyclable products and made from wood grown in sustainable forests.
The logging and manufacturing processes are expected to conform
to the environmental regulations of the country of origin.

Hodder & Stoughton Ltd
338 Euston Road
London NW1 3BH

www.hodder.co.uk

This novel is dedicated to my brothers of the Arm Chair Lodge: high school classmates, teammates and lifelong friends. The countless weekends of role-playing taught me how to tell a great story.

SCOTT SIGLER

HOW IT BEGAN . . .

For a hundred thousand years, the machine traveled in a straight line.

The Creators had launched it into space along with many others, *countless* others. The others also traveled in a straight line, but each one in a different direction. It wasn't long, relatively speaking, before the machine could no longer detect the others, before it could no longer detect the place from which it had come, before it could no longer detect the Creators themselves.

Alone, the machine traveled through the void.

It would have flown in that same straight line for all eternity were it not for a faint trace of electromagnetic radiation known as a *radio wave*.

Analysis was instant and definitive: the radio wave was not naturally occurring. It was artificial, proof of existence of a sentient race other than the Creators.

For the first time, the machine changed direction.

It moved toward the source of this signal so it could fulfill its sole purpose: find the species that generated the signal, then assist the Creators in wiping that species from the face of existence.

As it traveled, the machine detected more and more transmissions. It studied the signals, learned the languages, assigned meaning to the images. In doing so, the machine defined its target: a race of small, hairless bipeds that lived on a blue planet orbiting a yellow star.

Some twenty-five years ago, the machine reached Earth. Stored inside the machine were eighteen small probes. Each probe was about the size of a soda can, and each probe could cast over a billion tiny seeds adrift on the winds. If these seeds landed on a sentient individual, a *host*, they could analyze the individual's composition and send that information back to the machine. The machine could also send information to these seeds: in particular, how to make the seeds hijack the host's biological processes.

At least, that was the theory.

The first six attempts failed altogether. The seventh successfully produced minor changes in the hosts, but did not reach the level of modification necessary for the machine to complete its mission.

With each successive attempt, the probe gained more and more knowledge about the hosts' biology. By the twelfth attempt, the machine could reprogram the hosts' bodies to produce new organisms. The goal of those organisms: build a massive structure — a gate — that would allow the Creators to bend the laws of physics, to instantly deliver an army directly to the blue planet.

But the hosts fought back. They found the organisms and destroyed them.

The machine kept trying. Each attempt, however, cost another irreplaceable probe. Fourteen . . . fifteen . . . sixteen. Every attempt involved a new strategy, and yet the hosts always found a way to win.

On the seventeenth attempt, the hosts discovered the machine. They gave it a name: *the Orbital*. And once again, the hosts defeated the Orbital's efforts.

The Orbital had no backup. No help, no resupply. Seventeen attempts, seventeen failures. The eighteenth attempt was the machine's final chance to stop the hosts. Failure meant the hosts would have hundreds of years, perhaps *thousands*, to improve their technology. They had already made feeble-yet-successful attempts at escaping their planet.

If the hosts developed far enough, they might reach the stars. And if they did, someday, they might encounter the Creators, and — possibly — *destroy* the Creators. That was the very reason for which the Orbital had been built: to find burgeoning races and help the Creators eliminate them before they could become a threat.

During the first seventeen tries, the Orbital had come very close to success. That meant some of the earlier strategies were worth replicating. And yet in the end, each of those strategies had failed, which meant the Orbital also had to try something new, had to feed all its collected data into this last-ditch attempt.

No more gates.

No more efforts to conquer.

For the eighteenth and final probe, the Orbital's goal became singular, simple and succinct:

Extinction.

But before the Orbital could launch that probe, the hosts attacked. Over a hundred centuries of existence came to a brutal end as dozens of high-velocity depleted-uranium ball bearings tore the machine to pieces.

Pieces that splashed into Lake Michigan.

The eighteenth probe, however, remained intact. Nine hundred feet below Lake Michigan's surface, this soda-can-sized object hit the lake bed and kicked up a puffing cloud of loose sediment. As the object sank into the muck, the sediment settled around and on top of it, making it invisible to the naked eye.

The U.S. government searched for the Orbital's wreckage. Many pieces were found. The soda-can-sized object, however — a tiny speck of alien material resting somewhere among 22,400 square miles of lake bottom — remained undiscovered, undetected.

Until now.

BOOK I

THE BIG WATER

THE BLUE TRIANGLE

Candice Walker stared at the tiny cone of hissing blue flame.

She couldn't do it.

She *had* to do it.

Her chest trembled with the held-back sobs. *No more . . . no more pain . . . please God no more . . .*

Pain couldn't stop her, not now. She couldn't let that happen. She had to get out, had to make it to the surface.

She had to see Amy again.

Candice looked at her right arm, still not quite able to believe what was there, or, rather, what *wasn't* there. No hand, no forearm . . . just a khaki, nylon mesh belt knotted tight around the ragged stump that ended a few inches below her elbow.

The knot's pressure made the arm feel almost numb. Almost. The belt's end stuck up like the rigor-stiff, stubby tongue of a dead animal, flopping each time she moved.

She again looked at the acetylene torch's steady flame, a translucent, blue triangle filled with a beautiful light that promised pure agony.

I can't let them get me again . . . do it, now, Candy . . . do it or die . . .

When the pain came, she couldn't let herself scream; if she did, they'd find her.

Candice lowered the flame to her flesh.

The blue jewel flared and splashed, blackening the dangling scraps of skin and arm-meat, shriveling them away to cindered crisps of nothing. Her head tilted back, her eyes squeezed shut — her world shrank to a searing supernova point of suffering.

Before she knew what she was doing, she'd pulled the flame away.

Candice blinked madly, trying to come back to the now, trying to clear the tears. The bubbling stump continued to scream.

Do it so you can see your wife again . . .

Her mouth filled with blood — she'd bitten through her cheek. Candice looked at her shredded arm, gathered the last grains of strength that remained in her soul. She had to keep her eyes open, had to *watch* her arm or she'd bleed out right here.

See your job and do it, Lieutenant. DO IT!

Candice lifted her severed arm, opened her mouth and bit down hard on the belt's flopping end. She tasted nylon and blood. She pulled the belt tight, then brought the blue jewel forward. Flame skittered, seemed to bounce away at strange, hard angles. The sound of sizzling meat rang in her ears, partnering with a hideous scent of seared pork that made her gag, twisted her stomach like a wrung-out towel.

This time, she didn't look away. Blood boiled and popped. Skin bubbled and blackened. Bone charred. And the smell, oh Jesus that smell . . . she could *taste* the smoke.

She heard grunts. She heard a steady, low growl, the sound of an animal fighting to chew its foot free of the iron-toothed trap.

The torch slid from her hand, clattered against the metal deck. The blue jewel continued to breathe out its hateful hiss.

She pulled the scorched stump close to her chest. Her head rolled back in a silent cry — *How much more? How much more do I have to take?*

Candice forced herself to look at the charred mess that had once been connected to a hand. A hand that could draw and paint. A hand that had almost sent her to Arizona State to study art before she made the choice to serve her country. A hand that had touched her wife so many times.

Blisters swelled. Her flesh *steamed* like a freshly served steak, but the bleeding had stopped. Drops of red oozed up through the blackened stump's many cracks and crisp edges.

Her right hand was gone . . . so why did her missing fingers still feel the fire?

With her remaining hand, she reached inside her uniform's shirt, felt her belly where she'd hidden her drawings — *still there.*

Candice reached for the door that would take her out of the submarine's tiny, steel-walled trash disposal unit. She couldn't hide here forever. She held her breath, knowing that just lifting the TDU door's lever would make noise, might bring her shipmates.

She closed her eyes again, searching for the strength to go on. *Amy, I will never quit. They won't get me they're all out to get me they're all trying to murder me . . .*

Candice slowly lifted the lever.

The door opened to a dark passageway, empty save for the few wisps of smoke that filtered in from the fire she'd set in the engine room. The gray bulkheads, piping and electrical conduit looked no different than they had for all the months she'd served here.

Everything was the same; everything was different.

To her right, the wardroom where she had eaten countless meals.

To her left, the crew's mess: pitch-black, all the lights smashed and broken.

Candice reached to the small of her back, drew her pistol. She'd shot two men dead; how many additional crew had she killed with her act of sabotage? She wished the answer was *all of them.*

She had to reach the dry deck shelter. The surface . . . she had to get to the surface.

Sweating, shivering and bleeding, Candice stepped out of the TDU.

She almost slipped when a cracking voice sounded over the intercom.

"This is the . . . the captain."

Candice froze as if he was actually in the passageway with her, as if he could see her. It was his voice, familiar from so many months, yet *not* his at the same time. He fought to get the words out.

"Man Battle Stations Torpedo. I say again, man . . . man Battle Stations Torpedo. That . . . that is all."

She flinched at the harsh *click* of the PA shutting off. Torpedo launch? Against who? There wasn't an enemy out there, wasn't anyone at all except for . . .

"No," she said. *"No."*

She'd disabled the sub's ability to escape; she hadn't disabled its ability to *fight.*

Escape. They were coming for her . . . she had to escape.

Candice held her severed arm close to her chest, her right shoulder shrugged up almost to her ear. She moved down the passageway, waiting for each step to bring one of her tormentors running.

If she could get to the forward escape trunk hatch that led to the dry deck shelter, if she could get into one of the SEIE suits, then she could make it to the surface. The dry deck shelter was amidships, just aft of the control room and attack center. To reach it, she would have to walk through the crew's mess, past all the dead bodies.

And some of them, she knew, weren't *all the way* dead.

Candice felt a vibration under her feet: the torpedo tubes flooding, the final step before launch. Only seconds until Mark 48 ADCAPs shot out at fifty-five knots, heading for ships that had no idea what was coming.

She walked into the darkness of the crew's mess. An aisle ran down the center. Small, four-person booths lined either side. In those booths, she could make out lumpy shadows, the still forms of corpses, the crimson shade of dried blood.

This was where they had tried to bring her.

A dim light filtered in from up ahead, shone down from the open, overhead escape trunk hatch.

Her eyes adjusted enough to make out something on the ground just in front of her.

A severed head.

And she recognized it: Bobby Biltmore, an ensign from Kansas.

Congrats, Bobby — at least you're actually dead.

She stepped over the head and kept moving through the aisle, waiting for one of the corpses to rise up and grab her, pull her under a table, do to her what they'd done to the others.

The smell of rot, fighting for dominance against the scent of her own cooked flesh.

Only a few more feet to go. The shadows seemed to move, to take shape and reach out for her. Her hand tightened on the pistol's grip, squeezed hard enough to somehow force back the scream building in her chest and throat.

Candice Walker felt another vibration.

Fish in the water . . . torpedo launch. The targets wouldn't just sit there, they would fire back. That meant the *Los Angeles* only had minutes to live.

She focused on the light ahead. A ladder led up to the escape trunk hatch. The ladder usually hung from brackets on an adjacent bulkhead — someone had connected it.

Candice reached the ladder and started up, her only hand holding the gun, using her elbow and smoldering stump to keep her balance as exhausted legs pushed her higher.

She climbed up into the cylindrical escape trunk: empty, thank God. At five feet in diameter, there wasn't much space, but she didn't care — salvation lay one more ladder up, one more hatch up into the dry deck shelter.

That hatch, too, was already open.

She stayed very still. She saw someone walk by the hatch. She saw a face, a flash of color. Wicked Charlie Petrovsky. He was wearing a bright-red SEIE suit: *submarine escape immersion equipment.*

Candice Walker's pain didn't vanish, but it took a backseat to the rage that engulfed her. Was Charlie like her? Or was he like them? Either way, it didn't matter — she needed that suit.

The sub vibrated again. Another torpedo had just launched.

It wasn't fair. It *wasn't fair!* She'd done more than anyone could ask. She wanted to *live.*

Candice sniffed once, tightened her grip on the pistol, then quietly started up the ladder.

WICKED CHARLIE PETROVSKY

Wicked Charlie Petrovsky came to.

He lay on the floor of the dry deck shelter, bleeding from a bullet lodged in his neck. He kept his eyes closed, didn't make any noise — he could hear her moving around nearby.

Candice Walker: the woman who had shot him.

Charlie was a guitar player. That was why he started calling himself "Wicked Charlie," because he was wicked-awesome on the six-string. He'd known it was kind of douchey to give himself a nickname, but everyone liked him and he could flat-out *shred* on his vintage Kramer, so the moniker stuck.

None of that mattered anymore, though, because he knew he'd never play another note.

So *cold*. His eyes fluttered open to a view of Bennie Addison. Bennie's eyes were also open, but they weren't seeing anything because Bennie Addison had an exit wound above his left eye.

Charlie heard footsteps, heard the *zwip-zwip* sound of someone walking while wearing thick, synthetic fabric. She was somewhere behind him. The DDS was a squashed, metal tube some thirty-five feet long but only five feet wide — she'd have to step over him to reach the rounded door that led into the small decon chamber. The divers used it to clean themselves up after returning from a search, to make sure they didn't bring any of the outside in.

The sound came closer, then feet stepped down in front of his face; right, then left, both encased in the SEIE suit's bright red, watertight boots. He heard muffled crying coming from inside the sealed hood.

Charlie stayed very still. If he moved, she would shoot him again. Couldn't risk that; he was on a mission from God. He couldn't complete God's work if he was dead.

He didn't dare to look up, but he knew what she was doing — opening the door so she could step through, close it behind her, then flood the decon chamber. Once that chamber flooded, she could exit it and enter the water.

She was heading for the surface.

That was wrong. *Charlie* was supposed to be the one heading to the surface. God said so. God told him where to go, and what to do when he got there.

Wicked Charlie Petrovsky would not fail God.

Candice stepped into the decon chamber. The heavy door clanged shut behind her.

Charlie waited until he heard the door wheel spin, sealing the chamber tight.

He pushed himself up on his hip. He felt his own blood coursing down his shoulder. He pressed a hand hard against his neck. He didn't have long to live, he knew that. That he'd survived at all was a miracle, the hand of God obvious and undeniable.

Charlie tried to stand. He could not. One hand on the cold deck, the other pressed against his bleeding neck, one foot pushing him along, Charlie crawled toward a life vest hanging from a bulkhead. He awkwardly reached it, slid first one arm through, then his head. His shivering, blood-covered hands fumbled with the straps.

Would God be mad at him?

The answer came immediately.

He heard a *whump* that shook the air a split second before the DDS's starboard bulkhead ripped inward. A hammer blow of jagged metal tore into him, as did a simultaneous blast of high-pressure water that slammed him against the far wall, shattering bones on impact.

Not that Charlie felt it. He would never feel anything ever again.

The Orbital had watched. The Orbital had learned.

Its first infection vector had been rather simple in concept: spores that floated on the air, released by the Orbital from its position some forty miles above the earth. Those spores hijacked the host's stem cells, reprogrammed them, turned them into microscopic factories. The factories punched out parts that self-assembled into *triangles*. Left unchecked, those triangles grew into *hatchlings*.

The shotgun approach of a high-altitude release meant that most spores were wasted. They blew into areas of low population, got stuck on the ground, or simply fell into wet areas where they crumbled into bits of nothing. When spores *did* land on a host, they worked well, but a hatchling couldn't make more hatchlings. Nor could a hatchling spread the contagion by infecting additional human hosts.

So the Orbital had changed strategy.

It created a new design: the microscopic *crawlers*. Crawlers didn't hatch out of a host. Instead, they migrated into the host's brain, reshaped it, modified the host's instincts and behaviors. A crawler-infected host could make new crawlers to infect *other* hosts. Unlike the hatchlings, crawlers could reproduce. They could *spread*.

The crawler method of contagion worked on a one-to-one basis, something a blond-haired little girl named Chelsea Jewel had once referred to as "smoochies." Smoochies created the capacity for an ever-expanding army of infected, but the method was slow. It didn't allow for continued, mass infections to occur.

It was Chelsea — not the Orbital — who solved that problem.

She created a third mode of transmission: turning her own mother into an obscenely bloated gas-filled bag containing millions of spores. At some point this swollen host would burst, scattering spores onto the wind like dandelion seeds carried by a summer breeze. The method was similar to the Orbital's original infection strategy, but the swelling host was already on the ground — that meant better odds for a higher rate of transmission. Each spore could infect a host with triangles, or with crawlers, or it could turn that host into yet another gasbag that would burst and continue the cycle.

Before the Orbital was shot down, its logic processes determined it needed yet another mode of transmission, something that allowed for infection by touch alone, or — more important — by a vector that lingered in areas of high contact where multiple potential hosts could be exposed. As part of that strategy, the Orbital also wanted one additional key element: that this new vector could continue to infect long after the host died . . .

The swirling, churning, angry water spun Wicked Charlie like an insect dropped into a boiling pot, sucked him out of the submarine and into the cold, silent black.

His body seemed to hang for a moment, motionless, as if he were that same insect trapped in dark amber. Then, the life vest began to rise, bringing Charlie along with it.

His body floated toward the surface.

Charlie's flame of life finally flickered out. His systems shut down, a cascading effect that should have ended all activity in his body.

Should have.

His stem cells had been hijacked to produce crawlers. These microorganisms had instinctively followed his nervous system, using it as a pathway to reach his brain. There they had collected, altered their shape and *changed* him.

A very specific type of his stem cells, however, had been reprogrammed to make something never seen before the infection that overwhelmed the *Los Angeles*.

That special type: *hematopoietic stem cells*, also known as *HSCs*.

HSCs have the ability to produce any type of blood cell. Charlie's HSCs had been hacked to produce one specific creation, a modification of something common throughout the human body: *neutrophils*, more commonly called *white blood cells*.

White blood cells are a critical part of the immune system. They hunt down bacteria and other foreign matter, engulf and destroy the things that could hurt us. Neutrophils are *amorphous*, meaning they are without form. They move like amoebae: reaching out pseudopods, finding their path, then the rest of their shapeless bodies follow along.

When Charlie's mutated neutrophils detected a severe lack of oxygen in his blood, the microorganisms reacted as they were programmed to react. They weren't sentient, at least not by themselves, but the lack of oxygen told them that their host was dead — time to prepare to abandon ship.

The Orbital had watched humans respond to its infection iterations. It had measured humanity's reactions, its processes and equipment, and it had prepared a new strategy to deal with both.

Charlie's neutrophils secreted chemicals that would harden into cysts, cysts to help protect them from the decomposition chain reaction that would soon turn Charlie's body to mush. Protect them for a little while, at least — hopefully long enough for a new host to come along.

That done, the neutrophils "turned off," entering a static state beyond even hibernation. From that moment on, only specific physical cues would cause the microscopic organisms to reactivate, to shed their cysts and seek out a new host.

Those cues? Vibrations. Movement. *Regular* movement, the kind only exhibited by living beings. Until they detected such signals, the neutrophils would remain motionless, almost as dead as the tissue that surrounded them.

THE END

REPUBOTHUGGY: Like anyone would ever believe Gutierrez's "little green men" bullshit and the work of his "scientist whore" Montoya. they should find those spics and shoot them liek the traitor that he is.

JAMES U: (in reply to REPUBOTHUGGY) A republican would say something like that, which shows your lack of education. Thanks for trying, though. Maybe you should read a book.

J-C-DOOMTROOPER: (in reply to JAMES U) I bet I read twice as many books as you, lib-tard, and the ones you read are full of pictures. I read philosophy, stratgy, history and the most importan book of all THE BIBLE!!!!!!!! Detroit got nukes because it was a soddham and gamhora and it was God's will.

CAROL B: (in reply to J-C-DOOMTROOPER) Stupidtrooper, you can't even spell, which is so typical of people who think the Bible (a.k.a., the "story-book") is real. Your words show how stupid you actually are, so good job on that.

"Margo?"

Margaret Montoya reflexively closed the laptop. It shut with a sharp *click*. She felt instantly foolish; caught in the act, she'd reacted without thinking when simply closing the web browser window would have done the job.

Clarence Otto stood in the doorway of their home office. He glanced down at the laptop in front of her.

He frowned. "Torturing yourself again?"

"No," she said. "It was just some research."

His eyes narrowed. "Really?"

Margaret felt her face flush. She knew better than to try to lie to him, especially about that.

She glanced at the clock next to the computer — he'd left work a bit early.

His black suit still looked pristine on his tall, thick frame, as sharp as when he'd left that morning. To anyone else, he probably looked all buttoned up, the kind of man who didn't have to get off a bar stool to leave the place with three new phone numbers. But Margaret had known him for six years — four of those as his wife — and she saw the telltale signs of a long day: the tie just a bit askew; lines at the corners of his eyes because when he got tired, he started to squint; the slight discoloration on the collar of his white shirt, because he always sweated a little even in air-conditioning; the slight, damp gleam on his forehead that made his black skin glow.

Clarence walked into the office to stand next to her. She stared at the closed laptop. He reached a hand down to her chin, gently tilted it up until their eyes met.

"We talked about this," he said. "We've been to therapy."

She snapped her chin away. "And that was a waste of time, just like I told you it would be."

Margaret searched his eyes, searched for the love that used to be there. She didn't find it. Truth was she hadn't seen that for a long time, hadn't felt his warmth. Its absence made her feel far colder than if she'd never known it at all. Now when he looked at her, it was with pity. Sometimes, even contempt.

He tapped the closed laptop. "This is what you do all day," he said. "You read the comments of uneducated idiots who have no idea that they're only alive because of what you did." He looked her up and down. "And I see that you also followed the therapist's advice about waking up, getting showered and dressed?"

She'd forgotten she was still wearing the same ratty blue sweatpants and long-sleeved University of Oregon T-shirt she'd slept in. She'd meant to shower, but that thought had slipped away sometime during the second or third blog post she'd read. Was she angry at Clarence for calling her out on that, or at herself for not doing something so utterly basic?

"What I wear is none of your business. And I have to do *something* with my time — It's not like you're ever around."

He tapped a fingertip against his sternum. "I *work*. You know, that thing that keeps a roof over our heads?"

She laughed. Even as she did she heard how hateful and dismissive it sounded. He was supposed to be on her side, not riding her ass.

"You think your job keeps a roof over our heads, Clarence? Oh *please*. We never have to work another day in our lives. We *saved the world*, remember? Uncle Sam will give us a check anytime we ask, just to keep us quiet."

Margaret stood, stared at his face. He was a full foot taller than she was. Once upon a time, she'd loved that — now it was just annoying to always have to look up.

"You don't work because you *have* to," she said. "You work because you're so goddamn naive you actually think you still make a difference."

He said nothing. She saw the veins pulsing in his temples. They popped out like that when he clenched his jaw. He clenched his jaw when he was trying to control his temper.

"I *do* make a difference," he said softly. "And so did you, before you decided to hide from the world. Before you decided to quit life."

He controlled his anger, as always; his discipline enraged her. The world threw hate at her day in, day out, yet off to work he went, leaving her to face everything alone. She felt a thick rage bubbling in her stomach and chest, a physical, *tangible* thing with a life of its own. She had to dial that back, or once again she would feel like a helpless participant who could only watch as someone else used her mouth to say awful things.

"*Quit?* Is that what you call it? Well, fuck you, Clarence."

He nodded, a tired gesture that said, *And there it is, right on cue.*

The same argument as always, flaring up faster each time.

Margaret pointed her finger, her weapon of choice. She pointed it right in his face because he hated that, because if a man did that to him he'd probably hit that man but he couldn't hit her, would *never* hit her. She shook the finger as she talked, almost daring him to lose control, a part of her hoping that for once, just for *once*, he'd show real emotion.

"You don't know what it's like," she said.

Margaret looked to her desk, to the framed pictures of the people she'd lost. A picture of Dew Phillips in a jacket and tie just like Clarence's, although Dew's looked like he'd been wearing it for days. Dew's crescent of red hair looked similarly disheveled; he stared at the camera as if he was just waiting for an excuse to beat the shit out of the photographer.

Next to Dew's frame, a picture of Margaret sitting at a table with the short, pale-skinned Amos Braun, warm smiles on both of their faces, arms around each other, half-empty glasses of beer in front of them. Five years on and the photo didn't make her think of the good times: she could only see his expression of panic, the life fading from his eyes as his blood sprayed against the inside of a biohazard suit visor.

And the final picture: a framed cover of *Sports Illustrated*. A massive football player dressed in the maize-and-blue uniform of the University of Michigan, tackling a white-jerseyed player wearing a silver helmet with crimson dots. Dirt and grass streaked the Michigan player's oversized arms. The block letters at the bottom of the cover read: "So good it's SCARY: Perry Dawsey and the Wolverine D lead Michigan to the Rose Bowl."

Perry. Tough, brave, tortured both physically and emotionally. Every night she dreamed of his last moments on Earth — those final few seconds before she'd killed him.

Those three men had died on her watch. So had Anthony Gitsham, Marcus Thompson, Officer Carmen Sanchez and a dozen other people she'd met, along with an entire city of people she had not.

"You *can't* know what it's like," Margaret said.

He rolled his eyes. "You going to tell me again how you *killed a million people*? You didn't kill them, Margaret."

She felt the scream tear at her throat, felt her face screw into a nasty, lip-curling mask.

"I'm the one who told them to drop that bomb! I'm the one who made those people die! *Me!* But you wouldn't know what that kind of responsibility is like because you're just a goddamn *grunt*."

This was the part of the dance where he'd say something like *just a grunt? I'm not as smart as you, so I don't matter?* and then she would tell him he was exactly right, because that would hurt him and she *wanted* to hurt him. She didn't have anyone else to lash out against.

His eyes narrowed to black slits. His skin gleamed brighter, because the arguments always made him sweat. He took in a nostril-flaring breath. *There* it was, the anger she wanted to see.

She waited for his usual response.

He didn't deliver it.

The big, held breath slowly slid out of his lungs — not as a yell, but a sigh of defeat. And he didn't even look angry anymore. He didn't look hurt, either.

He looked . . . *spent*.

Clarence stared at the floor.

Margaret felt a pang of alarm; something was wrong, more wrong than normal — Clarence Otto *always* looked people in the eye, as if he was a lighthouse perpetually flashing confidence, forever broadcasting a constant message of Alpha male.

Margaret felt hot. Her left hand pulled at the leg of her sweatpants: *tug and release, tug and release, tug and release.*

"Margo," he said, his voice barely a whisper. "I can't do this anymore."

Her hand speeded up: *tug and release, tug and release, tug and release.* He was going to say the words she constantly hoped he would say, the same words she never wanted to hear.

He cleared his throat, an oddly soft noise from a man of his size.

"Us," he said, the single syllable loud, definitive. "I can't do *us* anymore."

She took a step back, a step so weak she almost fell. And still, he stared down.

This man, this tall, strong man who had served his country in one form or another for twenty years, this black man who had put up with anything he'd had to in order to climb the ranks of the white-run CIA, this lover who had once put her on the back of a motorcycle and raced her out of Detroit while the world went crazy around them — now this man could not look at her.

That tiny inaction said more than any words ever could. Clarence had already made up his mind. He had made the decision days ago, probably, and had been waiting for the right moment to tell her. Knowing him, he'd been waiting for a chance to be kind, to at least *try* to be kind, but she'd forced it out of him. She'd been a self-involved bitch and backed him into a corner.

"Honey . . ." she said. There was more to the sentence, but she lost it. The single word hung in the air, lonely and impotent.

She thought of their early years together, their happiest years, and how they'd squandered much of that with days and even weeks apart due to her marathon sessions in the lab or his other assignments. She thought of how they'd console each other by saying they had all the time in the world to catch up, because they were *married*, because they were *together*.

Now it was all gone.

Clarence sniffed. He blinked back tears. "I'm getting older, Margo. I want a wife who's *here*. I want a family."

"I can't," she said instantly, feeling better for the briefest moment because this was another familiar argument. "I can't bring a child into this world."

A world of death and violence. A world of constant hatred. And she was too old, too old for a baby . . . those excuses and a hundred more.

Clarence sniffed again. He wiped the back of his hand against his eyes. "I know you can't," he said. "I accept that. Once I was willing to give up children if I could have you" — he looked up, spread his hands to indicate the room where she spent almost all her time — "but you're not *you* anymore, Margo."

She shook her head. "Honey, you don't—"

"Stop," he said sharply, the word a slap that landed in her soul instead of on her face. Then, softer: "You know me. You know I wouldn't start this unless it was already finished. I love you. I always will. You didn't *kill* millions, you saved *billions*. I tried to help you realize that. But you know what? It's just not something you want to hear."

Margaret spent much of her time hating him, *wanting* him to go, but now that he'd brought the idea out of the shadows and into a squirming reality, she suddenly, *desperately* wanted him to stay. She couldn't have let this slip away.

"I won't give you babies, so you're leaving me," she said. "That's all I am to you? Just a breeding factory?"

She'd used that argument before, and it had always worked. This time, however, his eyes hardened.

"You're not a breeding factory," he said. "You're not a *wife*, either. We don't even make love."

This was about his goddamn *dick*? Her hands clenched into fists. "We just had sex a couple of days ago."

"Two *weeks* ago," he said. "Only the second time in the last four months."

It seemed like more, but she knew better than to argue with him. He probably kept a calendar somewhere, tracked the actual days. That was often the difference between the two of them: Margaret *reacted*, Clarence *planned*.

He weakly waved a hand at the laptop. "You don't want me because *that* is your lover. You *want* the hurt and the misery. You *want* to read the awful things people say about you."

She felt a stinging in the back of her eyes, and a hard piece of iron in her chest where it met her neck. "They despise me," she said. "I deserve it."

The sadness faded from his eyes, replaced by conviction. That look stabbed deeper than his angry stare ever could — it was done.

"You don't deserve to be hated," he said. "But I'm done being your punching bag. If you can't love yourself, I won't spend any more time trying to convince you why you should. You've given up on life. I haven't. I need someone who'll fight by my side, not roll over and wait for death. I need a *soldier*. That's what you were, once . . . but not anymore."

She felt her hands gripping her shoulders, felt her body start to shake. Her rage had vanished. The puppeteer that made her say horrible things had fled the field of battle.

"But Clarence . . . I love you."

He shook his head.

Margaret wanted to go to him, hold him, have him hold her, but a barrier had sprung up between them, a distance that might as well have been miles.

His cell phone buzzed. He pulled it out in an automatic motion, so fluid and fast it was more muscle memory than conscious thought.

"Don't answer that," she said. "Please . . . not now."

He looked at the screen, then at her. "It's Longworth."

"I don't care if it's Jesus. Not now, Clarence, *please*."

He stared at her for another moment. The phone buzzed again. He answered.

"Yes sir?"

Clarence listened. His eyes widened. "Yes sir. Now is fine."

He put the phone away.

She felt numb. Not cold, not hot, not even angry or sad — just *numb*. "You just told me you're abandoning me, and now you're going to go to *work*?"

"I'm not going anywhere," he said. "Murray will be here in fifteen minutes."

The director of the Department of Special Threats was coming to their house. At three-thirty on a Wednesday afternoon. It was important, but she didn't care.

"You know I don't want anyone here," she said. "Why didn't he have you drive in?"

Clarence took a step closer. "Because he's coming to see *you*."

She felt a cold pinch of fear. There could be only one reason Murray wanted to see her:

It was starting again.

GIRLS, GIRLS, GIRLS

Such a tough choice: sit in the sun and watch girls in bikinis, or spend the afternoon rolling up forks and knives in napkins? Steve Stanton had opted for the former.

He'd slipped away from the restaurant earlier that morning while his mother, father, uncle and cousins were prepping the day's vegetables, pot stickers and egg rolls. Steve held advanced degrees in robotics, artificial intelligence and computational science, yet his family wanted him to snap the stems off green beans and prepare a hundred sets of flatware for the customers who couldn't figure out how to use chopsticks? He wasn't doing it, especially on a day like today.

Instead, Steve had brought a lawn chair out to the narrow, run-down park that ran along the St. Joseph's River. He'd also brought his laptop. That, connected through his cell, gave him the Internet. His father didn't know cell phones could do that: if the man came looking for Steve, he'd start in the coffee shops that offered free Wi-Fi.

Steve gazed up at blue skies, soaking up delicious warmth. For once, the November clouds had failed to appear. Gulls called constantly, both close and distant. He looked at the boats either heading out onto the endless horizon of Lake Michigan, or returning to port. A century-old, black-iron bridge hovered over the river, ready to turn ninety degrees and connect the railroad tracks on either side should a train come along.

His father would never look for him here, not in the park while an unseasonal sun blazed down. Steve normally avoided the sun. He'd inherited his mother's light complexion. As she had done back in China, she made a point of staying as pale as possible; dark skin was for laborers, for fieldworkers. Steve didn't care about his color. He stayed covered up because he had no intention of dying from skin cancer. Shorts and a T-shirt might have been more comfortable than his sweatshirt and jeans, but the long sleeves and hood blocked the sun's rays.

Butt in the lawn chair, laptop on his knees, Steve slid his sleeves a little higher so he could type unencumbered. Not that he was typing all that much; three girls were also taking advantage of what might be the year's last sunny day to stretch themselves out on a blanket laid upon the grass. They all looked to be in their midtwenties, about Steve's age. His eyes kept flicking away from his screen's engineering reports and oceanographic research to the girls, to their long hair, to their tan skin gleaming with oil.

He ached to talk to them. But those kinds of girls didn't want a guy like him. Girls like that wanted the captain of the football team, not the captain of the chess club. Girls like that didn't care that he'd earned two doctorates before he'd turned twenty-one, could have earned at least another three if he hadn't been forced to keep his discoveries secret.

And anyway, those kind of girls didn't go for first-generation Chinese American nerds. As smart as he was, talking to women made him feel stupid. It made him feel *small*.

The girls back at Berkeley had liked him. Well, not girls who looked like *that*, but at least they were girls. Here in Benton Harbor, Michigan? Women wouldn't give him the time of day, let alone their phone numbers.

For all Steve's brilliance, he was wasting away in this shit hole of a town in a shit hole of a state, waiting for a moment to serve his people and his country — a moment that was never going to come. He couldn't use his education, his rather significant set of skills, couldn't do anything that might draw attention. Not until the Ministry of State Security decided there was nothing in Lake Michigan worth finding.

His eyes followed the curve of the middle girl's ass, took in the smooth skin, the way the sun kicked off a soft reflection from the curve's apex.

She looked up, caught him staring. He turned away instantly, tapped random keys on his keyboard, focusing on the screen like it was the only thing in the world. He heard the girl laugh. Just her, at first, then the other two.

He felt smaller than ever.

A trickle of sweat rolled down his temple, but he knew the heat wouldn't last. Weather.com said the first big fall storm was on the way in. Early effects were due in about a half an hour. The encroaching front would soon chase away the girls with the long legs and tight butts, while Steve would be nice and warm in his heavier clothes. By tonight, everything would be freezing and wet.

Why did people live in Michigan, anyway? Winters full of cold and snow.

Trees shed leaves that turned into a brown paste on the roads. When the summer finally came, it brought with it sweltering, cloying humidity that seemed to suck the sweat right out of your body.

He wanted out of this washed-up excuse of a small city, wanted to leave this frigid state for good, to go somewhere the sun never hid behind clouds or vanished for weeks on end. He wanted to go back to Cali, to Berkeley. He had friends there, people who understood him. And if he couldn't go back to California, he wanted to go to his *real* home.

He wanted to see China for the first time, experience the nation of his people, see where his parents and ancestors had come from. Even his last name — Stanton — that wasn't *his*. The MSS had ordered his parents to change their names when they arrived in America. More for his sake than theirs, as it helped establish their son as just another American boy.

What Steve wanted never seemed to matter, though. The MSS wouldn't let him go to China. Not that he ever talked to anyone who was actually *from* the MSS — just their messengers, their errand boys.

So warm. Steve's eyelids drooped. Maybe the girls stopped laughing at him, maybe he just dozed off.

A shadow fell across his face.

Steve looked up to see a wrinkled old man looking down at him. Well, if it wasn't the MMS's main messenger.

"Bo Pan," Steve said. "Haven't seen you in a while."

Bo Pan nodded once.

Steve sighed. "You're blocking my sun."

Bo Pan looked down, realized he was casting a shadow. He quickly stepped to the left.

"Sorry, sorry," the man said.

Bo Pan wore secondhand jeans, secondhand sneakers and a Detroit Lions sweatshirt that was probably *third*-hand, if not fourth. With wispy hair around the temples of a bald head, and eyes that were deeply slanted even by Chinese standards, Bo Pan didn't look like a threat to anything but the grass on some rich white dude's lawn.

Steve sat up, turned, put his feet on the sparse, cool grass and packed dirt. "There's nothing new to report. But you know that. Here to check up on me?"

Bo Pan shook his head. He looked out at the river, squinted at the sun, then took in Steve's chair.

The old man frowned. "You look comfortable. Are you enjoying yourself?"

Steve smiled. "I am, actually. It's a beautiful day for a pimp like me."

Bo Pan's mouth pursed in confusion. For someone who had spent decades living in America, he understood little of the culture and *none* of the lingo.

"Do your mother and father know it's a beautiful day? I saw them working away in the restaurant."

Bo Pan hadn't come around in, what . . . three months? Three months without a peep, and the first thing he had to communicate was a guilt trip?

Steve eased back in his chair. He took his time, milking the motion just to annoy Bo Pan.

"My mother and father don't need me today."

"You are lazy," Bo Pan said. "You have grown up like them."

Like them: like an American.

Steve glanced over at the girls. He couldn't help it. As if being a semi-heliophobic nerd sitting with a laptop wasn't enough of a turnoff, now he was hanging out with a hunched-over, fiftysomething old man.

The girls were pulling on sweatshirts of their own, stepping into form-fitting jeans. The temperature was dropping.

"I'm not lazy," Steve said to Bo Pan. "I'm efficient — my work is done, remember?"

The old man shook his head. "No longer. We have a search location."

Steve sat up. He forgot about the girls, forgot about the sun.

"A location?"

The older man smiled, showing the space where his front right incisor once resided.

A location. Five years of effort, millions of dollars spent — Steve didn't know exactly how much, but it was a *lot* — the whole reason his family and the People's Party had hidden him away in this inflamed hemorrhoid of a town, and now it was finally his moment to shine. He didn't know what to think, how to feel. Afraid? Excited? After all this time, was it finally his turn?

"A location," Steve repeated. "How did we get it?"

Bo Pan shrugged. "The American love of money knows no bounds."

"No, I mean *how* did we, or they — or *whatever* — get the location? Satellite? Did someone properly model the entry angle? Did someone find . . ." His voice trailed off.

Did he dare to hope?

Gutierrez's green men. The story of the century. Steve's task: build a machine that could dive, undetected, to the bottom of Lake Michigan. Could there be actual *pieces* of an alien spacecraft?

"Wreckage," he said. "Did someone find *wreckage?*"

Bo Pan shook his head. "You don't need that information."

Steve nodded automatically, acquiescing to Bo Pan as if the man was something more than a simple go-between.

Wreckage. It had to be. Steve had finished work on the *Platypus* three months earlier. His baby was more a piece of art than a cutting-edge un-manned underwater vehicle. It sat in a crate like a caged animal, unable to move, unable to fulfill its purpose. Other than midnight test runs, there had been no point in putting the UUV to work. Unless Steve knew where to look, he couldn't have the machine go out and explore 22,400 square miles of Lake Michigan.

But now, they had a location.

The old man cleared his throat, dug his left pointer finger into the folds of flesh below his left eye, rubbed there. "When I last spoke with you, you said you had researched a local vessel that could take your machine far out on the water?"

Steve nodded. "JBS Salvage."

"A small operation, as I asked? Not a big fleet of ships?"

"Just two men," Steve said. "Only one boat."

"Good. And you check on them frequently?"

"Every week." A lie; a lie fueled by a stab of fear that maybe JBS had finally landed a job, that they wouldn't be available. It had been three weeks since he'd even bothered to see if their boat was still in port.

Bo Pan cleared his throat again. This time, he spit phlegm onto the dirt. "Can you talk to them right now?"

"Of course," Steve said, that feeling of foolishness growing. Why hadn't he checked every week? Bo Pan was right — Steve *had* been lazy. If they had to find another company to carry the *Platypus* to the target area, how long would that take? Days? Weeks?

Bo Pan's eyes narrowed. "You seem unsure."

"It's fine," Steve said. "I got this."

"And your strange machine . . . it *is* ready? There is nothing you need to tell me?"

Steve smiled: that was something he didn't have to lie about.

"My gear is ready to rock, playa."

Bo Pan nodded. "Good, good. They will be happy to hear that. If you hire the boat company today, how soon do you think we can leave?"

Steve felt a small burning in his chest. "We?"

Bo Pan looked away, embarrassed. "They want me to go with you."

Of course. There had to be something to diminish the moment. Steve would be stuck on a boat with this old man for days, maybe even weeks. Well, that was a small price to pay to finally put the *Platypus* to work.

And, at the very least, it was better than rolling up forks and knives in napkins.

"I'll go see JBS right now," Steve said. "Maybe we can leave in a day or two."

Bo Pan slid both of his hands into his sweatshirt's front pocket. He pulled out a thick envelope and a cell phone.

He handed the envelope over. "Tonight," he said. "Make them leave *tonight*."

Steve took the envelope. It felt solid, heavy, a brick of money.

Bo Pan then handed Steve the cell.

"Call me when you know," Bo Pan said. "Use this phone only. I am already prepared for the trip."

The old man turned and walked across the park grass, headed for his rust-spotted, ten-year-old Chevy pickup.

Steve turned back to face the water. The girls were gone. The wind was already growing from a stiff breeze into shirt-pulling gusts. November was supposed to be the worst time to be out on Lake Michigan.

Five years preparing for this day. No, more like *nine* considering that they'd recognized his intelligence early and sent him to Berkeley, readying him for a project that would require a brilliant, deeply embedded engineer. Embedded? That wasn't even the right word. Steve had been born right here, in Benton Harbor. He was as American as those girls, and yet he longed to serve a country he had never seen.

A lifetime of waiting for a chance to serve his people, his heritage, and now — perhaps — his moment had finally come.

He just hoped no one would get hurt.

DUTY

Sitting on the couch in her living room, Margaret felt newly aware of how much she had fallen apart.

Clarence sat on her left, as he if were really still by her side. That made him a liar. She wanted to hate him. He'd tightened the tie, dabbed the forehead, and once again looked like he'd just stepped out of the pages of *Government Agent Quarterly*.

In a chair across from them sat Murray Longworth, director of the Department of Special Threats. Or, as people in the know tended to call it, *the second-most-powerful agency you've never heard of.*

A black cane lay across Murray's lap, the handle atop it a twisted, brass double helix shape of DNA. Murray Longworth hadn't aged well. He looked frail, as if somehow he'd bathed in Detroit's nuclear glow and was slowly melting like a candle left sitting on a heater. His dark-gray suit was a little too big; Margaret guessed it had been tailored for him several years ago, several *pounds* ago.

A thick man in a black suit — a suit so indiscernible from Clarence's the two men might as well have been wearing matching uniforms — stood behind Murray's chair. A flesh-colored coil ran from a tiny, hidden earpiece to somewhere behind his neck. The man stared straight ahead, seeing everything and looking at nothing.

Three men in suits. She hadn't bothered changing. Her sweatpants had two small holes in the left knee and an avocado stain on the right thigh. She hadn't showered in three days. Margaret wondered if she smelled.

Murray forced a smile, his old, wrinkled face cracking like a windshield hit by a brick.

"Hello, Margaret," he said. "You look like a bag of assholes."

The man's penchant for pleasantries hadn't changed.

"And you look like an ad for a convalescent home," Margaret said. "Isn't there a mandatory retirement age in government work?"

Another smile, this one genuine. "I wish I *could* retire. My wrinkled old

ass should be in a fishing boat in Florida, catching redfish and croakers." The
smile faded. "Not everybody gets that choice."

Margaret felt a wave of guilt. Murray Longworth was over seventy, possibly even seventy-five. He worked ridiculous hours for a department that
barely existed on paper, a department tasked with anticipating and defeating
the country's next biological nightmare. He was right: he *should* be retired,
and yet he served every day while she sat on her behind and hid from the
world.

She crossed her left leg over her right, a move that would have looked
professional had she been wearing a dress.

"Murray, what do you want?"

He pulled a page-sized, brown envelope from inside his jacket.

"Nothing I'm about to tell you leaves this room," he said. "Yesterday, there
was an incident involving the *Los Angeles*, a nuclear attack submarine that was
part of Operation Wolf Head."

Operation Wolf Head. The task force assigned the duty of finding and
recovering any wreckage from the alien construct that had crashed into Lake
Michigan five years earlier. That construct had come to be known as "the Orbital" because, when discovered, it had been in a low, geostationary orbit that
defied the accepted laws of physics.

Margaret had known about the task force, as did most of the public. The
government couldn't hide the fact that they'd moved warships onto the Great
Lakes. But she hadn't known a nuclear sub was involved.

Neither, apparently, had Clarence.

"I thought the *Los Angeles* had been scrapped," he said. "And how could
you get it through the Saint Lawrence Seaway without being seen?" He
sounded annoyed, maybe even a little humiliated at being left out of the big-
boy loop: Mister Super-Agent wasn't privy to all the secrets, it seemed, and
that fact burned.

Murray tapped the edge of the envelope against his cane. "We converted
her into a search vehicle assigned with scouring the bottom. Slipped her
through the Saint Lawrence with a fake superstructure that hid the sail and
outline. Looked like just another tanker. What matters is that for five years,
the crew of the *Los Angeles* found nothing of note. Six days ago the sub's
commander reported a significant discovery. Two days ago, the flotilla lost
contact with the sub. Last night, the *Los Angeles* fired torpedoes at — and

sank — the guided missile destroyer *Forrest Sherman* and the Coast Guard cutter *Stratton*."

Clarence sat forward. "*Sank?* Heavy casualties?"

Murray nodded. "Two hundred and forty-four crew from the *Sherman* are dead. Fifty-seven from the *Stratton*. Seven more from the *Truxtun*, another destroyer, which was hit but remains afloat. We're assuming the entire crew of the *Los Angeles* perished — that's another hundred and twenty. In total, four hundred and twenty-eight dead or lost and presumed dead. Considering the number of wounded, we're still adding to the list."

Clarence sagged back into the couch.

Margaret suddenly wanted to go back upstairs and sit down at her computer. She could look at the blogs and read the comments, see if people were still talking about her — anything was better than hearing this.

Murray kept tapping the envelope against his cane, a *rat-tat-tat* beat that paced his words. "A third destroyer, the *Pinckney*, took out the *Los Angeles*. The *Truxtun* remains afloat, although it can't do much. Right now the survivors of the sunken ships are all on board the *Pinckney* and on the *Carl Brashear*, a naval cargo ship converted for Orbital-related research."

Clarence's face wrinkled in indignation. "You didn't evac the wounded to mainland hospitals? That's not— "

Margaret's left hand found Clarence's knee. An automatic gesture, a way for her to tell her man *relax*, even though he apparently wasn't her man anymore.

"The wounded can't leave," she told him. "No one there can."

Clarence blinked, then he got it. Any of those survivors — wounded or not — could be infected. He turned back to Murray.

"The media," Clarence said. "What's the cover story? How do you explain the battle?"

"We don't," Murray said. "The flotilla was in the upper middle part of Lake Michigan. The shore was twenty-five miles away to both the east and west, a hundred to the north and two hundred to the south. Nobody on land saw a thing. The battle occurred in a no-fly zone, so there was zero civilian air traffic. The sailors themselves won't be leaking the story, because right now no one leaves the task force — for the rather obvious reason that somehow escaped you."

Hundreds dead, just like that. A U.S. ship sinking other U.S. ships;

Margaret knew the infection could make that happen, could take over a host's brain and make him do horrible things.

"Cellulose tests," she said. "Any positives?"

She had to ask, even though she didn't want to know the answer. Inside a host's body, the infection built organic scaffolding and structures from cellulose, a substance produced by plants that was not found in the human body anywhere outside of the digestive tract. She and Amos had invented a cellulose test so accurate it left almost no doubt: if victims produced a positive result, it was already too late to save them.

"Two," Murray said. "Both from corpses."

Positive tests. Just the thought of it made Margaret sick.

The infection was back.

Murray offered Margaret the envelope.

She reached for it, an automatic movement, then she pulled her hand back.

"You don't want me," she said, her voice small and weak. "I . . . this is all horrible, but I put in my time. I can't go through this again."

Murray's lip curled up ever so slightly, a snarling old man who wasn't used to hearing the word *no*.

"Worst loss of life in a naval engagement since Vietnam, and it happened right here at home," he said. "Three ships destroyed, one damaged, about three billion dollars' worth of military assets gone, and we have no idea what really happened. So pardon my indelicate way of speaking my mind, Montoya, but *look* at the *motherfucking* pictures!"

He was going to *yell* at her? Like she was some intern who would jump at his every word?

"Get Frank Cheng to look at them," she snapped. "He's your fair-haired boy."

Murray nodded. "So you know Cheng's the lead scientist. I see you haven't completely tuned out."

She huffed. "It's not like Cheng makes it hard. He probably has reporters on speed dial so he can make sure his name gets out there. Send him to your task force. He might even bring along a camera crew."

Murray's eyes closed in exasperation. Cheng's desire to be recognized as a genius clearly rubbed the director the wrong way.

Clarence reached out and took the envelope. Murray slowly sat back —

even that minor motion seemed to cause him pain — and stared at Margaret. His fingertips played with the brass double helix atop his cane.

"Operation Wolf Head's primary research facility is on Black Manitou Island, in Lake Superior," he said. "That's where Cheng is. He made the case that he should stay there to provide continuity for the entire process, as opposed to being the first person to examine the bodies."

Margaret couldn't hold back a smirk. She should have known Cheng's desire to be quoted stopped at the edge of any actual danger.

"What a surprise," she said. "I guess you get what you pay for, Murray."

The old man's wrinkled hands tightened on the cane.

"I wanted to pay *you*," he said. "You said no. But that doesn't matter now, because I'm not the one asking this time — I'm here on direct orders from President Blackmon. She wants you on-site, immediately."

That numb feeling returned. For the second time in Margaret's life, a sitting president of the United States had asked for her. By name. She'd answered that call once, for Gutierrez; look where that had gotten her, gotten him, gotten *everyone*.

She heard a rattle of paper. She looked to her left: Clarence had taken the photos out of the slim envelope. He'd looked at them and was now offering them to her.

Margaret still didn't take them. She knew what would happen if she did.

"Printed pictures, Murray?" she said. "With your black budget you can't afford a fancy tablet or something?"

"Nothing electronic," Murray said. "Not out here, anyway. It's a lot harder to make paper go viral."

She thought it odd to hear someone that old use a term like *go viral*. Most people Murray's age barely understood what the Internet was.

Clarence put the pictures in her lap. She looked down, an instant reaction, saw the one on top, and couldn't look away.

It was a photo of a drawing: a man sitting in a corner, covered in some kind of bulky blanket. No, not *one* man . . . two . . . maybe even three. There was only one head, but sticking out from the blanket she saw four hands.

The original drawing looked water stained. Whoever had drawn it had done so quickly, yet there was no mistaking the artist's skill — the subject's open eyes looked lifeless, stared out into nothing.

Why were the men hidden under the blanket? No, it wasn't a blanket at all . . . it was a membrane of some kind, wrapped around dead bodies, parts of it attached to the wall, to the floor. It wasn't an impressionist's take; the artist had *seen* this, or at least thought he'd seen it.

"Murray, what the hell is this?"

"One of the bodies we recovered from the *Los Angeles* had that on her person," he said. "The artwork is good enough that we were able to confirm visual ID — the subject of the drawing is Ensign Paul Duchovny, who served onboard the sub. Obviously there are others in there with him, but since we can't see their faces we can't identify them."

"Did you send divers into the sub?"

"No one has gone near it," Murray said. "The sub is off-limits until we get our analysis team set up. It's nine hundred feet deep, so people can't go down without specialized equipment. On top of that, there's a radiation leak. We don't even know if it's safe to enter the wreck. Right now all our intel is coming from UUVs."

Margaret looked up. "UUVs?"

Clarence answered. "*Unmanned underwater vehicles.* Sometimes autonomous, like a robot, but most of the time they're controlled from a person on a surface ship."

Margaret again looked down at the picture. "Who drew this?"

"Lieutenant Candice Walker," Murray said. "She escaped the sub, made it to the surface. Unfortunately, she died before divers could get her to medical attention. She was just as crazy as Dawsey — cut off her own arm with a reciprocal saw just below the right elbow. She used her belt for a tourniquet and cauterized the wound, but it wasn't enough. She escaped the sub by wearing an SEIE suit, a bulky thing that lets submariners rise up without suffering pressure effects. We think her tourniquet came off when she was exiting the sub, or maybe while she ascended. Since she was in the suit, she had no way of tying the belt off again. Her picture is next."

Margaret flipped to the next page, then hissed in a breath. A dead girl wearing battered, blood-streaked dark-blue coveralls. A lieutenant in the navy, based on her insignia — a highly trained adult, although her face looked all of eighteen. The girl's right arm was a horrid sight: seared flesh and protruding, blackened bone. Extensive blood loss made her skin extremely pale. She had a bruise under her right eye and a long cut on her left temple.

Margaret thought of the first time she met Perry Dawsey.

He had been a walking nightmare. A massive, naked man, covered in third-degree burns from a fire that had also melted away his hair, leaving his scalp covered with fresh, swelling blisters. His own blood had baked flaky-dry on his skin. A softball-sized pustule on his left collarbone streamed black rot down his wide chest. His knee had been shredded by a bullet fired from the gun of Dew Phillips. And worst of all — even more disturbing than the fact that Perry clutched his own severed penis in a tight fist — the look on his face, those lips caught between a smile and a scream, curled back to show well-cared-for teeth that reflected the winter sun in a wet-white blaze.

Perry, mangled almost beyond recognition. This girl — correction, this *naval officer* — much the same.

Margaret shuddered, imagining a saw-toothed blade as a buzzing blur, jagged points scraping free a shred of skin or a curl of bone with each pass . . .

"Did the autopsy confirm she died from blood loss?"

Murray frowned. "You've been out of the game longer than I thought, Doc. We didn't do an autopsy yet. The *Los Angeles* had a mission to recover pieces of the Orbital. You remember the Orbital, right? The thing that made the most infectious disease we've ever seen, a disease that turned people into psychopaths? The thing that made little monsters that tried to open a god-damn gate to another goddamn world? The thing that forced us to nuke the Motor City to stop that gate from opening?"

Margaret felt her own lip curl into a sneer. "Yes, Murray, I *so* need you to fucking remind me about the *fucking* Orbital."

She felt a hand on her arm. Clarence, quietly telling her to ease down.

Murray leaned forward. He spoke quietly, trying to control his rage. "Apparently, you *do* need a reminder," he said. "Before Lieutenant Walker died, she admitted to sabotaging the engine room of the *Los Angeles*. She also admitted to shooting and killing two men. Her corpse and the second body, that of Petty Officer Charles Petrovsky, are in a Biosafety Level Four facility inside the *Carl Brashear*. They are infected with the same goddamn disease that could have wiped us all out five years ago, that made the crew of the *Los Angeles* fire on U.S. ships. So no, genius, we haven't done an autopsy yet. For that, we need the best. We need *you*."

Margaret cleared her throat. She'd asked a stupid question and been properly slapped down for it. "You said the *Los Angeles* found something?"

"Look at the last photo."

It was a photo of an object she didn't recognize, some kind of beat-up cylinder sitting on the gray, lifeless lake bottom. The diver or photographer had rested a ruler close by: the cylinder was about five inches long, two and a half inches wide. It was *frayed* in places, as if it were woven from a synthetic material; like fiberglass, maybe. Detritus and some kind of mold had taken root within the fibers, making the object look fuzzy, almost *alive.*

"This is from the Orbital?"

"Maybe," Murray said. "An unmanned probe discovered it six days ago. Five days ago, it was brought onboard the *Los Angeles* using the most rigorous decontamination and BSL-4 procedures known to man."

Clarence took the photo. "Not rigorous enough, apparently."

Murray nodded. "Three days ago, the *Los Angeles*'s commanding officer reported problematic behavior among the crew. We're sure that was the beginning of the infection incident."

Margaret could only imagine how horrible that must have been. A submarine, hundreds of feet below the surface . . . those people had been trapped in there, nowhere to run.

Clarence handed her back the photo. She stared at it, amazed that she was probably looking at an actual piece of alien hardware. The most significant discovery in human history — a discovery that had already delivered death and promised much more of the same.

"This object," Margaret said, "is it now onboard the *Carl Brashear?*"

Murray shook his head. "It remains in the *Los Angeles*. The sub was struck amidships. The object was in the forward compartment, near the bow. That area appears to be flooded, but otherwise intact. We're still dealing with fallout from the battle. Tomorrow or the next day, we'll figure out how to go down and get it out."

They were going to bring it up. Of course they were.

"Nuke it," she said. It shocked her to hear those words come out of her mouth, but it was the only way to be sure. Massive ecological damage was a small price to pay for ending the threat. "Do it now. *Today*, Murray, before it gets out."

Clarence cleared his throat, a tic of his when he was about to politely contradict her.

"Margo, that's a big step," he said. "The biggest. And it's not like we have a nuclear torpedo — they'd have to figure out how to deliver a nuke and put it right on the money."

Her eyes never leaving Longworth's.

"They don't have to deliver it because it's already there," she said. "Right, Murray? There's a nuke onboard the *Los Angeles*? Probably about five megatons, enough to completely sterilize everything in a hundred-yard radius?"

The corners of his mouth turned up in a small, wry grin; the master was proud of his pupil. He rubbed his jaw, looked off. Margaret sensed that he had already suggested nuking the site, maybe suggested it to the president herself, and he'd been overruled.

"Destroying it isn't an option," Murray said. "If we grab it now, at least we have a chance at containment."

He was a puppet speaking the words of his controllers.

"This isn't about *containment*," Margaret said. "The military wants it. They want to see if we can get some genuine alien technology. Great choice on the risk-benefit analysis, Murray."

He shifted in his seat. "Spare me a lecture, Doc. It's not my choice. I've got my orders. We need to know how that object affected the crew — is this the same thing we saw before or a new phase in the disease's development? Finding that answer could literally save the world."

Margaret looked down at the pictures. She tidied them up, then slid them back into the envelope.

She held the envelope out to Murray.

"I already saved the world," she said. "Twice. I can't, Murray . . . I just *can't*."

He struggled to stand. He leaned on the cane, took a step closer to her. His eyes burned with fury. She could see his too-white dentures.

"You hide in this house like a coward," he said. "You've seen horrible things? You've done your part? So have I. So has Clarence. So have thousands of other people, and they *keep on* doing their part. You have a knack for understanding this thing, Margaret. You are the only reason we stopped it last time. *You*. So how about you pull your head out of your ass, put your pity party to bed, pack a bag and come with me, because I don't care if you saved the world once, twice, or fifty fucking times" — he shook the cane head at her, the ceiling light glinting dully off the brass helix — "*your job isn't done*. You got the short end of the stick, Margaret. Maybe you're not a soldier, but you man the wall just like the rest of us."

Not a soldier. She looked at Clarence. For a moment, she wondered if he'd talked to Murray earlier, if they'd set that up together, but the look on his face said otherwise. Her husband was ashamed he'd said that to her.

She loved him. If this thing got out, he would die. So would she. So would everyone.

You got the short end of the stick, Margaret.

Murray was right. She hated him for it.

"I'll go," she said.

Clarence stood. "We'll be ready in thirty minutes."

"*Hell* no," Margaret said. "The area is possibly contagious. There's no benefit to putting you at risk."

I can't take seeing you every day; I can barely even look at you right now.

Clarence started to say something, but Murray *clonked* the bottom of his cane on the floor.

"Stop this," he said. "You two handle your relationship issues on your own time. Otto is going with you."

She turned on the old man. "Hold on just a damn second. If you want me there, then you — "

"*He's coming,*" Murray snapped. "Doc, you are the only choice for this job, but forgive me for being an insensitive prick when I say that you might not be playing with a full deck. Otto has been taking care of you for years. He's the best qualified to keep you focused."

"Great," Margaret said. "So you're assigning a babysitter?"

"I'll assign a midget with a whip if that's what it takes to keep you from reading blog posts about yourself for fifteen hours a day."

Margaret fell silent. Murray knew all about how far she'd fallen. Of course he knew. Clarence had probably told him.

Murray reached out and took the envelope from her.

"Get packed," he said. "A car will be here for you in fifteen minutes."

HIGHWAY TO HELL

Cooper Mitchell stared at the accounting program on his computer screen. He willed the numbers to change. The numbers didn't cooperate.

The force is not strong with this one . . .

He looked at the company checkbook. Specifically, he looked at the check stub, frayed edges lonely for the check that should have been there.

"Goddamit, Brockman," Cooper said. "How many times do we have to go through this?"

There was no information on the check stub, of course — Jeff never bothered to do that. Maybe this would be one of the lucky times when he hadn't spent that much, when he actually came back with a receipt, when his impulse purchase wouldn't make their account overdrawn. Again.

Cooper rested his elbows on the messy desk, his face in his hands. The dented, rust-speckled metal desk took up most of the small, cinder-block office. The "Steelcase Dreadnaught," as Jeff called it. It weighed some 250 pounds. Cooper could barely budge the thing; Jeff had once picked it up by himself, held it over his head just to prove that he could. The desk had been here when they'd bought the building and would probably be there when they sold it.

Which, if they didn't get a client soon, would be within weeks.

Their building bordered the St. Joseph's River, but the office's only window didn't offer that view. Instead, it looked out onto a bare concrete floor. The place had been a construction company garage once; maybe the window was where the foreman watched his people toil away, loudly growling *get back to work!* every time someone slacked off. The tall, deep shelves lining the walls were filled with diving gear (some functioning, most not), welding rigs, heavy-duty tools and other equipment. He and Jeff hadn't used some of the pieces in years, but in the underwater construction business you never got rid of something that was already paid for. Never knew when you might need it.

In the middle of the shop floor sat Jeff's pet project: an old, sixteen-foot racing scow that he had been meaning to fix up for the last five years. The boat, of course, had been purchased with one of the mystery checks. That check had bounced. Jeff still got the scow, though. Since the day they'd met in the third grade, the man could talk Cooper into damn near anything.

Jeff had put in all of eight or nine hours on the scow before he got bored with it, moved on to the next shiny object. But not a day went by when he didn't talk about making it pristine, selling it for a huge profit. Jeff loved the thing. Cooper wondered if someone would buy it as-is. Maybe it could bring in enough to make that month's payment on JBS's only ship, the *Mary Ellen Moffett*.

Maybe, if anyone was buying. In this economy, no one was.

Through the window, he saw the building's front door open. Jeff Brockman walked in, carrying a blue SCUBA tank under his left arm. A few brown, windblown leaves came in with him, one sticking to his heavy, shoulder-length hair of the same color. From his right hand dangled an overstuffed white plastic bag — take-out food.

Cooper forced himself to stay calm. A new tank? Maybe Jeff had found it. Maybe he hadn't spent money they didn't have on equipment they didn't need.

Yeah, and maybe Cooper would suddenly find out he was a long-lost relative of Hugh Hefner and had just inherited the Playboy Mansion.

Jeff Brockman strode into the tiny office, blazing a smile that said *I totally hooked us up!*

"My man," he said. "Wait till you hear the deal I just scored."

Cooper pointed to the open checkbook. "A deal you paid for with that?"

Jeff looked at the checkbook, drew in an apologetic hiss.

"Oh, right," he said. "Sorry, dude. I know, I know, you told me a hundred times. I'll fill in the stub thing right now." He looked around for space on his desk to set the food. "The receipt's in my pocket. I think. Or maybe I left it at the dive shop."

Cooper stared, amazed. Jeff moved a stack of bills aside, cleared a space to set down the bag. Through the strained plastic, Cooper counted five containers — had to be enough food there to feed a half-dozen grown men. And the odor . . . Italian. Fuck if it didn't smell delicious.

"It's not about the stub," Cooper said. "Well, yeah, it's about that, too, but, *dude*, we don't need a new tank!"

Jeff looked the part of rugged entrepreneur: the hair, the two-day stubble, the wide shoulders, and the blue eyes that made meeting girls at the bar so easy he didn't even have to try.

He smiled. "Coop, buddy, I got a *great deal*. We'll need to replace my tank in a couple of years anyway, so I actually *saved* us money."

Cooper stood up, slapped his desk hard enough that the thick metal *thoomed* like a cheap gong.

"You don't *save* money by *spending* it, Brock!"

Jeff's good humor faded away. His expression hardened. They hung out together all day, most every day, and that familiarity made Cooper forget that Jeff had thirty pounds and four inches on him, made him forget that Jeff carried layers of muscle built over a lifetime of construction and demolition jobs, made him not really see the little, faded scars on Jeff's face collected from the fights of his youth. That expression, though, made Cooper remember those things all too well.

"Coop, I own half of this company. I think I can take a little money to treat us once in a while, bro. I don't need permission to write a check."

"No, what you do need is enough *money in the checking account* to *cover the check*. I can't believe you'd be so stupid."

Jeff nodded. "Stupid, huh? Was I *stupid* when I convinced my brother to get you into that medical trial? Was I *stupid* when I somehow kept this business going while you were in the hospital for *six months*? Maybe it was just a miracle we didn't go out of business, maybe it wasn't because I worked two goddamn jobs to keep us afloat so you could get your goddamn life back."

Cooper's face flushed. He looked away.

It was almost hard to remember what the lupus did to him: the fatigue, the swollen joints, the chest pain . . . all of it had threatened not only his ability to work, but his life as well. Jeff had stood by him. Jeff had called in all the favors he had with his brother, a doctor in Grand Rapids, to get Cooper into an experimental gene-therapy trial. The trial had *worked*. Most of Cooper's symptoms were gone. As long as he went in every three months for booster injections, the doctors told him the symptoms would *always* be gone.

Still, the past was the past, and if they didn't do things right, there wouldn't be a future.

"Come on, man," Cooper said. "You know I'm grateful for that, but it doesn't help our business right now."

Jeff reached up, flipped his hair back. "Saving your life doesn't help our business? You ever saved *my* life?"

Oh, now it was Jeff who wanted to forget how things had been? He wasn't the only one who could lay a guilt trip.

"Brock, my family is the only reason you *have* a life, bro."

As soon as Cooper said the words, he wanted to *unsay* them. There were some places friends just didn't go, no matter how mad they got.

Jeff and his brother had come from a broken home. When their father finally left them and their alcoholic mother, the boys had little guidance and even less help. Jeff's brother had been sixteen; he'd been old enough to make his own way, to attack life and take what he wanted. Jeff, however, had been ten years old — he'd been lost. Cooper's mom had all but adopted him, given Jeff love, support and discipline when his birth mother provided none of the above. Jeff had spent at least half his high school years sleeping at Cooper's place. To say the two of them had grown up together was more than just a figure of speech.

Cooper felt like an asshole. He could tell Jeff felt the same way. They'd both gone too far.

Jeff sighed. "Hungry?"

He opened the bag of food, offered Cooper a Styrofoam container.

One sniff told Cooper what it was. "Roma's green tomato parmesan?"

Jeff raised his eyebrows twice in rapid succession. "Who's your friend?" he said. "Who's your buddy? I am, aren't I?"

Cooper laughed. He couldn't help it.

"Just because you've got a dead-on impression of Bill Murray from *Stripes* doesn't mean we're not broke."

"Broke, schmoke," Jeff said. "Something will come up. You gotta think on the bright —"

From Jeff's pocket, his cell phone rang: the three-chord-crunch opening of AC/DC's "Highway to Hell."

He answered. "JBS Salvage, we got the skills if you got the bills. This is Jeff himself speaking." He listened for a few seconds. "You're right outside? Sure, come on in."

Jeff slid the phone back into his pocket and smiled at Cooper. "See? God provides, my son. A potential customer is coming in to talk to us."

They walked onto the shop floor just as the main door opened. In came a skinny Asian kid. Early twenties, maybe. All of five-foot-eight, with shiny black hair that hung heavy almost to his eyes. His dark blue hoodie had BERKELEY on the chest in block yellow letters. A gray computer bag hung over his left shoulder. From the way the strap dug into the sweatshirt, it looked like he was carrying a lot more than just a computer.

Jeff and Cooper walked around the racing scow to meet the man.

"Hi there," Jeff said. "Can we help you?"

The kid smiled uncomfortably. "Uh, yes. Are you Mister Brockman?"

Cooper had expected to hear an accent, Chinese or Korean, Japanese maybe, but not a trace.

Jeff flashed his trademark grin. "Depends on who's asking," he said. "If you're a bill collector, my name is Hugo Chavez."

The kid stared, blinked. "Chavez?" He shook his head. "Oh, no, I'm not a bill collector. My name is Steve Stanton. I want to hire your boat."

Jeff looked at Cooper. Cooper knew what his partner was thinking — this kid certainly wasn't the type who worked in the marine construction and salvage industry. Cooper shrugged.

Jeff offered his hand. "Jeff Brockman." The kid shook the hand, winced a little at Jeff's overzealous grip.

"Ah, sorry," Jeff said. "Sometimes I don't know my own strength, know what I mean? This is my partner, Cooper Mitchell."

"Nice to meet you," Cooper said, shaking the kid's hand. "What kind of work do you need?"

Stanton adjusted his computer bag. It was so heavy he had to lean to the side a little to balance himself.

"My boss is looking for Northwest Airlines Flight 2501."

Cooper felt a spark of excitement, of hope — if this kid was some kind of treasure hunter, he might have money for the job. No one was going to find Flight 2501, but that didn't matter if he could write a check that wouldn't bounce.

"It went down in 1950 over Lake Michigan," Stanton said. "It was a DC-4, flying from New York to Minneapolis, had to— "

"Reroute due to weather," Jeff finished. "We're familiar. Fifty-eight people died, worst crash in American history at the time, blah-blah-blah, and so on and so forth. It's the Flying Dutchman of the Great Lakes. No one has found the wreckage."

Steve looked surprised that Jeff knew about the disaster. If this kid thought he'd discovered something unique, he didn't know a damn thing about the Lakes culture.

"No, no one found the wreckage," he said. "Or the bodies."

Jeff smiled and looked to the ceiling. This wasn't his overeager *whatever it takes to win your business* smile, but rather his *I smell bullshit and you're wasting my time* smile. Cooper wanted to strangle his friend: *just play along, you idiot*.

"Got news for you," Jeff said. "After all this time, there ain't gonna *be* no bodies."

Steve Stanton laughed, the sound short and choppy, overly loud. "That's the point," he said. "That's why the insurance companies never paid out to the families of the crash victims, because no bodies were found."

This was a play for insurance money?

Cooper's hope sparked higher. "You don't look like a lawyer, Mister Stanton."

"I'm not, but my boss is," Steve said. "He's gathered a bunch of descendants together and is ready to file a *huge* lawsuit on their behalf. All kinds of compound interest and stuff, it's gonna be *mad* stacks."

Mad stacks? Cooper looked at Jeff. Jeff shrugged: he didn't know what it meant either.

"Money," the kid said. "A *lot* of money."

That Cooper understood.

"But Northwest isn't even around anymore."

Steve nodded. "No. Delta is, though. They bought out Northwest, and they've got deep pockets."

Jeff ran his fingers through his hair, lifted it, let the heavy strands drop down a few at a time.

"People have been looking for 2501 for decades," he said. "*Experts*, people who make me look like I know nothing, and trust me, buddy, I know a *lot*. Besides . . . if it's in the deep water, like below three hundred feet, we just don't have the equipment for that."

Cooper felt a pain in his jaw — he was grinding his teeth together. Couldn't Jeff just be a *little* dishonest for once?

Steve Stanton smiled. "I don't need you to find it, or go down and get it.

I'm an engineer. I designed a remotely operated vehicle that can cover a lot of ground faster and better than anything that came before it. You guys take me out for a few days, maybe a week, we let the ROV survey the bottom for a few days, see if we get lucky and make my boss happy."

Jeff sighed, crossed his arms. He tilted his head a little to the right, an expression Cooper knew all too well. Jeff was about to show Stanton the door. Cooper had to do something, fast, something that would change Jeff's mind.

"It would be expensive," Cooper said. "Jeff's well-known reputation as a navigator, his expert knowledge of the lake, and the weather is going to be a factor, of course, and—"

Steve Stanton reached into his sweatshirt pocket, pulled out a neat, bank-bound bundle of hundred-dollar bills. He held it up.

"Will this get us started?"

Cooper stared at it. So did Jeff. *That* certainly wasn't going to bounce. The bills smelled new. They smelled even better than the green tomato parmesan. That bundle alone would make the payment on the *Mary Ellen* and catch them up on three months of back utilities.

"Let me guess," Jeff said. "That's a *mad stack*?"

Steve laughed his too-loud laugh. "This one isn't even a little ticked off, man. What will it cost to hire you?"

Before Cooper could speak, Jeff gave a number that was triple their normal rate. Cooper froze — Stanton could turn around and hire a boat from one of the big companies for half that. Jeff was actually *trying* to price JBS out of the job.

Steve Stanton swallowed, licked his lips. He looked nervous. Maybe he wasn't authorized to pay that much?

"Okay," he said. "If we can leave tonight, you're hired. I'll pay for the first week in advance."

Cooper Mitchell was a shitty poker player, and he knew it. Always had been. He tried to stay perfectly still, wondered if any tells showed how bad he wanted this job.

Jeff, however, was an amazing poker player. Probably because he didn't know how truly full of shit he was, and he believed whatever story poured from his mouth at that given moment.

"Tonight," he said, shaking his head. "There's a storm coming in right now. Tonight's not a good idea. Listen, I appreciate you wanting to hire us, but I have to be honest with you, you're better off—"

"I'll double your rate," Steve said. He looked like he might start hyperventilating. "But only if we leave tonight."

Six times their normal day rate? And he'd pay a full *week* in advance? This was it, this was the job that could turn everything around.

Cooper looked at Jeff, waited for his partner to accept the job.

But instead, Jeff shook his head.

"I think you might want someone else," he said.

Cooper reached out, grabbed his best friend's elbow.

"Jeff, can I talk to you in the office for a moment?" The words came out cold. Jeff looked down at Cooper's hand.

Cooper let go, tilted his head toward the office. "*Now*, please."

Jeff sighed, smiled at Steve. "Would you excuse us a moment?"

The two partners walked into the cinder-block building within a building. Cooper shut the door.

"Brockman, what the fuck, bro?"

Jeff shook his head. "Dude, the job is bullshit."

"What do you mean *it's bullshit*?"

"I quoted him a metric fuck-ton of money, he didn't blink," Jeff said. "For that kind of scratch, he could hire the bigger companies all up and down the coast. And *cash*? And *Flight 2501*? Come on, man, that's never been found and it's never gonna be found. It's like he's trying to entice us with, I don't know, the thing that has the most *glory* attached just in case the cash isn't enough."

"Who cares? Glory or no glory, someone wants this computer nerd's little toy out on the water. Maybe Mister Stanton doesn't know what a normal rate is."

Jeff let out a half-huff, half-laugh. "*Mister Stanton*? He's half our age, man."

"Is that what this is about? That a twenty-five-year-old kid can come in here with enough cash to make us jump?"

Jeff looked away, scratched at his stubble. Yeah, that was the problem. Part of it, anyway. Both Cooper and Jeff were pushing forty. Every day, they grew more and more aware that they had no money in the bank. No wives. No children. They'd been in business together for two decades. They'd passed up going to college to be the captains of their own ship, literally, and they were one letter from the bank away from having nothing to show for it. Their big plans for a fleet had never materialized.

Cooper had changed his ways: partied less, paid more attention to the books, the business, changed his diet . . . whatever it took to grow up, to accept that his youth had passed him by. Jeff refused to let go of his. Cooper wasn't even sure the man *could* let go.

Jeff begrudgingly nodded. "Okay, that bugs me. But that's not why we need to pass, bro. This is too good to be true. It's skunky."

Skunky: Jeff's word for a superstitious belief that if something didn't feel right, it was bound to go wrong.

"You don't do the books," Cooper said. "We're in a lot of trouble, dude. We need this gig."

Jeff bit at his lower lip. "I'm telling you, we should take another job."

"You want another job? How does busing tables at Big Boy sound? Because that's where we'll be if we pass this up."

Jeff looked down, stared at his work-booted toe scraping a circle against the concrete floor.

"It's skunky," he said. "I'm telling you."

For as long as he could remember, Cooper had trusted his friend's instincts. Although they were partners, Jeff was the de facto leader — but where had that gotten them?

Cooper put his hand on Jeff's shoulder. "Dude, I'm begging you. Just this once, will *you* trust *me?*"

Jeff inhaled a long, slow breath that seemed too big for his lungs. He let it all out in a whoosh.

"Okay, I'm in," he said. "We're going to need a third guy. With this kind of money we could stop hiring under the table."

Cooper shook his head. "Let's use José. We still haven't paid him for the last two jobs. We owe him."

Jeff tilted his head back. "Damn, I forgot we haven't paid him."

Of course Jeff had forgotten. Cooper had what he wanted, so there was no point in digging on Jeff for that.

Jeff smiled, clapped his hands together, rubbed them vigorously.

"José it is," he said. "Let's go tell Mister Stanton he's hired himself a boat."

INFLUENCE OF THE SONOFABITCH

Choices had been made.

The Orbital had never possessed true sentience. That didn't mean, however, that it didn't have a logic process. It still had to *think*. It had to create questions, evaluate those questions, form hypothetical strategies and use the data it possessed to evaluate probable results.

The Orbital had limited resources. Some of those resources needed to be used in an attempt to create new weapons, new strategies. Logic also dictated, however, that some resources needed to be used on three existing, proven designs: *hatchlings*, *crawlers*, and *mommies*.

Hatchlings moved fast. They could build up or tear down defenses. They could swarm, they could attack. They could *kill*.

Crawlers turned humans into murderers that slaughtered their own kind. Crawler-infected humans could still use weapons, vehicles and tools. They could work together, take and give orders, function as an organized force. And perhaps far more important, a crawler-infected human could infect others.

Mommies had been created by Chelsea — *not* by the Orbital, but that didn't matter. The design turned humans into spore-filled gasbags. Mommies couldn't fight or build, but they were an extremely efficient vector for mass infection.

Those designs filled specific roles. All three were included in the Orbital's last salvo.

But they weren't enough.

The Orbital needed new troops, new weapons. It had to create something . . . *better*.

The pure, brute force of the "sonofabitch" had defeated the Orbital's early attempts. The Orbital had learned from that and would use similar tactics in one of its final designs. This fourth design wouldn't just affect the host's brain; it would overwhelm the host's entire body, *transform* it, providing strength, rage, aggression, toughness, brutality . . . a fitting monument to the only human who had dug hatchlings out of his own body. Were the Orbital capable of emotion, that fourth design might have been the product of spite. Or, possibly, of *hatred*.

Brute force had stopped the Orbital's attempts, but so, too, had intelligence. The fifth design would harness the human intellect, shape it, turn it into a weapon. The most brilliant humans would be transformed into *leaders*, generals that could manage the war long after the Orbital had perished.

To protect such a vital strategical asset, the Orbital had spent much of its remaining days finding a way to hide these leaders — not only could they direct a growing army, they could also function in a covert role, hiding among the humans until the right time to strike.

Three proven designs. Two designs as-yet untested when the Orbital crashed into Lake Michigan.

The Orbital would never know just how successful those last two designs turned out to be.

THE SITUATION ROOM

Murray Longworth had a dream.

That dream consisted of a giant bonfire, a bonfire made from the long, heavy, wooden table that sat in the White House's Situation Room. Throw in the wood paneling as well; that would burn up real nice. Not the video monitors that lined those walls, though — he would set those up around the bonfire and play some shit on them that had nothing to do with saving the world: a Zeppelin concert, maybe some playoffs for whatever sport was in season, a few cartoons, perhaps, and — for sure — at least three screens playing constitutionally protected good old-fashioned American porn. He'd have a keg. He'd hire some strippers a third his age to sit around in bikinis and laugh at his jokes. He'd warm his old bones in the heat of that bonfire, get crocked, and celebrate the death of the room he hated so much.

"Murray?"

He blinked, came back to the moment. He was in that very Situation Room of his brief daydream, but there was no bonfire, no keg, and no porn. Images of Lake Michigan played across the screens. Instead of strippers, he was looking at some of the only people who knew the entire history of the situation, from Perry Dawsey's naked run for freedom right up to the sinking of the *Los Angeles*.

"Murray?"

The president of the United States of America had called his name. Twice. Sandra Blackmon stared at him. She wore a red business suit. She always wore red. She did not look happy with him. In his defense, the only time she *did* look happy was when the news cameras were on her. There were no news cameras in the Situation Room.

Murray sat up straighter. "Yes, ma'am," he said, waiting for his mental playback loop to retrieve the question his conscious mind had missed. Forty years of marriage had developed that skill, the ability to make part of his brain record words even when he wasn't paying attention at all. His wife would ask, *Are you listening to me?*, and Murray could regurgitate the last ten or fifteen seconds of what she'd said. The same skill came in handy during these meetings.

His playback loop brought up her question: *Did you get Montoya?*

"Yes, Madam President," he said. "Doctor Montoya is on her way to the task force. She'll report to the *Carl Brashear*, where we have the remains of Lieutenant Walker and Petty Officer Petrovsky."

President Blackmon nodded, just once. Murray thought the motion made her look like a parrot.

"Excellent," she said. "Lord willing, maybe Montoya can find something that other person you have running the show could not. What's that man's name again?"

"Cheng," Murray said. "Doctor Frank Cheng."

Blackmon nodded once. "Yes, Doctor Cheng. Why isn't he on the *Brashear* already?"

Murray's teeth clenched. "Doctor Cheng is at Black Manitou Island, overseeing preparation for the delivery of any samples that Montoya sends out for more detailed analysis."

Blackmon's mouth twisted to the left, a tell that she wasn't buying it. Most people bought into Cheng's grandstanding bullshit. Murray did not. Neither, apparently, did President Blackmon.

"Fine," she said. "He can stay there and *prep*. I wanted Montoya on the case, and she is, so we'll put our full trust in her."

If Murray could have lived out his bonfire fantasy, he knew some of the people in this room would eagerly join him. Others, no. These were among the most powerful people in the country: the chairman of the Joint Chiefs of Staff, the national security advisor, the secretary of defense, the director of homeland security, the secretary of state . . . the nation's decision makers, gathered together to help President Blackmon chart a path in this dangerous time.

She turned to the chairman of the Joint Chiefs, Admiral Samuel Porter.

"Admiral, you're absolutely certain the *Los Angeles* didn't succumb to enemy actions? Our regular enemies, I mean. I want the world to know that we are ready to strike back against *anyone* who thinks we are weak."

Sam Porter took in a deep breath. He looked down. No matter what the situation, he took his time answering a serious question. His pale skin made Murray think the man had been a submariner himself, an extended absence from sunlight causing his body to jettison any color as unnecessary baggage. Maybe Porter had even spent time on the *Los Angeles* as he moved up the ranks.

"Madam President," the admiral said, "we have no indication of any terrestrial forces in the Great Lakes area, or anywhere on the American theater. We have firsthand accounts from the *Pinckney*. There is no question here — American forces attacked American forces. This is, officially, the worst friendly-fire incident in U.S. history."

Blackmon pursed her lips, held them there as she thought. Fifteen years ago that same expression might have looked alluring. Now it showed the lines around her mouth, at the corners of her eyes.

Like Porter, Blackmon took her time to think things through. She didn't rush. That made the two of them get along quite well. For the bystanders, however, watching them converse was like watching paint dry.

Blackmon had swept to power amid anti-Democratic fervor aimed at President Gutierrez, who had made the fatal mistake of trusting in the intelligence of the American people. An alien pathogen had turned regular Joes and Janes into psychopaths, had spawned a nightmarish version of little green men, and Gutierrez told the people the truth.

What an idiot.

Half the country hadn't believed him then. Even less believed him now. Blackmon had been merciless in her campaign, citing Gutierrez's inability to keep the country safe, hammering on the fact that, as president, he'd "allowed" the worst disaster in American history. Those things alone should have been enough, but she'd gone one step further. Without coming out and actually saying it, her allusions and insinuations made her stance clear: since God created everything, and the Bible was the immutable word of God, and the Bible didn't talk about aliens, well, then there couldn't *be* aliens — therefore Gutierrez was lying.

Murray had watched, stunned, as a man who told the truth was washed out of office by a nation that didn't want to believe humanity was not alone in the universe. Blackmon hadn't rallied just the Bible thumpers. No, you couldn't win in America anymore if you only paid attention to the religious Right. You also needed the Koran thumpers, the Talmud thumpers, and the thumpers of all moldy old books suitable for thumping. She found a way to gather all of those people into her fold without alienating her Christian base.

Countering her strategy, practically every scientist in the country stood firmly behind Gutierrez. They trotted out papers and studies and formulas that proved he was telling the truth, yet that didn't matter.

When it comes to politics and tragedy, in the end people need someone to blame.

A nation aching with loss and reeling with disbelief had chosen Blackmon. Piousness and ultraconservative views felt like the perfect counter to the science-minded liberal who ran the show when a mushroom cloud blossomed over Detroit.

When the landslide election results came in, Murray had hoped Blackmon's religious rhetoric was just a way to get her into power. It was politics, after all — say whatever you have to say to get elected. But Murray had come to realize that her brilliant election strategy wasn't a show.

Sandra Blackmon *believed*.

In closed-door meetings like this, President Blackmon accepted that America had nearly been invaded by some kind of strange force. She also acknowledged that Gutierrez had played the only card available to stop a disaster that could have taken out the entire Midwest, possibly the nation, maybe the entire world. The problem was, she didn't believe that force came from somewhere other than Earth. Most of the time, she acted like the attack had to have come from another country: Russia, China, maybe even India (for which she had an inexplicable hatred).

Sometimes, however, the president of the United States of America said things that made it sound like she thought the attack was *Satanic* in nature. The fact that she might believe that, and she had her finger on the button? The thought made Murray's balls — what were left of them, anyway — shrivel up into little fear-peanuts that tried to crawl up into his belly and hide.

Blackmon turned to André Vogel, a man who — in Murray's humble opinion — should have walked around with a coating of slime all over him and his fancy clothes.

"Director Vogel," she said. "What about spies? Any more information on Lieutenant Walker's background? Could she have been turned?"

"It's possible," Vogel said. "So far, however, we have nothing."

Murray knew that people sometimes said his department, the Department of Special Threats, was the second-most-important government organization you'd probably never heard of. The first? The Special Collections

Service. Part NSA, part CIA and all black-budget, Special Collections existed well outside the framework of official government business. André Vogel was exactly the kind of shifty motherfucker needed to run it.

"Walker seems to be as red, white and blue as they come," Vogel said. "Naval Intelligence and the FBI are looking into the entire crew of the *Los Angeles*, Madam President. That's a big job. But if a foreign power is at the root of this, we *will* find out."

Typical Vogel-speak: casually mention the difficulty of the task, but also promise results.

Blackmon leaned back in her chair. "What about the Chinese? The NSA reported there was chatter shortly after the attack. Can we be *sure* the Chinese weren't involved?"

Vogel shook his head. "No, Madam President, we can't be sure. We're listening. They know something crashed into Lake Michigan five years ago. President Gutierrez informed the whole world that we had visitors, so it's easy for the Chinese to put two and two together. Regardless, though, they can't *do anything* with that knowledge. Even if they had a sub within a hundred miles of our coast, they couldn't get it through the Saint Lawrence Seaway and into the Great Lakes."

"They've got *money*," Murray said. Heads turned to look at him, eyebrows raised because he'd spoken out of turn. He ignored them all, just stared at Vogel.

"The Chinese have more money than they know what to do with," Murray said. "Do we really know for sure they couldn't just quietly hire locals to go down and get the thing?"

Vogel smiled, looking smug. "The probable crash site is seven hundred to nine hundred feet deep. You need specialized gear for that. The intelligence community has been consistently monitoring all domestic companies that have the right kind of equipment, with a special eye on Lake Michigan outfits, of course. Canadian and Mexican companies as well. The navy task force made short work of discouraging filmmakers, reporters, documentarians, even conspiracy theorists from venturing into a maritime exclusion zone."

He sat back, gave his bald head a quick, damp rub. "The only way anyone could steal our alien technology, which we haven't even secured yet, would be to invade the United States of America and occupy Michigan, Wisconsin and Minnesota."

The man knew his business, no doubt, but after all this time he *still* didn't get the big picture.

"I'm not talking about stealing it," Murray said. "I'm talking about *touching* it. We just lost a nuclear sub, a destroyer, a cutter and over four hundred brave men and women. That didn't happen by accident. If the wreckage was somehow contaminated with any of the contagious shit that forced us to nuke Detroit, then the Chinese don't have to *get* the thing out of the country, they just have to be dumb enough to go down and *try*. That alone could be enough to goat-fuck us right in the ass."

"That's *enough*," President Blackmon said.

Murray didn't know if she'd had that voice of unquestionable authority before she took over as commander in chief, but she sure as shit had it now.

"This briefing is over," she said. "I think Director Vogel has clearly illustrated that the site is protected against espionage. He's doing his job. Murray, you do yours. Find out what turned the crew of the *Los Angeles* into traitors, and find out fast."

DAY THREE

NIGHT FLIGHT

Margaret's belly wanted to be sick, but Margaret was in charge of such things and she was *not* going to let this helicopter ride make her throw up.

She'd spent most of the last three years sequestered in her house. Now here she was, at 4:00 A.M., in a loud-as-hell helicopter streaking across the black surface of Lake Michigan, strapped tightly into an uncomfortable seat and wearing an ill-fitting helmet. Her soon-to-be-ex husband sat next to her, a constant reminder of her failures as a wife.

How had Murray talked her into this?

Maybe it hadn't been Murray at all. Maybe it was because the infection had returned, and she couldn't stand aside while others fought that evil for her.

Before "Project Tangram," before she and Amos stumbled onto something that would turn out to be one of humankind's biggest and worst discoveries, she had been an epidemiologist with the CDC. She hadn't been a "nobody," by any stretch, but no one had really known who she was.

The infection changed all that.

She moved from a back room to the front line. She had become *the one*, the person who figured it out, who stopped it. Doing so had cost so many lives; it had destroyed hers as well.

She should have been a celebrity, a hero. She should have been an icon of the scientific world. Instead, she had suffered so much in the past five years. *Lost* so much. She wasn't going to let that be for nothing.

You will not win. I WILL beat you.

The pilot's voice came over the headphones built into her helmet.

"We're coming up on the task force," he said. "We're on high alert, so this will be a slow approach as they make sure everything is okay. If you look out the port side, you can see the task force coming up pretty quick."

Margaret readjusted her loose helmet as she looked. Rain pounded against the helicopter's windshield. She could see no stars, nothing but black above and below. Then, in the distance, she saw the glow of lights.

Warships, on the Great Lakes. And the concept of *lake* didn't really register — she couldn't see land in any direction, not even the distant sparkle of cities or towns.

As the helicopter closed in, the faint lights of the four gray ships became more clear. The ships were big . . . so big they seemed to ignore tall, black, undulating swells that could have dragged normal boats to the bottom. The longest of the gray ships looked boxy, like a cargo hauler. Two others were nearly as big but had the sleek lines of combat vessels. One rode tall in the water, pristine and impressive, while the other listed slightly to port, parts of its superstructure blackened and twisted. It took her a moment to realize the two ships were identical, a before-and-after image representing the effects of combat. The smallest of the four didn't look like any ship she had ever seen.

Margaret pulled on Clarence's sleeve and pointed at the identical pair's undamaged ship. She tried to lean into him and cracked her helmet against his. He reached up, tapped the helmet's microphone sitting directly in front of her mouth.

"Oh," she said. "Sorry." She didn't need to yell over the helicopter's engine to be heard. She pointed out again. "What is that?"

"That's the *Pinckney*," Clarence said. "Arleigh Burke class guided missile destroyer. It's the flagship of the flotilla. The one that's listing is the *Truxtun*. The one that looks like a tanker is the *Carl Brashear*. That's where we're headed. It's about seven hundred feet long, so your motion sickness should settle down once we're aboard."

She hadn't told him she felt ill. He just knew.

Margaret gestured to the final ship, the smallest of the four. Its long, thin, pointed nose widened near the base, flaring out into the superstructure, which itself led to a flat, square back deck. The ship's steeply sloped sides reminded her, somewhat, of the old Civil War ironclads, and yet the vessel's overall appearance was that of a spaceship from a science fiction movie. On the back deck, she saw two helicopters, ready and waiting.

"That's the *Coronado*," Clarence said. "It's new. It's called a littoral combat ship."

"So it literally does combat?"

"Not *lit-ER-al*, *lit-OR-al*," he said. "It means *close in to shore*. That's where SEAL Team Two is."

Guided missile destroyers. Littoral combat ships. SEALs. This was the equivalent of putting a floating flag in the middle of Lake Michigan and tell-ing the rest of the world *this is ours, and if you even look this way, you're going to get a black eye.*

How typical. Five years after what could have been the extinction of the human race, and her government chose to rattle its saber instead of working with other countries to share the biggest scientific discovery in history.

And yet as impressive as three of the four ships looked, she realized that just a day ago there had been a total of seven: two more on the surface, one below. Somehow, the infection had taken them out.

I will beat you.

The helicopter suddenly plummeted, an elevator with the cable cut. Just as quickly the drop ended with a hard rattle that bounced her in her seat and jostled her loose helmet.

"Sorry about that," said the pilot's voice in her earphones. "The wind is pretty tricky. Turbulence is going to be rough as we come in to land. Hold tight."

Something seemed to slap the helicopter's left side. Margaret's stomach let out a brief-but-intense prepuke warning. She started to look for something to throw up in, but Clarence was already offering her an open barf bag.

Margaret held it to her mouth as she discovered that she was not, after all, in charge of such things. She kept throwing up as the helicopter descended toward the *Carl Brashear.*

MUTUALLY ASSURED DESTRUCTION

Steve Stanton stood at the rail of the *Mary Ellen Moffett*, wondering if the phrase "freezing your nuts off" was less a figure of speech and more an accurate scientific possibility.

He stared out at an endless black surface, not that he could see all that far at 5:00 A.M. on a starless morning. November wind tore at his raincoat. Five-foot swells slapped against the hull, splashing icy spray into his face. He'd been out on the lake dozens of times while testing the *Platypus*, but until this moment he had never, in his entire life, been in a place where he couldn't see land. He felt like a shivering speck in the middle of nowhere, like a satellite surrounded by the expanse of space.

Bo Pan stood next to him. The old man had already thrown up over the rail once. He looked like he might soon do so again.

It was hard to believe that just twelve hours earlier, Steve had been sunning himself in a lawn chair. As soon as the *Mary Ellen Moffett* left the dock, the temperature had plummeted twenty degrees. The growing wind dragged it down at least another fifteen. The Gore-Tex foul-weather gear he'd bought (with some of Bo Pan's wad of cash, thank you very much) was rated for temperatures well below this, and yet still Steve felt wet and cold. When he got back, he'd write a stern letter of complaint to the manufacturer's customer service department.

Steve found himself caught between excitement and fear. Despite years of preparation, it seemed impossible to believe that he was here — to possibly acquire a piece of something created by an extraterrestrial race.

"Bo Pan," Steve said in a whisper that was lost on the wind. He leaned in closer and spoke louder. "Bo Pan, do you really think the location is accurate?"

Bo Pan shrugged. He looked miserable, but resigned to the misery, like a wet sheep patiently waiting out a hailstorm. Bo Pan hawked a loogie, spit it over the side. The man had cornered the market on phlegm.

"I do not know," he said. "I was told to bring you here, and to launch your creation that way." He pointed starboard, to the north.

Steve stared out. Maybe his destiny was out there, nine hundred feet below the surface. He could be the one to find it, to bring it back for the glory of China. If what lay on the bottom provided new technology, if it was or helped create a weapon, his country needed it. Hard times were coming to the world. America would not give up her place at the top without a fight. The People's Party had spent decades preparing for that final shift to ascendancy — it wouldn't be fair if a chance find gave America some kind of accidental edge.

Steve knew his history: when America had an advantage, it used that advantage. The atom bomb against Japan. Logistics and manufacturing against Germany. A superior air force against Iran, Libya and Bosnia. The shock and awe tactics against Iraq. When America fought with one hand tied behind its back, as it had in Vietnam and Korea, it lost. When it used everything it had, when it let the generals decide strategy, America *always* won.

China was gaining, gaining fast, but America still had the best tanks, the best planes, the best ships. Chinese armed forces claimed technical superiority, but as an engineer Steve knew such claims were a steaming pile of bullshit. Even with the largest manufacturing base in the world and an entire government dedicated to developing a high-tech military, China was still a decade away from being able to fight on equal terms. If war came, America would use everything it had: including alien technology, maybe even that psycho disease President Gutierrez had talked about.

Sure, Gutierrez had warned everyone to be on the lookout for symptoms. Steve remembered the president's endless "T.E.A.M.S." public service commercials, the acronym that told the populace to watch for *triangles*, *excessive anger* and *massive swelling*. People knew what to look for, yet the disease had never reappeared — at least as far as the public knew. Did America have it stored away somewhere, like the anthrax or smallpox it also wasn't supposed to have?

If America possessed a weapon, America would use it.

The only way to keep the balance, to properly protect the land of his ancestors, was to make sure China had the same weapons. If Steve found something his nation could use to defend itself, he would become a legend. In America he could get rich, sure, but he'd always be thought of as nothing more than *that smart Asian guy*. In China, they would build statues of him.

He would be a national hero.

Bo Pan gagged, then leaned over the rail and threw up again. Steve grabbed a handful of the older man's coat, just to make sure he didn't tip over and drop into the water. After a few heaves, Steve pulled Bo Pan back.

The man wiped the back of his mouth with his sleeve. "Sorry," he said. "Sorry."

Steve wished he could have come alone. Or, if they *had* to send someone with him, maybe someone better than this useless, seasick messenger.

Noise came from farther back on the deck. Cooper Mitchell and a short Mexican man named José were following Jeff Brockman around the deck. Bo Pan had been agitated that Cooper and Brockman brought another crewmember. Steve couldn't figure out why — you had to have enough people to run the boat, after all.

José was all of five-foot-five, wiry, with a heavy mop of black hair and a face so happy it looked like he had to concentrate to show anything but a smile. He seemed to look up to Brockman, both literally and figuratively.

Brockman was always first to laugh, first to scowl, first to talk, as if he felt compelled to drive every conversation and every action. He was fun to be around, but Steve suspected that Cooper was the only reason Brockman had a business at all.

The three men checked the straps securing a pair of long, custom-made shipping crates. The bigger of the pair was five feet high and wide, fifteen feet long. Inside lay Steve's baby, the *Platypus*. The second crate was smaller, only about four feet long and lower to the deck. It held another of Steve's creations, one he hoped he wouldn't have to use.

Bo Pan watched the commotion as well. "How soon can we put your machine in the water?"

Steve's brain automatically looked for a reason not to do that, checking for something he'd missed, something he'd forgotten, but there was nothing. He was prepared.

"Right now, I suppose," he said.

Steve watched Brockman and Cooper. He waited for something to happen. After a few minutes, he realized he was waiting for Bo Pan to tell Brockman to get started. But Bo Pan wasn't in charge.

Steve was.

It was all on him, and him alone. Now he *really* wished Bo Pan's handlers

had sent someone else. As strange as it felt, Steve was now a real-life spy —
the future of his country might actually rely on how well he handled the situation. No pressure, right?

He cupped his hands and shouted. "Hey!" The men looked at him. "Can we get it in the water?"

Brockman looked out at the horizon, as if gauging the wind and the waves, then he glanced at Cooper. Cooper nodded.

Brockman gave Steve a thumbs-up. "We're on it, boss!"

They started unstrapping the crate.

Steve spoke, and three men jumped into action?

Maybe being in charge would be kind of fun.

LITTLE GREEN MEN

Clarence Otto sat in a chair in front of the captain's desk, waiting for Captain Gillian Yasaka to arrive. Margaret sat in a chair to his left. She stayed quiet, kept her thoughts to herself. Clarence couldn't blame her.

The trip from the landing deck to this tidy office had been disturbing, to say the least. The wounded seemed to be countless. Every open space held prone sailors stretched out on tables, on cots, even lying on the floor with nothing more than a thin blanket to give them some padding. Some of the wounded slept. Others moaned, tossed and turned, overwhelmed by hideous burns on hands, arms and faces. Some of these men would be scarred for life.

Margaret had tried to stop a half-dozen times, her years as a medical doctor compelling her to do something, to help those in pain. Clarence had had to keep her moving, gentle steady pushes that reminded her she had to think of the bigger picture — there wasn't enough time to help any of them, let alone all of them.

The *Brashear*'s overcrowding made Clarence nervous. People packed that tight would speed the spread of any contagion. One infected person would quickly turn into ten, into a hundred. Maybe that was why Margaret was staying quiet, because she was worried about the same thing.

Yeah, right.

If the woman he'd married was still in there, somewhere, Clarence didn't know how to find her. He'd tried. He'd tried to understand her, to help her, tried to deal with years of constant crying, constant sadness, the obsessive reading of blog posts and comments. He had tried to stay calm while being her endless punching bag, the target of a rage she couldn't control. He had tried to be there for her, guide her through all of it.

At what point does a man say *I've had enough*?

Did he have to give up any chance at happiness in exchange for spending his short life watching her wither away? *For better or worse* looked great under the showroom lights. Once you drove it off the lot, it was a different story.

He couldn't fight for Margaret if Margaret wouldn't fight for herself.

She sat in her chair, stared straight ahead. Did she still love him? No, probably not — truth was she hadn't loved *anything* for years. She still needed him, absolutely, but the way a crippled man needs a crutch, or the way a drunk needs a bottle. Still, as messed up as she was, Clarence knew that Margaret Montoya was the person for the job. The *only* person. His love for her had faded, but not his belief; she could figure this out, she could stop it.

He would play his role. He'd make sure she ate, make sure she slept, because she forgot to do both when she lost herself in research. He'd fetch her coffee. He'd clean her clothes. Whatever it took; when the *real* shit hit the fan, Margaret Montoya took center stage, and Clarence was fine with that.

Captain Yasaka entered. Clarence stood up instantly, faster than he would have liked — leftover reactions from his days in the service. At least he didn't salute.

Margaret stayed seated.

Captain Yasaka — actual rank of *commander*, but operating under the honorary title of *captain* like the commander of every ship in the navy — was as neat and clean as her stateroom. Her graying black hair was pulled back in a tight bun, and her dark-blue coveralls looked like they had been pressed and then hung on a mannequin protected behind a plateglass window. Her belt buckle was the only thing that outshined her shoes. She stood all of five-six, but Clarence could tell that she had the presence needed to make tall boys quake in their boots if they failed in their duties.

All her meticulous grooming, however, didn't hide her exhaustion, a certain slackness to her face. Yasaka looked like she hadn't slept in days. She probably hadn't.

"Doctor Montoya," she said. She shook hands with Margaret, then Clarence. "Agent Otto."

Clarence nodded. "Captain."

Yasaka gestured to Clarence's chair: *sit, relax.*

Clarence sat, as did the captain.

"My apologies for making you wait," she said. "We're on full alert, and there were things that required my attention."

Clarence waited for Margaret to speak. It was her show, after all; he was just the wingman. When she said nothing, he spoke for them both.

"Yes, ma'am," Clarence said. "We understand."

"I need to make this short," the captain said. "I have a ship full of wounded, and I have to report about this meeting to Captain Tubberville over on the *Pinckney*. He's the task force commander. So I can answer your questions, but please, let's get to it."

Margaret nodded. "I need to know what happened," she said. "The timeline. Timelines are very important."

Yasaka's jaw muscles twitched. "Six days ago, at twenty-one-fourteen hours, an ROV from the *Los Angeles* located an object of interest. The ship commander dispatched a diver to recover that object. The diver wore an ADS 2000, the atmospheric diving suit required for such depths. He disembarked from a dry deck shelter modified for decontamination. The diver recovered the object, then returned to the DDS. While still wearing the ADS, he was sprayed in bleach to kill any possible external contaminant before reentering the ship proper."

Margaret leaned forward. "The ROV spotted something special? Sending out a diver was unusual?"

"Not at all," Yasaka said. "In fact, this was the six hundred and fifty-second time a diver from the *Los Angeles* had performed that task. Every two or three days, on average, the ROV saw something the onboard crew couldn't identify. Whenever that happened, Captain Banks sent out a diver."

Clarence wondered if the repetitive, uneventful nature of their job had made the divers sloppy.

Yasaka continued. "At twenty-one-fifty-five hours that same day, the *Los Angeles* notified us that the object was a significant discovery."

Margaret looked at Clarence, then at the captain. "So if they thought it was significant, why wasn't it brought up to the *Brashear*? I was told this ship has a full BSL-4 research lab."

Biosafety Level Four . . . Clarence hated those words. The most stringent safety procedures known to man, used for work with lethal, highly contagious airborne diseases like Marburg and Ebola, shit that could kill millions. BSL-4 suits — the kind Margaret wore to study the alien infection — had positive pressure: if something poked a hole in the suit, air pushed *out* instead of *in*, because contact with even a single, microscopic pathogen could mean death.

"My ship's facilities are fully compliant," Yasaka said. "We've brought up fifteen objects over the last five years. Scraps of Orbital hull, mostly. Bringing potentially contaminated items up from nine hundred feet below is dangerous, Doctor Montoya, and *expensive*, so the *Los Angeles* was retrofitted with a small lab of its own. Standard procedure was to make sure an object was not of terrestrial origin before sending it up."

Margaret looked angry, annoyed. "So they found an alien object and they just *held on to it* for a few days?"

Yasaka nodded. "If they had found an alien body, or something that was clearly made by little green men, that would have been different. What they found looked like a strange can, so they prepped it and waited until they had enough data to merit the *extensive* procedures required to send something to the surface."

Margaret wasn't the only one getting annoyed; Clarence could see that Yasaka didn't appreciate Margaret's intensity. The captain had a ship full of wounded. Her crew had probably recovered hundreds of dead bodies from the *Forrest Sherman* and the *Stratton*. This wasn't the time for Margaret to grill Yasaka about procedure. Clarence's job of helping Margaret included stepping in when she was about to burn a bridge.

"So it was business as usual," he said. "You would have probably ordered the object to be brought up, but you didn't get the chance. What happened next?"

Margaret leaned back in her chair, tried to relax. She'd picked up on Clarence's cue, knew she needed to back off a little.

Yasaka folded her hands on her desk. "Three days ago, the *Los Angeles* reported erratic behavior among the crew. A fight involving a few injuries. I'm afraid there wasn't much detail. Captain Banks made his scheduled daily report, but he seemed . . . strange. Agitated, but not angry. He didn't exhibit any of the behaviors associated with the Detroit disease, nor did any of his crew send a message that they suspected he might be infected."

That surprised Clarence. "I'm sorry, Captain, you're saying that the crew could contact the *Brashear* without the captain's knowledge?"

She nodded. "The navy knows what could be down there, Agent Otto. Procedures were in place that would allow anyone to raise a red flag if something seemed amiss with anyone on the crew, including the captain."

"But no one raised a flag."

"No, they didn't," Yasaka said. "We now believe that the captain *was* infected, and he either sabotaged the red-flag system before anyone could use it, or put guards at the various red-flag stations, preventing anyone from calling up. His report about the fight was the last communication we received from the *Los Angeles*.

"At twelve hundred hours on the day of the battle, we attempted to perform our daily, scheduled communication with the *Los Angeles*. We received no response. Sonar told us the *Los Angeles* was just sitting there at eight hundred feet, not moving at all."

Yasaka paused. She licked her dry lips, then continued. "We were trying to figure out what to do next when the *Los Angeles* fired on the *Forrest Sherman*. No warning. At that range, the *Sherman* had no chance. The *Pinckney* was the first to respond — Tubberville ordered counterfire, but the *Los Angeles* managed two more torps before she sank. One hit the *Stratton*, sinking it, and the other damaged the *Truxtun*."

The captain sat back in her chair. She stared off at some invisible thing in her stateroom. "Since then it's been a nonstop process of recovery and aid." Her voice was low, haunted. "I've got a hold full of dead sailors stacked up like goddamn firewood. We've been ordered to burn the bodies — their families don't even get to say good-bye."

She shook her head, blinked rapidly, sat up straight. "One of my recovery teams — in full BSL-4 diving gear, before you ask — found the bodies of Lieutenant Walker and Petty Officer Petrovsky and brought them aboard. Those divers are in containment cells for observation and won't be released unless you give the green light. Walker and Petrovksy are the only two crewmembers recovered from the *Los Angeles*, which means over a hundred bodies are still on the bottom. I pray to God that we haven't missed any."

Clarence wasn't a religious man, but he'd match that prayer. One severed hand, floating to the surface, escaping detection, bobbing toward shore . . . if that happened, all the containment efforts could be for naught.

"We've sent UUVs down to get eyes on the *Los Angeles*," Yasaka said. "They only came close enough to get visual confirmation that she's destroyed. The *Brashear* has two ADS suits onboard. Tomorrow, we're sending a diver down to try to recover the object."

Clarence's stomach churned. Margaret already had to autopsy the infected bodies. If Yasaka's divers succeeded, Margaret would also have to deal with the object that had started this whole slaughterfest.

The captain stood. Clarence rose immediately. Margaret stood as well.

"I have to get back to my crew," Yasaka said. "Doctor Tim Feely is waiting for you in the research facility, belowdecks."

"He's an M.D.?" Margaret asked.

"Degrees in genetics and bioinformatics, actually," the captain said. "But the man sure as hell knows his medicine. He saved a lot of lives in the battle's aftermath. He's a civilian researcher from Special Threats, Doctor Montoya, like you. Hopefully you'll get along, because you're going to be here for a while. I've been told Walker and Petrovsky — and the object, if we find it — are too risky to ship to the mainland."

Margaret nodded. "That's right. Every bit of travel, every exchange, there is a small chance that something will go wrong. A plane crash, a car wreck, a helicopter's emergency landing . . . if even the tiniest speck of the pathogen gets out, it could spread too fast to contain."

Yasaka sighed. "And then we start dropping nukes."

Clarence saw Margaret look down. Her face flushed. He knew she'd taken that the wrong way, that she thought Yasaka was blaming her for Detroit, blaming her just like the rest of the world blamed her.

"Right," Margaret said. "If it gets out, we start dropping nukes again." She looked up, stared back at Captain Yasaka. "It's been five years. If the disease had the ability to swim away from this location, it would have done so by now. This task force is a floating isolation lab. We have to make sure nothing leaves."

Yasaka nodded, slowly and grimly. She knew the stakes. Clarence recognized the look in her eyes — Yasaka didn't think she would ever set foot on land again.

Clarence hoped she was wrong.

If she wasn't, he and Margaret would die right along with her.

CASA DE FEELY

Margaret thought the lower areas of the *Carl Brashear* were much like the top floor — or *deck*, or whatever they called it — a lot of gray paint, a lot of metal, neatly printed warning signs all over the place.

After the meeting with Captain Yasaka, a twentysomething lieutenant had been waiting for her and Clarence. The lieutenant had led them out of Yasaka's stateroom, past the wounded packed into every available space, and had taken them amidships to a door guarded by two young men with rifles. The men carefully checked her ID, Clarence's and even the lieutenant's, someone they clearly already knew.

Very meticulous, very disciplined.

The lieutenant held the door open for them.

"Doctor Feely will take it from here," he said. "Just go down the stairs."

Clarence thanked the man. Margaret said nothing. Clarence went down first. Even on a secure ship, he wanted to make sure it was safe for her.

The steep, switchback flights were more ladder than stairs. The same gray walls, but no wounded here because there was nowhere to put them. Margaret found the descent eerily silent.

The last flight opened up to a small room. Gray walls lined three of its sides. A white airlock door made up the fourth. Through a thick window in the middle of the door, Margaret saw a short man reach out and press an unseen button. She heard his voice through speakers mounted on top of the airlock.

"Welcome-welcome-welcome," he said. "Casa de Feely is happy to have you, Doctor Montoya."

Feely had thick, blond hair that seemed instantly out of place in a military setting, although judging from the way it stuck up in unkempt bunches he clearly hadn't washed it in days. Maybe he had a pair of holey sweatpants just like she did. If not, hers would have fit him: they were the same height, although she probably weighed a bit more than he did. His brand of skinny came from lack of sleep and lack of food rather than exercise. The thing that really caught her attention, though, were his eyes — alert but hollow and bloodshot.

She'd seen eyes like that many times, when looking in the mirror after a forty-eight-hour on-call stint from her doctor days, or during the marathon sessions she and Amos had put in when they'd tried to cure the infection.

Clarence rapped his knuckles against the glass.

"You going to let us in?"

"Absolutely," Feely said. "Just as soon as you take my little prick."

Clarence scowled. "Excuse me?"

Tim pointed down. "At your feet," he said. "Cellulose test. Be a pair of dears, won't you?"

At the base of the door were two small, white boxes, each about the size of a pack of cigarettes. Clarence picked one up and opened it. He looked, then showed the contents to Margaret: sealed alcohol swabs and a metal foil envelope.

She opened the envelope, expecting to see the cheek-swab analysis device she and Amos had invented. Instead, she saw a simple, six-inch plastic tube, white, with three colored LEDs built into it: yellow, green and red.

Margaret held it up. "You don't use the swab test anymore?"

"You've been on vacay for a while, I take it," Tim said. "Yours was susceptible to false-positives if the test subject had recently eaten plant material. Considering the level of concern in this joint, I didn't want some guy getting shot because he had a piece of spinach stuck in his teeth. The one you're holding is a blood test. Spring-loaded needle. Just press it against your fingertip."

Clarence huffed. "Are you serious? We just got here."

Tim nodded. "While I may have the natural good looks of a late-night TV host, I assure you I'm serious. I'm negative and I mean to stay that way."

Smart thinking. Margaret thought of a line she'd read in a book once: *perfect paranoia is perfect awareness*. She liked Tim already.

Margaret opened an alcohol swab, rubbed down the pad of her thumb, then pressed the tube's tip against it. She heard a tiny *click*, felt a sharp poke. She lifted the tube, looked at it: the needle had retracted. A small smear of her blood remained on the unit's flat end.

The yellow light started to flash. She had a brief, intense flash of fear . . . *what if she'd already caught the disease?* What if the light turned red? The yellow flashing slowed. The tiniest mistake could make her change, turn her into a killer, it could—

The green light blinked on.

Margaret let out a long breath she didn't know she'd been holding. She was right back in it again, dead center in the hot zone.

Clarence picked up the second box, repeated Margaret's actions. In seconds, his test flashed green.

The airlock door slid open with a light hiss of air. The blond man stepped out. He all but ignored Clarence in his rush to offer Margaret an overly excited handshake.

"I'm Tim Feely," he said. "Biology, mostly, but also regular-old doctorin' when it's needed."

His hands felt soft.

"I'm Margaret Montoya."

He threw his head back and laughed. A genuine, *I don't care what anybody thinks* laugh. In a bar or on a date, this one would be quite the charmer.

"I *know* who you are," he said. He turned to Clarence. "As if I don't know who she is, right?" He turned back to Margaret, his moves twitchy, like a bird's. "*Everyone* knows. You're the woman who saved the world. Thanks for that, by the way."

He wasn't being sarcastic — he meant it, said it with real admiration. On the Internet and the news talk shows, no one thanked her. But this man had.

Tim bowed with a flourish, gestured toward the airlock. "Come one, come all, to the midnight ball. *Fuck* am I glad to have some help down here."

"Thank you," Margaret said. "That's quite a welcome."

"I try, I try," Tim said. He tilted his head toward Clarence. "Who's the stiff?"

Margaret noticed that Tim was trying — and failing — not to stare at her breasts.

"Agent Clarence Otto," she said. "My husband."

Tim looked Clarence up and down, and not in the same way he'd scoped out Margaret.

"Nice suit," Tim said. "Not many suits in lab work. I don't suppose you can do anything down here that's actually helpful?"

"You never know," Clarence said. "Sometimes shooting people is a useful skill."

Tim rolled his eyes. "Oh, great, an action hero. That will come in handy among all the dead bodies. Come on in. Let me give you the tour. After you, m'lady."

She stepped into the airlock, faced an interior door. Clarence and Tim followed. Margaret glanced around, saw drains in the floor and the familiar nozzles and vents — the airlock doubled as a decontamination chamber.

"The lab complex has a slightly negative internal pressure," Tim said as he shut the exterior door and cycled the airlock. "Anything punches a hole in the wall, outside air comes in, any cooties we might have don't go out. Plus when you need that extra-clean feeling, this baby gives you a little chlorine, a little sodium, a little oxygen . . . all the things a growing boy needs."

Clarence's nose wrinkled in a look of confusion. "What are you talking about?"

"Bleach," Margaret said. "The nozzles spray bleach."

Clarence looked annoyed. Maybe he felt dumb for not getting Tim's reference. Clarence hated to feel dumb.

The internal door opened. After so much battleship gray, Margaret was surprised to see white walls and floors. Framed prints added color, as did potted plants.

"This is the living section," Tim said. "All the comforts of home while floating on an inland sea."

The place looked like the lobby of a small, posh hotel: couches, chairs, a table with a chess set ready for play, a huge, flat-panel monitor up on the wall. Soft overhead lighting made things look, well, *cozy*. It didn't feel like being on a military ship at all.

The decor seemed to bother Clarence. "Nice," he said. "Good thing you don't have to put up with the same conditions as the enlisted men who are taking care of you."

Tim nodded, missing the dig. "Tell me about it, brother," he said. "This place makes the time somewhat passable."

He walked to a picture mounted on a wall. It was an emergency escape diagram, a long, vertical rectangle broken into three squares. The top was labeled *Living Quarters*, the middle *Lab Space*, and the bottom one *Receiving & Containment*.

Margaret noticed that all escape routes led back to the airlock they'd just exited. Just one way in, and one way out.

Tim pointed to the top square.

"That's where we are now," he said. "Living Quarters consists of ten small bedrooms, communal bathrooms, the room we're standing in — I call it the Rumpus Room, by the way, because who *doesn't* want to have a Rumpus Room — a kitchen with our own food supply, and a briefing room that doubles as a whoop-ass movie theater."

He pointed to a green icon on the right side, on top of a line that divided the Living Quarters from the Lab Space below it. The Lab Space square contained three long, vertical rectangles. Margaret recognized the symbols: research trailers, ready-made modules that could be hauled by a semi or shipped as cargo. She felt a shudder — the trailers were probably similar to the Margo-Mobile where her friend Amos Braun had died a horrible death at the skinless hands of Betty Jewel. The rectangle on the left was labeled *Morgue*, the one in the middle *Analysis*, and the one on the right *Misc*.

Tim tapped the green icon. "This is the second airlock, the one that leads to the lab section, another step down in negative pressure. *Keep them pathogens where they belong*, my grandmother always used to say. Suits are in that airlock." He turned to Clarence, smiled. "*Real* suits, my friend, the kind that matter."

Clarence ignored the gibe.

Tim turned back to the map, traced his finger down through still another green icon. "This airlock leads from the lab space to the Receiving and Containment section. That's where they brought in any material recovered by the *Los Angeles*. It's a cool setup, you'll dig it. It's also where we keep any living subjects, which includes the two navy divers who retrieved the bodies of Walker and Petrovsky."

He rubbed his hands together. "So, y'all ready to get to work, or do you want to take a little nap before we go in? Maybe powder your noses? I have a little single malt in the theater, if you want to wet your whistles."

"No," Margaret said quickly. "I don't need a drink. The bodies, are they affected by the black rot?"

That was the thing that made it so difficult to work on infection victims.

The crawlers set off a chain reaction that caused cell death on a massive level. An unrefrigerated body could decompose in just thirty-six hours, becoming little more than a mass of sludge that sloughed off the skeleton.

Tim shrugged. "Walker's body is okay, but Petrovsky is already showing signs of liquefaction. By tomorrow I think he'll be blood pudding."

Like always, a ticking clock held sway over everything.

Margaret nodded. "Then let's get to work."

FAKE FUR

"What the *fuck* is that thing?"

Jeff Brockman had such a way with words, although Cooper had to agree with the sentiment.

The *Mary Ellen Moffett*'s deck lights lit up Steve Stanton's strange machine. The lights wouldn't be needed for long: the sun was only minutes from sliding up on the horizon, its glow already turning the low-hanging clouds a pinkish-orange. Five-foot swells continued to rock the boat, but at least the wind had finally died down. When the sun did rise, Cooper hoped the temperature might climb into the double digits.

Breath frosting from their mouths, Cooper, Jeff, José, Steve and Steve's buddy Bo Pan stood in a loose circle, staring down at the cargo they'd hauled out to the middle of Lake Michigan.

When Steve Stanton had spoken of his ROV, Cooper assumed he knew what to expect: a boxy metal frame, about six feet wide and tall, maybe ten feet long, yellow ballast tanks on top, a couple of turbines in the back and a pair of robotic arms in the front. Throw in a camera suite and a long-ass cable, and you were in business.

But *this*?

For starters, it wasn't yellow. It was covered in elephant-gray material studded with little points, kind of like acoustic foam. Ten feet long, sure, but there was nothing boxy about this contraption. The ROV's front end came to a streamlined point. From there, it flared wide with the outline of a fish before tapering down again to a pair of flippers in the rear, like those of a Cape fur seal. On each side was a wide fin, like that of a penguin.

Jeff stared down at it. He crossed his arms, frowned.

"It's fuzzy," he said. He looked at Stanton. "You made an ROV with fur?"

"It's an antiturbulence material," Steve said. "Helps adjust the water flow for greater speed. Once it gets wet it looks very different."

Cooper reached down and gently poked one of the furry points with a finger — felt like a stiff foam.

Steve shot out a panicked hand. "Please don't touch!"

Cooper stood, held up both hands, palms out. "Wow, sorry."

The kid blinked, looked around, saw that everyone was staring at him. He forced a smile.

"The material is just delicate is all," he said. "My bad, I should have asked everyone not to touch it earlier."

Cooper felt Jeff glaring at him. Jeff had that suspicious expression on his face again — the ROV was beyond state of the art, something altogether new, and that bothered him. Jeff subtly held up his hand, thumb rubbing against his fingertips: *that thing looks like big money.*

Cooper nodded. Of course Steve had money; he was part of some lawyer's class-action lawsuit. Millions of dollars on the line. Cooper felt bad for the people who now ran Delta Airlines; this was going to wind up being one high-toned bitch of a lawsuit.

José craned his head around, looked at the ROV from all sides.

"Hey, Jefe Steve," he said. "Where do you connect the control cable?" José insisted on calling everyone *jefe*, Spanish for *boss*. He looked around the deck, as if he suddenly realized he was missing something. "And where *is* the cable? Is that in the other box?"

He started toward the smaller of Steve's two boxes, the one still strapped to the deck.

"Please don't touch that one, either," Steve said. Again, the words were rushed, nearly panicky.

Jeff glared. Cooper felt uncomfortable — the customer was acting very strange.

Steve shook his head, forced another smile. "There isn't a cable. The *Platypus* is remote controlled to some extent, but mostly autonomous."

Autonomous? An *unmanned underwater vehicle*; a robot. Cooper winced: that meant it cost exponentially more. He looked at Jeff, who was already shaking his head, lips pressed together in held-back anger.

"You told us you had an ROV," Jeff said. "Now you're telling us this is a UUV?"

Steve's eyes widened. He glanced over to Bo Pan, just for the briefest second, but Bo Pan kept staring at the deck.

Cooper was losing his patience. Jeff could still blow this job if he kept being difficult.

"Jeff, it's all good," Cooper said. "UUV, ROV, ABC, whatever, let's just get it in the water, okay?"

Jeff looked at Cooper, looked at the machine. He nodded.

"Yeah, okay," he said quietly. Then, his booming *I'm the boss* voice returned. "Cooper, man the crane. José, get ready to get wet. Mister Stanton, if you'll point out the right way for us to hook up your machine so we don't break it, we'll get her in the drink and you can do your thing."

Everyone moved into action. Everyone except for Bo Pan. As Cooper headed to the *Mary Ellen*'s crane, he noticed Bo Pan watching Jeff, then watching José. Then, his eyes locked with Cooper's.

For just a moment, Bo Pan didn't look like the old man who had come aboard. His eyes were hard, cold . . . *dangerous*. Then the expression vanished — he looked out to the water, hawked a huge loogie and spat it over the side.

Just some old dude along for the ride. Right?

Cooper felt a shiver that wasn't from the cold. He shook off the sensation, then got to work.

KILLER MATH FOR $200

Testing units weren't the only thing that had changed in the last five years.

Margaret stood in the second airlock with Tim and Clarence. The three of them wore BSL-4 suits.

At first, the suit had seemed familiar. Like those she'd worn before, it was made of airtight Tyvek, a synthetic material. A heavy-gauge seal secured the oversized helmet onto the suit, and the helmet itself had a tall, wide, clear, curved visor that gave her full range of vision.

The visor itself, however, was something out of a movie.

"This is crazy," she said. "So much information."

"You'll get used to it," Tim said. "Before you know it, it'll be second nature."

She looked at him. She could see him through her visor, but her eyes also tried to register the information playing on the *inside* of it — the visor was a full-on heads-up display, scrolling data about the airlock and a medical report about the two divers in observation. She was wearing a computer screen in front of her face.

"My eyes are trying to focus on two things at once," she said. "It's giving me a headache. How do I just get rid of it for now?"

"Just reach up and grab it," Tim said. "Then swipe it to the side."

She reached up to grab something that wasn't there, and she felt ridiculous doing it, but when her hand "closed" on the display window of airlock information, that window trembled slightly, indicating she had it. She moved her hand to the right, out of her range of vision, and let go. The window was gone. She repeated the process for the medical report.

"Wow," she said. "That's easy."

Tim nodded. "I'll walk you through menu selection in a little bit. Any data we have in the system, you can call it up right in front of you. There's even an all eye-track mode, so if you've got your hands full, you can still get whatever you need. A blink-pattern lets you record video, another lets you send it my way. You can even send me dirty movies, if said movies have some scientific importance."

How nice: even in the middle of nowhere with a scientist who clearly respected her, Margaret still got harassed. She decided to chalk it up to an inappropriate sense of humor. What choice did she have, really? Tim would be working at her side for the indefinite future. She had dealt with shit like that all of her professional life. If he did more of the same, she'd say something, but for now she wanted all of their focus on the problem at hand. She let it go — Clarence, though, did not.

"Nice comment, Feely," Clarence said. "You know I'm standing right here, yeah?"

"Like I could miss it," Tim said. "Okay, time to see the good stuff."

He opened the internal airlock door and they stepped out. In here, it was even harder to remember she was inside a ship.

On her right, she saw the three long, modular lab trailers. They were lined up length-wise, side by side. Sealed corridors connected them, both on the near side and on their far ends. At the end closest to her, another trailer ran horizontally, atop and across all three.

Tim pointed to the three lower trailers, calling out names as he did. "Closest to us is the miscellaneous lab, where you've got a little bit of everything. The one in the middle is for tissue, chemical and metallurgical analysis. That beauty on the end is the morgue — what I lovingly call the *hurt locker*. That's where the bodies of Candice Walker and Charlie Petrovsky are stored.

"Walker was almost dead when they brought her in. It was too late to help her. I was able to isolate crawlers from her, though, and some of them are still alive. Petrovsky's are all dead, but I have samples isolated for you just the same."

He pointed to the trailer lying crosswise atop the other three. "That's a control room. From there, you can see down into the other three. The control room also has a mini airlock and its own wee little bathroom, so if Secret Agent Man wants to stay involved but take off his suit, he can do that in there. Shall we start with the bodies?"

Three trailers, each capable of comfortably supporting four or five people working simultaneously, and yet Tim was the only one here. And along the same lines, the facility had ten bedrooms — nine of which had been empty before Margaret and Clarence had arrived.

"Doctor Feely," she said, "where is the rest of the staff?"

Tim flung his gloved hands up in annoyance. "They're all pursuing their disciplines at other facilities or at the research base on Black Manitou Island. When they first brought me in, I was part of a ten-person staff. Year after year, as the navy didn't find anything significant, the rest of the staff found ways to conduct their research off the ship. But believe it or not, one guy can do the majority of the grunt work down here. Most of the equipment is automated, and all of it is the best money can buy."

"You're still here," she said to Tim. "Why aren't you on Black Manitou?"

His bloodshot eyes narrowed. He looked at the wall. "I worked there a few years ago when it was a civilian biotech facility, before DST took it over. I'm not allowed to talk about what we were working on, other than that it involved technologies for rapid growth. There were some . . . accidents." He gave his head a little shake. "Anyway, I don't ever want to go back. It's safer here."

Safer *here*, on a task force dedicated to working with a vector that had the potential to wipe out the human race. Margaret wondered just what kind of *accidents* Tim was talking about. Whatever the reason, he had chosen to stay down here, mostly alone. He was a shut-in, just like she was.

"What have you worked on all that time?"

"Lots of stuff," Tim said. "My tan, mostly. Oh, and trying to engineer a new strain of yeast, *Saccharomyces feely*, to secrete the infection's self-destruct catalyst so we'd have a weapon if the disease ever struck again."

"*Saccharomyces feely*," Margaret said. "Naming it after yourself?"

Tim grinned. "Don't hate the player, girl . . . hate the game."

This one was quite full of himself.

Regardless of what he named the strain, it was a worthwhile pursuit. When a victim died, the infection triggered two chemical chain reactions that combined to leave scientists with nothing to study.

The first reaction: uncontrolled apoptosis. Apoptosis was the normal process of cell destruction. When a cell has damage to the DNA or other areas, that cell, in effect, commits suicide, removing itself from the organism. The infection modified that process so it didn't shut off — a cell swelled and burst, spreading the chain reaction to the cells around it, which then swelled and burst, and so on. Within a day or two, a corpse became little more than black sludge dripping off a skeleton.

The second chain reaction had the same effect on the infection's cellulose structures. Instead of apoptosis, infection's cells produced a cellulase. Cellulase dissolved cellulose, the cell swelled and burst, spreading the cellulase catalyst to surrounding cells, and so on.

The Orbital had hijacked human systems; Tim was trying to turn the tables and do the same to the Orbital's creations.

"Speaking of *grunts*," Clarence said, appearing to refer to Tim's comment about *grunt work* but intending it as a slap-back at Margaret's insult, "What does *Saccharomyces* mean?"

"Yeast," Margaret said. She felt her face heat with shame. No matter how bad she and Clarence fought, there was no valid excuse to insinuate he wasn't smart, that his work didn't matter. When she was fully rational, she knew that. Problem was, that man made her irrational far more often than she cared to admit.

She tried to shake it off, turned to face Tim. "Yeast, that's smart. Modify their germline DNA so that subsequent generations produce that cellulase catalyst, and you've got an endless supply of something that kills the infection. Any luck?"

Tim shook his head. "Close, but no cigar. I was able to get the yeast to produce the catalyst, but that catalyst is toxic to the yeast as well. The engineered yeast die before they can reproduce, so we don't even get a second generation, let alone the massive colonies needed to secrete the amount of catalyst we'd need."

Clarence fidgeted in his bulky suit, pulling at the blue material, trying to make it settle on him better.

"So, Doctor Feely, it's just you down here," he said. "Captain Yasaka mentioned you also helped with the wounded. How much sleep have you had?"

Tim frowned, made a show of counting on his gloved fingers. "Let's see, carry the one, divide by four, and . . . Alex, the question is, *what is zero?*"

That didn't surprise Margaret, not with the number of wounded up above.

"No sleep," Clarence said. "You on drugs or something?"

"If by *drugs* you mean Adderall, Deprenyl and/or Sudafed — mostly *and*, though — then yes, I am on drugs."

Margaret saw Clarence taking a deep, disapproving breath. She put her gloved hand on his arm.

"Clarence, relax," she said. "Any doctor pulling a triple shift might do the same."

He turned to her, disbelieving. "Have you?"

"More times than I can count. I had a life before I met you, you know. And apparently a life *after*."

If he wanted to make snide comments, she could do the same. The words caught him off guard, stung him. They also piqued Tim's interest. Margaret wanted to kick herself for the slipup, for exposing personal problems at a time like this. She had to stay on point.

Tim grinned at Margaret. "Come on, it's the scheduled time to give my little prick to the two divers. After that, we can touch bodies. Dead bodies, that is."

Clarence sighed again, and Margaret couldn't blame him.

GOD'S CHOSEN

Chief Petty Officer Orin Nagy had always dreamed of serving in the navy. The big ships, seeing the world on Uncle Sam's dime, the service, the career — he had wanted all these things.

He hadn't wanted to murder people, though.

Until now.

Now, he wanted to murder a *lot* of people. Ever single person he saw, in fact.

The biosafety suit made him sweat. It also bounced his own voice back to him when he talked, made him sound strange.

"Lattimer, John J.," he called out, reading from the list on the clipboard as he'd been instructed to do. "Cellulose test."

Four wounded men were lying on the floor in the corner of the bunk room. They were too wounded to do work, but less wounded than the men who occupied the actual bunks. Second-degree burns covered one man's arm. Another sailor had a red-spotted bandage wrapped around his head, something straight out of a shitty war movie.

Orin wanted to shoot them. Stab them. Maybe stomp down on their throats and watch them suffocate to death. But for now, he had to keep up appearances.

"Lattimer, John J.," he said again. "Which one of you is Lattimer, John J.?"

The one with the head bandage raised his hand.

Orin pulled a cellulose testing kit out of the bag slung over his shoulder, handed it over. Orin knew he wasn't human anymore, but he could still appreciate the irony that *he* was one of the sailors testing people to see if they were infected.

His turn was coming soon enough. He'd managed to dodge his last test, when he'd already realized God had chosen him. Orin had pretended to fall, jabbed the end of his testing stick into a sleeping man. It worked: his test administrator had been distracted, had been counting down names on the list, looking for the next testee. If it had been business as usual aboard the

Brashear, the administrator would have been eyes-on, carefully watching the results. But it wasn't business as usual; God had seen to it to place *hundreds* of extra men onboard, many severely wounded, creating confusion, making people lose focus.

Still, Orin knew that he probably wouldn't be able to fake his way through the next test. They, the *humans*, they would find out about him, and they would try to kill him. That test was scheduled in two hours.

In thirty minutes, his shift in the suit was up.

That would give him ninety minutes to touch as many people as he could, to spread the gift that he'd been given.

Then, maybe, he could answer that burning, churning need in his chest. He could finally *kill*.

TESTY-TESTY

The final airlock cycled. Clarence stepped out first, took in a large area hemmed in by the now-familiar white walls. In front of him were two rows of high-ceilinged, ten-by-ten glass cells stretching to the back of the room.

A man stood in each of the two closest cells: a black man on the left, a white man on the right, both wearing gray hospital gowns. They were just there to be observed, but that didn't make it any less of a prison. Both men seemed fit and healthy, arms lined with lean muscle.

Each cell had a small steel desk, a steel chair beneath it, and a plastic-covered mattress that lay on top of a stainless steel bed. A tablet computer sat on each desk — the divers' entertainment and reading material, perhaps. Other than that there was nothing, save for a steel toilet that looked to be a raised hole without plumbing.

In a third cell, behind that of the white man, Clarence saw an Asian man lying motionless on the bed. Medical equipment surrounded him, a techno-logical monster clutching at him with wires and sensors, looking inside him through tubes up his nose and IVs in his arms.

Through their clear cell walls, the two standing men watched Clarence, Margaret and Tim. The men looked afraid. They watched. They waited.

To Clarence's right, past the line of glass cages, was an open space ringed with gleaming steel tables, clamps, saws, robotic arms . . . various equipment to prepare material brought up from the lake bottom, he assumed. The reason for the prep area was clear: to receive material from yet another airlock, this one the biggest he had ever seen. It was the width of a two-car garage. Nozzles and vents lined the ceiling; everything in this room here could be sprayed down, disinfected in a rainstorm of bleach.

Margaret walked to the aisle that ran between the two rows of cells. The cell doors opened onto that aisle — *if* they would ever be opened, that was. Clarence knew those men might very well die in those cells. A flat-panel monitor was mounted at the left side of each cell door. On those monitors,

Clarence saw the familiar spikes of an EKG, various other numbers revealing the physical state of the men inside.

How much did these men know? Did they truly understand why they were being held?

"They look okay," Clarence said.

"They do," Tim said. "They're tested every three hours, all negatives so far. The rest of the ship is tested every six hours. Including me. And, now, both of you."

He pointed to the cell with the prone man. "That fellow, on the other hand, is unfortunately brain-dead. Ensign Eric Edmund. Couldn't exactly call him *okay*."

Margaret stepped into the aisle between cells. "Was Edmund also a diver?"

"No," Tim said. "Injured in the battle. He's a gift from Captain Yasaka, in case I need a living subject for my yeast experimentation."

Clarence felt his anger flare up. He spun to face Tim.

"*Experiment?* Brain-dead or not, that's a serviceman in there, not a *gift*."

Tim didn't bother to hide a look of contempt. "Agent Otto, Ensign Edmund isn't coming back. If he wasn't in that cell, he'd have already been put in the incinerator along with the other dead bodies. Machines are the only thing keeping him alive."

"Alive for your research," Clarence said. "Which you already told us was a failure."

Tim rolled his eyes. "How about you use that oversized melon of yours for something other than a hat rack? We have no idea what we'll need. If we have to experiment, it's Edmund or some other sailor, maybe one who's *not* brain-dead."

"What's the matter, Feely? Don't have the balls to experiment on yourself?"

Feely shrugged. "I didn't enlist, big fella. If you're dumb enough to sign your life over to Uncle Sam, then Uncle Sam gets to decide what happens to you."

Clarence moved closer, stared down at the smaller man. "I was *dumb enough* to enlist, you asshole."

He'd assumed his size would intimidate Feely, that his position with the DST might make Tim rethink his opinion of servicemen — but Tim just smiled an arrogant smile.

"You were a soldier? And here I was thinking you had a particle physics degree in your pants — maybe you're just glad to see me."

"*Enough*," Margaret said, her words loud enough to rattle the speakers in Clarence's helmet. He turned, looked at her, and felt instantly foolish — this was no time to let someone like Feely get a rise out of him.

Margaret glared at them both. "If you two want to have a pissing contest, save it for later. Doctor Feely, if it weren't for Agent Otto, you wouldn't be here. I didn't save the world all by myself, you know. Give him the respect he deserves."

Clarence had a brief moment to feel justified, to feel that Margaret was backing him up, before she turned her anger on him.

"And you, Clarence, *wake up* — before this is over, we might have to do far worse things than experiment on a man who's already gone. Now, if the two of you are done posturing, can we get to work?"

Clarence's anger shifted instantly into embarrassment. He nodded.

"Sorry," Tim said. "From now on, I'll be sugar and spice and everything nice."

Feely was still being a smart-ass, but Clarence thought he heard a hint of sincerity in there.

Margaret reached out, tapped at the left-hand cell's panel. "They've been in here for" — she tapped again — "thirty-eight hours."

"Correct," Tim said. "Your notes described an incubation period of between twenty-four and forty-eight hours before infected victims start to show symptoms. So if we're lucky, these men are in there another two days, just to be sure."

The black diver spoke. "I find your definition of *luck* somewhat wanting, Doctor Feely."

The white diver rested his forehead against the inside of his cell wall. "Oh, man . . . two more days?"

Tim walked back to the airlock door and opened a cabinet mounted just to its left. He pulled out two cellulose test boxes, then returned to the black diver's cell.

"Master Diver Kevin Cantrell, meet Doctor Montoya and Agent Otto," Tim said. "How about you show them our fun little drama called *it puts the lotion in the basket*."

Tim placed the box in a small, rotating airlock mounted in the clear door, then moved his hands in midair. It took Clarence a second to remember Tim was using his suit's HUD to control things. The airlock turned. Cantrell opened the white box, pulled out the foil envelope inside.

He stared at it like it was a living thing, something pretending to be still until it was ready to bite.

"Your title is wrong," Cantrell said. "I prefer *The Merchant of Venice*."

"Venice," Tim said. "What's that got to do with anything?"

Margaret answered. "It's Shakespeare — *If you prick us, do we not bleed?*"

Cantrell glanced at her, then at the testing unit, then looked at her again, stared hard.

"Lady, are you . . . are you here to kill me?"

A direct question, but it didn't make sense. Clarence noticed a slight gleam on Cantrell's forehead. He was perspiring a little . . . did he have a fever?

Margaret answered in a calm, measured voice. "Mister Cantrell, why do you think I want to kill you?"

Clarence understood: she thought Cantrell might be showing signs of paranoia, one of the main symptoms of infection.

Cantrell blinked rapidly, sniffed. He forced a smile, gestured to the walls around him.

"I'm a guinea pig, ma'am," he said. "It's a logical question."

Before Margaret could ask another question, Cantrell removed the white plastic tube, pressed it against the tip of his right pointer finger. The yellow light started flashing immediately.

Clarence watched, tension pulling his body forward, making his hand itch to draw his weapon — a weapon he didn't have. He felt naked. He needed to get a rig that would let him wear a holster over the suit. Was Cantrell's light about to turn red? Was a piece of thick glass all that separated Margaret from one of the infected?

The flashing yellow slowed, then stopped and blinked out.

The green light turned on.

Clarence's body relaxed slightly, a tight spring uncoiling halfway. Maybe these guys still had a chance.

Cantrell carried his test — box and envelope and all — to his toilet. He tossed everything down the open hole. Clarence heard a soft *whump:* an incinerator flaring to life.

The other diver slapped on the glass of his cell, making Margaret jump.

"Ma'am, you got to get me out of here," he said to her. "We're fine, the tests keep coming up negative, we're *fine*."

It took Tim only two steps to cross the aisle. He put the other box in the airlock, rotated it through.

"And this fine gentleman is Diego Clark," Tim said. "Clark, how about you quit with the whining and make with the pricking?"

Clark looked at the test box like it was poisonous. He then looked up at the cluster of nozzles mounted in his cell's high ceiling. Some of the nozzles were stainless steel, others were brass. The brass nozzles reminded Clarence of something, but he couldn't place what. The stainless steel ones he recognized, as he'd seen them in the MargoMobile — they were for knockout gas, in case Tim and Margaret had to go in and work on a dangerous infection victim.

Clark slapped the glass again. "Let me *out*! We were just doing our jobs, we shouldn't be locked up! This is horseshit! Where's my CO? Where's my lawyer?"

"Less talky-talky," Tim said, "more testy-testy."

Clark opened the box and removed the foil envelope, then threw the box down and stomped on it.

"When I get out of here, Feely," he said, "I'm going to shove one of these straight up your ass."

"As long as you buy me dinner first," Tim said. "Now do the damn test."

Clark again looked up to the ceiling, then shook his head.

"Ain't gonna burn *me*," he said.

Burn. That triggered Clarence's memory. He again looked up at the cell ceiling, and understood why the brass nozzle seemed familiar: it looked like a flamethrower. Clark was right to be afraid — his cage could be instantly turned into a fire-filled oven that would burn him alive.

Tim sighed, clearly bored with the drama. He slowly raised a finger toward the flat-panel controls of Clark's cell.

"You're getting tested," Tim said. "You can either be conscious for it, or I can knock you out and give it to you myself. Your choice."

Clark instantly shook his head. Whatever Tim used as knockout gas, it clearly had unpleasant side effects. Clark tore the foil envelope open, took the time to use the alcohol swab — which Cantrell hadn't bothered with, Clarence realized — then stabbed the end into his finger.

The yellow light flashed faster, then slowed.

Then, stopped.

The red light came on.

No one said a word. Clarence stared, stunned into thoughtlessness. The man had looked fine.

Cantrell broke the silence. "'If you poison us,'" he said quietly, "'do we not die?'"

Clark raised the testing kit to eye level, his wide stare locked on the steady, red light.

Margaret shook her head. "No," she said. "No . . . we *won*."

Tim finally reacted. He moved his hands in front of his face, accessing something on his HUD.

"Clark, Diego L., tested positive for cellulose," he said. "Administering anesthesia."

He tapped the empty air. Something up above beeped. Clark looked up, eyes wide, body shaking.

"Don't light me up, man," he said, "don't . . . light . . ."

He sagged to the floor. He didn't move.

RUNNING DRUGS

"Hey, Jefe Cooper."

José spoke quietly, but Cooper heard the words loud and clear. He tried to ignore them. He was sleeping, after all.

"Hey, Jefe Cooper."

Cooper lifted his head, opened his eyes. Smiling José was kneeling next to the bed. He was close, almost leaning over Cooper, but the tiny half-stateroom didn't leave much of an option; it was already too cramped for just one person, let alone a second.

José offered a steaming cup of coffee. "Ah, you're awake," he said, as if it was a lucky coincidence.

"I am now," Cooper said. "And I don't want to be. I haven't slept all night, man. Is everything okay?"

José shrugged. "Probably. But . . . can I show you something?"

Cooper flopped his face back into the pillow. "Does it involve me getting up?"

José laughed, but it seemed forced. "Why, is there something of mine you want to see while you're lying in bed?"

"Good point. Aren't you supposed to be on the bridge?"

"I am," José said. "But I think this is really important."

Cooper sat up quickly. "Is Jeff . . ."

His voice trailed off. He was about to ask if Jeff had the helm, but the loud snoring from the other side of a thin wall told him Jeff was out cold. When they'd bought the *Mary Ellen*, Jeff had built a wall dividing the ten-by-ten captain's stateroom into two equal five-by-ten rooms. He'd put in another door, even installed a second sink so they would each have one. Partners, fifty-fifty all the way, as they'd been since childhood. While it gave Cooper the luxury of a small amount of privacy, it also meant he heard everything that went on in Jeff's stateroom. What Jeff did more than anything else in there was snore. Loudly.

Cooper took the cup of coffee. "You left the bridge unattended. This better be fucking important, dude."

José nodded quickly, placatingly. "Yes, Jefe Cooper, I know. Maybe it's nothing. Come up to the bridge, okay? And . . . and don't wake up Jefe Jeff, yet, okay?"

"Why?"

José shrugged. "I need the money from this job. If I don't get it, my family will get kicked out of our house."

That meant the problem had something to do with Stanton. Jeff seemed one more incident away from insisting on turning back, killing the contract and dumping Stanton and Bo Pan back on shore. José needed the money — so did Cooper, so did Jeff.

"Okay," Cooper said. "But you do know how ridiculous *Jefe Jeff* sounds, right?"

José smiled, shrugged. He slid out of the stateroom and into the corridor.

Cooper took a sip of the coffee, set the mug on his half-desk. He stood, slid his feet into his shoes. He was already dressed — in bad weather, you had to be ready to move quick.

He left the stateroom, stopped in front of his best friend's door. It felt wrong to not wake Jeff up, involve him in this, but Jeff just wasn't thinking clearly. Cooper would handle it. If it turned out to be anything important, he'd wake Jeff right away.

Cooper headed up. José was waiting for him on the *Mary Ellen*'s small bridge. Cooper stepped inside, shut the door behind him. The bridge had only a little more room than his stateroom; on the *Mary Ellen*, everything was nice and cozy.

"Okay, what's this about?"

"Jefe Stanton's robot ship," José said. "Something you need to see from when it launched."

He turned to the sonar unit and started to call up a recording.

"You woke me up to show me sonar of the customer's ROV?"

"UUV," José corrected.

"Right, UUV, whatever."

Jose finished loading the recording. He played it. Cooper leaned in to look at the sonar readout, and as he did, he grew angry.

The *Platypus* was ten feet long, not quite two feet wide at its widest point, a long, thick eel of a machine with flippers at the end and the sides. It was *artificial* — metal and carbon fiber, materials that bounced back sonar loud and strong. The image on the sonar recording didn't look artificial at all.

"Goddamit, José, that's a sonar signature from a fucking *fish*. This is what I get for letting an illegal Filipino play with expensive equipment."

"Putang ina mo," José said.

"What's that mean?"

"It means you have pretty eyes, Jefe Cooper."

"I'm quite certain that's *not* what it means," Cooper said. "Just because you don't know how to work the equipment doesn't mean you can insult me."

"And calling me an *illegal* isn't an insult? I'm an undocumented worker."

José paused the playback. His finger reached out, rested below the screen's time readout. Cooper saw it, made the connection — the recording was from the time of that morning's launch.

Cooper leaned in. "What the hell?"

"This is when the *Platypus* was right next to the boat," Jose said. "Watch as it starts to move away . . ."

He hit "play." The sonar signal faded, then vanished. Cooper looked at the time readout: only ten seconds had passed.

"That can't be right," he said. "Ten seconds after it started moving, it wasn't even thirty feet away from us."

At a distance of thirty feet, something artificial the size of the *Platypus* should have been a bright white signal.

José paused the playback. He looked at Cooper. For once, the man wasn't smiling.

"That's not just *expensive* equipment, Jefe Cooper. That's *stealth*. Military-grade, maybe. Is Stanton running drugs or something? What if the Coast Guard comes out here?"

Cooper finally understood José's concern.

"Steve Stanton is not running drugs," Cooper said. "We won't get busted by the Coasties. You won't get deported. You're fine."

José looked at the paused recording. He hit "play" and again let it run. It showed nothing. He looked up at Cooper again.

"And no gang war? No one will shoot at us?"

"No gang war," Cooper said. "We're safe. I promise. Just . . ." Cooper couldn't help looking at the screen again, noting that the time stamp was thirty seconds into the *Platypus* launch — the thing should have still been kicking back sonar like mad. "You were right to tell only me. Jeff will just get all fired up, and it's nothing. Between us, right?"

José nodded, raised his hands in a gesture that said, *You told me what I needed to hear.*

"Okay, Jefe Cooper. Sorry to wake you up." He stood and walked to the door.

"No problem," Cooper said. "You go on, get some sleep. I've got the helm."

José left.

Cooper sat, feeling mixed emotions.

Stealth. Military-grade.

If Jeff found out . . .

Cooper shook his head. Jeff wouldn't find out. So the customer had expensive equipment, *crazy* expensive, so what? That wasn't Cooper's business, and it wasn't Jeff's business, either. They were getting paid like kings to facilitate Steve Stanton's search for the Flying Dutchman of the Great Lakes.

Jeff's instincts and decisions had almost put the business under. It was Cooper's turn to call the shots. A few more days, a week at the most, and this would be over.

THE BODIES

"Margo," Clarence said, "you okay?"

Margaret heard his voice through the speakers in her wide helmet, but also from outside the suit. Clarence was right behind her, in a BSL-4 rig of his own.

She'd tuned out, got lost in her memories. *Amos . . . Dew . . . Betty Jewell . . . Chelsea . . . Perry.* The mind-ripping horror of it all. No, she wasn't okay. Not even close.

"I'm fine," she said. "Just give me a minute."

She hadn't been on the *Carl Brashear* for more than a few hours, and there was already one person infected. The divers had done something wrong, exposed themselves somehow.

Margaret was already far behind in the race.

To center herself, she took a long look at the trailer Tim called the *hurt locker*. The place had been designed with volume in mind. Ten metal tables were lined up in parallel, running down the trailer's length. Each table had its own rack of analysis equipment. Maybe the engineers assumed the *Carl Brashear* would have a full complement of scientists when the shit hit the fan.

She reached up, checked the hose connected to her helmet: secure, no problems. When moving from trailer to trailer, the suits used internal air supplies. For working in one area, however, ceiling-mounted hoses provided breathable air.

Two of the metal tables held corpses of Candice Walker and Charlie Petrovsky. Tim was already working on Petrovsky, taking samples from all over his body.

Margaret couldn't put it off any longer: she had to get to work, figure out what had happened. One of those bodies — or both — had infected Diego Clark.

"Clarence, I need you to talk to Cantrell," she said. "Clark's diving gear was BSL-4 rated. We have to figure out how he got infected."

"I can do that," Clarence said. "I've read his report, seems like everything was solid."

She'd also read the report, hadn't seen any mistakes. "Maybe he missed something. Maybe the suits malfunctioned, somehow."

"Maybe," Clarence said. "I'll find out. Do you need anything before I go talk to him?"

She shook her head. From her helmet's speakers, she could hear him breathing. He was there with her, like he always was, like he had been since he'd been assigned to her when all of this began nearly six years earlier. What would life be like without him? And how had she managed to let a man like him slip away?

Margaret had to get her head in the game. She couldn't rely on Clarence to be her crutch anymore.

"I'm fine," she said. "Just go, Clarence. Talk to Cantrell."

She walked toward the bodies.

Candice Walker had suffered horribly, but Charlie Petrovsky had it even worse. His entrails were mostly missing, as was his left hip and the leg that would have been attached to it. His left arm looked fine, but his right was a ribbon of flesh made bumpy by the broken bits of bone beneath.

The rapid decomposition had started in, giving his skin a gray pallor. Large black spots dotted his torn flesh. Smaller black spots peppered his body — Tim was right, within the next twenty-four hours that unstoppable chain reaction would turn Petrovsky into a pitted skeleton and a puddle of black slime streaked with gossamer threads of green mold.

Candice Walker's naked body had yet to show the black rot. She had died later than Petrovsky, obviously, but her rapid decomposition would soon start to show. Margaret noticed some small pustules on Walker's left thigh, right breast and right shoulder.

Margaret had seen similar pustules on Carmen Sanchez, the Detroit police officer whom she had studied as the infection raged through his body. The pustules were likely full of crawlers, modified so they could be carried away on the wind when the skin broke open. If the crawlers landed on a host, they would burrow under the skin and start modifying stem cells to produce more of their kind.

Stripped of her uniform, Walker looked barely out of her teens. She could have been a giggly college freshman killed in a spring break drunk-driving accident. Could have been, except for the sawed-off arm.

Margaret closed her eyes as a memory flared up, powerful and hot and so real it felt like it had happened only moments earlier.

Amos . . . his gloved hands grabbing at his throat but unable to reach it because of the Tyvek suit, blood trickling from a hole in that suit and also jetting against the inside of his visor, pulsing from a severed artery . . . Amos falling as Betty Jewel rose up from her examination table, pulling at the cuff that kept her there until her skin sloughed off and her bloody hand slid free . . .

"Doctor Montoya," Tim said. "You okay?"

Margaret opened her eyes. Tim was looking at her, a scalpel in one gloved hand, a petri dish in the other.

"Sorry," she said. "I'm fine."

"And I'm a six-five power forward for the Knicks. Call me Baron Dunk-O-Lition."

Margaret stared at the man for a moment, then laughed. As far as laughs went, it was a small, pathetic thing. *Half* a laugh, really — but it was a sound she hadn't made in years.

"You're a funny guy, Baron," she said. "You told me you collected live crawlers?"

"Correctamundo," Tim said. "From Walker. I didn't have much time when the bodies were brought in here. There were too many wounded that needed my help. But I isolated fifty crawlers from her, four of which are still alive."

Margaret was impressed; in a crisis situation, with sailors dying up above, Tim had done what was needed with the dead before he tended to the living. Maybe he did say inappropriate things, but in crunch-time this man seemed to excel.

"Let's do Petrovsky first," she said. "We'll start with the brain."

"Sounds good. I'll get the Stryker. Let's crack some skulls."

AWAKENING

Motion.

Vibrations from a bone saw, the regular probing of fingers and hands, these things resonated through the body.

These vibrations, these *movements*, triggered an ingrained, automatic response inside the cyst-encased neutrophils. They turned *on*. They secreted a new chemical, one that dissolved the shells protecting them against the forces of decomposition.

Newly exposed to the apoptosis chemicals, the neutrophils didn't have much time. Some of them didn't make it: caught in blobs of caustic rot, they died almost immediately. Others pushed up, pushed out, crawling through Charlie's muscle, through his subcutaneous layer, through his dermis, then his epidermis and finally gathered just beneath the squamous epithelium — the skin's outermost layer.

There they would wait, wait until they felt the pressure of another surface coming into contact.

When that happened, the neutrophils would cling to that new surface.

Then they would simply follow their programming, and do what they were made to do.

THE FULL RIDE

Clarence hated the suit. It made him feel clumsy, awkward. He'd strapped a holster to the outside of his thigh, but if things went south he wasn't even sure if his gloved fingers could fit through his weapon's trigger guard. Far more significant, though, was the fact that he might be just one tiny rip away from suffering the same fate as Diego Clark.

He hated the suit, true, but the heads-up display thing was amazing. He had Cantrell's service record right in front of him, at the left edge of his vision. All he had to do was turn his head and read.

Clarence exited the airlock and walked to Clark's cell. He stood in front of the clear door, staring in.

The mattress had been removed. Incinerated, probably. Clark lay on his back on the bed's metal surface. Metal-mesh straps across his chest, hips and thighs held him tight to the bed's metal surface, as did thick restraints around his wrists and ankles. All that was overkill at the moment — an IV ran into Clark's right arm, a steady flow of drugs keeping him unconscious.

A voice from behind: "Makes me want to enlist all over again."

Clarence turned to look at Kevin Cantrell. He was leaning against the wall of his cage, forearm and forehead pressed against the glass. The front of his clear cell looked directly into the front of Clark's.

"Look at that poor bastard," Cantrell said. "Years of service, and he'll die horribly." The diver tilted his head to the right, toward Edmund, who lay in his bed and would never wake again.

"Or him," Cantrell said. "Good to know that the fucking navy can heap disgrace upon misery and use our bodies like we're laboratory mice. I mean, doesn't all this just make you want to sign up?"

"Already did," Clarence said.

Cantrell raised his eyebrows, nodded. "Oh, that's right, your little spat with Doc Feely. You enlisted. You're one of *us*, right? Let me guess . . . Marines?"

"Rangers," Clarence said. "Then Special Forces. Got shot at plenty, but no one strapped me to a table. I need to talk to you."

Cantrell shrugged. "It's not like my calendar is all that full at the moment."

The man seemed different than he had just a little while earlier. He was calmer. Relaxed. He hadn't exactly been freaking out earlier, nothing like that, but he'd seemed tense, jittery.

Clarence tilted his head toward Clark. "Sorry about your friend."

"A real shame," Cantrell said. "Seems inevitable, though. The pathogen obviously had some kind of reservoir that allowed it to maintain viability all these years. The *Los Angeles* likely found that reservoir. Clarkie drew the short straw."

Clarence raised his eyebrows. "You seem to have a good grasp of what's going on. At least I think you do, because I'm not entirely sure I understand what you just said."

Cantrell shrugged. "I know me some biology. I was premed at Duke."

"Jesus. Not the typical life story of a serviceman. How the hell did you wind up in the navy?"

"Fighting, I'm afraid," Cantrell said. "I was an angry young black man raging against the inequities of life, even though I'd grown up in the suburbs and had a full ride."

"You had a full ride to *Duke*? You must have been one hell of a baller. Point guard?"

Cantrell laughed. "If you were white, I'd call you racist. It was an *academic* full ride."

"Oh." Clarence actually *did* feel a little racist, which was a strange sensation. "What did you do to get the academic full ride?"

"Perfect score on the SAT."

Clarence hadn't even known that was possible. He'd taken the SAT once upon a time. His score was less than perfect, to say the least.

"You had college for free, but couldn't keep your nose clean. Book smart, but no common sense?"

Cantrell nodded. "No concept of perspective, actually. But close enough."

"So you enlisted?"

"I did," Cantrell said. "I was out of options. Thought I'd do the GI Bill and save up enough to actually pay for college on my own, but I wound up in diving school and fell in love with it. I'm sure you're surprised to hear this, Agent Otto, but in the navy there is no such thing as a dummy diver. You have to be *smart* just to get in, and *smarter* to stay alive. In our job, one mistake can get you killed." He tilted his head toward Clark's cell. "Or get you infected, apparently."

Clarence knew that Cantrell might also be infected, might be just one of Tim's *little pricks* away from getting a death sentence of his own.

"I read your report," Clarence said. "I didn't see any opportunity for Clark to get infected, but it would help if you walked me through what happened when you guys picked up the bodies."

Cantrell thought for a moment, scratched absently at his throat.

"Okay, sure," he said. "When the shit hit the fan, Clarkie and I were ordered to suit up and search for bodies from the *Los Angeles*. We knew that meant a chance of handling infection victims. Our suits are aquatic BSL-4 arrays — positive pressure, completely internalized air, solid seals, similar to what you're wearing now, only more streamlined for movement. A modified Seahawk flew us out to the target areas."

"Modified? How?"

"Special lift cage," Cantrell said. "Same thing we used to retrieve material of interest from the *Los Angeles*. ROVs from the *LA* bring up these sealed, decontaminated containers, we collect the containers, get in the lift cage, the Seahawk drops the lift cage near the *Brashear*'s port side."

Cantrell pointed behind him, through his clear cell, across the prep area with its stainless steel instruments, to the wide, horizontal airlock door.

"The *Brashear*'s cargo crane picks up the cage and puts it right there," he said. "In we go, divers, cage, ROV, even the cable the crane uses to connect to the cage. *Anything* that could possibly touch the sample container, or touch something that touches the container, gets fully deconned. The airlock seals up, completely fills with bleach, destroying any biocontaminants. When the bleach drains, the inner airlock door opens and we take the container to the prep area. Then we go *back* into the airlock, get another dose of bleach, then the crane brings us up on deck."

The decon procedures seemed thorough. And yet, something had still gone wrong.

"So on the night of the attack, the Seahawk takes you and Clark out," Clarence said. "What was different?"

"You mean other than the screaming, the blood and the fires?"

Clarence paused, nodded. "Other than that."

"The 'Hawk's pilot spotted a flasher on Walker's SEIE suit," Cantrell said. "Into the drink we went. She was alive when we found her, mumbling about the people she'd killed and how she'd sabotaged the *LA*."

"So you touched her?"

The diver rolled his eyes. "No, Agent Otto, we sat back and told her she had nice titties. She was still alive. We were trying to save her."

"Do you remember what she said?"

Cantrell stared back. "You've got my report right in front of you. Read it for yourself."

The man didn't want to repeat the words. Why not?

"But do you remember? Can you tell me?"

Cantrell sighed.

"Yeah. She said, *I took out the reactor*. Then she said, *They bit me. I killed them. I shot two of those bastards.*"

Clarence read from the statement. Cantrell had it word for word.

"Okay, so what happened then?"

"The 'Hawk dropped the collection cage," Cantrell said. "Clark and I put Walker inside, then got in with her. We were just about to return to the *Brashear* when the pilot spotted a second body. Clark and I went back into the drink. Petrovsky was eviscerated, among other significant damage. We loaded him into the cage."

A cage normally meant for two divers and a container had four people in it, two of them infected. Clarence wondered if there was something to that.

"Did you continue to search for bodies?"

Cantrell shook his head. "Command wanted the Seahawk to return and look for survivors from the *Forrest Sherman*. No part of the helicopter had touched us or the bodies, if that's what you're wondering. The 'Hawk dropped our cage into the water, *Brashear*'s crane took us up, we got in the airlock just like normal. This time, however, there were two man-size, airtight containers waiting for us. We loaded the bodies into the containers. Feely was talking to us at that point. We went through the bleach bath, then carried the body containers to the morgue trailer."

Clarence called up Feely's report. Cantrell's recall matched the report exactly, as if he were reading directly from it. All except for one thing.

"It says here that when you entered with the bodies and went through the decon bath, you smelled bleach."

Cantrell paused. "Of course I smelled it," he said. "They bathe us in it. The suits smell like it when we're done."

"I'm not talking about when you're done. You're quoted in the report as saying, *I smelled bleach during decon step. Maybe a seal leaked.*"

Cantrell's eyes narrowed. Was that a look of . . . anger?

"That is not accurate," he said. "Maybe I typed it wrong."

"So you *didn't* smell bleach when you and Clark were submerged in the decon tank?"

Cantrell shook his head. "Not that I recall."

Clarence reached out into air, called up Clark's report on his HUD.

"Clark also reported smelling bleach," Clarence said. "He was worried the suit would fill up with it."

Cantrell clapped his hands together once, spread them out. "There you go, Agent Otto. Clark told me that right after we finished. I was exhausted. I must have put his words down as mine."

Clarence studied the man. That explanation sounded perfectly logical. A battle, a high-risk recovery of infected bodies . . . that kind of stress could lead to significant fatigue, the blurring of memories. But Cantrell seemed to have a near-photographic memory of the event, all except for that one detail.

Had the vector somehow got inside Clark's suit through a broken seal or a tiny tear that also allowed in a small amount of bleach? If Cantrell was now *lying* about smelling bleach, he was doing so because he knew evidence of a tear would lengthen his time in the cell. Or could he actually be infected and trying to protect himself? So far, though, Cantrell had tested negative.

Clarence felt he was missing something . . . but what?

"Let's go over the entire day again," he said. "You don't mind, do you? Like you said, it's not like you're going anywhere."

PHOTO BOMBING

Margaret had thought diving back into this world would be hell. She'd thought working on the bodies of infection victims would further stir up the ever-present memories of Amos Braun, of Perry Dawsey, of Dew Phillips, of Detroit and everything else that had turned her life to shit.

But she didn't think about any of those things.

In fact, almost as soon as she began the examination, those thoughts faded away. She didn't think about anything *but* the work. And, most important, she didn't think about Clarence.

In that way, at least, donning a BSL-4 suit and standing next to a body that had the potential to wipe out the human race was kind of . . . well, it was kind of *nice.*

She slowly ran her gloved hand over Candice Walker's body. A meticulous search. She had Tim's report up on the right side of her visor. She was getting the hang of the eye-track navigation; as she found torn pustules and other marks on Candice's body, she checked to see if Tim had logged them. Maybe he'd missed something. Or, maybe something had grown after he'd completed his initial exam.

Margaret heard a rattle: the heavy, compact Stryker bone saw moving against a prep tray. Tim was cleaning Petrovsky's powdered bone and that thick rot from the blade, preparing to use the device on the skull of Candice Walker. Petrovsky's rot was accelerating now. Most of his skin looked black and wet, and it was already sloughing off at his left shoulder to show the sagging, decomposing muscles beneath.

Tim stopped, looked up. "Uh, Doctor Montoya? What are you looking for?"

"Triangles," she said, turning her attention back to Walker. "I'm looking for any skin growths that would show triangle infection."

"I checked for that. She doesn't have the triangles or any Morgellons fibers indicative of a fizzle."

A *fizzle*, Amos's name for an infection that didn't quite take hold, resulting in red, blue or black fibers growing out of the host's skin.

Margaret stopped and stared at Tim. "You don't mind if I look again, do you?" She wasn't going to have Feely second-guessing her. She already knew his report showed no growths on Candice, but something didn't add up. Triangle victims often cut into themselves, but Candice didn't have triangles. She had crawlers; crawler hosts didn't mutilate themselves. So why had Walker cut off her own arm?

Tim met Margaret's gaze. He slowly raised a gore-slimed, gloved hand in front of his visor, making a monotone noise as he did. When his hand moved in front of his eyes, he made a crashing sound, held the hand still.

The world is in danger, and this asshole is playing games?

"Tim, what are you doing?"

"Raising my blast shields," he said. "Your death stare will not take me down, Vader."

For the second time that day, she laughed. There were two dead bodies on the table, both infected with a potentially world-killing pathogen, and Tim Feely made her *laugh*.

He lowered the hand just enough for his eyes to peek over. "Am I safe?"

"For now," Margaret said. "Stop playing." She pointed to the ravaged stub of Walker's severed arm. "Your initial report said she did this to herself?"

He nodded.

"How do you know?"

Tim started tapping at the air. He was calling something up on his HUD, but the action still seemed odd; it made him look crazy.

"Here's how," he said. He grabbed the air in front of his face, made a tossing gesture in Margaret's direction. Inside her visor, Tim's report shrank down to a tiny icon at the lower left. Her vision filled with a series of images.

A reciprocal saw, the long device so ubiquitous in the construction field: red, industrial-plastic handle, just big enough to hold with one fist; the same plastic on the saw's thick body, where the other hand would cup it from underneath; the blade guard and finally the blade itself, eight inches long, designed to slide back and forth so fast you couldn't even see its jagged points.

Margaret reached out into the air, swiped left to right. The next picture showed Candice Walker's left fingers wrapped around the saw's handle. The saw lay across her chest, the blade against the severed stump of her right arm. Margaret looked through her visor, down at the real thing, then refocused on the image — if Candice had cut herself, the angle of the wound was exactly right.

The third picture showed a close-up of gouges in Candice's ulna — a failed cut, one that hadn't gone through. The saw blade sat neatly in the groove, a perfect fit.

She swiped again to see the fourth and final picture: a smiling, biosafety-suited Tim Feely holding the saw and leaning down by Walker's face. He was giving a thumbs-up.

"Feely, you really are an asshole," Margaret said. "You play with the dead?"

He shrugged. "There was no one else to play with. But now you're here." He waggled his eyebrows.

Another crass innuendo. Maybe that was his way of dealing with the pressure of the situation. Or . . . or maybe he was actually interested. Either way, she didn't have time for it.

Thoughts of Tim Feely's advances faded away. The missing arm still didn't add up. If Candice had the crawlers, and crawlers that took over her brain, then why did she mutilate herself when no other known crawler host ever had?

"There's something different about Walker," Margaret said. "Are you finished processing Petrovsky's brain?"

Tim nodded. "I am. It's turning into black goop, but there was enough to see that it was riddled with the crawler mesh. If that ever happens to me, hopefully your hubby will put me down like the dog that I am."

She didn't know if Tim was serious about that request or just talking to deal with the stress. He had no way of knowing Clarence had done exactly that to infection victims in the past, and wouldn't hesitate to do so again.

Margaret stroked Candice Walker's hair one more time. In a few moments, Tim would slide a scalpel across the back of her scalp, then flip the scalp down over her face so he could use the Stryker saw to open her skull.

She heard a *click* in her helmet speakers, then, Clarence's voice.

"Margaret, can you and Doctor Feely hear me?"

"I can," she said. She looked at Tim, who gave a thumbs-up. "So can Tim."

"Good," Clarence said. "Listen, I'm finished with Cantrell's interview. There's some things I want to talk about."

"So get in here," Margaret said.

"Uh, can I report from the control room? This suit, I've been in it for two hours."

Tim rolled his eyes.

"Yes, but make it fast," Margaret said. "We'll keep working until you're ready. Tim, call up the images of crawlers from both Petrovsky and Walker. Let's take a look while we wait."

RED HOT MOMMA

For most of the last five years, Tim Feely had enjoyed collecting a huge paycheck and not doing a whole lot to earn it. He worked hard at whatever anyone asked him to do — well, at least he made it *look* like he was working hard — but he had harbored a hope that this infection crap was over forever, and that his black-budget gravy train would last for decades.

Obviously, he'd been wrong. This shit was *real*. If the infection got out, it could literally end the world. Like it or not, he was smack-dab in the middle of it.

But it wasn't all doom and gloom: he got to work with Margaret Montoya. *The* Margaret Montoya. She didn't understand what a legend she had become in scientific circles. For reasons Tim couldn't fathom, she seemed to be concerned with what regular people thought, people who knew nothing about science, nothing about how her genius had saved their uneducated asses.

Plus, she was *fine*. Margaret wanted to pretend that she and Clarence were solid, but Tim sensed friction. A marriage cracking at the seams, if it hadn't already shattered. Tim liked his women older, smart and powerful: Margaret was all three. He was helping save the world, sure, but that didn't mean he couldn't keep the game afoot. Pursuing a sexy woman gave him an edge, helped distract him from worrying about the fact that he'd probably never leave this ship alive.

While that pansy Agent Otto got out of his suit, Tim made good use of the time.

"Okay, Doctor Montoya," Tim said, "I've queued up the images of dead crawlers from Petrovsky and Walker. Ready for the side-by-side comparison?"

"I am. And please, call me Margaret."

"Can I call you *Red Hot Momma*?"

"You may not," she said. "The crawlers, please?"

Tim eye-tracked through his HUD menus, called up the prepared video, then grabbed and tossed it at Margaret so that both of their visor displays showed the same thing: a side-by-side progression of dead crawler images. Walker's were on the left, Petrovsky's on the right.

Margaret made a clucking sound with her tongue as she thought. "Walker's crawlers, they're in an odd state of decay. Almost like they were . . . *melted*."

At first glance, the crawlers all looked similar to oversized nerve cells: each consisted of a large, roundish end with *dendrites* that extended, split, and split again like tree branches; a long, thin central body, or *axon;* and finally a tail end that spread out in thin *axon terminals*. Closer examination, however, revealed that the crawlers were actually made up of modified muscle cells that could *reach*, that could *grab* and then *crawl* toward the brain.

Tim had been far too busy to do any comparative analysis. Lives had been at stake. As he looked at the images side-by-side for the first time, he saw immediate differences.

"Walker's aren't decomposing the same way as Petrovsky's," he said. "Petrovsky's crawlers have spreading clusters of black spots, starting small and expanding, like a banana that's just starting to go bad. With Walker's, the cell damage looks uniform, like something is affecting them all at once. You hit the nail on the head — they look like they're melting. You didn't see anything like that in your prior work?"

Margaret shook her head. "No, we didn't. We studied Carmen Sanchez through the whole crawler-infection process. Nothing like this in him, or in Betty Jewell, and she was in an advanced state of the apoptosis chain reaction. This . . . this is new."

She reached out, manipulating her images. Tim eye-tracked through his menu, altering his display so he saw exactly what she saw. Margaret had zoomed in on Walker's crawler.

"Uniform damage," she said quietly. "These crawlers started out alive, moving, then something made them start to dissolve." She reached out again, wiped away the images from Petrovsky. Only Walker's remained. "You said you also extracted live crawlers from Walker. Can I see them?"

Tim menued through to the video he'd recorded. "Let me get one on visual."

The image came up. Still moving, still twitching, still *reaching*. He placed it side by side with the dead, melted crawler.

Margaret stared at the two images for a moment. "Walker's crawlers are *significantly* different. I've never seen this form before."

Tim felt his face flush with embarrassment that he hadn't spotted it himself. Unlike all the other crawler images, this one didn't have the spreading axon terminals at the tail end, just a long, thin body and the dendrite arms on what he presumed to be the top — and even that part was unusual. Where a normal crawler's dendrite arms looked like a stubby tree with many branches, the living sample only had five arms of varying lengths.

Margaret's eyes changed focus. Instead of seeing the images inside her visor, she looked through them to stare at Tim.

"Feely, why the hell didn't you tell me they looked different?"

His face flushed deeper, but this time with anger. "I didn't notice. There wasn't time to do any in-depth work."

She put her hands on her hips, a gesture that looked oddly out of place for someone wearing a bulky biosafety suit.

"Didn't have *time*? Are you kidding me?"

Tim stabbed a finger toward the ceiling. "Maybe you didn't get the memo, Montoya, but there was a goddamn *battle* up top!"

Her hands slid off her hips. She looked surprised, as if it had never occurred to her that he could blow up at someone. Well, he had, and he couldn't stop the volcano of frustration and grief that came blasting out.

"I did what I could," he said. "There weren't enough hands to go around. I had to make snap decisions. If I took too much time to save one man, three others would die."

The ship's doctors, overwhelmed. Bodies all over the deck. He'd been covered in blood . . . the smell of burned flesh, the screams, people begging for help . . . all the drugs in the world weren't going to erase those two days. His anger faded. He saw the faces of men who had looked at him, looked *right at him* when he was already writing them off because they were too far gone.

And then there was Murray's order to collect some crawlers and seal them up for shipment to Black Manitou. Tim had done that the day of the battle, grabbing a few samples from Petrovsky and sending them on. He knew he should have fought that order, but all he wanted to do was satisfy Murray's request so he could get back to the wounded. Murray had sworn Tim to secrecy on that — Tim couldn't tell anyone, and in truth, he was ashamed of caving in and didn't *want* to tell anyone.

"I worked two days straight to save as many as I could. The only time I stopped was when Yasaka had two men drag me — literally *drag* me — down here to do some basic sample gathering on Walker and Petrovsky. And when I came down, I made sure not to touch the bodies, *at all*, just on the off chance I might bring contagion up with me when I returned to the wounded. I only used needles to gather samples, and I gathered those samples as quickly as I could. Know why? *I had more important things to do than play with corpses.* So no, Margaret, I didn't pay that much attention to the motherfucking crawlers."

Margaret sighed. She looked sad.

"I apologize," she said. "I should know better. We have so little time to get this work done. I'm sure I'm missing things, and there are tests we should be running that just have to wait because we don't have the resources. Everything is hurried, rushed, and you had it even worse with all the wounded. I'm sorry you had to go through that."

He could see she meant it. The sincerity of her response made his anger fade away as quickly as it had erupted.

Tim shrugged, feeling the bulk of his suit on his shoulders when he did.

"You're really sorry?"

She nodded.

"Sorry enough for apology sex?"

"Not that sorry, no."

"Oh well, worth a try."

Margaret shook her head, a sad dismissal of his feeble attempt. She focused on the images in her HUD.

"These new crawlers from Walker . . . where exactly were they inside her body?"

"The pustules," Tim said. "That was the fastest and easiest place to get a sample, so I started there. I collected crawlers from other areas as well, but all of those were dead. And, come to think of it, all of the dead ones look the same as those I collected from Petrovsky."

Margaret frowned. She reached out, turning the image of the living crawler, looking at it from multiple angles. "Sanchez had pustules, but what was in them didn't look like these. So we know that Walker definitely had the old kind of crawlers, the ones we saw back in Detroit, the same that are in Petrovsky, but she *also* had this new kind."

Tim studied the images on his own HUD. The new crawlers reminded him of a microorganism he'd seen way back in his undergrad days.

"They kind of look like hydras," he said.

Margaret nodded. "Yeah, a little bit. As good a name as any for the variant." She stared. The tip of her tongue traced her upper lip. "So the hydras and the crawlers were in Walker at the same time, but only the crawlers were melted."

Tim watched the real-time image of the hydra, watched it reach and move, searching for something to grab onto. Walker's crawlers had melted; Petrovsky's, Sanchez's and Jewell's had not. Her hydras were the only known variable.

"Maybe the hydras killed the crawlers," he said. "Something they secreted, perhaps."

Margaret thought about that for a moment. "Possibly. But . . . *why*? Crawlers and hydras are on the same side, so to speak."

"Maybe it's a new design," Tim said. "The first round of infections — with Perry Dawsey and the other early victims — they only had the triangular growths. But later on, when Detroit got crazy, you saw the crawler-based infections, and even that woman you said blew up like a puffball."

The look on Margaret's face made it clear she didn't want to remember that moment.

"The disease seemed to adapt," she said. "We stopped the triangles. In the following outbreak the disease expressed itself in at least two new ways."

Tim closed his eyes, let his brain work through the details, hoping he could find that spark of inspiration. "We've had no new activity since the Orbital was shot down. Now we find a piece of the Orbital, and *blammo*, we've a third new form. So it's reasonable to hypothesize that all the designs originated with the Orbital. You stopped the first attempt, the Dawsey-era infections, so it retooled and tried again with the things you saw in Detroit. You stopped *that*, so maybe it was already making additional changes when it was shot down. Maybe the hydras are that new design."

Margaret bit at her lower lip. "Maybe. But that doesn't explain why hydras would kill crawlers. Why would the Orbital make something that kills something *else* the Orbital made?"

Tim didn't have an answer for that. He felt like he was on the right path, although he couldn't see where that path ended.

"Well, the hydras aren't an accident," he said. "The infection reprogrammed Walker's body to make them."

Margaret's eyes stared off, seemed to lose focus. Her lips moved slightly, like she was talking quietly to herself.

"An accident," she said. She closed her eyes, kept mumbling to herself like a student trying to work out a complex math problem. Tim wasn't even sure if she knew he was there anymore.

"Tim, what if *was* an accident. Or rather, a mutation. Maybe there was something different about Walker's body, about the way her cellular factories reacted to the infection's reprogramming." Margaret blinked rapidly, raised her eyebrows — her eyes again focused on him. "Can you get Walker's medical records?"

"Of course. What do you want to know?"

"Start with her medical history. Maybe there's something unusual in her system that wasn't in the other victims."

Tim called up Walker's records, scanned through the usual list of military checkups, inoculations, physicals . . . then found exactly what Margaret was looking for: something unusual.

"She had lupus," he said.

Margaret shook her head. "That can't be it. I can't see how an autoimmune disease would affect the crawlers. They hijack stem cells to produce copies of themselves."

Tim looked deeper in the record. When he found the next difference, he felt his heart start to hammer.

"Jesus, Margaret . . . Walker underwent HAC therapy to treat the lupus."

Margaret narrowed her eyes, not understanding. "What's HAC therapy?"

That question surprised Tim. She hadn't just tuned out from life, she'd tuned out from medicine altogether. She wasn't even reading research journals.

"HAC is *human artificial chromosome treatment*. It's an experimental way to treat genetic defects. The process introduces a new chromosome into stem cells. The end result is stem cells with forty-*seven* chromosomes instead of the normal forty-*six* that all cells are supposed to have. The forty-seventh chromosome probably has a myriad of immune system modulators meant to reprogram cells to stop the autoimmune effects of lupus — new transcription factors, genetic code to modify gene response, et cetera. In some cases HAC even introduces fully artificial gene sequences."

Even as he said the words, it struck him how similar the process sounded to the Orbital's infection strategy: targeted changes to the host's DNA, altering the processes created by millions of years of evolution. Was humanity that far away from harnessing the very technology that threatened to wipe it out forever?

Margaret's eyes narrowed. Her nostrils flared. Normally, she looked like she couldn't hurt a fly, but now her expression was that of a predator.

"An artificial chromosome in stem cells," she said. "Maybe the Orbital's technology can't properly integrate that forty-seventh chromosome."

She nodded, slowly at first, then gradually faster.

"This therapy," she said. "Where did Walker get it?"

"Let me check." Tim read through Walker's records. "Looks like a clinic within the Spectrum Health System in Grand Rapids, Michigan. Cutting-edge stuff, only ten people in the trial."

Margaret thought for a moment. Her excitement seemed to grow.

"Correlation isn't causation, but this is one *hell* of a correlation," she said. "We need to see if these new, larger crawlers colonized Walker's brain, like the older ones colonized Petrovsky's. Let's find out right now."

Tim walked to his prep tray and lifted the compact Stryker saw, preparing to cut into Walker's skull.

PREPROGRAMMING

Perhaps a thousand modified neutrophils had reached Charlie Petrovsky's squamous epithelium. Most of them died there, wiped out by the evergrowing apoptosis chain reaction that steadily turned Charlie into a pile of black sludge.

Some, however, held on to life, held on just long enough for a gloved hand to brush against Charlie's skin.

When that gloved hand moved away, a dozen neutrophils moved with it.

They emitted a new chemical, an airborne signal that announced their presence to any other neutrophils that might be near. If a neutrophil detected that chemical coming from mostly one direction, it moved in that direction: *flow, reach, pull . . . flow, reach, pull.* If it detected roughly equal amounts of the chemical coming from multiple directions, it stayed where it was. This simple process created an instant implementation of quorum sensing, of individuals using a basic cue to communicate as a single individual.

The microscopic neutrophils had a relatively massive area to cover. The equivalent, perhaps, of a dozen mice scattered onto an area the size of a dozen football fields. Much ground to cover, and yet the neutrophils had been designed for this very action.

Three were too weak to make the journey. They expired along the way, leaving nine that found each other, amorphous blobs pressing in on each other.

At the center of this shifting pile, three neutrophils underwent a rapid physical change. They altered their internal workings to produce a caustic chemical, a chemical specifically preprogrammed by the Orbital some five years earlier. This trio pressed themselves flat against the Tyvek material of the gloves upon which they rode. The trio started to swell, to fill with fluid, until — following those same, preprogrammed instructions — they sacrificed themselves by tearing open their own cell walls.

The caustic chemical spilled onto the Tyvek: just a microscopic drop, something not even visible to the naked eye, but enough to weaken the material, to create a tiny divot.

Another neutrophil flowed into the divot, then repeated the process, deepening the hole. Then another, and another.

The chemical burst of the last one was enough to punch all the way through.

Pressurized air flowed out, an infinitesimal, nearly immeasurable amount, sliding past the flat bodies of the seventh and eight neutrophils that climbed through the microscopic hole all the way to the glove's inner surface. These, too, began a phase change — their bodies quickly split into dozens of tiny, self-contained particles.

Those particles flaked away, scattered like an invisible shower onto the skin of the person wearing the gloves. There the particles began to burrow.

The Orbital had watched. The Orbital had learned. It knew of the primitive-yet-effective technology the humans had developed to protect themselves from infection. Drawing on the knowledge of a vastly superior technology, the Orbital had prepared a way to defeat this protection.

The last neutrophil sensed that its fellow microbes had succeeded. It underwent the final portion of the preprogrammed dance. It slid into the microscopic hole and began to swell, bloating until it pushed against the sides.

Air stopped flowing out of the glove.

That final neutrophil hardened, then died, fulfilling its role as nothing more than a plug in a hole so tiny it would take an electron microscope to see it, if anyone ever looked.

And no one ever would.

IT'S ABOUT CANTRELL

Clarence needed a shower. At least he was out of that suit. Built-in air conditioner or not, when he wore it, he sweated like a whore in church — probably less from any heat and more because of what waited just outside of the thin material.

He sat in the small control center that looked down through the clear roofs of the three science modules. The console in front of him and the walls on either side were packed with computers, monitors and communication equipment — neat, tidy, space-conscious military design. The built-in microphone in front of him let him speak to people in the modules; speakers in the console let him hear them talk.

Through the control center's glass, he saw Margaret and Tim working away. They'd pulled Candice Walker's scalp down over her face. The inside-out flesh looked bone-white, smeared with tacky blood. Tim was cutting into her skull with a handheld saw.

Clarence had been in the BSL-4 suit for about two hours, total, and had been counting the minutes until he could get out of it. He didn't know how Margaret and Feely managed it so well; the two of them would probably be in their suits for another eight to ten hours, at least. They had both opted for devices that allowed them to urinate and defecate while still in the suit.

You told her she's not a soldier. You can barely keep your suit on for ninety minutes but she can piss and shit inside of hers for twenty-four hours straight if she has to.

Not that Clarence hadn't faced his own fair share of awful conditions. In Iraq, his unit had been pinned down. Waiting for support, he and his buddy, Louis Oakley, had hidden behind rocks, suffering 120-degree heat while dreading that the next bullet would hit home. Lou-Lou took a round to the head. He died instantly. Clarence had lain there for the better part of a day, unable to move away from the corpse, willing his body to press closer to the ground. Louis had looked on, unblinking.

Clarence shook his head, came back to the moment. No time to get lost in those memories.

He finished up the notes from his interview with Cantrell. Margaret preferred her information summarized, the most-important stuff bullet-pointed right up top. If she needed info beyond that summary, she would ask.

At times, being in a relationship with a woman who was clearly much, *much* smarter than he was felt a little intimidating. In their day-to-day life it hadn't been noticeable — she was a woman, he was a man, things worked out. But when it came to talking politics, finances, history, or — God forbid — science, the gap in their IQs became clear. At least he knew more about football than she did. Or, at least that's what she let him believe. He was never really sure about that one.

Clarence turned on the microphone. "Margo, is now still a good time?"

She and Tim stopped what they were doing, looked up. Margaret nodded.

Tim had a shit-eating grin on his face. "Suit's a little stuffy, eh, fella? You want me to go to the kitchen and fetch you a nice glass of lemonade to cool you off?"

Clarence ground his teeth in embarrassment.

"Or some talcum powder," Tim said. "Maybe your bottom is damp?"

Margaret reached out, slapped Tim lightly on the shoulder. He stopped talking, but the grin didn't go away. Was he actually posturing, trying to impress Margaret? At a time like this, the guy was hitting on her?

Just hope we never step into the ring, you little runt. We'll find out who's the better man.

"Margo," Clarence said, "verbal or send it to your HUD?"

She tapped her visor. "HUD. Tim's as well."

Clarence did as he was asked.

Both Tim and Margaret read through the info playing on the inside of their visors.

"Fancy," Tim said. "It's like Cliff's Notes for Holy Shit the World Is Going to End Theater. Bullet points? Please, Agent Otto, don't spend any time going into actual detail."

"Tim, cut it out," Margaret said, still reading. "This is how I want my data. Clarence knows what I like."

That line shut Tim up. He glared up at the control booth. Clarence knew

Margaret hadn't meant anything sexual by the reference, but he couldn't help but give Tim a little nod that said, *Awww yeah, I know what she likes, and you never will.*

Margaret tapped the air, shutting off the report.

"The bleach thing is interesting," she said. "Is anyone checking their suits for holes or malfunctions?"

"I asked Captain Yasaka if someone could test them," Clarence said. "She's going to have the nonquarantined divers run a pressurized rate of fall test as soon as they can, probably first thing tomorrow morning. The divers pressurize the suit and watch the gauges, see if there is a loss greater than expected. In other words, fill it with air and see if it leaks."

"The holes could be small," Tim said. "The crawler spores are tiny. We're talking microns, here. Gauges might not show pressure loss from something that size."

Clarence nodded. "Correct, which is why if they don't find a leak that way, they will then go for a full submersion test. They need our airlock for that, the big one that leads outside the ship."

Margaret waved a hand dismissively. "Any hole so small the pressure test won't show it is too small to worry about. I mean, a spore or a crawler would have to randomly land on that tiny hole, and somehow fall *through* that hole when the suits are pressurized to push air *out*, and then still land on skin."

Her eyes again focused on the report displaying inside her visor.

"You emphasize Cantrell's intelligence," she said. "Why?"

"When he told me what happened, it was almost a word-for-word rendition of what he wrote in his incident report," Clarence said. "He remembered what he said perfectly, all except for smelling bleach. It strikes me odd he has perfect recall for everything save for that one detail."

"So you think Cantrell is lying," Tim said.

Clarence wasn't sure what he was thinking. Something just didn't seem to add up.

"Maybe, maybe not. Another thing about that report struck me as odd. When he and Clark reached Walker, one of the things she said was *they bit me*. Did you guys find a bite mark on her body?"

"None," Tim said. "But just because we didn't find one doesn't mean Clark and Cantrell were lying about hearing her say that."

Clarence rubbed his face. He already felt so damn tired. "Yeah, that's a good point. But the bleach discrepancy still bothers me. Maybe Tim should test him again."

Margaret tapped the report back on, read something, tapped it back off. "It's been thirty-six hours since Cantrell was exposed," she said. "If he was infected, he'd have probably come up positive by now. Even if he's got a longer incubation period than we've seen in the past, he's being tested every three hours so we'll find out soon enough. He's scheduled for his next test in twenty minutes. Clarence, can you take over the testing duties? I need Doctor Feely here with me."

Clarence looked at Tim.

Tim nodded: *Awwww yeah*.

Clarence ground his teeth. "Sure, Margo," he said. "I'll make sure Cantrell is tested every three hours."

She turned back to the table. Tim got to work; Clarence heard the bone saw's whine even through the control room's security glass.

Then, Margaret turned back. She stared up at Clarence.

He had seen that look on her face before. She had figured something out, or was just on the edge of doing so.

"Margo, what is it?"

She looked down at Walker's corpse. Margaret lifted the severed arm, stared at it.

"The bite," she said. "Walker claimed to be bitten, but there are no bite marks. What if she was bitten on the arm?"

Tim stopped cutting into the skull. "You're thinking she cut off her own arm not because she was infected, like Dawsey, but because she thought it would *prevent* her from being infected?"

"Maybe," she said.

Tim set the saw on a tray. He reached out into the air and started calling up information.

Clarence tried to imagine himself in Walker's shoes. A submarine full of people, some of them turning into killers, killers that worked together like those soldiers in Michigan did during the last outbreak . . . and nowhere to run.

"It can spread from a bite?" he asked.

"Probably," Margaret said. "Some of the infection victims had growths on the tongue that could spread the contagion. But what matters is if Walker *thought* it could spread from a bite. Maybe she saw her friends being turned into murderers, maybe she did anything she could to not become one herself."

"Like a zombie movie," Clarence said. "You think she got bit, panicked, did what she thought might keep her from becoming one of the bad guys?"

Tim shook his head. "Timeline doesn't add up for that," he said. "She cut off that arm around thirty-eight hours ago. Based on the state of her crawlers, she was already heavily infected by that time. She was already . . . what's the word I want . . . oh, she was already *converted*. Why would she cut off her own arm if one of her own kind bit her? Hell, Margaret, why would one of them bite her at all? The Converted all work together, like ants in a colony."

"My point exactly," Margaret said. Her eyes were sharp, full of sudden assuredness. "The *Converted*. That's an excellent term. Candice Walker had crawlers, absolutely, but she was *not* converted. Feely, get that brain out, and get it out now."

Steve Stanton was done with the cold weather. The small stateroom he shared with Bo Pan wasn't toasty by any stretch of the imagination, but it was easily thirty degrees warmer than it was up on deck. Plus, no wind. *Plus*, no ice-cold water spray.

Maybe he should have hired a bigger boat. The guest stateroom was smaller than his freshman dorm room back at Berkeley. It was cramped to begin with — sharing the space with Bo Pan made it miserable. Bo Pan didn't do much, mostly just sat in his bunk. Sat and *watched* Steve type code.

A small table built into the wall held two of Steve's three laptops. The other rested on top of the blankets of his bunk (he got the top bunk — he was the "boss" of this trip, after all).

Cooper had warned him that spending too much time belowdecks could lead to seasickness, but so far Steve had felt no ill effects. If anything, the constant rocking motion made him hungry. He chewed mouthfuls of Doritos, which he washed down with swigs of Diet Coke. He felt Bo Pan staring at him. Steve kept typing, tried to ignore his bunkmate.

"Disgusting," Bo Pan said. "I do not know how you eat such garbage. We have paid to rent this boat. They would let me use the little kitchen. I could cook you something."

Steve tipped the bag of Doritos toward the old man. "Breakfast of champions, Bo Pan. Want some? Blazin' Buffalo & Ranch, can't go wrong."

Bo Pan's face wrinkled in disgust. He looked away.

Steve shrugged and reached in for more. Imagine the dichotomy: Bo "King of Phlegm" Pan calling someone else *disgusting*.

"Your machine," Bo Pan said. "Do you have its twat yet?"

Steve's eyebrows rose. "Uh, its *what*?"

Bo Pan leaned back slightly, confused. "Twat. Is that not what you call it? The Twatter messages your machine sends?"

"Ah," Steve said. "Twitter. It's a *tweet*, not a *twat*. Big difference."

The old man waved a hand, a gesture that might as well have been sign language for *get off my lawn*. "Have you received any?"

"Not yet. I'm sure it will *twat* at any moment."

Using Twitter to send and receive messages from the *Platypus* had been an act of genius, if Steve did say so himself. Twitter boasted five hundred million accounts sending up to three hundred million tweets a day. It added up to an overwhelming amount of data flying across the Internet, 140 characters at a time. The typhoon of content was a perfect place for hiding messages, especially if they corresponded with a code held only by the receiver and the sender. *Get in the kitchen and make me some pie* might be an innocuous quote from a TV show, but if Steve sent it from his account, @MonstaMush, to @TheMadPlatypus, his lovely machine would know it was time to return to the launch point.

There were over a thousand such tweet-based commands stored in the *Platypus's* memory. Steve had programmed his baby to surface periodically and log on to the Internet by using a communication method ubiquitous throughout the United States: cell-phone signals.

Even though the UUV's sonar-dampening "fur" made it practically invisible to sonar, the U.S. naval assets in the area still made surfacing dangerous; Steve had to limit the number of surface trips the *Platypus* could make.

He called up a bathymetry map of Lake Michigan. Different bands of color represented different depths: reds and yellows for zero to 50 feet, greens into greenish-blue to 150 feet, blues through 300. There hadn't been a color for depths beyond 300 feet, because Lake Michigan's average depth was 279 feet. So Steve had programmed more: blue-purple to purple for 300 to 500 feet, purple to dark purple for 501 to 800 feet, dark purple to black for the deepest spots the lake had to offer.

The *Platypus's* destination? The blackest spot on the map. Bo Pan's coordinates were in a spot known as Chippewa Basin, the very bottom of which was 923 feet deep.

"How solid are these coordinates?" Steve asked. "I'll program a search field. It would help to know how far out I have to plot for."

The old man shrugged. He shrugged a lot.

"I only know what I have been told," he said. "It is the same location the

American navy has. That means ROVs and divers will be in the area. You had better hope your claims of near invisibility are accurate."

Steve rocked slightly back and forth. He tried to control his excitement. Not just excitement, but also fear, stress and anxiety. He believed he'd constructed the most advanced UUV ever created. Manufacturers and fabricators in a dozen countries had provided parts, had unknowingly helped him build the *Platypus*. He'd had a huge budget to make his creation, but there was another organization with a far bigger checkbook: the U.S. Navy.

The navy had remotely operated vehicles. The navy had unmanned vehicles. The navy had some of the best minds in the world creating, designing, building. But the navy had one limitation that Steve did not — the navy itself. Proposals, funding, approvals, bidding, construction checks, supervised tests . . . dozens of administrative layers and miles of red tape that slowed down the creative process. Steve suffered through none of those things.

The *Platypus* incorporated the best components. Some were prototypes from other designers, things that had yet to enter beta testing, let alone hit the market. Others, Steve had designed himself. The biggest advantage, however, was that Steve had designed the *Platypus* for one purpose and one purpose only — military contractors had to make machines that could do multiple things in order to serve multiple masters.

If Steve's creation went up against black-budget DARPA machines, which would come out on top? Could he really out-invent the world's largest buyer of weapons?

Bo Pan hawked a loogie, spat it into his cup with a wet *plop*. He smiled. "You seem nervous."

Steve felt instantly insulted. "Nervous? No. Just excited. Well, a little nervous. We don't know what the navy has. If something goes wrong with the *Platypus* and it can't surface to send a signal, we'd never hear from it again. We'd never know what went wrong."

The old man's smile faded. "Do you know how much money was spent on your machine?"

Steve shook his head.

"Guess," Bo Pan said. "I am curious if you are even close."

Steve didn't really want to think about how much money he'd wasted if his machine had failed and was lying on the lake bottom, but he closed his eyes and mentally walked through what he knew about the components and the materials used to make them.

"Um . . . eighteen million?"

Bo Pan laughed. The sound made Steve more nervous. Something about that laugh made his stomach pinch, made him *afraid*.

"Eighteen million," Bo Pan said, shaking his head. "You have no idea. The cost is *one hundred and ten* million. Rounded down."

A staggering sum. It didn't seem real. It seemed like Monopoly money.

"One hundred and ten million," Bo Pan repeated. "If your machine does not return, Steve, then you have wasted not only our investment in *you*, but also all that money."

Steve turned back to his computer. Still no tweet from the *Platypus*.

One hundred and ten million dollars . . .

"I'll write some more code," he said. "I'll make sure we are not discovered."

Bo Pan nodded. "That is good. You do that while I make some calls."

The old man pulled out his cell phone. He lay back in his bunk and let Steve get to work.

CLEAR YOUR MIND

Margaret tried not to hold her breath as she watched Tim Feely slice into Candice Walker's brain. She was right, she *had* to be right; it was the only thing that fit the observed data.

Tim separated the left and right hemispheres, then made horizontal slices across each. When he was done, the thing that had made up Walker's personality, stored her memories, comprised everything that she was, lay on the dissection tray like a pair of strange, gray loaves of sliced bread.

Tim looked up. "I don't know what to make of this. In the other infection victims, including Petrovsky, the crawlers create fibrous structures in the brain. I found hydras in Walker's brain, but none of those structures. She didn't have any crawlers in there, either — melted or otherwise. Petrovsky's brain was packed with the things. Aside from the presence of the hydras, Walker's brain looks perfectly normal."

Margaret felt an electric surge of possibility, powerful enough to make her fingers and toes tingle. She leaned in and eye-tracked through her HUD controls, calling up magnification, labeling and enhancement. The visor showed Candice's brain in far greater detail than Margaret could have seen with the naked eye.

She looked for the visible, telltale signs of brain infection: a latticework of crawler threads, each thinner than a human hair, spreading through the obifrontal cortex, amygdala, and hippocampus.

There weren't any.

Tim seemed dumbfounded. "Walker tested positive for cellulose. I found hundreds of crawlers in her spinal column alone. Why didn't her crawlers make it to her brain?"

Margaret didn't know, but one hypothesis loomed large. Her heart hammered, her face felt flushed. She heard herself breathing rapidly.

"Tim, is there any evidence of the black rot in Walker's brain?"

He shook his head. "No, none." He looked at Walker's body. "In fact, I haven't observed any apoptosis on her at all — according to the normal timeline, we should be seeing that by now. She's just not rotting like Petrovsky and the other infected victims."

Melted crawlers . . . no rot . . . no growths in the brain . . .

The observations pointed to one obvious conclusion, a *glorious* conclusion.

"Candice was infected by crawlers, but *not* under their control," Margaret said. "The hydras are clearly different, and we have to assume they stopped the crawlers from colonizing her brain."

"Calm down, Red Hot Momma," Tim said. "You look like you might pass out. Take it easy."

She turned on him, so fast she almost stumbled.

"I *can't* calm down, Tim. Don't you see what this means?"

Margaret drew in a sharp breath, held it, tried to stop her body from shaking. For years she had dealt with the hard truth that there was no known method of preventing the alien infection from penetrating new hosts, from hijacking stem cells to make whatever bioparts it needed. If her new hypothesis about Candice Walker was right, there might finally be a way.

"Your engineered yeast," she said. "You've taken genetic information out of the crawlers, put it into the yeast. You can get your yeast to produce the catalyst that kills the crawlers."

"Sure," Tim said. "But like I told you, the catalyst kills the yeast as well. So it's a dead end."

"*Was* a dead end. The hydras survive an environment that kills the crawlers, Tim. If we can figure out *how* they survive it—"

"Maybe we can put that survival trait in the yeast," Tim finished, his eyes wide with renewed energy. "Then we could generate huge colonies of yeast that would produce the catalyst . . . an endless supply of something that kills crawlers dead."

Margaret reached out, grabbed Tim's shoulder. If they weren't in the suits, she might have kissed the man.

"Tim, I think the hydras made Candice *immune* to the infection, to the crawlers, to all of it. We still don't know what the hydras are, what else they can do to a host, but if we can figure out how they survive when crawlers die, and if we can reproduce that ability . . . maybe we can make *everyone* immune."

GET LICKED

Chief Petty Officer Orin Nagy didn't know much about the original infection.

Like everyone else in the world, he'd been glued to the news when that disaster hit. He'd watched reports of Detroit's blistering end and the aftermath that followed. He'd heard the endless public service announcements hammering home the acronym "T.E.A.M.S." Like everyone else, he knew the methods of transmission: get infected by a spore, or get licked — yes, literally *licked* — by a host.

But since then, God had created new vectors.

Orin didn't have to lick people. All he had to do was *touch* them. He didn't know how he knew this, he just knew. Touch them, and a few days later, they would be his kind.

An even greater illustration of God's perfection and power? He didn't have to always touch people directly — if he touched a surface, then someone else touched it shortly after, that alone could be enough to spread God's love.

Soon, the humans would come for him, try and make him take the cellulose test, but he wouldn't be where they expected him to be. It was time to wander. Surrounded by a ship full of people who wanted to kill him, he would stay out of sight as best he could. He would avoid attracting attention.

The longer he went without being caught, the more people he could touch.

CHEMISTRY

Before Tim could find out how the hydras survived when the crawlers melted, he had to identify what, exactly, melted those crawlers.

To solve this puzzle, he had to find the key differences between two human corpses. Both bodies had come from an identical environment: the *Los Angeles*. Although there were significant variables — one was male, the other female, with additional differences in size and genetic background — for all intents and purposes those two bodies were the same. One had suffered the infection's final-stage brain modification, the other had not.

That made Tim's job theoretically simple: all he had to do was identify something in Candice Walker that was not in Charlie Petrovsky.

He stood alone in the analysis module, running tests on blood, tissues, organs, even bone. Chemical breakdown, mass spectrometry, DNA analysis, any test he and Margaret could think of for which they had the equipment onboard — and they had a *lot* of equipment.

She checked in with him every fifteen to twenty minutes, a hyper Latina with the newfound energy of a chipmunk on meth. She was working with the hydras, trying to figure out what they were. Just another Orbital weapon? Or, possibly, something else.

Margaret wasn't the same person who had arrived, what, just a scant fifteen *hours* earlier? She'd shown up ready to work, certainly, but not like this: now she had a nuclear reactor for a soul that made her tireless, unceasing.

Tim wanted her more than ever. He'd worshipped Margaret Montoya from afar, mesmerized by the intellect he'd seen reflected in the words and recordings of her Detroit research. The word *genius* didn't do her justice.

His visor display started flashing an icon: the blinking, red exclamation point of an alert. Tim eye-tracked to it, called it up.

Four hours after he'd begun his comparative analysis between Petrovsky and Walker, the *Brashear*'s computer had identified a significant discrepancy in mass spectrometry. Walker's blood showed a massive spike of an unidentified chemical compound that wasn't present in Petrovsky, not even in trace amounts.

Whatever it was, she had a *ton* of it in her system. Was this compound related to the hydras? Was it the reason the hydras lived and the crawlers died? Or was it why Walker didn't suffer the black rot?

And why was this mystery chemical so concentrated in her blood?

Her blood . . .

Petrovsky's tissue . . .

"Fuck," Tim said. "Why didn't I think of that before?"

He activated his comms. "Margo, you there?"

She answered immediately. "Yes, Tim. You okay?"

"I'm fine," he said. "Shittyballs, I'm way more than *fine*. I need you to find the least-rotted bit of Petrovsky."

"Uh, sure," she said. "You want to tell me why?"

"You'll see soon enough."

At least he *hoped* she would.

THE *LOS ANGELES*

The stateroom felt ice cold, but Steve Stanton couldn't stop sweating.

He sat at the tiny table, drinking Diet Coke and eating Doritos, hoping his two laptops would give some signal. *One hundred and ten million dollars . . .* was that investment sitting dead on the bottom of Lake Michigan?

Bo Pan spent his time either sleeping or on his cell phone. Steve didn't know who Bo Pan was talking to, but the conversations revolved around more aunts, uncles, nephews and nieces than one man could possibly have. It didn't take a rocket scientist to figure out that Bo Pan was sharing information about Steve's work, getting details about the activities of the nearby navy ships — Steve and the *Platypus* had their code; Bo Pan and his handlers obviously had theirs.

"Steve, it is late," Bo Pan said. "You told me your machine would contact us an hour ago." The old man lay in his bunk, spit cup in hand, bushy eyebrows framing black, emotionless eyes.

"Relax," Steve said. He tried to sound confident. "It might be staying below because of high levels of navy activity. Sometimes this is more an art than a science."

Bo Pan picked his nose. "I see," he said as he wiped a booger on his jeans. "Then perhaps we should have spent all that money to get you an art degree."

The coldness of Bo Pan's voice made Steve swallow, which drove a flake of Dorito into his throat. Steve tried to wash it back with Diet Coke, but coughed before he could get it down. He managed to turn his head and spray caramel-colored foam onto the wall instead of onto his computers.

Bo Pan huffed. "Breakfast of champions. I can't wait to see how you handle your dinner."

Steve managed to flip the old man the bird as he brought his coughing under control.

Bo Pan seemed . . . different. He'd always acted like a beaten-down laborer, a man who'd spent his life taking shit from everyone. Since the *Mary Ellen* left the harbor, however, he seemed more self-assured, in control.

No, no . . . Steve was just stressing out, imagining things. Bo Pan was Bo Pan. Had to be. It was Steve who had changed. In all his years of work, pursuing whatever development he thought might add to the *Platypus's* effectiveness, he'd felt invulnerable. He'd felt *brilliant*. None of that had been real. This, however, was reality: a boat that never sat still, an old man watching his every move, a machine that refused to respond, and a nation's investment in him about to go bust.

He didn't feel brilliant anymore. He felt incompetent.

Bo Pan pushed himself up on one arm.

"Steve, it seems you are telling me you don't know where your creation is, but I know you cannot be telling me that."

A coldness in that voice, and *steel*. No *sorry, sorry* this time. Steve shivered.

"The sensor algorithms determine where the *Platypus* goes, so it isn't necessarily moving in a straight line," he said. "If it has to go around or through anything, that causes delays, and if it sees any American UUVs or divers, it knows to swim away and come back later. Could be any minute now. Or it could be hours. The UUV is programmed to *not* be seen, Bo Pan. I can't—"

A laptop let out a beep. Bo Pan sat up straighter. Steve put the chips aside, brushed his orange-dust-covered fingertips against his shirt, then pulled the laptop closer.

A tweet.

@TheMadPlatypus: Dizzy in the hizzy.

Steve sagged in his seat, felt the anxiety flood away in a crashing waterfall of relief.

"It's the *Platypus*," he said. "It's signaling."

He watched a string of tweets come pouring in. Seemingly normal language — mostly about "hot bitches" and "keg stands" — told him the story.

Bo Pan leaned in. "Is it working?"

Steve smiled. "Hell yeah, it is." The *Platypus* had found the location. Steve read the tweets, trying to figure out what had taken so long. There it was:

@TheMadPlatypus: Mean muggin' AT-ATs all over the damn place.
 Fuck the Empire.

Navy ROVs.

Holy *shit*, it was really happening.

@TheMadPlatypus: Stick in the mud is big like a pickle.

It wasn't just the ROVs . . . the *Platypus* had found a big object on the bottom. *Too* big.

"Something is off," he said. "When the alien object came down, there was enough observed data to calculate its size as roughly equivalent to a small refrigerator, like the kind I had in my dorm. But the *Platypus* found something exponentially larger."

Bo Pan nodded slowly. His eyes seemed electric.

"Do you have pictures?"

Steve huffed. "Does a bear shit in the woods?"

The old man's forehead wrinkled with confusion. "What are you talking about?"

"Yes, I have pictures."

"Show me," Bo Pan said. "And prepare yourself. There is some other information I have not told you."

Steve sighed. The old man was being cryptic. Whatever.

That feeling of failure faded away. Steve had done it — he felt strong once again, ready for the next step.

The *Platypus* couldn't send straight video. That was too much bandwidth; even if his encryption held, the size of that signal and the location it came from could alert the navy ships to the *Platypus*'s presence. Instead, his machine took low-bandwidth snapshots — one frame every twenty seconds — and routed each one through a different secure server.

"Here we are," Steve said, and called them up on the screen.

The first picture showed something green, blurry. That meant it was a pale color, brightly reflecting the low-light camera's illumination.

"Can't make that out," Steve said. "Lemme get the next one."

He called the image up, and froze: the face and torso of a corpse.

A sailor. A *navy* sailor.

Puffy face. Black sockets where the eyes had once been, eyes probably eaten by fish that had also picked at the skin, tearing holes and leaving strands of flesh dangling weightless in the water. Body bloated, so swollen it had burst the zipper at the belly and neck, leaving only a bit near the collar still fastened. Pale skin glowed an obscene white-green.

"Bo Pan, what is this?"

"More pictures. Let me see."

The next image showed a long shape. Gray, perhaps? The one after that, yes, *gray*, large, maybe ten feet tall or even taller, rising up at an angle. Definitely artificial.

When Steve saw the next picture, he felt his heart drop into his stomach. He realized, finally, just how dangerous this game was.

The gray image rose up at an angle. Flat, with slightly curved sides. At the top, a white, three-digit number glowed a bright green.

The number: 688.

"A submarine sail," Steve said. "Is that . . . is that a *nuclear* sub?"

Bo Pan leaned in closer, so close Steve could smell his unwashed odor. The old man seemed . . . gleeful.

"The *Los Angeles*," Bo Pan said. "There was a battle. It sank."

Steve hadn't asked questions, hadn't tried to understand the situation; when Bo Pan said the word *location*, Steve had jumped. How naive. How *stupid*.

The next picture came up. The *Platypus* was moving closer to the sub. Another corpse. Some kind of bulbous, sausage-shaped metal construct behind the sail, bent and torn, a man-size round door still sealed but the construct itself ripped open. And there, stuck on that jagged metal, a leg — just a leg, no body. Inside the ruined construct, Steve saw an inner hatch sitting open.

This was almost a thousand feet below the surface. Could there be survivors?

"A battle," Steve said, his voice a husky whisper. "Between who?"

"The Americans. They shot at each other."

Steve couldn't think. Why hadn't he asked more questions?

The final picture showed blackness: the *Platypus* moving over the submarine to the other side. Then, a wider shot of the sunken ship; from this angle, it looked bent, like a loaf of French bread kinked in the middle. A huge gash marred the hull, metal shards bent violently inward.

Bo Pan pointed to the gash.

"There," he said. "Can your machine go inside?"

Steve stared. What had happened? Why had the navy destroyed its own vessel? If the navy would slaughter everyone on the *Los Angeles*, it wouldn't think twice about sinking the *Mary Ellen Moffett*. He started to shake. He was in danger. This little excursion might get him killed.

"*Steve*," Bo Pan said sharply. "Can it go in inside?"

Steve tried to clear his thoughts, tried to focus. He examined the tear in the hull.

"No, that's probably not a good spot," he said. "The metal is too torn up, too jagged. The *Platypus* could get hooked on a shard, get stuck."

"Then go back to the picture of the dry deck shelter."

Steve started to ask what that was, but then he knew — the sausage-shaped construct behind the sail. He called up that image.

"There," Bo Pan said. "Could it go in there?"

A hole large enough for two men to walk through . . . the open inner hatch . . . far enough away from the torpedo damage that the corridors would be flooded, but mostly intact . . .

But if the *Platypus* went in and got stuck, and the navy captured it, could any of the advanced tech lead back to Steve? What would happen to him if it did?

"We need to leave this alone," he said. "The data shows there are American ROVs in the area."

He felt an iron-hard hand grip his shoulder. Steve's body scrunched up from the sudden pain.

Bo Pan bent close. When he spoke, Steve felt the old man's breath on his neck.

"I said, *can it go inside*."

"Yes, sure," Steve said in a rush. "But it's like a maze in there. Without a deck plan, the *Platypus* might get stuck. We'd never get her back."

Bo Pan stood straight, lifted up his bulky Detroit Lions sweatshirt to reach into his jeans pocket — when he did that, Steve saw the handle of a small revolver.

A gun?

Bo Pan had a *gun*?

Steve realized he was staring, turned quickly to lock his eyes on the laptop screen.

"Steve, what is wrong? You seem startled."

The tone in Bo Pan's voice made it clear: *I know you saw the gun, and now you know who is really in charge, yes?*

"I'm fine, Bo Pan. Fine."

"Good."

The old man offered Steve a folded piece of paper.

Steve took it, started unfolding it. Even as he did, he wondered if this might be the end of him. Once he looked at it, would he know too much?

He found himself looking at a detailed deck plan of the USS *Los Angeles*. Under the title were the words *Modified: Operation Wolf Head.*

Bo Pan flicked the paper. "This cost your country a great deal of money." He pointed to the sub's nose. "There. The Tomahawk missile tubes were removed and a lab was installed." He slid his finger to a small box with an X drawn on it. "And *that* is their containment unit. Tell your machine to look there, and bring us whatever is inside."

Steve turned in his chair, stared at the older man. Bo Pan still looked like some rich white man's gardener, yet here he was with classified information that had to go way beyond top secret.

"The alien artifact," Steve said, "that's what's inside the containment unit?"

"Hopefully," Bo Pan said.

"This is a bad idea. The submarine was hit by a torpedo. Even if the alien artifact is inside, it could be broken into a hundred pieces, and each piece might have that contagious disease that turns people into killers. We should just *go*. The navy will be angry if they find us looking in there, and—"

The slap rocked Steve's head back. He stared, wide-eyed, hand cupping his now-stinging cheek. He hadn't even seen Bo Pan move.

The old man stared down at him. "You are wasting time, Steve Stanton. Do you think you are the only intelligent person on the planet? The X on the paper represents a locker, a locker built to withstand a direct hit from almost any kind of weapon. Inside that locker is a piece of alien ship stored within an airtight container that has already been decontaminated. If the locker is not damaged, the container can be brought onto this ship with no danger to any of us."

The sting of the slap faded to mild heat. Steve gently rubbed at his cheek. It hurt. He'd made a mistake by following orders and not asking questions, but he wouldn't be bullied into making an even bigger one.

"No," Steve said. "I'm done with this." He turned to his laptop, fingers reaching for the keys. "I'm telling the *Platypus* to return to—"

A cold pressure pushed against his temple. He felt a mechanical *click* that sent a slight vibration through his skull — Bo Pan had put the revolver against his head and cocked the trigger.

Steve couldn't move.

"If the container makes it to shore, *you* make it to shore," Bo Pan said. "Do you understand?"

Just a pull of the trigger, one tiny motion, and his brains would splatter all over the cabin. Steve stayed oh-so-still, lest a shiver or a twitch make Bo Pan's finger squeeze.

"Yes, I understand."

The pressure against his temple went away, leaving the cool spot in its wake.

"Good," Bo Pan said. "And your other machine, the snake, it can destroy an American ROV?"

The snake had been in the second crate. It hitched a ride on the *Platypus* the way a remora hitches a ride on a shark. It was made up of nine metal-shelled sections connected together by rubber seals. Each section had a battery-powered motor inside. The nine motors worked in synchronicity to create a waving motion: the three-foot-long robot could slither across land like a snake, or swim through water like an eel.

Each metal-shelled section also held twenty grams of C-4. If the snake swam near a threatening object, it could detonate all nine charges at once.

"Steve, I asked you a question. If it needs to, can the snake destroy an American ROV?"

Steve's body vibrated with fear.

"Yes, of course," he said. He wasn't sure if it could or it couldn't, but he wasn't about to say that to an angry old man holding a gun. "If the snake can wrap around one of the navy's ROVs, it can detonate and crush the thing like a tin can. But if you're thinking of using it on the locker that holds the alien object, Bo Pan, I can't guarantee it won't destroy everything inside."

Bo Pan shrugged. "The Americans will try to retrieve the container. When they do, they will open the locker for us. That is when your machine will take it. I will tell you what I want it to do. I talk, you program, understand?"

Steve turned to his computer, suddenly relieved to dive into his work, to give his brain something to think of other than Bo Pan's gun.

THE BARRIER

Clarence sat in the observation module. He watched a monitor, trying to make sense of the video Tim and Margaret were so excited to share with him. It was time-lapse footage, two side-by-side bits of Charlie Petrovsky's rotting flesh. Five hours compressed into fifteen seconds let Clarence immediately see a significant difference.

He looked over the console, down into the Analysis Module where Tim and Margaret stared up at him, waiting.

"Okay, I watched it," Clarence said. "The one on the left is rotting faster than the one on the right. What's it mean?"

Tim turned to Margaret, half bowed, lowered his arm in a sweeping gesture: *after you, madame*. Margaret mocked a curtsy, which looked ridiculous in her bulky suit.

To say their mood had changed was an understatement; they thought they were on to something big.

"The sample on the left is the control," Margaret said. "That's Petrovsky's tissue, getting hit hard by the black rot. The one on the right is also his tissue but was treated with a solution that contained Walker's blood."

Clarence glanced at the footage again. "Walker's blood stops the black rot?"

This time Margaret turned to Tim, bowed, made the *after you* gesture. Tim kept form and mocked a curtsy of his own — a little better than Margaret's, Clarence had to admit.

"Not Walker's blood, exactly, but a chemical that's in it," Tim said. "I found a compound in her blood that wasn't present in Petrovsky. We then detected that same compound in the few living hydras we have left. Ergo, the hydras make it. The compound is a catalyst that alters the black-rot process — it turns *off* the part that makes human bodies undergo exponential apoptosis, but it doesn't do anything to the chemical that makes the infected tissues and microorganisms undergo their own chain-reaction decomposition."

Clarence had to play back the words in his head to make sure he wasn't oversimplifying what he'd heard. Could it be that straightforward?

"So it's a cure," he said. "It kills the infection, but leaves our tissue alone?"

Tim thought for a moment. "Sort of. It depends on how long the person has been exposed. See, the catalyst is a really *big* molecule. You know anything about the blood-brain barrier?"

Clarence hesitated for a moment, wondering if Tim was trying to make him look stupid in front of Margaret, but both of them seemed far too excited to be playing any games.

"No, not really."

"Think of it like a mesh," Margaret said. "It's a semipermeable membrane. That means things of a certain size can penetrate it, but things larger than that size cannot. It evolved to keep circulating blood separate from the extracellular fluid" — she paused, perhaps realizing she was going too far into detail — "to keep blood and other things separated from actual brain tissue. Blood can't go through the barrier, but oxygen diffused *from* blood can. So if things are small enough, they can slide through the mesh. If they're too big, they can't. Follow me so far?"

Clarence nodded.

Tim held out his hands wide, like he was talking about the fish that got away.

"The hydra catalyst is too large to penetrate the barrier," he said. "So to answer your question, the catalyst first works as an inoculant — if it's already in your system *before* you are exposed to the infection, any crawlers produced will die before they can reach your brain. It makes you immune. And if you've already *been* infected but the crawlers have *not yet* reached your brain, the catalyst can kill off those crawlers. Meaning, if you get infected right now and we get this catalyst in your system within twenty-four hours, it will probably cure you."

Clarence now understood their excitement. He was beginning to feel it himself.

"So if you take it soon enough, it *is* a cure," he said. "What happens after the twenty-four hours?"

Tim shrugged. "The crawlers need about twenty-four hours to form, find your nervous system and reach your brain. If enough of them get in, they rework your brain into the cellulose-based structures we've seen. At that point, it's too late."

Clarence looked at Margaret. "But you said Walker had hydras in her brain. Hydras can get in there?"

Margaret nodded. "They can, following the same path the crawlers do. We don't have much evidence to go on right now, but it seems possible the hydras travel to the brain instinctually, because they are so closely related to the crawlers. But there's a difference — the hydras don't seem to alter brain tissue. They're just *there*."

As far as cures went, alien organisms in the brain didn't seem all that encouraging.

"Say the crawlers get to the brain first," Clarence said. "They start changing everything around, and then the hydras get there. What happens then?"

Margaret glanced at Tim.

"The hydras probably keep secreting their catalyst," he said. "Since they're on the other side of the blood-brain barrier, and so are the crawlers, any crawlers exposed to the catalyst will die. Any cellulose-based structures probably dissolve."

"Which means what to the host?"

"Death," Tim said. "It means death."

For a few minutes, Clarence had dared to hope that it was all over, that if some poor soul was infected, he or she could be saved with a shot or a pill. Life didn't work that way, it seemed. Still, at least now there was *something* to fight with.

"Impressive work," Clarence said. "So what happens next?"

"Tim goes to work on genetically sequencing the hydras," Margaret said. "He isolates the genetic code that makes the catalyst, inserts that bit of code into the genome of his yeast, and the yeast produces the catalyst."

That sounded impossible.

"Feely, you can really do that?"

Tim shrugged. "It's how insulin is made for diabetics. The DNA that makes insulin is inserted into bacteria, the bacteria secrete the insulin, which is harvested and purified. When the bacteria reproduce, the subsequent generations have that same inserted DNA. Boom, you have a permanent, insulin-producing population.

"The basic technology is decades old. I've spent the last two years inserting crawler coding into my fast-growing yeast, so at this point it's just plug-and-play. The only question is if my yeast will survive the new coding. If so, we'll have *Saccharomyces feely* producing the catalyst inside of a few hours."

A few *hours*? Clarence fought down his immediate reaction. He wasn't going to get his hopes up this fast.

"Let's hope you're right," he said. "What do you need to make this happen?"

Now Tim glanced at Margaret. She looked away, looked down.

"We need to make more hydras," she said. "And there's only one way to do that."

HUMAN EXPERIMENTATION

Margaret had killed one of the hydras to analyze it. Another had died on its own; she assumed the last two surviving hydras couldn't be far behind.

Time was running out.

Candice Walker was dead, as was everything inside of her. There were no more hydras to be had from her corpse.

Margaret entered the clear cell of Eric Edmund. She carried a small tray holding an alcohol swab and a syringe. She set the tray down on Edmund's stomach. She had to remind herself that the man was brain-dead. He would never recover.

Edmund's *self*, all that he had ever been, that was gone forever . . . but his body lived on. His heart pumped, his blood flowed, his cells divided. The human body was the hydras' natural environment. There, hopefully, they would modify Edmund's stem cells, make copies of themselves — they would replicate.

Margaret picked up the alcohol swab and wiped Edmund's shoulder, cleaning her target area. She set the swab down and lifted the syringe. She stared at it through her visor. Just one CC of saline, and inside that fluid, a pair of passengers.

Only two left.

A slap on the glass. She turned to see Cantrell, staring at her, the lighter skin of his palms resting on the clear wall. His eyes . . . he looked like he was trying to control his anger.

"Doctor Montoya, what are you doing?" Cantrell smiled. He looked at the syringe. "Don't you need permission for something like that?"

How could he know what she was doing? He didn't know; he was just being difficult.

"Not your concern," she said.

Cantrell frowned, spoke sweetly. "Awww, Doc, of course it is. He's in the cell next to mine. What if something breaks? What you do to him could affect me."

"You have nothing to worry about," Margaret said. "You're not infected, Cantrell."

The smile returned. A chilling smile.

"Then let me out," he said. "I keep testing negative . . . just let me out."

Those eyes, so intense, so *angry* even though his voice sounded smooth and calm.

Why was she wasting time with him?

Only two left . . .

Margaret slid the needle into Edmund's shoulder, then pushed the plunger all the way down. The saline emptied into his arm.

That was that. She could only hope those hydras were as reproductively efficient as the crawlers that had taken over Betty Jewel, Carmen Sanchez and so many others.

All Margaret's energy drained away. She felt hollow. The biosafety suit suddenly seemed so heavy. If she could just get out of it for a little bit, maybe rest her eyes.

She heard the click of someone coming onto her channel.

"Margo," Clarence said. "Where are you?"

"Detainment."

"What are you doing there?"

"I'm working, Clarence. What do you want?"

"The diver is going into the *Los Angeles* in forty-five minutes," he said. "I thought you'd want to watch."

She did want to see that. Maybe the diver would come across the subject of Candice Walker's final drawings, the three men in the membrane. Forty-five minutes . . . enough time to decon, get out of the suit, grab twenty minutes of sleep.

She turned to leave, felt Cantrell's eyes upon her. For just a moment, she froze — he looked like he wanted to kill her — and then the moment was gone.

Cantrell walked to his bed and sat.

Margaret picked up her tray and left Edmund's cell.

FOLLOW-THROUGH

When he'd been ten years old, Orin Nagy's father finally showed him how to properly swing a baseball bat. It was all in the hips, his father had said. Twisting them at the right moment brought your body around, maximized your swing velocity. Arm strength mattered, sure, but the *real* power came from the hips. The hips, and following through.

The same advice held true for swinging a pipe wrench.

Orin swung, Orin *twisted*, bringing twenty pounds of unforgiving metal to bear on the motherfucker that wanted to make him take the cellulose test.

The man's biosafety suit offered little protection. The heavy wrench caved in his right temple like a hammer slammed into a ripe melon.

And, just like the good boy he'd once been, Orin followed through.

The man dropped like a bag of wet shit.

Daddy would have been proud.

Orin heard men screaming angry things. He saw another one raising a pistol. Orin let the follow-through carry him all the way around in a fast 360-degree turn. As he came out of that turn, he swung again, more overhand axe-chop than smooth baseball swing. The results were much the same: the wet *crunch* of a crushed skull.

The gun went off. A pair of bodies slammed into Orin, dragged him to the ground.

He fought, because God commanded he do so, and also because before he died he wanted to kill just one more of the cock-sucking pissant humans that he hated so fucking much . . .

140 CHARACTERS

Six miles clear of the navy flotilla and fifty feet below the empty, roiling surface of Lake Michigan, the *Platypus* hovered, motionless save for the slight back-and-forth tug of the waves high above. It might have been a dead fish. It might have been a log.

A clamp released, freeing a fist-sized piece of plastic. The plastic floated upward, trailed by a thin cable. Forty feet . . . thirty . . . twenty . . .

The plastic reached the surface, bobbed there. It extended a telescoping antenna that was no thicker than a pencil at the base, little more than a stiff wire where it topped out four feet above the water.

The *Platypus* floated, unmoving, waiting for instructions.

A signal came in: a tweet. Then another. Five 140-character alphanumeric messages in all. Each message called up commands stored in the *Platypus*'s memory.

The *Platypus* retracted the antennae, then reeled in the plastic float. The machine tilted down, started to swim. A hundred feet down, then two hundred, then three hundred.

Ten feet from the bottom, the *Platypus* leveled out. It called up the recorded bearing that would lead it back to the *Los Angeles*. It followed the lake floor's contour, going deeper and deeper as it closed the distance.

The *Platypus* scanned for any signal, any communication, ready to adjust its path based on the presence of other craft.

A half mile out, it detected pings from a powerful sonar almost a thousand feet above: signals from a surface ship sent to submerged vessels. The *Platypus* couldn't read those messages — they were encrypted — but the signals themselves alerted it to a danger of detection.

Steve Stanton's creation slowed to a crawl. It sank to the bottom, resting its underside on Lake Michigan's thick muck. It used its side fins as arms rather than paddles, pressing against rocks and sand and mud to pull its body slowly forward.

It detected light, light coming from yellow shapes. The *Platypus* stopped moving, ran the visual data through pattern analysis programs. It quickly identified the shapes as U.S. Navy ROVs.

The *Platypus* shut down everything but its detection systems.

Eventually, the yellow shapes moved away, away and *up*, taking their light with them. When that light dropped below a certain level, the *Platypus* started a timing subroutine. If the light didn't come back after four minutes, it would proceed.

Infrared cameras searched and found none of the moving objects it was programmed to avoid. Sonar continued to sweep the area, but the *Platypus*'s furry foam coating absorbed those signals, let almost nothing bounce away. What little echo escaped would show as nothing more than a fish.

The *Platypus* moved forward again, slinking across the bottom toward its goal.

So far, the machine had done nothing remarkable: *Move toward an obstacle; search for unobstructed space; enter unobstructed space; repeat while moving toward the preprogrammed target location*. To a robotics engineer, such maneuvers were child's play, part of freshman robotics classes — *high school* freshman classes, that is.

The *Platypus* swam closer to the *Los Angeles*. Lined up next to the 362 feet of the wrecked sub, Steve Stanton's 10-foot-long, narrow robot kind of did look like a fish. A *tiny* fish.

Rear fins undulated slowly, pushing the *Platypus* toward the crack in the dry deck shelter. Small internal motors activated, pulling the machine's sides in tighter. As it slid through the crack, it hit something soft — the severed leg that had once belonged to Wicked Charlie Petrovsky.

From the black shoe, which was still tied, up to midthigh, the leg looked normal. Wet, but normal. From the midthigh up, however, it was a study in damage. A jagged shard of bone stuck up from streamers of pale, bloodless muscle. The impact with the *Platypus* made Charlie's leg spin in a slow-motion circle, shreds of tissue marking the curve like morbid little comet tails.

Just as the *Platypus* moved past, the fleshy mass of Charlie's thigh spun into the sonar-eating foam, kicking up a small cloud of Charlie meat that danced in the robot's wake.

The leg bounced away.

The *Platypus* moved to the open hatch that Bo Pan had spotted several hours earlier. In it went. It swam past motionless bodies, moved around wreckage, squeezed through doors that had been bent and torn by a torpedo's lethal shock wave.

Steve Stanton's creation quickly found the submarine's nose. It entered. It located the locker that stored its objective. Recent programming told the *Platypus* to wait here, wait for someone or something to come and open that locker.

It used infrared to scan the room: measuring, calculating, searching for the best place to hide. Empty racks lined the walls. Airtight cases that had once rested on those racks now gently bobbed against the ceiling.

The *Platypus* flapped all its fins, gently but firmly, turning as it did. It swam into the empty racks and wedged itself down near the floor, nose aimed into the room in case it sensed a threat and needed to move quickly.

A threat, or, an opportunity.

For the second time, the *Platypus* shut down almost all its systems. No lights, no motors, nothing but a camera lens that was — ironically — shaped like a fish eye.

It watched.

SCARY PERRY

She knew she was dreaming, because she'd had this dream before. So many times. That didn't make it any less gutting.

"Hello, Perry."

Perry Dawsey smiled.

They stood on an empty street in a desperate, run-down area of Detroit. It was the last place she had seen him alive. The bloated, Thanksgiving Day Parade float of a woman had just burst, scattering a dense, expanding cloud to float on the light breeze. The cloud was made of dandelion spores, little self-contained crawlers that would instantly infect whomever they touched.

They had touched Perry.

He was going to die. He knew that.

"Hey, Margo," he said.

"Hey," Margaret said. The words in the dream were always identical, both her part and his.

"I got Chelsea," he said. His smile faded. "The voices have finally stopped, but . . . I don't think I'm doing so good. I've got those things inside of me."

I've got those things inside of me, he'd said. What he hadn't said was: *again.* What he hadn't said was: *It's not fair. I fought hard. I won. And I'm going to die anyway.*

His face wrinkled into a frown, a steady wince of pain.

"It hurts," he said. "Bad. I think they're moving to my brain. Margaret, I don't want to lose control again."

They: the crawlers that were already working their way up his nervous system, heading for his head. There, they would spread their interweaving tendrils. They would take him over, *change* him, and destroy who he was in the process.

"You won't," she said. "They won't have time."

And now her gift to him, his reward for standing tall in the face of absolute destruction, for being the one person willing to fight no matter what the odds.

She heard a growing whistle — the sound of an incoming artillery shell. A small shadow appeared on the ground between their feet, a quivering circle of black.

Perry stared at her. His smile returned, a smile of exhausted disbelief.

"Holy shit," he said. "Are you nuking me?"

"Yes," she said, because there was nothing else to say.

The shadow-circle grew larger, engulfing their feet, then spreading until they were both standing in its shade.

A wet laugh joined Perry's corpse smile. "Dew said I'm like a cockroach, that nothing can kill me. I don't think physics is on my side this time, though."

He was dead twice over, yet still he cracked jokes, for *her*, a last effort to lift some of the blame from her shoulders.

Perry coughed. Little hatchlings shot out of his mouth, fell to the ground. They righted themselves and sprinted away, out of the shadow and into the light.

They wouldn't escape. Nothing would.

Perry wiped his mouth. His blue eyes bore into her.

"How long do I have?"

"About fifteen seconds," she said.

Then she started to float away, leaving Perry behind.

He looked up. "No shit? That's kind of fucked up."

The bomb's shadow spread faster, throwing the buildings on either side of the street into deep blackness. Perry stood in the shadow's center, his blond hair and blue eyes still as bright as if the sun reached down and set them alight.

Margaret floated higher. Perry looked smaller and smaller.

He cupped his hands to his face and shouted: "Margo?"

Shooting up into the sky, she shouted back: "Yes?"

She saw the bomb now — as big as the city itself, a cartoony thing that would crush Detroit by impact alone even if it didn't detonate.

Perry drew in a huge breath, and screamed his final words.

"Thank you for saving my life!"

The giant bomb exploded. The mushroom cloud rose up far beneath her feet. It wouldn't reach her. She wouldn't feel the effects.

She was safe: it was only other people who died.

"I'm sorry," she whispered. "I'm so sorry."

• • •

Margaret Montoya opened her eyes. She'd failed Perry. She'd failed Dew Phillips. She'd failed Amos Braun.

She sat up in bed, trying to remember where she was. A bed, clean sheets that smelled faintly of bleach, heavy blankets . . . her room aboard the *Carl Brashear*.

A nap, a *short* nap that had done nothing to ease her exhaustion.

She wanted to watch the diver go into the *Los Angeles*, but she could barely move. Maybe it was time to take Tim up on his offer for Adderall. She'd had four hours of sleep in the last twenty — every hour of sleep was a lost hour of analysis and research.

Margaret pushed herself out of bed. She could watch the diver's efforts while she waited for the initial results from Tim's yeast modification. *Saccharomyces feely*. That was the answer, it *had* to be.

The hydras were a fascinating development, but largely unknown. What effect would they have on a living host? They might wind up being as bad as — or worse than — the crawlers that they killed. Tim had found his living hydras inside pustules on Walker; that was one way the crawlers spread. Would the hydras also *puff* out, microscopic bits floating on the air until they landed on a new host?

If so, the hydras could become an airborne contagion.

Tim's yeast, on the other hand, carried no such threat. He'd ramped up the growth rate somehow, making it reproduce two to three times faster than most yeast. It wasn't contagious — and even if it was, it was just yeast with a piece of the hydra's coding: no threat of any kind. Still, she had sent Murray a message to look into the Spectrum Health HAC study. If one participant in that study produced hydras, other participants might as well. She couldn't afford to overlook any possibility that could provide a potential weapon.

Margaret stood. She felt old, she felt creaky. She'd watch the diver, then maybe take one of Tim's pills.

Tired or not, the work wouldn't wait.

POSITIVE THOUGHTS

Tim Feely walked down the white corridor, toweling off his hair as he went. Amazing what a shower could do for the soul. His flip-flops flapped against the floor. He wore a thick, white, terrycloth robe, a gift from Captain Yasaka. That poor, poor woman; she commanded an entire ship's worth of sailors, day in, day out, but sometimes a girl just needed someone else to take charge.

Tim wondered if Margaret Montoya was that kind of woman in the bedroom. Or did her boudoir policies stray into the dictatorial realm? He certainly couldn't see Clarence Otto as the kind of guy who let his lady boss him around. Maybe that was the problem. Maybe Margaret was too aggressive for Tall, Dark & Don't Threaten My Manhood. If Margo wanted to call the shots, that wouldn't bother Tim in the least.

If the ladies liked it, Tim liked it — a simple philosophy that opened up a world of possibilities.

Could he land Margaret? Why the fuck not? He felt on top of the world, he felt like a king. He'd isolated the hydra's catalyst-producing gene sequence and inserted it into his fast-growing yeast, which was now happily diving away. It remained to be seen, however, if the modified yeast actually produced the catalyst, *and* if that catalyst actually worked.

From everything he'd seen so far, it would. Which meant — Tim Feely might very well have just saved the world.

And if *that* don't get you laid, nothing will.

Tim entered the briefing room. Margaret was sitting in one of the room's ten theater-style chairs. Clarence stood off a bit to the side. He'd lost the suit coat, thank God. He wore jeans and a black T-shirt. A T-shirt that was too tight, in Tim's opinion. Well, maybe Margaret was tired of all those muscles. Fuck but that Clarence dude was put together, though.

Margaret saw Tim enter, raised her glass of wine. "Doctor Feely. I found the liquor cabinet and helped myself. You don't mind?"

He gave her his best seductive smile. "Don't mind at all."

Clarence saw the smile. He scowled.

Tim dialed the smile back a few notches, from *leering* to *slightly-more-than-friendly*.

Margaret gestured to the room, clearly hoping to change the subject. "This theater is really something."

Tim could imagine how the room took newbies by surprise. In addition to cushy seats that faced a ten-foot screen, there was a fridge full of beer, plenty of snacks, and a liquor cabinet packed with the best liquid treats a boy could buy.

"Don't forget there was a full staff here for years," he said. "Uncle Sam wanted his pet scientists to be happy."

Clarence let out a snort. "Yeah. And the people who actually do the work of running the ship? What do they think of your little private theater?"

Tim waggled his pointer finger side to side. "Please to *no-no-no*," he said. "The entire science module is off-limits to the rank and file. I doubt people who hot-bunk would appreciate we brainiacs living in the lap of luxury."

"Right," Clarence said. "That doesn't bother you at all?"

Tim walked past Clarence to the liquor cabinet. The half-empty bottle of Adderall was right on top. Correction, *half-full:* Tim was an optimist, after all. He opened the cabinet and pulled out the bottle of Oban 2000.

"Clarence," Tim said as he poured a glass, "it's not my fault other people didn't get a doctorate."

"No, I suppose it's not," Clarence said. "Just like it's not your *fault* that you get to live in freedom."

This guy *had* to have an American flag tattooed somewhere on his body.

Margaret waved a hand. "Boys, don't rain on my parade with your political differences, okay? If Tim's yeast culture takes off, we may very well have this thing beat. I'm in the mood to enjoy my break, because soon we have to get back to work."

Tim nodded. "I agree. Tomorrow's going to be a big day."

Margaret shook her head. "I'm talking about *tonight*, Doctor Feely. As soon as we watch the diver enter the *Los Angeles*, we'll get back at it."

Tim had a moment to hope she was joking. The look in her eyes said she wasn't.

"Ah," he said. "I see."

Good thing he had enough stimulants to go around. Better living through chemistry.

He sat in the chair next to Margaret, feeling Clarence's stare on the back of his neck as he did. Tim sipped his Oban.

The image on the big screen showed a cone of dimly lit water, featureless save for an occasional bit of flotsam that glowed like a tiny star in the diver's light, then gone as the camera passed it by. Numbers played out at the bottom of the screen, showing the descending depth: eight hundred feet and counting. Another hundred feet or so, and that light would play off the wreck of the *Los Angeles*.

Up until the shit hit the fan, Tim had spent most of his time in this very room, watching downloaded movies and TV shows, playing video games, just generally dicking around and wasting taxpayer money. What else had there been to do? Sure, he'd worked on his yeast, trying to engineer a genome that would successfully produce a little-understood cellulase. Trying, and failing; he'd had no crawlers, no samples, nothing to go on but a mass spec analysis that clearly wasn't 100 percent accurate. He'd collected a six-figure paycheck, come up with bullshit to put on his weekly reports and generally kicked back and lived the good life of a government employee flying under the radar.

Now, however, he had something he *could* use: an actual cellulase, and plenty of it. On the one hand, it made him furious to see how close he'd been to getting it right. On the other, if the new line of *Saccharomyces feely* succeeded, his work could make the human race immune to a disease that made the black plague look like postnasal drip.

Tim raised his glass toward Margaret. She frowned, but begrudgingly reached out her wineglass and *clinked* in a quiet toast.

Like him, she had showered. Her black hair hung heavy and damp, but she looked fantastic. When she'd arrived, she'd been drowning in a bizarre notion of self-pity. Well, no more — her eyes blazed with intelligence, with life, and a persistent smile hovered at the corners of her mouth. She looked good even inside a BSL-4 suit; outside of one, she looked fantastic.

Tim could see more than a few lost weekends with that one. As long as Captain Yasaka didn't find out, of course. It was always a good rule of thumb not to incur the jealousy of a woman with keys to the weapons locker.

"I should make popcorn," Tim said. "You guys want popcorn?"

Neither Margaret nor Clarence responded. Their attention stayed fixed on the screen.

The number at the bottom of the screen ticked up to 850.

"The diver will be there soon," Tim said. "We'll get a look at this debacle."

"It's not the diver," Clarence said. "This is from a camera mounted on the nose of a Blackfish 12, the navy's high-end UUV. The 'Fish is going down ahead of the diver to get a fresh rad reading."

Tim drained his glass. He thought about asking Clarence to fetch him a refill, but he wasn't really in the mood to get his ass kicked. He started to stand.

Margaret put a hand on his arm. "Doctor Feely, you're not getting another drink, are you?"

Tim stopped halfway out of his chair. "Uh, the thought had crossed my mind."

She shook her head. "I'd appreciate it if you didn't. We go back into the lab in a little bit."

Tim sighed, sat down and watched the screen. The Blackfish's lights played against a far-off, ghostly image. Finally, the submarine.

His hand tightened on his empty glass. *The submarine . . . Walker, immune . . .*

"Wait a minute," he said. "We think Walker was immune, right?"

Margaret nodded.

"So then why did she sabotage the sub's engines? Why did she cripple it if she *wasn't* a psycho?"

"The answer is simple," Clarence said. "Maybe not for someone with a *doctorate*, but simple enough for a veteran."

Tim turned to look at Clarence, saw the man's self-confident smirk.

"Do tell, Agent Otto," Tim said. "Edify me with your worldly wisdom."

"The disease wants to spread, it *always* wants to spread," Clarence said. "If the captain was one of the Converted, he'd head for the nearest major port so he could spread his infected crew among a dense population."

Margaret's eyebrows rose. "Chicago. They were heading for Chicago. Candice stopped them."

Clarence nodded. "Lieutenant Walker knew her duty. She knew what she had to do to protect the country."

Tim huffed. Clarence was right, obviously, which Tim found annoying.

Patriotism could drive people to sacrifice themselves. That, too, was damn annoying, because it flew in the face of survival of the fittest. Stupid people could be convinced to die for the greater good. The *greater good* was always someone who would live on because of — and long after — that sacrifice. Soldiers die, generals retire.

On the screen, the wrongly angled sail of the *Los Angeles* loomed into view. Lights played off more flotsam. Tim knew a lot of that detritus was composed of sailor bits, bodies either torn apart by the torpedo strike or picked at by scavengers.

The number 688 glowed a bright white.

The PA system clicked on: a too-loud, mechanical voice that broke the moment's magic.

"Doctor Feely, line one for Captain Yasaka. Doctor Feely, line one for Captain Yasaka."

Tim glanced at the wet-haired Margaret Montoya, felt like he'd been caught at something — did Yasaka know he was ogling his fellow scientist? He stood and strode to a phone mounted on the wall. He lifted the handset, as always marveling a little at the archaic cord that ran from it to the wall unit.

He pushed the number "1."

"This is Doctor Feely."

"This is the captain." Yasaka's voice. Not the voice that on some nights said *take me*, or on extraspecial nights said *please, Daddy*. This was her command voice.

"Captain, how can I be of service?"

"Are you with Doctor Montoya?"

"I am."

"A petty officer just killed two of my crew," the captain said. "He tested positive, as did two other men who were bunking near him. We have a total of three positives."

Tim's body went ice cold.

"Three . . . *positives*?"

"So far," Yasaka said. "Security will deliver these men to cells in your lab. I suspect they won't be the last."

DIVER DOWN

Clarence sat in the lab's control room module, looking down at Tim and Margaret who were working away in their big-helmeted suits.

They'd rushed out of the extravagant theater, desperate to get back to work. Clarence had watched them both pop some pills — apparently, now wasn't the time to let fatigue get the better of them.

As for himself, he'd suited up and overseen delivery of the new prisoners: Orin Nagy, the killer, as well as Conroy Austin and Lionel Chappas, both of whom had tested positive. Cantrell now had company.

The deck crane had lowered the men down to the *Brashear*'s big side airlock, accompanied by six biosafety-suited guards. Clarence had watched everyone go through the bleach-wash decon process, watched the infected men be placed in clear cells, watched the guards reenter the airlock for their final decon.

The side airlock was the only safe way to bring the infected into the holding area, but it was also needed for the submersion tests on Clark's and Cantrell's suits. The first test, the pressurized fall test, hadn't detected any leaks; if the suits had holes, those holes were microscopic. Margaret didn't seem that concerned about it, but Clarence would still push Captain Yasaka to do the submersion test. With Yasaka's crew redoubling efforts to find any infected, the best Clarence could hope for was to see the test run tomorrow night, or, at the very latest, the following morning.

The mood had changed, to say the least. In the extravagant briefing room, he'd sensed Margaret's subdued elation — she thought they had the infection beat. Not today, of course, but so soon that a few more weeks would make no difference. Now, however, the infection had spread to the general crew. Three positives would quickly multiply. Yasaka's best efforts couldn't stop the spread, not with so many people packed on the *Brashear* and nowhere to send them. The captain could only hope to slow the contagion, give Margaret and Tim time to come up with a solution.

And if they didn't find that solution? This would end with an F-27 Eagle dropping a firebomb on the entire task force. *Carl Brashear* would join the *Forrest Sherman*, the *Stratton* and the *Los Angeles* at the bottom of Lake Michigan. Would Clarence and Margaret still be aboard if that happened? Maybe. If Murray Longworth wasn't sure that he and Margaret were clean, he'd torch them without a second thought.

Clarence couldn't do anything to help Tim and Margaret. What he could do was pay attention to the diver entering the wreck of the *Los Angeles*.

On the counter in front of him, Clarence had diagrams of the *Los Angeles*'s layout. He watched the diver's progress on the console's small screens. It was quite different from the deep-water dives he'd seen on the Discovery Channel: no rust, no colorful clusters of barnacles and anemones, no schools of bright fish. The *LA* had sunk only three days earlier — just a broken, gray hull sitting on a lifeless lake bottom.

The control room's speakers carried the chatter between the diver and the *Brashear*'s crew.

"Diver One, status? How you doing, Tom?"

"Diver is okay," came back the answer. "Goddamn cold down here, feeling it in my joints right through the suit. Request permission to start cutting."

"Permission granted, Diver One."

Seconds later, the screen blared brightly. Clarence looked away.

The diver's awkward high-pressure diving suit made him look like a cross between a morbidly obese man and a heavily armored beetle. Five round, blue segments made up each arm, connected together by oscillating rings that allowed limited movement. There weren't even hands, just blue spheres tipped by black pincers.

The legs were similar to the arms, all connecting to a white, hard-shelled torso, as did the bulbous helmet. A boxy red backpack housed the oxygen supply and CO_2 scrubber, which could give the diver up to forty-eight hours of life support. An ADS rig was one of the few things that could make a space suit look dainty by comparison.

The suit was far too bulky to fit through any of the *Los Angeles*'s external hatches. Cutting directly into the nose cone might put the alien artifact at risk. The diver would use an underwater torch to cut through the hull of the torpedo room, then move through that wider space into the nose cone.

The bright light faded from the screen.

"Diver One, cut complete. Removing hull."

Clarence saw a large, oval piece of metal drop away from the submarine's curved hull and *thump* into the lake bottom, kicking up a slow-motion cloud of flotsam.

"Diver One, proceed into the torpedo room."

"Roger that, Topside. Moving into the torpedo room."

Clarence inched closer to the screen.

Almost immediately, the diver's light revealed three uniformed corpses that hung motionless in the water. Rigor held arms away from bodies, as if the dead were waiting to give someone a hug. There was at least *some* animal life at this depth — even though no fish were visible, the ripped flesh of hands and faces betrayed their presence.

"Topside," the diver said, "you seeing this?" His voice sounded tinny. Clarence could hear the man's breathing increase.

"Roger that, Diver One," the dive master said. "Nobody said it was going to be pretty. You're almost there. Just get the job done."

"Roger," the diver said. "Moving in."

Clarence could imagine the diver's stress. Nine hundred feet below the surface — a depth that would kill him without the suit — he was surrounded by corpses while violence and uncertainty swept across the ship above him. The diver, *Tom*, he had to have giant balls of steel.

Technically, Clarence was the current representative of the scientific team. If needed, he had an override button he could hit and speak directly to the diver. If any major issues popped up, Clarence could route the diver-cam view to Margaret's heads-up display, let her decide what needed to be done.

The dive master's voice sounded loud and clear in the speakers. "Diver One, move forward through the torpedo room to the nose-cone airlock."

"Roger that, Topside."

"Diver Two," the dive master said, "position yourself at the entrance point and maintain safety of Diver One's umbilical."

"Diver Two, confirmed," came a third voice, the voice of a woman.

Of course they were using a safety diver. Oddly, that made Clarence nervous — the *Brashear* only had two ADS 2000 rigs. If something went very wrong on this dive, there was no way to get another person down to the wreck without flying in additional suits. Even on a rush order, that might take a day or more.

"Topside, Diver Two," the woman said. "Feeding Diver One's umbilical."

The ADS onboard air meant the divers didn't need air tubes. What they did need, however, was a communication cable a thousand feet long — if Tom cut his on some jagged piece of wreckage, the *Brashear* would lose his visual and audio signals.

On the screen, Clarence saw racks of long, gray torpedoes. A body sat there, ass on the deck, back against one of the racks, chin hanging to chest as if the man was only taking a catnap.

"Topside, Diver One," the diver said. "I have reached the nose-cone airlock. It's open."

Clarence looked at the sub's schematics. The nose cone had a small external airlock, for loading material from the outside directly into the negatively pressurized minilab, and it also had an internal airlock, allowing the science crew to enter the lab from the ship proper.

"We see it, Diver One," the dive master said. "Proceed."

The images on the screen blurred: the diver turning, slowly pulling in the slack on his umbilical cord. He turned again, then stepped through the airlock door into the small area beyond.

The room looked tilted, of course, about a thirty-degree slant down and to the right. Every wall had racks. Most of the racks were empty — they had been meant to hold small, airtight cases, cases that now bobbed against the ceiling. The cases held various scientific equipment: microscopes, voltage meters, hardness-testing kits and a dozen other devices that might help in identifying alien material.

"Topside, no bodies here, room is empty," the diver said. "Moving toward the objective."

He turned to the right, his light moving past the empty racks.

Clarence saw something. He slapped at his "override" button.

"Wait! Look left again!"

The dive master's voice came back angry and impatient. "Who's on this goddamn channel?"

"This is Agent Clarence Otto. Sorry. Listen, Tom . . . I mean, *Diver One* . . . can you turn to the left again?"

The dive master spoke again. "Diver One, stand by! Agent Otto, this is dangerous work. We finish the recovery first. Diver, stay with the mission par—"

A no-bullshit female voice cut in. "This is Captain Yasaka. Facilitate any and all requests of Agent Otto, as long as those requests do not compromise diver safety."

Clarence waited through a short but uncomfortable pause.

"Aye-aye, Captain," the dive master said. "Diver One, do as Agent Otto asked."

"Roger that, Chief," Tom said. "Diver turning left."

The image on the screen slewed left again.

"Look down," Clarence said.

The diver did. The image of a black shoe appeared.

"Just a shoe," Tom said. "It's stuck in some kind of brown stuff, looks like sediment has leaked in through a crack somewhere."

Clarence remembered when Murray had come to his house, remembered the picture drawn by Candice Walker.

"Move closer," Clarence said. "Pan up a little bit."

"Diver moving closer," Tom said. "I don't . . . wait, I think there's a foot in that shoe, and the leg is buried in the . . . oh my God. Are you guys seeing this?"

"Uh . . . roger that," the dive master said. "Stand by."

Clarence leaned closer to the monitor. Wedged between a pair of equipment racks was a body. Unlike the sitting-down-and-napping body in the torpedo room, however, this one was encased in something, something attached to the hull, the deck, even crusted up over the equipment racks. Tom's light played off of a brown, bumpy surface that covered the unknown sailor's torso and half of his face while leaving the mouth and nose unobstructed. The right eye stared, wide and forever frozen open. A left hand stuck out from the brown mass, fingers curled in a talon of death, just a bit of blue shirtsleeve still visible. Clarence saw a *second* left hand — there were two people in there. At least. Just as in the drawing made by Candice Walker.

"Diver One to Topside, what the hell is this?"

Tom's voice sounded ragged, like he was becoming overwhelmed.

"Ignore it, Diver One," the dive master said. "Proceed to your objective. Tom, stay cool."

Clarence could barely blink, barely breathe. Tom again turned right, toward the room's main storage locker. It looked like a horizontal, flat-topped freezer, the kind usually kept in a basement, only this one was military gray instead of the white. Inside, Clarence knew, was the soda-can-sized object the *Los Angeles* crew had collected days earlier.

Tom moved slowly toward it.

On the locker, a tiny keypad glowed green — it had its own power supply, which was obviously still functioning.

"Topside to Diver One, great work, we're almost home. Prepare to enter access codes." The dive master read off the sixteen-digit code. Tom read it back. Clarence saw Tom extend his suit's pincer hand. The pincer ended with a stiff rubber stud, small enough to press the keypad digits.

The last button drew a *beep* from the crate, audible over the speakers. The keypad's glow shifted from green to orange.

The crate's lid slowly rose on a rear hinge, pushed up by steel pistons on either end. The diver's lights shone on a small, black, cylindrical container. It wasn't much bigger than a travel mug.

Hidden inside of that, a piece of an alien spacecraft.

"Topside, Diver One, I see the objective."

"Visual confirmed, Diver One. Retrieve the objective and then exit the vessel."

The hard blue spheres — inside of which were Tom's hands — reached into the crate, toward the objective. The black pincers opened wide, ready to grab the black tube, then paused.

"Diver One to Topside, I know I was briefed that this is safe, but . . . well, are you *sure*?"

"Diver One, retrieve the object," the dive master said. "It's safe, Tom, just don't pretend you're making a James Bond martini, okay?"

Tom actually laughed, a sound thinned by the electronics but still full of a grateful relief.

"Yeah, *shaken not stirred*, you got it."

The diver's pincers closed on the container, rubber grips locking down on the curved, black surface. He lifted it free of the storage locker.

"Topside, Diver One — objective acquired."

Something black darted across the screen, a split-second flash that made Clarence think of snakes, worms, eels.

The image on the screen shifted, blurred, the diver turning as fast as he could.

"What the *fuck* was that?" Tom's voiced peaked his microphone, making his words crackle with static.

"Diver One, calm down," the dive master said, his tone cool and collected — of course it was, he wasn't the one in a dark tomb nine hundred feet below the surface, surrounded by dead bodies.

Clarence's hands clenched into involuntary fists. He wanted to reach down and somehow grab Tom, drag the diver to safety.

The image skewed as Tom turned, looking for the source of that unknown movement. His lights lit up the same empty shelves and slightly bobbing boxes, the same motionless dead men covered in crusty brown.

"Topside, Diver One — I think I saw something moving in here, maybe a fish. Moving to exit the . . . it's on my suit! Goddamit, there's not supposed to be—"

The screen turned to white noise.

"Diver One, status?"

No answer.

Clarence closed his eyes, tried to stay calm. So close . . . what had happened?

He heard the dive master's disembodied voice in the control room's speakers. "Diver One, status? Talk to me, Tom."

There was no response.

"Diver Two, we've lost contact with Diver One," the dive master said, his voice still supremely composed, infuriatingly so. "Proceed inside immediately to Diver One's location. Move forward with caution — it's possible Diver One tripped a booby trap."

"Topside, Diver Two, entering the sub."

The dive master continued to calmly issue orders, sending the remaining UUVs to the *Los Angeles* and getting rescue divers into the water.

The image on Clarence's screens shifted from static to the entrance hole and then the torpedo room, the view of Diver Two's camera nearly an exact replay of what Diver One had seen just minutes earlier.

Suddenly, the image shook violently, filled with bubbles and bits of falling metal. The diver slewed right, making the view tilt.

"Topside! Large explosion in the nose cone! Wreck is unstable!"

"Diver Two, exit immediately. Repeat, exit immediately."

Clarence heard the diver scream, saw a flash of something coming down from above. The image slewed the other way, the horizontal now vertical and the vertical horizontal as the diver fell to her side. He heard a *crunching* sound, painfully loud in the speakers.

"Diver Two, get out of there," the dive master said, his voice at last carrying a shred of urgency, a hint of emotion. "Exit immediately."

"Topside . . . I'm stuck . . . oh my God, my visor is cracked, water is coming in, get me *help*, get someone down here—"

Another *crunch* far louder than the first, then, no sound at all.

The sideways view didn't waver. The diver had been crushed, but her helmet camera remained on, continued to send signals up the umbilical to the *Brashear* far above.

Clarence sagged back in his chair. He felt cold, distant, as if it were all happening somewhere else. Two divers dead. Both ADSs destroyed.

And, worst of all, the artifact was still down there.

FOREIGN POWERS

Murray hated the Situation Room, but at least that felt comfortable, felt *familiar*. The president's private sitting room didn't feel familiar at all. He'd been here twice before, both times to deliver bad news to former presidents; the kind of news that couldn't wait until morning.

The room could have been in any house, really, any house of someone with money and status. Murray and Admiral Porter sat on a comfortable couch. Murray knew he looked wrinkled, disheveled — he'd been napping on a cot when the news had come in. His staff had brought him fresh clothes, but he'd done little more than throw them on. Porter, of course, looked neat and pressed, not a wrinkle on his uniform.

The sitting room was right next to the president's bedroom. Blackmon seemed sleepy, which was no surprise — she'd been woken up only fifteen minutes earlier.

"An explosion," she said. "What was the cause, Admiral?"

"Unknown at this time," Porter said. "Possibly sabotage, a booby trap left by the infected crew of the *Los Angeles*."

Blackmon's tired eyes turned to Murray. "Is that what you think?"

"It's a possibility, Madam President," Murray said. "Once the *LA*'s engines blew, the infected crew could assume that sooner or later divers would come down to retrieve the artifact. Booby traps fit the mentality of the infected, to some degree, although the infected would be most interested in spreading the disease. The explosion was definitely internal, however, which does make crew sabotage the most-likely cause."

He stood — slowly, his aching hips and a stabbing pain in his back keeping him from doing it otherwise — and handed the president a photo taken by one of the Blackfish UUVs. The front end of the *Los Angeles* had blown open like some cartoon cigar.

Blackmon studied it. "Admiral, would that destroy the artifact?"

"Possibly," Porter said. "The last report from the diver said he had removed it from the main, hardened storage locker. If that is accurate, it's doubtful the smaller container holding the artifact itself could have withstood such an explosion."

Blackmon set the picture in her lap. "When will we know for sure?"

"Another ADS is en route," Porter said. "It will be at least twelve hours before we can get a person down there. The UUVs have scanned the area, but found no sign of the container. Considering the damage, that's not surprising."

She looked at the photo again. "Could it have been survivors? The *Los Angeles* also had one of those deep-sea suits, did it not? That, or someone in an air pocket? Or could the disease modify human biology enough for people to survive down there?"

Porter shook his head. "Not likely. At that depth, the pressure is twenty-eight times that of sea level — nitrogen narcosis would quickly kill anyone not locked into a sealed area or wearing an ADS. Those suits have at most forty-eight hours of life support, and the *Los Angeles* sank four days ago. Any normal human being in that crew is definitely dead."

Porter looked at Murray to answer the final part of the question.

"The disease can change physiology, but not to that extent," Murray said. "Pressure is still pressure, Madam President."

She nodded. "All right. Now for the obvious question — could this have been a deliberate attack by foreign agents, allowing them to seize the artifact?"

Murray had known that question was coming. Truth be told, he wanted to hear the answer himself.

Porter thought carefully before responding.

"It's absolutely a possibility, although less likely than the booby trap. Recon flights are out around the clock. Coast Guard ships have been called in to patrol the five-mile perimeter around the task force. It is highly doubtful any sub could swim undetected beneath that perimeter, and nothing on the surface could get past it unseen. The *Pinckney* reported no sonar sightings, nothing was detected by the UUVs and ROVS, and neither of the deceased divers reported anything unusual until they entered the nose cone."

Murray wasn't a naval expert, but Porter seemed confident in the measures taken.

Blackmon eased back in her chair. "So, sabotage," she said. "That's the most likely answer. But if something *did* get through our lines . . ."

She didn't finish the thought. She didn't need to.

"Every agency is on alert," Porter said. "Homeland, TSA, everyone. Not that this changes anything — they've been on alert since the *Los Angeles* went down."

Murray had his doubts. Anyone talented enough, *resourceful* enough, to snatch an artifact from nine hundred feet down — right out from under the nose of the U.S. Navy — would have no problem getting past airport security, or just putting the thing on a truck and sending it to Mexico.

At any point on any path of transport, infection could occur.

"Well," Blackmon said, "for once, I find myself rooting for sabotage."

Murray couldn't agree more.

WELCOME ABOARD

Ten clear cells. Four empty. Six occupied.

Three new subjects. Margaret tried to think about them in those terms, as *subjects*. But unless Tim's cellulase-secreting yeast acted like some kind of miracle cure, those men were death-row inmates.

She stood in the airlock that led from the lab space to the containment area. She looked through the door's window, stared at the men in the cells. Clarence stood on her right, Tim on her left. They quietly waited for her to think things through.

Thirty hours since she and Clarence had landed on the *Carl Brashear*. Barely more than a day, and things were already collapsing.

The men in the clear cells weren't alone — two positives had been found on the *Pinckney*, the infected men discovered because they opened fire on their shipmates, killing three and wounding two. Unlike the *Brashear*, however, the *Pinckney* had no containment facility: Captain Tubberville had ordered the immediate execution of the infected men and the incineration of their bodies.

Obviously, Petrovsky and Walker hadn't been the only ones to come up from the *Los Angeles*. Others, or at least pieces of others, had floated to the surface, contagious flesh mingling with swimming survivors of the *Forrest Sherman* and the *Stratton*. Or could it have been something else? Maybe a gas-filled puffball corpse breaking the surface and then opening up to spill spores across the task force?

The cause almost didn't matter: what mattered was that the task force had become infected. This was going to end in a giant fireball. The only real question was, would *anyone* get out alive?

"The killer, Orin Nagy, the test missed him," Margaret said. "I didn't think false-negatives were possible."

"They're not," Tim said. "He must have found a way to skip his test, or use someone else's blood."

Margaret turned to Clarence. "Yasaka has strict procedures in place. How could someone dodge a test?"

"I don't know the specifics," he said, "but there's hundreds of extra men on this ship. It's very confused up top, no matter how disciplined Yasaka's crew is. If someone smart tried hard enough, they could probably duck a test. Maybe even two."

That didn't make the cellulose test worthless, exactly, but not far from it.

"Maybe more are ducking it," Margaret said. "There's got to be another way to look at the task force's population as a whole, try to get an idea of just how fucked we are."

Tim raised a gloved hand. "I can get Yasaka to give me access to onboard medical records. I'll set up a biosurveillance algorithm. Maybe there's common symptoms reported early, before the infection reaches the stage where it's detectable and then contagious. If there's a spike in a certain symptom — say, headaches — we might get an idea of how many people are infected but not yet testable."

Biosurveillance . . . she hadn't thought of that. Maybe Tim's background in bioinformatics could make a difference.

"Do it," Margaret said. "But make sure your yeast cultures are the first priority. What's the status of those?"

"Modified yeast is growing like wildfire," Tim said. "Population-wise, we're succeeding, but it remains to be seen if it has any impact."

Tim didn't sound jovial anymore. The light had faded from his eyes. He, too, was good at math, and math said he was standing in what would wind up being his tomb.

"We need to split your cultures," Margaret said. "As soon as we're finished here, give half to Clarence so he can ship it to Black Manitou."

Tim didn't answer right away. Margaret knew he could read between the lines, knew she was confirming his fears that they were all doomed.

"Sure," he said. "I guess that makes sense."

Clarence cleared his throat. "I assume sooner is better than later?"

"Yesterday was already a week too late," Margaret said. "Get ahold of Murray, make it happen. Right now, Tim's cultures are the most valuable thing on the planet."

"Will do," Clarence said. "What about those new crawlers you injected into Edmund? The hydras. Do we need to get those to Black Manitou as well?"

Margaret looked into the containment area again, toward the cell that held Edmund.

"We'll find out soon," she said. "I'm going to take samples from him right now, see if the hydras replicated."

Aside from Tim's yeast, the hydras were the only other real hope. The yeast would live in the intestine, secreting cellulase into the bloodstream, cellulase that would, hopefully, melt any infection. But Tim's yeast wouldn't survive in there indefinitely: normal gut flora would outcompete it, the very nature of the gut itself would kill it, and so on. To maintain effectiveness as an inoculant, people would have to ingest regular doses of the stuff.

Hydras, on the other hand, reproduced on their own. Like the crawlers, they hijacked stem cells, made those stem cells produce more hydras. As far as Margaret could tell, hydras would provide *permanent* immunity from the infection — no booster doses needed.

But with that possibly permanent immunity came a larger problem: Margaret still had no idea what else the hydras might do. Using them might very well be trading the devil she knew for the one that she didn't.

"Okay," she said, "let's get in there."

She opened the airlock door and stepped into the containment area. Four hospital-gown-clad captives looked at her.

Clark was still sedated and strapped to his bunk. Triangles were beginning to show; pale blue shapes beneath his white skin.

Edmund, of course, wasn't ever getting up again.

Cantrell stared out, eyes only for her. She'd done nothing to the man, but he couldn't hide his hate for her. She didn't know why and didn't have time to worry about it.

Margaret looked at the three new men.

Men? Of course they were men, although two of them looked like boys. Especially the one who cried silently, tears wetting his young cheeks.

He was in the cell next to Edmund. How old was this boy? Nineteen? Maybe twenty, tops? Had Margaret made different choices in her life, he was young enough to be her son, just like Candice Walker was young enough to have been her daughter.

Margaret closed her eyes briefly, gathered herself. There was no time for those thoughts.

"Clarence, which one was the killer?"

Clarence pointed his gloved hand at a thick-chested man in the second cell in the left row, the one just past the prone Clark.

"Chief Petty Officer Orin Nagy," Clarence said. "Killed two men with a pipe wrench. They were trying to give him the cellulose test."

Nagy stood ramrod straight, fists at his sides, staring out at Margaret with rage-filled eyes and a smile that promised pain. He had a salt-and-pepper buzz cut. Blood trickled from a purple welt on his forehead. His gown's short sleeves revealed arms knotted with long muscles, skin dotted with faded tattoos. He looked like a navy man from a '60s movie.

He didn't seem to notice the wound on his head. Margaret felt fear just looking at the man, at meeting his dead, psychotic stare.

"We'll need to put him under and dress his wound," she said, then gestured to the crying boy. "And him?"

"Conroy Austin," Clarence said. "The last one is Lionel Chappas. Both of them were found on the same testing sweep that triggered Nagy's attack."

She turned to Tim. "Is the outbreak just on the *Pinckney* and the *Brashear*? Any infected on the other two ships?"

He shook his head. "The *Truxtun* and the *Coronado* haven't reported any positive results. That's not surprising for the *Coronado*, though — the crew and the SEALs onboard haven't been allowed to interact with anyone at any point. They weren't even allowed to help rescue people after the battle. The task force has upped the cellulose testing schedule to every two hours. Captain Yasaka reported that there are new deliveries of testing kits being flown here to make sure we don't run out."

The *Pinckney* had 380 crewmembers. That ship alone now required forty-five hundred tests a *day*. That would wreak havoc on the crew's sleep, causing people to be tired, irritable . . . sloppy. But if the increased testing caught any other infected personnel before they became contagious, then maybe there was still a chance.

Maybe, but she doubted it.

"Tim, as soon as you split the culture for Clarence, split it again. Four ways. Keep one as a new starter culture — we're going to use the other three on the three new men, see what happens."

She had no idea what effect ingesting the yeast would have on someone who was already infected. There was a possibility it could kill off the infections growing inside of them, though, and that was reason enough to try.

Tim turned to face her. "Three doses for them, or three doses for *us*? They're already infected — we don't even know if the yeast will do that much for them. But we get that yeast in *our* system, right now, and within a few hours we'll have enough cellulase in our blood that the infection probably can't take root. If we do become exposed, the infection is stopped before it even starts. A dose now will last us about a week, I think, but by the end of that week I'll have cultured far more and we'll be able to take booster doses. It makes way more sense to take it ourselves, Margo."

Was he right? Did it make sense to use themselves as guinea pigs? She'd been witness to what the disease did to people: she would kill herself before she let it change her. Tim was offering another alternative. But there wasn't enough yeast right now to give herself a dose *and* to know if it might be a cure for those already infected. Every second mattered.

"These men are infected *now*," she said. "If there's a chance the small amount of yeast we have will help them, we need to do it. Besides, that's data we need to capture and send to Black Manitou before . . ."

Before it's too late is what she started to say.

Tim's eyes narrowed with frustration. "It's too late for them. *We* are the ones that can stop this thing, Margaret. *We* are the ones that need to live, not a bunch of grunts."

She winced at the use of that word. She'd called Clarence the same thing. Margaret looked at Clarence, saw the sadness in his eyes — but he didn't object to Tim's statement. She knew Clarence was doing his own kind of math: the military math of acceptable losses, of choosing the greater good. He didn't care about himself, she knew, but he obviously wanted her and Tim to be protected, to keep working as long as possible.

Margaret had tuned the crying boy out, but he suddenly grew louder. The suit comms were on a private channel — the young sailor couldn't hear Tim's statement of doom, but perhaps he'd read the look on Clarence's face.

Two options, neither of which promised success: save herself, or try to save these men? She clenched her jaw tight, and made her decision.

"Gas the cells, knock these men out," she said. "We know the infection has mutated. One or more of these men could have the strain that makes those strange cocoons. We put them under, get samples from all of them before we administer the yeast."

Tim shook his head. "We need to get the hell off this boat is what we need to do. We're still clean. Can't Secret Agent Man call in an evac for us? Let's get out of here before some psycho kicks in the door and swings a wrench at *our* heads!"

She took two steps toward him. She meant to stand face-to-face, but forgot about the clear visors, which *thwapped* together.

"Feely, we need to see exactly what strains these men have. We'll get tissue samples from each of them, then you divide the yeast, just like I told you to. In a day or two, you'll have enough yeast for us to take it ourselves. We need to act now, because these men can't wait."

"What we need to do next is save our own asses, Margaret."

"How about we save the *world*, Feely? Can you stop being a selfish little prick long enough to focus on that?"

He couldn't hold her stare. He looked off, sniffed, then nodded his head.

"Voice command," he said. "Feely, Tim. Activate gas in cells three, five and six."

The men couldn't hear him, but they knew something was up. Austin and Chappas stood. Chappas pounded on the glass, screaming to be let out. The scream didn't last long. Colorless, odorless gas filled their tanks. Within seconds, Chappas and Nagy slumped to the floor.

Margaret looked at Austin Conroy. The boy was still crying, his cheeks puffed out, his lips pursed into a tight little pucker. He was holding his breath. Wet, pleading eyes stared at Margaret.

Tim looked away. Margaret did not.

The boy held on for almost thirty seconds, but his crying broke his lips apart and he drew in an unwanted breath. His sobs slowed, then stopped. He fell back onto his bed.

"All right," Margaret said. "Let's get to work."

That bitch was crazy.

Tim prepared the yeast culture for Clarence. Sure, that had to be done; it only made sense to get it to Black Manitou. Maybe someone could re-create his work from data alone, maybe not — sometimes getting that first engineered organism to produce was more art than science. He'd spent years perfecting his skills and techniques. Douchebag Cheng might fuck it up if he had to re-create from scratch, so sending him an already successful culture, yeah, that was the right thing to do.

But test the yeast that remained on a bunch of poor fuckers who were already infected, instead of just taking it themselves? Crazy. Margaret was willing to sacrifice her own safety for a shot at helping those guys. Maybe Tim had been wrong about her — maybe she and Mr. Flag Waver really did belong together, living happily ever after in the Land of Idealism & Platitudes. He sealed up the fist-sized canister for Clarence. Inside was enough living yeast to start a hundred new colonies.

That left the remainder to be divided four ways: one quarter to continue the base colony, and one quarter each for Nagy, Austin and Chappas.

Tim stopped. Why didn't Margaret want to use some on Clark, the man who was already showing triangle growth? Clark was a lot farther gone than anyone else. Maybe she was going to drain the hydras from Edmund, put those in Clark.

He eye-tracked through his visor menu, called up the surveillance feed from Clark's cell. One look showed it wouldn't be long now. Six bluish triangles with inch-long sides were clearly visible under his skin, a slit near each point running toward the center.

Four days into Clark's infection. The timeline seemed to vary slightly with every victim — every host's body responded differently — but if the general track record held true, those triangles would hatch *today*. Clark's containment cell would be home to six hatchlings, their inch-high triangular bodies supported by long, black tentacle-legs.

Then what? Someone would have to go in there, put the hatchlings into smaller cages. Those cages would be shipped to Black Manitou. Cheng's group would study them, look for weaknesses.

And Clark? He'd just be dead.

Tim licked his lips. He had an overpowering urge to get off this ship. But if he did, what then? If the infection somehow reached the mainland, then Tim was fucked anyway. *Everyone* was fucked.

He looked at his yeast, the result of years of work combined with the dumb luck of Candice Walker's bizarre immunity. His yeast secreted the killer cellulose that slipped through the gut barrier to enter directly into the bloodstream. Theoretically, anyway — *Saccharomyces feely* had yet to be tested.

A human trial. That's what was needed. An *uninfected* human trial.

He again focused on the video feed of Clark. Tim didn't want to end up like that, with things growing inside of him, things that would rip out of his body, tear him to pieces.

Tim eye-tracked the menus, zoomed the camera in on the triangle embedded in Clark's right shoulder. A gnarled, nasty thing. A living, blackish-blue cancer just beneath the skin.

And then, the slits vibrated . . . they opened.

Three eyes, black as polished coal, seemed to stare right into the camera, seemed to look right at Tim. Alien eyes, *demonic* eyes, eyes filled with murder.

Tim nodded.

"Yep, that does it," he said. He reached out, wiped his hand right to left, clearing the video from his view.

"Yes indeedee dodee, that certainly fucking does it right fucking *there*. Fuck you, Mister Triangle, fuck you right in your fucking *face*, fuck you very much."

Tim returned to dividing up the yeast into four cultures of equal size. He knew what he had to do. If Margaret didn't like it, well, then that was just tough shit.

TWATTER

Twenty-five miles south of the task force, the *Mary Ellen Moffett* rocked gently from three-foot swells. Compared to most of the trip since leaving Benton Harbor, Steve Stanton considered it damn near a dead flat calm.

He watched his laptops. Bo Pan was lying on the bed. Steve didn't want to look at him. Maybe the old man had the gun pointed at Steve's back; maybe it was better not to know for sure. Steve felt sick, twitchy — the stress was grinding him down.

If the *Platypus* didn't make it back . . .

A laptop beeped.

"Contact," Steve said.

Bo Pan scooted out of his bunk, stood at Steve's right. Steve leaned a little to the left, an instinctive reaction that he checked before he fell off the edge of the chair.

The old man bent closer. "Did it get the container?"

Steve pointed to the screen.

@TheMadPlatypus: Bottle in hand at the microphone stand.

"It got it," Steve said. "Holy shit, it got the thing."

Bo Pan thumped him in the back. "Genius! Steve, you are a *genius*!"

Steve laughed, the giddy feeling that rolled through him undeniable and unquenchable. For just a moment, he forgot about the old man with the gun, forgot about the danger of an alien disease. Had he really just beaten the entire U.S. Navy? Everything had gone according to plan. The *Platypus* had the small container holding the alien artifact and had left behind ten pounds of C-4 to blow the submarine's nose to bits and cover its tracks.

Bo Pan thumped his back again. "This is very good. Are there movies? Can Twatter show us what the *Platypus* saw?"

For the first time, the old man had used the proper name for Steve's creation.

"Yes, but we shouldn't send the movies," Steve said. "You told me the navy had stepped up activity, remember?"

Bo Pan nodded. He'd made several short, intense cell-phone calls about an angry uncle from Cleveland, which was his handler's code name for navy ships.

"Then we should wait," Steve said. "The *Platypus* will reach our boat in a few hours. The military has to be scanning for any kind of communication. If we broadcast anything before the *Platypus* gets here, there's a chance the military will pick off that signal."

And if they did, what then? Could they triangulate, find the *Mary Ellen Moffett*? Steve was an American citizen . . . the thought had never crossed his mind before, but would he be tried for *treason*?

The moment of elation passed. He'd achieved his objective, but what now? Bo Pan was standing right next to him. Bo Pan, the man with the gun. And as for beating the world's superpower? Maybe they'd trace this back to him anyway, somehow, no matter how good he'd made his encryption.

Steve wanted to go back to the family restaurant. He wanted to see his mother, listen to his father talk about how hard things had been when he was a kid. Steve wanted to roll forks and knives in napkins, snap the heads off a thousand green beans. He didn't want to go anywhere near his creation ever again.

"Bo Pan, when you have the container . . . can I go home?"

The old man laughed. "Soon, my young hero. Go tell the owners of this boat that as soon as the *Platypus* returns, we are leaving."

Steve looked up at the smiling old man.

"Leaving? For Benton Harbor?"

Bo Pan shook his head. "No. For Chicago."

GAMBLING

Clarence stood in the airlock of the control room, fumbling with the bio-safety suit's awkward seals and latches. He just wanted to get the thing off and sit down for a few minutes.

He'd carried the canister of yeast out of the living quarters, gone up the long stairs to the upper deck, all the while wearing the suit. Yasaka had positioned armed guards around him, even established a kill zone — approach Clarence Otto, and you would be shot. He'd carried the yeast to the helipad, handed it directly to a similarly suited man in a waiting Seahawk helicopter. That man had given Clarence something in return: a small, gray, airtight case.

Only when the Seahawk lifted off had Clarence looked around and taken in the dozens of men and women — all exposed to the open air — staring at him like he was a visitor from another world. He was even wearing a space suit, so to speak. They stared because they knew that he was safe, and they were not.

New case in hand, Clarence had headed back down. Decon through the living quarters airlock, keep the suit on while entering the lab area, decon again, climb to the control room airlock, decon a third time, and finally he was free.

He fell more than sat into the console's comfortable chair. The gray case still had some bleach and disinfectant beaded up on it. Clarence brushed the wetness away, then opened it.

Inside, a bulky cell phone.

"Aw, Murray, you shouldn't have."

He'd seen this kind before. The bulkiness came from the encryption hardware loaded inside. The phone bypassed all ship communication, used the normal cell-phone signal available this far from shore. Sometimes spy hardware used secret satellites, gear that cost millions, and sometimes it just used what was available.

He flipped it open. It had one number programmed into it. He dialed.

On the other end, the phone rang and rang. Clarence was patient. He closed his eyes, almost fell asleep — just like that, almost nodded off — then stood up, bounced in place trying to chase the fatigue away.

On the other end, Murray Longworth finally answered.

"Took you long enough," he said. "Did you stop to jerk off before calling me?"

"Twice," Clarence said.

"The vaccine on its way to Black Manitou?"

"It's not a vaccine," Clarence said. "But yeah, it's on the way."

"Good. I've seen reports from Yasaka and Tubberville. The task force is compromised. I want to hear it from you, Otto — what are the odds of this thing being fully contained?"

Clarence closed his eyes. He felt for the chair, sat back down. Murray was the hangman, and he was giving Clarence just enough rope to make the noose. Murray did not play games. He wouldn't hesitate to put the entire task force on the bottom if it meant stopping the infection's spread. That Murray asked him — not Tubberville, not Yasaka, but *him* — was a high honor, a mark of ultimate trust; trust that Clarence Otto would tell the truth no matter what the cost.

"The odds are zero," he said. "Margaret and Doctor Feely both think the genie is out of the bottle and we can't put it back in. Even if their inoculant works, there's no way they can make enough in time to stem the tide."

Clarence didn't have to see Murray to know the old man's head dropped, that he probably rubbed at his eyes as he tried to deal with the news.

"Damn," the director said. "I was truly hoping it wouldn't come to that."

That was as close as Murray Longworth would come to an apology. And why should he apologize? He'd made the right call. Command meant that you put people at risk. Sometimes, you sent them out knowing full well they wouldn't come back.

"Had to be done, sir," Clarence said. "Yasaka and Tubberville might surprise us, but you need to prepare for the worst."

"I'll make arrangements," Murray said quickly, which meant he'd already mapped out a contingency plan. He'd likely had that plan in place before he'd ever sat in the living room and asked for Margaret's help.

"Now the hard question," Murray said. "How about you and Margaret? Are you . . ."

That was a first: Murray didn't know what to say. The almost expression of actual sentiment was almost touching.

"Negative so far," Clarence said. "So's Feely. If the shit hits the fan, we *must* get them out of here so they can continue their work."

"Don't be an idiot," Murray said sharply, an automatic rebuke. Then, softer: "You know I can't let anyone who's been exposed fly back to the mainland."

"Then keep her at sea," Clarence said. "Has the *Coronado* followed orders to steer clear of any other task force ships and personnel?"

Murray fell silent. The lack of response answered Clarence's question: the *Coronado* remained an infection-free place to stash Margo and Feely.

Finally, the director spoke. "SEAL Team Two isn't a taxi service for your wife, Otto. The SEALs are my insurance policy. If the command structure of any ship becomes infected, their mission is kill those people. You think I'm going to take a chance that they could become compromised just to keep Margaret alive?"

Clarence closed his eyes. All this talk of life and death — at least he was no longer in danger of falling asleep.

"Sir, Margaret is too great an asset to waste. She's working on more than just the inoculant. If you don't want to lose her, then give me direct contact with the *Coronado*. If things go bad, I can get her off the *Brashear*."

"And what if she's infected and doesn't know it? Better yet, what if *you're* infected, and you use the *Coronado* to shit all over the mainland?"

"I'm afraid you'll have to gamble."

Murray huffed, a sound that turned into a laugh of disgust. "Gamble." *Gamble* with a disease that can make us extinct?"

"That's right," Clarence said. "You know Margaret is worth the risk."

He waited through a long pause.

"All right, Otto. I'll get you in contact with the *Coronado*. But the ride is for a *clean* Margaret Montoya. If you find out she's infected . . ."

Clarence licked his suddenly dry lips. *For better or for worse.*

"Director, if it comes to that, I'll do us both."

"Good man," Murray said. "I'll be in touch."

A NEW HOPE

Margaret double-checked the time in her visor's HUD, just to confirm what she already knew; yes, it had been only eight hours since she'd injected *two* microscopic hydras into the body of Eric Edmund.

They had multiplied.

Samples taken from his spinal column showed a few hydras, as was to be expected. What surprised her was Edmund's blood: there were already *thousands* of them in his circulatory system. They thrived in there, reproducing at a rate that defied logic, even strained the limits of her imagination. The hydras reprogrammed stem cells to make more hydras, which then reprogrammed additional stem cells, creating an exponential population increase. If he had thousands inside of eight hours, within twenty-four he would have *millions*.

Then what? Would they keep reproducing until there were billions? *Trillions*? Would the hydra population in his body expand until it overwhelmed him, until it started to damage him?

She had no way of knowing, other than to just watch Edmund.

What *were* the hydras? Were they friend? Foe? Or were they neither, just a parasite that used the human body? And if she dared to hope, what if they weren't a parasite at all — what if they were symbiotic, something that could live inside the human body without harming it while at the same time protecting against the infection?

The hydras had kept Candice Walker from becoming one of the infected, from becoming *converted*, but that didn't mean the new microorganisms were harmless, purely beneficial things. They found their way into the host's brain — the human brain hadn't exactly evolved with room for passengers.

Charlie Petrovsky had finally been consumed by the black rot. Other than a pitted skeleton, there was nothing left of him to study. Complete liquefaction just three days after death.

Candice Walker, on the other hand, still showed no sign of the infection's rapid decomposition.

Margaret eye-tracked through her HUD menus. She directed a micro-scope to lock onto one of the hydras in Edmund's blood sample. Its waving tendrils reached out, blindly feeling for something to grab, to pull itself forward.

Walker's stem cell therapy had introduced something new, something the Orbital hadn't encountered before. Her infection had modified some of her normal stem cells, which probably produced the crawlers Margaret had seen so many times before. But some of the hacked stem cells must have had that artificial chromosome — was that what produced the hydras? A variant so different that it didn't recognize the original crawlers as "self"?

The new hydra strain reproduced at a phenomenal rate, but so far didn't seem to damage the host in any way. Walker had only had the hydras for three or four days, at most — there was no telling what might have happened had they continued to grow inside of her.

So many unknowns, but there was one fact that Margaret couldn't deny: the hydras secreted a catalyst that killed off earlier strains of the infection — strains that damaged the human host, even killed it.

"You're protecting your environment," she said to the microscopic image on the HUD, as if it could hear her, as if it could think about her words. "Walker was your world . . . when she died, most of your kind died as well. You're something *new*. You aren't a means to the Orbital's ends at all, are you?"

The hydra didn't answer. It kept reaching, kept pulling.

Margaret felt her stomach churning. One too many of Tim's Adderalls? The excitement at discovering a new form of life? Or was it that the hydras' potential went *way* beyond Tim's yeast? Walker's pustules had contained hydras, hydras that might become an airborne contagion spreading from person to person, all across the globe, promising permanent immunity to the Orbital's infection.

A different kind of pandemic.

Margaret shook her head. Too risky. Too many unknowns for something that had been created, after all, by the Orbital's alien technology.

An alert popped up in her HUD: Tim Feely was calling her. She eye-tracked to the icon and connected. His face appeared in a small window in the upper-left corner of her visor.

"Margaret, I'm finished processing the samples taken from the three new victims. Can you join me in the analysis module? I think you better take a look."

"On my way," she said.

Tim's face blinked out.

So little time . . .

SQUARE-JAWED MAN

Tim knew that if he made it out of this alive, he was changing careers. Janitor, maybe. At a grade school. Mopping floors, scrubbing out toilets, cleaning up puke — he'd be the happiest employee around.

Two doctorates. A lifetime of advanced learning. His work on Black Manitou had been a part of one of the most revolutionary projects in human history, and now here he was neck-deep in another. And where did all that put him? Right in the crosshairs of disaster.

"Tim? Hello?"

His head snapped right, toward Margaret. Clarence was with her; he'd suited up for once, decided to join the party.

Margaret smiled at him. "Tim, you okay?"

He wasn't. He never would be again.

"Yeah, I'm fine." He wanted to rub the crust from his eyes, but the goddamn suit meant he couldn't touch them.

"Looks like our three new hosts give us a mixed bag of infections," he said. "Brain biopsy shows crawler material in Nagy. He's already converted, obviously. The samples from Chappas show signs of those dandelion seeds you documented in Detroit, so it looks like he's on his way to becoming a puffball."

Margaret nodded slowly. "All right. And what about Austin?"

Conroy Austin, the boy who had cried right up until he'd been gassed.

"His body is changing on a scale unlike anything you documented before," Tim said. "Your earlier research showed the infection seems to concentrate on specific areas of the host's body, so the altered stem cells are packed in tight. Like a supply chain — the closer the factories are together, the faster and easier it is to combine the parts, right?"

Margaret nodded.

Tim called up an image and shared it with both Margaret's and Clarence's headsets.

"The infection is hitting Austin *everywhere*, and all at once. The poor bastard. It isn't just rewriting his stem cells . . . it's rewriting *him*."

"To make what?" Clarence asked. "Maybe that encased man that Walker drew, could that be happening to Austin? We saw a man like that in the *Los Angeles*'s nose cone, too. We've got video of it."

Margaret reached out, started grabbing and poking at the air. She fumbled her way through a directory that only she could see, then she made a tossing gesture Tim's way. The video popped up on his helmet screen. Tim recognized it: the encased man from the sub's lab.

"We already watched this," Tim said. "There's no way to figure out what that covering material is, not from video of this quality."

"Don't look at the cocoon," Margaret said. "Look at the temporomandibular joint."

Clarence leaned in. "The *what*?"

"His jaw hinge," Tim said as he reached out, zoomed in on that part of the video. With the poor lighting, the glowing bits of particulate floating in the way, at first the body looked perfectly normal. But . . . something was off. He adjusted the contrast, making the dark areas absolutely black, the brighter areas varying shades of light gray.

Tim saw what Margaret had seen. "Holy *shit*. The TMJ, his mandible, they're *massive* — they look too damn big for his head. And the masseter . . . it's at least four times normal size."

The man's entire skull looked *distorted*, like a sculpture more finished on one side than on the other.

Margaret reached out again, adjusting what she saw. "This sailor, he was getting bigger."

"Impossible," Tim said. "He can't get visibly *bigger* if he's not ingesting massive amounts of food. Even if the infection is hot-wiring his system somehow, it can't make something out of nothing."

"He doesn't have to eat, at least not in the way one usually does . . . he's not alone in there." Margaret again shared what she was seeing.

Tim looked at the new image. She had zoomed in on the torso. Tim saw her focal point: two left hands. There was another body under the membrane. Was Margaret saying that one person was *absorbing* the other?

"Fuck this," Tim said. "Honestly? I don't even want to know what's going on in there."

Margaret turned to Clarence — she, apparently, *did* want to know.

"Clarence, from a military perspective, what do you think it could be? Clark has triangles, which turn into hatchlings that can build gates. Crawlers turn people into killers that can protect the hatchlings. Puffballs are for mass infection. What role would could this new thing play?"

Clarence shrugged. "I couldn't tell you."

Margaret sneered. "Then *guess*, goddamit. You're the *soldier*, remember?"

Tim leaned back, stayed quiet. There was so much emphasis on the word *soldier* it clearly had a special meaning for the two of them.

Clarence raised his eyebrows, nodded, an expression that said *you got me there.*

"Okay, let me think this through out loud," he said. "Believe it or not, I'm not that worried about a new gate. A dozen satellites have been launched since Detroit, and their only job is to scan for gate signatures. If the infection gets out and the hatchlings try to build one, we'll know in plenty of time to blow the hell out of it. Besides, Murray is pretty sure they *can't* build one without the Orbital. It acted as some kind of telepathy hub, letting them work together like ants in a colony."

Tim focused on the image of the two left hands. Did one of them look . . . shriveled?

"So you think whatever is forming under that membrane might act as a new communication device," he said. "A walking cell-phone tower or something?"

"Maybe," Clarence said. "Or, possibly, the Orbital thought like a general. The units it had on the battlefield didn't get the job done, so maybe it wanted something new."

Margaret closed her eyes, hung her head. "It doesn't matter," she said. "We have three doses of the yeast, we give one each to Nagy, Austin and Chappas. Then we see what happens."

It was time to fess up, and Tim knew it wouldn't be pretty.

"We have two doses," he said. "Not three."

Margaret's eyes narrowed in confusion, then widened in understanding.

"*You* took a dose?"

Tim shrugged. "If it's any consolation, it tasted like a baboon's ass speckled with hot bat guano."

Clarence's gloved hands noisily curled into fists. "You disobeyed orders."

"Oh, what*ever*," Tim said. "I'm not military, you goon, and what are you gonna do, cut it out of me? We can't waste all of it on those guys when we don't even know if it will help them. We need to know if it works on the *un*-infected, and that's me."

They were angry, sure, but Tim knew he had done the right thing. Not just the right thing, the *smart* thing. He wasn't going to take any shit for it. He was ready to stand his ground, argue his case.

What he *wasn't* ready for, however, was Margaret's reaction.

She started to cry softly. Tears glistened on her cheeks — she couldn't reach inside her helmet to wipe them away, so on her cheeks they stayed.

"Fine," she said. "Since we don't have the resources to treat them all, we choose two for the yeast."

She looked up at Tim, her wet eyes screaming of hopelessness and anguish.

He felt small, insignificant.

"Nagy and Chappas," she said. "Edmund's blood is packed with hydras — we'll try that on Clark since Clark is already so far gone. We'll apply Edmund's blood to Clark's skin. We already know the hydras can replicate if they're injected directly into the body. This method will let us test if they can also spread by exposure to blood, and, if that works, what impact they have on someone who has triangles."

She was writing Clark off, and with good reason. His triangles couldn't be cut out. Tim had taken X-rays, seen the spiked triangle tails wrapped around Clark's heart, lying against his arteries. Removing the triangles would kill him.

Nagy and Austin, however, were in the early stages of infection. It was worth a shot to see if the yeast could cure them.

Clark, Nagy, Chappas . . . that left one.

"What about Austin?" Tim said. "The kid who was crying. Are you going to expose him to the hydras?"

Margaret sniffed sharply. Her expression changed — she was done crying.

"We're not treating him at all," she said. "We have to know what we're up against. We have to let Austin's infection run its course, so we can see what he becomes."

She turned and walked out of the analysis module. Clarence stared at Tim for a few moments — maybe because of Tim's selfish choice, or maybe just because Tim had made his wife cry — then followed her out.

HOMECOMING

Cooper stood on the deck of the *Mary Ellen Moffett*, waiting for the *Platypus* to close in.

He was experienced and sure-footed, yet the screaming wind and the rough water made him hold the rail to keep from falling overboard. Steve Stanton's machine had brought with it bad weather, the worst of the trip so far. Stanton and Bo Pan stood close by, watching carefully.

Cooper turned to José. "You ready?"

The Filipino was wearing only swim trunks, flippers, a mask and a snorkel. He gave Cooper a thumbs-up. How in the hell the little man could tolerate frigid temperatures was beyond Cooper's knowledge.

"You sure you don't want a wet suit? That water will freeze your balls off."

José smiled. "I am married with two children. I haven't seen my balls in years."

With that, the short man sat on the rail, put his hand tight to his mask and fell backward to splash into Lake Michigan. He surfaced in seconds. He grabbed a buoy that held a cable lead, then turned and swam toward the blinking light of Steve Stanton's UUV.

The *Platypus* sat low in the water. The fuzzy, gray, wet material blended in with both the water and the cloudless night, making it look like a sea monster that might suddenly attack José.

José put his hands on the foam surface, pulled it in close. The cable lead had a hook on it, which he threaded through an eyebolt sticking out of the *Platypus*'s back. José yanked the connection to make sure it was secure, then gave Cooper a thumbs-up.

Cooper looked up to the crane's tiny pilothouse, where Jeff was waiting. Cooper flashed a thumbs-up of his own. Jeff nodded, then worked the controls.

The winch whined as it reeled in the cable, lifting the UUV high. Water poured down from the machine's foam covering, first in a triangular downpour, then a thick stream, then drips and drops as the crane pivoted, bringing the UUV over the *Mary Ellen*'s deck.

Jeff lowered the machine. Seconds after the *Platypus* touched down, a wave caught the *Mary Ellen* broadside, tilted the boat severely and splashed a high spray of water across the deck. The *Platypus* skidded starboard, heading for the edge.

Cooper rushed forward, one hand on the rail to keep his balance. With the other, he grabbed at the wet, gray machine — he couldn't get a firm grip on the slippery surface. Then Bo Pan was there, throwing himself on top of the *Platypus*. Steve grabbed the tail; his feet slid out from under him and he fell hard on his ass, but he held on tight.

The two men seemed to have it; Cooper took a quick look to make sure José was safe — he was, already climbing up a rope ladder — then pulled the *Platypus* toward its storage crate. Jeff came out of the crane cabin and also grabbed hold.

Another wave rocked the *Mary Ellen*, but four men gripped the UUV and it wasn't going anywhere. They slid it into the custom-built storage crate, then locked the crate shut. Cooper and Jeff strapped down the lid.

The *Platypus* was secure.

Cooper smelled something. He looked at his hands, then sniffed them — *ugh*, like dead fish, or worse. He wiped his hands against his jeans.

Bo Pan had something in his hands: a black tube, about the size of a travel mug. The old man unzipped his jacket and stuffed it inside. He headed for the door that led below, moving as fast as he could in the rough conditions.

Steve followed close behind.

Cooper felt a strong arm slap down hard around his shoulders.

"Hey, Coop!" A smiling Jeff screamed to be heard over the wind. He sniffed his free hand and wrinkled his face in disgust. "Coop, that thing smells like your old girlfriend's cooch." Jeff started laughing, as if he'd just made the wittiest statement in all of history.

"Funny," Cooper said. "Let's get out of this mess. Time to head for Chicago. And dibs on the shower."

Just a few hours more, and the *Mary Ellen* would be free of her strange guests. Cooper and Jeff could head back to Benton Harbor, pay off a shitload of debts, and they'd never have to worry about this whole strange incident ever again.

HATCHING

It wasn't fair.

No time . . . no time . . .

Margaret knew she had the tools to beat the monster, to put a sword deep into its heart, but the monster was already breeding, already spreading.

She stood in the containment area, walking up and down the aisle. Ten clear cells, each with an occupant, all unconscious. Full house. Four more tests had turned up positive on the *Carl Brashear*. The men had been delivered to the clear holding cells. Another six positives reported from the *Pinckney* — those sailors were dead, executed on the orders of Captain Tubberville, their remains already incinerated.

Although all the captives were unconscious, their bodies continued to change. Austin's metamorphosis had kicked into high gear. Even worse, Clark's triangles were hatching.

Tim had bailed, said he had other things to do. She was done arguing with him. Clarence, however, was there, right by her side.

"Margaret," he said, "are you *sure* you have to watch this?"

She nodded. "I do."

Someone had to be there with Clark, even if he was so doped up he had no idea what was going on. She'd exposed him to Edmund's hydra-filled blood, naively hoping for a miracle. The hydras had begun to reproduce almost immediately. She didn't know what, if anything, would happen next.

"Clarence, if you don't want to watch, I understand."

He shook his head. "If you're going to endure it, then I'll endure it with you."

A noble gesture coming from a man who had left her. That was his nature, though — he'd have done the same for anyone he was assigned to.

Her heart raced. Maybe that was from the Adderall, not the situation, but the situation was enough to give anyone a coronary.

Austin lay on the floor of his cell. Brown fibers were sprouting from all over his young body, slowly crawling across his skin, sticking to both the metal grate deck and the clear glass walls. If she stood still and watched carefully, she could see those fibers moving, see new fibers pushing out of his body. It was like looking at time-lapse footage of a growing plant. At this rate, he'd be covered in a matter of hours. She was uploading a live feed of that to Black Manitou, making sure the information would survive even if things got really bad.

She was also sending live video of Clark. His triangles had started moving a few minutes ago. Blinking, twitching and jiggling as the tentacle-legs hidden inside him started to flex, to push, trying to drive the creatures out of the man's body.

Margaret had seen a hatching once before, when three of the monsters had torn out of a woman named Bernadette Smith. Clark's hatching seemed different . . . like something was wrong. The black eyes that had stared out with visible hate, visible *intelligence*, now widened, shut tight, widened again.

Almost as if the creatures were in pain.

The triangles started to lurch, to push against Clark's pale skin. Out and back, out and back, a little farther each time, stretching his skin so taut it reflected the lights from above.

He lay there, unconscious thanks to the anesthesia — a mercy for his final moments.

Clarence shook his head. "This is awful." His voice cracked with the strain. The horror show had gotten even to him. She reached her left hand out to the side, slowly, until it brushed against his. Without hesitation, he held her hand tight, their gloved fingers linking together.

The triangles jumped harder, so hard the man's prone body shook, made his straps *snap*, made the solid metal table rattle like a snare drum.

This was the reason Perry Dawsey had cut into himself, over and over. He'd sensed this was coming and done what no man could do, what Clark hadn't had the chance to do.

One of the triangles stopped jumping. It was on Clark's left abdomen. The man's skin sagged like a sock with a tennis ball inside. The hatchling wasn't moving. Its eyes looked . . . *lifeless*.

The one on his shoulder started to vibrate.

Her fingers clamped down tighter on Clarence's.

The shoulder triangle's eyes widened, bulged . . . then one eye *popped* in a tiny splash of black and green. The triangle kept twitching but no longer pulled against the stretched and torn skin. It spasmed like a moth caught in a spider's web.

She looked at a third, this one on his muscular thigh . . . it was *swelling*.

"It works," she said, barely able to believe the words herself. "It's the hydras, has to be . . . they're killing the hatchlings."

The sound of fists pounding against glass startled her, made her jump away. Clarence didn't let go of her hand.

Chief Petty Officer Orin Nagy, the man who'd killed two people with a pipe-wrench, stared out. Madness wrinkled his face into a twisted mask. He'd been gassed and should have been under for at least another two hours — how the hell had he woken up?

He pointed at her.

"Your little trick won't work on me, *bitch!* I know you put something in my belly, but you know what? I'm fucking fine, thanks for asking!"

Had his crawlers overcome the anesthesia? Counteracted it, somehow?

A slight pull on her hand — Clarence, pointing into Clark's cell. The hatchling on Clark's thigh had swollen to water-balloon proportions, triangular sides bowed outward against taut skin.

Skin and triangle alike ruptured, spurting purple and black and red a foot into the air before it splashed down on top of his thigh, sticking like thick mucus.

Then another *pop*, and another.

Then, nothing. No motion at all, not from Clark, not from his triangles . . . just the slow, oozing drip of blood and viscous fluids pattering down to the floor of his cage.

"Jesus," Clarence said. "What do we do now?"

She had failed to save Clark, but his death wasn't in vain — now she had a weapon, even if she did not yet understand how to use it. His death had served a greater purpose.

Margaret turned, met the crazed stare of Nagy. His death would also serve a purpose. And in truth, the man he'd once been had died days before.

"I'll tell you what we do now," she said. "We find something that will put

Nagy under, and we dissect his brain so we can see if Tim's yeast did anything to him."

She smiled. Only a little, but she couldn't help it. She hoped the infected still had some degree of communication, at least a shred of their inexplicable telepathy. She wanted them to know she was about to kill Nagy . . . first him, then *all* of them.

SELF-MEDICATION

Tim knew what was going on in the cells. That didn't mean he had to watch. If his yeast inoculant didn't work, that could very well be *him* in one of those cells, with some jackass doctor or scientist calmly watching monsters tear out of his body. Maybe they would take notes. Maybe they would frown sadly at his imminent demise.

For the moment, his talents were best used elsewhere. He sat alone in the analysis module, taking advantage of the opportunity to examine his bio-surveillance results. He'd set up two algorithms: the first to scan the medical records of the seventeen confirmed positives, look for any commonalities or recent trips to the ship doctor; the second to analyze prescriptions and over-the-counter sales of medicine taskforce-wide.

Six of the seventeen infection victims had visited ship doctors. There could have been more than that — all medical staffers were impossibly overworked taking care of the wounded, and there was no way of knowing if they'd properly tracked visits.

Of those six, though, there was an instant commonality: they had reported to the infirmary with complaints of headaches, body pain, sinus drip, and sore throats. Minor things, especially at a time like this. The docs had prescribed ibuprofen and cough suppressants. Basic treatments for common ailments. So common, in fact, that most people with aches and a sore throat wouldn't talk to a doctor at all — they'd just tough it out.

Tough it out, or, self-medicate.

He called up his second algorithm, the one that data-mined records of all medical supplies across the entire task force.

When the results came up, he felt a cold ball of fear swell up in his stomach, felt a panicked tingling in his balls.

He had to tell Margaret.

Margaret and Clarence sat in the theater/briefing room, waiting for Tim to come in and deliver his urgent news.

She had just watched a man die, yet she felt . . . *excited*. Walker's hydras were a weapon, a *contagious* weapon. They spread via contact with blood. If pustules formed on Edmund, she would test those as well but she already knew that would also result in contagion.

The hydras killed the infection, but what else did they do? Hopefully she would have enough time to study that, find out what the side effects might be.

So far, Tim's yeast had produced no noticeable effect on Chappas. It was several hours into the test, yet they had no way of knowing what the catalyst's effects might be, if there were any at all. Maybe they'd get lucky with Chappas; maybe the yeast would cure him.

She'd dissected Nagy's brain herself, found it thickly webbed with the crawler-built mesh. Tim's hypothesis seemed correct: once the crawlers reached the brain, it was too late.

But that didn't change the possibility that the yeast could inoculate the *un*infected. Sooner or later they would have to test that theory. Since Tim had selfishly helped himself to part of the first precious batch, Margaret wondered if he might volunteer. Somehow, she didn't see that happening. Tim was an excellent scientist, but he was also a coward. He didn't have an ounce of Clarence's self-sacrificing nature.

Speak of the blond-haired devil: Tim rushed into the room, more wide-eyed than ever. He smelled of sweat. He carried a laptop, information already displayed on the screen.

Margaret stood. Her legs ached. Her whole body ached. "So what's this critical information, Tim?"

He handed her the open laptop.

"I found a significant indicator for infection," he said. "We can probably detect outbreaks across larger populations, and do it even *before* victims would test positive for cellulose."

Margaret looked at the screen: a chart showing purchases of cold medication? Clarence came up to stand by her side, read as well.

At first, she didn't understand the significance, but then it clicked and clicked *hard*.

Clarence shook his head. "I don't get it," he said. "People buying cough drops and ibuprofen shows that they're infected?"

"Not on an individual basis," Tim said. "But in the bigger picture, yes. It's how the CDC can spot a flu outbreak, based on an abnormal spike in sales of medicine that treats flu symptoms. Seventeen people on this flotilla have tested positive so far — shortly after the battle, six of them reported coldlike symptoms of headaches and body pain."

Margaret read through Tim's numbers; they painted a frightening picture.

"Ibuprofen could be meaningless," she said. "People are working hard, they're beat-up, stressed, but look at this — the *Pinckney*'s ship store is out of Chloraseptic, Robitussin and Sucrets. Almost out of Motrin and Tylenol."

"Inventory for those items was at eighty-five percent the day before the *Los Angeles* attacked," Tim said. "Two days after the attack, inventory on pain meds *and* cold meds dropped to fifty-five percent. Three days after the attack, those supplies were at about thirty percent. Today — four days after the attack — the supplies are gone. Those supplies should have lasted six months or more."

He sniffed, whipped the back of his hand across his nose. His bloodshot eyes stared out. Tim was in bad shape.

"The *Brashear* isn't as bad," he said. "But consumption is clearly up. If I'm right, the *Pinckney* is badly infected and the *Brashear* is close behind."

Margaret noticed that Clarence was staring at Tim. Not in disbelief, or in surprise or admiration, but in *suspicion*.

"Tim," he said, "you have a runny nose?"

Margaret felt the room grow cold. Clarence's hand had drifted near the pistol strapped to his left side.

Tim, however, didn't seem to notice. "A little," he said. "I'm kinda wired and worn out, you know? Fuck-all long days it's been."

Then he, too, saw Clarence's stare, and understood. Tim leaned back, held up his hands.

"Don't get crazy, big fella. I just tested negative like ten minutes ago. Besides, the yeast probably made me immune."

"*Probably*," Clarence said. "But if you were already infected for more than a day or two, the yeast doesn't do anything, right? You were here during the attack, treating dozens of sailors. You could have been exposed."

Margaret reached out, put a hand on Clarence's arm.

"Just test him again," she said. "Remember, he'll test positive well before he's contagious to us, so calm down. I doubt he's infected."

Clarence raised his eyebrows: *how do we know that?*

"I've got the sniffles, too," she said. "And my body hurts all over."

Clarence took a step back, giving himself enough space to watch both her and Tim.

Margaret sighed in exasperation. "Clarence, for fuck's sake. Tim and I are working around the clock here — at some point, the body breaks down. You get the sniffles, you get headaches. So how about we all test now, together, just to be sure? We can test again every time we step out of the suits."

Clarence relaxed slightly, almost imperceptibly, but he wasn't convinced.

"Okay," he said. "But unless you're in your suits, I need you two to stay away from each other. And both of you keep your distance from me, got it?"

She let out a sarcastic huff. "Good to see you're consistent."

Now he looked only at her. There was hurt in his eyes. She wanted to take those words back, but she couldn't.

Clarence put both hands on his face, pressed hard, rubbed. He lifted his head, blinking rapidly, sniffing in a big breath.

"If Tim's theory is right, we have to assume well over half of the *Pinckney* is infected, about to convert and become violent. I need you both to suit up and finish whatever you're doing in the lab. Get samples of your work packed up and ready to travel on a moment's notice."

Margaret had been thinking only of numbers, but Clarence's urgency drove home a harsh reality: the *Pinckney* was a heavily armed warship, one that might soon be overwhelmed with the Converted.

THE SEAL

Paulius Klimas had never seen a cell phone quite like the one that had been handed to him by the captain of the *Coronado*. It was a bit smaller than the satellite phones he'd carried into at least a dozen missions, and ridiculously heavy for its size.

The captain had asked Paulius to his stateroom, provided the phone, then left, giving Paulius privacy. That alone indicated some important shit was about to go down. The first call to the new phone had come from none other than Admiral Porter himself. That call had lasted all of three minutes, long enough for Porter to stress that the safety and future of the United States was on the line, and that Paulius was to facilitate in any way possible the next person who would call.

Maybe that finally meant some action.

When the battle had occurred four days earlier, he and his men had been ordered to do nothing. The *Coronado* hadn't launched boats to rescue the drowning, hadn't welcomed the wounded aboard. *Zero contact*.

As other ships sank, as flaming oil spread across the water, Paulius had watched sailors fighting for life and he had done *nothing* to help them. He and his men from SEAL Team Two could have put their three Zodiacs into the lake, could have grabbed dozens of sailors from the water, could have saved many lives — he had never felt so ashamed of following an order.

But he had obeyed. He had made sure his men obeyed.

Paulius understood the order, even if he didn't agree with it; so far, no one on the *Coronado* — SEAL Team Two included — had tested positive for the infection. He and his men were a contingency plan, to be used in a worst-case scenario.

And now, it seemed, that scenario had arrived.

The *Pinckney*, the *Brashear* and now even the damaged *Truxtun* had reported positive tests, incidents of violence and murder, even the execution of military personnel. Porter's call meant it was almost time to act.

The phone buzzed. Paulius answered.

"This is Commander Klimas."

"Hello, Commander," said a baritone voice on the other end. "This is Agent Clarence Otto."

Paulius nodded. Yes, *finally*, there would be a role to play.

"Agent Otto, I have been instructed to follow your orders."

"Good," Otto said. "What have you been told so far?"

"That you control the package, and that the package is our highest priority."

The package, in this case, was a person — one Dr. Margaret Montoya, and whatever she might be carrying. Tim Feely and Agent Otto were to be rescued as well, if possible, but Dr. Montoya had become the focus of Klimas and his team.

"Excellent," Otto said. "I need you to prep for an extraction."

"Understood. When?"

"Soon. We're hopefully finishing up some research here, but we may have to bug out at any moment."

Three people from a ship that was already known to be compromised. When Paulius went after them, he'd probably take all twenty SEALs under his command, bring the package back to an isolated ship with a crew of fifty. Just one infected person could mean the death or conversion of everyone on-board.

"May I ask as to the state of health for you three? I'll come get you if you're halfway down a crack leading straight to hell, but I'd like to give my people the best possible chance of making it out of this alive."

"Are you asking if you should be wearing CBRN gear?"

The acronym stood for *chemical, biological, radiological and nuclear*, and applied to the bulky biohazard suits military forces wore when any of those four threats were present.

"They do get in the way a bit," Paulius said. "If possible, we'd rather go with our usual attire."

Paulius heard the man breathe in deep through his nose, let it out slow. A thinking man, perhaps. If so, that was a good sign.

"All three of us are negative at the moment," Otto said. "But be ready to adapt. Listen, Commander, I want something to sink in. If I call you, the people you're bringing out and the material they are carrying could save the world. That's not a figure of speech. It's literal."

"Admiral Porter told me we were saving the USA. Now it's the world. Go figure. If we fail to extract the package, what's the worst-case scenario?"

"Extinction," Otto said. "The entire human race, gone. If any of your men signed up to be heroes, Klimas, this is their chance."

Agent Otto sounded like an okay guy. Maybe he had a service background. He didn't sound like a bullshitter, but he was still a suit — bullshitting and suits went hand in hand. His words, however, stirred Klimas's soul; no one joined the SEALs to push pencils.

Saving the world? This was as big as it got.

HEADING FOR PORT

Cooper sat in the bridge of the *Mary Ellen Moffett*, guiding the ship toward Chicago at eight knots. The wind had picked up to forty miles an hour. Waves hammered the boat. It was two in the morning, the storm blocked out all stars, and snow swirled madly — his visibility was damn near zero.

At a time like this, Lake Michigan was the wrong place to be.

The weather forecast said the storm would die down in a few hours. Once it did, he could make better time, probably hit Chicago sometime that afternoon.

Everyone else was asleep. As well they should be — the job was almost over, and the weather had made everything about as difficult as it could be.

Cooper yawned. He drank a little coffee; it was already cold, but he didn't care. He just needed to stay alert for three more hours, then Jeff would take over and Cooper could get some sleep. If all went well, he'd wake up just in time to help dock the *Mary Ellen*. Then he and his best friend would be rid of Steve Stanton and Bo Pan. They wanted off in Chicago? Well, that was just fine.

After that sweet good-bye, Cooper and Jeff could hit the town. A couple of days in the Windy City would be just the thing. José could come, too, if he opted to go out for once instead of rushing back to his family, as usual.

Look out, Chicago . . . the boys are about to be back in town.

BATTLE STATIONS

"Hey, Margo," Perry said. He smiled, that smile that would have made it rain endorsement-deal millions had he fulfilled his destiny in the NFL.

"Hey," Margaret said.

"I got Chelsea." Perry's smile faded. "The voices have finally stopped, but . . . I don't think I'm doing so good. I've got those things inside of me."

His face wrinkled into a frown, a steady wince of pain.

"It hurts," he said. "Bad. I think they're moving to my brain. Margaret, I don't want to lose control again."

I'm so sorry I failed you, Perry . . . I tried so hard . . .

"You won't," she said. "They won't have time."

The same dream, the same lines, and now, the same sound — the whistle of a bomb rushing downward to kill him.

A small shadow appeared on the ground between their feet, a quivering circle of black.

Perry stared at her. Then, he looked to the sky. "That doesn't sound right, does it?"

The whistle; it had always been a consistent sound, growing steadily as the bomb fell, but this time it sounded intermittent . . . on, then off, on, then off.

Perry leaned in close. "General quarters, Margo — all hands man your battle stations."

Margaret jerked awake. She was trapped, held down, something wrapped all over.

Cocooned.

Margaret blinked, reeled from the stab of terror that flooded her chest. No, she wasn't in one of the fleshy brown cocoons . . . she was in her biohazard suit.

She was in the lab.

The sound of an alarm filled the air, audible even through her thick suit, a high-pitched *whooop . . . whooop . . . whooop* that told her things had gone bad.

She was sitting at a workstation next to the butchered body of Candice Walker. Margaret had fallen asleep, right on the keyboard. On the screen, an endless line of BBBBBBBBBBBBBBB stretched from the top to the bottom.

She heard Tim's voice in her helmet speakers.

"Margaret! Get up! We're under attack!"

Under attack? That didn't make any sense. Who would attack them on Lake Michigan?

A hand grabbed her arm, gripping hard against the blue synthetic material, jerked her around. Tim Feely, eyes wide and nostrils flaring behind his clear visor. He held a metal canister in each of his gloved hands.

"That's the combat alarm," he said. "What do we do?"

A voice bellowed over the speaker system, making them both jump.

"General quarters, all hands man your battle stations."

The blaring alarm returned at full volume.

The floor suddenly bucked up beneath them, tossing them into the air. Margaret landed on Candice's body — both she and the corpse fell to the floor. Monitors, tools and equipment rattled down all around them. Margaret found herself staring into Candice Walker's empty skull, the concave impressions of where her brain had once been reflecting the lights from above.

Candice . . . the hydras had made her immune . . .

The hydras. Margaret had to save the hydras.

She jumped to her feet, as did Tim. A canister had fallen to the debris-cluttered floor. He picked it up and clutched it to his chest.

Margaret pointed at the canister. "That the yeast or the hydras?"

Tim flashed a glance at it. "It's the yeast." He looked down, around, a move made awkward by the bulky helmet. "The other one has the hydras . . . where is it?"

A cold vibration in her chest; if they lost that canister, she'd have to go back into the holding cells — in the midst of all this insanity — and draw blood from Edmund. She turned, looking for the canister amid the fallen equipment and scattered supplies. The morgue module looked like an earthquake had thrown it to and fro. Candice's body lay on the floor, half on and half off an overturned autopsy table.

An excited voice blared from the ship's speaker system.

"All hands to battle stations, we're under fire from the Pinckney. *Repeat, under fire from the* Pinckney. *All hands to battle stations! This is not a drill. Repeat, this is not a drill."*

The ship lurched again, hurling her across the module. She slammed into a wall, felt her head bounce off the inside of her helmet. Lying on the floor . . . left shoulder stinging . . . someone yelling . . . she smelled smoke.

How could she smell smoke? She was in the suit . . .

The stinging in her shoulder. She looked, saw a piece of torn metal jutting out, blood trickling down the blue synthetic fiber of her suit. A hole . . . six inches long, ragged . . .

She was exposed.

Hands pulled her up, hands far stronger than Tim Feely's. Margaret found herself staring at Clarence. He, too, was wearing a suit, but there wasn't a mark on it. He had his pistol holster strapped to his right leg.

"Margo! You okay?"

She glanced at her shoulder. No, she wasn't okay.

Clarence pulled her close, looked at the shard of metal. "It's not deep. Hold on." He reached up, grabbed it, gave it a light tug — the sting intensified for a second, then eased off.

He put his left arm around her, placing that hand on her wound and squeezing, applying direct pressure even as he urged her toward the door.

"Come on," he said. "We're moving. We've got to reach the side airlock."

Margaret planted her feet.

"The hydras," she said. "There's a canister of them around here — we have to find it!"

The floor lurched beneath her again, a concussion wave slapping like the hand of a giant. Stunned, she started to fall back, but Clarence held her up.

"No time," he shouted. *"Move!* Feely! Get your ass up and follow me!"

Margaret didn't have a chance to see if Tim was okay, because Clarence all but dragged her to the ruined door. The door and walls alike were bent and shredded, white surfaces streaked with sooty black. Small fires flickered wherever they could find purchase.

Clarence raised his foot and lashed out, kicking the door open. He led her from the morgue into the analysis module, which was in better shape, straight through it to the miscellaneous lab and finally out of the trailers altogether.

He turned right, pulling Margaret along, headed for the airlock that led into the receiving and containment area.

Then Tim was next to her, the yeast container still pressed to his chest. Something had split his helmet visor. Blood poured from his forehead down the left side of his face, making his left eye blink spasmodically.

The airlock looked intact.

She planted her feet. "No! What if the explosions broke the containment cells? Those men could be out! My suit . . . I could be exposed."

Clarence pulled his pistol from its holster, pointed it at the ground.

"Tim, get that door open," he said. Tim ran to it.

Clarence pulled Margaret forward. "Margo, we don't have a choice. We either get into the water so the SEALs can rescue us, or we go down with the ship. We don't have long before strike fighters blow everything to hell."

Fighters. Murray had pulled the plug. He was going to fire-bomb the *Brashear*, the *Pinckney*, the *Truxtun*, send all of it — metal and man alike — straight to the bottom.

Tim opened the door and they all moved inside. He sealed it up, started the pressurization cycle. As air hissed in, he looked at her arm.

"Shit," he said. "There's sticky tape in the processing area inside the big side airlock. We can seal this up."

The airlock finished cycling. Clarence opened the door to reveal a smoke-filled mess. Sodium hypochlorite sprayed down from the ceiling; she smelled it instantly, filtering through the tear in her suit. The automatic decon procedures had kicked in, and she instantly saw why — the containment room had taken a direct hit.

Something had blown a hole in the white wall and slammed into the clear cages, ripping apart the middle cells. Bodies and parts of bodies — some red and raw, others blackened and smoldering — lay scattered among foot-thick, spider-webbed shards of glass.

She saw Conroy Austin's severed head, a sleepy look on his young face. Something had torn it from his shoulders. It had come to rest on the bloody, ragged neck, temple pressed against a broken chunk of cell. A rain of bleach wet his hair to his scalp. Bits of brown material clung to his cheeks.

The two cells closest to her had avoided the worst of the damage, but thick cracks lined their walls. The cell on the left held Clark's hatchling-ridden corpse, still strapped to the metal bed. But the cell on the right,

Cantrell's cell . . . it was empty. The cracked door hung open, its flat-panel monitor black and still.

Where was he? He'd tested negative all the way through. Could he come with them?

Clarence released her shoulder. He stepped out of the airlock door, pistol in both hands, barrel in front of him. He moved to his right along the bulkhead wall that separated the containment room from the lab area, keeping the metal to his back. Bleach rain drizzled on his suit, ran down it in rivulets.

He looked back at her, reached out his left hand and curled his fingers inward: *follow me.*

Tim gently pushed Margaret's back, urging her forward. She stepped out and followed Clarence. Bleach beaded up on her visor. She quickly reached her right hand up and held her left shoulder, covering the hole in her suit as best she could.

Clarence kept moving to his right, eyes on the shattered cells in front of him. He reached the empty prep area just inside the wide exterior airlock. The endless rain splattered off the stainless steel equipment. He looked back at her, urgently waved her forward.

She stumbled toward the garage-door-sized airlock. Tim ran past her, head still tilted down as much as he could manage, his blue suit wet and gleaming.

The bleach smell grew stronger — some of it had leaked into her suit. It wouldn't be long until the fumes made her lungs burn. Clarence had to get them out fast or she'd be as good as dead.

Tim reached a keypad to the right of the airlock. He punched in a code. The heavy door let out a hiss of compressed air, then slid open.

Margaret stared out into a nighttime blizzard. Through the whipping snow she saw shimmering lights — the *Pinckney* looked like a mystical fortress rising from the depths. Snaps of orange and yellow dotted the sky, muzzle flashes lighting up like the sparkle of cameras in a dark arena.

Fresh air blew in hard, making the bleach spray in any direction but down.

"Oh shit," Clarence said. He grabbed her, held her tight. "Tim, hold on!"

From the rear of the shimmering, gray leviathan that was the *Pinckney*, Margaret saw a billowing cone of fire and heard a simultaneous blast that hammered her ears. The deck bounced beneath her. She fell, landing on top of Clarence's thick chest.

A roar overhead; Margaret looked out and up, saw a bulky helicopter moving through the whipping snow, away from the *Brashear* and toward the *Pinckney*. Something flashed from under the helicopter's stubby wing. A missile shot forward trailing a rope of glowing smoke. The missile closed the distance in two seconds: a fireball erupted from where the *Pinckney* had just fired.

"Margaret, hold still."

Clarence, shouting to be heard over the alarm and the explosions. She turned to see something moving toward her face. She closed her eyes, trusted him, felt that something tug down around her neck and shoulders, pushing her suit against her skin.

A life jacket.

"Look at me," Clarence said.

She opened her eyes. Bits of snow and ice clung to her visor, sliding down the glass along with the spraying bleach. Through it, and through his visor as well, she locked onto his intense eyes, his *commanding* eyes.

He shouted. She listened.

"The jacket will keep you afloat," he said. "We have to jump. You'll hit and go under, but you'll pop right up."

She heard a ripping sound, looked to the source — Tim Feely, wrapping sticky tape around his back and belly, over and over again, fastening the yeast container to his stomach.

Clarence ran to the wall and grabbed another life jacket. He pulled it around Tim's head even as the smaller man kept taping. Clarence fastened the life jacket as Tim cut the tape and tossed the roll away.

Through the wind and the spray and the sound of gunfire, Margaret heard something to her right — the labored breathing of a man in pain.

She turned and saw Cantrell coming for her, not even ten feet away, black skin wet from the bleach rain, his squinting eyes red and swollen.

In his hands, a fire axe.

She took a step backward, away from the man. "Clarence!"

He was there, instantly, stepping between her and Cantrell, pistol raised and firing.

Margaret kept backing up as the first round made Cantrell twitch to the right. The second bullet blew out the side of his head. He fell like he had no bones at all, face slapping on the metal deck.

She took one more step back to stop her momentum, but the foot hit empty air.

The fall lasted forever and less than a second, a moment of nothingness before she slammed into the water.

All noise ceased instantly; someone had turned off the volume. In front of her, *blackness*.

Cold hit her hard and from all sides. Her body went rigid. Her breath locked in her chest. Then, sudden heat across her skin as her suit automatically tried to compensate for the drop in temperature; she felt it everywhere but her shoulder — there, a creeping, icy death as water poured in.

She had a sensation of rushing upward, saw tiny, wavering lights, then her helmet-covered head popped back into the noise of war. Gunfire and screaming, the roar of flames, the concussive pulse of explosions so powerful that air slapped against the water. The surface reflected the firework flashes from above.

In front and behind, towering ship hulls rose up like smooth, impenetrable castle walls. Swells lifted her and dropped her.

She felt that numbing cold, that clutching snake wrapping around her feet — water pouring in through the tear in her suit, filling up her boots.

Margaret turned sharply, trying to lift her left shoulder out of the water. She dipped into a deep trough. From her right came a new roar as a black monster tore free from the top of the wave, kicking out a spray of water that sparkled orange from the reflected fire above. The black shape crested, almost flew, then came down hard in another splash of molten orange.

Not a monster: a black *boat*, a raft, packed with men who looked like robots, dark bulky shapes and smooth helmets and huge guns mounted to the raft itself.

A line of splashes burst up in front of her face. *Bullets*, someone shooting at her from up on the *Brashear* or the *Pinckney*. As one, the boat's gunners aimed up: the black monster breathed fire.

The boat rapidly slowed to a stop near her, its bow wave pushing her back. A black man — no, a man wearing blackface — pointed a black rifle at her, screaming to be heard over the gunfire. "Identify yourself!"

"Muh . . . muh . . ." Her jaw chattered so hard it hurt her teeth.

"Identify yourself!"

"Muh . . . Margaret . . . *Montoya!*"

The point of the rifle lifted. The man leaned forward and reached, grabbed her life jacket and pulled her toward the boat.

"I'm Commander Klimas," he said as he yanked her up. "Stay down and *don't move.*"

She felt a strong hand push her, not to harm her but rather to hold her still. Margaret found herself in the bottom of the raft, lying against a soaked and shivering Tim Feely. Most of his suit had been cut away. A black blanket covered his shoulders. His bloody scrubs clung to his body. He clutched the container of yeast tight to his chest.

The deafening guns continued to roar, to spit tongues of flame up at the sky. Shell casings rained down, bouncing off her visor, landing in the boat or hitting the surrounding water where they vanished with an audible *tsst.*

She saw a knife move near her face, then a rapid tugging on her suit as someone cut it away in long shreds. A long, heavy blanket was thrown on top of her, tucked around her shoulders.

The boat shot forward, smashing against the tall waves, rolling her against black-booted feet. She sat up, knees to her chest, pulling the blanket close to try to fight off the cold that rattled her body.

"Where is Clarence?" She screamed to no one, to everyone. One of these men had to know. "Agent Otto, where is he?"

The unmistakable *plunk-plunk-plunk* of bullets smacking into the boat.

Something hammered into her right thigh, made the muscles numb — she was trying to get her bearings when the numbness quickly faded, replaced by a branding-iron pain that seemed to singe her femur.

Wincing, fearing the worst, she opened the blanket to look at her leg. Blood poured from the wound, hot against her ice-cold skin, matting her scrubs to her thigh. She grabbed the thin fabric of her pants and *ripped* — a long gash ran from a few inches below her hip down to midthigh. The bullet hadn't penetrated, only grazed her.

A man landed hard in front of her, black face tight in a grimace of agony, left arm across his chest, left hand clutching at the back of his neck. Blood poured out from between his fingers, looking just as black as everything else.

She forgot about her leg, lurched forward to help the soldier.

"Tim! Come here!"

Tim stuffed the yeast canister into his scrub top, then leaned over the wounded man, trying to keep his balance as the boat rose up and smashed down again and again and again. Tim's hands probed the back of the man's neck.

Margaret wiped her cold, bloody fingers against her soaked scrub top, then slid them along the man's throat, looking for additional wounds.

"Clear and breathing," she said. "How bad is the wound?"

"The bullet took out most of the posterior musculature on the right," Tim said. "The jugular and carotid were spared, but he has significant hemorrhaging from the wound. I think the brachial nerve plexus is gone." Tim sounded calm, of all things. Margaret briefly wondered why he'd gone into research — the man had been born for this.

Gunfire roared around her. She sat up higher, hands searching the man's combat webbing for something that felt like a flashlight.

Again a hand came down from above, grabbed the back of her neck, tried to force her flat. Her palms pressed against the bottom of the boat.

"Stay *down*!"

The boat hit hard against a wave: it felt like driving a car into a wall. The hand came off her for a second. She pushed up and swung her right elbow back as hard as she could, felt it *clonk* into something both hard and soft.

"I'm a doctor, goddamit, *let me work!* And give me a fucking light!"

Plunk-plunk-plunk, another string of bullets stitched across the small boat.

She felt the hand reach down again, but this time it pressed something against her chest: a small flashlight. Margaret flicked it on and scanned the man's body; he might have other wounds that were even worse.

The boat hammered across the waves, repeatedly rising up hard then dropping to *smash* against the concrete surface.

She found nothing.

"No additional wounds," she said, then handed the light to Tim.

That strong hand on her yet again, on her shoulder this time. Klimas, the SEAL who had pulled her in, knelt next to her.

"Agent Otto is in the other zodiac," he said. "He's okay."

She felt a burst of relief, albeit a brief one — she had her hands full trying to save a life.

Tim adjusted his grip on the wounded soldier. "He's still breathing, he's moving his legs, and I think the major vessels are intact. He can survive this if we can control the bleeding."

"Cease fire," another voice called out. "Cease fire!"

The gunfire stopped, leaving only the driving snow and the howling of the wind.

Klimas stood. "Recovery complete," he said. "We're clear."

From high above, she heard the loudest sound yet. She looked up in time to see a flicker of flame heading behind them, toward the *Pinckney* and the *Brashear*.

A missile.

She looked away just before it hit and became a deafening, temporary sun that lit up the surface of Lake Michigan.

The task force was done for. Captain Yasaka, Cantrell, Austin, Chappas, Edmund, all the crew from both ships and the *Truxtun* as well — all gone.

So, too, were the last of the hydras.

A black-gloved hand dropped a black canvas pouch in front of her. It was about twice the size of a paperback. She looked up, saw the black-faced Klimas looking down.

"Trauma kit," he said. "Save him."

She nodded.

Thoughts of Clarence, the battle, the dead, the hydras, even the awareness of her shivering body and her own wound faded away as she and Tim Feely went to work.

THE SELECTION PROCESS

In the deepest points of Lake Michigan, the water temperature remains steady at just a few degrees above the freezing point.

The intense cold hadn't stopped the apoptosis chain reaction from affecting the *Los Angeles*'s dead crew, but it had slowed the process enough so that plenty of rotting meat remained on their bones. Meat, for example, that was on the severed leg of one Wicked Charlie Petrovsky.

When the *Platypus* ground its way past that leg, slimy flesh sloughed off onto the machine's acoustic foam covering. This coating of partially rotted tissue contained thousands of cyst-encased neutrophils.

As the *Platypus* returned from its mission, the regular, mechanical vibrations of its fins and inner workings caused the neutrophils to come out of hibernation. The microscopic organisms shed their cyst coats and prepared for the touch that might give them a host. When Cooper Mitchell, Jeff Brockman, José Lucero, Steve Stanton and Bo Pan worked to secure the *Platypus* to the deck, Charlie-slime smeared onto exposed skin — the neutrophils found their new homes.

The five men had no idea what had happened. They had no idea what was coming next.

The neutrophils secreted chemicals to make microscopic fissures in the hosts' skin, then slid through those fissures, penetrating deep inside. The little bits of crawling infection sought out stem cells, tore them open and read the DNA within.

It was there, at that initial point of analysis, that the neutrophils chose the role of each host.

One host had a genetic disposition for increased size — significant height, heavy bone density, above-normal muscle mass — so the crawlers in that host programmed stem cells for one of the two new designs.

Another host's genes showed significant indicators for high intelligence. *Extremely* high intelligence. For this host, the neutrophils chose the other new design, a design that would be the true masterpiece of the long-lost Orbital's bioengineering efforts. The neutrophils rapidly changed their form, shedding cellulose to become a microorganism made from normal human proteins. Then, they converted stem cells to produce millions of copies of themselves. From there, all would head straight for the host's brain.

The genetic makeups of the final three men were unremarkable. They were *normal*. For those three, the crawlers chose between three random options — these men would become a *kissyface*, turn into a *hatchling factory* or swell up with gas, soon to pop and spread the infection wherever their spores would reach.

In twenty-four hours, one of the hosts would become contagious. In forty-eight hours or so, all of the hosts' brains would start to change. Sometime past seventy-two hours of incubation, they would start to recognize each other, realize that they were all members of a new species, a species above and beyond humanity.

Roughly ninety-six hours after infection — in just four days — they would not only recognize each other, they would start to work together.

Work together . . . to *spread*.

A LITTLE PRICK

Margaret slowly awoke. Darkness, save for the lights of medical equipment. She lay on her back, blankets pulled up to her chest. She started to rise, but a bodywide ache froze her in place.

"Oh, man," she said.

The last time she'd felt like this was the day after her first Boxercise class — *everything* hurt. This was what she got for years of sitting on her ass. But at least her muscles had served her well enough to get out; she was alive, which was more than could be said for most of the poor souls on that task force fleet.

She was in what looked like yet another trailer. A kind of trailer, anyway — this one was small, barely big enough for two field hospital beds, cardiorespiratory monitors, ventilators, a rack of IV pumps, a spotlight, and compact cabinets packed with supplies. An IV line ran into her arm.

A man lay in the other bed. She didn't recognize him. Margaret did, however, recognize the wound area — this was the SEAL she and Tim had worked on. They had saved this man's life. That felt good. It seemed ridiculous to feel that way, considering the hundreds of bodies now at the bottom of Lake Michigan, and yet, it *mattered*.

She slid her hospital gown down over her shoulder. As she'd suspected, not that bad of a wound at all. Eight stitches. Could have been so much worse.

Could have been and probably was: she'd been exposed. She might test positive in a day or two, possibly even less considering she didn't know how long she'd been asleep.

Margaret flipped the blanket from her leg, looked at her thigh. It had been neatly dressed. Black ink on the white bandage . . . was that writing? She slowly lifted her leg for a closer look.

For a good time, call Tim.

Margaret laughed, and even *that* hurt.

The trailer door opened. A man stepped in. He wore fatigues printed with a pixilated digital pattern of gray, black and blue. Nice-looking man: pale, pink skin, a heavy jaw and a chin that would have got him work in Hollywood were it not for his beady eyes, which seemed to be just a bit too close together. His right eye had a bruise under it.

The man shut the door. He took off his camo hat and held it behind himself with both hands. He stood between the beds, mostly because there wasn't enough space to really stand anywhere else. He stared at her, as if he expected her to know who he was.

"Hello," Margaret said. "Is there something I can do for you?"

He smiled. "Don't recognize me without my makeup?"

The voice brought it home — it was the SEAL who had yanked her out of the water, covered her body with his own as bullets rained down around them.

"Klimas, wasn't it?"

He nodded. "Yes, ma'am. Commander Paulius Klimas. How are you feeling?"

"Sore."

He nodded. "I can imagine. You went through quite an ordeal. I have a message for you from Director Longworth. He sends his best and said that Doctor Cheng is making excellent progress cultivating the yeast. He also said you're to rest, and that he'll video conference with you tomorrow. Which you can do right from the *Coronado*, by the way."

Ah, that's where she was.

"I don't remember coming aboard."

"You passed out," he said. "Right after you and Doctor Feely" — Klimas nodded to the unconscious man in the hospital bed — "stabilized Levinson here."

Passed out? Blood loss, fatigue, concussive damage, shock, stress . . . probably a combination of all of it.

"How is Doctor Feely?"

"Fine," Klimas said. "He treated your leg. He was rather insistent about it, actually. He's been sleeping ever since. Agent Otto is awake though, and he asked about you. Would you like me to bring him in?"

Why, so he can whisper more lies about how he loves me?

"Tell him I'm fine," she said. "I don't want to see him. How long have I been out?"

"About sixteen hours, ma'am."

That word, *ma'am*: it made her instantly feel old.

"Call me *Margaret*, please. Do I look like a *ma'am* to you?"

He shrugged. "Except for the people under my command, every woman is a *ma'am* and every man is a *sir*. It's not my fault I was raised right. And please, call me *Paulius*."

She nodded once. "Very well. Paulius, I want to thank you and your men for rescuing us. It might not mean much, but I owe you. If I can repay your bravery, I will."

He laughed lightly.

"That's odd," he said. "I was just about to say the same thing to you." He nodded toward the unconscious Levinson. "He'd be dead if it wasn't for the bravery of you and Doctor Feely."

Margaret felt suddenly uncomfortable, embarrassed. "*Our* bravery? You came in like something out of a movie. I'd have drowned without you. Or been shot. Or blown up. Or burned. Take your pick."

Klimas shook his head. "When the bullets fly, most people hide behind us. Trust me, I've done this before. Margaret, you *took a bullet*, then — under enemy fire — you and Doctor Feely saved my man's life. That's behavior I would have expected from a trained SEAL, not a civilian."

She knew a man like Klimas wouldn't make light of comparing someone to a SEAL. His words seemed to make her more aware of the ache in her thigh.

"I didn't get *shot*," she said. "Well, I did, but . . . are you a Monty Python fan?"

Klimas smiled. "'Tis just a flesh wound?"

She nodded.

"You got shot," he said. "End of story."

He grew serious, leaned forward just a bit. His eyes carried a certain coldness. Commander Paulius Klimas was polite, sure, but he was still trained to take life whenever ordered.

"You saved one of ours," he said. "If you need us, we'll be there."

His intensity frightened her. These weren't just words — she knew that if she was in trouble, this man would kill for her.

Klimas stood straight, smiled. The moment of gravitas was over.

"Besides," he said, "I *know* you're a fighter." He pointed to the bruise under his right eye.

She remembered lashing out, her elbow hitting something. Her face flushed red. "I did that?"

"First shiner I've had in years."

"Oh my God, I'm so sorry!"

He laughed. "Don't worry about it. Is there anything I can do for you? Anything you need?"

She was hungry. "A sandwich would be good."

"I'll get food in here for you right away. Anything else?"

Margaret gestured to the small trailer around them. "What is this room?"

"It's called a *mission module*," Klimas said. "Instead of building everything in as a permanent part of the ship, the *Coronado* has space for modules that serve different purposes. This one, obviously, is a medical module. My unit has several — bunk modules, weapons maintenance, mission prep, that kind of thing. We've cleared out a bunk module for you, so you'll have private quarters."

She shook her head. "Absolutely not, I can't put your men out."

He held up a hand to stop her. "Normally, you'd get a stateroom, but we're restricted to the hold in hopes of providing some separation between us and the crew."

"You mean between the crew and anyone who had contact with me, Clarence and Doctor Feely."

Klimas shrugged. "Tomato, tomahto. We're in this together now. At any rate, the decision has been made — if you don't sleep in the bunk room, it will sit empty."

"Thank you, Commander. At least I know chivalry isn't dead."

His expression changed. For the first time, he looked uncomfortable.

"There's one more thing," he said.

Her eyes shot to his hip, to the holster there and the pistol in it. She hadn't given it a second thought . . . until now.

"You have to test me, right?"

Klimas reached into a pocket of his fatigues and pulled out three white boxes. The number surprised her.

"Three?"

He nodded. "One for you, one for Levinson and one for me. All my men are testing every three hours. If you don't mind, I'd like you to go first."

He offered her one of the white boxes. She stared at it. There was only one door into the mission module; by standing between the beds, Klimas had blocked the only way out. If she tested positive, he would kill her.

But if she did see that red light, did she really *want* to live?

She reached out and took the box.

"Let's get this over with," she said.

Seconds later, she stared at the blinking yellow light. Slowing, slowing . . .

Green.

Klimas smiled. "Only twenty-three more or so to go, right?"

She ran through the math in her head. "Yeah, three days ought to do it. We'll know by then."

Margaret sagged back into the bed. She still felt exhausted — the unexpected moment of intense fight-or-flight response hadn't helped.

Klimas opened another box, cleaned Levinson's finger, then pressed the tester against it. Yellow, yellow, yellow . . .

Green.

"Two down," he said. "My turn."

"Maybe you should give me the gun."

He opened his testing unit. "Don't worry about that. If we see red, I step out that door and everything will be taken care of."

Yellow . . . yellow . . . yellow . . .

Green.

He gathered the boxes and testing units like nothing unusual had just happened, like he was cleaning up after a late lunch.

"Margaret, you still look pretty beat. If you'd like to move to your bunk module, you could get more sleep."

He held up another white box: this one full of small, circular Band-Aids.

She nodded. "Yeah, I'd like to get out of here." She removed the IV, wiped up the drop of blood and applied one of the bandages.

"Lead the way, Paulius."

He opened the door for her. She stepped out onto the deck. She was in some kind of a cargo hold, much smaller than what she'd seen on the *Brashear*. Other mission modules were lined up end to end along the hold wall.

Margaret noticed a SEAL standing about fifteen feet from the door she'd just walked out of. A young man, black. The name on his left breast read *BOSH*. He had a gun strapped to his chest, barrel angling down. She'd seen that weapon before, recognized it: an MP5.

He had both hands on the weapon. Bosh must have been the one who would have *taken care of everything* if Klimas had tested positive.

"Margaret?" Klimas said. "This way, please."

She followed him toward a module. From the outside, they all looked the same. She cast a glance over her shoulder; Bosh was following, hands still on his weapon.

Margaret suddenly hoped the testing units were as accurate as Tim claimed — if her next test mistakenly returned a false-positive, she might not have time to ask for a second chance.

Klimas held a door open for her. As Margaret stepped in, she saw Bosh take up position outside the module. Inside were two sets of stacked bunks, gray blankets wrapped so tightly around the mattresses you could bounce a quarter off them.

"Take your pick," Klimas said. "I'll have that sandwich brought right out. Someone will check on you for your next test. Until then, I'll ask that you stay in here."

She nodded. He left, closed the door behind him.

Margaret sat on the first bunk. It seemed to pull her in, drag her down. With a U.S. Navy SEAL ready to execute her standing right outside, she fell asleep almost instantly.

PAY THE MAN

"It is necessary," Bo Pan said. "We'll take them one at a time."

Steve Stanton could barely breathe. His head throbbed. He was already responsible for killing one man, at *least* — and now Bo Pan wanted to murder three more?

"No," Steve said. "I won't be a part of this."

Bo Pan's eyes narrowed. As always, the two of them were alone in the tiny stateroom. Bo Pan stood in front of the closed door. If Steve tried to force his way past, would he make it? Would the old man shoot him down?

"Steve, you have done your nation a great service, but our work is not over yet."

Steve tried to speak with volume, with intensity, but his throat hurt, felt painfully scratchy — all that came out of his mouth was a cracking whisper, the voice of a boy rather than that of a man.

"We don't have to kill them. They have no idea what's going on. Just give them their money and they'll leave."

Bo Pan's nostrils flared. He drew a breath, ready to give a lecture.

Steve spoke first. "If you kill them, I'll tell."

The words sounded petulant, childish, but it was all he could think to say.

Bo Pan's head tilted forward until he stared out from under his bushy eyebrows.

The footage from the *Platypus* replayed over and over again in Steve's thoughts. Not the low-res pictures taken every twenty seconds, but the full-speed, high-def footage stored on the machine's internal drives. The dark footage of the man entering the *Los Angeles*'s nose cone, light beaming from a bulky suit that looked like it belonged to like a fat astronaut . . . the look of surprise on the diver's face as the *Platypus* shot in, cut the umbilical cord and then snatched the small, black container . . . a brief instant of that expression shifting to horror as the snake curled around his bulbous helmet.

Steve hadn't seen anything else, because the *Platypus* was already slithering quietly through the wreck, leaving the diver behind to die in an explosion of C-4 that likely blew the sub's nose cone wide open.

That diver's blood was on Steve's hands.

He'd thought only of himself. He'd programmed what Bo Pan told him to program, because he'd just wanted to go home.

Bo Pan wanted more death: Steve would not allow that to happen, even if saying *no* meant dying himself.

Steve sat very still, wondering if he'd die right in this very room, among empty cans of Coke and crinkly bags of Doritos.

And then, Bo Pan's face softened. The old man relaxed. He let out a sigh.

"As you wish," he said. "We would not have achieved this without you, Steve. We will pay them, then we go on our way."

Steve blinked. "You mean it?"

Again, the words of a child. He was in the middle of an international incident, had just defeated the U.S. Navy, was trying to stop the murder of three innocent men, and he sounded like a boy whose mother had just promised him a new toy.

Bo Pan nodded. "Yes. You are right. It would just cause too many problems. They don't know what is going on, so it is not worth the risk. We will dock and I will leave."

Which brought up another problem — Steve wanted to be as far away from Bo Pan as possible.

"Am I supposed to go with you?"

"No. You will return to your parents."

Steve was going *home*. In a day, maybe a little more, he'd be sitting at the restaurant, eating his father's cooking. Could it be true?

Bo Pan smiled a grandfather's smile. "I am sorry you can't come with me right now. Soon enough, however, you will be welcomed in China as a hero."

The old man thought Steve still wanted glory, when all Steve wanted to do was hide and forget this had ever happened.

"Okay," Steve said. "I understand."

Bo Pan took out his cell phone. He awkwardly typed in a message, one slow thumb at a time. He sent the message, yawned, then put the phone away.

"I have arranged transportation," he said. "Four men will be waiting for us when we arrive at the dock to help us with the *Platypus*. A truck will take you and your machine back to Benton Harbor."

Four men? The *Platypus* wasn't *that* heavy. Steve and Bo Pan could move it on their own — crate and all — and had done so many times.

Bo Pan rubbed his face. He sat on his bunk, laid his head on the pillow.

"I am going to sleep," he said. "Don't make noise."

The old man started snoring almost immediately.

Steve tried to stay calm. He felt a fever coming on, but he didn't have time to get sick. He was probably safe. *Probably*. Bo Pan still needed him; just because they'd found one alien artifact didn't mean there weren't more on the bottom of Lake Michigan, and only Steve and his *Platypus* could recover those artifacts if they were discovered.

But Bo Pan didn't need Cooper, Jeff or José.

Steve stared at Bo Pan for a few minutes, made sure the man was actually asleep. Then, he sat down at his little table. His fingers started working the laptop's keys: *quietly*, so quietly.

The storm outside was finally dying down. They would be in Chicago in a few hours.

He had to act fast.

KNOCKIN' AT THE DOOR

Heat.

She felt it through her biosafety suit. Angry wind scattered loose papers across the crumbling asphalt and the cracked bricks that made up the road's surface. At the end of the street, she could see the wide Detroit River — steam rose up from it, *heavy* steam, because the water was boiling. Abandoned buildings on either side of the street seemed to sag slightly, like they were exhausted, like the heat had taken the masonry and paint to just a few degrees below the melting point.

This wasn't right. Why was it so *hot*? The bomb hadn't hit yet.

She started to sweat suddenly, not in droplets but in *buckets* that poured off her, dripped down to fill the boots of her sealed suit.

Sweat pooled around her ankles . . . her shins . . . her knees.

Her hands shot to the back of her neck, clawing at the helmet's release clasps. Sweat pooled to her thighs.

If she drowned in her dream, would she ever wake up again?

Gloved fingers searched for the clasps, darted back and forth, hunting desperately . . . but there were no clasps.

Sweat rose past her belly button.

"Hey, Margo."

She stopped moving, looked out the curved visor to the huge man who had suddenly appeared before her. Dirty-blond hair hung in front of his electric-blue eyes, even down past that winning smile.

"Hey," she said.

The sweat tickled the base of her throat.

"I got Chelsea," he said. His smile faded. "The voices have finally stopped, but . . . I don't think I'm doing so good. I've got those things inside of me."

She started to tell him that she didn't care, that she really didn't give a *fuck* about his goddamn problems, but when she opened her mouth to speak, it filled with the hot, salty taste of her own sweat.

The level rose to her nose.

Perry reached out a hand. A triangle point pushed the skin of his palm into a pyramid shape, its blue color dulled by his nearly translucent flesh.

The sweat rose above her eyes, *stung* them, turned Perry into a shimmering vision.

Margaret heard a squelching sound, felt something hit her visor. She couldn't see Perry — all she saw was a wiggling, bluish-black creature: an inch-high pyramid with tentacle-legs twice as long as the body, plastered to her visor like a still-twitching bug splattered on a windshield.

The legs squirmed, spreading Perry's blood across the clear surface.

Margaret's lungs screamed at her: *breathe, you have to breathe!*

The hatchling's tentacles wrapped around the back of her helmet. The triangular bottom of the pyramid body had little teeth that sank into the visor's plastic, *bit* and *pulled* and *ripped*.

It tore open a hole. The sweat started to lower. She felt it drop to her forehead, then her eyes. She blinked away the sting, holding on desperately, waiting for it to drop below her nose.

When it did, Margaret drew in a gasping breath.

The hatchling scurried down her suit. It hit the ground and ran for the sagging buildings.

Perry's smile returned.

"It hurts," he said. "Bad. I think they're moving to the brain. Margaret, I don't want you to lose control."

"You won't," she said, the words familiar and automatic even though so much of the dream had changed. "They won't have time."

Perry's smile widened. "I didn't say *my* brain." He put his hands on her shoulders, gave them a brotherly squeeze. "I said *yours.*"

She heard a banging. Not the whistle of a bomb, not this time, but rather a banging as if someone had a gong and was hammering the whole city at once, *bang-bang-bang.*

"Somebody knockin' at the door," Perry said. "Do me a favor, open the door, and let 'em in."

Bang-bang-bang!

Margaret sat up, aching muscles voicing their complaint before they started shivering, shaking so bad that her back hurt and her teeth clacked. Her head throbbed. She needed water. Her throat felt so dry, so sore.

Her dream was *always* the same — why had it changed?

The sweat filling her suit . . . just like the icy lake water had done when she fell out of the *Brashear*. Her brain had brought the real-life trauma into the dream. And what Perry had said, that was just a reflection of her own fear of infection.

That was why.

That *had* to be why.

Her dream suddenly came to life again as the same *bang-bang-bang* sound made her jump.

No, not *bang-bang-bang* . . . a *knock-knock-knock*.

"Doctor Montoya?"

Klimas, calling through the door.

"Oh, sorry," she said. "Come in."

The door opened. He leaned in, beady eyes staring, smile playing at the corners of his mouth.

"Ah, you're dressed," he said. "That saves some awkwardness. It's time for your third test."

She realized there was a plastic-wrapped sandwich on a plate, sitting on a small table that folded down from the wall. She didn't remember anyone bringing it in.

"My . . . third?" The words cut at her dry throat. "I didn't take a second."

Klimas nodded. "Yes, you did. Passed with flying colors. You don't remember?"

She shook her head. "No."

"Well, you were pretty groggy," Klimas said. He offered her the all-too-familiar white box. "Please put this to good use, then Doctor Feely said you need to see something."

A white box. A foil envelope inside. Inside of that, Tim Feely's little prick.

I didn't say my *brain . . . I said* yours.

The dream, so different. She shook her head, chasing away the thought so she could focus on the present.

"How long was I out this time?"

"Six hours or so," Klimas said. "Feely said you could skip a test. Not like you're going anywhere, right?"

Six hours . . . she'd slept for sixteen before . . . that made twenty-four hours or so since the battle on the *Brashear* . . .

Could infection symptoms start in twenty-four hours?

Margaret blinked. She was being ridiculous. The battle, the abuse to her body, a dip in the icy waters of Lake Michigan, her wounds — she was just run-down, out of shape. Maybe she'd caught a basic, run-of-the-mill common cold.

There was one way to find out.

She reached out and took the box. With practiced motions, she swabbed the base of her thumb and poked herself with the tester before she had time to think about what she was doing.

Then, she stared at the flashing yellow light. Flashing slower . . . slower . . . slower . . .

Green.

She sagged sideways onto the bunk.

Klimas stepped forward, caught her. "Margaret, you okay?"

She nodded, weakly. He helped her sit up straight. "I'm fine. Couldn't be better."

He patted her shoulder. "That's a good soldier. So come on, get up. Doc Feely said you've rested enough."

He stepped back to the door and held it open for her. She stood, let the blanket slide away. She wore fatigues. When had she put those on?

That's a good soldier. She was dressed like one. In the past few days, she had sure as hell *acted* like one.

Fuck you, Clarence. I'm better off without you.

Margaret walked out of the mission module and onto the cargo bay's gray metal deck. Loud male voices filled the area. A row of closed mission modules lined the far side. In front of her, she saw three neatly stowed black boats, the same ones the SEALs had used to rescue her. In front of the boats, two Humvees on metal pallets that were chained to the deck.

Behind the boats lay an open area filled with around twenty armed men wearing camouflage uniforms. In the middle of them, wearing fatigues that were too big for him, stood Tim Feely. He'd set up a makeshift lab of some kind. Metal table, and a big metal pot that hung from an improvised tripod made of plastic poles and duct tape. Beneath that pot, three Bunsen burners cast up small, blue flames. A tube ran from each burner to a blue tank strapped into a dolly.

Clarence stood at the far edge of the circle. He was staring at her. He wore a gray T-shirt, fatigue pants and black combat boots. She wondered what he was thinking. Maybe he was thinking how he'd fucked up, how he was now alone. Maybe he thought she'd want to take him back.

Some of the soldiers sat on crates or chairs, others leaned against cargo and bulkheads, still others just stood there. They were talking and laughing. She saw an open crate, boxes of infection testing kits inside. Used testing units littered the area; what lights she could see glowed green. The men were checking themselves. She knew exactly what would happen if one of those units glowed red.

Three of the men raised cups to their mouths and drank. Their faces scrunched up in disgust. One of the men — Bosh, who had been prepared to shoot her — bent over at the waist, as if he was about to vomit. As men do, the others all hooted and hollered, playfully mocking him for being weak.

A short man with the worst excuse for a mustache she'd ever seen leaned in, shouted at Bosh.

"Oh come *on*, D-Day," the man said. His name patch read *RAMIEREZ*. He was shorter than everyone present except for Tim.

"Admit it," Ramierez said. "This isn't the first time you've had some random, hot goo in your mouth."

"Only his mom's," said another man, this one big enough to make Clarence look small, almost as big as Perry Dawsey had been. His name patch read *ROTH*. "Especially when she had the clap!"

The other men laughed loudly, relishing Bosh's discomfort. He gagged again and almost lost it, which made them shout at him even more.

Bosh stood, his big eyes watering. "Oh my *God*," he said. "I'd rather lick the pus from an infected camel taint than taste that again."

Klimas cleared his throat loudly. The men all reacted immediately, their eyes snapping first to him, then to Margaret.

"Gentleman," he said, "we have company."

The men immediately straightened, quieted down. They all grinned at her, beaming with admiration — all except Bosh, who looked quite embarrassed.

Tim gave a dramatic bow. "M'lady, welcome back." He stood straight. "Good to see you tested negative."

She nodded. If she hadn't, she would have died in her bed, and everyone knew it.

Bosh took a half step forward. "Ma'am, I'm sorry if that comment was offensive."

He looked mortified. Somewhere, out there, was a mother who had taught this young man to always be a gentleman, probably backed that up with several swats to a younger Bosh's behind.

Margaret couldn't let him suffer. "It's okay. I actually like camel-taint pus in my martinis, but it's an acquired taste."

The soldiers laughed, and the tension evaporated.

Clarence didn't smile. He just stood there, staring.

The stink of Tim's kettle drew her attention. She walked up to it. It steamed a little. Inside, she saw a thick, light brown broth. It wasn't boiling, but whitish bubbles clung to its surface.

She looked up. "Good thing you brought that yeast with you, I see."

"Lucky me," he said. "Who'd have thunk it?" He looked like the cat that ate the canary. He'd risked his life to bring the yeast with him. She'd thought he'd wanted to save it for research purposes, to make sure a second colony existed outside of Black Manitou, but this made more sense and meshed with his selfish personality — if he was going to be immune on a ship full of heavily armed soldiers, he wanted to make sure they were just as immune as he was.

"You brewed up quite a batch," she said. "And I see you have no compunction about giving these men something that's completely untested?"

Tim shook his head, a gesture that said, *Don't even try to judge me, sister.*

"Their choice," he said. "Come on, Margo, the *worst* that can happen is they get a wee bit gassy."

He had a point. Tim had ingested the concoction over twenty-four hours earlier, and he seemed fine. Worst-case scenario, really, was that it might make people a little sick. Best-case scenario: immunity from the horrific infection.

Klimas stepped closer. "As I said earlier, Margaret, my men and I came into direct contact with you, Tim and Agent Otto. If any microorganisms survived the bleach spray, then we were also exposed. Considering we just had to shoot at our own countrymen, we chose to take our chances with Doctor Feelygood's camel-taint pus."

Margaret's eyebrows raised. "Doctor *Feelygood*?"

Tim nodded, a huge grin on his face, the grin of a nerd who knew he'd been taken in and genuinely accepted by the coolest kids in school. "That's right," he said. "Seems Commander Klimas is a fan of Mötley Crüe."

Tim dipped the ladle into the smelly broth. He poured the contents into a cup and offered the cup to her.

"All my genetic tinkering has given this vintage quite the lovely bouquet," he said. "Hints of chocolate and elderberry, I think."

The soldiers watched, waited for her reaction. All of a sudden she found herself in a bizarre variation of a fraternity hazing ritual — *drink if you want to be one of us.*

Margaret took the cup, felt the broth's warmth through the plastic. Inside, thick bubbles floated on the milky yellow surface. It smelled like wet gym shoes stuffed with wilted cabbage.

She looked around the room. "To the SEALs," she said, and brought the cup to her lips.

They shouted in encouragement as she tipped her head back, letting the whole cup's contents slide into her mouth. She sensed the warmth a moment before she experienced the taste. Her stomach heaved and she gagged, but the men were watching her — if they could do it, so could she.

Margaret pinched her nose shut, braced herself, and started swallowing. It took three gulps to get it all down.

She gagged again, but nothing came up. She lifted the cup high, laughing at how close she'd come to vomiting.

Klimas was the first to smile wide and pat her on the back. He wasn't the last. Everyone did.

Everyone except Clarence. He just lowered his head, turned and walked deeper into the cargo hold.

NEUTROPHILS

Bo Pan slept. His body did not.

Thousands of crawlers worked their way up his nervous system, following the electrochemical signals along the pathways, heading ever closer to the source of those signals: the brain.

But the crawlers weren't the only microorganisms moving through his body.

Hundreds of thousands of neutrophils navigated in a different direction, moving down his arms, searching for his hands. In particular, for his fingertips.

There they would stay until Bo Pan touched something: a tabletop, perhaps, or a door handle, maybe a mug or a glass. The neutrophils could survive on that surface for a day or two, three at the most. If fortune smiled upon them, someone else would touch that same surface long before their time expired.

And when that happened, the neutrophil would *stick*, it would *burrow*, and it would go to work on its new host.

THE EVER-PLEASANT DR. CHENG

One of the *Coronado*'s mission modules was a small teleconference center. Paulius referred to it as the "SPA," an acronym for "SEAL Planning Area."

Margaret sat at the room's conference table, Tim to her right, Clarence across from her. A flat-panel monitor hung on one end of the module, the image split down the middle: on the left, Murray Longworth in Washington; on the right, Dr. Frank Cheng in the research lab on Black Manitou Island.

Murray looked like he hadn't slept in days. But then again, he always looked that way. His tailored suit hung looser than she remembered it, as if he'd lost even more weight in the three days since Margaret had last seen him.

Three days? Had all this happened in just *three days*?

Murray's body looked like it might fail him at any moment, but his eyes burned with undiminished intensity. He was close to winning, and he knew it.

As for Cheng's fat face, Margaret could barely stand to look at it. While she had hidden away in her home, Cheng had been climbing the ladders of both the CDC and the Department of Special Threats. In the CDC, he was the director of the National Center for Emerging and Zoonotic Infectious Diseases. That made him the top dog there for dealing with the alien infection. If Tim's yeast worked, if it provided immunity, Cheng would be a shoo-in to become the CDC's next overall director.

As for the Department of Special Threats, the organizational chart wasn't as neatly defined. Murray put people into roles as needed. There was no doubt, however, that Cheng was the DST's number one scientist. Frank Cheng answered to Murray Longworth, to the president of the United States, and to no one else.

All Cheng's power and status could have been hers. All she'd had to do was take it, but she'd chosen the coward's way out.

Or maybe . . . maybe Cheng had tricked her somehow. Had he? And had someone helped him?

Margaret looked across the table, at Clarence. Clarence, who had allowed her to stay home all that time. Had he worked with Cheng to keep her out of the picture?

She chased away that random, illogical thought, wrote it off to exhaustion. She rubbed her eyes as she listened to Cheng speak.

"We are making progress," he said, his fat face split by an arrogant smile of self-satisfaction. "I've perfected the genome of the YBR yeast strain."

Tim held up a finger. "*Excuse* me? The *what* strain?"

Cheng's smile faded. "The YBR2874W strain, Doctor Feely. *Properly* named — Y for yeast, B for chromosome two, R for right arm, 2874 for strain number and W for coding strand."

Tim slapped his hands on the table in an exaggerated bit of outrage. "Oh no you don't, Chubby. Naming goes to the discoverer or creator, and I be both. We already have a *proper* name, you blowhard, and that *proper* name is *Saccharomyces feely*. But you can call it the *Feely Strain*, if you like. Note the repeated emphasis on the word *Feely*, as in, *you feel what I'm cookin'*?"

The teleconference screens let people in different parts of the world make actual eye contact, let Cheng look Feely right in the eyes.

"Naming nomenclature is an established practice, Doctor Feely," Cheng said. "Many researchers are involved in this project. We wouldn't want to disassociate them from any credit by putting only your name on it."

And with that, it was instantly clear that Cheng's decision *was* about disassociating someone. He intended to take the credit for Tim's brilliance, for Margaret's discovery of the new cellulase, for *everything*, even though he'd been safe on Black Manitou Island while Margaret and Tim had been shot at, nearly blown up and almost drowned. Cheng couldn't grab all the glory if the strain was named after Tim.

Tim leaned back in his chair. He smiled, laced his fingers behind his head, and looked at Murray's monitor.

"Director Longworth, perhaps you should arbitrate this disagreement," he said. "As our impartial third-party observer, who is right? Cheng . . . or *me*."

Murray stiffened. Tim seemed so confident, almost as if he had something on Murray, or as if the two had worked out a backroom deal.

The director waved a hand in annoyance. "Fine. Cheng, you wouldn't have had anything to work on in the first place if it weren't for Feely's work. The yeast already has a name, so use it and let's move on."

Tim rocked slowly in his chair, smiling wide at Cheng.

Cheng's fat cheeks quivered with anger. "Very well. We've initiated an intensive incubation program to increase the yeast cultures that were delivered yesterday. We've also, as I mentioned earlier, altered the genome to create additional strains — some of which, I might add, show far more potential to be our magic bullet."

Margaret wasn't surprised. Cheng was a climber and a glory grabber, no doubt, but he was no fool and he had a small army of scientists at his disposal. Creating multiple strains was the logical approach. The more weapons they developed, the better chance of having one or two that would devastate the enemy.

"Developing variant strains is mandatory, Doctor Cheng," Margaret said. "But that doesn't address mass production. How are we going to make enough of this stuff to dose over seven billion people?"

Cheng's easy, arrogant smile returned. Margaret knew he'd come up with an original idea, one he'd be entitled to claim as his own.

"Breweries," he said.

Margaret's eyebrows raised . . . not just an original idea, a *brilliant* original idea.

Clarence looked from Cheng to Murray to Margaret — he didn't understand what Cheng was talking about.

Tim leaned back in his chair, surprised. He looked almost disappointed that Cheng had thought of it and not him.

"That's great," he said. "How many breweries are involved?"

Now it was Murray's turn to smile. "Most of the breweries in America, Canada and Mexico are onboard. President Blackmon's been on the phone nonstop with beverage company executives. Believe me, she's quite convincing."

Tim shook his head slowly. "Well, spank my ass and call me Sally," he said. "Cheng, I always thought you were a smelly, stupid douchebag with the integrity of a five-dollar whore, but you know what? You're not stupid at all."

Cheng started to give a nod of thanks, then stopped, unsure if he'd just been insulted.

Clarence looked at Tim, then to the screen, then at Margaret again, anywhere for an answer. "Sorry, can someone tell me what's happening? Breweries?"

Tim slapped the table again. "*Beer*, man. People have been using yeast to make beer for, shit, well since before we started recording history. We don't need to build production facilities for" — he turned to look at Cheng — "for *Saccharomyces feely*" — Tim turned back to Clarence — "because all over the world there are places already equipped to brew yeast cultures around the clock. Those places are called *breweries*."

Cheng's face was reddening. Tim had refused to let the man have his moment of triumph; Cheng couldn't help but chime in.

"And the distribution infrastructure is already in place as well," he said. "Most of the breweries have either their own bottling facilities or direct contracts with them, fleets of trucks, dedicated distribution centers — they can brew it, bottle it, and ship it."

No wonder Murray thought he was going to win.

"Sounds good in theory," Margaret said. "But will it work for the entire planet?"

Murray waved a hand in annoyance. "Do you mind if we focus on the USA first, Margaret? This is a massive effort, yes — one of the biggest projects in our nation's history. Fifty of the largest breweries already have starter cultures. Each of those fifty is delivering subcultures to at least ten more. In two days, we'll have fifteen hundred American breweries producing inoculant. We can make everyone who drinks it immune."

"*Temporarily* immune," Margaret said. All eyes turned to her.

"Let's not forget that one dose doesn't last forever. Tim's inoculant is good for . . ." She turned to Tim. "For how long?"

His eyes glanced upward in thought. He pursed his lips, tilted his head left, then right.

"Oh, about a week," he said. "Then it's going to fully process through the body."

Margaret nodded. "A week. So you're not just talking three hundred and twenty million batches for the good ol' USA, Murray, it's three hundred and twenty million batches a *week*. If the disease gets to the mainland, the inoculant can slow the disease's spread — but it can't stop it altogether."

Cheng huffed. "Unless the disease breaks out in the next three weeks, we'll have enough repeat doses for everyone in North America."

Margaret shook her head in amazement; Cheng was really starting to piss her off.

"This disease could give a fuck about borders," she said. "If you don't get regular doses to the entire world, you're looking at a disaster of epic proportions. This is about logistics as well as production. Across the planet, one person in seven is starving not because the world doesn't produce enough food, but because we can't get food to all the people. And you really think that you can get a regular supply of this to *everyone*?"

Cheng's face turned red with anger. "Yes, that is exactly what I think. This event will bind the human race together."

Margaret saw the expression on his face, understood it — he was annoyed because she doubted his ability to save the planet. He wanted to see *his* face in the history books.

Careful what you wish for, Cheng . . .

"We can't even bind *Americans* together, let alone the world," she said. "And what are your plans for the people who refuse to take it, like the idiots who refuse to vaccinate their own children? What do you do when the companies that are so helpful now decide that they've done their part and they have to go back to business as usual?"

Cheng's face furrowed into a tight-lipped scowl. "Doctor Montoya, this *is* the answer to the problem. We will find a way."

Margaret wanted to grab his fat cheeks with both hands, twist his head, make him whine like the little weakling he was. She wanted to slap him.

"We have a chance at a *permanent* solution," she said. "What about the hydra organism? There were ten people in that human artificial chromosome clinical trial — have you tracked down the other nine?"

Cheng leaned back. The scowl faded. He looked smug, like he'd defeated her argument merely by letting her say it out loud. He waited.

Murray answered her question.

"The president doesn't like the hydra solution," he said. "She doesn't like the idea of introducing one unknown disease to fight another. And as you pointed out, it's possible that the hydras are an airborne contagion — if we use them, they could spread uncontrollably and we have no idea what they might do. President Blackmon told us to focus on the yeast. If Cheng's . . . excuse me, if *Feely's* inoculant works, there's no need to expose the population to an unknown organism."

Her face felt hot. Now Murray was against her as well?

"*Blackmon* doesn't like it," she said.

Margaret knew what was happening. Cheng was sabotaging her work, whispering in the president's ear. Margaret felt an intense anger welling up inside of her.

She stared at Cheng. "So the president doesn't like it, eh, Cheng? And who gave her the idea that the hydras were so godawful dangerous, huh?"

Cheng's eyes sparkled with delight.

"You did, Doctor Montoya," he said. "Your reports labeled the hydras an incalculable risk."

She blinked. Her reports *had* said that.

"But . . . but that was before," she said. "Surely you're not so incompetent you can't see what we're up against. We still don't even know if Tim's yeast works. And if it does, what if the disease evolves to beat it? We have to at least pursue the hydras as an alternate solution."

Cheng shrugged. "We have some people seeing if they can track down other patients of the HAC study, but to be blunt, I don't put much credence in your theory, Doctor Montoya. I hardly think infecting people with your contagious *space worms* is a viable solution."

She reached her fist high and brought it down hard, pounded it on the table like a gavel.

"That's the *fucking point*," she said. "The hydras are *contagious*. If it is airborne, and I think it is, it will spread from person to person without your fucking bottles and goddamn *distribution routes*."

Cheng leaned in, sure of himself. He had all the power and he knew it, relished it.

"We'll look into it, Doctor Montoya. I appreciate what you've done so far, believe me, but there's little you can do while you are isolated on that ship. My team is on the front lines. We'll manage it from here."

She stood so suddenly her chair shot from under her. "The *front fucking lines*? I'd like to come up there and see you face-to-face, you miserable, fat *fuck*. I'd like to cut off your motherfucking *balls* and *fucking feed them to you*. Would you like that, you stupid cunt?"

A hand on her shoulder: Clarence, reaching across the table, looking at her in shock and concern.

"Margaret, take it easy."

She blinked. Her words played back in her head. Her face flushed red. Everyone was staring at her. She slowly sat back down.

Clarence turned to face Murray's screen.

"Director Longworth, Doctor Montoya is under considerable stress."

Murray nodded. He looked less than pleased.

"I can see that," he said. "Doctor Montoya, get some rest. Doctor Cheng, assign more people to look at that stem cell therapy, as Doctor Montoya requested."

Cheng couldn't hide his smirk. He stared right at her.

"Of course, Director Longworth," he said.

"Good," Murray said. "That will be all."

His side of the screen blanked out, leaving just Cheng's face.

"Good day, Doctor Montoya," he said. "Enjoy your time away."

"Go fuck yourself," Margaret said, then she stormed out of the mission module.

PORT

Cooper and José worked to tie the *Mary Ellen Moffett* to the long pier. Jeff was in the pilothouse, managing the fine maneuvering that brought the ship into place.

Waiting at their slip were three vehicles: a white van, a long, black limo and a pickup truck. Four Chinese men stood outside the white van. They wore jeans and sweatshirts, very nondescript, but Cooper wouldn't have wanted to bump into any of them in a bar. Hands in pockets, shoulders shrugged against the cold — they clearly hadn't understood that the temperature at the docks was usually the same as the temperature out on the water. Maybe they were here to help Steve and Bo Pan?

The pickup truck's doors opened and two men — properly dressed against the cold in work jackets and insulated pants — stepped out. They had the burly look of dockworkers. They approached the *Mary Ellen*. Cooper had no idea who these men were, either. He noticed that when the dockworkers came forward, the Chinese men shrank back, just a little bit.

The limo was the most interesting of all: a man in a chauffeur suit — the driver, obviously — stood in front of it, a drop-dead-gorgeous woman on each arm. The women were laughing and smiling, but also shivering beneath thick fur coats. Past the hem of their coats, Cooper saw sparkly dresses and high heels.

The hanging bumpers on the *Mary Ellen*'s port side ground against the seawall.

Cooper was about to greet the two approaching men when a voice called out from behind him.

"Wait!"

He turned to see a bundled-up Steve Stanton rushing out of the cabin door. Steve ran across the deck, two overstuffed laptop bags strung around his shoulders. And not far behind Steve, Cooper saw Jeff descending from the bridge.

Steve slid to a stop, pointed at the dockworkers. "I hired these men," he said in a rush. "And a bonus for you!" He pointed to the limo. Or maybe at the girls, Cooper wasn't sure.

"A bonus?"

Steve nodded hard. "Yes! For such a good job. I have two nights at the Trump Tower for everyone! All paid for. The limo will take us there."

Jeff joined them, a wide smile on his face.

"Stop the presses," he said. "Did I hear you say you bought us two nights at the Trump Tower, and a limo ride with some girlies?"

Steve nodded furiously. He seemed overly hyped up. Stressed, maybe? His eyes kept darting to the cabin door. Was he waiting for Bo Pan?

"My way of saying *thanks*," he said. "And maybe we can all get a beer after we check in?"

Cooper frowned. "You're there, too?" Cooper just wanted to be rid of the guy who bothered Jeff so much. Although at the moment, Jeff couldn't stop smiling, couldn't quit looking at the girls.

Again Steve's eyes flicked to the door. He looked at Cooper, forced a smile.

"I need a break, too," Steve said. "If I can hang out with you guys tonight, I'll pay for one more day at our agreed rate. I really think I should, uh, be around you for a while."

Cooper started to say no — he'd had his fill of Steve Stanton and this weird job — but Jeff put an arm around Steve's shoulders and gave the smaller man a friendly, solid shake.

"Hell yes, you can hang out with us," Jeff said. "Thanks for the gift, Steve! We appreciate it. Coop and I will show you all the good spots in town. Won't we, Coop?"

Hours earlier, Jeff had wanted to get as far away from Steve Stanton as possible, and now he wanted to be the kid's best friend? A couple of nights in a five-star hotel — and a limo loaded with some high-class ladies — could have that effect.

"Sure," Cooper said. Cooper pointed up to the two dockworkers, who were standing at the edge of the pier, waiting for instructions. "Steve also hired these guys to help us unload."

Jeff slapped Steve's back, then invited the dockworkers aboard. He led them to the crane and gave them the rundown on how they'd off-load Steve's crates.

Steve glanced to the cabin door again, and this time he froze. Cooper looked as well — Bo Pan was quickly approaching, a duffel bag over his shoulder. Inside of it, Cooper knew, was the case recovered from the lake bottom. Bo Pan looked like he was trying to control his temper.

"Steve," the old man said, "what is going on?"

Steve took a step away.

"I hired help for unloading," he said.

Bo Pan looked to the dock, saw the white van, pointed at it. "We have help."

"They're not union," Steve said. "We have to hire union labor in Chicago, right, Cooper?"

Cooper glanced at the Chinese men near the white van. They were edging closer, like they wanted to approach but were waiting for instructions. Bo Pan looked furious.

Cooper thought of pointing out that they could have unloaded themselves, and therefore didn't need to hire help — union or otherwise — but Steve looked more than on edge . . . he looked *afraid*.

Steve was the one in charge, wasn't he? Or had this all been some kind of strange sham all along? Was Bo Pan the one who called the shots? And if so, just how much trouble was Steve in?

"Steve is right," Cooper said, following an instant instinct to protect the kid. "If you hire labor to unload, Bo Pan, they've got be union. This is Chicago, my friend."

Bo Pan's bony hands clutched into fists. Anger smoldered in his wrinkled eyes. He looked to the dock.

"I see," he said. "And the limousine? And those women, standing there, watching us . . . are they *union*, too?"

"Steve gave us a bonus," Cooper said. "In fact, Mister Stanton, why don't you wait in the limo? We'll be off-loaded in just a moment."

Steve shook his head. "Uh . . . I'd rather stay on the ship with you and Jeff until everything is finished."

That line made Bo Pan even angrier. He coughed up a wad of phlegm, spat it onto the deck, then started climbing out of the slightly moving boat onto the pier. Two of the Chinese men ran over to help him. One took the duffel bag. The man handled the bag delicately, reverently.

Bo Pan and the men got in the van, which quietly drove down the dock toward the pier gate.

Cooper turned to Steve.

"Want to tell me what that was all about?"

Steve shook his head. "No. I do not." The kid looked like he might puke at any moment. He reached into his coat pocket, pulled out a banded stack of hundred-dollar bills and handed it to Cooper.

"Another part of your bonus."

Cooper looked at it, dumbfounded. Another *mad stack*, another ten grand, just like that.

Steve started climbing out of the boat. Cooper had to help him, thanks to two computer bags, one of which was stuffed with two laptops.

As Steve walked to the limo, Cooper wondered what had just happened. He'd try to get it out of Steve later, if, indeed, Steve was really going to hang out.

Cooper turned, waved to José. The Filipino came running over.

"Yes, Jefe?"

"Big surprise," Cooper said. "We're all staying in the Trump Tower for the next two nights. All free, big guy."

José's smile faded. "A tower?"

"A hotel," Cooper said. "Big one. Fancy as hell, from what I hear. Steve paid for it. We even get a limo ride." He nodded toward the long, black car, the shivering girls.

José coughed, then sneezed. He wiped his nose with the back of his hand.

"Bless you," Cooper said. "You okay?"

José shrugged. "Coming down with something. I think I'll just go home. I miss my family."

Cooper wanted to talk him into coming but could see there was no point. José missed his family, true, but he was also always paranoid of anything that involved giving ID or being around lots of strangers. The man was so hard-working, so at home on the boat; it was easy to forget that once on land, he didn't have the same rights and privileges that Cooper and Jeff enjoyed.

"Okay," Cooper said. "You need a ride anywhere?"

José shook his head. "My cousin is coming to get me. It's just a two-hour drive to Benton Harbor, no problem."

He coughed again, much harder this time. His eyes watered.

"Damn, dude," Cooper said. "Maybe you should swing by a hospital and get that checked out."

José cleared his throat, shook his head and smiled; he thought Cooper was joking.

Cooper felt like an idiot for the second time in as many minutes — José was as afraid of hospitals as he was of hotels. He probably feared that a trip to the hospital might turn into a visit with the INS. A ridiculous fear, Cooper knew, but then again he never had to deal with such concerns.

Cooper peeled off twenty one-hundred-dollar bills from the stack, handed them to José.

"Tell your cousin not to drive like a goddamn illegal, will ya?"

José's face lit up in surprise. He put the money in his pocket. "Sometimes, Jefe Cooper, you're a good guy — for a racist asshole, I mean. Thank you."

"You're welcome," Cooper said. "Great work. Now help get Steve's crap off the boat, okay?"

José jogged over to join Jeff and the two dockworkers, who were already unloading Steve's crate.

A tickle flared up in Cooper's windpipe, a tickle that quickly turned into a small cough. He cleared his throat . . . felt a little scratchy.

Well, he wouldn't let a little cold stop him from having one grade-A bitch of a good time.

Windy City? Here we come.

FREQUENT FLIERS

Bo Pan put a bottle of water and a tin of Sucrets on the counter.

The cashier grabbed it, ran it across the scanner, spoke to him without looking up.

"Hello, sir," she said. "How are you today?" Her name tag said *Madha*. She held out her hand. "That will be seven fifty-five."

Bo Pan adjusted the strap of his carry-on bag so he could get at his wallet, then handed over the money. When he did, his hand touched hers.

Neutrophils detected contact, reversed their grip, letting go of Bo Pan and clinging to Madha instead. In two days, she would kill her husband by driving the point of a clothes iron into the back of his skull.

"Would you like a bag, sir?"

Bo Pan shook his head. "No, thank you. I am fine."

She offered him his change. "Thank you for shopping at Hudson News."

He took his money, moved to the magazine rack. Bo Pan pretended to look at the covers showing bright cars, men with too much muscle or women showing too much skin. Americans certainly loved big breasts.

He tried hard to stay calm — his contact was late. His plane boarded in ten minutes.

What if Ling didn't show?

He unwrapped a Sucret and popped it into his mouth. Cherry flavor. He liked that. His throat was scratchy, and it felt like he had a fever coming on.

Bo Pan heard the rattling of wheels rolling along the concourse's tile floor. He looked up just as Ling rolled a dolly into Hudson News. The dolly held five blue plastic trays, each loaded with soft drinks. Ling met Bo Pan's eyes but didn't acknowledge him in any way.

Ling rolled his dolly of drinks toward the glass refrigerator.

Bo Pan turned quickly to follow; when he did, he bumped into Paulette Duchovny from Minneapolis. Bo Pan's hand came up immediately, reactively touching Paulette's bare forearm.

"Oh!" he said. "Sorry, sorry."

Three hours from that moment, Paulette would be back in Minneapolis. Two days after that, she would infect seven other people, including her son, Mark, and her daughter, Cindy. Mark and Cindy would lock up the house and stand guard as Paulette transformed into something that was not fully human. Before the sun set on the fourth day, Paulette Duchovny would do what a voice in her head told her to do — she would murder a family of five in their home, ending the slaughter by gutting a three-month-old baby.

Paulette smiled at Bo Pan. "That's okay, no problem."

He nodded again, then walked to the refrigerator. Ling was already there, the glass door pinned open by his dolly. He was pulling bottles of Coke out of the plastic bins, then reaching into the refrigerator to place them behind the bottles that were already there.

Ling saw Bo Pan, then took a step back and gestured at the open refrigerator. "Go ahead, sir."

"Thank you," Bo Pan said. He grabbed a Coke.

"Oh," Ling said, then reached down to the floor and picked up a black fanny pack. The pack's pouch looked like it held something cylindrical, perhaps about the size of a travel mug.

He offered it to Bo Pan. "You dropped this."

Bo Pan's heart hammered in his chest. It couldn't be this easy to get an object past the TSA. It simply *could not*. The CIA was here, somewhere, they were watching, waiting for him to take it. They would start shooting at any moment.

Bo Pan took the fanny pack. As he did, his left pinkie touched Ling's right thumb.

In three days, Ling would be dead, a leaking bag of fluid slowly sloughing off of a prone skeleton. The infection would not properly work with his particular physiology, and he would slowly dissolve in a chain reaction of apoptosis. But before he died — and after he became contagious — Ling would stock a total of twenty-two airport refrigerators. He would leave mutated neutrophils on over three hundred bottles, neutrophils that would be nicely refrigerated until a hand touched them, or a pair of lips brushed against them.

Bo Pan turned and walked away, waiting to hear screams of *get down on the floor!* But all he heard were the normal sounds of an airport. He walked to his gate just as his group was boarding.

The last thing Bo Pan did before getting on the plane was to hand his ticket to Enrique Calderone, who lived in the Boystown area of Chicago.

In three days Enrique would grab a kitchen knife and chase his lover through their apartment building, slashing him on the shoulder, the forearm and the temple. His lover would run, leaving a long trail of blood, before finding a fire axe, which he would swing at Enrique's stomach, burying the blade in Enrique's ribs just under his left arm. Enrique would bleed to death a few feet away from his building's laundry room.

As for the people on Flight 245, some of them would prove to be unlucky as well. By the end of the two-hour flight to Newark, seven of them would have touched a surface previously touched by Bo Pan. His neutrophils would already have penetrated their new hosts' skin, would already be cutting open stem cells, rewriting DNA and starting the cycle anew.

Two of those people were on their way home to New York City. They would take the PATH train to Penn Station, then get on the F-train, one of them headed to the Upper East Side and the other to Queens.

Another passenger would transfer to a flight to North Carolina.

Another would board an El Al flight to Morocco.

A fifth was catching a red-eye to London.

The final two, like Bo Pan, were heading to Beijing.

He took his seat, almost giddy with success. He wore Ling's fanny pack in the front. The pack would never be out of his sight or his touch.

After twenty-two years in America, he was finally going home. In fourteen hours, he would land as a national hero.

Unfortunately for Bo Pan, his body would not be able to handle the infection's final transformation changes. He would not become one of the "Converted." The process was already weakening an artery in his right temple, creating an aneurysm. In fourteen hours, yes, he would land as a hero of the people. In fifteen hours, that artery in his head would rupture, causing a stroke — he would die of a hemorrhage.

Bo Pan's infection, however, would live on. Live on in the most densely populated nation on the planet.

THAT TODDLIN' TOWN

Steve Stanton didn't know how to handle his hurricane of emotions. Bo Pan would have killed Jeff, Cooper and José, probably with the help of those men at the dock. That alone felt terrifying. Add to that Steve's guilt over the death of the navy diver. Steve's creation killed the man, killed a soldier who wanted nothing more than to serve his country — just like Steve had wanted to do. Which, in turn, stirred up confusion; just which country *was* Steve's, anyway? He'd grown up American. He'd never even *been* to China — how could he count that distant nation as his home?

Fear, guilt, confusion and a final emotion that, in contrast, made the others all the more intense: happiness.

He was out having a blast with Jeff Brockman and Cooper Mitchell, two men who in their younger days probably picked on and ridiculed guys like Steve. They had no idea that he'd saved their lives, and Jose's as well. The five unexpected witnesses Steve hired — the two girls, their driver and the two dockworkers — had forced Bo Pan to leave the *Moffett*'s crew alive.

By now, Bo Pan was on a plane to New York, then London, and finally Beijing. He would probably never come back. Why would his bosses take the chance that Bo Pan could make a mistake, be picked up and interrogated, when they could just keep him in China and know his secrets would forever stay safe?

And if Bo Pan's bosses sent Steve another handler? Well, Steve was the only one who could maintain and operate the *Platypus*, which meant he was probably safe. As for Cooper and Jeff? Now that Bo Pan had escaped the country with his prize in hand, Steve couldn't think of a logical reason why someone would want them dead.

Still, Steve knew he would spend the rest of his life wondering if someone would come for him . . . and his parents, maybe. Someone who would want to tie up loose ends and silence anyone who knew anything.

Cooper and Jeff had picked up on Steve's troubled thoughts and applied what seemed to be their cure-all for any affliction — drinking. The three of them sat in a booth at Monk's Pub. This was their third stop of the night; Steve was already drunk. They'd had Old Style beer at a dive bar called Marie's Riptide Lounge, then moved on to far more fancy trappings and expensive scotch at Coq D'Or and finally landed at Monk's. Steve had lost track of the drinks he'd consumed. Three beers . . . or was it four? And those two shots . . . had they contained more than the standard one and a half ounces of liquor? Based on the way his head was swimming, it seemed like they had.

Monk's was packed. Music blared. People laughed, shouted to be heard over the high level of noise. Steve wondered if it was loud enough to damage his hearing. One night wouldn't do that much damage, he figured. Besides, tonight he wasn't some nerd hanging out with his parents and family at the restaurant, he was *partying*. And the girls . . . so many girls, black and white and Asian and Hispanic, wearing jeans and tight sweaters or more revealing outfits they'd hidden under heavy winter coats. Steve glanced over to the bar, to a blond girl with glasses he'd been staring at earlier.

She was staring back at him. She smiled.

Jeff smacked Steve in the arm.

"Too bad about those limo ladies, my friend," Jeff said. He wore jeans, a black belt and a black AC/DC concert T-shirt that showed off his lean biceps and muscle-packed forearms. "I can't believe you hired actual models instead of escorts. I mean, they *were* escorts, sure, but not *escort-escorts*."

A tap on his other arm: Cooper. He also wore jeans, but with a gray sweater that made him look like a college professor.

"Jeff is a sad panda because you didn't hire hookers," Cooper said.

"I'm not *sad*," Jeff said. "Just saying a little limo-shag is never a bad thing. Hey, Steve-O, you going to pick out something to eat, or what? We need to get some food in you or you're going to pass out on us, and there's *way* more drinking to be done!"

Steve picked up the menu sitting on the table in front of him. He tried to concentrate on it, but it blurred in and out of focus.

"Maybe a burger," he said. "Cooper, are you having a burger?"

Jeff laughed. "A burger? For that hippie? Maybe there's some grass in here for him to graze on."

Steve looked at Cooper. Cooper shrugged.

"I'm a vegetarian," he said. "Jeff can't quite comprehend why anyone wouldn't want to consume the flesh of animals raised as captives and then butchered, screaming in agony."

Jeff crossed his arms, affected a look of utter disgust. "Dead animals are God's gift to man. Beef is delicious. Bacon tastes good. Pork chops taste good."

The waitress appeared, carrying three beers.

"You boys ready to order?"

Cooper closed his menu. "Roasted vegetable salad, please."

"Cheeseburger," Jeff said. "Make it moo."

Steve stared at his menu, but the words again fuzzed to the point where he couldn't read them.

The menu suddenly flew from his hands. Jeff had yanked it away and closed it.

"Stanton, enough rinky-dinking around," he said. Jeff turned to the waitress. "My man here is having a cheeseburger, medium. And may I say, your eyes absolutely *sparkle* in this light."

The waitress winked. "Smooth talker. Won't get you out of giving me an obnoxious tip."

"Don't worry," Jeff said. "My tip is always oversized."

The waitress shook her head, but she had to hold back a laugh. If Steve had said a line like that, he would have been slapped. Not that he could ever actually say something like that in the first place.

The waitress walked off.

Jeff pointed to Steve's glass. "Get at that beer, bitch! It ain't gonna drink itself!"

Cooper rolled his eyes. "By *bitch*, he means *Mister Stanton*."

"Here," Jeff said, picking up his glass, "let me show you how a *real* man does it." He tipped the glass back and drank the whole thing in one pull. He set it down hard enough on the table to make the other drinks slosh a little. He belched.

"*Boom!*" Jeff pointed at Cooper's mug. "Coop, get to gettin'! You, too, Steve-O! Knock it back!"

Steve glanced to the bar, to the girl, saw that she was still watching, still smiling. He didn't want the girl to think he was a wimp, so he lifted the glass.

"I have to drink the whole thing?"

Cooper shook his head. "No, you don't." He shot Jeff a stern look. "This isn't a frat party, right, Jeff?"

"Phi-drinky-drinky," Jeff said. "What's the matter, Steve? Are you a *puh-puh-puh*-pussy?"

Steve looked at the full glass of beer in his hand. If Jeff had done it, then so could he. He tipped the glass back. He swallowed once, twice, then his throat got so *cold* but he kept swallowing. Jeff screamed "*go-go-go*" as Steve drained the glass and set it on the table.

Jeff raised his arms high. "Winnah!"

Cooper rolled his eyes again, but clapped lightly. "You two can hang out all night. Clearly you've got the same testosterone problem."

Jeff stood. "Boys, don't go anywhere." He walked to the bar, leaving Steve and Cooper alone.

"So, Steve," Cooper said, "you having a good time?"

Steve nodded. His head felt all heavy and loose. "Yes. But I think I may have drunk too much."

"I can see that. I'll make sure you get back to the hotel safe. Now, you want to tell me what was going on back on the *Mary Ellen*?"

Steve felt the elation drain from his body. Why did Cooper have to bring that up now?

Cooper leaned across the table. "If Bo Pan is messing with you, maybe Jeff and I can help."

He looked so honest, so open. Steve thought about telling him the whole story, right there and then.

And then Jeff returned, the girl with glasses at his side. Jeff slid in next to Cooper, the girl with glasses sat down next to Steve.

"Boys, meet Becky," Jeff said. "Becky just so happens to be one of my favorite names."

Cooper seemed to forget all about the discussion; he looked hungrily at Becky. "A lovely name to accompany a lovely face," he said.

Becky laughed, covering her mouth with her hand. Her blond hair bounced and swayed.

Jeff and Cooper seemed so at ease with girls, so natural, like they'd done this a thousand times.

Jeff reached across the table and grabbed Steve's shoulder.

"Steve, Becky and I have a bet," he said. "She bet me that you can't drink a shot of Jäger."

Cooper groaned. "Jesus, Jeff, what are you trying to do, kill our boss?"

Jeff slapped the table. "She didn't think our boss could drink his shot! I said, Becky, you are a dirty whore with the diseased snatch of a smelly pirate hooker!"

Steve's jaw dropped, but Becky laughed even harder. She looked at Steve, smiled a sexy smile.

They were calling him *boss* . . . for Becky's benefit? To make him seem more important in her eyes?

The beautiful girl put her elbows on the table, leaned closer. Her shoulder touched Steve's.

"You guys are *way* older than he is," she said. "Are you *sure* he's your rich boss, or are you running a line on me?"

Cooper put his hand on his chest. "Madam, you offend me. I assure you, Mister Stanton has more money than we could count in a week. Maybe even *two* weeks. It's just that much. Not only is he smart, well-off, *insanely* good-looking, staying at the Trump Tower because he's fancy and fine, but he's also an adventurer — we're back from several days at sea."

Steve held up a finger. "It was a lake."

"Several days at *lake*," Cooper said. "Right you are, boss."

The waitress returned, plunked down four shot glasses filled with black liquid. Those were *definitely* more than one and a half ounces.

Becky smiled at Steve. "The bet is that if you can drink one of these, I have to kiss you."

Steve stared. He swallowed. "And if I can't?"

Becky leaned even closer. "Then you have to kiss me."

Yes, this was really happening. Drunk or not, this was really happening.

Steve grabbed the glass, tilted his head back and poured it all in. His mouth rebelled almost instantly — *how awful!* It tasted like moldy licorice. It burned going down. He felt his stomach roil, but he wasn't going to throw up in front of the prettiest girl he'd ever spoken to.

He turned the glass over and set it on the table, the awful taste still clinging to the inside of his mouth and his nose as well.

Becky put her hand on his chest, pushed him lightly until his back pressed against the booth seat. She turned to her right, then raised slightly and slid backward into Steve's lap.

"You win," she said. She kissed him, slow and warm. Steve's body seemed to melt. Becky's hand held the back of his head as her tongue slid into his mouth. He felt himself grow hard instantly, knew that she felt it, too, and she didn't move away. He heard Jeff screaming something supportive yet obscene, but Steve's world narrowed to the kiss, to the girl.

This was the greatest night *ever*.

As Steve, Cooper and Jeff partied, they couldn't know what was happening to their bodies. Jeff, in particular, couldn't know of the microscopic, amoebalike organisms on his palms, his fingertips. He couldn't know that on everything he touched — and every*one* he touched — he left these moving vectors of disease.

A waitress picked up a glass: *contact.*

The bartender put his hand on the bar where Jeff had done the same only moments earlier: *contact.*

A drunk man bumped into Jeff, then they shook hands to make sure no one was upset: *contact.*

Jeff made out with a woman who had put in a long day at the office and just needed to blow off some steam: *contact.*

That night, two dozen people would leave the bar with crawlers already burrowing under their skin, already seeking out stem cells . . .

. . . already changing them into something else.

BOOK II

CHICAGO

DAY SIX

MEN WITH GUNS

"Hey, Margo," Perry said. "Aren't you going to say hello? That's what you're supposed to say at this point — *hello.*"

Her mouth moved.

"Hello, Perry."

Perry Dawsey smiled.

The bomb screamed its war cry of descent. Margaret tried to take a step forward, but couldn't move her foot. She looked down. What little blacktop remained atop the decades-old brick street had melted, all shiny and black, a stinking, gravel-strewn mess that trapped her like an ancient animal in a tar pit.

Hot wind whipped madly, making roofs sag and smolder. Her blue hazmat suit slowly dripped off her, running down her body to puddle along with the liquid tar.

Perry drew in a deep breath through his nose, seeming to soak up the hot wind and the fetid air. He looked around.

"This is where I caught Chelsea," he said. "The voices stopped, but you know what? It didn't matter. Those things were already inside of me. Nothing I did made any difference. I shouldn't have fought them, Margo — I should have *welcomed* them."

Her suit melted away, leaving her naked. Stabbing pains rippled across her skin, the hard sensation of long needles sliding into her muscles, her organs.

Perry frowned. "Margo, what's wrong?"

"It hurts," she said. "Bad."

He nodded knowingly. "I think they're moving to your brain. I know you don't want to lose control, but it will be okay."

The pains grew worse, driving to her bones, *through* her bones and into the marrow inside.

"I . . . I'm not infected," she said. "The tests . . . I took the tests . . ."

Perry reached out his right hand, cupped her naked breast. His skin felt icy cold, a knife-sharp contrast to the blast furnace that roiled around them.

"The Orbital traveled across the stars," he said. "It could rewrite our DNA. It could turn our bodies into factories that made the things it needed. Did you think it wasn't smart enough to make changes, Margo?"

Her skin bubbled like the street's boiling tar. She fell to her knees.

Perry stood over her, gently stroking her head. Her scalp came away in bloody, wet-hair-covered clumps that clung to his huge hand.

He squatted in front of her, put a finger under her chin, lifted it until she looked into his blue eyes. Then, he gave his finger the smallest *flick* — her jaw tore off, spiraled away.

Perry smiled. "Did you *really* think it wasn't capable of beating your silly little test?"

A shudder brought her awake. She sat up, pulled the blankets and sheets tight around her. She was alone in the tiny bunk room.

She was on the *Coronado*. She was here with Tim, with Clarence, with Paulius and his SEALs.

She was safe.

Or was she?

Outside that door stood a man with a gun — a man who would murder her if her next test blinked red.

And Clarence . . . she couldn't trust him. He'd worked with Cheng to keep her out of the project until it was too late, until Cheng got all the credit. Tim Feely had also helped Cheng, gone behind Margaret's back, sabotaged her work. She had put her life on the line and the three of them — three *men* — had conspired to push the only woman out, to make sure she got no credit. No, not three, *four*, because Murray *had* to be part of it.

Now that breweries were kicking out millions of bottles of Feely's yeast — and how convenient the strain was named after him and not her — did Murray even need her anymore? Maybe that man outside with the gun wouldn't stay outside for long. Maybe he was already planning on how to put a bullet in Margaret's brain, maybe he was . . .

Her thoughts trailed off. Her *paranoid* thoughts. Perry had been paranoid. All the infection victims had been.

Paranoia.

A sore throat.

A headache . . . body pains.

She had all the symptoms.

The incubation period was around forty-eight hours. Her suit had been ripped during the battle, but that was just *twenty* hours ago — even if she had contracted the infection, she wouldn't be showing symptoms yet. She *couldn't* be infected . . . could she?

No, she couldn't, because she'd ingested Tim's inoculant and introduced his modified yeast into her system. That should have killed the crawlers long before they could reach her brain.

A knock at the door.

"Margaret?"

Klimas. Coming with another test.

She couldn't move. She couldn't speak.

The door opened. Klimas stepped inside, a smiling assassin with a black eye.

No preliminaries; he just offered the box. And why not? The drill was old hat. Klimas knew she wasn't infected. She'd tested negative so many times already.

But how could that be?

Her hand reached out on its own, took the box. She didn't want to die, not like this, not with a bullet to the head . . .

She ripped open the foil, used the cool, wet cotton to clean her finger. She pressed the tester against her fingertip, felt the tiny sting of the needle punching home.

Yellow . . . blinking yellow . . . slowing . . . slowing . . . slowing . . .

Green.

Klimas nodded. "Good to go. Thanks."

He took the blinking test and the empty box from her, then walked out. He shut the door behind him.

Margaret's body shuddered with both relief and terror — she was alive, but she was infected. *Had* to be. But why hadn't it turned red . . .

Did you think it wasn't smart enough to make changes, Margo? Did you really think it wasn't capable of beating your silly little test?

She shook her head.

"No," she whispered. "Oh God, no."

Cantrell . . . he'd tested negative over and over again, but when he'd escaped his cell he'd come after her, tried to kill her. Cantrell . . . the one with the genius IQ, just like her. He'd been infected the whole time, right under their nose.

The Orbital had created a new organism — an organism that the test didn't detect.

And *she* had it.

She had to tell someone, warn everyone. She had to tell Klimas . . . but if she did, he'd kill her on the spot. If she didn't, she'd convert, become one of *them*. But maybe she wouldn't . . . this new organism, it was untested, unproven. Maybe she wouldn't convert.

And, maybe she was just being crazy . . . the test turned *green*, not red, GREEN.

She was okay. She wasn't infected.

She *wasn't*.

A PRAYER FOR THE DYING

Murray sat on a couch in the Oval Office. In front of him was a table loaded with neat folders. Beyond that, a chair that held President Blackmon. They were alone.

They had spent the last hour in the Situation Room — along with Admiral Porter, the secretary of defense and a few other big hitters — debriefing about the *second* naval disaster to occur on Lake Michigan in the last six days. At the end of that meeting, Blackmon had asked Murray to join her.

For the first thirty minutes of that second meeting, her personal staff had been present, helping plan and explain the logistics of the immunization effort. It was the largest public health effort in the nation's history, so there were a *lot* of logistics.

Then, Blackmon had asked everyone to leave. Everyone except Murray.

This wasn't the first time he'd been alone with a president. Going on four decades, now, Murray had been summoned to this office to discuss things that could have no record of being discussed.

Blackmon had her left leg crossed over her right, the hem of her stiff dress suit perfectly positioned over her left knee. In her lap, she had an open folder. Blackmon preferred paper over electronics whenever it was convenient — one of the few things about her that Murray found admirable.

She shut the folder and looked up at him. "The first delivery of inoculant will be here tomorrow afternoon. Deliveries to military facilities will start arriving tomorrow night, and it will take a week before we reach them all. The first civilian deliveries are scheduled to arrive in major cities two days from now. I'm burning every last scrap of political capital I have on this, Director Longworth, so I have to put you on the spot — I want to know what Cheng saw when he tested it on his crawlers."

Now Murray understood the reason for the one-on-one meeting. In the wake of the *Los Angeles*'s attack, Murray had given Captain Yasaka a clear order — send Tim Feely down to the lab to process the bodies and have him package tissue samples to be sent to Black Manitou. Feely had been in such a rush that he'd only prepared samples from Petrovsky; an unfortunate choice, considering Margaret's insistence that Walker's hydras might be humanity's final solution.

The end result: crawlers *had* escaped the task force, because Murray had orchestrated it.

The transport had been risky, of course, but had gone off without a hitch. Cheng's team had a brain-dead woman on Black Manitou Island, which they were using to cultivate the crawlers for research and testing. Crawlers and test subjects alike were locked down in conditions that made BSL-4 precautions look about as difficult to pass through as airport security. Cheng and his team were just as sequestered on their island as Margaret, Clarence and Feely were on the *Coronado*.

Murray could count the people who knew about the Black Manitou crawlers on two hands — and leave three fingers to spare. And that number included the president and himself. Murray hadn't even told Margaret. Apparently, neither had Feely: something the man seemed to think was a favor to Murray. Feely had called in that imaginary marker during the argument with Cheng over who got to name the yeast. Murray could give a wet shit about the name of the damn stuff, so Feely got what he wanted. Besides, that had pissed off Cheng, and Murray hated Cheng.

"Doctor Cheng tested the inoculant directly on the crawlers harvested from Charles Petrovsky's corpse," Murray said. "The substance dissolved the crawlers with one hundred percent efficiency. However, his team euthanized the subject and performed an autopsy — the inoculant had no effect on removing the infection from her brain. As Montoya and Feely predicted, once the infection reaches the brain, it's too late."

"So it's not a cure, and we still don't know if it prevents infection," Blackmon said. "Can we test it on lab animals? See if it really does inoculate them?"

Murray shook his head. "The crawlers only survive in humans, Madam President. We don't know why. They don't even survive in primates."

Blackmon nodded. She fell silent, stared off.

Murray waited. He already knew what she was going to ask.

She looked at him. "The SEALs on the *Coronado* took the inoculant yesterday, did they not?"

Murray nodded.

Blackmon sighed. Murray had seen that before, too — a leader's reluctant acceptance that he or she had to put someone directly in the line of fire.

"We need a volunteer," she said. "Get one of those SEALs to Black Manitou, inject him with the crawlers. We have to know for sure if this actually works."

She wasn't fucking around. But to directly expose a serviceman to that risk . . . the soldier Murray had once been bristled at the thought.

"Madam President, we have a little time to keep testing the—"

"*Now*, Director Longworth. We've already turned a huge sector of our economy over to making the inoculant. If it *doesn't* work, then we have to put all resources behind Doctor Montoya's hydra theory."

Murray nodded again. The president was right, of course — protecting a single soldier wasn't worth the wait. Four sunken navy ships and over a thousand dead sailors were ample enough evidence for that.

"I'll take care of it, Madam President."

"Thank you, Director Longworth."

He'd been dismissed. He left the Oval Office.

The president had given him an order. Maybe one of Klimas's men would actually volunteer. Knowing those crazy-ass SEALs, they probably all would.

Murray hoped the inoculation worked.

Hell, for once, he'd even *pray*.

THE HANGOVER

Steve Stanton threw up. Again. At least this time he'd made it to the toilet.

When his stomach finally relaxed, he slumped down on his butt. He wondered how much dried urine from hotel residents past he was now sitting in.

It wasn't the first time he'd gone drinking, but he'd *never* partied that hard before. Now, he was paying the price.

His head pounded so bad it hurt to move. His throat felt sore. His body ached.

Becky had left a few hours earlier. Sometime around noon, if he remembered correctly. What a night.

He, Steve Stanton, had gone out to a bar, met a girl and got laid. He could hardly believe it.

But now, oh, man . . . his *head*.

He had to stand up, then make his way back to bed. He'd sleep the day away, or at least try to.

Tomorrow, maybe, he'd feel better.

THE HANGOVER, PART II

Cooper took the wet washcloth off his forehead, flipped it, then gently set it back in place, sighing as he felt the fabric's coolness against his skin.

He was getting too old for this shit. He was certainly old enough, *experienced* enough, to know what awaited him at the business end of ten beers and six shots.

Cooper glanced at the room's other bed. It held one occupant: the waitress from Monk's. He didn't remember Jeff bringing her back with them, nor did he remember hearing anything during the night. He didn't remember seeing her when he'd stumbled to the bathroom for the washcloth. How far gone did he have to be to not know his best friend was tagging a hot waitress just a few feet away?

A loud, sawing snoring sound came from the foot of the beds, by the TV on the dresser. Cooper slowly lifted himself up on his elbows. There was Jeff, buck naked, lying on the floor on top of his jeans and AC/DC shirt.

"Strong work," Cooper said.

He lay back and closed his eyes, tried to manage his throbbing head. It hurt to swallow. Had he been screaming all night? He wasn't sure, because he couldn't really remember anything after that sixth beer.

Yes, he was old enough to know better. After he slept this one off, he'd make changes. Sure, he'd promised himself the same thing a hundred times before, but this time would be different.

Maybe Tim wasn't so unlucky after all.

He'd worked on Black Manitou long before it had been a government-owned facility. That had been his first job out of college, working for a civilian biotech company engaged in questionable research. That research had gone south: people had died in horrible ways. He'd almost died himself.

After that, he'd taken the job with the Operation Wolf Head task force, preferring the isolation of a military ship on the water to the memories of what he'd seen on land. He hadn't actually thought the infection could return. He'd felt protected, safe.

But that hadn't lasted.

The infection's reemergence and all the death that came with it made him think he was some kind of doomed soul. And yet, that math didn't add up.

How many people had died during his time on Black Manitou? He wasn't sure, but that number paled in comparison to the task force disaster, to five ships and over a thousand corpses resting at the bottom of Lake Michigan.

Yet he had survived . . . *again*. He was one of only three people to make it out alive. On top of that, he was now one of the few people in the world immune to that alien bullshit.

Probably immune, anyway.

For now he was as safe as safe could be, sitting at a table in the *Coronado*'s cargo hold, sipping Lagavulin with three SEALs who had taken quite a shine to him.

"Let me get this straight," said D'Shawn Bosh. "You're saying you can tell if people are infected by how fast Tylenol sells?"

Tim nodded. "Basically, yeah. I can even do it from here on the *Coronado*. Klimas set me up with a laptop that ties into the TSCE."

The *total ship computing environment* gave him ridiculously high-speed Internet access, even though they were floating in the middle of an inland sea.

Bosh smiled. "Well, look at my man, here — *TSCE* — like he's been in the navy all his life."

A day ago, a comment like that would have embarrassed Tim, made him wonder if these big, dangerous guys were mocking him, but not now. They *loved* him. He'd helped save one of their own. He'd done it under fire. It shocked him as much as it did anyone else, but when the shit had hit the fan he'd actually been *brave*.

Whatever bravery Tim had, however, paled in comparison to the man he'd helped save. A few hours earlier, a helicopter had taken Roger Levinson off the *Coronado*. Tim knew there was only one reason to do that: a human trial to test the inoculant against direct exposure to the crawlers kept on Black Manitou. No one else knew that, except for Levinson and probably Klimas, Levinson's commanding officer. Their fellow SEALs didn't know the mission, they only knew that Levinson had volunteered for some secret duty. *Volun-fucking-TEERED*. The courage and self-sacrifice needed to do that . . . Tim couldn't quite process it.

Saccharomyces feely would soon be put to the ultimate test. If Tim's solution didn't work, Roger Levinson would become infected. If that happened, Tim knew, everyone and everything was screwed.

Calvin Roth, the big one, drained his shot glass, set it down on the table. "What I don't get are all the little critters floating through people's bodies. We drank your nasty-ass yeast to protect us from crawlers, which are part plant, part *us*, but then there are also hydras, which maybe *aren't* part plant, but *are* part us . . ."

He shook his head, pushed his glass over to Ramierez. "Fill me up, Ram. I need another shot to understand this shit."

Ramierez dutifully filled the glass. Tim had to concentrate to not stare at the man's patchy, pencil-thin mustache.

"You're not that far off," Tim said. "You drank the inoculant, which—"

"Camel-taint pus," Roth said, raising his glass.

Ramierez raised his own. "I'll drink to that. Knock 'em down, boys!"

Tim drained his glass, felt his throat burning. He set his glass on the table and made an educated guess that these men would drink to just about anything.

"Like I was saying, you guys drank the inoculant. That means even if you did get exposed to the infection when you rescued us, you're fine, because the inoculant wipes out the infection if you take it within twenty-four hours of exposure. And if you weren't exposed, now you're safe as long as you keep taking the inoculant doses every couple of weeks. If you get exposed from here on out, you technically still get infected, and the infection *will* modify your cells to make crawlers or other things, but those things will dissolve before they can do any damage because of the catalyst that's in your blood."

Bosh nodded. "It's like if we had to dive into a vat of acid to assemble a bomb. All the parts of the bomb are there, but we don't last long enough to put them together."

Tim clapped and leaned back, almost fell over his chair. He was drunker than he thought.

"D-Day, you nailed it!"

The men had insisted Tim call them by their first names, or their nicknames: *D-Day*, *Ram* and plain-old *Cal*.

Ramierez shook his head. "I don't get it. The hydras kill the infection. Why are we fucking around with this yeast when we could just, I don't know, *pre*-infect ourselves with the hydras?"

Tim raised a finger. "Ah, a good point, my man. Two reasons. First, we don't have any hydras — they went down with the *Brashear*. Second, even if we did have them we wouldn't use them. Once the hydras get into your body, they start reproducing. We don't know if they'll stop at a certain point, or if they will keep on reproducing until there are so many of them they damage you, maybe even kill you."

"Reproducing," Roth said. "Little animal things in your blood, fucking away. Like a microscopic orgy?"

Tim laughed. "While I admire that analogy more than you will ever know, my extralarge friend, the hydras reproduce asexually. That means they don't have to mate to produce offspring."

Roth shook his head in disgust. "That's as fucked-up as a football bat."

Ramierez leaned in, the half-full bottle in his hand. "They do it with themselves because they can't get laid, just like Cal."

Roth drained his scotch, set the glass down. "For that, little man, you get to fill my glass. And I do it with myself because I'm just that damn good."

"Hear hear," Ramierez said, and poured another round of shots.

None of the fun seemed to have sunk into Bosh. To him, this was obviously serious business.

"It's all so fucked," he said. "I'd rather have an enemy I can see. Alien microbes? Modified yeast? Just give me something I can shoot."

Ramierez nodded sagely. "Wiser words were never spoken, D-Day. Come on, boys, around the horn again. Let's see those glasses."

Everyone pushed their shot glasses toward Ramierez. He filled all four. The SEALs raised theirs and Tim followed suit. The men let out a loud *hooyah*, and they drank. Half of Tim's shot slid down the side of his face. The glass slid out of his hand. Shoddy workmanship, apparently — go home, shot glass, you're drunk.

That, or *he* was drunk. Drunk, and *safe*, isolated from everything, surrounded by trained killers who thought he was the bee's knees.

Tim *was* lucky, after all. If that luck held, he could just stay right here, in this very safe place, until Cheng's grand plan ran its course.

A HUSBAND'S ROLE

Clarence Otto stood on the *Coronado*'s rear deck. No wind for a change, just the oppressive cold. He stared out at the setting sun, wondering what might happen next.

He'd survived. Margaret had survived. Tim Feely had survived. Black Manitou was leading the effort for mass production of inoculant. By any measure, Clarence had succeeded in his assigned mission. Murray would probably try to give him a medal for the effort.

But Clarence didn't want a medal . . . he wanted Margaret.

Onboard the *Carl Brashear*, the woman he'd fallen in love with had returned. She'd been decisive, insightful, tireless and brilliant. She'd been her old self, her *fighting* self.

And now? Now she wouldn't see him.

All day long she'd stayed locked up in her mission module. He'd tried to get in to talk to her, but through the closed door she'd told him to go away. She sounded scared. She sounded *alone*.

For the last five years, whenever she'd felt those emotions she had come to him. He had comforted her, or at least he'd tried. She was his wife. His job was to protect her, help her through any problem no matter how great. At the end of the day, no matter how he sliced it, that was a mission he'd failed.

The sun finally ducked below the water, leaving only the residual glow of pink clouds to reflect against Lake Michigan's tall waves.

Maybe tomorrow he could talk to her. Maybe he could make it all up to her.

If he worked hard enough at it, if he apologized enough, then maybe . . . *maybe* . . . they could repair the damage they had done to each other.

Maybe they could be together again.

ACTUALIZATION

Clarence Otto had to die.

They *all* had to die.

All of them . . . all the *humans*.

Margaret had turned off the lights in her bunk module. She sat alone in the dark, thinking. She finally understood. Why had she fought against this for so long? It was so *obvious*. People had turned the earth into a cesspool of hatred and waste, had taken the gift of winning evolution's grand game and pissed it away.

She got it now. She *understood*. The Orbital had tried to fix things, it had tried to do . . .

. . . to do . . .

. . . to do *God*'s work.

Not the God she had thought she'd known in the naiveté of childhood, or any of the thousands of randomly invented supernatural beings that caused people to slaughter each other throughout history. No, a *real* god. A god with the power to send ships across space. The power to change human beings into something else, something new.

Something *powerful*.

Humanity had shit all over this planet.

It was time to remove humanity, time to let the world start over.

Margaret *hated* them. She wanted to walk out of her little cabin and stab the first person she saw. Maybe find a wrench, bash them in the head again and again until bone cracked, until she saw the bloody mess that was their brains.

She wanted to kill Clarence.

She wanted to kill Tim.

She wanted to kill the sailors, the SEALs, sink this fucking ship and put them all on the bottom so they would never hurt anyone ever again.

Margaret stood. The thought of taking life thrilled her, infused her with excitement, made her vibrate and bubble with pure energy.

Who would be first?

She reached for the door handle, then stopped.

They outnumbered her. If she killed one of them, maybe even two or three, the rest would certainly get her. She couldn't let that happen, because she was meant for something greater.

Margaret's former self had tried to second-guess the Orbital, tried to figure out what strategy would come next. She'd never even considered its latest tactic: create an infectious agent that the cellulose kits didn't detect.

An infectious agent that turned brilliant humans into converted *leaders*.

Leaders who could pass undetected among the humans. Leaders who could infiltrate human organizations. Leaders who could gather the troops of God together, make them operate as an organized unit.

Margaret could do all of those things. She had been chosen for it.

How ironic that Clarence turned out to be right after all: Margaret Montoya wasn't a soldier — she was a *general*.

All she had to do was bide her time and wait for her army.

She wasn't contagious. Her infection gave her that knowledge. No tongue triangles, no blisters with dandelion seeds, nothing that could reveal her true nature. That made perfect sense: if she showed those telltale symptoms, the humans would kill her. *Not* being contagious was actually a form of camouflage.

For now, while trapped on this ship, she had to blend in. She couldn't kill anyone. She couldn't do anything out of the ordinary. She had to wait. She had to be . . . *calm*. Like Cantrell had been back on the *Brashear*. Not at first, no; he'd been jittery, paranoid. He must have been very close to finally realizing his role, just as Margaret now realized hers.

The Orbital must have engineered new crawlers that could penetrate BSL-4 suits. That was the only logical answer. It wouldn't take much, just a microscopic hole, barely detectable if it was even detectable at all. Was that how Clark and Cantrell had become infected? Yes, that made sense, and when they were submerged in bleach, maybe the pressure change caused a tiny bit to leak through . . . that explained why they both reported smelling it.

But if the crawlers had worked their way through her suit, why hadn't they worked their way through Tim's? Why wasn't he converted?

Because he'd ingested that yeast. Her exposure had to have come from Petrovsky's body. Tim had worked on Petrovsky as well, had also been exposed, but he'd taken the yeast within twenty-four hours of that exposure. Margaret hadn't ingested the inoculant until the next day . . . at least forty-eight hours after the likely exposure.

What a difference a day makes.

Margaret wanted to laugh. She wanted to scream with joy. The precautions and preparations of the thing she used to be had been useless against the glory of God's plan. How foolish her former self had been, how *arrogant*, to think she could outsmart such a power.

But that didn't matter anymore. God had chosen her.

Margaret reached for the door. She opened it. Time to join the others. Not to hurt them, not to drive a knife into their throats, but to simply pretend she was one of them.

If she played it smart, sooner or later she'd make it to the mainland. She'd find others like herself. She would organize them into an army of God.

Then the carnage would begin.

STATISTICALLY SIGNIFICANT

The small table still smelled slightly of spilled scotch. A few SEALs were walking around the cargo hold, checking various things and keeping busy, but Tim had the table to himself; plenty of room for his laptop and a cup of coffee.

On the laptop, a video-chat window showed the face of Kimber Lacey, a CDC staffer who'd been assigned as his mainland liaison. Tim could access the databases remotely, but it helped to have a direct contact at the CDC's headquarters in Druid Hills, Georgia.

"Doctor Feely, the latest results of your data-mining algorithm are coming in," Kimber said. She had big, dark eyes and deep dimples at the corners of her mouth.

"Kimber, I have to wonder about your life choices."

She looked concerned. "What do you mean?"

"I mean with a face like that, why aren't you in Hollywood making movies?"

She shook her head, but also blushed a little. "Doctor Feely, can we just go over the results?"

"Sure. Let's hope there aren't any."

"Let's hope."

A pattern of medication consumption had revealed the *Pinckney*'s advanced level of infection. If the vector had somehow escaped the flotilla and made it to the mainland, the same consumption patterns would likely hold true. Through Kimber, Tim had programmed the CDC's database to track spikes in the purchase of cough suppressant, pain medication and fever reducer.

Kimber typed with her mouth open. Damn, that girl had pretty lips.

"Here we are," she said. "They just came in. Let's see . . ."

She stopped talking. She just sat there.

"Kimber, what is it?"

She blinked, looked up at the camera, those dark eyes widening with fright.

"There's a geospecific spike," she said. Her words rattled with tension. "I read a nine hundred percent increase in cough suppressant, eleven hundred in pain meds, and a *two thousand* percent jump in fever reducer."

Tim said nothing. He didn't have to, because the numbers said it all — the infection had escaped quarantine. Could Cheng's team on Black Manitou have fucked something up? That seemed impossible; Tim had seen the facilities there, knew how foolproof they were. Then how? Had something floated away from the *Los Angeles*, drifted for miles until it was picked up by some random boater?

He swallowed. There was still hope; maybe this was an isolated outbreak. A small town in Wisconsin, perhaps, something that Longworth's semi-illegal DST soldiers could isolate and quarantine.

Tim closed his eyes. Before he spoke, he gave in to superstition.

God, please don't let it be a major city . . .

"Where?"

She didn't want to say it any more than he wanted to hear it.

"The one I just read you, that's the biggest one . . . it's from Chicago."

Tim's balls felt like they wanted to shrivel up and hide somewhere in his belly. *Chicago* — the third-largest city in America, the very heart of the Midwest.

"The *biggest* one? There are others?"

She nodded. "Statistically significant spikes in Benton Harbor, Michigan, Minneapolis, Minnesota, and" — she looked straight into the camera, dead into Tim's eyes — "New York City."

Minneapolis? Chicago? *New York?* It was already too late: nothing could stop it from spreading.

"Send me the data."

He looked at the numbers himself, hoping Kimber had suddenly contracted a case of the stupids, hoping she was wrong.

She wasn't.

Forty-odd hours had passed since the *Pinckney* and the *Brashear* went to the bottom. The statistical spikes indicated the Chicago infection had begun shortly after that battle.

The second-largest spike came from Benton Harbor, a town on the east coast of Lake Michigan. That infection looked to have started just a few hours after Chicago's began, New York's and Minneapolis's three to four hours after that.

It had begun in Chicago. Benton Harbor was only two hours away . . . based on what Tim knew of incubation periods, someone could have driven there from Chicago. That matched what he saw in the data. But New York? A twelve-hour drive. The level of spikes indicated New York was only six to eight hours behind Chicago in the level of infection.

That meant one thing and one thing only: a carrier had been in an airport.

MURDER

Steve Stanton sat up and turned on the light. He squinted, blinked. Was it still night? The heavy curtains shut out all traces of the outside. He looked at the alarm clock on the little nightstand next to his hotel bed: 11:52.

He squinted, saw a little red light at the bottom left of the time, next to white letters that read "AM."

Eleven fifty-two in the morning. He'd slept all day, all night, and into the next day. Were hangovers supposed to last this long?

He reached to the nightstand and grabbed the bottle of Chloraseptic he'd paid a bellboy to bring him. He opened his mouth, sprayed the cooling, numbing mist against the back of his throat.

It helped a little.

Steve wondered how Cooper and Jeff were doing. Maybe they'd already checked out of the hotel and were headed back to Michigan.

He'd wanted to tell Cooper what had really happened, maybe get some help in case Bo Pan came back. Steve had worked it all out in his head the night before, thought he was safe . . . but maybe he wasn't. Should he call the police? If he did, would that put his family in jeopardy? And for that matter, would the police turn him over to the CIA? Maybe even send him to China?

But . . . what if *Cooper* had contacted Bo Pan? What if Cooper and Jeff had given Bo Pan Steve's room number . . . what if all three of them were on their way to kill Steve right now?

He sucked in a big breath. That was a crazy thought. It didn't even make sense. How could Cooper reach Bo Pan? Steve didn't need to make up illogical fears about Cooper and Jeff, not when there were plenty of very real things to worry about.

Like the small matter of a dead navy diver. *Murder.* An act of war.

Some "hero" Steve had turned out to be.

What was he going to do? Maybe he was missing something, not thinking it through because he felt so awful.

He sprayed again, letting the cool feeling spread through his throat. That was enough for now. He needed rest.

Steve put his head back down on the pillow. He closed his eyes.

The hero slept.

LEADERSHIP

Murray had never heard the Situation Room this quiet. The only sound came from a few monitors that played newscasts at low volume. He couldn't hear anyone typing. No one talked. No one cleared their throats. No one even moved.

Blackmon folded her hands together, rested her forearms on the tabletop.

"How did it get off the flotilla?"

When she got mad, when the cameras weren't around, her stare burned with intensity. She looked *predatory*.

"We don't know, Madam President," Murray said. He wasn't going to sugarcoat it.

The predator's stare bore into him.

"Three cities," she said. "Chicago, Minneapolis, New York. Is that all?"

"And western Michigan," Murray said. "Doctor Feely thinks there will be more. He thinks a carrier went through one of the Chicago airports."

She still had that *presidential look* about her, but how long would that visage stay at the fore? The disease had broken quarantine, spread to three areas of very dense population. Things were about to get bad in a hurry, and on *her* watch — she couldn't blame Gutierrez for this one.

"Do we know who the carrier is? Can we trace the travel pattern?"

Murray shook his head. "No, Madam President. At this point we have no idea who the carrier is, or where the carrier went."

Hands still folded, Blackmon tapped her left pointer finger against the back of her right hand.

"What do Doctor Cheng and Doctor Montoya think?"

Murray felt a little embarrassed.

"Doctor Montoya is still on the *Coronado*, so she can't help us much right now." Margaret was there, and mad as hell. She had predicted the infection would escape, said they needed to be preparing a "hydra strategy," and Murray hadn't backed her play. After all the times she'd been right, he'd doubted her: now he was paying the price.

Margaret was out of the picture, which meant he had to rely on the man who, frankly, wasn't in her league.

"Doctor Cheng thinks we're now in a race against time," Murray said. "The vector is in the wild. He said the patterns show it's highly contagious, on a level unlike anything we've ever seen. The only thing we can do to mitigate exposure is to inoculate as many people as possible, as fast as possible."

Blackmon stared at Murray like she wanted to pin the blame on him. But she knew as well as he did that she couldn't politic her way out of this one. Americans were going to die: what remained to be seen was how many.

The president turned to Admiral Porter. "What's the status of inoculating our troops?"

The first batches of inoculant had come to Washington, of course. Murray had drank a bottle of the nasty stuff himself. The military was next in line. If the people with guns became converted, that would create another level of problems.

Admiral Palmer rattled off a litany of bases. The biggest of them — Fort Hood, Norfolk, Fort Bragg, and a few others — were inoculating their own troops and already creating starter cultures for other bases. Within three days, five at the most, every soldier, sailor and airman on U.S. soil would be protected. That was, of course, if the infection wasn't already spreading through some of those garrisons.

"We've also ordered all bases on foreign soil to lock up tight," Porter said. "No one in and no one out. They're already constructing their own culturing plants. As soon as starter cultures are available, we'll ship them. We project eight to ten days until all foreign bases are fully inoculated."

Blackmon turned to Nancy Whittaker, secretary of the Department of Homeland Security.

"Nancy, what's the status of our domestic inoculation production?"

The military took care of its own logistics. For everything else, inoculation management fell to Whittaker. So far, she had been unflappable — it didn't seem to faze her that the health and safety of an entire nation had somehow fallen into her lap.

"Trucks are already shipping finished product on the East Coast and in the Midwest," Whittaker said. The former Georgia governor had never bothered to train away her drawl. "Seattle started brewing almost immediately — fifty thousand doses have already been delivered to final FEMA distribution points. In the next twenty-four hours, Madam President, we believe all participating breweries will at least be at fifty percent production capacity, and full distribution will be under way in all major cities."

Blackmon's deadly gaze swept the room.

"Twenty-four hours," she said. "How many Americans will already be infected by then?"

No one had an answer. Murray couldn't even guess, so he stayed quiet.

Blackmon stared down at the table, stared so hard Murray had to wonder if the table could feel as intimidated as he did.

"We have to slow the disease's spread," she said. "Shut down air travel."

All heads turned to a short, fat, bald man who stood in the corner of the packed Situation Room. As secretary of transportation, Dennis Shaneworth needed to be present but wasn't important enough to merit a seat at the table.

"Right away, Madam President," he said. "Chicago, Minneapolis and New York?"

Blackmon looked at him. "Shut it down *everywhere*. Cancel all civilian passenger flights immediately. Allow cargo flights *only* if they are needed to distribute the inoculant. Do it now."

The room's silence vanished as hands flew to phones and people scrambled to carry out her orders.

Murray felt a spark of hope. So far the only data they had was a run on drugstores for cough drops and pain reliever. Some politicians would have waited a half-day, maybe more, just to be *sure* a shutdown was necessary. He hadn't expected Blackmon to move so decisively.

She again looked at Murray. She curled a finger at him, calling him over. Murray stood and walked to his commander in chief.

"Chicago," she said quietly. "That's the start of this?"

Murray nodded. "The word is *epicenter*, Madam President."

She let out a slow breath. Up this close, he saw the fear in her eyes.

"Chicago is the epicenter," she said. "Should I have Whittaker prioritize inoculant shipments there?"

"Yes," Murray said. "As much as she can spare. Doctor Feely figures we're in day two of the exposure. But" — he leaned closer, so only she could hear him — "Madam President, may I be frank?"

"You mean there's a time you show restraint?" She closed her eyes, as if that might protect her from more bad news. "Yes, tell me."

"According to Feely's statistical models, the majority of Chicago's population is either already infected, or will be before we can help. My honest opinion is that the city is fucked."

Her eyes opened. The predator's stare faded away, at least as much as it could for her.

"Find ways to increase production, Murray," she said. "I want a list of any factory in the United States, Canada or Mexico that cultivates yeast, for any purpose. We'll find a way. I won't give up on Chicago."

Blackmon sat straight, faced the room. That brief moment of genuine empathy vanished.

"I'm declaring a federal emergency under the Stafford Act," she said. "I want SecHHS and FEMA to put together a task force to run this inoculation. Let's get Congress and SCOTUS notified. Director Longworth" — she again turned to face him — "is Montoya safe to travel?"

He shook his head. "Cheng quarantined the *Coronado* for two weeks, to make absolutely sure no one onboard is infected. Margaret needs to stay there."

The president silently mouthed the word *dammit*. "Then get me Cheng. I want him here."

She turned to Porter. "Admiral, I want the Joint Chiefs and the National Security staff to notify Congress of my intent and desire for a total mobilization of reserve forces."

Blackmon took in a breath as if to make a grand statement, then seemed to remember something. She again turned to her chief of staff and spoke quietly, but Murray was close enough to hear.

"Get the speechwriters. In two hours I want to address Congress, and I want every network carrying it live. Prepare that footage Montoya sent of the sailors from the *Brashear* — people need to see what this plague does to the human body. Go."

The chief of staff scurried off.

Blackmon put her shoulders back and her chest out — more true leader than pure politician.

"Ladies and gentlemen, if we don't act *now*, we are quite possibly facing a worst-case scenario. The nation is counting on us."

Murray started dialing: he had much do and little time in which to do it.

ALL CHANNELS

Jeff lifted his head from the pillow. "Dude, is that the president? Get that Republicunt off the TV, will you?"

Cooper nodded. His head felt heavy, full of the same goop that he blew out of his nose every five minutes.

He used the remote to change the hotel TV's channel, from Channel 3 to Channel 4 — and there, again, was President Blackmon. Channel 5: Blackmon. Channel 6: Blackmon.

"She's on all the big networks," Cooper said. He tried ESPN, only to find the same thing. "Holy shit, dude — she's on *all* the channels."

"She's a stinky, hate-filled, nasty—"

"Hold on a sec," Cooper said. "This has to be something big."

Jeff propped himself up on one elbow to watch.

"I already feel like a bag of assholes," he said. "And now this? I hope it's not another Detroit. Hey, Coop, you feel sick?"

Cooper gestured to the pile of Kleenex on the little lampstand next to his bed. "Yeah. I do." He pressed the "volume" button.

". . . an unprecedented threat upon our great nation, and one that requires unprecedented action. My fellow Americans, we are mobilizing a swift and thorough response. I am in constant contact with the world's leaders. Every nation on earth is working together to win this battle."

The camera angle shifted, panning across a half-bowl of applauding politicians. Was that Congress? Cooper could never remember if that was the House, the Senate, or if they all met in some special room for things like this. What he did know was all the politicians looked the same: rich fuckers who raped the system, the only differences between them being ties and dresses of red or blue.

A news ticker ran across the bottom of the screen:

. . . INFECTIOUS AGENT THAT RESULTED IN THE DETROIT DISASTER IDENTIFIED . . . SCIENTISTS HAVE DISCOVERED WAY TO INOCULATE AGAINST THE INFECTION . . . PRESIDENT BLACK-

MON CLAIMS "DISEASE WILL BE WIPED FROM THE FACE OF THE EARTH" . . .

"Holy shit," Cooper said. "It is another Detroit."

Jeff flopped his head back into the pillow. "Told ya. Holler if they say *Chicago* — otherwise, I don't give a shit. I'm going back to sleep. I feel like I got face-fucked by a rabid buffalo."

The applause died down. Blackmon continued.

"Even as I speak to you now, factories all over America are collaborating in the largest unified manufacturing initiative since World War II. Distributors, shipping companies and grocery store chains are all cooperating with FEMA to bring you the medicine that will keep you safe. Over five hundred corporate sponsors have signed up to fund this initiative. More join the cause every hour. We are faced with a challenge to not only our country, but to every person on our planet. With God's help, America is taking the lead to protect the human race."

The audience cheered again, louder this time. At least some of them did. Cooper didn't follow politics, but it looked like only the Republicans were standing. The still-seated Democrats applauded politely.

Cooper looked at Jeff. "Protect the human race? Is this even bigger than Detroit?"

Jeff shrugged. He didn't seem to notice the yellow bit of snot dangling from his nose.

The applause faded. Politicians sat back down. Blackmon continued.

"I can't stress this enough," she said. "The surgeon general and the Centers for Disease Control urge you to cooperate with local distribution centers to get the treatment. The emergency broadcast system will be transmitting delivery days and locations. There *will* be enough for everyone. Until you receive your medication, limit contact with others and stay indoors as much as possible."

Blackmon made a fist and banged it once on the podium. "All the naysayers who claimed that American manufacturing was dead are about to see how wrong they were. Other nations are following our lead, producing their own medicine, and what they are producing began *here*. American ingenuity is gone? I . . . don't . . . *think so*."

The Republicans stood. They roared their approval. Some of the Democrats begrudgingly stood as well.

Jeff let out a huff. "So the world is in danger, and she turns it into a campaign speech. This from a woman who doesn't want universal health care? Whatever."

Blackmon held up both hands, gave the crowd her trademark half-smile. She looked confident and excited, but not too much of either. The applause died down again.

"Let me say I do not fault my predecessor, or his party, for allowing things to come to this point," she said. "These are exceptional times not only in the history of our nation, but also of the world. Together, we will forever end the greatest threat the planet Earth has ever faced."

"Man, she's good," Cooper said. "Something new is happening and she still manages to imply that Gutierrez opened up Pandora's box in the first place."

"She's been president for two years," Jeff said. "Whatever happens now is on her."

"Yeah, right. *Four* years into Gutierrez's term, you were still blaming his Republican predecessor for the crappy economy. Give me a break, Jeff — with you, the Republicans are always at fault and the Democrats never do anything wrong."

Jeff raised a hand, gave a thumbs-up. "Now you're understanding how things work, bro. Turn that thing off."

Turn it off? There was some kind of world-shaking shit going down, and Jeff wanted to nap?

On the TV, Blackmon grew more serious. More solemn. "Now, I must show you some very disturbing footage. This footage underscores the reason we must all work together in this inoculation effort. This is footage from—"

"*Coop!*"

Cooper jumped; Jeff had screamed the word. Cooper turned.

Jeff propped himself up on one elbow. "I told you to *turn it off*. You trying to fuck with me or something?"

His lip curled up, like it was all he could do to not stand up and smash Cooper's head into the TV. Cooper didn't know what to say.

Blackmon continued to babble, but Cooper wasn't paying any attention. He used the remote to turn the TV off. "Dude, just take it easy, okay?"

Jeff's lip returned to normal. He blinked a few times. The hate left his eyes.

"Oh, wow, man," he said. "Sorry about that. This bug has me in a shit-ass mood, I guess."

Cooper shrugged. "Don't worry about it." He felt a wave of relief — for a second, he'd thought his best friend was going to get out of that bed and come at him.

Jeff rubbed at his face. "No, it's not okay. I can't talk to you like that. Sorry." He looked up and forced a smile. "So that shit they were talking about on TV, that medicine. When do we have to take whatever it is they're passing out?"

"I don't know," Cooper said. "You want me to turn the TV back on?"

"No. Whatever it is, it's not going to be here in the next six hours. I'm going to get some more sleep. Really awesome vacation in the Windy City, eh?"

"My kind of town. Old Blue Eyes was full of shit, if you ask me."

Jeff laughed, which quickly turned into a heavy, ripping cough that curled his body into a fetal position. Cooper plucked a pair of Kleenex from the box and offered them. Jeff had his left hand over his mouth, but reached out with his right to take the tissues. He pressed them to his mouth as the cough racked him again. He rolled to his back.

"Aw, *fuck*, Coop — that shit hurts."

Jeff pulled the Kleenex away from his mouth and looked at it. Amid a glob of greenish-yellow were bright streaks of red.

"Dude," Cooper said, "that's not good."

Jeff balled up the Kleenex and tossed it away. He waved a hand as if brushing away Cooper's thoughts.

"Ain't the first time I've coughed up a little blood, bro. Don't worry about it." He rolled to his side, rested his head on the pillow. "I'm going back to sleep. Turn off the lights, man. If you make any more noise, I'm going to hurt you."

Cooper froze. Was Jeff joking, or threatening? It didn't sound like a joke. Cooper stared for a moment, once again suddenly aware of the size difference between them. Jeff was bigger, stronger . . . and Jeff knew how to fight.

Cooper slowly reclined on the bed, careful not to make too much noise. Maybe he didn't feel like he'd been face-fucked by a rabid buffalo, but he sure as hell didn't feel like singing and dancing, either. He was exhausted; sleep would be good.

And maybe when he woke up, Jeff would be back to normal.

GUINEA PIG

Paulius Klimas sat at the SPA's conference table. He stared at a blank screen, waiting for a call. Once the call began, he'd get one minute. Even that much was a blessing, a courtesy done for him by Murray Longworth.

Paulius had lost men before. Five so far, all on missions that had never been announced, never been recorded. Every one of those deaths had been hard. Each time he'd questioned his leadership abilities, wondered if he could have done something different to bring that man home alive.

But this was the hardest of all.

Longworth had needed a volunteer. Since Levinson couldn't fight, Paulius gave the man first dibs. Levinson understood that if he didn't go, another SEAL would go in his place.

So Levinson had accepted.

Now, Paulius was about to hear the results.

The screen flared to life. He found himself looking at Levinson: in a hospital bed surrounded by clear glass walls, but bright-eyed and smiling.

"Commander," Levinson said. He saluted.

Paulius returned the salute. Some of his pent-up stress bled away.

"You look good for a lab animal," Paulius said. "What have they told you?"

"Looks like that awful crap Doctor Feelygood brewed actually works. I'm eighteen hours in. If I was infected, I'd probably have a sore throat, fever and aches, but I feel fine. Other than where I was shot, I mean. That still hurts like a bitch. They said painkillers could mask infection symptoms, so this little piggy gets none."

More of the stress eased. Paulius hadn't realized he'd carried the pressure in his chest — it suddenly felt much easier to breathe. Levinson seemed fine. More than that, the mission to recover Feely, Montoya and their research had turned out to be critical after all.

Even though the infection had somehow escaped the task force, he and his men had made a difference.

The screen beeped: time was up.

Paulius saluted. "Your courage is immeasurable, Roger. If you don't turn into a plant, drinks are on me."

The wounded man returned the salute. "As long as it's something besides what Feelygood makes, I'll take you up on that offer."

The image blinked out.

Paulius stared at the blank screen. He and his men had twelve more days of quarantine, as did Feely, Otto, Montoya and the *Coronado*'s crew. He'd given his men a few hard-earned days off, but no more — it was time to start combat drills.

He and his SEALs were immune. If the shit hit the fan, they might be called upon once again.

They would be ready.

DAY EIGHT

#TAKETHEMEDS

@DrDurakMerc

Don't be a sheeple! Trust the government to give you your shots?
Then you get what you deserve.

@ARealGirl

What the fuck is wrong with you anti-vaxers? This disease turns
people into MURDERERS. Drink the fucking inoculant already,
or you'll kill us all.

@TwistahSistahBB5

I don't get this hostility — if you want to take their drugs, take
them, if I don't want to, that's my choice! It's a Big Pharma trick.

@BadAstronomer

Hey, antivaxers, heard of a thing called "the news"? You know,
those fancy moving pictures that keep showing what happened
on the *Brashear*? #TakeTheMeds

@BootyHooty912

You don't want to drink your gunk? Shit, dawg, give it here — I'll
put it next to my Glock, which you'll see again when you change.

MANIPULATION

She had to find a way to control the men.

Margaret sat with her back against the mission module's thin, metal wall, her thighs parallel to the ground, her feet on the floor — the *chair position*. Her thighs burned. A fight was coming: she needed to be strong.

At the count of one hundred, she bent forward, extended her body and started doing push-ups.

One . . . two . . . three . . . four . . .

Math. The most basic language of the galaxy. The language created by God. Not the human god, or god*s*, but the *real* god.

Sixteen . . . seventeen . . . eighteen . . .

If the men on this ship had converted, she knew she would have been able to control them. They would have followed her, did whatever she said; God had made it that way. But the men weren't converted — they were merely human.

Human, yes, but trained killers. Dangerous.

Thirty-four . . . thirty-five . . . thirty-six . . .

She was smarter than they were. She could find a way to make them do what she wanted. If she started now, when the right time came she could play them against each other. Or, at least, she could stay alive long enough to find her own kind.

Fifty-nine . . . sixty . . . sixty-one . . .

Her arms and chest burned. She ignored the pain. Years spent hiding away had made her soft. She needed to make her body *hard*.

Clarence would be the easiest to manipulate. She knew what motivated him — the simple sentiment of a soon-to-be extinct species: he *loved*.

One hundred two . . . one hundred three . . . one hundred four . . .

BIG PHARMA

EXCERPT FROM THE WEBSITE "BEYOND TOP SECRET"

By SmrtEnough2See

For decades the government has been the pawn of Big Pharma, funneling billions of taxpayer dollars to companies that produce improperly tested drugs and vaccines. And now that same government is telling you that you *must* take this new "inoculant" drug for the mysterious "alien infection"? An infection that has not been proven to exist? And a drug that has not been properly tested, even by the rubber-stamping Big Pharma pawn known as the FDA?

The government "tested" the drugs and vaccines that gave our children autism. Our friendly overlords aren't even bothering to *pretend* to test things anymore.

And now our government says we *must* take this untested "medicine." If we don't, why, we'll become murderers! We'll kill our own families!

How frightening, and how convenient.

Until the government publishes the science behind this claim, *do not believe the lies.*

Demand information. Demand *proof.*

THE WEST COAST

The Situation Room was getting crowded.

Murray tried not to stare across the table at the latest person to join the party. Dr. Frank Cheng looked like the cat that ate the canary: smug, self-satisfied and quite impressed with his new place of importance.

You don't even realize you're choice number two, jackass — if Margo wasn't stuck on that ship, she'd be here instead.

Murray, Cheng, Admiral Porter, André Vogel, the president and a standing-room-only crowd of other directors, assistants and important people listened to Nancy Whittaker, secretary of homeland security, describe the massive inoculation project.

"The West Coast response was phenomenal," Whittaker said. "All major breweries and ninety percent of independents have cultures and are either in full production or close to it. Bakeries all over the country have joined in. They're collaborating with any bottling facility they can find. We estimate that eighty-five percent of the populations of Seattle, Portland, San Francisco, Oakland, San Jose and San Diego are inoculated. The Los Angeles basin is lagging behind at around sixty-five percent."

The speed of the national response boggled Murray's mind. In all his years of service he had never seen the nation unify for one cause like this. Not for 9/11, not for oil spills or tornadoes, not for hurricanes or superstorms.

Maybe it was because most disasters were *regional* — a flooded Long Island had little impact on Arizona or California, didn't affect the farmers in the Midwest and the plains states, didn't bother anyone in the Great State of Texas. The news covered such tragedies, people donated to the Red Cross, then everyone who wasn't in the disaster zone went on about their daily lives.

The infection outbreak, on the other hand, affected *everyone*.

Some people remained oblivious, as people often do, but the majority of Americans understood the situation's stark reality: this was the potential death of their nation. Americans were banding together to fight it tooth and nail.

Banding together thanks to the leadership of President Sandra Blackmon.

Murray had thought her an idiot, a Bible-thumping figurehead, but her ideology and personality seemed tailor-made for just this situation. Demons were at the door; Americans wanted a defender armored up in good old-fashioned religion.

Whittaker finished her report, but she didn't sit down. She shifted uncomfortably, like a high schooler who had to tell her strict parents she'd been caught screwing in the parking lot.

"Spit it out, Nancy," Blackmon said. "I heard your good news, now give me the rest."

Whittaker cleared her throat. "Madam President, while the distribution is going well, there is a growing problem. On multiple websites and in social media, people are broadcasting a message to *not* take the inoculant."

Blackmon's face wrinkled in doubtful confusion. "Is this a religious reaction? I know the Muslim community isn't thrilled we're using breweries, but my people are in direct contact with Islamic leaders and we're overcoming that."

Whittaker shook her head. She cleared her throat again, giving Murray a moment to wonder who could be so bug-shit crazy they wouldn't take the inoculant.

"The objections are anchored by the antivaccine crowd and the alternative medicine movement," she said. "Almost without exception, both groups are using every communication vehicle they have — websites, blogs, email lists, social media — to tell people that this is, quote, a *Big Pharma trick*. I have some sites to show you."

Whittaker called up websites on the Situation Room's main monitor. Murray saw page after page with headlines that painted the inoculation effort in terms of government abuse, a capitalist power grab, grand Illuminati conspiracy, even mind control. Who could be so bug-shit crazy? These people, that's who.

Blackmon stared blankly.

"People are actually *listening* to this? These are just fringe movements. How many people are we talking about?"

Whittaker shrugged. "It's impossible to say at this time."

Blackmon threw up her hands. "But this doesn't make any sense! We broadcast *video* of those brave sailors, the cocooning, that horror show of the triangles. We *showed* that!"

"The most common reaction is that the videos are fake," Whittaker said. "Hollywood special effects, CGI . . . they say all the data is fabricated."

Blackmon shook her head. Wide-eyed and open-mouthed, she had never looked less presidential.

"But that isn't even *sane*," she said. "What possible motivation could we have for *tricking* three hundred and thirty *million* people into drinking the inoculant?"

"To create dependence," Whittaker said. "That's the most common claim. Other theories involve nanotech that will let the government target people who oppose official policy, or that the inoculant will let the shadow governments control politicians and the military, or just to make everyone dumber and more docile. All of these are variations on ideas that have been around for years and applied to everything from agriculture to chemtrails to broadcast television. Our urgent message that everyone *has* to take the inoculant plays right into the conspiracy theorists' existing structures."

Blackmon sat quietly for a moment as she thought it over.

She looked at Cheng. "The people who refuse to take the inoculant . . . what are their chances of contracting the disease?"

Cheng leaned back, stroked his chin. The little fuck was actually milking the moment, pausing for drama's sake. Murray cursed the misfortune that kept Margaret away.

"We estimate that the infection rate will be around ninety percent for anyone who isn't immunized," Cheng said.

Blackmon straightened in her chair. She nodded, accepting the difficult news.

"I see," she said. "All right, let's face reality — Doctor Cheng, if some people refuse to take the inoculant, and the infection spreads to these people, won't they just die off?"

Cheng sat forward, eager. "If only it were that simple, Madam President. This disease doesn't kill people, it turns them *into* killers."

The fat man stood, addressed the room as if he were an actor on a grand stage.

"This denial will create pockets of people susceptible to the disease, true, but keep in mind that even if we had one hundred percent acceptance from the populace, there is no way to inoculate *everyone*. We've seen it time and time again with pending natural disasters, where people don't get the warning message despite our best communication efforts. If we inoculate, say, ninety percent of the population, ten percent of the population can still become infected — that's up to thirty-three million Americans behaving like the infected victims we've already documented. It would create untold havoc."

Murray remembered the rampages of Perry Dawsey and Martin Brewbaker. Colonel Charlie Ogden had led a company of converted soldiers into Detroit, cut off all roads, shot down commercial jets, brought that city to its knees. Every infected person became a mass murderer — if *millions* of people became infected . . .

Blackmon looked around the room. "Can we *force* the inoculation on those who won't take it voluntarily?"

Whittaker nodded. "Legally, yes. Local and state public health organizations have the right to require vaccination via the precedent of *Jacobsen versus Massachusetts* — sometimes individual freedoms lose out to the greater need — but it's doubtful we can do that on a national scale. Even if we had every police force working with us, we can't organize a door-to-door campaign for the entire country."

Blackmon's predator gaze swept the room, looking for prey.

"I must not be hearing this right," she said. "Are all of you telling me that we just have to *wait* and see if American citizens get infected, then suffer whatever damage they inflict until we can kill them?" She slapped the table. "Unacceptable! I want alternative plans, and I want them in four hours. Cheng, what about Montoya's hydra strategy?"

Cheng froze. He looked left and right, saw that everyone was waiting for his answer. He licked his lips.

"Um, we're working on it."

Blackmon slapped the table again. "*How long?*"

Murray was just as much at fault as Cheng for this, but he couldn't help take a tiny bit of satisfaction at watching the attention whore suffer. *You wanted the big time, hot shot? This is what it's really like.*

Cheng had no choice but to meet the president's burning gaze.

"We have to locate the individuals who had that experimental stem cell therapy," he said.

Blackmon's nostrils flared, her lips pressed into a thin line. The most powerful human being on the planet had eyes only for Cheng.

"I'm gathering you've found none so far," she said. "And the only way that could happen is if you haven't actually *looked*."

She turned on Murray, pointed at him. "This is on you, too, Longworth."

"It is," he said. "I'll take charge of the search personally."

"Director Vogel," Blackmon said. "You're now in charge of that search. I don't care what you have to do to find those people. Get the details from Murray and make it happen."

Vogel nodded. "Yes, Madam President."

She turned her attention back to Cheng. "From what you've told me, the hydra strain could be just as bad as what we're already dealing with. But if this spins out of control and my choices are hydras or the destruction of the United States of America, you know goddamn well which one I'll pick."

Blackmon sat still for a moment, gathering herself. Murray wanted to crawl across the table and kiss her. He looked around the room, saw similar sentiments etched on the faces of America's elite; at that moment, no one gave a rat's ass if Sandra Blackmon was Republican or Democrat, civilian or a vet, male or female. She was the right person in the right place at the right time. Everyone *believed* in her.

She took a breath, visibly calmed herself. "The hydra strain is one contingency plan, but that's not enough. I want everyone working on worst-case scenarios. I want to know just how bad it can get, and I want to know what we're going to do if it gets that way."

In the face of an utter catastrophe, it defied logic that Murray felt optimistic — and yet, he did. It wouldn't be easy, and he knew many would die, but they were going to beat this thing.

They were going to *win*.

MISTER BLISTER

Cooper took another bite of his egg-white omelette. Room-service break-fast, and it tasted damn good. He wasn't sure if it was thirty-seven dollars good, but this was on Steve's tab so he didn't really care.

He still felt crappy — exhausted, weak, like his whole body was rebel-ling against him — but at least his appetite had returned. He was turning the corner. One more good, long sleep, and he'd be right as rain.

Jeff, on the other hand, had gotten worse.

"Buddy-guy, you got to eat something," Cooper said. He pointed his fork at the hamburger sitting on the tray in front of Jeff's bed. "Feed a cold, starve a fever, bro."

"Got a fever, too," Jeff said. "Dude, I hurt so goddamn bad."

His eyes were swollen, almost crusted shut.

"Jeff, I know you don't want to see a doctor while you're on vacation, but—"

A loud *thump-whoof* came from outside the curtain-covered window, fol-lowed by the faint, constant cry of a car alarm.

Cooper put his fork down and walked to the window. He opened the heavy curtains, looked down to wintry Wabash Avenue far below.

"Jeff, come take a look at this."

Jeff did, groaning as he pushed himself out of bed and joined Cooper at the window.

Fifteen floors down, flames billowed out of a black-and-white cop car. One cop lay on the pavement, unmoving, his heavy winter jacket on fire and billowing up greasy black smoke. Another cop stood near the car, aiming his pistol at running pedestrians.

"Holy *shit*," Jeff said again. "I think he's—"

Filtered by the distance and by a thick window that wouldn't open, the cop's firing gun sounded like the tiny *snap* of bubble wrap.

A woman fell face-first onto the slushy sidewalk. She rolled to her back, holding her shoulder.

The cop turned, aimed at a running man: *snap*. The man kept running, angling for a brown delivery van parked half up on the sidewalk. *Snap*. The man stumbled, slammed into the van's side. He slid to the ground.

The cop strode toward him with a steady, measured pace.

"Jesus," Jeff said. "That cop . . . he's killing people."

Cooper heard sirens approaching; thick, long echoes bounced through downtown Chicago's city canyons.

The cop reached the fallen man, pointed his gun at the man's head. Cooper couldn't breathe — fifteen stories up, there wasn't anything he could do but watch.

Then, the cop put the gun away. He knelt down and put his face on the fallen man's, held his head in what looked like a passionate kiss. The man kicked and struggled, but the cop kept at it, ignoring the feeble punches that landed on his shoulders and back.

Jeff shook his head. "What the fuck? Johnny Badge shoots him down, now he's performing mouth-to-mouth?"

Cooper didn't say anything. The burning cop car continued to pour black smoke into the sky, the greasy column rising up right in front of their window. The woman was crawling across the sidewalk, a trail of blood marking her path.

"That's some pretty fucked-up shit," Cooper said.

Jeff coughed again, even harder than before. Half bent over, he walked to the bed and flopped down.

"Fuck it," he said. "I gotta sleep. Turn out the lights, bro."

Seeing Jeff on the bed made Cooper's own crippling fatigue hit home. The excitement had made him briefly forget how bad he hurt, but there was no escaping it.

"It'll be on the news soon," Cooper said. "Got to be, bro. We'll find out what happened then."

He looked out the window again. The cop was still bent over the fallen man. Two other people had come up to help, but Cooper couldn't make out what they were doing from so far away. Across the street, two women clashed in a hair-pulling chick-fight. Friday night in downtown Chicago. That toddlin' town.

Cooper jumped as something smashed into the wall next to him, shattered in flying pieces of black and clear plastic — the alarm clock.

"Coop, I *told* you to turn out the *fucking* lights!"

Jeff stared hatefully at him through swollen, red eyes, his mouth open, the tips of his wet, white teeth visible behind cracked lips. His face looked . . . different, somehow. If Cooper had bumped into this Jeff on the street, he would have barely recognized him.

Angry Jeff was back. And just like before, Cooper's instincts screamed at him to do nothing that might set his friend off.

"Calm down, dude," Cooper said softly. "I'll get the lights."

Cooper pulled the curtains tight. He moved slowly to the light switch, flicked it off. Darkness engulfed the room — even the alarm clock's red glow was gone. A tiny bit of light filtered through the top of the curtains.

"I can hear you," Jeff said from the darkness. "Your loud-ass breathing, Cooper, I can *hear you*."

Now he was breathing too loud? Cooper wasn't about to go to sleep if Jeff might wake up at any moment and beat the living hell out of him. Cooper wanted out, and he wanted out *now*.

"Jeff, brother, maybe I'll just go downstairs and let you sleep."

He started to edge toward the door.

"Coop?"

Cooper stopped cold. Jeff's voice, but normal again. Normal, and *scared*.

"Don't go," Jeff said. "Just . . . just stay here, okay? I hurt awful bad."

Cooper felt a pull of emotions. The fever was making Jeff delirious, maybe even dangerous enough to do something violent, but he was also afraid and in pain. For Jeff to actually *ask* Cooper to stick around? That man never asked for help. That meant he was in bad shape.

"It's okay," Cooper said. He quietly returned to his bed, feeling his way through the darkness. He lay down. "It's okay, Jeff. I'll be here. Just go to sleep."

"You won't bail on me?"

Cooper felt a rush of love for his friend. They'd known each other their whole lives — like he could *ever* bail on Jeff Brockman.

"Hell no," Cooper said. "I got your back. Just sleep. I'll be here."

Moments later, Jeff started snoring.

Cooper adjusted in his bed, but felt a pain on his right shoulder. He quietly sat up, craned his neck to get a look. In the faint light, he saw he had a blister of some kind. Small, reddish, straining the skin like it had liquid inside. Liquid, or . . . *air*?

He pressed a finger against it, slowly at first, then harder. It *squished* in, but didn't pop.

Cooper rubbed at the area, then lay down. If it was still there tomorrow, he'd deal with it then.

For now, however, the more sleep, the better.

BECOMING MORE

Steve hurt.

He didn't mind the pain. Something was happening . . . something *wonderful*. He wasn't afraid of Bo Pan anymore. He wasn't afraid of anyone, or anything.

He lay in his dark hotel room. He heard noises outside — sirens, faint screams, something that might be a gunshot — but he didn't care. None of those things concerned him.

He wasn't going back to Benton Harbor. He'd never see his parents again, but that, too, was okay, because — somehow — his parents were no longer *his*.

They weren't his parents any more than some chimpanzees were his parents. Related? Sure, but vastly separated by different states of intelligence, different states of awareness.

Steve closed his eyes. He would sleep a little more. And he knew, he *knew*, that when he awoke, he would be a new man.

THE FRONT DESK

Yelling from outside the room.

Cooper yawned. He sat up in bed. The room was pitch-black. He was still coming out of sleep, but damn, he felt a hundred percent better. Just *not* being sick made him instantly happy, giddy at feeling normal once again.

Another yell from the hall.

Then, silence.

Cooper thought of the scene on the street: one cop burning, another cop shooting a man then making out with him, a woman crawling across the sidewalk, leaving a trail of blood.

He sat very still, listening for anything, hearing nothing.

What time was it?

That question made him remember Jeff throwing the clock against the wall. Sick Jeff. *Angry* Jeff.

Cooper quietly felt around the nightstand, searching for his cell phone. He found it, turned away from Jeff so the light wouldn't cause problems, then checked the time — 8:45 A.M. He'd slept through the night.

Had Jeff slept, too?

Cooper slowly moved his phone so the display's illumination lit up the bed next to him.

It was empty.

He turned on the nightstand lamp. He blinked at the sudden light. On the floor below the TV, Jeff's AC/DC shirt and his jeans: gone.

Cooper quietly stood, walked to the closed bathroom door.

"Jeff," he said in a whisper. "There's some shit going down in the hall."

No answer.

Cooper opened the door — the bathroom was empty.

Where the hell was Jeff?

He quietly walked to the room's main door, careful not to make any noise. He leaned into the peephole and looked out.

There was a teenager lying there, bleeding from a gash in his forehead. The kid moved weakly, unfocused eyes staring up at nothing.

Cooper automatically reached for the door handle, but stopped when he saw a flicker of motion. Through the peephole's fisheye lens, another teenager stepped into view. Then another.

One grabbed the fallen one's feet, the other reached under his shoulders. They lifted.

Cooper again started to open the door, to see if he could help, but one of the teenagers turned his head sharply.

Wild eyes stared right at Cooper.

He felt a blast of fear, something that rooted him to the spot — he dare not move, not even to step away from the peephole.

Was the teenager looking at him? No . . . no one could see through a peephole, not from that far away. Maybe Cooper had made a noise.

Not knowing why the teenager scared him so bad, Cooper stayed perfectly still. He didn't even breathe.

The boy said something to his friend. They carried the fallen one down the hall, out of sight.

Cooper ran to the hotel phone. He stabbed the button marked "front desk." The phone on the other end rang ten times before a woman answered.

"Hello, this is Carmella."

"I need security," Cooper said. "No, just call the cops. There was a hurt kid up here. Maybe there was a fight. They took him."

"And I give a shit, why?"

Cooper blinked. "Uh . . . didn't you hear me? I think that kid was hurt. He had a head wound."

"There's a lot of that going around," the woman said. "Fuck you very much." She hung up.

Cooper stared at the handset for a moment, then felt stupid for doing so and put it back in the cradle.

He looked at his cell, dialed 9, then 1, then paused: those cops in the street, shooting people. Were more cops like that? Maybe *all* of them? Maybe calling 911 wasn't such a good idea.

He heard sirens coming up from the street. He walked to the window and pulled back the heavy curtains. For the second time in a handful of seconds, what he saw stunned him.

Chicago burned.

He saw flames rising high from the windows of two skyscrapers. Down on the street, people scrambled in all directions. There were four fire engines, but only one had a crew that was trying to fight the fires. The other three trucks seemed to be abandoned. And no, people weren't *scrambling* down there, they were . . . chasing . . . they were fighting.

A black car turned the corner, completely out of control. It skidded across cold pavement and skipped up onto the sidewalk, where it plowed into an old man. The man flew back a few feet, then vanished below the still-moving black car.

Cooper heard the now-familiar, distant *snap* of a gunshot, but he couldn't see where it came from.

Chaos down on the street. Bloody teenagers in the hall. The front desk lady didn't sound like she was dealing with a full deck. Jeff, gone. And Steve Stanton . . . was Steve okay? Cooper vaguely remembered Steve was on another floor, but he had no idea what the room number was.

He couldn't worry about Steve right now. Finding his best friend was all that mattered.

Cooper looked at the nightstand, seeing if Jeff had left his cell phone — it was gone. He looked to the room's lone chair: Jeff's coat was there, Cooper's piled on top. It was freezing outside . . . maybe Jeff was still in the building.

He dialed Jeff's number.

On the other end, Jeff's cell rang. And rang.

"Shit, bro, pick up."

On the seventh ring, Jeff answered.

"Coop?"

A surge of relief at hearing his voice.

"Jeff, dude, where are you? Shit is going *off* outside. I don't know what's happening but we need to bail the hell out of Chicago. We have to get to the *Mary Ellen* and get out of here."

Jeff said nothing.

"Jeff, talk to me — where are you, man?"

"Not . . . sure."

His voice sounded so deep, racked with pain and confusion.

"Jeff, just tell me where you are. I'll come get you. Are you in the hotel?"

"Hotel?"

"Yes, the Trump Tower, where we're staying? Are you in the building?"

Cooper waited for an answer. Jeff sounded like he was on the edge of passing out.

"Yeah," he said finally. "Uh . . . basement."

"Basement? Good, Jeff. *Where* in the basement? Focus, brother, *focus*. I'll come get you. Look around and tell me what you see."

"It hurts," Jeff said. "Coop, it *hurts*."

"Okay, I hear you, but tell me where you are, buddy. You—"

The phone went silent, the connection broken.

Cooper immediately dialed again. The phone rang and kept ringing until voice mail answered.

"This is Jeff Brockman of Jeff Brockman Salvage, and if you've got the bills, we've got the skills. Leave a message and we'll get back at ya, pronto."

The message beeped.

"You stupid *dickhead*! Call me back the second you get this, and *tell me where you are*."

Cooper hung up, then immediately called again, only to get voice mail for the second time.

The basement. That narrowed things down, at least.

Cooper got dressed. As he did, he caught a reflection of himself in the room's mirror. That blister on his shoulder was gone, just a red spot now. He took a closer look; no, not gone, broken open. A shred of weak, torn skin dangled from the edge. No wetness, though . . . it looked like something had puffed it up like a balloon, then the balloon *popped*.

He quickly examined himself in the mirror. He had more of the blisters: on his chest, his hip, below his right knee. Something leftover from whatever had made him sick? An allergic reaction to detergents in the hotel's sheets?

The blisters didn't hurt, and he didn't have time to worry about them. He dressed. He grabbed his coat and also Jeff's for good measure — if they had to go outside in the bitter Chicago cold, they'd both need to stay warm.

Cooper walked to the door, reached down to open it, then stopped. He looked out the peephole again, half expecting the teenage kid to be staring right back at him.

Nothing there.

Nothing except for a little red streak on the far wall, where the first teenage kid had fallen.

A streak of blood.

Cooper took a deep breath, steeled himself.

He opened the door and stepped into the empty hall. He had to find Jeff. Jeff first, then maybe the two of them could track down Steve. Until then, Cooper hoped Steve Stanton could fend for himself.

FOLLOW ME

Steve Stanton strapped on his two laptop bags stuffed with three laptops. He stepped out of his room on the Trump Tower's seventeenth floor.

Anger coursed through his body, set every muscle cell on edge. He felt an almost overpowering urge to smash a human's head in, find a brick and crack the skull open so he could get at the brains, pull them out, *stomp* them and . . . .

His own thought played back in his head: *smash a HUMAN's head in*.

Why had he thought of it like that? Why hadn't he thought of the word *person*, or *man* or even *woman*?

Why? Because Steve Stanton was no longer human, not at all — humans were the enemy.

He heard a scream coming from the right, around a corner and farther down the hall. He walked toward that scream.

Steve turned the corner. He saw a shirtless, middle-aged man dressed in tan slacks. The man's belly hung over his belt. He wore no shoes. He stood above a woman in a torn, red dress. Steve assumed the two red sandals scattered nearby belonged to her. She was on her butt, one hand behind her, the other raised up, palm out.

"Morris! Stop hitting me, for God's sake!"

In response, the man — Morris, Steve assumed — reared back and kicked the woman in the thigh. The woman let out another scream. She rolled to her hands and knees and tried to crawl away. Morris reached down and grabbed her right ankle, yanked her back. The woman fell flat on her stomach, arms out in front of her.

Morris grabbed her hip and flipped her over. Before she could say another word, he pressed his bare foot hard against her neck. His face scrunched into a confused mask of rage. She twisted, turned her lower body, tried to kick. She grabbed at Morris's foot, clawed at it, her purple fingernails leaving crisscross streaks of ragged red on his skin — but the foot did not move.

The man leaned lower, rested his forearms on the knee of the leg pressing down on her neck.

"How about that toilet seat now, Cybil? How about that *fucking goddamn cunty toilet seat now*, you ball-busting, dried-up-pussy bitch? I guess you shouldn't have nagged me about putting it down, huh? *Huh?*"

Steve walked closer. The man seemed entirely focused on the struggling woman. There was a bluish triangular growth on the man's chest, under his skin just left of the sternum. And another on the right side of his belly.

Steve stopped cold: something in the air . . .

A smell.

He breathed deep into his nose; he recognized that scent even though he'd never smelled it before. He sniffed again . . . the man had the scent, but not the woman.

The triangles, that smell . . . he is my kind, he is me.

The man — Morris — was staring at Steve.

"Hi," Morris said. "You, uh . . . you want to help with this?"

In that instant, so many things became clear. Morris was nothing but an ugly husk meant to carry infinite beauty, beauty that would soon break free of his body, leaving him a dead shell.

Morris was stupid.

Steve was *smart*.

"You'll do what I tell you to do," Steve said.

Morris didn't take his foot off the squirming woman's neck, but his eyes narrowed as he tried to understand.

He nodded. "Yeah," he said. "Yeah, you're right. I'll do what you tell me to do."

The woman yelled, fought with renewed energy. She clawed and ripped. Her fingernails turned Morris's foot into a ragged mess that splashed blood on her face and chest.

This man would do what Steve said. Steve *felt* it.

So much happening all at once. Steve thought back on a lifetime of not standing up for himself, of staying quiet, of avoiding conflict or embarrassment. His circumstances had denied him his birthright. He was brilliant. He was a *genius*. His destiny was more than wrapping knives and forks in fucking napkins.

Steve Stanton had been born to *rule*.

He nodded toward the woman. The *human* woman.

"Morris," Steve said, "do something about her."

Morris looked down at his bloody mess of a foot. He pressed it down harder — the woman stopped fighting. She drew in wet, broken hisses of air.

The man looked back to Steve, hope blazing in his wide eyes. "Can I kill her? She was always bitching about *everything*. Like the goddamn *toilet seat*. Like she's such a helpless princess she can't reach a finger out and tip the goddamn thing forward? Can I kill her? Can I?"

Steve stepped closer and looked down at the woman. Her wide eyes pleaded for help. In those eyes, Steve saw fear. She was afraid, because she wasn't him, and he wasn't her. She was *human*.

"Kill her," Steve said.

Morris pumped a fist like he'd just scored a goal in hockey.

"Fuck *yeah*!" He screamed down at his wife. "You shoulda been nicer to me, you nagging bitch! *You shoulda been nicer!*"

He raised the bloody foot, then slammed it back down again heel-first into her throat. She grunted. She stiffened. Her arms and legs twitched.

Morris stomped again and again. Steve watched.

The woman stopped moving. Wide, dead eyes stared out. Her throat was a real mess.

Steve took off his laptop bags, set them on the floor.

"Carry those," he said. "We have to find more friends. And after that, I think we need to find a place for you to lie down." Steve reached out, his fingertips tracing the firm outline of the hard, bluish triangle on the man's chest.

"Tomorrow, I think," Steve said. "Tomorrow, something wonderful happens to you."

THE BOILER ROOM

Cooper moved down the concrete-and-metal stairwell. He kept one hand on the rough, unfinished walls. In the other, he carried Jeff's coat.

He moved slowly. He didn't want to make any noise, because every time he passed a landing he heard *plenty* of noise coming from beyond the heavy, reddish-brown metal doors.

Yelling. Shouting. Screams of rage. Screams of pain. And *laughter:* the kind of laughter only insane people made.

Three times he'd heard another kind of sound, a sound that damn near made him piss his pants. Twice from below and once from above, he'd heard the sound of a metal door opening and slamming against a landing wall, the echoing of a laughing/screaming/giggling/yelling man or woman running into the stairwell. Cooper had held his breath, waiting for them to come his way, but all three times he'd been lucky and they'd gone in the opposite direction.

He reached the first floor. Past the heavy fire door, he heard more noise than he'd heard on any floor before it. He briefly thought about opening the door and taking a peek, but a line from some old book popped into his head — *when you look into the void, the void looks back into you,* or something like that.

All that mattered right now was tracking down his friend. Together, they would find a place to hide until the cops or the National Guard or whatever came to make everything safe again.

Cooper moved down another flight to what had to be the basement level, then down again until the steps ended on a flat, concrete floor. He'd reached the subbasement. Might as well start here and work his way up. Cooper put his ear to the landing door's cool metal — he heard nothing.

He thumbed the door's lever, quietly pulled the door open.

The empty hallway looked like a service area: more concrete floor, but here it was smoother, slightly polished. White walls with bumpers on the bottom, black marks on the walls where carts had scraped against them.

He stepped into the hallway, slowed the automatic door's closing until it clicked shut with the tiniest *snick* of metal on metal.

Cooper looked at his cell phone. Still one bar. He dialed Jeff's number. He held the phone to his ear only long enough to make sure it was ringing, then lowered it, pressed it against his thigh to mute that sound.

For all the commotion going on upstairs, it was very still down here. Still and quiet, like a tomb.

He listened. He held his breath.

Come on, dude, where are you?

And then, very faint, a sound so thin he wondered if he was imagining it: the crunching guitar chords of AC/DC's "Highway to Hell" — Jeff's ringtone.

Cooper turned in place, trying to nail down the direction. There, halfway down the hall, a pair of white, windowless metal doors. He walked to them, looking left, looking right, listening for any sound that might warn him of company.

Somewhere around a corner, a door smashed open, echoing through the concrete hallways. Cooper heard a man screaming in anger.

"... *cut you* ... *cut you up* ... *run, motherfucker!*"

The yelling grew louder. Shit, the man was coming his way. Cooper thumbed the left-hand door's latch and yanked it open. He quickly stepped inside a poorly lit area, quietly pulled the door closed behind him.

He turned, letting his eyes adjust to the low light — and when they did, he found himself facing a smiling, bald man sitting on a folding metal chair.

A single overhead light lit up that man's white shirt, played off his pink head. He wore a patterned tie loosened at the neck. Black slacks, sleeves rolled up to his elbows. The clothes and his beer gut screamed *conventioneer from Wisconsin.*

"Hello," the man said.

"Uh," Cooper said. "Hi."

Cooper quickly looked around, got his bearings. He was in a boiler room. On his right, two big metal tanks on concrete footings. The tanks needed a fresh coat of paint — gray enamel bubbled here and there, had been scraped away in others. The size of the tanks held his attention for a moment: it figured a large hotel like this would need a ton of hot water, but that wasn't something you thought of when you checked into the Trump's swank lobby.

Farther back in the room, just one other light glowed. There were dozens of dangling light fixtures, but none of them were on; most of the bulbs looked broken.

The man stood. His chair slid back an inch, the scraping sound echoing off the boiler room's concrete walls. He took in a long, slow breath through his nose, then exhaled out his mouth in a cheek-puffing expression of relief.

"Can I help you?" he said.

His eyes . . . there was something off in them. The man radiated excitement, like he wanted to jump and dance and scream, yet he stood stock-still.

"Uh, no, thanks," Cooper said. "I'm just looking for my friend."

The bald man smiled. He nodded. "A friend of yours is a friend of mine. We're all friends now, right?"

Cooper didn't know what to say. What was this man's deal? Something about his eyes, how they glowed with intensity, with . . . *joy*. Joy, yes, but something else as well — this man looked more than a little crazy.

The *dangerous* kind of crazy.

"Sure, buddy," Cooper said. "We're all besties, whatever you want. My friend is six-two, about two hundred pounds, looks like he's forty." Cooper tapped his own left shoulder. "Brown hair about to here?"

The smiling man smiled some more. His front right tooth looked chipped. There was a fresh cut on his lip, the flesh torn and exposed. Cooper wondered if the two wounds happened with the same punch.

"I've seen a lot of people," the man said. "A lot of people came down to the basement. Some left. Some stayed."

Cooper quickly looked left, right — were there others down here? He'd been scared in the stairwell, but he'd been alone. Now his stomach pinched and twirled. His hands shook. This was a bad scene, as bad as bad got. He had to get out of there, but he wasn't leaving without Jeff.

He lifted his phone to dial Jeff's cell again but saw that he had zero bars — no connection in the boiler room.

Cooper put the phone in his pocket. "See anyone wearing an AC/DC T-shirt? A black one?"

The bald man nodded. "Oh, sure! That guy's here. He's resting."

Cooper's heart raced. He could get his friend and get the hell out of there, leave this two-cards-shy-of-a-full-deck Wisconsinite behind.

Cooper forced a smile. "Can you show me? I'd appreciate it."

"Sure," the bald man said. "We're all friends now, right?"

"All friends," Cooper echoed. "Total BFFs."

"Huh? Bee-eff-eff?"

"We're friends, I mean," Cooper said. "Show me?"

The man walked deeper into the poorly lit basement, past the gray boilers. Cooper hesitated. This was a mistake. He was going to follow a strange, whacked-out man into Freddy Krueger's home turf?

You fucking owe me, Jeff. I hope you're okay, so I can kill you myself.

Cooper followed the bald man in the blood-speckled white shirt.

As he walked, he scanned left and right again . . . and he saw shapes. Shapes back in the shadows, where the floor met the wall, around and even underneath the boilers. The shapes were . . . *people*? Sleeping people covered in dark blankets, maybe?

There were two more smaller boilers beyond the first pair. After the last boiler, the white-shirted man stopped and turned. He smiled that *something-is-wrong-with-me* smile, then gestured toward a bulky shape, covered in a blanket, resting at the base of the cinder-block wall.

It took Cooper a moment to see something in that shape, to see a person's face.

Jeff's face.

His best friend in all the world, his business partner, his *brother*, and yet the sight of him suddenly repulsed Cooper. Jeff's face looked . . . *bigger*. Swollen, sweaty, with big threads from that blanket clinging to his jaw, his cheeks. And the body beneath that blanket . . . bloated, misshapen . . . *too large*.

Something deep inside of Cooper told him to stay the fuck away from Jeff. No, not just *stay away*, more like *turn and haul ass out of there.*

No. He would not leave. That was his friend. Jeff was sick. *Really* sick, obviously, something way beyond drinking himself halfway into a coma and finding a quiet place to pass out.

Cooper took a step closer, leaving the strange man facing his back.

Those threads on Jeff's face . . . they weren't threads.

Because it wasn't a blanket.

Jeff was *encrusted* in some kind of dark-brown clay, or maybe a stiff foam. His eyes were closed, his mouth was open. The material curved up over his left cheek, split into tendrils that threaded up into his hair: a twisted delta of that strange mud cupped Jeff's head like a mother cradling a child.

Then, Cooper saw something that took his mind a moment to register. Half covered by that material, there were *two* left hands. No . . . *three* of them. There were two people in there with Jeff, two small people. Cooper saw a shoeless, skinless foot sticking out, a foot with black, shriveled skin . . . almost like the foot of a mummy.

Cooper's chest tightened and tingled. Was Jeff *dead*?

No, his lips were moving, just slightly — he was still breathing.

"Jeff," Cooper said. "Bro, can you hear me?"

"Of course he can't," said the bald man. His words faded away into the boiler room's shadows.

The situation hit Cooper with a sudden, gripping clarity — a city going crazy and he was in a dark basement, a strange man with a psycho grin standing right behind him. Had this man put Jeff here? Had he covered Jeff and those other people with this brown goop?

Cooper turned, looked at the chipped-tooth smile. He pointed down at Jeff.

"What is that stuff all over him?"

The man shrugged. "I dunno. That's how it's done, I guess. I'm just supposed to watch and make sure they're safe."

"Safe from what?"

The man's eyes narrowed. He sniffed again. Twice, like a dog checking something out. "Safe from people who are not our friends."

Friends. Out of the bald man's mouth, the word sounded heavy, important. It sounded . . . *religious.*

Cooper squatted in front of Jeff, forced himself to reach for his friend — then he pulled his hand back. What if that brown shit was some kind of disease? What if it was contagious? Could it be part of what Blackmon had been babbling about on TV? He had to call an ambulance. But if he did, would one come? The world outside had melted down. Cooper couldn't count on help from anyone; Jeff needed him, and needed him right now.

Cooper reached out with his index finger, pointed it, poked the tip into the brown material. It felt like a crunchy sponge.

"Hey," said the man behind him. "You're not supposed to touch that. *Never* supposed to touch that!"

Cooper stood and turned. "You said you didn't know what this crap is."

The man's smile faded. "Maybe I was wrong."

The hair stood up on Cooper's neck. To his left, the bulky, hot boiler. To his right, heavy shadows that hid the rest of the basement. This crazy fuck blocked his path to the door.

"Uh, wrong about what?"

"About you being my friend."

The man's hands shot out, reaching for Cooper's neck. Cooper flinched away — his heels hit Jeff. Cooper fell backward against the cinder-block wall, slid down it until his ass landed on the pile of bodies. He tried to scramble up, but the bald man's hands slammed into his throat, wrapped around his neck.

Strong thumbs pushed hard into Cooper's windpipe. He couldn't breathe. The man leaned in hard, his weight keeping Cooper pressed down on Jeff, the other bodies and the crunchy material that covered them.

"Just give us a smooch," the man said. "It'll be okay."

He opened his mouth and bent closer.

The overhead lights cast the man's face in shadow, but not so much that Cooper couldn't see the wide eyes, pupils so big they looked like dimes, the strand of spit stringing from the upper lip to the lower, and the man's tongue — pink, dotted with tiny, blue triangles.

What the fuck oh God oh God!

Cooper's hands shot up and grabbed the man's face. Thumb tips drove deep into the man's eyes with a *pop* and a *squelch* and a burst of hot wetness.

The man released Cooper's throat, flailed at Cooper's hands. Cooper shoved him away. The man fell back into the aisle, his ass landing on concrete, his hands covering ruined eyes that spilled blood onto his white shirt. The sound he made . . . it was like an obese cat crying for food.

Cooper coughed, drew in air, pushed himself to his feet. His wet thumbs were already cooling in the basement air. He quickly wiped them off against his pants legs, horrified at what was on his skin.

He had to get out of there.

Cooper turned to face his friend. Jeff hadn't moved a muscle. Neither had the other two people hidden beneath the brown material.

"*Jeff!* Dude, *wake the fuck up!*"

Cooper went to grab Jeff's shirt to shake him, actually touched the brown stuff before his hands retreated on their own as if they'd touched a man-size spider.

Gloves, he needed gloves, something to cover his hands. No, too late for that — he already had flecks and chunks of the brown stuff on his fingers, and he could feel pieces of it on his neck and face.

Cooper fought back revulsion as he grabbed at the brown material and tried to pull it off his friend. It was some kind of membrane, a thick sheet that didn't want to be ripped free. Little tendrils were anchored tight to the cinder block like roots of crawling ivy. It felt like touching wet wood, so black and rotted that it *squished* more than *crunched*. Cooper pushed his fingers through it, down around Jeff's shoulder, and *yanked* — Jeff remained covered in the membrane, but at least Cooper had pulled him free of the wall.

Cooper felt two strong hands lock down on his right ankle. He started to turn, to kick out, but before he could, he felt the hard sting of something biting his calf through his jeans.

He looked down to see the bald man: hollow holes for eyes, white teeth locked on dark denim that was already growing darker with spreading blood.

Cooper raised his right fist high, twisted as he brought it down on top of the man's head. The man quivered, but didn't let go. Cooper reached down with both hands and gripped hard on the back of the man's neck. He *yanked*, felt a deeper pain as the man's teeth tore free.

Cooper flung the man onto his back, straddled him, then wrapped his hands around the man's throat and *squeezed* and how do *you* like it motherfucker squeeze just *keep squeezing* and never stop and never stop until you *die motherfucker until you* DIE!

The man's blue-dotted tongue stuck out. He made noises that might have been a desperate effort to draw air. The bloody mess of two ruptured eyes still managed to squint in agony, eyelids sagging in against the negative space.

Cooper felt the man's life slip away.

So he squeezed some more.

He didn't know how long it was until he felt his hands weaken, the muscles exhausted, until they could no longer keep up the crushing pressure. Cooper stood, chest heaving. He heard the sound of his own ragged breaths.

Had he just *killed* someone?

No-no-no, the man couldn't be dead, this couldn't be happening, it wasn't real *it wasn't real*.

What was going on? The craziness out in the streets, in the hotel, and now this? And Jeff . . .

Cooper stumbled back to his friend. Jeff still hadn't moved. He lay there, covered in that blasphemous rot.

The sounds of metal doors slamming open echoed through the room. The boiler blocked a view of the door, but the sound of shoe soles slapping against concrete told Cooper people were coming, fast.

He had to hide. There was only one place *to* hide. Cooper quickly and quietly slid between Jeff Brockman and the wall.

Jeff's body felt *hot*, as if his fever had magnified a hundred times. Cooper slid down on his right side, pulled on Jeff so his friend's back once again rested against the cinder-block wall.

Cooper tried not to think about the other two people under the membrane . . .

Rushing footsteps coming closer.

It was a shit hiding place it wouldn't work they were going to *kill him* and *strangle him* but it was all he had.

Through a small rip in the membrane, he could see part of the concrete floor, could see the foot and leg of the dead bald man.

Maybe it's dark enough, maybe they won't touch Jeff because they're not supposed to touch NEVER *supposed to touch, maybe—*

Three sets of feet stepped into view: red sneakers; a pair of shiny, polished shoes; a pair of brown loafers. The heels of the polished shoes rose up — someone was kneeling over the bald man's body.

"He's dead," a voice said.

"Where's the killer?" said another.

The feet moved. Shoes pointed in new directions as people looked around the boiler room

"I don't see anyone," the first man said.

"Should we check the cocoons?" said another.

"Check them for what? We don't even know what's happening in there. We're not supposed to touch."

"*Never* supposed to touch," a woman said.

The first voice spoke again. "Someone who is not a friend is around here somewhere. Let's go tell Stanton."

Stanton? Had Cooper heard that right?

The shoes moved away, slowly, but it only took a couple of steps before they were gone from Cooper's view.

He lay there, under his best friend and the two people packed in with his best friend, all of them covered in God knew what, trying not to make the slightest noise that would bring men who wanted to kill him, kill him because he wasn't a *friend*.

Cocoon.

That's what they called the membrane, a fucking *cocoon*? What did that mean?

A cocoon . . . a caterpillar turning into a butterfly . . . was Jeff changing into something else?

Cooper closed his eyes, tried to breathe as quietly as he could. If Jeff *was* changing, what would he become?

And how long did Cooper have before it happened?

THE INTERNET

Murray bit into a chicken sandwich, his mouth filling with the punchy taste of aioli and Gouda. Things were going to hell in a handbasket, but he could say one thing for the White House — someone here sure knew how to cook.

They all ate. The chief of staff had insisted, making sure everyone got what they wanted, making doubly sure that Blackmon didn't skip her meal of a BLT and fries.

As Murray chewed, he watched the big monitor at the end of the Situation Room, the one mounted opposite the president's seat at the head of the table. The left half of the monitor condensed the developing situation into a handful of ever-changing estimates:

IMMUNIZED: 26%
NOT IMMUNIZED: 66%
UNKNOWN: 8%
FINISHED DOSES EN ROUTE: 62,000,000
DOSES IN PRODUCTION: 71,300,000

The right half of the monitor showed a map of the United States. Each state was a shade of gray. The more doses delivered, the darker the state became.

The same map used colors to denote outbreaks. Philadelphia, Boston and several other cities glowed yellow, indicating high numbers of early-stage cases. That meant people were infected but had not yet turned violent.

Other cities glowed orange, showing areas with spiking cases of assault, murder, property damage, et cetera. Those cities — Baltimore, Pittsburgh, Milwaukee, Columbus — were just beginning to tip over to the worst color of all: red.

Four red areas glowed ominously: Grand Rapids, Minneapolis, New York City and Chicago.

And at the bottom of the monitor, white letters on a black bar that stretched across the bottom of the display:

INFECTED: 530,000
CONVERTED: 78,500
DEATHS: 1,282

Those numbers were estimates, a best guess compiled from city reports, the CDC, FEMA and other organizations responsible for tracking the disaster.

Things were bad. Things would get much worse, but the important numbers were on top: *26% immunized, 133 million doses en route or in production.* America was rallying to the cause. When it was said and done, this would rate as the worst disaster in American history, by far, but the tide was already turning.

Murray actually let himself believe that, right up until André Vogel rushed into the room. The normally calm, cool and collected Vogel looked anything but. He had a cell phone held against his left shoulder, using his suit jacket to mute it.

Murray put down the sandwich.

"Madam President, I have bad news," Vogel said. "Our embassy in China was just attacked. Ambassador Jane Locker is reported dead, along with seven other staffers."

Blackmon's mouth pressed into a tight circle. "What happened?"

"We're not sure," Vogel said. "A staffer got a call out that they were under attack and that the ambassador was dead, then the signal cut off. We're unable to reach anyone at the embassy."

Blackmon stood. "Attacked by *who?*"

"A mob of civilians," Vogel said. "Enough to overpower the Chinese guards and our embassy security forces. That's all the intel we have at the moment."

Blackmon spread her hands, palms up: *are you kidding me?*

"Then get me *more intel*, Director Vogel," she said. "I have to know what happened."

Vogel took the cell phone off his shoulder, pressed it to his ear. He held up a finger to Blackmon — *one moment* — then spoke quietly. He nodded, put the cell phone in his pocket.

"I wanted to confirm it before I told you," he said. "We can't reach representatives of the Chinese government. And I mean we can't reach *any-one*. China's communications grid is offline. Broadcast, telecom, satellite — nothing is going in or coming out. They've even shut down their part of the Internet."

Murray had lost his appetite. The world's only other nuclear-armed superpower had just gone dark. He waited for the president's response.

"There has to be something," Blackmon said. "I need to speak with them."

Vogel nodded. "Of course, Madam President. The NSA is working on it, highest priority, but as of this moment, we have no way of communicating with the Chinese government."

Blackmon sat back down. She picked up a french fry, stared at it. She took a bite. Everyone waited as she chewed and thought.

"Director Longworth," she said, "tell me again where you think our patient zero traveled to when he left Chicago."

Murray pushed his sandwich away. "Analysis shows the carrier was likely in O'Hare four days ago. London is reporting an outbreak, which means the carrier probably stopped there. The itinerary that best fits the outbreak pattern is Delta Flight 305, which flew from O'Hare to LaGuardia, then to Heathrow, then to Beijing."

Blackmon turned in her chair, stared at Vogel.

"You said no foreign power could get to the *Los Angeles*, Director. Yet here we are with an infection pattern that points straight to Beijing, and that government has just shut off all communication. If an operative got the artifact and took it back to China, and if he showed his new prize to high-level officials, then we could be looking at infected government leaders."

Vogel started to sweat.

"Madam President, as I said, it would be virtually impossible for anyone to reach that artifact, let alone take it out of the country. A more likely scenario is that Chinese leadership sees a spreading, global infection and they're nailing their windows shut. They want to stop any other carriers from getting in, or make sure the world can't watch how they choose to handle any localized infection. Probably both."

Admiral Porter politely cleared his throat.

Blackmon spoke to him without taking her eyes off Vogel. "What is it, Admiral?"

"Madam President, if the infection has somehow taken over the Chinese leadership, we obviously have to prepare for that. However, if Director Vogel is right and the Chinese are isolating themselves for their own protection, they may decide to take preemptive measures."

Blackmon spun her chair back around: the admiral had her full attention. "What kind of preemptive measures?"

Porter pointed to the monitor showing the map of America, with its red and yellow major cities.

"We're already significantly infected," he said. "If I were the Chinese, I'm not sure I'd wait for the infection to rage across Europe and America until it eventually reaches my borders. I'd consider surgical strikes to eliminate infected populations while I still could, before the disease spread so far it can't be stopped."

The way Porter delivered it, it made perfect sense. Murray felt a chill in his chest — with the fate of the world on the line, Porter's take actually sounded like a logical strategy, an almost *inevitable* one.

Blackmon laced her fingers together. "Admiral, do you really think the Chinese would *nuke* us to mitigate this disease?"

Porter nodded. "I do, Madam President. After all, we nuked *ourselves* to accomplish the same goal."

The chill spread to Murray's stomach, to his throat.

Porter stood. "Madam President, we have to assume this is a genuine threat. Whether we're facing an isolationist China or one now controlled by rogue elements, we have to show that we're ready to defend ourselves. I recommend we immediately move to DEFCON 3."

DEFCON stood for *Defense Readiness Condition*. The system had been in place since 1959, implemented as America adjusted to the threat of nuclear war.

DEFCON 5 was the normal level, the lowest state of war readiness.

With a change to DEFCON 3, the mobilization and response times for select air force units were shortened, often quite significantly. Some combat missions could be launched on fifteen minutes' notice. Since the end of the Cold War, America had only reached that level on September 11, 2001.

DEFCON 2 was the step just below nuclear war. *All* armed forces were ready to deploy and engage on six hours' notice. The nation had reached DEFCON 2 just one time: during the Cuban Missile Crisis in 1962.

And then the real troublemaker: DEFCON 1, also known as "Cocked

Pistol." It meant nuclear war was imminent, that the end of the world was just a presidential order away.

The room waited. Blackmon took her time, but she didn't flinch, didn't show any sign of the stress overtaking her.

She turned to face Murray.

"Director Longworth, everything I've been told indicates the infected are mindless killers. Could they do more? Could the Converted actually take over a government?"

He wanted to say no because he didn't want to believe any of this was happening, but his job was to tell the ugly truth.

"Based on what we've seen so far, they could not," Murray said. "However, Doctor Montoya reported there were major changes in the way the disease behaved. I can't rule out the possibility that the Chinese government is now under control of the Converted."

Blackmon put both hands flat on the table. "Admiral, take us to DEF-CON 3."

FEET

A gunshot woke him up.

Cooper Mitchell knew enough not to move, not to make a sound. All he did was open his eyes. The boiler room was even darker than when he'd entered. Another bulb had been broken.

How the fuck had he fallen *asleep*? Had he heard the shot, or dreamed it? It had been so faint, probably from somewhere out in the hall.

There were more noises now, noises he definitely wasn't imagining, coming from *inside* the boiler room. Soft sounds of surprise, perhaps of pain.

Cooper didn't move. Jeff (and his blanket-buddies) remained on top of him, still breathing, everyone covered by the ripped, tattered brown membrane. Cooper could only see a foot or so above the floor; his view consisted of the dead bald man and some of the far wall. The boiler blocked any view to his left.

Jeff's body still felt hot.

Coop had to pee. Real bad.

The sound of shuffling feet. More groans of pain. A noise like a yawn, if that yawn came from a gravel-voice demon.

Something moved across Cooper's limited field of vision: *feet*. Walking near the dead bald man. Feet that were too large for their loafers, so big the leather seams had split. What little light there was showed a glimpse of skin inside those splits . . . not white skin, not black or brown or tan, but . . . *yellow* . . . the color of bile mixed with sour milk.

I am so fucked, so utterly fucked.

And then, something spoke.

"WHERRRRRRE . . . ?"

The deep, drawn-out word eased through the boiler room, an audible shadow of blackness. Something about the sound resonated deep in Cooper's chest and stomach — he felt a fear so primitive it shut down everything, left room for only one thought: *to move is to die*. He recognized the word, but that voice . . . it wasn't human.

A second voice answered.

"BASE ... MENT?"

An even deeper tone, somehow more terrifying than the first.

Cooper's bladder let go. He was barely aware of the wet heat that spread through his crotch down his right hip, along the part of his right thigh that pressed against the concrete floor.

"COME," said the first voice. "FIIIND ... SOMEONE."

The yellow feet shuffled away. Cooper couldn't see where.

He was shaking. His body trembled so bad it made Jeff's body tremble as well.

The boiler room door opened, closed.

Cooper listened as the door's echo faded to nothing.

A long-held breath slid out of his lungs. He tried to move, but he could not. He lay there, in his own urine, shaking so badly he could barely think.

What was happening? What had made those people *yellow*? Gutierrez's PSAs about "T.E.A.M.S." had never said anything about that.

Triangles, excessive anger and massive swelling.

Cooper stuck his tongue out and felt it, checking for hard bumps, then yanked his fingers away — those fingers had touched the membrane covering Jeff. He swallowed automatically, before he thought to stop himself from doing so.

Was some of that shit now *inside* of him?

He had to find a place to wash up. He was in a boiler room ... there had to be a sink down here somewhere. He could wash his hands, clean up the piss. Cooper slowly slid out from under Jeff. He listened carefully for any sound coming from the hallway, for any hint of sliding yellow feet.

Nothing.

He crept to the edge of the boiler, peeked around the curved edge: he saw no one, just the closed, white doors that led out into the hall.

In the hall, the yellow people could be waiting ...

Cooper quietly walked deeper into the boiler room's shadows. His eyes continued to adjust. He froze when he saw another unmoving, membrane-covered man. This one was standing, wedged against a vertical pipe. So tall ... six-six? Six-seven? Tall, and *thick*, like an NFL lineman, but also lumpy, just like the cocooned Jeff.

Next to the encased man, Cooper saw a metal sink, the industrial kind.

What faint light there was reflected off something on the floor, something wet . . . water from the sink? A puddle, a thick puddle, running up to the shoes of the cocooned man.

Shoes . . . four of them.

Cooper looked closer. Near the head, a flap of membrane hung down. It was brown, but only on the outside — the inside looked wet-black. Behind the torn membrane, something *white*.

Cooper's eyes finally adjusted to the limited light. He was staring at a skull smeared with globs of rancid black. The white bone beneath the rotted flesh looked pitted and pockmarked, like someone had sprayed it with acid.

The membrane-covered man had a lump on his left side, below the chest. The lump, it was the shape of a person . . . a *shriveled* person, as tall as Cooper but thinner than a death-camp victim.

This can't be happening . . . none of it . . .

Cooper moved to the sink. He watched the membrane-covered man out of the corner of his eye as he turned on the hot water. He saw soap on the sink's edge, used it to scrub his hands until they stung. He pulled handfuls of paper towels from a dispenser on the wall and used them to clean the piss from his pants.

He finished and turned off the water. He was dabbing himself dry when he heard a metallic click — the sound of the boiler room door, closing.

Cooper turned quickly, expecting to see something coming down the aisle toward him, but all he saw was the closed door. Had another of the creatures left?

Jeff.

Cooper looked left, to the base of the wall, to his friend . . .

. . . the membrane, disgusting and tattered and torn, lay in a rumpled heap on the concrete floor.

Jeff was gone.

REPRODUCTIVE RIGHTS

"I'm pregnant."

The words stunned him. Clarence Otto stared at Margaret, but he wasn't really seeing her. He wasn't really seeing anything.

His lungs didn't work. The little air he still had in them came out in a single syllable:

"What?"

Margaret hadn't talked to him for almost four days, not since the video-conference with Cheng and Murray. She'd hidden in her private mission module. She hadn't even come out for meals. The SEALs waited on her hand and foot, bringing her whatever she needed.

And then, not even fifteen minutes ago, that tall black SEAL, Bosh, had found Clarence up on the helicopter deck, told him Margaret was waiting to speak with him in the conferencing module.

Clarence had entered. She had pointed to a chair, told him to sit. He had. Before he could even say *how are you*, she'd hit him with that mind-numbing news.

"I said, *I'm pregnant*." Margaret stared at him. She wasn't smiling, wasn't frowning.

Pregnant. His wife, the woman he still loved, pregnant with his child.

"That . . . Margo, that's fantastic."

She crossed her arms over her chest. "Is it? Is it really *fantastic*, Clarence? Then I wonder why being a single mother isn't at the top of every little girl's lifelong wish list."

Single mother? What was she talking about?

"I'm right here," he said. "This is great. I mean, it's a shock, but it's great."

She pointed at him. "You're not *right here*, Clarence. You left me, remember? And irony of ironies, you left me *because I wouldn't have a kid*."

Everything he'd ever wanted — the woman he'd fallen in love with, a child, a *family* — right there in front of him. He'd waited so long for her, then made an agonizing decision. Would he lose his dream because he hadn't been able to wait just a little bit longer?

"I know," he said. "I did leave you, you're right. But that was before."

She smiled. "Oh, *before*? You mean when I was a total mess? Now that your *old Margo* has returned, you want a do-over on abandoning your wife?"

No, that wasn't what he . . . well, yes, he did want that. He never would have left *this* Margaret.

"Things have changed," he said. "Think about it — we can be a family."

She crossed her arms again. "If I decide to keep it."

Clarence sagged in his chair. *If I decide to keep it:* those six words carved a deep chasm, with her on one side and him on the other. And that decision, the fate of his unborn child . . . that lay on her side of the line.

"Margaret, you can't even think that." He tried to sound authoritative and conciliatory at the same time. All he managed to do was sound small, weak.

"Don't tell me what to think," she said. "This isn't exactly an ideal world for a newborn, now is it?"

Margaret had always been pro-choice. So had Clarence. But now he had *no* choice. He had never felt so powerless.

He couldn't read anything in her eyes.

"We can make it work," he said. "We'll stay together. That's what you wanted."

She nodded. "Right. What I *wanted* — past tense. It's only been a few days, Clarence, but maybe me coming back to my normal self happened because you weren't there to smother me, stifle me." Her eyes narrowed. "You weren't there to trap me in that house, to leave me alone all goddamn day, to . . ."

Her words trailed off. She closed her eyes, gave her head a tiny shake. Then she looked at him. Her expression softened a little, but there was still a hardness in there, and also something . . . vacant.

"I'll think about it," she said. "But it goes without saying that you better take good care of me, Clarence. You've got a lot of making up to do."

She was going to make him grovel? The proud man inside wanted to turn around and walk out; the father-to-be inside, the *husband* inside, made him keep his ass right in that chair, made him nod.

"Whatever it takes," he said. "Anything you need, Margo — anything."

SOFIA

Cooper Mitchell stared down the barrel of a gun.

A woman held it. She was twentysomething, young enough to still be called a *girl*. She'd tied her black hair back in a loose ponytail. A look of anger and pain swirled in her dark eyes.

The girl's right hand clutched her right side, where blood turned her yellow shirt a disturbing reddish-orange. She looked pale and weak. She held the black pistol in her shaking left hand.

"Don't move," she said. "Don't you fucking move."

Cooper's hands came up. He stayed as still as he could. He'd never had a gun pointed at him before.

He'd waited in the boiler room, hoping Jeff might return, but not for long — not after he found other cocoons in the shadows. Cooper had gathered up Jeff's coat, then wandered the basement, looking for his friend, looking for a weapon.

When he'd turned a corner, he'd almost walked right into this gun-slinging girl.

Cooper bent a little, lowered his shoulders, tried to look as unthreatening as he could.

"Don't shoot," he said. "Please, put that down. I'm not one of them."

Assuming she would know what *them* was, that he hadn't hallucinated the whole thing, that he hadn't dreamed about his best friend wrapped up in a membrane, hadn't imagined strangling a triangle-tongued man to death, hadn't made up the people with inhuman voices and swollen, yellow feet.

Her trembling aim stayed fixed on his face.

"Mister, if you think I'm going to put this down, you're fucking retarded."

"Fine, just try to not aim it right at me, okay? The way your hand is twitching, you might kill me by accident."

Her eyes shifted to the gun. Her eyebrows raised — she hadn't realized she was shaking.

She lowered the gun, rested it against her thigh. She sagged a little to the left; her foot slid over quickly to maintain her balance. She was exhausted. How much blood had she lost?

The girl jutted her chin at him.

"Stick out your tongue," she said.

The man in the boiler room, with the triangles on his tongue . . . she'd seen the same thing and was guarding against it. That meant she was *normal*.

"Thank God," Cooper said. "Lady, you don't know what I've—"

The gun snapped up again, the barrel's tiny, black hole a window into death.

"Your *tongue*, asshole."

And then Cooper realized that he had no idea if he had triangles on his tongue or not. He rubbed it against the roof of his mouth, trying to feel bumps . . . he couldn't feel anything, but did that mean they weren't there? And if he had them, was he going to wind up like the bald guy?

Give us a smooch . . .

She moved her right foot back, widening her stance. She straightened her arm. She moved with confidence, like she'd done it before — this girl knew how to use a gun.

Her hand stopped trembling. "Last chance, mister."

Cooper closed his eyes. He stuck out his tongue.

"Open your mouth wider," she said. "Stick it out farther."

He did. He wondered if he'd hear the *bang*, or if everything would just end.

The girl let out a sigh of relief.

"Okay," she said. "I guess you're okay. Just don't come near me. And if you try for the gun, I'll put you down."

Cooper's heart thudded fast and loud, each *pump-pump* raging through his ears and temples. He opened his eyes.

"Sure," he said. "We need to get out of this hallway, find a place to hide."

She nodded. Her gunfighter's stance had sagged. Her eyes fluttered. She took a step back, then stumbled.

He rushed forward without thinking, his right arm sliding around the small of her back, supporting her.

"I got you," he said. "I got you."

For a moment, her strength gave out completely; he was the only thing holding her up. Then she stood, pushed him away. She didn't point the gun *at* him, but it was close enough.

"I told you to *stay away*."

His hands returned to the palms-up position. "Sorry. You were going to fall."

She started to say something, but somewhere in the basement a door opened, *slammed* open — the sound echoed through the hall. He couldn't wait for her anymore.

"Lady, I'm finding a place to hide. Come with me if you want."

He walked away from the noises, down the concrete hallway. They were still in a service area — laundry, storage, linens, maybe a kitchen. At the end of the hall he saw double doors, a rectangular window in each.

Cooper walked to the doors, looked through the glass . . . a carpeted hallway. He didn't see any movement.

The noises from behind grew louder.

He pressed the metal latch that ran horizontally along the door — unlocked. He pushed the door open and stepped through.

His feet fell silently on the carpet. Little brass plaques hung to the right of the closed, wooden doors lining both sides of the wide hall.

He turned to call for her and almost knocked her over.

"Hey, chick with the gun, mind not sneaking up on me, for fuck's sake?"

"Sorry," she said. Then her hand was on his back, half urging him forward, half leaning against him for support. "Hurry, someone is coming."

Cooper walked to the first door on his left. He pushed it open — inside, darkness, save for the light from the hall flooding in, illuminating a dozen tables covered with white tablecloths and surrounded by folding chairs.

He forced himself to enter.

Three steps in, he heard a soft *click* and the room lights suddenly flickered on. His eyes adjusted instantly, ready and expecting to see something coming for him, but nothing moved. A carpeted wall on the left, one of those sliding dividers on the right. The room was about twenty feet wide and forty feet deep.

Some of the tables had open laptops on them, along with pens and pads of paper embossed with the Trump Tower logo. Open bottles of water, half-full cups of coffee . . .

. . . and a body.

A bloody *mess* of a body, a man, still wearing a black suit, facedown, arms spread out across blood-streaked carpet. His head looked dented, smashed and cracked beneath a wet mop of black hair. In front of him lay a folded metal chair, the side of the seat streaked with blood and matted with bits of that same hair.

Cooper heard the door quietly close behind him.

"We have to hide," the girl said. "Fast, they're coming."

He heard noises outside the door, had images of a horde of villagers storming down some gothic German street, torches raised high as they came to kill the monster — except *he* was the monster they wanted dead.

Hide? There wasn't any place *to* hide. He was in a hotel conference room.

"Please," the girl said. "I . . . can't stand. Help me."

He turned to look at her. So pale. The pistol hung heavy in her grip, as if it was all she could do to keep it from falling to the floor.

So easy to take it from her . . .

He pushed the thought away, moved to the back of the room. He tipped two of the round tables on their edges, tops facing the door. Tablecloths fell into wrinkled piles. The tables' metal legs kept the round tops from rolling.

The end of the world had come, and his defense against the boogeymen was a child's fort.

He rushed back to the woman. "Come on," he whispered. "We can lie back here. If they do open the door, maybe they won't see us and they'll move on."

He helped her walk behind the tables.

She stared down at them doubtfully. "This is the best you can do?"

"I left my army tank in my other pants."

He helped ease her down gently. As soon as she sat, he saw her relax, the last of her fight slipping away.

The girl looked at him through half-lidded eyes. She whispered: "What's your name?"

"Cooper," he whispered back. "Yours?"

"Sofia."

"That's a sexy name."

He gave his head a sharp shake. What the hell was he doing? Was he hitting on this girl? *Now*? Or maybe it was a nervous thing, an impulse to make this insanity feel at least a tiny bit normal.

"That's funny," she said, "I don't feel all that sexy right now."

The noises outside the room grew louder. Whoever it was, they were coming close. It wasn't just the sound of people talking loudly — Cooper heard doors opening.

Sofia lifted the gun again, but this time butt-first. She offered him the handle.

He took it. His hand slid around the grip, his finger felt the cool reassurance of the trigger.

The room's lights went out — the sensor that detected motion didn't pick up their movements from behind the tables.

Cooper made himself as small as he could. Gun in hand, he waited.

The room door flew open, letting in dim light from the hall. Cooper gripped the gun tighter . . . should he pop up and fire? No, no he would wait just a moment more, maybe the person would leave.

On the other side of the overturned table, just fifteen feet away, someone was standing in the doorway.

Cooper waited.

Seconds later, that angular swath of light narrowed, narrowed, blinked out accompanied by the door latch's soft *click*.

Cooper leaned to the side, peeked out under the edge of the round tabletop.

It was too dark. He couldn't see anything.

His right hand held the gun out in front of him. With his left, he reached up above his head and waved.

The lights blinked on: the room was empty.

"They're gone," he whispered.

She leaned against him. "Thank God."

Sofia slid down to her side, rested her head in his lap. He started to stroke her hair, an automatic movement. Then he realized that while she had checked him for triangles, he had never checked her.

"Your tongue," he said. "Let me see it."

She didn't complain. She looked up at him, opened her mouth wide and stuck out her tongue.

Normal.

"Thanks," he said.

She put her head back in his lap. He resumed stroking her hair. They were two strangers trying to deal with the incomprehensible, finding small comfort in physical contact.

"Cooper, you got a phone?"

He nodded. "You?"

"Battery's dead," she said. "I called 911 about a hundred times. No one answered. I called all my people, same thing. Think maybe I could use yours to call my son?"

Cooper pulled his phone out of his pocket: his battery icon showed one bar out of five. Not much power left. He handed it to her.

She took it, gratitude in her eyes. She slowly dialed a number, put the phone to her ear.

Cooper watched, waited. Sofia's face held only a shred of hope, a shred that didn't last long. Cooper heard the mumbled words of someone's voice mail, then the *beep*.

"Baby, it's Momma," Sofia said. "I'm still alive. If you get this, call me at this number, okay? Please, baby. I love you."

She disconnected but held the phone to her chest. "I'm sorry to ask this, but do you mind if I hold on to it? I . . . I just wouldn't want to miss the call, if it comes in."

Cooper started to say no, but who was he going to call? Jeff wasn't answering. Neither was 911. Cooper didn't know a soul in Chicago. If it gave this woman some comfort to hold on to the phone, that was fine, as long as they stuck together.

"Sure," he said. "Listen, I'm not a doctor, but maybe I should look at your wound."

She nodded. She reached down to pull up her bloody shirt. He helped her.

Cooper had never seen a gunshot wound before. He wasn't sure what he was looking at, what he was looking *for*, but despite the blood it didn't seem that bad. The bullet hadn't gone *through* her as much as it had ripped off a chunk of her side.

He gently put a finger near the wound, not on it, and pressed.

She hissed in pain. "How's it look, Mister I'm Not a Doctor?"

He shrugged. "Don't really know. Don't think you're going to die, but we need to stop the bleeding."

Cooper looked around, saw the piled-up tablecloth. He grabbed a handful and dragged it over.

"Sofia, this is going to hurt."

"Can't hurt any worse than it already does. Go for it."

He gently laid the tablecloth on her side, then pressed down. Her body stiffened. She hissed in an angry breath.

"*Shit*," she said. "Guess I was wrong."

"Direct pressure," Cooper said. "I have to—"

"I know, I know. Just talk about something else, okay? You from around here?"

"No," he said. "Michigan."

"Lions fan?"

"Unfortunately, yes. All my life."

"Sucks to be you," she said. "Go Bears. I work here. Front desk, hospitality."

Cooper remembered calling for security after seeing the wounded teenage kid outside his room.

"Did you work with a woman named Carmella?"

He felt Sofia nod.

"I think she's infected," Cooper said. "I called down earlier, she said some awful things."

"That doesn't mean much," Sofia said. "Even before this started, Carmella was a real bitch."

They sat in silence for a moment. The lights clicked out, once again drenching them in darkness.

"So," she said, "what brings you to town?"

"Work. I mean, a postwork celebration kind of thing. We work on a boat and just finished up a big job."

"We?"

"My partner and me."

"You gay?"

"The other kind of partner." Cooper thought of telling her about the cocoons, but if he did, she might think Jeff was something to be shot, not someone to be saved. "He was gone when I woke up this morning. I can't find him."

They fell silent for a moment. He stroked her hair, felt her relax a little more.

"This shit is insane," Sofia said. "I heard the president was saying something about it a couple of days ago, but I have two jobs — who has time to follow politics, right? Yesterday morning we got a delivery of that inoculant gunk she was talking about. It was meant for the rich guests. I sneaked a bottle, drank it. Maybe that's why I'm not sick."

Cooper remembered the speech, remembered Blackmon talking about some kind of medicine.

"Is there any more of that stuff here?"

He felt her shrug. "I don't think so. Most of it got delivered to the top floors, the suites."

Blackmon's medicine had arrived in time to help make a difference, and the one-percenters got priority? It infuriated him, but he knew he shouldn't be surprised: some things never change.

He felt Sofia's blood cooling in the damp tablecloth.

"How'd you wind up getting shot?"

She paused, seemed to gather herself.

"This morning, all this shit was going on outside," she said. "Explosions, fires. These two pigs came in. We thought they were there to take care of things, you know? But they just started shooting people. Peter, a guy who was working with me, they shot him in the head. They got a couple others too, I think. I don't know for sure, because I ran."

She sounded a little guilty, as if she should have gone all Rambo on two trigger-happy psycho cops.

"You're alive," Cooper said. "You did what you had to do."

He felt her shrug again. "I guess. One of them shot me just as I reached the stairs. He followed me down. He cornered me. He . . . I think he was going to rape me or something."

Cooper remembered the bald man . . . *give us a smooch.*

"He tried to kiss you? That why you wanted to see my tongue?"

He felt Sofia nod.

"Asshole was crazy," she said. "He tried to pull me close . . . he had both hands on my shoulders. He was so strong. I kicked him in the balls and it didn't do anything. I think he laughed, like it was a fun game or something. He came at me again . . . he stuck his tongue in my mouth. I felt those fucking bumps. They stung."

Cooper tried not to flinch, to jerk away. He realized he'd made a huge mistake. Just because her tongue looked normal didn't mean she wasn't infected. She claimed to have taken the inoculant, but how did he know she was telling the truth? Was she going to change? Was she changing that very second? Would she attack him the way the bald man had?

He looked down at her, a dark, warm shape in his lap. She was a danger . . . he had a gun. All he had to do was put a bullet in her, then he'd be safe for certain.

But Sofia seemed normal. He *needed* normal. Maybe she wasn't lying about drinking the stuff from the government. Maybe she was fine.

Maybe.

"I think your bleeding is slowing down," he said. "How do you feel?"

"You mean aside from being shot?"

He nodded. "Aside from that."

"Fine, I guess," she said. "If you don't count the fact that you're jamming your fist into my bullet wound."

He wanted to hear the rest of her story. "So how did you get away from the cop?"

She paused. He felt her arm slide around his back, felt her pull herself tighter to him. She was tough, no question, but there was still a frightened woman in there, a frightened woman who wanted comfort.

"He was forcing me to kiss him. He had his hands on my shoulders. His gun was in his holster. I grabbed it."

For the first time, Cooper actually looked at the flat-black pistol in his hand. The faint, red light of the Exit sign played off the black barrel, enough for him to read the engraving on the side: *SPRINGFIELD ARMORY U.S.A.*, along with the stylized letters *XDM*.

Cooper had never owned a gun. He'd been to a firing range three times in his life, all three times with Jeff, all three times just for fun. He hadn't totally forgotten how to work a pistol. He pushed the release lever, slid the magazine out. On the back of the magazine, he saw two vertical rows — tiny dots that looked gold if a bullet was in there, black if there wasn't. He counted seven spots of gold.

"Holds sixteen rounds," Sofia said. "After the cop, other men tried to get me. I only missed twice. One in the chamber, so you've got eight left."

He turned the weapon this way and that, looking for an orange dot.

"Where's the safety?"

"Trigger and back-strap safeties," she said. "Don't worry about them. Just hold the gun tight, give the trigger a smooth pull." Her voice dropped to barely a hiss. He heard anguish in her words. "It will shoot, trust me on that."

The gunshots he'd heard while in the boiler room . . . how many of those had been hers? He'd killed the bald man with his bare hands. She'd killed people with this gun.

"It's okay," Cooper said, unsure if he was consoling her, or himself. "You did what you had to do. So did I."

And in that moment, he knew he was in this with Sofia all the way — whatever the fuck was going on, they would face it together.

He kept pressing the tablecloth against her side, even though his arm was starting to tire. It had to hurt her, hurt her bad, but in seconds she started to snore.

Cooper Mitchell sat in the darkness, this brave stranger's head in his lap, wondering what the hell they should do next.

#APOCALYPSE

@Ticonderagga:

OMG, my neighbor just went ape-shit and attacked his wife! Pittsburgh PD shot him dead. Can't believe this is happening.

@PickleThruster10:

15-car pileup on I-80 South. Looks like a guy cut in front of a tanker truck. Traffic at a dead stop — not going anywhere. #FuckingTraffic #AsianDrivers

@LongIslandIcy-T:

If anyone gets this, we're trapped on roof at W139th & Amsterdam. Cops aren't responding to 911. This guy is trying to kill us! Please send help!

@AlabamaCramma:

Explosions in downtown MLPS. News coverage spotty, says 30-40 dead, many more injured.

@Boston_Police:

Emergency notice: 24-hour curfew in effect. Stay in your homes. Do not let anyone in. Do not go into public areas. Do not approach police officers.

@WhiteSoxChum:

Where the FUCK is the nat guard? Riot in street. I see dead bodies. Where are the cops? This is insane.

@BACOemergency:

Power is out throughout Baltimore. No ETA on recovery. Conserve cell phone power. Fill all available pots with water. Do not drink tap water after 5pm.

THE CITY OF LIGHTS

Murray watched it unfold on the Situation Room's big monitor. The estimates were changing: some for the better, some for anything but:

IMMUNIZED: 43%
NOT IMMUNIZED: 50%
UNKNOWN: 7%
FINISHED DOSES EN ROUTE: 70,115,000
DOSES IN PRODUCTION: 58,653,000

And, at the bottom:

INFECTED: 976,500 (1,800,000)
CONVERTED: 250,250 (187,000)
DEATHS: 13,457 (30,000)

They'd added parentheses to the bottom numbers, representing global totals. The outbreaks of America and England were already producing cataclysmic numbers. China remained silent; that nation's numbers could only be estimated based on limited satellite data and the stories of the refugees trickling into Myanmar and Vietnam. No refugees were hitting Japan, however — the Japanese Maritime Self-Defense Force sank anything that came near the coast. Murray didn't know if those casualties were counted in the tally.

As for France, well . . . the number of *deaths* in parentheses would need to be updated.

Paris burned.

The screens showed different angles of a city ablaze. Fire raged, consuming buildings both classic and new. The dancing orange demons cast tall, flickering spires up to the night sky, spewing pillars of smoke into the blackness above.

Motherfucking *Paris*.

Some of the shots were from helicopters, some from the ground well outside the city proper, and two came from satellites. The scenes reminded Murray of watching the *shock and awe* of Desert Storm, but it was even worse than that — this level of destruction hadn't been seen since World War II, since Dresden: he was watching a firestorm.

The unthinkable scenario had begun just a few hours earlier. There was no chance of controlling it. The French government had stopped giving death toll updates. The president, his cabinet, and much of the legislature had fled the city, hoping to set up somewhere else, to maintain government, to keep the head attached to the snake. Everyone who *could* get out of Paris probably already had.

Those who remained in the city were either dead or about to die. Black, white, Arab. Native sons and daughters. Immigrants. Today there was no confusion about French identity — burned bodies all look the same.

"This can't be happening," André Vogel said. When China shut off communications, Vogel's veneer of confidence had shattered and hadn't returned. "The fire crews . . . where are the fire crews?"

"They're dead."

All eyes turned to Pierce Fallon, the director of national intelligence. Fallon always had a seat at the table — he just didn't say much unless he was asked, or unless he knew exactly what was happening. He was as unassuming as he was quiet, the kind of man who could effortlessly fade into the background.

"Those flames will rage until there's nothing left to burn," Fallon said. "We have multiple reports of firehouses being attacked at noon, Paris time. Assault and murder of fire department personnel, destruction of vehicles and equipment, fires set to the stations themselves. This drew an immediate police response, but armed gangs were waiting to ambush the police."

He paused as something exploded on-screen. Another building collapsed.

"At twelve-thirty P.M., Paris time, there were reports of attacks on petrol stations, stores, anything that would burn fast and spread the fire to neighboring buildings," Fallon said. "With the city's fire response crippled, the results" — he gestured to the screen, where the Eiffel Tower looked like a black spike jutting up from the flames of hell — "were quite predictable."

Blackmon looked shocked, a rare crack in her emotional armor. "You're telling me this was a coordinated attack?"

Fallon nodded. "No question, Madam President. We estimate about a thousand insurgents were involved."

A single word instantly changed the tone of the room: not *infected*, or *converted*, but *insurgents* — an organized force.

"One thousand," Blackmon said. Her shoulders drooped. "The city stood for centuries. Just *one thousand* people destroyed it."

Murray's soul sagged with the hopelessness of it all. No invading force. No trained army. Paris had been destroyed by people who knew the city's streets, the routes, knew how the police acted, knew where all the fire stations were — Paris had been destroyed by Parisians.

Blackmon turned to Murray. "A coordinated strategy," she said. "Can that happen here?"

Once again, he was out on a limb, giving his best guess at something not even the smartest people he'd ever met could understand.

He gestured to the monitor. "Right now, we're looking at a feed from CNN. The entire world is watching the same images we are. These Converted are obviously more organized than we've seen in the past. We have to assume some of them are watching this, and are seeing a strategy that works. If their goal is to destroy, now they know how."

Blackmon put her hands on her face, rubbed vigorously. She lowered them, blinked and raised her eyebrows.

"Get the word out to law enforcement in the major cities — and *especially* Chicago, New York, the places most heavily infected — that they need to protect fire stations."

People started to talk, to protest, but the president held up her hands for silence.

"I know every police force is already spread thin," she said. "But if a city can't fight fire, then we lose that city. Even if it's a couple of cops in each firehouse, at least that gives us a chance."

She put her hands on the table, leaned heavily. She looked at the image of a burning Paris.

"Not here," she said. "Not on my watch."

THE COOK

Cooper Mitchell awoke to darkness. Darkness, and the sound of a cough. A cough that wasn't his — and wasn't Sofia's, either.

He was on his back. He'd bunched up his coat as a pillow. Sofia lay next to him, her head on Jeff's folded coat. Cooper could feel her breathing.

The cough again . . . a *man's* cough, coming from inside the dark room.

Cooper had a moment of panic — where was the gun? His right hand slid out snake-strike fast, feeling for the weapon, found it almost immediately. He flexed his fingers on the pistol grip, then sat up.

Another sound: a light snore. Like the cough, it came from the other side of the overturned table.

Was it a man? Was it one of the yellow things?

The conference room's door remained closed; no light from the hall, just the red glow of the Exit sign.

Cooper swallowed. He drummed up what courage remained in his quivering chest.

He stood.

The room lights flickered on, illuminated the familiar white-tableclothed tables, chairs, the dead man in the suit — and a new body. A man, facedown, wearing a cook's uniform.

The cook's chest rose with a breath, then spasmed with another cough. *Sleeping.* Maybe he and Sofia could slip out of the room without waking him up.

Cooper knelt back down. He slid the pistol's barrel into the waist of his pants. He reached down slowly, then simultaneously slid his left hand behind Sofia's head and cupped his right over her mouth.

She feels so hot . . .

Her eyes opened wide. Her hands shot to his, grabbed and scratched. Her legs kicked and she let out a muffled scream. Cooper fell to the floor next to her, put his mouth to her ear, spoke so quietly his words were nothing but breaths.

"It's me, Cooper! Be quiet — one of them is in the room."

Sofia went rigid. Her unblinking eyes stared at him.

She was burning up. A fever. Not as bad as Jeff's had been in the boiler room, but still, a bad one.

Cooper let go of her head. He helped her to her feet. She winced as she stood. He pointed to the man in the cook's uniform.

She leaned in close, spoke in a hissing whisper. "Is he asleep?"

"I think so."

"Shoot him."

"What? No, we need to get out of here. If we shoot him, it'll make noise, maybe bring others."

The sleeping man coughed again, this time much harder, the lung-ripping sound pulling his body into a fetal position.

Cooper thought about throwing Sofia over his shoulder, making a run for the door. He thought about it a moment too long: the cook sat up.

Cooper drew the pistol and pointed it at the man's chest.

Just shoot him, just shoot him now — but what if he's not one of them?

The man had reddish-brown spots all over his white uniform. Cooper knew those stains weren't from preparing some dish in the kitchen.

The man looked at the gun. Then at Cooper. Then at Sofia.

"Are you guys friends?"

That word again. *Friends.* When the bald man had thought Cooper was his friend, everything had been fine. Maybe Cooper could bullshit his way through this — maybe he wouldn't have to murder this man.

"We're friends," Cooper said. "We're all friends here."

The man wiped his white sleeve across his nose; the fabric came away streaked with red. Sweat gleamed on the cook's face and forehead. He sniffed deeply, the sound choked by snot clogging his sinuses.

"I'm all stuffed up," he said. "Can't smell a thing. If you're a friend, why you pointing that gun at me?"

The man had obviously come in here looking for a place to sleep. He hadn't bothered to look behind the tables — Cooper and Sofia had been lucky.

"My name is Chavo," the cook said. "What's yours?"

Chavo. Cooper hadn't wanted to know the man's name, hadn't wanted to think about him as a person.

"Don't worry about our names," Cooper said. "How long have you been in here?"

Chavo shrugged. "Since sometime last night. We were taking care of business." He smiled when he said it. *Taking care of business* meant *killing people.*

He stuck out his tongue, showing the blue triangles that dotted the pink surface. The man's smile widened as his tongue slid back into his mouth.

"See? I can prove I'm a friend."

Cooper felt Sofia squeeze his arm.

"Shoot this fucker," she said.

Chavo started coughing again, his fist at his mouth, his body nearly convulsing, yet his eyes never left Sofia.

He pointed at her. "She's not a friend."

The man lifted his right knee and planted his foot as if to stand.

Cooper leveled the pistol at Chavo's face.

"Don't you fucking *move.*"

Sofia's fingers dug into his left bicep, so hard they felt like dull metal needles that couldn't quite penetrate the skin.

"*Shoot* this fuck," she said. "Waste him before he calls for help!"

Her hands let go of his bicep; Cooper felt them grabbing for the gun.

He used his free arm to keep her away. "Sofia, *stop!*"

Chavo stood and ran for the door. His hands reached for the horizontal bar, hit it, knocked the door open.

He made it one step out before the gun fired twice, *bam-bam*, the second shot surprising Cooper even more than the first.

The man lurched forward, landed hard on his face and chest.

Cooper felt stunned . . . he'd just shot a man in the back. He hadn't thought, he'd just done it.

Chavo wasn't dead. His arms came up, hands pressed against the floor — he started to crawl. Two spots of red spread across the back of his white uniform.

Cooper saw Chavo's chest fill with a big breath, saw the man's head tilt back . . .

"Kill*lll* them! They're in here!"

He shouldn't be able to scream, I shot him in the back, he should be dead . . .

Sofia yanked the gun from his hand.

She limped toward the door, one hand pressed to her side, the other holding the pistol.

Chavo crawled a little farther. His belly left smears of blood on the carpet.

Sofia reached him. She put the gun to the back of his head and fired. Chavo's face flopped onto the carpet. He stopped moving.

Cooper ran to Sofia, stood next to her. Blood soaked into the carpet beneath Chavo's face — or what was left of his face — a thick stain that slowly spread outward.

Sofia sagged against Cooper, weakly held the gun up for him to take. "You've got five bullets left," she said. "Try not to be . . . be such a pussy . . . okay?"

She started to fall; he slid an arm around her waist, held her up. He could feel her heat even through her clothes. He had to get her to a hospital, find a doctor or something.

Cooper took the gun from her hand. He stared down at the dead man.

Then, he heard the roar.

It was a sound both human and not, a sound that carried through the hall. It came from somewhere off to the right. Then, from the left, a man answering with a guttural shout.

Cooper again looked at Chavo's body. The blood streaks pointed back to the door, like an arrow that said *the people you want to kill are in here*.

He pulled Sofia tighter. "Come on, we have to move."

She seemed to gather the last of her strength. She gently pushed away, stood on her own two feet. "Move where?"

Where? Good question. Whatever was coming would check this room, check the nearby rooms as well. If he and Sofia were going to survive, they had to find something better . . . maybe find a car and get the hell out of Chicago, maybe reach the *Mary Ellen*.

"Hold on a second," he said, then ran back into the conference room and grabbed the two coats. He shrugged his on, offered Jeff's to Sofia.

"Outside," he said. "We have to go outside."

Sofia rubbed her face. She nodded. "Well . . . shit. Had to happen sooner or later, I guess."

She put on Jeff's coat. Cooper slid under her shoulder and helped her forward. He held the gun tight as the roars grew louder.

SERMON ON THE MOUNT

Steve Stanton stood tall, his hands resting lightly on the balcony's marble railing. Wide stairwells descended on the left and the right, but his followers were packed in so tight Steve couldn't see a single step. Below, a sea of reverent faces gazed up at him. Skylights above shone a pale yellow, letting in the scant late-morning sunlight that managed to penetrate the winter storm blowing outside.

He was in the Art Institute of Chicago, a place dedicated to the beauty of the human race. With the help of the people packed in to hear him, to *follow* him, he would destroy that beauty, and that race as well. This place was a fitting cathedral for the newly born flock to hear his message.

The Converted murmured in anticipation, in excitement. They waited for him to speak.

Until just a few days ago, Steve hadn't believed in a higher power. Now he knew one existed, and knew that this divine being had chosen him to lead — *when God stands with you, no man can stand against you.*

The people on the stairs, the faces down below, they were all God's children, but they were not all the same. Some had the mark of the triangle on foreheads or cheeks. Others of that type had no visible marks, because clothes hid their blessings.

Even if the signs were hidden, Steve could just *look* at a person and know their caste.

Those marked with the triangles were *hatchling hosts*, walking incubators who were soon to give up their lives for the glory of God's very first creation.

Then there were the *mothers- and fathers-to-be*, people already swelling with God's love. Soon they would be moved away from the city center to areas where humans huddled in offices and stores and apartment buildings. When these parents blossomed, the winter wind would carry spores to places that the Chosen could not reach.

The *triangle-tongues* made up the main body of Steve's growing army. Stable and reliable, but also vicious, hungry and *smart*. Not as intelligent as he was, of course, but capable of thinking for themselves, able to follow orders to the letter or problem-solve when those orders no longer made any sense.

A scant few of the faces below belonged to *leaders*, people closer to Steve's own intelligence. Like him, these individuals showed no outward sign of any kind. Yet, they had something inside of them, something that called to the other castes, made the hatchling hosts and triangle-tongues and parents-to-be *want* to follow, made them *need* to please and obey.

And God's final creation: the *bulls*. Steve didn't know who had first used that nickname, but it fit perfectly. Something to do with local sports teams, apparently. There were very few bulls so far; many had perished during the conversion process, either in their cocoons or shortly after hatching. Whole-scale restructuring of the human body carried a high risk of failure.

Steve had ordered his few "finished" bulls to stay out of sight for now. Bulls were harder to control. They were more violent than even the triangle-tongues. The last thing Steve needed was fighting among the people.

Soon, however, he'd let his bulls run.

All of these castes would do anything he said. They would obey. They would kill. If he asked them to, they would *die*.

He raised his hands; they fell silent.

"My friends," he said. "This is the start of something wonderful."

His words echoed slightly off the stone walls, making him feel far more grand, far more powerful. His speech carried the will of God.

"You have been chosen," he said. "Every one of you feels this in your heart, just as I do. You used to be workers and bosses, teachers or policemen. You used to be shopkeepers and soldiers. You served in a hundred other roles. What you were before no longer matters, because now we are *one*."

The smiles, the nods, the wide-eyed stares of bliss. They knew. They *believed*.

"Everyone here understands that humans are the enemy, that they must be destroyed," Steve said. "We will accomplish that, but we can't act like animals. The American military will strike back, and soon. They will start with the cities where the violence is out of control, where it is clear our people have taken over. We can't help those other cities. We can only help ourselves. Therefore, as we accomplish our goals, we have to draw *as little attention as possible*."

Heads nodded. Some put hands over hearts. Some even cried. The power of God flowed through Steve Stanton.

He had seen the news coverage of Paris. He had to make sure his followers didn't do anything stupid like that. Cities *mattered*.

"Spread the word — do *not* destroy power facilities. Leave all power lines and transformers alone. Do not destroy any communication. Telephone lines, utility poles, cell-phone towers, leave them all be. And *no more fires*. If any of you see a Chosen One setting a fire, kill that person and make an example of them. Am I understood?"

A thousand heads nodded.

"We will use their own communication systems against them," he said. He pointed to his ear. "The humans are listening. Only the heads of individual groups may have a cell phone. *Do not* talk about being Chosen on phones, on the Internet, or in emails. I will distribute code words that you will pass on to others by face-to-face meetings *only*. If I need to make everyone act at once, we'll broadcast those code words. We must be careful so that the outside world doesn't suspect our numbers."

The heads nodded faster, more intently. They understood.

"As you spread through the city, find others of our kind. Tell them about me, tell them I am in charge. If you find humans who are not converting, *kill them*. Who here has served in the military?"

Along the descending stairs and down on the main floor, forty-odd hands rose.

"Excellent," Steve said. "All of you, come up and meet with me when I dismiss the rest. Everyone else, when you leave here, find me more soldiers. Ask for military experience, and ask *specifically* for anyone who served in a reserve unit in this area. If there are weapons in or around Chicago, we need them."

Steve again put his hands on the cool, stone railing. He leaned forward, letting the motions come naturally, letting the intensity build. His past, the shy, awkward thing he'd once been, it all seemed a bad dream. Power coursed through him. He could control the Chosen Ones as easily as he'd controlled the *Platypus*.

"The world is about to change, forever," he said. "We will make this city *ours*. Soon after that, the entire country." He stood straight. He raised his arms, spread them wide. "When the Chosen in other cities are tearing themselves apart, tearing their *cities* apart, Chicago will stand tall. From here, we will *rule*. The time of humanity is over, Chosen Ones — *your* time has come!"

Their roaring cheer filled the open space, echoed off the marble walls, made Steve's skin ripple with goose bumps.

This thousand would spread through the streets, gathering others of their kind, killing any who were not. In a day, this city would be under his control.

Chicago was only the beginning.

THE TRUMP TOWER

The fire stairs had seen him safely down. Cooper prayed they would see him safely up. It was smarter than taking the elevator, anyway: who knew what those doors might open up to?

Sofia couldn't climb the steps on her own. That burst of strength she'd used to kill Chavo was already a distant memory. Cooper kept his left arm around her waist, helping her along. His right hand stayed locked on the cool, comforting feel of the pistol.

Two switchback flights led from the subbasement to the basement level. Another pair would lead to the ground floor. He'd helped her up six steps to the first landing, halfway to the basement level, and his legs were already burning.

"Cooper . . . I'm not doing so great."

"You have a fever," he said. "Maybe your wound is infected."

"That fast?"

He shrugged. "Beats the hell out of me. I think we have to find a drugstore or a hospital, get you antibiotics."

There had to be drugstores close by. He could find her some medicine, then maybe they could make their way to the *Mary Ellen*. Jeff was nowhere to be found, and — Cooper hated to admit it — after seeing that empty cocoon membrane, he was no longer sure he *wanted* to find Jeff.

He helped Sofia up another step.

"Just a little more," Cooper said. "Make it to the ground floor, then we'll peek into the lobby and see if the coast is clear."

Two heads peered around a white stone corner. Cooper stared into the Trump Tower's long lobby. On his right was the forty-foot-long, twenty-foot-high glass wall that looked out onto Wabash Avenue. Outside, big clumps of snow whirled down from a sky that was almost the same yellow as the feet he'd seen in the boiler room.

Directly in front of him stretched the modern, white marble floor that led to the registration desk . . . or at least what was left of it. Body parts littered the lobby. Puddles of tacky blood pooled around corpses, bloody footprints leading away in various directions.

He took all that in at a glance, because he could really focus on only one thing.

Hatchlings.

Twenty of them, maybe thirty. Cooper had seen shaky footage of hatchlings before, part of Gutierrez's T.E.A.M.S. program. The video had been taken by soldiers in the woods just before the creatures attacked. But to see the things in person . . .

They stood around two feet tall. Three thick, twitching tentacle-legs made up half of that height, legs that attached to the bottom points of a three-sided pyramid covered in gnarled, glossy-black skin. And in the middle of each triangular side, a vertical, black eye. Purplish lids blinked rapidly, pushing in from the left and the right sides, keeping the eyes wet and clean.

The hatchlings crawled on everything: furniture, body parts, the splintered wood of the shredded front desk, even chipped and cracked white stone walls that four days earlier had been a spotless, polished marvel. The monsters lowered their bodies to these various surfaces. They jittered and shook perversely, like misshapen dogs humping wood and glass and marble. As they shook, Cooper heard crunching sounds, grinding noises.

He watched one of the hatchlings rise up on its three tentacle-legs. It climbed on top of a hard, knee-high, uneven mound that ran the inner length of the lobby's floor-to-ceiling glass wall. The creature vibrated: clumpy damp material squirted from its bottom.

It was *shitting.* That mound . . . it was *all* solidified shit. The thing vibrated one more time, squeezing out the last bits, then the graceful tentacle-legs carried it to the torn reception desk.

No, not *torn . . . half-eaten.*

Sofia's hands clutched at Cooper's arm. She stood half behind him, using him as both protection and support.

"Fuck me," she said. "I never believed they were real. I thought that news footage was special effects bullshit."

Cooper nodded, neither knowing nor caring if he'd ever believed or not. The past didn't matter, because he could see just how real they were.

Sofia tugged at his coat. "What are they doing?"

"I don't know. Maybe they're making a bulwark or something."

"A *bulwark*? What the fuck is a bulwark?"

"Like a wall," Cooper said. "Something to stay behind during a gunfight."

"You a soldier or something?"

"History Channel. Watch enough World War Two documentaries and things sink in."

The sound of roars suddenly echoed through the lobby, filtering in from somewhere deeper in the hotel. Cooper couldn't be sure where the roars were coming from — if he and Sofia were going to get out of the hotel alive, they had to go right through the little poop-making monsters.

His hands felt sweaty. He raised the pistol, started to aim at the closest creature.

Sofia's hand rested on his forearm.

"Don't," she said. "Five bullets. We have to conserve" — she ran out of breath in midsentence; she was farther gone than Cooper had hoped — "our ammo."

If he fired off a round, would the hatchlings scatter? Maybe . . . or maybe they'd attack, like they had in the video, swarm in, chew him up alive and then shit him out to make more of their little fortress.

He looked at Sofia. "I can shoot one, see if they run. What else can we do?"

"We could . . . just walk out," she said. She closed her eyes, tried to deal with the heat washing through her body. "We don't fuck with them, maybe they don't fuck with us. Chavo didn't attack you . . . maybe these things won't, either."

Cooper's throat felt tight. A pinching feeling churned in his guts.

Sofia raised a weak hand, pointed to the glass wall.

"The street is right there," she said. "If we stay any longer, we'll . . . we'll run into something worse than those little monsters."

Another roar — the closest yet — seemed to punctuate her words.

She was right. They didn't have time to find another way out.

Gun in his right hand, his left arm around Sofia's waist, Cooper stepped out from behind the corner and walked toward the front door some forty feet ahead.

The twenty hatchlings stopped moving. Cooper paused. They all turned their bodies so two of their eyes looked his way, focused on him.

Sofia slipped, just a little. He caught her, held her up.

Now or never . . .

He started walking again. Sofia did her best to carry her own weight and keep pace.

The pyramid creatures watched.

The long, glass wall passed by on Cooper's right. At the end of it, past the reception desk on the left, was the revolving door that opened onto the street.

He was halfway to it when, as a unit, the hatchlings suddenly went back to their work of humping, grinding and shitting.

Cooper and Sofia reached the revolving door. They stepped inside, pushed, walked with it until it opened onto the sidewalk of the Trump Tower's curved entry drive.

A strong, icy wind clawed him, ripped at his coat. Sofia's hand came up to shield her eyes and face. He and Sofia stepped forward.

The two of them stared out at a war zone.

Burned-out cars lined Wabash Avenue, including the cop car he'd seen on fire just a few days ago. Or was it hours? He wasn't sure. Powdery snow swirled along the pavement, in places stopping and sticking, turning into long, thin, white fingers that stretched over the blacktop.

Across the street to the left, a black-glass skyscraper towered high above. Cooper didn't know the name of it. It had caught fire at some point. The building look like a tall, sparkling cinder.

And everywhere . . . *bodies.*

Some were bloated, their swollen bellies stretching shirts and popping buttons. Some were missing arms or legs. Some had their stomachs ripped open or their heads smashed in. The clothing of the corpses rippled and snapped in time with the unforgiving wind. Pools of blood had frozen into snow-speckled red glass.

Pillars of smoke rose across the city skyline, abstract streaks of wavering grayish-black brushstrokes on a canvas of glowing yellow and orange.

Five days ago, Chicago had been . . . well . . . *Chicago*. Now it was a slaughterhouse.

Beneath the wind's undulating howl, he heard no car engines, no honks, no tires squishing across slushy concrete. No talking, no yelling . . . no *people*. The lack of city sounds jarred him almost as much as the hatchlings had.

"Fuck," Sofia said.

"I know," Cooper said. "Oh man oh man, this is so messed up."

"Not that. I mean it's *cold*."

Cooper nodded. The wind stung his face. Wind like this could burn you, make your skin crack and peel worse than eight hours in the sun. He started shivering. Had to be five or ten below out here, way worse with the windchill. He was lucky he'd brought Jeff's jacket, or there was no way Sofia would have lasted more than fifteen minutes out here.

The coat meant that her wound and infection might kill her before the cold did. He had to help her.

"You know of any drugstores in the area?"

Sofia nodded. "There's a Walgreens up on Michigan Ave, by Pioneer Court."

"How far is that?"

"Two blocks east, a block north."

Not far. He squeezed Sofia a little tighter, trying to reassure her. "And if we can't get into that Walgreens, what else can you think of?"

She thought for a moment. "Northwestern Memorial Hospital is a little farther north, on Huron. If we can't get in, we keep going right up Michigan Ave. There's another Walgreens at East Chicago, I think . . . seven blocks north from here. Can we find a car?"

"No use right now," Cooper said. "Even if we found one that worked, the street is too clogged with wrecks. For now, we walk."

"I was afraid you'd say that. Cooper, I'm cold."

He stuffed the pistol into the back of his pants. He bent, scooped Sofia up, held her in his arms as if they were about to walk across the threshold.

"Romantic," she said, her voice barely audible over the winter wind. "You . . . you know we're gonna die, right?"

Cooper pulled her close, kissed her forehead: even that felt scorchingly hot.

"We'll make it," he said. "Just give me directions."

She pointed to the right. "North on Wabash."

Sofia leaned in and kissed him on the cheek, then rested her head on his shoulder. She was shivering even worse than he was.

Cooper adjusted her in his arms. He headed north.

A GAME OF TAG

Admiral Porter relayed the news, somehow keeping his voice as emotionless as that of a traffic reporter.

"Seismic readings indicate a nuclear detonation in south-central Russia," he said. "Approximately twenty megatons, believed to be of Chinese origin."

Murray's stomach did flip-flops. A nuke. A goddamn *nuke*. It changed the game in every possible way. Not only was the world up against a disease that turned humanity against itself, the disease had apparently learned how to push the button.

The staff of the Situation Room looked as sick as Murray felt. Everyone except for the Joint Chiefs and the president. Porter and the other generals exuded grim determination — like it or not, this was their moment. Blackmon just looked pissed.

"I don't understand," she said. "This came out of nowhere. If it was an ICBM, we should have seen the launch."

Porter nodded, took his customary pause before answering. "That's because it wasn't an ICBM. Our guess is a Type 631 missile fired from a truck just south of the Russian border, between Kazakhstan and Mongolia. Truck-fired missile range is over four hundred kilometers, enough to reach Omsk, Novosibirsk or possibly Krasnoyarsk."

Murray didn't know any of those cities. How big were they? Which one had been hit?

André Vogel pressed a finger to an earpiece in his right ear. He dabbed at his now constantly sweaty, bald head with a handkerchief.

"We've got a bird bringing up visuals on the region," he said. "We should have satellite imagery on the big screen in a few seconds."

The Situation Room fell silent. All heads turned to the monitor that showed fifteen American cities lit up in yellow, another eight in red. Smaller red and yellow spots dotted the country — violence was radiating from the big cities, spilling out across the nation.

The map of America blinked out, replaced by a high-angle view of a mushroom cloud billowing up over a glowing landscape. Murray saw the hall-marks of a major metroplex: a river cutting through the middle, clusters of tall buildings, roads snaking out to suburbs, then to forest and farmland.

A single word at the bottom identified the city.

"Novosibirsk," Blackmon said slowly and carefully, as if she wanted to respect the newly dead by properly pronouncing the name of their now-destroyed home. "How many people?"

Admiral Porter answered her. "Third-largest city in Russia, behind Moscow and St. Petersburg. Population, one-point-five million."

On the screen, the mushroom cloud continued to rise. Murray found himself wishing that this was a joke, the prank of some sick, twisted fuck.

It wasn't.

"My God," Blackmon said. "This is really happening." She did her hands-rubbing-the-face thing, then blinked rapidly, worked her jaw as if trying to get a bad taste out of her mouth. "Do we detect any other launches from the Chinese?"

"Negative," Porter said. "All ICBMs are still. The Chinese aren't warming anything up that we know of. It could have been a rogue element. Possibly the truck crew was converted — they could have launched on their own."

Vogel dabbed at his sweaty face with a sweat-soaked handkerchief.

"We've got full satellite coverage now," he said. "If there's another truck launch, we'll see it happen."

Blackmon laced her fingers together. She was trying to stay calm, to show confidence, but the fingers gripped too tightly, made the skin on the back of her hands wrinkle and pucker.

"Director Vogel," she said, "I need you to find a way for me to talk to Beijing."

Vogel leaned on the table. "We're trying everything we can, Madam President. We're starting to get satellite images from China's largest cities. Several of them show major fires. Communication seems to be down all across the country. They can't talk to us, and far as we can tell it looks like they can't even talk to each other."

Blackmon seemed to realize her hands were strangling each other. She extended her fingers, moved her hands apart, dropped them to her lap.

"Get me in touch with *someone* who can make decisions in China," she said. "And get Morozov on the line. Right now."

Bodies scurried into motion, hands picked up phones — at least four people jumped on the task of trying to reach Stepan Morozov, the president of Russia.

Paris, a cinder. London in chaos. Gun battles in the streets of Berlin. Reports of Converted wreaking havoc in South America, Northern Africa, India and Pakistan. Every continent felt the effects. All except for Australia, the leaders of which had been smart enough to shut down all travel three days earlier.

Blackmon turned to Porter. "Admiral, what's the condition of the Seventh Fleet?"

Maybe Murray wasn't up on his Russian geography, but he — like everyone else in the room — knew exactly what Blackmon was asking. The Seventh Fleet operated as a forward force near Japan, a constant presence of power some sixty ships and three hundred aircraft strong. The Seventh was America's sheathed saber in that region.

"Seventh fleet is at REDCON-1," Porter said. "They are prepared to defend any hostile action and are available for offensive operations."

Blackmon nodded her approval. "Make sure fleet command knows they have clearance to shoot down anything that comes near them. From here on out, we err on the side of an international incident as opposed to losing even a single ship."

"Yes, Madam President," the admiral said. He turned to his assistants, setting in motion another miniflurry of activity.

Vogel looked off, put his hand to his earpiece. He turned to Blackmon.

"Madam President, we have President Morozov on the line. He called us."

An assistant placed a red phone on the table in front of Blackmon. It was an old-fashioned thing, a handset connected to the main phone by a curly cable: the "hotline," a piece of equipment that for five decades had served as a last resort to stop nuclear war.

Blackmon took a deep breath. She picked up the handset.

"President Morozov, America expresses its deepest condolences at this tragedy."

She paused, listening. Her eyes widened.

"Stepan, don't do this," she said. "That attack probably wasn't ordered by the government. China is dealing with the same problems you are — you *know* they wouldn't risk a war with Russia. If you retaliate, all you'll do is kill innocent people."

She listened. Her eyes closed. That was it, just her eyelids closing, and everyone in the room knew Morozov's answer.

Blackmon opened her eyes. They burned with anger and frustration.

"The United States objects in the strongest possible terms," she said. "The world is on the edge of collapse. This will push us even closer."

There was a pause, then she hung up the phone.

Blackmon took a moment. The room waited for her. She squared her shoulders and spoke.

"President Morozov feels compelled to retaliate. What will Russia's likely target be?"

Vogel rubbed at his bald scalp, rubbed *hard*. "Probably a city comparable in size to Novosibirsk," he said. He tapped at his keyboard, glanced at the main monitor as he did. "The closest Chinese city would probably be . . . Ürümqi."

The image on the screen shifted, showing a city nested between three snowcapped mountain ranges. At the center, the word *Ürümqi*. If Murray hadn't heard Vogel say it, he would have had no idea how to pronounce it.

Blackmon nodded once, as if she knew the city of Ürümqi was the only obvious answer. "And that city has one-point-five million people?"

"Closer to *two*-point-five million," Vogel said. "Three-point-five in the prefecture, so the death toll would depend on what weapon the Russians use."

Murray shook his head in amazement. Three-point-five million: about the size of Los Angeles, America's second-largest city.

Blackmon's hands clenched together again. The world's most-powerful human being had no power at all to stop a massive slaughter.

"Admiral Porter, how would Russia strike that city?"

"Tupolev bomber," Porter said. "Likely a Tu-160 flying out of the Engels-2 air base near Saratov. You can bet it's already in the air. It will launch a Kh-55 cruise missile, probable warhead yield of 200 kilotons."

A series of concentric circles appeared on the screen, overlaying the city. The center circle was a bright red, surrounded by one in red-orange, which in turn was surrounded by orange, and finally a ring of yellow. More words appeared on the screen, showing districts or suburbs, Murray wasn't sure:

Qidaowanxiang, Ergongxiang, Xinshi, Tianshan, Shayibak and more. The names all fell within the bands of color. Murray didn't know those names, probably couldn't even pronounce them, but the names made everything more real.

People lived in Xinshi, people lived in Qidaowanxiang . . . people who were probably going to die.

Vogel turned to Admiral Porter, looked at all the Joint Chiefs.

"We have to do something," Vogel said. "Do we have any resources in the area? A carrier, anything?"

The air force admiral started to speak, but Blackmon cut him off.

"We do nothing," she said. Her voice was cold, unforgiving. If her heart felt anything, she refused to let those emotions reach her brain.

Vogel looked shocked. "But Madam President, a strike could kill *millions* of people! We have to try to stop it!"

Blackmon stared straight ahead. "Russia has been attacked and will retaliate. If we try to intervene, we . . ."

Her voice trailed off. She closed her mouth, licked her lips. She gathered herself, continued.

"If we intervene, Russia could interpret that as an act of war. America is in dire straits — we can't risk doing anything that would put our troops in conflict, and we *cannot* risk nuclear weapons being launched at our shores. Russia has the right to defend herself."

Vogel slumped back into his chair. He was stunned, just like most of the people in the room, just like Murray. Wasn't the president of the United States supposed to be able to reach out and stop injustice?

And yet, Murray knew Blackmon was making the right call. If the USA stuck her nose in the middle of this fight, the next mushroom cloud might rise over Miami, Seattle, Phoenix . . . any number of American treasures. Blackmon had no choice other than to make sure Russia didn't see the United States as an enemy.

Admiral Porter cleared his throat. "Madam President, if I may offer a suggestion?"

She waved her hand inward: *go ahead*.

"We think the Chinese nuke was launched by a rogue element," Porter said. "However, it is also very possible that the government was testing Russia, seeing if the infection had impacted Russia's ability to respond to attack."

"Russia's ability has not been affected," Blackmon said. "Which the Chinese are about to find out firsthand."

Admiral Porter nodded. "Of course. But, if China actually *was* testing Russian resolve, their next test could be against us. We need to prepare our own retaliatory response. The Chinese — or whoever is running things there — will see us preparing for launch. They'll know the United States is ready to hit back."

Three nuclear powers at play, inches away from an all-out exchange. If Murray had wondered how things could get any worse, now he knew.

Vogel knocked twice on the table. "Porter is right," he said. "The Chinese will see us preparing. So will the Russians, just in case they get any bright ideas while they're lobbing nukes into China."

Murray shook his head. "Are you warmongering assholes really this obtuse? You want to make things *worse* by spinning up our birds?"

The admiral glared at him. Vogel chose to look elsewhere.

The president raised a finger. "Director Longworth, let's keep this civil."

"Sorry, Madam President."

She turned back to Porter.

"Admiral, you're sure about this? You really think prepping for launch will be interpreted as a warning and not a threat?"

There was a gleam in the admiral's eye. Maybe Murray was imagining that, but this man — all the Joint Chiefs, for that matter — had spent a lifetime training and preparing for a situation this severe.

"China has already used a nuclear weapon," Porter said. "Russia is about to do the same. The seal is broken, Madam President. It's a lot easier to justify the second strike than it is the first."

Russia would launch at China, maybe one of them would launch at America, and then America would launch at *both* — just to be sure — and then . . .

Murray stood up. The action seemed to surprise the other people at the table. It even surprised him.

"This is what it wants," he said, the words rushing out. "These people, the Converted, they aren't monsters. They aren't zombies. The destruction of Paris made that clear. The bomb that hit Novosibirsk — if it wasn't the Chinese government, it wasn't truly *rogue*, either. That was a calculated attack, because this disease *wants to kill us all*. Vogel, put our disease tracking numbers back on the screen."

Vogel did so. Murray pointed at the top number.

"Sixty percent immunized," he said. "Soon to be seventy, then eighty. We're in the lead, and the other industrialized nations are close behind. Don't you see? We've stopped the spread. We'll have millions of infected to deal with, sure, but we've *stopped the spread*. The Converted . . . they can watch the news just like we can. They know the score. We've checked the contagion, so now they're looking for other ways to take us out. We just so happen to have tens of thousands of *other ways* in the form of nuclear missiles. Don't you get it? We're beating them now because we're organized, because we have communication — if a nuclear shooting match starts, all that goes away. They want to *destroy* us. If they start a nuclear war, then we do their work for them."

Vogel turned sharply, his hand shot to his earpiece: new information. The room hushed, waited for him.

"Seismic readings indicate a one-hundred-kiloton detonation in China," he said. "Probable epicenter . . . Ürümqi. Returning to satellite coverage."

The main monitor switched back to the image of Ürümqi, only now the city couldn't be seen — a billowing mushroom cloud roiled up, blocking any view of the city center. The shock wave expanded out, a ring of dirt and debris widening at supersonic speed.

Blackmon stood up, rested her hands on the table. She leaned forward, her predator's stare locked on the scene of mass destruction.

"Admiral Porter is right," she said. "We need to send a clear signal. We need to make sure the Russians and the Chinese know what will happen if they attack. Take us to DEFCON 2."

THE STREETS OF CHICAGO

It could have been an Old West ghost town, complete with howling wind. Skyscrapers in place of beat-up wooden shacks, snowdrifts instead of rolling tumbleweed, but it was just as desolate, just as empty.

Some of the traffic lights were on, some were off. Most buildings sat dark. A few random windows glowed against the darkening sky.

Vehicles littered Michigan Avenue's six snow-swept lanes. Some of the cars, trucks and buses looked fine, save for smashed-in windows and dented doors, while others were crumpled, knocked on their sides or even resting upside down with snow accumulating on their upturned tires and dark underbellies. Many were burned-out husks, blackened and misshapen from long-dead fires.

Light from the setting sun slipped through the packed, gray clouds, reflected off the tall skyscrapers. Broken windows looked like missing teeth, black spots marring the smooth glass faces.

Winter wind ate at Cooper and Sofia, cut into jeans and slacks, drove through coats to chill their bones and bellies. The snow kept falling, met in the sky by whirling bits of burned, blackened paper. Everything smelled like a day-old campfire. Icy flakes melted against skin, stuck to hair, clung on Cooper's four-day stubble.

So many dead. Blackened corpses sat inside of blackened cars. A cindered bus sagged from the heat that had scorched it. A scattering of five corpses spread out from its twisted door — people who made it out of the vehicle, but still succumbed to the flames. Bloated and frozen bodies lined the sidewalks, lay between the ruined cars that filled and blocked the streets. It was as if God had picked up a graveyard, turned it upside down and rattled it, scattering the dead like a child dumping out a box of toys.

Cooper began to hear occasional sounds through the wind — a clank of metal, distant tinkles of breaking glass, the screams of the hunted and gleeful cheers of the hunters. He stayed close to the buildings on the west side of the street, trying to be as inconspicuous as possible.

Nothing came out to stop him, but he and Sofia weren't entirely alone. Here and there, Cooper saw the little pyramid-shaped monsters, sometimes scurrying across the street from one building to another, sometimes through ground-floor windows where they built their walls of solidified shit.

He also saw flashes of movement from deep inside buildings, through smashed storefronts and from behind windows higher up the towering buildings. He was being watched, watched by something bigger than the hatchlings.

Cooper had carried Sofia north on Wabash and cut east on Hubbard. At Michigan Avenue, he looked south. The snow-covered Michigan Avenue Bridge led over the Chicago River. He wondered if they should go that way instead, but Sofia tugged on his jacket to get his attention.

She raised a shaking hand, pointed at a twenty-story building a half block up on the left.

Fire had raged through the smooth glass tower, covering what windows remained with waving patterns of soot. At the bottom of the building, he saw a broken overhang that once had shielded Chicagoans from rain or snow. It, too, was twisted and blackened by the fire. A warped script *W* and one *e* were all that remained of brass letters that had spelled out "Walgreens."

Cooper's heart sank. He kept walking, kept carrying Sofia. Maybe the fire damage was only superficial.

It wasn't.

Nothing remained of the drugstore. Through broken and blackened glass, Cooper saw melted metal shelves and powdery paper ash. The smell of burned plastic poured out of the place as though it was still actively ablaze.

Sofia shivered in his arms.

"Shit," she said.

Cooper nodded. "I guess we go to the hospital next. Let me take a little rest."

He looked around, saw a nearby car that had smashed into a bus. The car's windows remained unbroken, intact. He carried Sofia over to it. He used the hand under her knees to open the driver's door, then bent, his back straining as he carefully set her on the driver's seat.

His whole body seemed to sigh in relief. Sofia weighed all of a buck-ten — not much to hold for a few moments, but an awful lot to carry across the city.

"I'm slowing you down," she said, her weak voice barely audible over the wind. "Why are you doing this for me?"

He thought for a moment, searching for an answer.

"Because of my mom," he said finally. "She'd want me to help you."

A not-so-distant scream from behind, a woman's scream, echoing through the empty streets. Cooper looked back the way they had come, his hand moving on its own, reaching for the cold handle of the gun stuffed into his pants.

Two long blocks away, he saw a woman at the base of the bridge. Her hands clutched to her shoulders as if she was trying to compress herself, make herself too small to see. Chicago's skyscrapers rose up into the gray evening sky around her. She stood in the middle of the street, looking to her right, then turning right, then looking right again, then turning again, spinning in place in a stop-start motion. The wind blew snow at her, probably cutting right through her thin blouse.

For a moment, Cooper wondered why she hadn't worn a coat (didn't she know it was freezing outside?) before he realized she had probably fled some hiding spot, had run just to stay alive.

He saw movement: two other people approaching the woman. A tall man, wearing a red down jacket, and a woman wearing a blue snowsuit. They must have come out of the surrounding buildings. They closed in, and suddenly there were four more people — sliding out of ruined cars, walking through doorways.

They had the woman surrounded.

She kept turning, first her head, then her body.

"Don't just stand there," Cooper said quietly. "*Run.*"

The woman didn't move. The six closed in on her.

And then, on the bridge, coming from the south, through the falling snow and scattering bits of paper, Cooper saw something else.

Something . . . *huge*.

He felt Sofia's fingers clutch tight at his jacket. The raw intensity of her words hit his ears like a siren, even though they were barely more than a whisper.

"What the fuck is *that*? Cooper, *what the fuck is that*?"

Cooper didn't know, didn't *want* to know. It was a man . . . maybe. Sickly yellow skin, no jacket, an upper body that was far too wide for legs that would be gigantic on anyone save for an NFL lineman. And the *head* — Cooper couldn't make out much other than a neck that was as wide as impossibly wide shoulders, a neck that led up to a face hidden behind a blue scarf wrapped around the mouth and nose.

The woman let go of her own shoulders, finally turned to run, but it was too late; six people grabbed her. She screamed and jerked, tried to fight, but the others held her fast.

The man in the red jacket stood in front of her, reached into his coat, pulled out a long butcher knife.

Cooper thought about drawing his gun, taking a shot, maybe he could get lucky from this far out—

—and then it was too late. The man in the red jacket drove the knife into the woman's belly, slid it *up*, like a butcher slaughtering a pig. The woman didn't even scream, she just stared. Stared, and *twitched*.

Her attackers tore into her. Cooper saw hands driving down, yanking, *ripping*, saw those hands come back bloody and full of dangling intestines or steaming chunks of muscle.

The five people started to eat.

I am not seeing this . . . I am not fucking seeing this . . .

A tug on his coat.

"Coop," Sofia said. "Get me the hell out of here."

He realized the gun was in his hand. He didn't remember actually drawing it.

"Yeah," he said. "Let's go."

He stuffed it once again into the back of his pants, then reached into the car for Sofia.

TIPPING POINT

From his little table in the *Coronado*'s cargo hold, Tim Feely studied the numbers. New York City, Minneapolis, Grand Rapids and Chicago were no longer providing consumer data. They were too far gone for that.

Elsewhere in the country, people were stocking up on whatever they could before it was too late. That panic skewed the consumer pattern information, but there was still enough data from which to draw conclusions.

Philadelphia: 9,000% increase in cough suppressants
Lexington: huge spikes in purchases of fever reducer
Fayetteville: All stores sold out of pain relievers

The list went on and on. Most of Baltimore had lost power the day before, so there was no additional data to be had there. Indianapolis, Huntsville and Birmingham were in the same boat.

As near as Tim could tell, most cities on the Eastern Seaboard had significant outbreaks. The Midwest was even worse. The West Coast showed some signs of infected activity, but the overall stats indicated those populations were mostly normal; they'd brewed the inoculant faster there, distributed it better, done a superior job at overcoming local objections. Although murder rates had skyrocketed, police departments remained in control of the West Coast and the Southwest — except for Los Angeles.

Riots and looting had cast LA into chaos. There was no information to discern if the violence came from the Converted, or if it had blown up due to the deaths that occurred because of the mayor's shoot-on-sight after-dark curfew.

Canada was also in bad shape. Montreal was ablaze, just like Paris. Tim didn't have consumer data on Europe, but news reports of burning cities and corpses littering the streets told the story just fine.

Pandora's box had opened. Just like the myth, evil things had flown out to infect the world. In that myth, the last thing to escape had been *hope*.

This time, Tim wondered if there was any hope at all.

COOPER'S CHOICE

Shadows moved within the darkness of a wintry Chicago night. Cooper stumbled more than he ran, the girl in his arms a heaviness that threatened to pull him down.

Just drop her . . . just leave her, she's going to die anyway . . .

They'd found the hospital to be a burned-out husk. When they'd come in for a closer look, something had found them, followed them.

Cooper had carried Sofia away, but that something had picked up their trail. They fled north. The storm that threatened to kill them also provided some cover: blowing snow helped them hide, masked their tracks and their sounds.

His arms burned, screamed for oxygen. Sofia hung low, near his thighs, his left arm under her knees, his right around her back. He stopped only long enough to heft her high again, up to his chest, then he continued up Michigan Avenue.

He felt her fingers clutch his jacket, pulling it tighter across his chest.

"They're coming," she said. "I can hear them. Run faster, goddamit!"

Cooper could barely run at all, let alone *faster*, but he heard them, too, heard their yells, heard the roaring of some misshapen thing.

He'd walked seven excruciating blocks — careful not to step on frozen body parts or broken glass — with the cold making his hands numb, making his fingers tingle, with Sofia's weight dragging at him, and now he was only a block shy of Chicago Avenue.

So he ignored the icy cold air that sucked deep into his heaving lungs, ignored the wind that made his face sting and burn. He moved faster.

Up ahead, on the other side of Chicago Avenue on both the left and the right, he saw gothic buildings made of white stone. They looked like castles, especially the one on the left with its octagonal tower that stretched thirty feet above. It was old, so old it had probably once towered over the surrounding buildings back when "tall" meant four or five stories. Now it was just a lost footnote in the city's sprawling skyline. A little castle . . . a little fortress . . .

Leave her and go hide. Go in the fortress, block the door, you can hold them off . . .

A tug at his collar.

"There," Sofia said. She pointed right: he saw the white WALGREENS lettering on a black overhang. Below it, a revolving door of glass in a curved metal housing. The store sat at the base of a tall, tan building. This place wasn't burned out. Cooper didn't see any activity in front of the store, or inside it. Maybe they could hide in there, killing two birds with one stone.

He reached the door: it was still intact, as were the glass windows on either side.

Cooper carefully carried Sofia into the rotating door, careful not to stumble and drop her or smack her head against anything. He pushed. It turned with a deep *swishhh*. Three steps later, he stepped into a miracle.

The lights were on.

There was no wind.

No heat, either, but without the windchill the place felt comparatively warm.

The doors might be intact, but this place hadn't escaped the disaster. Ten feet in lay a headless body. Ice crystals formed a strangely beautiful pattern in the blood that had spilled from the man's neck and spread across the hard stone floor.

Farther up the first aisle, between scattered bags of chips on one side and candy bars on the other, lay a second body, a woman. A look of disbelief had frozen on her face, maybe when her attackers had torn her right arm from her body, leaving the ripped sleeve of her blue jacket ragged and stiff with icy blood. That jacket remained buttoned under her chin, but open at the belly to show an empty cavity — her internal organs were gone.

"My God," Sofia said. "Coop, we gotta hide."

He nodded. He hefted her higher, or tried to, but his arms wouldn't lift her. He was damn near done. "Is the pharmacy in the back?"

"Yeah," Sofia said. "Straight back."

Cooper stepped over the bodies.

All through the aisles, products had been ripped off the metal shelves and tossed onto the floor. It didn't look like much had been taken, though — more a store-trashing rampage rather than people scrambling for supplies.

He stumbled on a box of candy, causing him to hit the shelves on his left, rocking them a little before they settled back down with a *bang*.

Sofia's face wrinkled in pain. She'd taken the brunt of that blow.

"Sorry," he said.

She said nothing.

Cooper kept moving. The fluorescent lights created the strange sensation that — aside from the bodies, of course — this place was still open for business, that the horrors outside had passed it by.

He reached the pharmacy counter. Instead of looking for the door, he set Sofia on the counter, then hopped over. When his feet hit the floor, his exhausted legs gave out beneath him. He fell in a heap on the tile, banging the top of his head against the corner of a rack that held hundreds of little plastic pull-out bins.

"Owww." Cooper rolled to his back, hands pressed to his new injury.

"Graceful," Sofia said. "Just . . . let me catch my breath, then I'll . . . start carrying you."

He lifted his head to look at her. She'd pushed herself up on one elbow to stare down at him. Jeff's big coat made her seem so small, so feminine. She looked like death warmed over — face gaunt, black hair stringy and frozen in clumps, eyes half lidded — but the left corner of her mouth curled into a shit-eating grin.

Back flat on the floor, muscles burning, chest heaving and head stinging, Cooper started laughing.

"Sofia, you're kind of a dick."

She nodded weakly. "I've been told that once or twice in my day. You mind getting me down from here?"

The brief moment of humor vanished. He fought his aching body and stood, gently lifted her from the counter, then set her down with her butt on the floor and her back against the inside of the counter. If anyone else came in the store, Cooper and Sofia wouldn't be seen unless the intruder came all the way to the rear.

She reached up and caressed his face. "Thanks, Cooper. I mean it. I'd be dead already if it weren't for you."

He didn't know what to say, so he just nodded. He turned to the pull-out bins, started filing through the paper envelopes inside of them.

"Amoxicillin, maybe? You allergic to that?"

"No idea," Sofia said. "I guess we'll find out."

He nodded. "I guess we will." He dug through the envelopes.

"Hey, Cooper . . . you feel okay?"

"You mean other than cold and exhaustion? Sure, I guess. Why?"

"You got some kind of big blister on the back of your neck."

He stopped flipping through the envelopes. He remembered the puffy, air-filled spot he'd seen on his shoulder.

"Don't worry," he said. "It's some kind of allergic reaction, I think. Hives or something. I haven't checked in a while, but I had them all over my body."

He reached to his neck, felt what she was talking about: a puffy blister the size of a small marble. He pressed on it, heard a soft *pop*, saw a tiny mist of slowly floating white. Sofia's breath scattered it away.

"Gross," she said. "Like a puffball."

Cooper nodded. "Yeah. That is kind of gross."

She gave a halfhearted shrug. "The least of my worries right now. Can you get me some water? I'm really thirsty."

He noticed her breath crystallizing when she talked. The store gave them shelter, but he'd have to find a way to get heat, fast.

He pulled out six of the plastic bins, slid them over to her.

"Look through those envelopes," he said. "We want amoxicillin, penicillin, shit like that. I'll get you that water."

He stood, looked over the counter and out into the store — still empty. The pharmacy door was off to his left. It opened into store's horizontal rear aisle. Most of the end-cap displays were untouched. If he'd needed a new mop head or a four-for-three bargain on Tampax, it would have been his lucky day.

He saw the refrigerators off to the left, still lit from within. He skipped the soft drinks, grabbed three bottles of water and an orange juice instead. One refrigerator contained sandwiches. He grabbed three.

The lights are on . . . the refrigerators are working.

In all the apocalyptic movies, the power was one of the first things to go. But not here in Chicago. With the city all but destroyed, wouldn't the psychos have hit a power plant? A transformer? Power lines, maybe? Apparently not.

He looked up and down the line of refrigerators. There was enough food and water to last him and Sofia for several days. And if they ate through all that, the shelves were still filled with dry goods, canned tuna, crackers . . . enough to last them *weeks*.

Long enough for the National Guard to arrive, to take control of the city.

An idea struck him. He jogged through the aisles, careful not to step on anything, looking for small appliances. In Aisle Six, he found what he wanted: an electric heater.

He juggled his loot as he walked back to the pharmacy door. If he could find a way to board up that front entrance, maybe board up whatever rear entrance the place had, they could stay here at least long enough for Sofia to get better.

Just to the right of the pharmacy door he found a waist-high wall of bandages and disinfectants.

He walked into the pharmacy and set the food and water next to her. She held up a white paper bag: amoxicillin.

"Good girl," he said. He opened a bottle for her and put it in her hands. He then opened the medicine, put two pills in her mouth. She lifted the water bottle — weakly, but on her own — and took a drink. Her eyes closed in relief.

"Oh my God," she said. "Thank you. I never thought water could taste so good."

He grabbed the box with the heater, slid it in front of her. "Unless you object, I'll just go ahead and plug this in for you."

Her eyes widened. She shivered. "*Heat*? Oh, Coop, if I wasn't so messed up, you'd totally get a blow job."

"Yeah? Well, then get ready for your panties to evaporate."

Cooper walked out, gathered an armful of peroxide, cotton balls and gauze wrap. He walked back to her and set the pile of medical supplies next to the pile of food.

She weakly lifted her water bottle, took another drink. "I've had better dates, but not many," she said. "Turn the heater on before I change my mind about fucking the living hell out of you."

"Yeah, all your bleeding and shivering is such a turn-on." Cooper ripped open the heater box. He looked at the cash register on the counter, followed the power cord down to an outlet. He plugged in the heater, turned it as high as it would go and pointed it at her.

The heater's fan spun up. The air came out, warm at first, then it quickly turned hot.

Sofia closed her eyes, leaned her head against the wall. "Oh, hell yes. Thank you."

Cooper gently opened Jeff's coat and pulled up Sofia's shirt to look at the wound. The edges were gray, almost black. It looked horrible. He had no idea what to do next.

He opened the bottle of peroxide, then a box of gauze strips. He poured peroxide onto the wound. Sofia hissed as the liquid fizzed into whiteness. He used the gauze to dab at the wound. He cleaned as gently as he could, wiping away blood both dry and wet. He used more gauze to cover the wound, then ran tape around her stomach and back.

"That's all I know to do," he said.

He smiled at her. She took a drink of water, smiled back.

Swishhhh.

They froze: the front door had just turned.

They heard footsteps.

A man's voice called out, and it was all Cooper could do to not piss his pants for the second time.

"Where are you, motherfucker? Are you in there?"

The voice sounded confident, aggressive; the voice of a man in a bar challenging another man to a fight.

Swishhh . . . swishhh . . . swishhh.

More noises. Feet moving, cellophane rattling, boxes falling. More than one man; maybe three, maybe four. Then, the sound of a low, *deep* growl.

Too deep to be human.

Sofia's hands snapped out: she grabbed Cooper's jacket, surprising him. He started to lean back, but she pulled him close.

"They're going to find us," she hissed. Her face was only inches from his, her skin red, the edges of her nose cracked and raw. "They're going to find us. They're going to *kill* us."

"Be quiet," he whispered back, trying to push her away. She was losing it. She was making too much noise. He had to get her out of there, had to get *himself* out of there.

"Sofia, let *go* of me!"

Out in the store, something hit hard against a shelf. The shelf must have tipped over, because it crashed onto the floor with a sound like a broken gong. Cooper heard people moving around, yelling at each other.

Sofia's puffy eyes filled with tears. She mouthed two words, over and over: *Shoot them!*

The noises in the store grew closer.

Cooper grabbed Sofia's wrists, pulled at them, tried to tear her grip from his coat.

He mouthed back to her: *Stop it!* She resisted for a second, even sneered at him, but he got his feet under him, then leaned away until her hands finally *snapped* free.

Out in the store, another rack fell over, the sound punching through him, shaking his atoms, letting him know the cannibals were coming and this panicking woman was going to get him killed.

He leaned in again, pressed his lips against her ear.

"Calm the fuck *down*. Just stay quiet, they'll leave, they'll—"

He felt Sofia's right hand on his hip, sliding around to his back . . .

The gun.

He leaned away hard, lost his balance. His ass hit the floor and he skidded into the heater, sending it clattering loudly into a wall.

Sofia scrambled to her feet. She tore off Jeff's coat and reached for the door handle, her open, bloody shirt flaring out behind her.

Cooper pushed himself to his knees and dove — his fingertips closed on the shirttail, then slipped free. He landed on his stomach as she opened the door and hobbled out into the store.

He jumped to his feet, drew the pistol as he rushed after her, just in time to see Sofia trip over an overturned rack. Her face bounced hard off the metal shelves. Blood poured instantly from a long gash across her forehead.

The blow staggered her, took away whatever adrenaline-fueled energy reserve she'd found. She flopped to her back, the tilted rack beneath her, the top of her head on the tile floor, her legs dangling off what used to be the rack's bottom.

She looked at him with glazed eyes.

But Cooper Mitchell didn't really see Sofia. What he saw were the six people standing there, three on either side of her, all staring at him, all hunched forward in clear aggression.

The same people who had killed that woman in the street.

Killed her, and *eaten* her.

Six people . . . and by the revolving door, mostly hidden by the racks of merchandise, that hulking form Cooper had seen coming across the bridge, head still wrapped in the blue scarf.

Five bullets; he couldn't get them all.

He was going to die.

They all held weapons: long knives, a fire axe, a machete, a tire iron. The woman in the blue snowsuit had a chrome-plated revolver in her left hand.

Cooper was too afraid to move. His pistol was pointed down . . . he had to raise it, had to do *something* . . .

The tall man in the red jacket took a small step forward, then stopped. The knife he'd used to kill the woman in the blouse caught the store's fluorescent lights.

Clean. The blade is clean. He took the time to clean it . . .

The man stared at Cooper. He lowered the knife. The others stood still. They weren't attacking.

Cooper looked at them. They looked at him, but they also looked at the gun in his hand.

"Help . . . me . . ."

The thin voice came from the floor, from Sofia. She weakly tried to roll to her stomach, but she didn't have the energy to even lift her legs. Blood coursed down her face, made a puddle on the floor.

Six people, one thing, five bullets . . .

And then another memory rushed up: Chavo, back in the hotel . . . Chavo, trying to sniff, asking if Cooper was a friend . . . asking Cooper why he didn't kill Sofia . . .

Seven of them, five bullets . . . I don't want to die . . .

Cooper's breath stopped. One thought overwhelmed him, one hope consuming every ounce of who he was.

He aimed his gun at Sofia's face.

She saw it. She didn't look dazed anymore. She lay inverted on top of a ruined rack of toothpaste and mouthwash. Her trembling lips formed the word *please*, but no sound came out.

I want to live . . . Sofia . . . I'm so sorry . . .

Cooper squeezed the trigger.

The gun leaped in his hand, rising up so fast it almost flew away. He blinked rapidly, the muzzle flash a strobe of green then red then white each time his eyes opened anew.

His vision mostly cleared. Glowing afterimages danced at the edges of his sight.

Sofia's left leg trembled sickeningly. Her left hand made clutching motions, half closing, then half opening.

The bullet had punched a hole in the right cheekbone, spraying blood across the white tile floor behind her head.

She blinked . . . her eyes locked on him, narrowed with recognition and realization, then relaxed. Her head lolled back.

She stopped trembling.

The six people looked at him.

You had to do it you had to do it you coward you murderer say something or they'll tear you apart you know what you have to say so say it say it now.

Cooper looked at each of them in turn, then he spoke: "She wasn't a friend."

The Tall Man nodded. The others smiled.

Seven of them and now only FOUR bullets . . .

Cooper fought the urge to turn and run. He knew he wouldn't make it far. He didn't know where the back door was, or if there was even a back door at all.

"She almost got me," he said.

The Tall Man looked down at Sofia, then back. "Then why were you carrying her?"

Cooper held up the gun. "She had this against my neck. She was hurt. I knew if I could keep her from shooting me long enough, I'd have a chance. She was going to come out of the office and shoot you guys, so I had to make my move."

The bulky man by the front door — the thing that was human and *not* human at the same time — walked forward. Seven feet tall, at least. In each hand it held some kind of long, white blade.

Do not run, they will kill you if you run . . .

It wore no shirt, leaving its pale yellow skin exposed — *yellow*, the color of pus, of coagulated grease. Whitish, black-rimmed rashes dotted its wide chest and bulging, bare arms. Thick fingers flexed, thin blood oozing from cracks and splits where fingernails had fallen off.

The white blades . . .

The thing wasn't *holding* them at all. The blades protruded from behind each wrist, jutted out from torn yellow flesh . . . and they weren't *blades*, they were *bones*: jagged, pale, as long as its forearm, wicked scythes tapering to hard, sharp points.

Its jeans had shredded at the thighs to make room for rippling muscle, turning the denim into dangling strips of fabric. Its shoulders were broader than any man's had a right to be, its neck easily thick enough to support the huge head. Long, thin patches of brown hair clung wetly to its scalp, a few more hung in front of its eyes.

It reached up a thick hand, bone-blade pointing to the ceiling, and its fingers pulled down the blue scarf.

. . . the face . . .

Cooper's reality warped and cracked.

"*Jeff?*"

The monster smiled, showing teeth that had grown wider at the base, and also grown longer, like fangs with the points chipped off.

"COOOO-PERRRR."

The Tall Man in the red jacket looked at the thing that used to be Jeff. "You know this guy?"

The monster nodded, a motion that made his massive shoulders dip up and down as if the thick neck couldn't quite bend all the way.

The Tall Man seemed pleasantly surprised.

"Well, that's just fucking titties and beer," he said. He smiled at Cooper. "You can join us. We're supposed to lie low. Stanton said to find the uninfected and get rid of them, but we're not supposed to burn or wreck anything."

That name again. Could it be a coincidence?

"Stanton? *Steve* Stanton?"

The Tall Man nodded. "Yeah. I actually got to meet him. The others haven't."

He said *got to meet him* as if it was the highest honor anyone could ever hope for.

It all fell into place. It all *clicked*. Stanton's machine had grabbed something from the bottom of Lake Michigan. The Detroit incident of five years earlier . . . the conspiracy theories that some alien ship had been shot down . . . Blackmon on TV, talking about the medicine . . . bringing the *Platypus* aboard the *Mary Ellen*, and everyone feeling ill shortly afterward . . . coming to Chicago . . . the city becoming a living hell . . .

Jeff, getting sick, and now he was . . . *that*.

Cooper didn't know what had happened, but he knew it had started when Steve Stanton walked into JBS Salvage.

So many people dead. A city in ruins. Stanton's work had killed hundreds, thousands.

But not Sofia . . . YOU killed her, didn't you?

Cooper shook away the thought. He had to think, had to get out of this alive. Knowing Jeff had earned respect from the Tall Man. Maybe knowing Steve would bring even more.

"I brought Steve Stanton to Chicago. Five days ago." Cooper nodded at Jeff. "He was with us."

The Tall Man took a step back. He looked at the others in an unspoken message of disbelief, then he looked at Jeff.

"*You* met Stanton?" The Tall Man said. "Why didn't you say so?"

Jeff nodded again, almost bowed, a motion that made the muscles under his sickly yellow skin ripple and twitch.

"COOOO-PERRRR, MY FRIEND."

Jeff smiled his shark-toothed smile. Cooper couldn't bear to look at him anymore. He stared down at Sofia's body.

You shot her you coward you murderer Jeff is a monster what the fuck what the FUCK you killed her and that's your fault but it would have never happened if not for Stanton . . . Sofia would still be alive . . . Jeff would still be Jeff.

Fear stabbed through him, made his breath rattle, filled his head with fuzz. He wanted to curl up, shut down, hide and pray these killers would just *go away*. But far more than that, he wanted to live.

Cooper slid the pistol barrel into the front of his pants. He left the handle out so they could all see it. He had watched them tear a human being apart. If they realized he was lying, he'd suffer the same fate — he didn't want them to forget he had a gun.

A gun with just four bullets.

He forced himself to look at the freakish thing that had been his best friend. Cooper would save one bullet for Jeff; he wouldn't let his friend suffer this horror.

The Tall Man brushed his hands together, as if he was dusting them off, done with the whole scenario. He knelt, patted down Sofia's corpse. He reached into her pocket, pulled out Cooper's cell phone.

"That's mine," Cooper said. "Give it to me."

The Tall Man stood. He shook his head. "Only group leaders get cell phones, and I'm the group leader."

He dropped the phone on the floor, then stomped down on it with his heel, smashing it.

"There," he said. He smiled at Cooper. "You'll come with us."

"Where?"

"To a hotel," the Tall Man said. "It's real close. This is pretty goddamn kick-ass, if you ask me. It will be great to have someone who knows Mister Stanton as part of our group."

Cooper didn't know what to do — if he tried to go off on his own, would they know he was lying? Would they know he wasn't a "friend"?

The Tall Man turned to Jeff. "Bring the woman."

Jeff, or the thing that used to be Jeff, walked forward, shreds of his jeans swaying with each step. He reached out with his right hand, slid the jagged, pointed bone-blade into Sofia's neck, drove it deep into her chest until his knuckles pressed against her shoulder. He lifted her as if she weighed nothing more than a bag of chips. Her arms and legs dangled limply. Her remaining blood slowly pattered down to the red-smeared floor.

Cooper stared at the woman he'd just killed. "Why are we bringing her?"

The Tall Man smiled. "It's going to be a long night. Fresh is way better than frozen. Don't worry — she has enough meat on her bones that we'll all get to eat our fill. Come on."

The Tall Man turned and walked toward the front door.

Cooper followed.

BOOK III

DEFCON I

IT GETS WORSE

IMMUNIZED: 65%
NOT IMMUNIZED: 29%
UNKNOWN: 6%
FINISHED DOSES EN ROUTE: 56,503,000
DOSES IN PRODUCTION: 38,913,000
INFECTED: 1,488,650 (10,350,000)
CONVERTED: 1,300,000 (1,689,000)
DEATHS: 86,493 (12,250,000)

The Situation Room was starting to stink. Too many meals eaten at the long table, too many people, not enough showers. Murray had left only to go to the bathroom and to sleep a few hours at a time. For once, the burden of age — not being able to sleep for more than four hours at a time — produced fringe benefits.

The rest of the world's infected estimate had surpassed the USA's and was expected to skyrocket in the next few days. While 65 percent of Americans were now immunized, there was no measuring how many people across the globe had received the Feely yeast strain. The best estimate was just 15 percent of the world's population.

That left six billion potential hosts.

Blackmon slept. While she did, everyone looked to Murray for answers. The disease was the thing, and he knew more about it than anyone else in the room. That meant when Cheng reported in from Black Manitou Island, it was up to Murray to ask the hard questions.

The man whose face stared out from the Situation Room's monitor was a far cry from the smug, arrogant ass that Cheng had once been. Gone were his illusions of glamour and importance. He wasn't looked upon as a genius that would save the country. The administration saw it a different way: instead of Cheng getting the credit for every life saved, he got the implied blame for every American death.

"Our models predict that one percent of the Chinese population is actually converted," he said. "Only ten percent is currently infected."

"*Only* ten percent," Murray echoed. "Doctor Cheng, China has one-point-four *billion* people. You're telling me you think a hundred and forty *million* Chinese people are infected?"

Cheng looked like he wanted to be anywhere but on this call. "That's our best estimate. In two more days, it could go as high as four hundred million infected, but by then at least a hundred million of those would be fully converted."

Admiral Porter shook his head. Somehow, the man never looked creased or sweaty. Maybe he changed his uniform every time he left to take a leak.

"Four hundred million," he said. "That's more than the entire population of the United States and Canada, *combined*."

Porter was thinking in terms of an enemy force, which was exactly the right way to think about it. A thousand had destroyed Paris — what could *hundreds of millions* do?

"Cities will be overrun," the admiral said. "If the numbers get that high, there's no way to get China back under control."

Cheng licked his fat lips, rubbed nervously at his jaw. "I'm afraid it gets worse."

His image shrank down to the bottom right corner. The screen now showed a map of China. The west side of the country was colored mostly in light blue with some swatches of dark blue and a few spots of green. The east side was mostly dark blue with larger areas of that same green. The middle was all a very pale blue, or white.

"This is a population map of China," Cheng said. "The majority of people live on the East Coast. The areas in green are more densely populated. Dark blue is still heavily populated but not as densely as the green. If the Chinese government focuses all or most of its efforts on saving the cities, the sparsely populated area in the middle could provide free range to millions of Converted. They could survive for months, if not years."

Murray shook his head. "The Converted won't last that long. They'd starve. It's not like they can go out and farm or something, not without being seen."

Cheng seemed uncomfortable, like he was holding something back.

André Vogel stood.

"The Converted don't need to farm," he said. "We just received a firsthand account from a field agent in Baltimore, uploaded before he died. I have images. They are . . . disturbing."

Murray waved toward the monitor. "We're all big boys and girls, Vogel. Put the damn pictures on the screen already."

The map of China faded, replaced by a picture of a dead woman. Murray heard people hiss in a shocked breath, heard one man gag.

The woman lay face-up, staring at the sky. She would have been staring, that is, if she had any eyes. Most of her face had been ripped away, leaving a skeleton smile streaked with rusty red and crusty black. Arms and legs all showed patches of exposed bone.

"Another dead body," Murray said. "So what?"

Vogel pulled out his handkerchief. "The agent said he saw Converted consuming this woman."

Consuming. *Eating.*

Porter sagged in his chair. "The ultimate infantry. God dammit. They don't need to grow food or forage — they eat what they kill."

Deathly silences had become a regular occurrence in the Situation Room. Now Murray sat through another one, taking a moment to think.

Even if as much as 25 percent of the Chinese population became converted, that still left nine hundred million bodies' worth of edible human-on-the-hoof.

Murray had harbored no illusions about the overwhelming magnitude of this situation, but now an even harsher truth started to hit home.

"Immunity alone isn't going to do it," he said quietly. "We have to find a way to kill these fucking things, *all* of them, or we're facing an extinction event — we'll be *gone*. Someone wake up the president. And get Margaret Montoya on this screen, right now."

BREAKFAST

As impossible as it seemed, Cooper Mitchell slept like the dead — right up until the smell of roasting meat brought him out of it. His mouth watered for a few seconds, then filled with bile when he realized exactly what that smell was.

Sofia.

He opened his eyes. The people sleeping just a few feet away: why did they think he was one of them? If they figured out he was not, then *he* would be the one sizzling over the fire.

He was in the small lobby of the Park Tower hotel. Before everything went to shit, this must have been an opulent place: marble floor, black-stone columns supporting a tastefully lit ceiling, art on the teak walls and glass display cases full of large, expensive fossils. Now it looked like he'd slipped back in time to when the Neanderthals lived in caves.

Wind blew in through the broken glass of the main entrance. It had been a revolving door once, but most of it had been torn away; Cooper guessed someone had rammed a truck through it, then driven off. As you came in that open space, feet crunching on broken glass, to the left were the trashed display cases and waist-high windows — shattered, of course — that opened up onto snow-covered Chicago Avenue.

He was as far away from those windows as he could get, maybe forty feet straight back, lying on the hard floor with his shoulder pressed up against the lobby's far wall. His new "friends" had built a fire here. A layer of smoke floated near the ceiling, swirling slightly from the wind that came in off the street. To his right were the remains of the reception counter, much of which had been torn away to keep the fire going.

He didn't want to be anywhere near the crackling flames, but the cold wouldn't let him stray far. That meant he had to stay close to the thick pile of hot coals, and to the makeshift spit the others had crafted from street signs.

On that spit, a naked, sizzling, blackened Sofia, a signpost shoved through her mouth, down her throat and out her ass.

The Tall Man slowly rotated her. He stopped for a second, raised a fist to his mouth as his body contracted in a wheezing cough. The skin at Sofia's right shoulder split. Juices bubbled out, dripped down to hiss against the coals, sending up a ribbon of steam that rose past her cooking body.

She counted on you. You told her you'd save her and you shot her you shot her you coward you murderer but I had to I don't want to die . . .

The skin on Sofia's head had shrunken, cracked, showed some of the white skull beneath. Someone had already eaten her eyes; empty sockets gazed out. And yet for all the damage, he still recognized her face.

Cooper sensed someone coming up from behind. He closed his eyes, pretended to be asleep. If he flinched, if he lost it and started running, they would know he wasn't one of them.

A hand patting his back, a friendly *thump-thump* that felt like being smacked with a heavy mallet. Each connection filled Cooper with an eruption of fear. His heart threatened to blast right out of his chest. He kept his eyes closed.

Stay still stay still don't flinch don't panic don't run . . .

Another *thump-thump*. Cooper couldn't fake sleep any longer. He opened his eyes — it was the Monstrosity Formerly Known as Jeff, crouching down on his heels. Jeff's pale-yellow face broke into a long-toothed smile.

"COOOOPERRRR."

Cooper came very close to shitting himself.

"Hey, Jeff," he said. What else *could* he say?

Jeff's horrid smile widened. A gnarled hand reached up — Cooper flinched, knew the bone-blade sticking out of Jeff's forearm would punch right through him, but then the pale, white scythe pointed to the ceiling. Jeff's gnarled fingers slid across his own scalp, lifted imaginary hair away from his swollen, yellow forehead. It was an instinctive motion, one he had made hundreds of thousands of times in his life, but his light-brown locks were no more. The fingers barely moved the few strands of hair that clung wetly to his scalp.

"COOOOOPERRRR . . . YOU HURT?" Monster Jeff rubbed his chest, then his stomach. "HURT INSIDE?"

Cooper glanced around the room, at all the others who had yet to rise. Were *they* sick? If so, should Cooper pretend to be the same way?

Jesus Christ save me get me out of this I swear I'll lead a better life Jesus please please please . . .

The Tall Man coughed again, worse this time, the convulsion making him double over.

Fake it be like them whatever it takes be like them . . .

"Yeah," Cooper said. "I hurt, Jeff. Inside."

He looked around at the band of murderous cannibals. Two were asleep. The other three sat near the fire, one sneezing, the last two coughing, just like the Tall Man was.

And those coughs . . . wet . . . powerful . . . familiar.

They sound just like Chavo did.

Monster Jeff stood. He turned toward the spit, his thick body blocking the firelight and casting a shadow across the marble floor. His left hand reached out; the bone-blade stabbed into Sofia's blackened butt cheek. He used the right-hand blade to slice at the charred corpse, then lifted his left arm — stuck on the point of his scythe was a chunk of whitish meat, still steaming and sizzling and popping.

Jeff turned, extended his left arm toward Cooper.

The hunk of meat dangled inches from Cooper's face. Juice dribbled down to the floor.

"EAT," Monster Jeff said. "FORRRR, STRENGTH."

Cooper gagged. In the same moment, he brought his fist to his mouth, hid the gag with a forced follow-up cough. He coughed again, made it as loud as he could, let everyone see it and hear it.

Fake it be like them whatever it takes be like them . . .

He looked over at the Tall Man, who was biting into a greasy handful of flesh. Chewing.

Be like them . . .

Cooper reached out and gripped the handful of hot meat, slid it off Jeff's hideous, pointy bone-blade — Sofia's flesh came free with a slight *squelching* sound and another bomb-run pattern of juice.

Jeff smiled his long-toothed smile.

Cooper Mitchell was going crazy. He knew it, he could *feel* it, because only a crazy murderer-coward would do this unforgivable thing to stay alive.

If he had to choose between sanity and death, he'd wear the straitjacket well. That was the price of life.

Cooper raised the piece of Sofia to his mouth. He hoped no one could see the tears that stung the corners of his eyes, or, if they could, that they'd think it was from the coughing.

He bit down, and tasted her.

BAT TWELVE

"Factories?" Blackmon said. "They're destroying our factories?"

Nancy Whittaker was the latest bearer of bad news, and her news was a doozy. If Murray hadn't been so bone-tired, he would have felt sympathy for the woman.

"No question, Madam President," Whittaker said. "Four hours ago, CNN covered an attack on a brewery in Bakersfield. After that, the Converted started attacking breweries, bakeries and transportation centers all over the country. The methods are different in each city, so it doesn't look like a coordinated attack. The news coverage must have given them the idea."

Blackmon slapped the table. "But we protected those facilities! We assigned police, National Guard, even what regular army we could spare."

"From what we can gather, the Converted know enough to attack in large numbers," Whittaker said. "In some places, they overwhelmed defense forces. In others . . ." Whittaker cleared her throat, tried to work out the final words. "In others, it appears that some Guard members and police were Converted themselves."

Blackmon's face reddened slightly. "How much production capacity have we lost?"

"Around sixty percent, so far," Whittaker said. "But the attacks are still under way. We assume we'll lose at least another twenty percent."

Blackmon fell back into her chair, as if an invisible hand had gently pushed her. She stared off.

Everyone waited. Murray didn't know what she would decide next. She'd pinned America's hopes on high levels of inoculation. The Converted were taking that option away.

"Director Longworth," she said. "How bad does this hurt us?"

Murray wanted to give her something positive, but there was no way to put a happy face on the facts.

"If our production is cut by eighty percent, our strategy isn't sustainable," he said. "We won't be able to produce enough of Feely's yeast. In a week,

maybe two, even the people we've already immunized will again be susceptible."

Blackmon sighed. She had moved heaven and earth to do the impossible.
With one simple, strategic shift, the Converted all but wiped out the gains
she had made.

"Director Vogel," she said. "What is the status of finding other patients
who had the same stem cell procedure as Candice Walker?"

"There were ten patients in the trial," Vogel said. "Eight — including Candice Walker — were from the western Michigan area, which is completely
overrun by the Converted. One other was from New York, and one from Germany. We haven't found any of them. We're doing the best we can, but I'm
not hopeful. We've put the word out to news organizations. Our best chance
is that one of the patients will see the story and contact us."

The president nodded, just a little, as if to say *that's less than helpful, idiot*.
She turned to Murray "Is Montoya on the line?"

"Yes, Madam President."

"Put her on the screen."

Murray did. Margaret appeared, sitting at the *Coronado*'s small conference table. She looked better than the last time Murray had seen her. Margaret seemed sharp, intelligent, with a serious stare that rivaled Blackmon's best.

"Hello, Doctor Montoya," the president said. "It's good to see you well."

"Thank you," Margaret said. "Truth be told, I've never felt better."

Blackmon put her hands palms down on the table, made slow circles as
she talked.

"Our inoculation strategy has suffered a setback," she said. "We might
not be able to sustain repeated dosing of those who have had a first round of
treatment."

Margaret nodded. "I'm not surprised. It was too big of a project to work.
I told you to pursue the hydra solution. You, Murray, Cheng — you didn't
listen to me."

"We didn't," Blackmon said. "And we're doing everything we can to track
down the other HAC stem cell patients. I ignored your advice once, Doctor
Montoya, I won't do so again. If we can't find those patients, what else can be
done?"

Margaret stayed still, showed little reaction, but Murray had known this
woman for years. Her eyes squinted a little, wrinkled at the corners. That only

happened when she laughed. Was Margaret trying to hold back a smile at all this?

"*What else can be done*," she said, mimicking Blackmon's words. "I gave you a solution, you didn't use it. Now it's too late. There are no other options. It's over."

Blackmon's demeanor darkened. "So you've given up? You, the undefeatable Doctor Margaret Montoya, you want us to just roll over and die?"

Margaret shrugged. "Ninety-nine-point-nine percent of all the species that ever lived on this planet were extinct before our ancestors even discovered fire. Extinction is the rule of life, not the exception. Humankind doesn't get a special exemption, Madam President."

Blackmon's lips tightened into a thin line.

"Doctor Montoya, I find it hard to believe God would let his greatest creation be snuffed out."

"You religious types have a saying, I believe," Margaret said. "*The Lord works in mysterious ways.* Extinction occurs because a species gets outcompeted for territory and resources — or just gets eaten. From observations and the reports we have so far, the Converted are faster, stronger and more ruthless than normal humans."

Murray noticed that Margaret had avoided the phrases *evolution* and *survival of the fittest*. Maybe she didn't want her message to get lost in the details.

The rest of the Situation Room seemed to fade into the shadows. Somehow this had become a battle of wills between Montoya and Blackmon.

"The Converted can't win," the president said. "We've got the weapons and the technology."

Margaret held up her hands, wiggled her fingers. "The Converted have *these*, just like we do. They can use the same weapons we use. And our high-tech tanks and planes give us an advantage only as long as there is gas to run them, places to repair them. Once the fuel and bullets run out, Madam President, this fight will come down to knives and spears and rocks. If that happens, humanity will lose."

The president's hands curled into fists, fists that pressed down on the table. The predator's gaze tightened — at that moment, she *hated* Margaret Montoya.

"You are *wrong*," Blackmon said. "I have faith that we will find a way."

"The wonderful thing about science, Madam President, is that it doesn't ask for your faith, it just asks for your eyes. In a week, you'll be looking at three-quarters of a *billion* psychopaths spread out across the world. Even the most powerful army on the planet can't handle . . ."

Margaret's words trailed off. She blinked, raised her eyebrows, shook her head a little. Murray had seen her do that before, too — Margaret did that when she'd been lost in a train of thought and wanted to come back to the present.

"Sorry," she said. "Listen to me, Madam President. Please. You need me there with you. I know we can find a way to beat this thing. I'm clean. I'm immunized. Fly me to D.C., *today*, and I'll be by your side."

That was the best idea Murray had heard all day. Cheng's fat ass could stay on Black Manitou. Margaret was right — the real brains of the operation belonged here, in the Situation Room.

André Vogel suddenly stood up, fingers pressed to his earpiece.

"Madam President, we just received actual footage of one of the larger forms."

Blackmon nodded quickly. "Doctor Montoya, we'll get back to you shortly."

Margaret started to say something, but Vogel cut her off. The monitor flashed with low-resolution video, black and oversaturated white — typical output from the cameras on combat aircraft.

"This is from Manhattan," Vogel said. "Seventy-Second and Columbus."

"Manhattan is cut off," Blackmon said. "Didn't we blow all the bridges?"

Vogel nodded. "Yes, Madam President, we did. A Pave Hawk helicopter was collecting reconnaissance footage and captured this."

The image on the screen looked slightly fuzzy, the signature of a camera pushed beyond its range. Still, Murray could easily make out a mixture of five- to ten-story buildings, the redbrick and tan concrete so common in New York.

Two people ran down the middle of the street, cutting in and out of the burned-out vehicles that littered the pavement. Farther back, a dozen others gave chase.

It was recorded, Murray knew that, but he silently willed the two front-runners to move faster.

More people poured out of doorways, alleys, some even from the interior of vehicles. They all joined the pursuers. The pack swelled to two dozen, then three, then *four*.

The distance between the hunted and the hunters shrank.

Vogel paused the playback. "The next voice you hear is the Pave Hawk pilot." He let the video continue.

The pilot keyed his mic, filling the Situation Room with the scratchy sound of the helicopter's engines and rotor.

"Command, Bat Twelve, I have two civilians being pursued by hostiles, request immediate permission to engage."

"Negative, Bat Twelve," came back an even scratchier voice. "You don't know who is healthy."

"I can fucking *see* it," said the pilot. "There are these . . . *things* . . . in the pack, chasing them, things that aren't human."

The image zoomed in on the pursuers. In the cluster of blurry, sprinting people, Murray saw something that was bigger than the rest. *Much* bigger.

Vogel paused the playback. On the screen, a hideous, out-of-focus creature was hurdling a Toyota. Shredded clothes, sickly yellow skin, a head and neck so big they made its face look disproportionately tiny. It carried some kind of long blade in each hand.

A wide-eyed Blackmon slid a hand into a pocket. It came out holding a gold chain, swinging slightly from the weight of a dangling gold cross.

"Jesus Christ," she said. "Satan walks among us. Let it play."

Vogel did.

The picture whipped back to the hunted. Murray saw that the woman had something clutched to her chest.

A baby.

The pilot spoke again. "Command, the woman appears to be carrying a child. Moving to engage."

"*Negative*, Bat Twelve," said the second voice. "Do not engage!"

Bat Twelve, apparently, wasn't interested in listening to orders.

"Right and left guns, engage the targets chasing the woman and child. You're cleared hot!"

The image vibrated slightly as the Pave Hawk's guns opened up. Long streaks of white shot out, slammed into pursuers, cars and pavement alike.

Some of the pursuers stopped moving, some scattered sideways, but most continued the chase. Among the crowd, Murray saw tiny flashes of light.

"Hostiles are returning fire," the pilot said calmly. "Where they hell did they get all those guns?"

The helicopter kept firing, but there were too many pursuers. Others came pouring out of doorways, cutting off any escape for the two — no, the *three* — hunted people. There was nowhere left to run.

The mob closed in from all sides. The man, woman and child vanished beneath a quickly growing pile of killers.

Vogel switched it off. The ever-increasing numbers of infected, Converted and dead took their normal place on the screen.

Blackmon stared. She scratched her right eyebrow. The Situation Room filled with another, familiar long silence.

"All those guns," she said. "Where did the Converted get all those guns?"

Murray laughed. He choked it down instantly, but he was so tired he couldn't help the reaction.

"Sorry," he said. "Madam President, we are the most well-armed nation in the world. There are a quarter-billion guns in the United States — the Converted didn't have to look far."

Millions of guns. Millions of Converted. Millions of *armed insurgents*. Could it get any worse?

As if on cue, Admiral Porter leaned forward again, a phone still pressed to his ear.

"Madam President, I regret to inform you that we have word from Fort Stewart and Hunter Army Airfield in Georgia. They each suffered coordinated attacks by a large number of Converted, and" — he paused, swallowed — "and significant numbers of soldiers stationed at those facilities assisted in the assault."

Blackmon's gold cross dangled.

"Reinforcements," she said. "Let's get them help. What do we have in the area?"

Porter shook his head. "Fort Stewart has *fallen*, Madam President. So has Hunter. Both facilities are now in enemy hands. The Third Infantry Division was stationed at Fort Stewart — that division has been destroyed. And we've also got word that Andrews AFB is under organized attack."

Murray's body sagged. Third Infantry, the *Rock of the Marne*, a unit that had fought in both World Wars, in Korea and Iraq, over fifteen thousand soldiers . . . completely wiped out. And Andrews AFB, where *Air Force One* resided, under attack. The base also housed the 121st Fighter Squadron, an irreplaceable asset.

But far more important than the base's aircraft was its geographical location.

Andrews AFB was just twelve short miles from Washington, D.C.

THE RESPONSIBLE PARTY

"COOOOPERRRR. SICK?"

Cooper wasn't sick. At least not physically; he'd eaten human flesh — what could be sicker than that?

Do what you have to so you can stay alive. Whatever it takes.

He sat cross-legged on a pile of clothes, probably gathered from one of the hotel rooms on the floors above. The fire warmed his face and chest. He held his gun in both hands. The barrel rested on his calves.

The Monster Formerly Known as Jeff sat next to him. It could almost have been a campfire scene, maybe a hunting trip to the Upper Peninsula, the two of them drinking Labatt, staring at the stars and talking about women.

Cooper wished the transformation had been more severe, that Jeff's face didn't look like *Jeff*, but the eyes, the nose . . . no mistaking his lifelong friend.

Jeff wanted to know if Cooper was ill. Cooper was trying to decide if he could put the barrel of his pistol to Jeff's ear and pull the trigger.

Shoot him shoot him but if you miss or don't kill him he'll kill you he'll eat you . . .

"COOOOPERRRR?"

"Yeah, Jeff," Cooper said. "I'm sick."

Other than Jeff, the cannibals were out of commission. They were sick, obviously hurting pretty bad. Even the Tall Man was down for the count.

Jeff reached a hand behind Cooper. Cooper froze . . . he tried to lift the gun, but he couldn't move a muscle.

Please God make this stop make him go away make him go away I want to live I want to live I—

Something touched his head. Something hard. Something *pointy*. The bone-blade. Jeff was going to carve him up, rip him to shreds.

Get up and run and fight shoot him shoot him no-no-no you'll miss you can't win play dead please God please don't let him kill me please.

Cooper started to tremble.

The thing touched his head again, only it wasn't the bone-blade at all . . .

it was Jeff's fingers, brushing from Cooper's temple to the top of his head. He felt the same thing a third time, and a fourth.

He's petting me. He thinks I'm sick and he's petting my head.

"EVERRRRYONE . . . HURTS. WILLLL GO FIND . . . HELP."

The fingers stroked Cooper's hair one last time, then Jeff stood. He lumbered to the front of the hotel lobby. He walked out the ruined rotating door and vanished into the night.

Cooper slowly stood. He scanned the ravaged, smoky lobby to see if any of the killers were looking at him.

They weren't. They were too busy dying.

The Tall Man's eyes leaked yellow fluid, not all that different in color and consistency from the phlegm coating his nose and mouth. He was still coughing, still sneezing, but was too weak to wipe the goo away.

Cooper walked closer. The man's rheumy eyes opened and closed, the stringers of yellow mucus that ran between his eyelids bouncing in time. His throat made a wet sound.

This was the man who ate Sofia.

You ate her too, you ate her too . . .

"I only had one serving, you *fuck*!"

Cooper took a step back: he'd just yelled at himself.

You are so fucking crazy you're going off the deep end man get control . . .

"Shut up, shut *up*!"

He scrunched his eyes tight. He rubbed the pistol barrel against his right temple.

You've got the gun use it use it . . .

Use it on the Tall Man? No need. The Tall Man didn't have much time left. None of these assholes did.

Or . . . maybe it was better if Cooper used it on himself.

He shook his head, shook it hard. No, he couldn't think like that. He could make it out alive. He *could*. But if he couldn't, if people like the Tall Man got him, if they were going to shove a stop sign up his ass and out his mouth, roast him over a fire . . .

Was eating a bullet better than just being eaten?

The Tall Man coughed again. Phlegm came up, but this time so did blood. A thick, dark-red glob clung to his chin.

He's coughing blood. Chavo was coughing blood . . .

Cooper heard yelling from the street. He held the gun against his thigh as he slowly walked to a broken window. He crouched, peeking just over the sill's jagged glass.

Outside, he saw two women sprinting for their lives. Behind them, seven or eight screaming people carrying knives, hatchets, one carrying a shotgun by the barrel as if it were a club. Running alongside the hunters were two hulking, pale-yellow creatures with tiny faces and rippling muscles. Were either of them Jeff? No, they weren't — Cooper would have recognized his friend, monstrous or not.

He couldn't help those two women. He hadn't saved Sofia, so he sure as *fuck* wasn't going to get himself killed over a pair of strangers.

He watched the pursuers, the ones who still looked like normal people. Why weren't they sick like the Tall Man and his crew? Why weren't they sick like Chavo?

Wind blew through the ruined window, scattering snow in Cooper's face. He walked back to the fire. No one had tended it for a while, nor tended to Sofia. Curls of orange heat wavered through the bed of coals, the flickering light playing off her blackened, burned, half-eaten corpse.

Cooper looked away. He had to get out of there, but he wasn't setting foot on those streets. No fucking way. Someone had to rescue him, someone with lots of guns, but who? Were news stations telling people how to get help? He hadn't seen a working TV since he and Sofia fled the Trump Tower. If he still had his cell phone, he could have tried reaching cops in other cities, maybe the army or the National Guard.

Then it hit him — he didn't have a phone, but his "group leader" did.

He walked back to the Tall Man.

"Your phone," Cooper said. "Give it to me."

The Tall Man stared up. His eyes narrowed in confusion — he was trying to focus, trying to see.

Cooper held out his hand. "Your phone."

The Tall Man blinked a few times. His eyes seemed to clear. He nodded. With great effort, he reached his right hand into his pants pocket and pulled out a flip-phone. He flipped it open with his right thumb. His left hand reached up to wrap around the top.

He twisted his hands and the phone *cracked* sickeningly, breaking into two pieces.

The Tall Man coughed, then laughed weakly. "I know now," he said. "I know you're not a friend."

Cooper wanted to stomp his face in. He wouldn't, though, at least not yet — the Tall Man was in great pain, and Cooper wanted him to suffer.

Cooper looked up at the ceiling. Most of the lights were out, broken by random psychos throwing random things for random reasons, but two of them shone bright.

The electricity . . . it was still on. Maybe he could find a hotel phone. If the power was on, maybe land lines still worked.

He looked at the registration desk, or what was left of it. The remains of three computers lay scattered on the broken wood. Computers . . . if he could get on the Internet, he could probably find out what was happening. He could find help. There had to be more computers around somewhere.

On the wall behind the registration desk, he saw a door.

A manager's office?

He walked to the door. He tried the handle: locked. Maybe the psychos hadn't been in there.

Cooper took another look around the lobby to make sure no one had gotten up, that no one was watching him.

No one was.

He set off to find something heavy.

WAITING . . .

Margaret Montoya sat on the bunk of her mission module. She had the lights off. The others thought she was sleeping, so they left her alone.

She'd handled that videoconference all wrong. She'd confronted the president with the harsh realities of life, had been unable to ignore Blackmon's superstitious, primitive tripe. Margaret should have pandered from the get-go, told Blackmon what the woman wanted to hear — anything to get an invitation to the White House. Margaret's rage had got the better of her, made her lose focus.

She could have gotten close enough to murder the president of the United States. Yes, Margaret would be killed in the process, but the act would further cripple America's ability to respond. A missed opportunity. Hopefully another of her kind, another *leader*, would figure out a way to get next to the president.

America would fall.

Then, the world.

If the opportunity came again, Margaret would seize it. For now, she worked on understanding God's plan, understanding the role of each caste.

The large, yellowish bipeds: that's what came out of the cocoons. The complete restructuring of an adult human body, creating a caste made to terrify, to destroy, to kill — a *soldier* joining the ranks of the hatchlings, puffballs, kissyfaces and leaders.

But without the Orbital, how would all these strains find each other? How could they work together?

The answer could be some kind of quorum sensing, the method hive insects, bacteria, and other nonintelligent life forms used to make what appeared to be conscious, intelligent choices: a bee colony "deciding" when to split into two smaller colonies and where to build the new nests; ants "deciding" how to best react to a threat; bacteria "deciding" to turn genes on or off based on population density. Chemical and physical cues led many individual organisms to act as a larger whole. The Converted clearly had a way of detecting one another and quickly forming cohesive units.

Maybe the crawlers provided a capacity to identify friend from foe. The best scientists in the world still hadn't figured out how the Orbital had communicated in real time to hundreds of infected individuals. That ability defied physics, yet she had seen it with her own eyes. If the Orbital could do that, it was reasonable it could also make a "Spidey sense" that let the infected know when they were near their kind.

Scent — could the explanation be that simple? A chemical on the host's breath, or exuded through his skin. Crawlers modified the host's brain: perhaps they adjusted the olfactory response, letting the Converted identify one another by smell alone. Maybe that was how Candice Walker had survived as long as she did. If this scent was a by-product of the cellulose, the Converted on the *Los Angeles* might have thought she was one of them, giving her more time to react, to plan.

Walker . . . now that Margaret understood a true God existed and guided its followers, she could only think of Walker in terms of another kind of religious figure.

Candice Walker had been the Antichrist.

The other patients from the HAC trial could also be Antichrists, the bringers of a plague that would wipe out Margaret's kind.

That was humanity's only hope, because without the hydras it was already over. The math didn't lie. She'd seen the numbers: *millions* of infected, *millions* of Converted. The exponential shift was already underway. In two weeks — three at the most — humans would be reduced to isolated groups, groups that couldn't trust one another because any one of them might be the enemy.

In four weeks, humans would be outnumbered.

In five weeks, *maybe* six, the only human survivors would be individuals hiding in the woods and mountains, living off the land.

And to think she'd been upset that she'd lost the hydra samples when evacuating the *Carl Brashear*.

Yes, God *did* work in mysterious ways . . .

She was more than willing to sacrifice herself if it sped up the change, if it brought the Converted to power. But if she was still alive when that change happened? Then she could start taking control. She would gather the most brilliant of her kind — the engineers, the physicists, the astronomers — organize them, figure out how to rebuild industry, how to create a civilization with one, unified goal:

Building more Orbitals, and sending them out into the galaxy.

THE EMPEROR

Steve Stanton's pencil was a blur as he finished writing his message. He handed the piece of paper to General Brownstone.

"Get that to the people."

She saluted. "Right away, Emperor!"

Dana Brownstone was a retired four-star general who had once run the U.S. Army Materiel Command. She was smart: a leader, just like him. Steve had big plans for her. She had already organized distribution of cell phones and weapons, created a detailed message-flow structure that improved Steve's ability to control over two hundred thousand Converted spread throughout the greater Chicago area.

Brownstone handed the paper to a runner.

"Make a hundred copies of that," she said. "Pass ten copies each to the primary level of cell leaders, have them pass it down to their sub-tens. Go."

The runner took off down the Institute of Art's wide steps. Steve would have to change locations soon. Too long in one spot made him a potential target for bombers, helicopters, or even inoculated commandos that might drop in.

Elsewhere in America, other leaders — who didn't seem to have Steve's special brand of foresight — were organizing large groups that destroyed everything they could find. The leaders who used the Internet for these "activist" calls to action were opening themselves up to the government's sniffer programs and computer analysts. Might as well put up a big, neon sign that said ENEMY OF THE STATE: DROP BOMBS HERE.

Steve knew too much to let that happen.

He still used phones and the Internet, of course, but only for messages coded to sound like the natural language of people panicking while the world collapsed around them. By using instant messaging, online forums, social media sites, texts, tweets, blog posts and comments — as well as the "sneaker net" of human feet — he could communicate with all his people while staying well under the government's radar.

Steve walked to a table where he'd set up his information lab. A follower sat at each of his three laptops, calling up websites, blogs, newscasts, anything that would give him the big picture.

The U.S. government had written off Manhattan. Minneapolis, too, by the looks of things, and — just a few hours earlier — Chicago. Paris was a memory. The British had barricaded London: no one in, no one out. That strategy hadn't worked in Chicago, and wasn't going to work there, either.

No info out of China. None at all. That was fine, because Steve could give a shit about China. He'd been born in America, and that was where he'd be crowned emperor.

The U.S. government had yet to pull the plug on the Internet. With several of the major networks down and more soon to follow — CNN showed nothing but color bars, ABC's feed was a constant hiss of static — the government needed the Internet to spread information to the uninfected: go here to be safe; stay away from these areas; here is your testing center; this place has inoculations available.

And, of course, monitoring the Internet was the government's main way to track down those large groups of Converted. Steve didn't mind that at all — anyone who could organize such a group was an eventual rival for power. If someone removed Steve's rivals for him? All the better.

He heard a cell phone buzz. Brownstone answered it, then held it out to him.

"Your uncle Sven," she said.

Uncle Sven was one of her names for the scouts who were hunting for higher-powered weapons. Pistols and shotguns just weren't enough.

Steve took the phone. "What is it?"

"It's Sven," said the voice on the other end — a bad attempt to sound panicked, but close enough. "I found out where Nate Grissom is, he's in town."

The scouts had found an armory. The "N.G." of "Nate Grissom" stood for "National Guard." A simple code, but with the country in a tailspin, no government analyst was going to figure it out — if anyone was even listening at all.

"Awesomesauce," Steve said. "Do you think you can take my cousins and go get him?"

"Yeah," the voice said. "I got inside info."

Inside info: that meant the scout's group included someone who had served at that facility.

"Okay," Steve said. "Then go get Nate."

Steve hung up. It was the third such call he'd received in the last hour. By morning, General Brownstone would be overseeing the distribution of military weapons.

THERE'S BAD NEWS, AND BAD NEWS

The wind had picked up, the fire had died down. The hotel lobby was colder than ever.

Cooper Mitchell lined up the bottom of the fire extinguisher, then jammed it down on the door handle. The metal *clinked* but didn't break.

He looked around, seeing if anyone or anything reacted. He remained alone except for the sick people lying around the fire.

He waited a few more seconds, just to be sure, then lifted the extinguisher again.

Clink, the door handle bent.

He drove the fire extinguisher down a third time: the handle ripped free and clattered against the floor. He slid his cold fingers into the hole, found the latch mechanism and pulled it sideways — he pushed the door open.

Inside was a tiny office, various calendars and work regulation posters tacked to the walls, just one overstuffed desk with a chair tucked under it. On that desk, various family pictures . . .

. . . and one black laptop, flipped open and waiting.

The screen was dark.

Cooper pushed the door shut behind him. The tiny room was much like the space behind the Walgreens counter. He thought of his last few moments with Sofia.

But she'll be with you forever now won't she because you ate her and you're digesting her and she'll be part of your muscles and part of your bones forever and ever and ever . . .

Cooper shook his head, tried to clear his thoughts.

A phone on the desk: he grabbed the handset, heard nothing. The line was dead.

He sat down in the desk chair. He was almost afraid to touch the computer. If it didn't turn on, he was out of options — he'd have to risk leaving on foot, all by himself against a city of cannibals.

Cooper tapped the space bar. The computer screen remained black for a moment, then flared to life.

Oh shit, it's working it's working . . .

He searched for a web browser icon. He found one, clicked it. The computer made small whirring noises. The Google home page flared to life. News, he needed news.

He called up *cnn.com*. The website's familiar red banner and white-lettered logo appeared. Below that, pictures of horror, of death, of a country on fire. Glowing headlines showed city names that read like a list of tourist attractions if you didn't count the words next to them, words like *ablaze, destruction, thousands dead . . .*

New York City.
London.
Minneapolis.
Berlin.
Philadelphia.
Boston.
Paris.
Miami.
Baltimore.

And, of course, *Chicago.*

"It's everywhere," he said. "Everywhere."

He clicked for additional news on *Chicago.* More stories appeared. All roads and highways had been blocked off, sometimes by trenches or collapsed overpasses, more often by miles of burned-out cars.

Cooper finally understood why the military hadn't come in to save Chicago . . . because the military had instead *blockaded* Chicago. At least that's what the news said. The military wasn't letting anyone in or out. The story said troops were preparing to reenter the city and take it by force: until then, all citizens were warned to remain inside, to not answer the door for anyone, not even family. Stay off the phones, don't overwhelm the cellular networks.

He nodded rapidly, yes, *yes* they were coming in, he just had to stay alive a little while longer . . .

And then he noticed the story's date. It was from yesterday. He started clicking through links, found that the *entire site* hadn't been updated in the last twenty hours.

Could CNN actually be down? The whole thing?

Cooper tried the Yahoo home page; it came up instantly with a huge, red headline:

CHICAGO: ABANDONED

"No," he said. He read the story, each word a crushing blow to his soul. "This *can't* be fucking happening."

The U.S. government had written off Chicago. No troops were coming in. Troops weren't even surrounding the city anymore . . . too much territory to cover. Those forces had been moved to protect cities that had not yet been overrun.

He couldn't be alone here, trapped with madmen and monsters.

Cooper kept searching, kept clicking, hitting the track pad so hard the desk vibrated. After five minutes of panicked reading, a story caught his eye:

GOVERNMENT WORKING ON BIOLOGICAL
WARFARE AGAINST CONVERTED

(Reuters) — Anonymous sources out of Washington, D.C., are reporting that the government is developing a biological weapon that will target the "Converted" who are raging across the country and are responsible for thousands of deaths worldwide.

An unnamed source said that the new weapon is actually a modified version of the pathogen responsible for creating the violent Converted in the first place. This "disease for the disease" is lethal to the Converted, but reportedly does no harm to people who have not yet been infected.

The modified version originates from people who have had a rare form of stem cell therapy known as "HAC-12b." When those patients become infected, the modified stem cells alter the nature of the pathogen, turning it into the biological weapon sorely needed to combat the Converted.

Anyone who has had this therapy should contact the government via the attached links at the bottom of this story.

Cooper couldn't breathe. He stared at the screen until the words blurred, until they moved on their own, jiggling on the screen like wiggly black cartoon worms.

Everything connected.

His stem cell therapy . . . no way, no *way*.

This disease began with whatever Steve Stanton pulled up from the bottom of Lake Michigan. Stanton apparently became some kind of Grand Dragon leader or something. Jeff got sick, turned into that *thing*.

Cooper got sick, too, but then he got better.

He thought back to the hotel, that first night with Sofia. Chavo had come in while they slept. Had Chavo already been sick, or did he get sick because he was in the room with Cooper?

When the Tall Man and his friends first caught Cooper and Sofia at the Walgreens, they'd seemed healthy. Then they'd spent the night in the hotel lobby with Cooper, breathing the same air as Cooper . . . and now those people were all sick, just like Chavo had been.

Cooper felt at the back of his neck. A shred of hanging skin, still there, left over from the blister Sofia had pointed out the day before. It had *popped* like a little puffball, squirted out a tiny cloud of white . . .

He forgot about the icy temperature, tore off his coat and shirt. He examined his body, found a dozen small, puffy spots filled with air, and at least another dozen that had already torn open.

It's me . . . I'm the reason . . .

Cooper rushed out of the office and back into the ruined lobby. He looked at the Tall Man, who was clearly dying. Two of the others were already dead, lifeless eyes staring out at nothing.

"I'm contagious," Cooper said. "I'm the reason they're dead." He looked to the blackened corpse above the dying fire.

"You hear that, Sofia? I got them for you. I got 'em good. I'm real sorry I had to eat you, *real* sorry. I just have to find a better place to hide, maybe a room upstairs, wait for the government to send people to save me, and then . . ."

His voice trailed off. Someone would come for him, sure, but what then? Would they lock him up and study him? The government barely gave a shit about civil rights when everything was fine; with the world going straight to hell, they would do anything they wanted with him.

Contacting the government, telling them he'd had the HAC therapy, that was his only chance to live. But he also had to find a way to make sure regular people knew about him, knew what he had inside of him — otherwise, he might vanish at the hands of the good guys just as easily as he could at the hands of the psychotic fuck-stains who had taken over Chicago.

The laptop . . . at the top of the screen, there had been a tiny, reddish dot . . .

. . . a camera.

Cooper rushed back into the office.

YOUTUBE

IMMUNIZED: 84%

NOT IMMUNIZED: 10%

UNKNOWN: 6%

FINISHED DOSES EN ROUTE: 30,000,000

DOSES IN PRODUCTION: 12,000,000

INFECTED: 2,616,000 (15,350,000)

CONVERTED: 2,115,000 (6,500,000)

DEATHS: 284,000 (14,100,000)

The Converted were coming.

Blackmon's people were trying to hurry her out of the Situation Room, but she was still the president and no one could make her go any faster than she wanted to. The time had long passed for her to be airborne, safely away from the rapidly deteriorating situation on the ground.

The army had reported contact with at least five large mobs of Converted in and around the city of Washington, D.C. The mobs seemed poorly organized, poorly armed, but they all had one thing in common: they had been heading for the White House.

Air Force One — known as *Air Force Two* just yesterday — had landed at Ronald Reagan National Airport, delivering Vice President Kenneth Albertson. The military maintained firm control of that airport. After Fort Benning and Andrews AFB had fallen, the Joint Chiefs had issued "kill zone" orders for all critical facilities. No matter who you were, infected or not, if you came within a hundred yards of a protected area, you got shot.

Blackmon was heading to the airport. Albertson was on his way to the White House to take her place. The American people knew him. With his face broadcasting from the nation's capital, it would remain clear that America had not fallen.

Not yet.

But Blackmon was a realist, and knew that worst-case scenario might come to pass. Elena Turgenson, the Speaker of the House, was third in the presidential line of succession. Blackmon had ordered her to Sacramento, to set up the next governmental seat in the eventuality that the Converted over-ran D.C.

Blackmon's aides were all ready to follow her out. They held stacks of paper, briefcases, and laptops. She had cleaned up for the trip: hair done up right and a freshly pressed red pantsuit gave her that hallmark *presidential look* once again. She was waiting for Vogel to finish talking on the phone. Someone had submitted info to the HAC site, and apparently linked to a video.

Vogel whispered something, nodded, then hung up.

"Identity confirmed," he said. "The subject is Cooper Mitchell. SSN and address are accurate. Facial analysis software registers a one-hundred percent match with DMV records. There is no question that this man was part of the HAC study."

Blackmon let out a little puffed-cheek *whuff* of air.

"We have a chance," she said. "Play the video."

A paused YouTube page appeared on the main monitor. The frozen image was a blur of blacks and grays. Murray couldn't make anything out.

"*YouTube?*" Blackmon said. "This video is *public?*"

Vogel nodded. "Yes, Madam President. It seems Mister Mitchell didn't fully trust our HAC form. He wanted to make sure everyone saw him, so he couldn't — I'm quoting from his submission form — *just vanish into a secret lab, you goddamn government shiteaters.* End quote. The video's play counter only shows three hundred and one views so far, which isn't much. We're still in control of this information."

Blackmon nodded. "Play it."

The image twitched and jumped, jostled by rapid movement. The face in the video belonged to the man holding the camera — Cooper Mitchell. He looked panicked, had the sunken eyes of someone who had flat-out gone over the edge. A week's worth of stubble. Skin red and cracked from exposure to wind and cold.

"It's *me*," Mitchell said. "They come around me and they die. It takes, uh, maybe like twelve hours or so, but they *die*."

He started laughing.

4 1 2 SCOTT SIGLER

The sound of that laugh made Murray's blood run cold. He'd laughed like that once, back in Vietnam, when he, Dew Phillips and six other men had heard the choppers coming to save them. Eight soldiers — all that remained from an entire company. They'd been overrun, covered in mud, fighting for their lives through the night in dark, sandbagged trenches. Murray had known his time was up, *known* he was going to die, right up until he'd heard those rotor blades slicing through the air. That sliver of sound had given him the strength to fight on.

The image jostled as Mitchell walked, but stayed centered on his face. The background moved madly around him.

"Just *look* at this," he said. "How fucked-up is this?"

The image skewed as he turned the camera around. Murray saw a fire pit topped with a pig mounted on a spit. At first, he thought the scene was somewhere outdoors — because that's the only place one *saw* fire pits — but then he realized it was inside the lobby of a trashed building.

Then, he realized it wasn't a pig.

"Jesus Christ," President Blackmon said. Her hand went to the cross hanging from her neck.

The image whirled to show a man in a red jacket, lying on his back. At first Murray thought this man was also dead, *had* to be dead from the tacky phlegm that coated his mouth and nose, but the man's eyes cracked opened. The eyelids looked nearly glued shut by strands of viscous yellow.

The man looked at the camera for a moment, then coughed hard. Blood bubbled out of his mouth.

"See that?" Cooper Mitchell said from off-screen. "Fucker is dying, man! *Dying!*"

The camera spun again, stopping on a prone woman. Her blank eyes stared out. Dried, bloody spittle flaked from the lips of an open mouth. On the woman's neck, peeking out from the jacket, Murray saw the shape that had marked the beginning of this horror show . . .

A triangle.

One of the triangle's slitted eyelids was slightly open — but instead of the glistening black Murray expected to see, there was a sagging, puckered, grayish membrane, like a party balloon that had almost fully deflated.

The shaking camera whipped around to once again focus on Mitchell. He leaned in close, until the screen showed only his wide, bloodshot eyes.

"*Dead! Dead as fuck! Because of me!* Someone come and get me, *please* come and get me, I make these assholes *die*! You want to save the world? Then you better fucking save *me*!"

The movie ended, leaving a blurred image of the too-close face up on the screen.

Blackmon looked shaken. Seeing an American citizen being cooked on a spit would do that to a person. She sat on the edge of the table, maybe to keep herself from collapsing. The polished surface reflected the bright red of her pantsuit.

"So this man could have Montoya's hydras," the president said. "Where is he?"

"Chicago," Vogel said. "Park Tower Hotel, downtown area."

Blackmon slid off the table, stood straight. She gave her pantsuit jacket a sharp tug downward, as if she were just about to go on camera.

"Admiral Porter, I want this man. What kind of resources do we have around Chicago?"

Porter shook his head. "We have nothing in that area, Madam President. All of Illinois is a mess. Converted have been spreading out from the Chicago-land area. We've got troops positioned at the nuke plants near Rockford and Wilmington, killing anything that comes close. Davenport and Champaign are part of that chain, trying to slow the spread from the suburbs. We could pull some of those forces, but doing so is going to widen the gaps the Converted can get through. Indianapolis is holding strong and I highly recommend we don't pull troops from there. Once we beat this thing, Madam President, we'll need those power plants and the industrial base of cities that weren't overrun."

"Screw the power plants," Blackmon said. "If we don't get this man, there won't be anyone left to *use* power."

The idea hit Murray fast, took him over and charged him up.

"The SEAL team that rescued Montoya," he said in a rush. "They're in quarantine on the *Coronado*. That ship could be off the shore of Chicago in hours, and it has two SH-60 Seahawk helicopters. The SEALs could go in, get Mitchell and bring him back out again."

Blackmon considered this. "Admiral? Will that work?"

Porter nodded. "Maybe. It's a damn good idea, but the city is overrun — a partial SEAL team probably isn't enough."

"Then get me something to back them up," Blackmon said. "Admiral, if we have any reserves at all, this is the time to use them."

Porter drew in a deep breath. Even at this late stage of the game, he wasn't going to rush things.

"We do have a few air-support assets on standby. The crews have been isolated from day one, so we know they're reliable. As for ground forces, I've got a Ranger company at Fort Benning. I was saving them for your security, Madam President. If *Air Force One* can't refuel in midair, or you have to land for whatever reason, that company will go to where you are, give you adequate protection."

She huffed. "My protection matters even less than those power plants, Admiral. Send the SEALs. Send the Rangers. Will that be enough?"

"It has to be," Porter said. "It's all we have left. We haven't seen the same organized forces in Chicago we've seen in Minneapolis or the New York boroughs, so this could work."

"God guide and defend our soldiers," Blackmon said. She addressed the entire room. "Ladies and gentlemen, I have to get to *Air Force One*. I have the utmost respect for your dedication and your bravery. The fate of our nation, of the entire world, hangs on us continuing to do our jobs. May the good Lord protect you all."

She finally let her handlers hustle her out.

Murray was sad to see her go. Not long ago he'd hated that woman, but when things were at their worst, President Blackmon was at her best. Now he'd get to see the VP in action — Murray didn't have high hopes. Albertson had been on the ticket because he could carry California. That, and probably *only* that, had put him in such a high place of power.

For now, however, Albertson didn't matter. Cooper Mitchell did. Murray had one card left, and now was the time to play it.

"Admiral, Clarence Otto is on the *Coronado*," he said. "He's Department of Special Threats. I think he should go in with the SEALs, manage the biological aspect."

Porter nodded. "That's fine. People, contact the *Coronado* and have it steam full speed for Chicago. Let's get the SEALs briefed." He turned to Vogel. "Show me that video again."

Vogel nodded, tapped some keys. The screen refreshed. It started to

play, then he paused it. He pointed to view-counter in the video's bottom
right-hand corner. In the time it had taken Blackmon to watch the video
and approve the mission to Chicago, the view-count had jumped from 301
to 15,236.

"Oh, shit," Vogel said. "I think it's gone viral."

VIRAL

Steve Stanton played the video for a third time. To think he'd actually saved Cooper Mitchell's life?

Now, he wanted to kill Cooper. Cut his belly open, pull out his intestines and make the man eat them. Have one of the bulls break his bones, one by one, while Steve danced to the music of his screams.

Four of Steve's high-ranking followers — three men and Dana Brownstone — stood before him. They all had the smart strain, like him. None of the four had challenged his leadership; those who had were already dead.

Although not at Dana's level, the men were all quite brilliant: Robert McMasters, the president and CEO of the energy company Exelon; Cody Hassan, who had apparently been an up-and-coming jazz musician; and Jeremy Ellis, a young geneticist who held multiple Ph.D.s. McMasters was hard at work on preserving the power grid. Hassan helped craft the messages to send through Brownstone's network. Ellis was already modifying facilities at the University of Chicago so he could study both the biology of the Chosen Ones, and how to defeat the humans' inoculation formula.

All four of them were afraid to make a noise. They all sensed Steve's fury. That, and their eyes kept flicking to the two huge bulls that stood behind him.

Three workers sat in front of his three laptops. All three screens showed the same YouTube video. Steve pointed to the middle screen.

"Cooper Mitchell shot this inside a building. Which building? What floor?"

Brownstone and the men said nothing.

Steve drew a black pistol from a thigh holster. The weapon had belonged to a cop. The cop didn't need it anymore; he had tasted delicious.

Steve aimed it at Hassan's face and pulled the trigger. The gun kicked in his hand. Hassan's head snapped backward. He dropped, probably dead even before his limp body hit the floor.

Steve holstered the pistol. "I said . . . *what building?*"

Brownstone shook her head. "We don't know, Emperor! The video quality is terrible. We can't identify any key structural elements. We think it's a hotel or an office building, but there's over a hundred and thirty *million* square feet of office space in the central business district alone. He could be anywhere."

Steve looked down at the man running the middle laptop.

"Refresh," he said. "And play it again."

The man did as he was told. As the window came up, Steve looked at the number of plays: 132,512. The views were climbing, fast. He didn't know if that was from uninfected watching it with a final sense of hope, his own kind watching it with a feeling of horrific dread, or a combination of both.

The video played. Steve wondered what Cooper would taste like. He'd never find out, of course, because Cooper was a walking plague.

If only he'd just let Bo Pan kill the man . . .

"Isolate his face from this video," Steve said. "Then print pictures. *Thousands* of pictures."

He turned to his four — correction, his *three* — top followers.

"Spread the word that everyone is to look for this man. Search every building, every office, every basement. If someone finds him, kill him on the spot, whatever it takes."

Ellis raised his hand. "Emperor, the people who kill him might very well contract the disease he carries and transmit it to the rest of us. If it's as contagious as it appears to be in the video, it could spread like wildfire through the Chosen Ones — it could eventually reach *us*."

That was a good point. Steve was glad he hadn't shot the scientist.

"Whatever group takes out Cooper Mitchell is to kill themselves immediately," Steve said. "They will go straight to heaven. They will be heroes. Now *move*. And send someone in here to clean up this body. Tell them to bring a mop."

ALL THE MARBLES

It made Margaret's skin crawl to be so close to them.

She, Clarence, Tim and Commander Klimas were packed into the same mission module where they had teleconferenced with Murray and Dr. Cheng. Margaret and Clarence sat on one side of the table, Tim on the other. Klimas stood in front of a screen that showed a map of Chicago.

He pointed out the landing area on the city's coast. "My team will OTB to Lake Shore Park on the city's east side and secure it as a landing zone."

Tim raised a hand. "OTB?"

"*Over the beach*," Klimas said. "The phrase covers the various methods we use. Sorry, I'll try to make the rest of this more civilian-friendly. We also have air support from two Apaches, three Predator drones, and — believe it or not — a B2 bomber."

"A B2?" Clarence said. "That's kind of overkill, isn't it?"

"Not if we find the Converted gathering en masse," Klimas said. "It's loaded with five-hundred-pound JDAM bombs, could take out a *lot* of them at once." He paused, cleared his throat. "It's also got, ah . . . well, it has a nuke."

They would never learn. Margaret knew the nuke had delayed things in Detroit, but the current situation showed that her kind could not be stopped. When the Converted rebuilt, they would just steer clear of any radioactive craters.

Klimas again pointed to the map.

"Once my team secures the LZ, Chinook helicopters will deliver the Ranger company, which is under the command of Captain Percy Dundee. We will then move about a half mile west to the Park Tower Hotel. SEALs lead and Rangers support by leapfrogging blocking positions at major intersections. If Cooper Mitchell is at the Park Tower, we grab him and get him out. We'll have close air support for the entire operation. Apaches will fly low and loud to intimidate the bad guys, and take out any organized force that might come to meet us. Easy as pie."

The video from Cooper Mitchell had changed the game. Margaret knew it was the real thing from the moment she'd seen it. He had the hydras — and from the looks of that video, they were far more contagious than she had thought. The Antichrist had risen again.

She had to find a way to kill him. If Klimas was successful, if he brought Cooper Mitchell out alive, then Margaret had no doubts of what would come next: in a few weeks, she and all her kind would be dead.

Clarence squirmed in his chair. "Why come in from the water and cross all that territory on foot? Why not take a Seahawk and drop in right on the hotel? I've moved through a half mile of urban terrain while under fire — it's risky, we'll lose people."

Klimas touched icons on the screen, zoomed the view in to a forty-five-degree angle that showed towering buildings. Margaret instantly saw the problem with Clarence's plan.

"Skyscrapers make for a lot of places the enemy can hide," Klimas said. "If the enemy is armed with something big enough, they can hit the Seahawk on the way in or on the way out. Lake Shore Park is a more secure place to land. Trust me, Agent Otto, SEALs and Rangers can get to that hotel in a hurry."

Margaret had seen those SEALs in action. Brave, smart, deadly, they moved without hesitation. She didn't know what type of resistance her kind would put up. Were the Converted in Chicago unified at all? Reports had come in from cities all over the world about organized bands, some the size of small armies, but there had been no such sightings in Chicago. As far as anyone knew, the city was in total chaos. If that were true, the SEALs might very well walk in, grab Cooper Mitchell and walk out.

She couldn't let them succeed. She needed to make sure Mitchell died. And while she was at it, she had an opportunity to eliminate another major threat: Tim Feely.

He was the brain behind the inoculation effort. If not for his work, her kind might already have taken over. Feely was too smart, too creative, and had too much knowledge of her former research. This trip would be the perfect opportunity to get rid of him.

Margaret stood. "I have to go with you. So does Tim."

Tim sat straight upright, looked at Margaret as if she was pointing a gun at his head.

Clarence stared at her in disbelief. "This is a high-risk operation. We can't be ferrying civilians."

Tim nodded. "Yeah, what he said. Oh, and also? Like *fuck* I have to go with you. Why would you and I go in, anyway? The SEALs grab this guy, bring him out, we draw the hydras from his blood, replicate them, and *boom* — we win."

"There are environmental factors to consider," Margaret said. "Mitchell's video indicates that the infected are dying, but we don't *know* that he's responsible for that. The sickness could be caused by something in that building's water supply, or in the air. If we bring Mitchell out only to discover that he's *not* the vector, we'll have wasted time and risked lives for nothing."

The three men in the tiny room looked at one another. Klimas didn't seem surprised; he was ready to back almost anything she asked for. Clarence, however, wasn't buying it.

"We can't risk you," he said. "We'll keep you in constant visual communication. The SEALs get Mitchell, they get samples from the dead bodies in the video, from the water and air, whatever else you want. Then they get the hell out."

She slapped the table. "Don't be stupid, Clarence. There's no guarantee Mitchell will be there. If he's not, we're left with those bodies. If the cause of death is something other than the hydra strain, tissue samples collected by untrained soldiers might not show us what did the damage. We need to examine the bodies where they died."

Clarence shook his head. He looked like he was losing control. "There's no way I'm letting a pregnant woman go on this mission."

Klimas and Tim stared at her. Their expressions changed instantly — with one word, she was suddenly fragile, a thing to be protected. Her strategy to hook Clarence had backfired.

She couldn't let him win.

"My body," she said quietly. "My choice."

Clarence crossed his arms. "*Our* child."

Margaret gathered herself, tried to remember what her weak, altruistic former self might have said. She concentrated hard, held her eyes open until they started to sting . . . she forced out a single tear.

"Wake *up*, my love. This isn't some men's rights debate. If this mission doesn't give us a weapon, we'll all be dead long before I could give birth. Don't you get it? This is the *end of the world*."

Klimas nodded. "She's right. This is for all the marbles. We need her expertise. If she wants in, she's in. Margo, how much time would you need on-site?"

Good question. If they found Mitchell, she needed enough time to kill him while not drawing attention to herself or exposing herself to his disease. She also needed enough time to kill Tim and not get caught doing it. She was willing to sacrifice herself to murder the president, but not to take out Tim Feely.

"At least overnight," she said. "Once we locate Mitchell, we test what we can while he's still in the same environment. We have to be *sure*."

Klimas's jaw muscles twitched. "Then we're no longer looking at a grab-and-go. We have to change the entire operation."

She nodded solemnly. "Then change it, Paulius. Whatever it takes."

Clarence stood. His body vibrated with anger.

"Klimas, are you kidding me? You think you'll last *overnight* in that place? As far as we know there's a hundred thousand Converted in the downtown area alone!"

Three quick knocks at the door, then it opened. The little SEAL with the horrible mustache peeked in.

"Commander, we're approaching the disembarkation point."

"Understood," Klimas said. He faced Clarence. "My decision is made. Margaret is coming."

Clarence slowly sat back down. He had lost and now had to contemplate his wife — whom he had abandoned — and his nonexistent unborn child going into hostile territory where the hostiles in question *ate* people. Margaret hoped he felt as miserable as he looked.

Klimas turned back to the screen. "The SEALs will still secure a landing area, as planned. The Ranger company will come in next. Once the LZ is secure, a Seahawk will bring in Doctor Montoya, Agent Otto and Doctor Feely."

Tim waved his hands. "Whoa, tough guy. Margaret wants in, that's fine, but I'm *out*. You get me? O-*u-t, out!*"

Feely was the final piece of the puzzle. Margaret *had* to get him to come along. What would push his buttons?

"Don't be a coward, Feely," she said. "I need you with me."

Tim shook his head, hard. "Fuck that. I've done my part!"

Margaret leaned across the table and slapped Tim's left cheek as hard as she could. The sharp *crack* sound filled the mission module. Tim stared, mouth open, eyes wide.

"You've *done your part*? The world is crumbling around us. We have one last opportunity to kill this thing."

He stood, hand still on his cheek. "I get paid to work in a lab. I don't get paid to ride a helicopter into the goddamn apocalypse. I've been shot at, almost drowned, and the last ship I was on got blown up by a missile. I'm not keen to add cannibalism to the list of threats on my résumé, understand?"

He turned toward the door.

Margaret was trying to think of another angle when Klimas gently put his hand on Tim's chest, stopping the smaller man from leaving.

"Hold on, Doctor Feelygood," Klimas said. "I know you're scared. So am I."

Tim huffed. "Ha. In this category, it's a safe bet that mine is bigger than yours."

Klimas smiled. "You've got me there. The SEALS get paid to do things like this, but we don't get paid to *fail*. If your presence increases our chances of succeeding, that's more important than your fear. That's more important than *you*. Everyone dreams of being a hero, Tim — this is your shot."

Tim shook his head. "I don't want to be a hero. I want to *live*. Margaret had it right — I'm a coward. It's what I've always been and what I'll always be."

"I'll get you out," Klimas said. "You have my word that I'll get you out safe. I know how much you respect Margaret. She wouldn't put you in danger on a whim."

Tim's resolve seemed to waver. He glanced at her.

Margaret looked down, did her best to appear contrite. "Sorry I slapped you," she said. His ego, the same ego that made him demand the yeast be named after him . . . that was his hot-button, she had to play to that.

"Tim, we've become a great team," she said. "If I had all the options in the world, I'd still pick you, but I don't *have* any other options. I can't do this without you."

Tim chewed at his lower lip, forgiveness already visible in his eyes. She almost had him.

He turned back to Klimas. "You gave your word. Does that mean the same thing it does when guys in war movies say it?"

"It means far more," Klimas said. "If anything comes near you, I'll kill it. I'm taking you in, I'm bringing you out."

Tim stared at him for a few more seconds, then looked down. "Shit," he said. "Okay, I'll go."

Margaret smiled.

In just a few hours, she could remove Cooper Mitchell, Tim Feely, then slip away to join her kind.

"Two more things," she said. "First, we still don't know the full impact of a hydra infection. Cooper Mitchell has them, but as far as we know they'll eventually kill him. Therefore, no one approaches Mitchell — and I mean *no one* — unless they are wearing full biological protection."

Going in was risky to start with. If she couldn't find a way to murder Tim and Clarence, she didn't want them coming back infected with a vector that could kill *her.*

She looked hard at all the men in the room. "Agreed?"

They all nodded.

"I'll make sure of it," Klimas said, his voice thick with that sickening *you can count on me* tone. "And the other thing?"

"I'm not going in there unarmed," Margaret said. "Would someone give me a crash course on how to shoot a gun?"

CASCADING FAILURE

Murray didn't remember the first time he'd seen the image of a mushroom cloud. He'd been two years old when a bomb named "Little Boy" had struck Hiroshima: at the time, he'd been far more concerned with his Lincoln Logs than with world-changing events.

Sixty-five years later, he'd seen his second, this one over Detroit.

Two days ago, he'd seen his third, then his fourth.

And now here he was in the Situation Room — the air thick with the scent of unwashed bodies, food and fear — watching his fifth and his sixth.

Vice President Kenneth Albertson sat in Blackmon's chair, his hand gripped white-knuckle tight around a steaming cup of coffee. He had all the trappings of a career politician: white, male, six-two, a full head of dark-blond hair (stylishly graying at the temples), perfect charcoal suit, red tie. Every time Murray looked at him, he thought that the right lipstick could make any pig seem competent.

The vice president said nothing. He wasn't alone in that reaction; a room full of people stared at the split-screen image of two mushroom clouds billowing up over dying cities. Movers and shakers, heads of shadowy departments and bit players alike, they all appealed to the irrational, illogical parts of their brains, hoping or even praying that their eyes deceived them.

Had Novosibirsk been the opening act? Was Murray watching World War III unfold?

"Xining, on the left," said some nameless assistant, there to stand in for one of the Joint Chiefs. "The right side is Lanzhou."

Murray didn't know those places. They looked big.

"How many?" he said. "How many people?"

"Uh, checking," the assistant said. "Xining has, or *had*, before all of this . . . two-point-two million."

The size of Houston, a little bigger.

"The other one," Murray said. "Lanzhou? How many?"

"Lanzhou has . . . Jesus." The assistant looked up, face ashen, drenched with despair. "It had three-point-six million."

Another Los Angeles, or maybe Chicago if you include enough suburbs.

Albertson's shaking hand raised the shaking mug to his lips. He took a sip. Only a little coffee spilled onto the table.

"Was it the Russians?" he said. "Why didn't we see these missiles when they launched?"

Admiral Porter rested his elbows on the table, hands pressed against the sides of his head. Even he, the stoic one, was worn down by the nonstop horror show.

"There wasn't a launch of any kind," he said. "That means the bombs had to be *driven* in. It wasn't the Russians this time — the Chinese nuked themselves."

Murray knew what those words meant. If the Chinese were desperate enough to bomb themselves, they wouldn't think twice about launching missiles against another nation.

The screen suddenly switched to an image of Blackmon. She had been sleeping aboard *Air Force One*. She wore red pajamas. Her hair was a tangled mess. Eyes narrowed by fatigue-fueled rage, she stared out, locking eyes with several people in that spooky, I-see-you-and-you-see-me connection enabled by the screen's telepresence.

"Tell me," she said.

Albertson stood. "Madam President, we—"

"Not you," she said sharply. The face on the screen turned, locked eyes with Murray. "*You*, Longworth. I want to hear it from you."

Murray felt all the eyes of the Situation Room upon him. Blackmon should have heard from her next in line, Albertson, or at least from Admiral Porter.

"Uh, sure," Murray said. "I mean, yes, Madam President."

"I want straight, simple language," Blackmon said. "Out of everyone there, you do that best. And if you need to curse to get the point across, I don't really care anymore."

Murray nodded. He recognized the look in her eyes, the anxiety at not being front and center, the desperate need for accurate intel. He again flashed back to his days in Vietnam, when *he* had been the one forced to make every decision and give every order. Men had lived and died based on what he told them to do. Back then, he'd relied on Dew Phillips, his top sergeant, to provide no-bullshit information, to help make those impossible choices.

Now Murray was playing that role to the president of the United States.

He quickly gave her the bad news, using the comparisons to Houston and Los Angeles so she understood the scope.

When Murray finished, Blackmon closed her eyes. Her lip quivered slightly. Murray hoped the president of the United States wasn't going to cry, because that would just be too goddamn much for him to take.

"Why, Murray? Why would the Chinese do this?"

"Those cities must have been overrun," he said. "Far beyond any hope of saving them. If this was an act of the Chinese government, I assume the goal was to kill as many of the Converted as possible before they could radiate to surrounding areas. If the government has fallen and the Converted detonated the nukes, then . . . well, I'm not sure those motherfuckers really need a reason."

Blackmon nodded. The lip quivered a little more.

"Any word from Beijing?"

"None, Madam President," Murray said. "If anyone is in charge, we don't know who it is."

Blackmon sat up straighter. She sniffed in sharply, regained her composure.

"All right," she said. "If anyone there is still watching us, waiting to see how we'll respond, we have to let them know that the United States of America is still ready to defend herself by any means necessary."

She looked away from Murray, took in the whole room.

"Admiral Porter, take us to DEFCON 1."

A GOOD DAY FOR A SWIM

Paulius Klimas's head broke the surface of Lake Michigan. His goggled eyes looked out at the empty sidewalk and eight lanes of Lakeshore Drive. A few streetlights were still working, enough to illuminate the burned-out cars blocking the entire road. Beyond, dark buildings rose high against a darker sky; only a few panes glowed with light.

Frank Bogdana surfaced off to Klimas's right, D'Shawn Bosh off to his left. Not far behind him, Luke Ramierez did the same.

Even if there had been anyone standing on that sidewalk, on the road, or in Lake Shore Park beyond, the four SEALs would have been all but invisible; just tiny, moving bumps of wetness in an infinite inland sea.

Paulius slid beneath the waves. He swam forward a good fifteen meters, pushing his M4 carbine in its shoot-through dry bag before him, then held his position underwater for another minute before rising up enough to peek above the surface. He again looked at Lakeshore Drive, the sidewalk, the park. Bosh and Bogdana did the same, searching for anything that might be a threat.

They saw nothing.

Paulius and his men moved forward. They would leave their rebreather gear below the water, fixed to the metal-and-concrete seawall. Whether they would need that gear again remained to be seen. If all went well, he and his men would fly back to the *Coronado* instead of swim.

Paulius reached the seawall. He removed his fins, slid his arm through them and gripped the handle of his still-bagged weapon. He shrugged off his gear, bundled it and left it clamped to the wall.

He and his fire team silently climbed over the seawall and onto the paved bike path that ran alongside Lake Shore Drive. They donned night-vision goggles and took up covering positions, protecting the other three fire teams as those men exited the water.

Paulius ordered squad two south and squad three north, to enter the buildings nearest to Lake Shore Park. Those units would climb six or seven stories and set up overwatch positions.

After those men were in place, squads one and four would make their way to the park. First, they would secure the park administration building. Then, they would secure the landing area for the arrival of four CH-47 Chinooks and an SH-60 Seahawk. The Chinooks carried the Ranger company — 150 men complete with mortars, heavy weapons and supplies, as well as some scientific equipment Margaret had requested. She, Otto and Dr. Feelygood would come in on the Seahawk.

Paulius took another minute to search for danger. He saw no movement. He knew he and his men were about to roll into a mission unlike any they could have prepared for, a mission where they would probably have to fire on Americans.

From here on out, however, they weren't "Americans."

They were the enemy.

INFORMATION IS A WEAPON

Steve Stanton stood alone in a twentieth-floor office, looking out at the mostly dark streets of Chicago. How to find Cooper Mitchell . . . that was really all that mattered at the moment. If Cooper infected any of the Chosen Ones, all Steve's careful planning could fall apart.

A knock at his door.

"Enter."

General Brownstone walked in, trailed by a teenage girl who was breathing so hard she could barely stand up straight. The girl had obviously sprinted hard to deliver a message.

"Speak," Steve said.

The girl stood, laced her fingers above her head, fought to draw enough air to get out her sentences.

"Helicopters," she said. "At Lake Shore Park. Five landed, soldiers got out. Two helicopters kept hovering the whole time. They looked mean."

Steve felt a flush of excitement. Maybe he wouldn't have to find Cooper after all — maybe the American soldiers would lead Steve right to him. Over half a million people had watched Cooper's video. That number obviously included people in the U.S. government who wanted to use Cooper as a weapon.

General Brownstone gently patted the girl on the back. "Good work, dear. Did you count how many soldiers got out of the helicopter?"

The girl nodded, blinked. "Yeah, about a hundred and fifty."

"A full company," Brownstone said. "Emperor, that's a serious force. And I'm certain the helicopters are Apaches. Considering what we know of the state of the country, this is a major allocation by the high command. Do you want me to arrange an attack?"

The Americans didn't have troops to burn, not if the ongoing coverage by Al Jazeera was to be believed (how that network kept reporting while the others had been wiped out, Steve didn't know: it was one of the few remaining sources for national news).

"No," he said. "They came for Cooper. We need to see where they go. Leave the soldiers alone for now, but watch them."

"And the Apaches?" Brownstone asked. "The Stinger missiles we acquired from the army reserve bases can destroy them."

"Where do you have those positioned?"

"Downtown. On the tallest buildings."

Steve thought it over. If he took out the Apaches, that would reveal too much about his strength. And, he didn't have many Stingers to start with.

"Leave the missiles where they are for now," he said. "Spread the word — I want everyone to stay well clear. I want these soldiers to think no one is opposing them. Once they reveal Cooper's location, we'll need to strike fast and strike hard. No mercy for them."

Brownstone saluted. She led the girl out of the office.

Steve returned to his view.

Now all he had to do was wait.

THE HIGHWAYS

IMMUNIZED: 88%

NOT IMMUNIZED: 7%

UNKNOWN: 5%

FINISHED DOSES EN ROUTE: 103,883

DOSES IN PRODUCTION: 214,591

INFECTED: 4,311,000 (25,625,000)

CONVERTED: 2,950,000 (12,120,000)

DEATHS: 500,000+ (28,000,000)

Murray had to admire the Converted's tactics.

There was no known general, no command structure to unify actions across the United States, but the Converted understood where they needed to attack in order to bring the nation to its knees. Like any good guerrilla force, their primary target seemed to be infrastructure.

Admiral Porter flipped from map to map, reading off a list of bad news.

"Highway 5 in California has severe damage north of Redding," he said. "It's been completely severed in several places."

André Vogel groaned in exasperation, leaned back in his chair. "I thought we had the West Coast under control. What, exactly, are they cutting the roads *with*?"

"Based on intel, anything and everything," Porter said. "Backhoes, bull-dozers, piles of cars set on fire, logs, rocks, even teams of people with shovels. And Highway 5 is just the start."

Porter changed the image on the main screen. The ticking death toll faded, replaced by a highway map of the United States. Hundreds of flashing red Xs showed where the highways were severed.

"We've lost communication with Reno," he said. "Flyovers show that all highway bridges have been destroyed. It's impassable. South of Lake Tahoe, Highways 50, 88, 4, 108 and 120 have all been cut. Highway 1 south of

Carmel, 101 south of Salinas, 5 near Mendota and 99 south of both Madera and Fresno, too."

Murray looked at the pattern of Xs. It wasn't hard to see what was going on.

"I'll be damned," he said. "They're trying to isolate the San Francisco Bay Area. They're cutting it off from the east and the south. How are the roads to the north?"

"The 101 at Eureka is out," Porter said. "North of there, air force sorties out of Fairchild and McChord AFBs, in conjunction with infantry from Fort Lewis, have wiped out any major efforts to cut the highways in Washington State."

There were some Xs in Washington and Oregon, but not as many. Something about that image bothered Murray.

Porter hit the remote control again, bringing a map of the entire United States. Red Xs dotted the Midwest on Highways 80, 70, 40 and 20, blocked various roads into major cities.

"The national situation is becoming untenable," Porter said. "Roads are heavily damaged, bridges are impassable if not outright destroyed. Rails are being cut. Military and off-road vehicles can easily get around these cutouts, but standard transportation — semis and other transport trucks — cannot."

Murray wondered if it would ever end, *how* it could ever end. Unless Margaret came through and recovered that bug from Cooper Mitchell, all the military could do was slow down the inevitable.

Vice President Albertson cleared his throat, surprising Murray — he'd forgotten the man was even there.

"We have to push them back," Albertson said. "What are we doing to secure the remaining infrastructure?"

Porter looked annoyed. "We *can't* push them back, sir. Even if we weren't at less than half our normal military strength, this country is so big we can't cover it all. We have to concentrate on defending specific transportation corridors. Outside of those and the main cities, the Converted will control everything else."

Albertson looked around the room, perhaps searching for someone to tell him what he wanted to hear.

"But that's giving up," he said. "We have to develop new tactics to defeat the insurgents."

Murray couldn't listen to the fool any longer.

"Mister Vice President, you're not hearing the admiral correctly," Murray said. "America is *too . . . damn . . . big*. The highway system consists of one hundred and seventeen thousand miles of road. These *insurgents* you're talking about were Americans. Many of them grew up in the very places they are attacking. They know the terrain, they know exactly what to hit. Now, would you *please* stop asking for things that are fucking impossible?"

It was only when Murray finished talking that he realized he'd just yelled at the vice president. He sat still and waited to be thrown out.

But Albertson didn't seem angry. Instead, he seemed to shrink in his chair.

He's such a pussy he'll let me yell at him — not exactly a prime candidate for the most powerful person in the free world.

Now it was Porter who cleared his throat. Murray sensed the man was about to drop something big.

"Mister Vice President," the admiral said, "at this time, it is the recommendation of the Joint Chiefs of Staff that we withdraw all remaining troops from Europe and the Middle East. We need those troops here at home. We also recommend moving all U.S. troops in South America to defend the Panama Canal and to cut off any and all access from that continent into North America."

Albertson stared. He sniffed once, scratched his nose.

"You want to coordinate with the Panamanians on that?"

Porter shook his head. "Sir, we recommend that our troops *seize control* of the canal. The Mexican border is too big to cover, but we can create a choke point at the canal. Then, when we start to regain superiority, we only have to contend with clearing out Mexico — South America will have to fend for itself."

Everyone looked to Albertson. He seemed lost.

"I don't know," he said. "Abandoning our allies . . . seizing the Canal . . . we need President Blackmon to make those decisions." He again looked around the room. "I asked someone to get her on the line for me twenty minutes ago. What the hell is wrong with you people?"

André Vogel pinched his ever-present phone between his ear and shoulder.

"We're still trying," he said. He put the phone back to his ear.

For the first time, Murray heard Samuel Porter raise his voice.

"*Mister Vice President*," the admiral said, demanding the attention of

Albertson and everyone in the room. "A decision *must* be made. We need to withdraw our troops from overseas, and we need to do it *now*."

Albertson's left eye started to twitch. He stared down at the table. "I'm sorry, only the president can make that call."

Vogel suddenly rose, stood up board-straight as if someone had connected his chair to a car battery. He looked like he might throw up.

"*Air Force One* . . . it's gone down."

All conversation ceased. The room seemed to dim, to go nearly dark save for a score of spotlights that lit up Vice President Albertson.

He placed his hands on the table. They were shaking.

"I see," he said. "When did this happen?"

"About fifteen minutes ago," Vogel said. "The pilot got a message out that there was some kind of commotion on the plane. He thought there was a Converted onboard, someone who dodged a cellulose test, maybe. He reported gunshots. Then fighter escort saw *Air Force One* go down. No survivors. President Blackmon is dead."

Those imaginary spotlights picked up in intensity. Their glare burned hot enough to make Albertson break out into a sweat.

Murray sagged back into his chair. He'd believed in Blackmon's ability to lead the nation out of this. Now she was dead, and with the nation at DEF-CON 1, Albertson was the commander in chief.

Admiral Porter broke the silence.

"Mister *President*," he said, putting emphasis on the second word, making it clear that the word *Vice* no longer applied. "From this moment on, you're in charge, sir. What is your decision about our overseas troops?"

Albertson's eyes looked hollow. The burden of leadership had fallen to a man who clearly couldn't handle it. Shaking hands lifted to tired eyes, rubbed them lightly.

"If you say so, Admiral," he said quietly. "Withdraw the troops."

Murray stared at Albertson. The man's very first command of his presidency? A confidence-building *if you say so*.

Maybe the Converted had already won.

URBAN TERRAIN

Oddly, Clarence thought of Dew Phillips.

Before Dew died, he had been at the tail end of his career. Truth be told, he'd been well past that. In his late sixties, Dew had been forced into intense physical action while managing, protecting — and occasionally even beating the crap out of — one "Scary" Perry Dawsey.

Clarence thought of Dew because five years ago Clarence had been the young buck on the team: fit, well trained and ready to rock. Now, *Clarence* was the one showing the wear and tear of age. Not that he was ready to retire, not even close, but being surrounded by twenty-five-year-olds in world-class shape made it obvious his best years were behind him.

Of course, the bulky CBRN suit didn't help at all. It was far less bulky than the full BSL-4 rig he'd worn on the *Brashear*, granted, but the fully enclosed suit still made it cumbersome to move around wrecked cars and through ankle-deep snow. His face felt hot inside the suit's built-in gas mask. The lenses over each eye cut off much of his peripheral vision; he found himself turning his head rapidly to make sure the Converted weren't sneaking up from the sides.

Clarence stayed close to Margaret. Two SEALs — the little one, Ramierez, and a swarthy man named Bogdana — shadowed them every step of the way. They and the other SEALs weren't wearing the CBRN gear. Speed, silence and agility were as much a part of the SEAL arsenal as their M4 carbines, Mark 23 pistols and Barrett M107 rifles. Margaret had argued with Klimas about it. She wanted everyone in the suits, but the commander had ended the discussion quickly. His support of Margaret only went so far, it seemed, and didn't include debates regarding his gear and the gear of his men.

Tim was currently twenty or thirty feet back, Klimas and Bosh constantly at his side. As soon as Clarence and Margaret stopped, Tim and Klimas would leapfrog ahead. That was how all the troops moved: one group stayed still, ready to provide covering fire, while another group advanced forward to take up covering positions of their own.

Two Apache helicopters flew high overhead, the roar of their engines echoing off skyscraper walls. On the ground, four SEAL fire teams were way out front, running recon. Behind them, the first Ranger platoon, then the civilians and their SEAL escorts, flanked on either side by the second Ranger platoon. The third Ranger platoon brought up the rear.

If the Rangers had objected to wearing the CBRN gear, they had lost that battle. With their urban-camouflage-pattern suits and hoods, their black rubber gasmasks and their rifles — mostly SCAR-FNs and Mk46s, with a few bulky M240B machine guns thrown in for good measure — the Rangers looked like extras from an apocalypse movie. That meant they fit right in with the surroundings.

Clarence could barely believe this was Chicago. Most of the lights were out, bathing the city in darkness. The place looked . . . *dead*. Soot-streaked snow covered the street, the sidewalks, abandoned vehicles and hundreds of frozen bodies. Footprints and well-worn paths through the snow were the only indication that anyone remained.

So many footprints, so many paths. There were people here, but where were they? The SEAL recon teams had reported zero contact. They had yet to even see a single soul.

Ramierez and Bogdana stopped behind a flipped-over BMW. Clarence crouched between them. So did Margaret, but she stepped on something under the snow and started to fall. Clarence reached out fast, softly caught her shoulders to keep her from hitting the pavement.

She slapped his arms away.

"I don't need your help," she hissed. "I'm not yours to protect anymore."

Before Clarence could answer, Ramierez leaned in from the right and held a finger to his lips. His eyes sent a message: *shut up before you get us killed*.

Margaret nodded. She looked back down the wide street, all but ignoring Clarence.

His wife, the mother of his child, she *despised* him.

Just get her through this alive, then you've got a lifetime to make things right.

He rose a little, peeked over the bottom of the overturned car. They were about to cross Mies van der Rohe Way, which would put them within a half mile of the Park Tower Hotel.

Ramierez slid down into a crouch behind the car's cover.

"Ramierez here, go," he said, not to Clarence but rather into the tiny microphone that extended down from an earpiece. "Yes sir. I'm ready."

The short SEAL looked at Bogdana.

"Frank, keep the package right here until I call for you," Ramierez said.

Then Klimas moved silently past. Ramierez slid around the front of the overturned car and followed his commander into the shadows.

KNOW YOUR ENEMY

Paulius and Ramierez approached a small firehouse. The building looked medieval — two stories of grayish-tan granite with small, faux turrets on the second-story corners. Its red roll-up door looked just large enough for one fire engine to enter or exit, but nothing was going in or out thanks to the long, white public transit bus that had smashed into it at an angle.

At the bus's rear end, almost to the sidewalk, stood two cops — one black, one white — both dressed in heavy blue coats, their fingers laced behind their heads. Their breath billowed out in expanding clouds that glowed thanks to a nearby streetlight. The men looked both hopeful and afraid. A black XDM automatic pistol lay on the snow in front of each of them.

They had their hands on their heads because two SEALs — Bosh and Roth — had M4s at their shoulders, barrels aimed at the cops' chests.

Paulius slung his own M4. He drew his sidearm, a 9-millimeter Sig Sauer P226 already fitted with a suppressor. He aimed it at the two cops as he came up on Bosh's right.

"Bosh, report."

"I saw these two exit the bus's rear door," Bosh said. "Thing is, advance recon looked through the bus to make sure there weren't any bad guys hiding there that could fire on the column. When they checked it, the bus was empty. Five minutes later, Rangers march through, these guys come out of it."

Paulius glanced at the bus. "There a hole in the front of it that leads into the firehouse?"

"I checked," Bosh said. "Didn't see any openings. I also did a walk around the firehouse, couldn't find a way in or out. The place is locked up tight, Commander."

Paulius glanced at the building's red-framed windows. In every one, behind broken glass he saw the dull glint of metal. The cops had fortified the place. Paulius had to keep his men moving — every second they spent here was a second wasted.

He looked at the cops. "What do you two want?"

The cops looked at each other, then back at Paulius.

The black cop spoke. "We want you to get us the fuck out of here. We've been in there" — he tilted his head toward the firehouse behind him — "for two freakin' days."

They looked normal, but the mission was here to rescue one man and one man only.

"We haven't seen anyone but you," Paulius said. "Why didn't you come out sooner?"

The white cop answered. "Right after Paris burned, we were ordered to protect the engine. We were inside the firehouse when things really went to hell. There were psychos everywhere, hundreds of them — they were *eating* people. We called for backup, for someone to come and get us, but no one's answering anymore. We didn't think we'd make it on the streets, so we kept quiet, boarded the place up."

"Then we saw you guys, you *soldiers*," the black cop said. "You came to rescue us, right? So how about you stop aiming that goddamn gun at my face and get us out of here?"

Paulius could imagine what it had been like to hide in that building, cut off from communication, while cannibals roamed the street. These guys were cops, public servants. Probably as brave as any soldier.

But he couldn't let them go. They had seen his entire force. If they were captured, they might talk. And, of course, they might already be infected. He could test them, but what was the point? The stakes were too high to take even the smallest of chances.

Paulius knew what he had to do.

God forgive me.

He pulled the trigger four times in just over a second. The suppressor made each shot sound like a snapping mousetrap. The first two shots hit the white cop in the face. The black cop had barely enough time to raise his eyebrows in shock and surprise before the next two rounds tore through his skull.

Both men dropped instantly. Blood mist hung in the air, slowly drifted down on top of them.

Paulius switched his mic to the "all units" frequency.

"Commander Klimas to detachment. No more delays. If anyone approaches the detachment, assume they are hostiles and put them down at a distance. Quietly. Make as little noise as possible. Repeat, as little noise as possible."

He turned to Bosh. "Let's move out."

THE PARK TOWER

I am going to kill you all, every one of you, I will wipe you off the face of the earth.

Margaret ran through the dark streets, doing her best to stay close to the nasty little soldier in front of her. Ramierez, his name was. What a fool — if she got the chance she'd slit his throat from ear to ear and bathe in his blood while he tried to draw air. And yet here he was, guarding her, clearly ready to risk his own life to protect hers.

The CBRN gear made it hard to move, but it would protect her from Cooper Mitchell's disease. Hopefully. The crawlers had found a way through her BSL-4 suit. The hydras might have that same ability. She would stay as far away from Mitchell as possible. She didn't know how she would kill him, not yet, but as a last resort she had the holstered Sig Sauer P226 strapped to her right thigh. She would just have to watch for her chance. Take out Mitchell, then slip away into the city.

She heard a short bark of gunfire, then another. She and Ramierez followed Clarence and Bogdana. They jogged past a car where CBRN-suited Rangers were setting up a tripod-supported machine gun, pointed back the way they had come. Other Rangers were manually pushing cars into a loose line. They were setting up a perimeter. She saw two soldiers running wires to small, green boxes that were labeled FRONT TOWARD ENEMY.

The Rangers' gas masks made them all look the same, made them look like the identical insects that they were.

Past the perimeter rose the seventy-story Park Tower Hotel, a pale tan spire reaching up to the black sky. Ramierez led her to the front of the building. She saw an arced glass awning that had once sheltered guests from the rain as they entered and exited. It wasn't sheltering anyone anymore — the only glass that remained stuck out in jagged shards. The body of a man dangled from a support beam. Icicles of blood pointed down from the ends of his fingers like stubby red claws.

Once upon a time, a rotating glass door had kept out the Chicago winds. That, too, was nothing but shattered glass and twisted metal.

Clarence approached and stood next to her. The mask hid most of his face, but not his eyes. He looked at her with a pathetic expression of hurt and confusion.

It would be nice if she could kill Ramierez. But to murder Clarence? That wasn't just a luxury — more and more, Margaret needed that as much as she needed to breathe.

Maybe her kind would descend upon this hotel and slaughter these soldiers. She would have them string Clarence up by his feet, cut him apart a piece at a time. She'd slice off his eyelids so he wouldn't be able to look away as people smiled at him and ate those pieces.

She stared back at him, not wanting to give him any satisfaction at all, not wanting him to think that things were okay between them. Until she had a chance to kill him, she wanted him to *hurt*.

He turned away, walked into the hotel. Margaret smiled a little, then forced that down. She was still surrounded by the enemy. She had to be careful.

She heard gunshots from inside the hotel. She heard men yelling but couldn't make out the words. Those sounds were lost as one of the helicopters roared overhead.

A bullet plinked into a car to her right. Then something hit her, knocked her face-first to the glass-strewn entryway, pinned her there — the soldiers realized she wasn't one of them anymore, they were going to kill her, slide a knife into her back, they—

"Sniper," Ramierez said. "Stay down, Doc."

From high above, the helicopter let out a new noise, a short-but-intense demon's roar. The faraway sound of tinkling glass smashing against concrete joined the cacophony.

Ramierez rolled off her, lifted her to her feet. He looked her up and down. "You okay, Doc?"

She nodded. "I think so."

Broken glass, I was rolling on broken glass . . .

"Ramierez, do you see any cuts in my suit?"

He gave her a cursory glance. "The suits are thicker than that, Doc, you—"

"Just look!"

Ramierez nodded, then checked her all over — placatingly, but also thoroughly.

She was entering a building crawling with the hydra strain. This place was death. Any cut, no matter how small, could spell the end.

"Looks clear," Ramierez said. "You're fine, Doc. And this lobby is secured, so you can relax."

She let out a genuine sigh of relief.

Ramierez led her deeper into the lobby, which looked even more like a war zone than the streets outside. She recognized details from the YouTube video: the fire pit, now spotted white with windblown snow; corpses that had frozen solid and still wore jeans and winter coats; the soot-blackened ceiling; the shredded reception desk. The only thing missing was the body on the spit — maybe some of her kind had come in here, decided not to let good food go to waste.

To the left of the fire pit, Rangers were unfolding portable tables and unpacking the equipment she'd asked for. Tim stood there, directing them, using what was left of the reception desk as the lab's main area.

Margaret looked around. The CBRN-suited Rangers seemed to be everywhere. They were setting up more of the tripod-supported weapons by the ruined door and also in the lobby's broken windows, creating a field of fire out onto Chicago Avenue. More Rangers were undoubtedly setting up similar positions all around the hotel. If her kind attacked, these soldiers would mow them down by the hundreds.

Other Rangers carried large weapons to the elevator, which, surprisingly, seemed to still be working. She saw Klimas conferring with the Ranger commander — Dundee was his name — at what looked to be a hastily constructed command center, complete with laptops and soldiers already working away on them.

She saw Klimas reach up to the small earpiece at his right ear. He stared off, listening, then said something she couldn't hear. He jogged to a stairwell door, calling out as he went.

"Ramierez, Bosh, Roth, with me! You too, Otto. We've got reports of hostiles in the building, so we're going straight for the package. Elevator gets us there the quickest, so let's move!"

On the way in, *she* had been "the package." Now that they had reached the hotel, that term referred to someone else: Cooper Mitchell. Klimas and the others were headed to the eighteenth floor. On the form he'd submitted online, that's where Mitchell had said he would be waiting.

In room 1812.

UNDER THE BED

Cooper heard a helicopter. It sounded big, *loud*, like military helicopters did in the movies. He also heard occasional blasts of gunfire. It had worked: someone was coming to save him. He just had to stay alive a little bit longer, and hope the rescuers got to him before the cannibals did.

The hotel still had heat. Anywhere but downstairs, where winter winds swirled snow through the lobby, the Park Tower remained well above freezing. At first, that had been a welcome discovery. Now, not so much.

If it were below freezing, the dead bodies up here wouldn't have rotted, *bloated*, and the corpse he hid beneath might have been frozen solid instead of turning into the wet, reeking mess that sagged down around him. The smell was enough to make him vomit, but to do that would be to make noise — to make noise was to die.

Die, or worse.

You ain't gonna eat me, motherfuckers, you ain't gonna eat me . . .

The motherfuckers in question were close. They were searching every room in the hotel. Earlier he'd risked moving down a few floors, just to keep checking his surroundings. On the fifteenth floor, he'd heard two men talking; talking about his YouTube video, talking about their search — for *him*.

It had seemed like such a good idea to upload that video, to make sure people knew who he was so the government couldn't just make him disappear. He felt so, *so* stupid now, but it had never crossed his mind that the video would make all the murderers in Chicago want to waste him.

Cooper had thought about running to a higher floor, but he'd waited too long and now he didn't dare. They were on the eighteenth floor. He'd barely had enough time to implement his next bright idea: dragging a sloughing corpse into room 1812 and hiding beneath it. His brain didn't seem to work right anymore. Too much stress, too much horror, he didn't know. He was smarter than this. He knew he was. If only—

Noises, coming from the next room. He moved slowly, adjusted the weight of the body on top of him, pressed his ear against the wall. He could hear muffled voices.

"Check under the bed," one said.

"Stop telling me that," said another. "There's no space under these beds."

Cooper started to shake. He slowly shouldered the corpse a little higher, so he could reach down to his back. Quietly, so quietly, he drew Sofia's pistol.

Ain't gonna eat me, Sofia, not like I ate you, no fucking way, I got four bullets left . . .

THE PACKAGE

It seemed so odd that the hotel still had power. Clarence was grateful for working elevators, though — climbing seventeen flights of stairs would have done him in. He was the only one wearing CBRN gear, which made him feel oddly out of place among Klimas, Bosh, Ramierez and Roth.

Beep . . . they passed the fifteenth floor.

"We're almost there," Klimas said. He reached to his chest webbing, pressed a black button. "Radio check, do you read?"

The three SEALs — Bosh, little Ramierez and the big fella, Roth — all nodded. Clarence nodded as well.

Beep . . . they passed the sixteenth floor.

"Bosh, cover the right," Klimas said. "Ramierez, the left. Roth, out and left. I'll go out and right."

Bosh and Ramierez knelt by their assigned corners, M4s pointed straight up. Noise suppressors attached to the barrels made the weapons look long and mean.

Clarence drew his Glock 19 from the thigh holster strapped to the outside of his suit.

"Where do you want me?"

Klimas raised an eyebrow. "You? I want you to stay out of our way and move when we tell you to move."

Maybe it was the impossible stress of the situation, or maybe his frustration with Margaret sitting squarely in harm's way, he wasn't sure, but Clarence felt a wave of annoyance.

"I know what I'm doing in a fight, Klimas," he said. "I was Special Forces."

Ramierez laughed and shook his head.

Klimas grinned. "Special Forces, huh? How nice. Know what you're not? A member of this team. You're here because Margaret doesn't want anyone exposed to Mitchell's hydras. You've got the CBRN suit so you can handle him. Other than that, kindly stay out of our way."

Beep . . . they passed the seventeenth floor.

•   •   •

Cooper heard the door open. A rectangle of hallway light filled the dark room, lit up the face of the bloated corpse on top of him.

"Gross," one voice said. "It stinks in here."

"Dead body," said the other. "Damn, it smells too far gone to eat."

Cooper couldn't see them. He heard their feet shuffling across the carpet . . . coming closer . . .

"Check under the bed," one voice said.

"Chuck," said the other, "if you ask me to look under the bed just *one more time* I will shoot you in your stupid *face*."

Something in the dead body *popped* softly, bringing with it an even more rancid stench. A trickle of fluid leaked out, ran down Cooper's forehead and onto the bridge of his nose. His left eye closed automatically as the foul liquid trickled across his eyelids.

Just go away just go away I don't want to be eaten . . .

The elevator doors opened onto the eighteenth floor. Bosh and Ramierez, both still kneeling, leaned out and aimed their weapons down the hallway. Bosh's weapon let out three snaps, *click-click-click*.

Klimas stepped out with his weapon pointed to the right, stock tight to his shoulder. Roth moved out at the same time, his weapon pointing left. Klimas fired his M4 once, another snapping *click*.

"Clear left," Roth said.

"Clear right," Klimas said. "Otto, with me."

Clarence stepped out. One body lay down the hall to the right. A woman, face up, dead eyes staring at the ceiling.

Klimas spoke quietly, firmly. "Bosh, take point. Let's move."

The SEALs did just that, moving without a sound, moving faster than Clarence would have expected; he found himself jogging to keep up.

As they passed the woman, Clarence looked down: three red spots were spreading across her chest. A fourth bullet had blown off the top of her head, splattering her brains across the carpet in a rough oblong. A black .38 revolver lay near her right hand.

Clarence checked off the room numbers as he passed them by —
1804, 1805, 1806 . . . Room 1812 would be down the hall, just past a left-

hand turn. Coming from that direction, he heard the faint sound of men's voices . . .

"The lights don't work," said the first voice. "All the bulbs is broke."

"You can see fine enough," said the second voice. "Man, look at that nasty body."

"That is *sooo* gross," said the first voice. "Move it so we can see if anything else is under that desk."

"No, *you* move it," said the second.

Cooper felt numb, like he wasn't even there, and maybe he wasn't . . . maybe this was all a fucked-up dream and he wasn't hiding under an oozing, rancid, bloated body, maybe he wasn't hiding from two men who would shove a signpost up his ass and slow-roast him over a bed of coals.

"Flip you for it," said the first voice.

"Okay," said the second. "Call it."

Go away just go away just go away kill myself kill myself now Jesus please help me please

"Heads," said the first voice.

"Asshole," said the second. "Hold my gun."

Cooper felt the dead body on top of him start to slide off. He raised Sofia's pistol and squeezed the trigger.

Clarence heard the roar of four quick gunshots — a pistol, sounded like a .40-cal.

Klimas's calm voice in the headset: "Go-go-go."

Bosh and Roth sprinted around the corner.

Cooper was still on his back, still covered in dead-person sludge, pointing his pistol up at the bearded face of a very surprised man. Cooper had fired four times — and *missed* all four times. His hands shook so bad that the gun looked like some poorly made stop-action movie.

"That's him."

The words didn't come from the bearded man, but from closer to the door. Cooper looked over — a man wearing a red-and-black knit Blackhawks hat cradled two weapons against his chest, a shotgun and a rifle.

"Holy shit," the man said. "That's *him*."

He fumbled with the weapons. He dropped the rifle, started to bring the shotgun up.

The rectangle of light from the hallway wavered as someone stepped into it.

Cooper heard a *click-click-click:* the man with the shotgun dropped. The bearded man turned to face the door. *Click-click-click:* he twitched, then fell to his back.

He lay side by side with Cooper. The man's chest heaved. His eyes blinked in surprise, but only for a few seconds — then they stared out at nothing.

"Clear!" a voice called out.

Another answered the same.

Cooper looked at his hand, saw the empty pistol was still in it, then shook his hand to let it drop. To come through all this and then to be shot . . . what if it was too late, what if they were going to shoot him anyway, and—

"Cooper Mitchell?"

He looked up, saw a man in a gas mask, covered head to toe in a heavy chem suit. Through the eye lenses, Cooper saw the man inside was black.

"Cooper Mitchell," the black man said again. "You're Cooper Mitchell?"

Cooper nodded.

The man reached down a gloved hand. "I'm Agent Clarence Otto. We're here to rescue you."

Cooper couldn't speak. His vision blurred as the tears started to flow. He reached out and let Agent Clarence Otto take his hand.

DR. FEELY'S BEDSIDE MANNER

Tim Feely had just finished setting up a centrifuge when the elevator opened. Two men stepped out: Clarence in his CBRN suit with combat webbing strapped to his chest and a pistol holster strapped to his thigh, and none other than the guest of honor himself — Cooper Mitchell.

Mitchell wore a tattered, filthy winter coat. Gray slime smeared his face, making the whites of his wide eyes seem all the whiter. The man looked crazy with a capital C. Hell, probably even a capital *Z* to boot.

Clarence guided Mitchell by an elbow, escorted him to Tim's impromptu examination area. It wasn't much: basic medical equipment set up on the reception desk's remains, a portable table stacked with the centrifuge, a microscope and some other lab gear . . . just things that could be carried in by hand. The Rangers had thrown in a cushy swivel chair they'd found in the office behind the reception desk.

Tim pointed to the chair. "Put him there, please."

Might as well make the crazy carrier of what could be humanity's salvation as comfy as possible.

Clarence eased Mitchell into the chair. Mitchell's eyes flicked everywhere: left, right, up, down. Yep, definitely a capital *Z*.

Tim also looked around. Where the hell was Margaret? She'd insisted on this mission. He saw her, over on the far side of the lobby — just standing there in a CBRN suit that was too big for her, staring at Mitchell, doing absolutely nothing.

Why wasn't she helping?

Tim felt a hand on his shoulder: Clarence.

"Feely, you want to get started, or what?"

Tim turned to look at the shell-shocked Mitchell. The man had been through hell. He'd worry about Margaret later. This man needed help.

"Yeah, I'm on it," Tim said. He moved to stand in front of Mitchell. "Mister Mitchell. I'm Doctor Feely. Don't mind this wacky suit, I assure you there is one damn-handsome man behind this mask. I'm going to examine you, okay?"

Mitchell suddenly stood up, his fists clenched, his body shaking with intensity. Tim took a step back.

"Examine me on the boat," Mitchell said. "Or in the helicopter, or plane or whatever the fuck you're using to *get me the hell out of here*."

Clarence stepped forward, put himself between Tim and the crazy man covered with rotten goo. Clarence had his gloved hands up, palm out.

"Mister Mitchell, please calm down," he said. "Doctor Feely just has to run a couple of tests."

Tim moved to the side, used his best soothing voice. "It won't take long, Mister Mitchell," he said. "You look very dehydrated. I'm going to put in an IV and get you some fluids, okay? While I'm doing that, I need you to tell me your recent history — when you came to the city, what happened after that."

Mitchell closed his eyes, shook his head so hard his cheeks wobbled.

"No-no-no," he said. "All you need to see is this."

He pulled at his jacket sleeve, slid it up until half his forearm was exposed. He pointed at a puffy red spot a few inches above his wrist.

"That," he said. "These things pop, and a day later, those motherfuckers die."

Tim tried to control his excitement. A pustule, the same thing he'd seen on Candice Walker . . . was that little blister full of hydras?

Slow down, Timmy Boy, do this right. Take care of the patient first, then go from there.

"I see," Tim said. "Mister Mitchell, do you mind if I call you Cooper?"

The man shrugged. "Uh, sure. I guess."

"Good, Cooper. Now just let me get that IV into you, okay? Your body needs fluids."

Cooper stared off, nodded slowly. "Okay," he said. "Okay, but I'm *not* crazy. I'm not."

"Of course you aren't," Tim lied.

As Tim ran an IV needle into the back of Cooper's wrist, the man started talking rapidly. His story began with a man named Steve Stanton and a trip out to Lake Michigan to find plane wreckage. Cooper's best friend

Jeff. Some guy named Bo Pan. A high-tech fish-bot. Arrival in Chicago. A night of drinking. A few days so sick he could barely move. Jeff, gone. The incident in the boiler room, where Jeff became something other than human. Fleeing the Trump Tower. Meeting a woman named Sofia, whom the bad guys murdered. The bad guys getting sick and dying. Making the video and waiting for help.

Tim felt for the man. Cooper had been through so much. Forget the capital C and Z, this guy was all-caps *CRAZY*, with some exclamation points to boot.

But Tim also sensed Cooper was leaving out a few bits of information — rather disturbing bits, based on what he *was* willing to share — but his babbling tale provided a quick overview on the hydra contagion's morphology. It was everything Margaret had hoped for and more: the ultimate weapon against the Converted.

Cooper's story ended with him lying under a decomposing body, which explained the slime. Tim felt suddenly grateful for the CBRN suit, which filtered out most of Cooper's rather pungent stench of death.

"That's everything that happened," Cooper said. "I told you what I saw, so now you can get me out of this city."

"Soon," Tim said. "We have a little bit of work to do here first."

Cooper's hands shot out, fingers clutching Tim's thick suit. He pulled hard, his face mashing into Tim's gas mask, their foreheads touching, the mask's lenses the only thing separating their eyes.

"Get me the FUCK out of here!"

Clarence stepped in fast and grabbed Cooper's wrists. An instant later, the man lay facedown with Clarence straddling his back.

Tim just stood there, not knowing what to do as Cooper thrashed and screamed.

"Get me out of here you assholes get me out of here please please I don't wanna die!"

"Calm down," Clarence said. "You're not going to die." He pulled zip strips out of a pocket in his webbing, and in a flash had Cooper's hands bound tightly behind him.

Clarence picked the man up off the floor and set him in the swivel chair.

Cooper Mitchell stared out for a second, then began to giggle.

"Die-die-die," he said. "Am I tasty? Death is die-die-*dielicious*!"

The man's screams echoed through the ruined lobby, seemed to make the Rangers skittish.

Clarence gave Tim's shoulder a light smack. "Would you shut this guy up?"

Tim reached into the medkit and found a vial of etomidate. He quickly prepped a syringe, then injected it into the IV line.

Cooper continued to struggle for a few seconds, but quickly lost energy. He babbled a bit more, then his head drooped.

Tim could agree with Cooper on one thing, at least: he also wanted to get the fuck out of Chicago

"Don't drug him too much," Clarence said. "We might still need to move on short notice. Now get to work and find out if he's got our magic bug."

Tim again looked across the lobby — there was Margaret, still watching, not making any movement toward them. If she moved any farther away, she'd be out on the sidewalk.

"Clarence, get Margo over here," Tim said. "This is supposed to be her show, man. We still have to thaw out the bodies from the lobby so we can get blood and tissue samples."

Clarence shook his head. "I'll get some Rangers to help you. Margaret told me she needs to examine the room where we found Mitchell. She said that's the best place to start for environmentals."

"What? But that doesn't—"

"Stop talking, start working," Clarence said. "I don't want to stay here a second longer than we have to."

Clarence walked to the elevator. Margaret joined him, as did the SEAL named Bogdana, who carried a limp CBRN suit under one arm. Just before the doors shut, she looked at Tim for a moment, then stared at Cooper Mitchell. Even through her mask, Tim saw Margaret's eyes narrow into slits of pure hate.

The elevator doors slid shut, and they were gone.

What was she doing? If she wanted to look for environmental factors, she should be starting in the lobby, where Mitchell had videotaped the bodies, where the Converted had died.

Tim shook it off. Margaret knew what she was doing. He turned back to the unconscious Mitchell.

"Well, Mister Mostly Unconscious, let's find that *magic bug* so we can get the hell out of here," Tim said. "I really don't want to be here long enough to find out if *I'm* die-die-dielicious."

Cooper Mitchell didn't say anything.

Tim got to work.

FLASH MOB

Steve Stanton shivered despite his thick jacket, snowpants, gloves and hat. The wind and the cold had both intensified when the sun went down.

He and General Dana Brownstone stood in the front of a public transit bus, looking through binoculars at the soldiers around the Park Tower Hotel. Just ahead of the bus, dozens of Chosen Ones stayed low behind a barrier made of cars, trash bins, doors and general refuse.

Hatchlings scurried in and around the objects, secreting a brown fluid that was quickly transforming the barrier into a solid wall. Steve's people had tested that material in several places through the city — it stopped all small-arms fire, probably stopped everything shy of a tank cannon.

Fortunately, the humans didn't have a tank.

General Brownstone lowered her binoculars. "The sun will be coming up in a few hours, Emperor. I recommend we attack before dawn."

Steve lowered his binoculars as well. He stared out at his people, and beyond them to the towering tan hotel rising high into the night sky.

"Maybe we should wait for morning," he said. "We have a mob, not a trained army. I don't want our people accidentally wasting bullets on each other."

Brownstone smiled. "Don't worry about that, Emperor. The humans were kind enough to put on uniforms."

Steve gave Brownstone an admiring look — he should have thought of that. Just shoot at the people in the uniforms and bulky suits. How much easier could it be?

He lifted the binoculars again. He could make out the heads and shoulders of a few masked soldiers peeking out from behind the line of ruined cars. To the right of an overturned VW Beetle, the few remaining streetlights played off the black barrel of a nasty-looking, tripod-mounted weapon. The human soldiers were heavily outnumbered, but they were special forces, well armed and clearly disciplined. They would kill Steve's Chosen People by the thousands.

Good thing he had *hundreds* of thousands.

And it wasn't like the Chosen Ones were some barbarian army armed with spears and knives: his people had guns, too — and he had special soldiers of his own.

He lowered the binocs, let them dangle against his sternum.

"How many fighting-capable followers have smartphones?"

"One thousand, two hundred and twelve," Brownstone said instantly. "Each phone is held by the head of a primary cell, and each primary cell has visual or foot-messenger connections to three secondary cells. We can quickly coordinate an infantry force of thirty thousand."

Steve held out his hand, palm up. Brownstone handed him a phone. He looked at the time: 3:33 A.M. Most of those thirty thousand Chosen Ones could reach this location within forty-five minutes or less. He called up Twitter, logged on to his @MonstaMush account. He typed in his message:

> Bottle poppin' 4am, party 4:10. #ChicagoFlashMob. Hug & hold #ChicagoVIP if u find him! Please RT!

He hit "send."

Brownstone looked at the message. "Aren't you concerned the human signal intelligence analysts will see that?"

Steve shrugged. "Nationwide, there's probably still a thousand tweets a second. *If* anyone sees it, they won't know what it means, and even if they somehow figure it out they won't be able to react soon enough."

Brownstone nodded. "If the humans have overhead surveillance, they'll spot our coordinated movement. We can expect air support to arrive quickly — predator drones, Apaches, possibly other aircraft we haven't seen yet."

"Let them come," Steve said. "Get word to the rooftops. From here on out, destroy whatever flies in."

Brownstone saluted. "Yes, Emperor." She exited the bus. She would carry Steve's orders to the masses.

He looked out the bus's door to the yellow-skinned bull hiding alone behind a burned-out Mercedes thirty feet away. The day before, that bull had come looking for Steve. It had made contact with dozens of Chosen Ones along the way, and not one of them had fallen ill. Jeremy Ellis had taken the bull straight to his biology lab, yet found no trace of disease. Ellis thought the bulls were not only immune to Cooper Mitchell's disease, they also weren't carriers of it.

"Yo!" Steve yelled to the bull. "Are you ready to find your old friend?"

Like a puppy called by its master, the massive creature took two hurried steps toward the bus before it stopped, remembering it wasn't supposed to get close.

"COOOOOPERRRRRR," the bull said. "FIND . . . COOOPERRRRR."

Steve smiled. God willing, Cooper Mitchell would die at the hands of his lifelong friend. The *mutated* hands, with those awesome bone-blades.

All things in due time. Steve checked the cell phone: forty minutes to go . . .

GAME CHANGE

Jackpot.

Tim lifted his head from the microscope. He wanted to drink scotch and screw and watch cartoons . . . maybe in that order, maybe not. He wanted to *party.*

Cooper Mitchell's blood contained *thousands* of hydras.

Tim had also found dead hydras in the frozen bodies that had been in the hotel lobby. Correlation wasn't causation, true, but the results pointed to one *motherfucker* of a correlation: Cooper Mitchell was Patient Zero. The *good* kind of Patient Zero.

I've got you Norman Bates bitches by the short and curlies . . . you're all gonna die.

"Cooper, you lovely, lovely bastion of microbial awesomeness, you might have just saved the world."

The man's story indicated he infected those around him almost immediately. The hydras debilitated individuals within just eight to twelve hours of initial exposure, killed them within twenty-four. What was more, Cooper said he hadn't touched any of the people who had found him in the Walgreens, yet at least five of the six had contracted the fatal pathogen. That meant the hydras *were* airborne, and were *highly* contagious; just being in the same room was enough.

It didn't matter what Margaret found up on the eighteenth floor, or anywhere else for that matter. The mission became one simple objective: get Cooper Mitchell out of Chicago and into a lab.

According to Cooper, only the "Jeff Monster" had survived the twenty-four-hour lethality. Tim had seen images of the big creatures, so different they looked more akin to gorillas than humans. That kind of large-scale physical alteration required large-scale genetic change: perhaps hydras took longer to affect them, or possibly didn't affect them at all.

But that wasn't Tim's problem. The hydras killed the other known forms — the dead in the Park Tower's lobby included two triangle hosts, two kissyfaces and one that had no marks of any kind yet died all the same.

He couldn't wait to tell Margaret. She'd want to double-check Tim's results, see for herself if he'd gotten it right. Of course, she'd actually have to come to the lab area to do that, actually have to stand next to Cooper Mitchell.

Which she wasn't doing . . . she hadn't even come *near* Cooper . . .

Margaret had been hands-on with Walker and Petrovsky. Years earlier, she'd personally done the work on Martin Brewbaker, Perry Dawsey, Betty Jewel and Carmen Sanchez. She'd been up-close and personal with infected both living and dead. Why would she go out of her way to avoid Cooper?

Because she knew that Cooper's hydras killed the Converted.

She knew, and she didn't want to die.

Tim slapped himself lightly on the sides of his masked head, *left-right-left-right*. Margaret couldn't be infected. She'd tested negative. She'd taken the inoculant, then tested negative some more. And besides that, she was *Margaret Montoya*, grand defender of the human race.

She tested negative . . .

But so had that diver, Cantrell, who had tried to kill Margaret during the escape from the *Brashear*. Tim had written Cantrell's behavior off to panic and confusion from the attack, the explosion that had blown his cell open, from breathing in a near-lethal dose of bleach. Why? Because Cantrell had shown no signs of infection.

That corpse in the Park Tower lobby, the tall one in the red coat, he had no signs of infection, either, yet his blood had been full of hydras all the same . . .

Tim lunged for the med kit. He tore it open, throwing things aside until he found what he needed: a cellulose tester. The unit would work on a dead body just as well as on a live one.

OBEY

Clarence stood in the doorway of Room 1812, waiting for a chance to be useful. Margaret wouldn't even let him help with little things like gathering samples or moving that nasty body. She was happy to let the SEAL, Bogdana, handle all of that.

Margaret was acting odd, even stranger than she'd acted on the *Coronado*. She had always wanted to be hands-on, yet now she was letting Tim do the dirty work? The *most important* work?

She said it was because of the baby: she wasn't taking any chances. Clarence wasn't about to argue with that. She shouldn't have come in the first place.

Margaret didn't touch anything in Room 1812. She insisted Bogdana wear the CBRN suit for this particular bit of work. Being unprotected on the streets was one thing, while handling a corpse was another. She directed his actions: move the rotting body; fill this vial; scoop up that slime; and on and on.

Clarence's headset crackled, followed by Tim's voice on the open channel.

"This is Doctor Feely." He sounded upset. "Clarence, are you out there? Talk to me, man."

Margaret's head snapped up.

Clarence reached to thumb the "talk" button, paused when Margaret held up a hand palm out: *stop right there*.

"Don't answer him," she said. "I need your help, right now."

He'd stood there for fifteen minutes with his thumb up his ass and *now* she needed him?

He held up a finger, asking her to be quiet as he thumbed the "talk" button.

"Feely, this is Clarence, go ahead."

"I found . . . uh, is Margaret with you by chance?"

"She is."

"Ah," Tim said. "Well . . . I found something. Can you come down here? Now? It's really important."

Margaret shook her gas-mask-covered head. Was she playing some kind of mind game? Was she craving protection, perhaps because of the baby, or was this another punishment for him leaving her? Whatever her reason, Clarence didn't have time to play along.

He thumbed the "talk" button again. "I'll be right down, Tim."

Margaret pointed to the floor. "I need you *here*. Do not go down there, Clarence, you hear me?"

Bogdana watched them both, the eyes behind his gas mask showing an expression of annoyed disbelief.

Maybe Margaret had good reason to be mad, but that didn't change the fact that Clarence had a job to do.

"Bogdana," Clarence said to the SEAL, "stay with Doctor Montoya until I check this out. I'll be back as quick as I can."

Bogdana nodded. "Yeah, I'll take care of the doc."

Clarence hesitated a moment, looked at Margaret's angry stare one more time, then jogged toward the elevator.

BALLS

Tim knew.

Margaret could tell from the sound of his voice. She didn't know how he'd figured it out, but there was no question — *he knew.*

She had to act now.

"Sorry about this, Bogdana, but I really need a skin sample from the genitalia."

The man's shoulders dropped. "Please tell me you're kidding."

Margaret shook her head. Her suit's gas mask wobbled just a little, despite the fact that she had it on so tight it partially cut off the circulation in her face.

"Sorry, but it has to be done."

She forced herself closer to the bloated corpse. A puddle of fluid stained the carpet beneath it — liquid from decomposition rather than blood. The man's penis and testicles looked black and shriveled, like a rotten avocado spotted with moisture.

"I need a sample" — she pointed to the decomposing member — "from right below his scrotum."

Bogdana shook his head, sighed. "My mother will be so proud that her only son is the military's highest-paid collector of fromunda cheese."

He knelt on both knees, then reached a gloved hand under the corpse's genitalia. He lifted gently, bent his head for a closer look.

Margaret quietly drew the Sig Sauer P226 from her thigh holster. She pointed it at the back of Bogdana's head and pulled the trigger.

SHOTS FIRED

Clarence exited the elevator and strode toward Tim's lab area. The little scientist jogged to meet him halfway, feet crunching on the broken glass and bits of charred wood scattered about the lobby.

"It's Margaret," Tim said. "I think she's infected."

Clarence stopped. What kind of bullshit was Tim trying to pull? Was the little coward looking for a way out?

Tim grabbed Clarence's arm, pulled him toward Cooper Mitchell. The man was moving again, head lolling as he struggled to wake up.

Tim looked back to the elevator, then around the lobby. He leaned in close.

"You heard me," he said. "Margaret is *infected*."

Clarence yanked his arm free of Tim's anxious grip.

"She's not. She's been with us the whole time. She drank the inoculant. So did I. So did you."

Tim nodded rapidly, continued to glance at the elevator. Clarence understood why — he was afraid Margaret might come down. He was afraid of *Margaret*.

"I know she did," Tim said. "The only thing that makes sense is she was exposed *before* we left the *Brashear*. By the time she drank the yeast, she'd already been infected for more than twenty-four hours, so it was too late to save her. Come on, man, she wouldn't come anywhere near Cooper. Does that sound like Margaret to you?"

All the pressure, the danger . . . Tim had lost it. He'd cracked.

"You're wrong," Clarence said, struggling to keep his voice level. "She's *pregnant*, you paranoid little shit. She doesn't want to take any chances."

"Are you kidding me?" Tim spread his arms, a gesture that took in the hotel, the city, everything. "Does this look like a sixth-grade field trip to the museum?" He pointed at Cooper. "She comes into this slaughterhouse no problem, then won't get near him? She's afraid of catching the hydras, Otto — she's afraid of catching a disease that *only* kills the infected."

No . . . Tim was wrong. He had to be.

"She tested over and over again," Clarence said. "She blew negative every time."

"So did Cantrell." Tim picked up a testing kit off the portable table and held it up. The light showed a steady green "So did the guy in the red coat, the one that Cooper said was the leader of his group of Converted. The guy who died from the hydras, just like the other infected. There's a strain the test doesn't detect, Otto, and Margaret has it."

Clarence stared at the testing kit. Green light. Margaret's tests showed green lights. She wouldn't go near Cooper. No, there had to be an explanation.

"The baby," he said. "She doesn't know how hydras might affect the baby."

"*Stop it*," Tim snapped. "We don't have *time* for denial. We have to—"

Klimas's voice came over their headsets.

"All personnel, Predator drones show heavy foot traffic headed our way," he said. "Movement on East Chicago, coming from both directions on Michigan, and *all* of it converging on our position. They aren't coming to swap spit and rub tummies, people. Man the perimeter, fire at anything that moves. It's game time."

How could they attack *now*? Tim said Margaret was infected . . . maybe she was just sick . . . the baby, making her act strange . . .

Clarence's headset let out a short burst of static as someone switched frequencies.

"Otto, this is Klimas, over?"

Clarence reacted automatically. "Otto here, go ahead."

"The shit is about to hit the fan. SITREP on the civvies?"

"Montoya is up in 1812 with Bogdana," Clarence said. "I'm in the lobby with Feely and Mitchell."

"Good," Klimas said. "Stay right there unless I tell you otherwise, or unless someone is shooting at you."

His wife was upstairs, and an attack was coming.

"I have to go get Margaret. I'll grab her and—"

"Negative, Agent Otto," Klimas said. "Stay *right where you are*. You are responsible for protecting Feely and the package. I'll have Bogdana bring Montoya down. Klimas, out."

Clarence closed his eyes, tried to think things through. The future of the human race was right next to him, sitting in a swivel chair, still partially sedated. But his family was seventeen floors above. Was Tim crazy?

Or, if Tim was right . . .

Clarence's headset came alive with Rangers and SEALs calling out targets, with the sound of weapons fire.

Then several voices at once, from both inside the lobby and over the comm link, calling the same word: *incoming!*

Clarence heard a muffled crash of glass followed by the *whoof* of billowing fire that filled the lobby with a sudden and angry orange light.

GAME ON

Paulius Klimas rolled across the snowy pavement, putting out the flames that danced up his thighs. Molotov cocktails rained down around him. The smell of burning gasoline filled the air. Mortars from inside the perimeter *thoooped*, weapons fired, men shouted out targets or screamed in agony.

Paulius slid up against the door of a burned-out Lincoln Navigator. He peeked around the front bumper, east down Chicago Avenue. Dozens of small flames arced through the air toward his position, spinning orange stars that would land and burst, spreading long ovals of flame. Off in the distance, he saw muzzle flashes coming from behind overturned cars on Chicago Avenue and on Rush Street, as well as from skyscraper windows in all directions.

Bullets plinked off the Navigator, punched through what glass still remained in the ruined vehicle. Molotovs hit every few seconds. Most of the improvised missiles fell short, but more than a few sailed over the perimeter to set the pavement afire.

He thumbed to his SEAL-only frequency and pressed the "talk" button.

"This is Klimas. Overwatch, locate and return fire, concentrate on enemy positions in the buildings on the corners of Chicago and Rush, Chicago and Michigan. Prioritize all high-elevation enemy snipers, repeat, all high-elevation enemy snipers. SITREP by squads, go."

The squads reported back: heavy concentrations of small-arms fire and Molotovs coming in from all directions. Most of the enemy troops had to be armed civilians. His marksmen would thin them out quickly, but just how big a force did they face?

Paulius switched to the Rangers' channel and listened in. Captain Dundee was already calling in air support. The Apaches would be here in minutes.

The hotel was so large, Paulius still had men going from floor to floor, securing the place one room at a time. He switched back to the SEAL channel.

"Interior personnel, sound off."

His men reported in. All but one — Bogdana. Were there still bad guys in the hotel? Had they taken out Bogs and Margo?

He switched channels again. "Civilians, sound off!"

Tim coughed, trying to clear the thick, greasy smoke from his lungs and throat. He'd lost his gas mask.

He pushed himself to his knees, but stayed behind the reception counter. The Rangers were putting out fires even as bullets whizzed into the lobby, splintering into the wood walls or taking chunks out of the black marble columns.

He saw Cooper Mitchell lying prone, struggling to rise. Tim threw an arm over the man, protecting him as well as he could.

Then the big form of Clarence Otto scrambled behind the ruined counter, aimed his pistol over it toward the hotel's front entrance.

Tim heard the short burst of static caused by someone coming onto the civilian frequency.

"Civilians, sound off!"

Klimas. In the background Tim heard the constant roar of gunfire and a wounded soldier screaming for help.

"Otto here," Clarence said. "Feely is with me, as is the package."

"Acknowledged," Klimas said. "Margaret, sound off."

There was no response.

"Margaret, *sound off*," Klimas said again.

Still nothing.

Otto crouched low. "Have Bogdana bring her down, Klimas, right now."

"No response from Bogdana," Klimas said.

Had Margaret killed the man? Tim didn't know if she could get the drop on a SEAL, but she was infected, he *knew* she was, and that meant she was capable of anything.

Clarence stayed low but took a step toward the elevator. "Klimas, I'm going to get Margaret."

"Negative, Otto, that's a—" Klimas stopped in midsentence. Gunfire filled Tim's headphones, so loud it made him wince. "I repeat, that's a negative. I'm sending Bosh and Ramierez to get her. Otto, *do not leave your post.*"

Clarence paused. Tim could see the man's eyes through the gas mask lenses, see the turmoil, the indecision.

"Affirmative," Clarence said.

Tim heard the click of Klimas switching off the channel.

Outside, the gunfire sounded constant, an orchestra of unending death. A bullet hit the centrifuge on top of the portable table, sending it spinning violently down to the marble floor.

Clarence shook his head. "I have to get her."

He again turned toward the elevator.

Tim reached up, grabbed Clarence's arm.

"Otto, stay *here*, goddamit! Don't you fucking leave us alone!"

Cooper Mitchell tried to roll to his hands and knees but lost his balance, fell back down to his side. He looked around, eyes blinking and unfocused.

Clarence grabbed Tim's wrist, pulled the hand free.

"I'm going to get my wife," he said. "Stay here with Cooper. The Rangers will protect you."

He sprinted for the elevator.

Tim felt lost. He looked at Cooper Mitchell, who was again trying to get to his hands and knees. Cooper . . . it was all about Cooper, about the microorganism he had in his body, in his blood.

Tim pressed his "talk" button. "Klimas, this is Feely, come in! Come in, Klimas!"

Klimas came back instantly, both his voice and the sound of gunfire painfully loud.

"Goddamit, Feely, stay off this channel!"

"Margaret's infected. Otto went to get her. I'm alone with Mitchell. Get us out of here!"

A bullet ripped through the portable table's metal leg — the table leaned to the right and fell on its edge.

"Feely," Klimas said, "do you have a weapon?"

"No."

"Then find one. Right now Mitchell is your responsibility. Protect him. The lobby is the safest place we have. That reception counter is decent cover, so stay behind it. I'll get someone to you as soon as I can. Klimas, out."

The frequency clicked off.

I am so screwed, so screwed . . .

A crash of glass, a *whuff* of billowing fire so close Tim felt the heat through his suit. He threw himself on top of Cooper to protect him from the flames.

So screwed, so screwed . . .

FREEDOM

Margaret paused on the stairwell landing of the fifteenth floor. She carefully checked her suit for tears and cuts: she couldn't take any chances now.

She had killed Bogdana, blown his brains all over that rotted corpse. To pull the trigger, to know *she* was the one to end that subcreature's miserable existence . . . it felt *glorious*.

Humans had pissed away their chance to live on this world. War, hatred, pollution, genocide . . . the true legacy of humankind. She hadn't taken a life; she had simply exterminated a pest.

After she'd killed Bogdana, she'd heard the battle erupt in the streets. A look out the window gave her all the motivation she needed to keep fighting — as far down Chicago Avenue as she could see, waves and waves of people hiding behind barriers, waiting to advance. The Converted, coming to save her.

But Cooper Mitchell was downstairs. *The Antichrist*. If her kind poured in like a tidal wave of blessed bodies, overwhelming the Rangers and SEALS, they might come into contact with that diseased piece of garbage; they might be exposed. If as few as four or five of them contracted his hydras and then faded into the night, mingled with others, that was enough to start an unstoppable plague. Margaret's people might be wiped out forever, leaving God's will unfulfilled. The humans could keep developing, keep building, until someday they reached the stars.

She had to stop that from happening. She had to kill Cooper Mitchell before her people could reach him. She had the gun. D'Shawn Bosh had shown her how to use it, how to take a shooter's stance, how to breathe out slowly, how to *squeeze* the trigger, never *pull* it.

Margaret didn't have to get close to Cooper to kill him: she just needed a clean shot.

A clean shot, and a distraction.

That fucker Feely had probably already told Clarence and the others that she was infected — they wouldn't trust her now, might even kill her on sight. She had to be careful, but she also had to move fast. The Converted onslaught would provide her the needed distraction. Everyone would be busy trying to repel the attack.

Kill Cooper Mitchell, then get to her people: that was all that mattered.

Afterward, she could figure out how to defuse humanity's last weapon. She had discovered the hydras; she could also find a way to destroy them. Chicago had universities, hospitals — she could cobble together a working lab. She'd saved humanity three times over, so why couldn't she do the same for her new tribe?

But first, Cooper had to die.

Margaret started down the steps.

THE EVIDENCE

Clarence sprinted down the hallway of the eighteenth floor, Glock 19 in hand, heading for the room where they'd found Cooper Mitchell. He leaned left to turn the corner without slowing, booted feet digging into the hallway carpet. He came around to the sight of a pair of M4s pointed his way. He tried to stop suddenly, knew in that moment bullets would rip him to shreds, but he was moving too fast — his forward momentum slammed him into the far wall.

He fell to the floor.

"*Drop the weapon!*" Ramierez screamed.

Clarence let the Glock fall from his hand to thump on the hallway's carpet.

Ramierez stayed in place, black M4 tight to his shoulder and aimed at Clarence's chest.

D'Shawn Bosh ran up, grabbed Clarence's sidearm, took two steps back.

"Montoya," Bosh said. "Where is she? She killed Bogdana."

That couldn't be true, *couldn't* be; there had to be hostiles in the building.

"You guys got it all wrong," Clarence said. "Margaret didn't kill anyone."

"Get your ass up," Bosh said.

Clarence stood.

Ramierez's aim didn't waver. He seethed with visible fury — if Clarence gave him a reason, he knew Ramierez would put him down.

Bosh pushed Clarence down the hall.

"Move," Bosh said. "See for yourself."

Clarence felt so lost, so disoriented. He didn't resist.

Another push on his back as he stumbled into Room 1812.

Clarence saw two bodies: the bloated thing that Cooper had hid beneath and, sprawled on top of it, Bogdana. A small hole in his CBRN suit, right at the back of his head, told the story.

"Point blank," Bosh said. "Bogdana's a SEAL, asshole — you think one of those gibbering idiots could have gotten that close to him?"

Clarence shook his head. No . . . not Margaret . . . she was immune, Clarence had *seen* her take the tests.

"We have to find her," he said. "She . . . she's in danger."

The words rang hollow, even to him.

Bosh tossed Clarence's pistol onto the bed.

"Ram and I are going to the fifth floor," he said. "Setting up a sniper position. Look for her if you want. But when you see her, if you don't shoot first, it was real nice knowing you."

The two SEALs ran off down the hall.

Clarence thumbed his "talk" button.

"Margaret, answer me."

He waited. No response.

"Margaret, please, *please* answer me!"

Nothing.

Clarence stared at Bogdana.

Bosh was right. Tim was right.

Margaret had done this.

She was *infected*.

The brutal reality hit home. He leaned against the wall. His wife, his love, the mother of his child . . . she was one of *them*.

The noise of the battle seemed to hit him all at once, the sounds of gunfire filtering up from the street. And not that far off, the pounding of helicopter rotors.

Why had she revealed herself now? Had she known this attack was coming, somehow? More of that infected telepathy, their hive-mind making them all move as one? Or was it simply because she realized that Tim had discovered her secret, that he was about to out her? But if that was the case, Margaret could have denied it — she tested negative, Tim would have had no proof.

Clarence looked at Bogdana. Had Margaret killed the man so she could slip away and join her kind?

The mission . . . the package . . . he had to focus on that. If he didn't concentrate on saving Cooper Mitchell, on making all of this worthwhile, he knew he'd go insane.

Clarence grabbed his weapon, turned, and ran for the elevator.

COCKTAIL PARTY

Flames soared from cars, trucks, delivery vans and buses, destroying any night-vision capability. Heat from a dozen fires chased away the winter night's chill. This wasn't a couple of indigs hucking a bottle to pretend they could fight back against the oppressors: this was a concentrated, planned, *sustained* attack.

From the north, south, east and west, men called for backup.

Paulius had no backup to send.

The Converted stayed behind their cover of burned-out cars and trucks, providing few targets to hit. When heads did pop up, the SEALs and the Rangers took them out. His overwatch had mowed down most of the enemy's high positions and were now picking off anything that moved.

The Molotov barrage had slowed since the attack began five minutes earlier, but still the bombs poured in, a constant symphony of breaking glass and billowing flame. The Converted had to be using a sling of some kind, something to hurl the gas-filled bottles farther than any man could possibly throw.

He clicked his "talk" button.

"This is Klimas, can anyone up top see what they're using to launch those Molotovs?"

"Negative, Commander," came back Roth's voice. "The bad guys put burning tires in front of their perimeter wall, too much smoke to see what's going on."

Through the flames and the constant gunfire, Paulius heard the roar of approaching helicopters. Apaches, lining up an attack run — these local yokels were about to get a rude awakening courtesy of chain-gun music.

He peeked out under the bumper of a delivery truck, looked east along Chicago Avenue. Many Molotovs had fallen short and crashed into the pavement. The flickering flames made the air waver and warp. Through that, Paulius saw bits of movement about thirty meters out, heads peeking above cars, shadows sliding from vehicle to vehicle.

Heads . . . and something else, something smaller, lower to the ground.

Roth's deep voice again: "This is East Overlook, we have large numbers of enemy infantry advancing on us from the east, on Chicago Avenue. Holy shit, boys, looks like *thousands* of them. Mixed units, people and those hatchling things."

Klimas switched to the Ranger channel. "SEAL commander to Captain Dundee. SEAL commander to Captain Dundee."

The Ranger commander answered instantly. "Dundee here, go."

"We have a battalion-sized force of infantry attacking from the east."

"Same from the north, south and west," Dundee said. "Drone video confirms."

"Weapons free," Paulius said. "Shoot anything that isn't us and maintain our perimeter."

"Roger that, Dundee, out."

Paulius switched back to the SEAL channel as a nearby Ranger opened up with a long burst from a 240.

"Weapons free, I repeat, weapons free. All but squad weapons use single fire. Make your shots count, boys — I don't think we brought enough bullets."

He clicked off, then leaned out past the front fender, just enough for the barrel of his M4 to aim down the street.

Three black hatchlings rushed toward him, running through the pools of fire rather than around them. Flames clung to their black pyramid bodies, curled around their tentacle-legs.

So fast . . . I've never seen anything that fast . . .

Paulius pulled the trigger twice, *pop-pop;* the middle hatchling went down hard. Another one dropped, either from a Ranger's bullet or from one of his overwatch men up on the fifth floor. The creature's forward momentum rolled it awkwardly beneath a burning car.

The third hatchling closed to within five meters.

Don't fire till you see the blacks of their eyes flashed through Paulius's mind right before he dropped it with another two-bullet burst.

The thunder of the Apaches' rotors echoed through the city canyons. The tone suddenly became more raw, more *real* as the first helicopter came around a building into plain sight, just behind the oncoming wave of attackers. Paulius heard the sharp snare-drum sound of M230 chain guns opening up.

A Molotov landed ten feet to his left, forcing him away from the front fender. He scrambled to the rear fender, looked around it. Through the flickering flames and the shimmering air he saw the enemy rushing forward.

Hundreds of hatchlings, and behind them, an endless wave of people.

As fast as he could, Paulius yanked grenades from his webbing and threw them at the oncoming mob.

STREETS OF FIRE

Frank Sokolovsky wondered if there could be anywhere colder than where he stood. Besides the roof of the John Hancock Building, sixty stories up, in the dead of night, with a Chicago winter wind whipping in at twenty miles an hour? That was some cold shit right there.

He had worked his way through college on the GI Bill. He'd served most of one tour in Afghanistan before an IED blew his left foot clean off. Frank had considered himself lucky — not only had he lived, he'd been given a medical discharge and gone home to Hyde Park, to his job as a shipping manager, to his wife, Carol, and their daughter, Shelly.

Frank had felt God's touch earlier than most. It came with pain, as did all things truly worth having. Carol knew something had changed. She knew even before Frank did, to be honest. He'd made some comment about disciplining Shelly. He still couldn't remember exactly what he'd said, but when he woke up the next morning, Carol and Shelly were both gone. That was too bad, because from that morning on he'd known exactly what he would have done to them both.

Frank had left his house and just wandered. His first kill had been a mouthy old lady. *Leave me alone*, the bitch had said. Can you imagine? *Please, no*, she had said. The nerve of some people.

He discovered new friends. Together, they found humans, killed them. Then word came of a true leader, a leader asking for everyone with military experience. Emperor Stanton and General Brownstone gave him a wonderful responsibility — a Stinger missile.

For two days, Frank Sokolovsky had frozen his ass off atop the Hancock. People brought him food. Once they'd brought him a whole arm, already cooked. There was probably half of that left.

Finally, though, the waiting was over.

He stood still, mostly hidden from sight, the Stinger on his right shoulder, watching the Apache fly down Michigan Avenue about thirty feet below his rooftop elevation. The helicopter's nose was tipped down, its 30-millimeter chain gun transforming the street below into a sparkling river of death.

The screaming war machine flew past.

Just before Frank pressed the "fire" button, he understood — without a doubt — that everything happened for a reason. He had needed money for college, so he joined the army. He'd served in Afghanistan, where he'd learned to fire this kind of weapon, where he'd suffered the injury that brought him home so he could become enlightened at *just* the right time. Anyone who considered that a coincidence was a fool. Frank knew the hand of God when he saw it, and for that guidance he whispered a fast prayer of thanks.

He pressed the button.

A Stinger launcher fires a FIM-92B missile: sixty inches long, twenty-two pounds. It is supersonic capable and can reach speeds of Mach 2.2. Frank's missile didn't attain that speed, because it was only in the air for three seconds — one second of flight powered by the launcher's ejection motor, which hurled the missile out into the predawn sky, and two seconds of flight powered by the missile's solid fuel rocket engine.

The FIM-92B penetrated right between the Apache's twin turboshaft engines. The warhead erupted, blowing both engines off the machine with such force that one flew three hundred feet to hammer into the glass and steel of Water Tower Place. The other engine clipped a building roof before comet-streaking into Chestnut Street, disintegrating into a cloud of tumbling, red-hot shards that shredded everything in their path.

In an Apache, the gunner sits in front, the pilot above and behind him, an armored wall between them. The explosion killed the pilot instantly. The armor kept the gunner alive long enough for the flaming helicopter to fall seven hundred feet to the street below, where he died on impact.

The wreckage smashed into the Converted running down Michigan Avenue, a rolling fireball that pounded flesh into paste. Pieces of the Apache broke off and crashed into stores, shattering glass, breaking walls and starting several fires.

Frank Sokolovsky stared down at his handiwork. He felt bad about where the helicopter had hit — how many of his kind had died? That was part of God's plan, though, and who was he to question God?

To the south, he saw another Apache start to climb. Maybe it had seen Frank's target go down and wanted to get some altitude, but it was already too late; a chasing flicker betrayed a Stinger fired from the roof of the Marriott on North Rush Street. Coincidentally, Frank and Carol had stayed in that very hotel on their honeymoon.

He laughed when the fireball engulfed the Apache. The Fourth of July was nothing compared to this. The flaming Apache banked and flew into another skyscraper, impacting at about the thirtieth floor. Frank didn't know the name of that building.

He shivered and set down his launcher. Unless someone brought him another missile, his work was done. He looked around. He'd fully expected that as soon as he fired, another helicopter would have swept in and killed him.

Maybe God had bigger plans for him. He'd head back inside, build a little fire and see if he could thaw out some of that arm.

Frank heard the Hellfire missile but he never saw it. By the time he turned around, the Predator-fired weapon detonated within fifteen feet of him, tearing him into three good-sized pieces that all sailed over the side of the John Hancock Building.

Fire danced around the Park Tower's ruined entrance. Icy, driving wind fed the flames. Clarence felt simultaneously hot and cold, and yet he also felt neither of those things: his mind focused on the battle, on the details that would keep him alive, let him find Margaret.

"Apaches are down," said a voice in his headset. "Bad guys have SAMs."

"Tell the Chinooks to abort pickup," said another voice. "If we lose them, the only way out is on foot."

Clarence had a Ranger on his left, two on his right, all firing at the attackers scrambling over the perimeter cars.

If only they'd extracted Cooper Mitchell as soon as they found him, then they wouldn't be facing this army of Converted. But Margaret had insisted staying was critical, and Clarence had believed her.

A voice on the open channel screamed for help. A burst of gunfire cut the scream short.

So much panicked chatter. Men shouted for help. It sounded like the Rush Street perimeter was about to be overrun.

Something whizzed past his ear. He instinctively jerked backward, so fast he fell onto his ass. He'd come within inches of taking a round in the face.

There weren't any reinforcements coming in. Air support was gone. The Rangers wouldn't be able to hold.

Clarence had to keep Cooper Mitchell alive.

He turned and ran into the lobby. "Feely! Get Cooper on his feet, we have to move!"

A maskless Tim shook his head hard so his spiky blond hair flopped back and forth. "No way! Klimas said to stay right here!"

Clarence ignored him. Cooper was sitting on the floor, looking around. Still groggy, but his eyes seemed normal, alert. Clarence knelt in front of him.

"Mister Mitchell, you with us?"

The man's eyes widened and blinked rapidly at the same time. Then they focused, locked on Clarence's.

"Yeah," he said. "I'm just a little fuzzy, maybe. And call me *Cooper*."

"Can you walk, Cooper?"

He nodded.

Tim leaned in. "Otto, we *have* to stay here!"

Clarence heard a hissing roar. His body reacted; he grabbed Tim and pulled him on top of a surprised Cooper, covering them both with his own body a moment before a crushing blast drove them all against the shaking floor.

FRONT TOWARD ENEMY

Paulius kept firing and reloading, his hands acting on autopilot while his brain tried to work out the rapidly deteriorating situation. They'd lost air superiority. Even with a significant advantage in firepower, they were outnumbered at least a hundred to one.

The snipers on the fifth floor were the only thing keeping the hostiles from overrunning Klimas's position. At their rate of fire, they'd run out of ammo in mere minutes.

Ranger-fired mortars *thoomped* every few seconds, followed by popping explosions out beyond the perimeter. The firing arcs were short enough that Paulius felt the concussion wave of each detonation.

The constant roar of the 240s, the pops of M4s and the barks of Benelli shotguns told him the perimeter remained intact. M23 grenade launchers countered the endless barrage of Molotov cocktails, filling Chicago Avenue with shrapnel.

And still the Converted came on, hatchlings and armed militants stepping over the shattered and still-twitching bodies of their comrades. Twenty meters and closing.

He thumbed his "talk" button.

"Claymores, *now*! Light 'em up!"

He'd barely finished his sentence before the powerful mines started detonating, each one a horizontal storm of seven hundred one-eighth-inch steel balls shooting out horizontally at a speed of twelve hundred meters per second. The enemy soldiers were packed in so tight Paulius could see the Claymores' blast patterns in the expanding cones of shredded bodies.

The advance slowed. The enemy suddenly broke, turned and ran, leaving behind hundreds of dead and dying. The little snow that remained on the street had turned into red slush, soaking up the blood that flowed down the sidewalk gutters.

Steve Stanton lowered his binoculars.

"Chickenshits," he said. "They're running."

General Brownstone nodded. "Too much enemy firepower. Looks like we inflicted some casualties, though. If I may suggest, Emperor, we should use the M72 light antitank weapons to target their snipers, and all our launched grenades to cover the second wave's advance."

That was the right call, and Steve knew it. He'd been hoping the first wave would overwhelm the human soldiers, but they were too well trained and too well armed.

"We don't have many of those M72s, General."

She nodded again. "Yes, Emperor. However, I'm certain the humans detonated all of their Claymores, and they have to be running low on ammunition. Our fast ground attack should breach their perimeter if we can clear out the snipers."

If the second wave didn't work, Steve's only option was to launch the third wave. That wave was supposed to be his containment wave, the troops that would kill anyone — Converted included — that came out of the hotel.

He didn't have time to think it through. The humans could send more helicopters at any moment, and his people had used up most of the Stingers.

The humans were running out of ammo, but so were the Chosen Ones.

He raised the binoculars. "General Brownstone, launch wave two."

Paulius ejected a spent magazine, popped in a fresh one. The enemy had fallen back, but they were still firing. He'd found new cover behind a white delivery truck. Bullets smacked into the metal body so fast it sounded like an off-rhythm drummer experimenting with a new song.

One Ranger lay dying to his left. Another to his right was already gone, or he would have screamed from the flames that engulfed his chest and arm.

An explosion came from the towering hotel above and behind him. Paulius looked up to see a cloud of thin smoke billowing from the fifth floor, window shards tumbling down to the street below. He saw a second explosion — a there-and-gone fireball blowing out a cloud of spinning glass, shredded insulation and torn metal.

He thumbed his SEAL channel.

"Overwatch, displace, rockets targeting fifth floor!"

Another explosion hit the hotel, farther to the right; three smoldering holes gaped wide, making the building look like a tree chopped at the base that might topple over and crash into the street.

The interior perimeter suddenly lit up with hard-hitting *snap* explosions that cast out waves of dirt and snow. Paulius threw himself face-first to the pavement — there wasn't much one could do against a grenade volley but lie low and pray.

A machine gun barked. A man shouting "Here they come again!" drew Paulius's attention back to the street.

He stayed on his belly, aimed his M4 under the truck, found his first targets: a pair of kids — *kids, dammit* — sprinting forward, each holding a kitchen knife. He took them out, two shots for the first, three for the second.

And then, Paulius saw something that his eyes couldn't immediately process: a taxi, sliding *sideways* toward the perimeter, toward *him*, smashing bodies aside, tires pushing up little waves of red slush. There was something behind that car.

Something *big*.

"All units, concentrate fire on that taxi!"

The taxi's doors blossomed with new holes as Rangers and SEALs alike focused their fire, but the vehicle was moving too fast — it was too late to stop it.

Paulius dove away from the delivery truck a moment before the cab crashed in. The truck toppled, smashed down on its right side. A Ranger who had been using the truck for cover didn't make it clear; the heavy vehicle crushed his left foot, trapping him.

Klimas rolled to his feet, came up ready to fire — and for the first time in his military career, he froze.

A *monster*. Eight feet tall, shoulders and chest rippling with thick coils of muscle. Molotov firelight played off wet, dark-yellow skin. Open sores dotted the body, some trailing visible rivulets of pus. The wide neck supported a huge, heavy-jawed head topped with spotty patches of tight, curly black hair. The face seemed toylike compared to the oversized body. Its mouth was full of long, thick teeth that could easily rip flesh from bones.

And sticking up from behind each clenched fist, a long, jagged, pointed arc of bone.

The trapped Ranger rolled to his back, stared up at the monstrosity only a foot away. The Ranger screamed.

The yellowish beast raised a bare foot, drove it down into the Ranger's stomach. The soldier's screaming stopped. His hands weakly gripped the long leg, then his fingers slid away and his arms fell limply to the wet pavement.

The monster leaned down and *roared*.

Klimas heard the telltale *thoop* of a grenade launcher. An explosion knocked the massive creature back, splashing his bloody entrails in a long streak across the white top of the overturned truck.

Gunfire brought Paulius out of it, gunfire aimed at him — a man and a woman sprinting around the delivery truck, the man firing a rifle, the screaming woman aiming a shotgun.

In less than a second, Klimas hit them each twice. The man dropped hard. The woman landed face-first and slid across the packed snow. Klimas fired twice more, aiming for her head, but his shots hit her back instead. As she slid, she raised the shotgun one-handed, screamed "*asshole!*" and fired.

He felt the blast smack into the left side of his chest and belly, felt a dozen needles dig deep as some of them found ways around the gaps in his body armor.

She slid to a stop. He put a bullet in her head, then looked up.

A dozen more hostiles poured in around the truck. Two of them tackled a fleeing Ranger. Another Ranger lay on the ground, screaming obscenities at the three people on top of him, one biting his face, another stabbing a knife into his right thigh over and over again. And just beyond the truck, Paulius saw two more of the yellow monsters rushing in fast.

His position was being overrun.

I promised Feely I'd get him out, and if I don't save him and Mitchell, then all this is for nothing.

Paulius turned and ran, tossing a flash-bang behind him. Up ahead, smoke billowed out of the hotel's entrance.

"All exterior SEALs, fall back to the hotel! Our mission is to get the civilians to safety. Someone find me another way out of that building!"

EVERYONE LOVES A PARADE

Steve Stanton really, *really* wanted to ride on Jeff's back, like Hannibal riding an elephant into battle, but that was a bad idea; there were probably still a few human snipers left in the Park Tower.

So instead of riding in glory, the emperor of Chicago walked toward the hotel. He walked slowly, and far back from the still-advancing second wave. Steve stayed a few steps behind Jeff so the bull's wide body would block any stray fire.

Hundreds of bodies lined the streets, victims of mines, snipers and grenades. Where dying flames didn't burn, the pavement ran red with blood.

As Steve advanced, his third wave came out of hiding. They slid out of cars, stepped out of doorways, all carrying weapons that had yet to be fired. They walked toward the hotel. There were *thousands* of them, so many and so thick it looked like a well-organized parade.

The third wave included most of the Converted who had been soldiers in their former lives. Each of them managed ten civilians. The soldiers communicated via hand signals, runners, cell phones, and most also had some form of radio or walkie-talkie that the scavengers had found in electronics, toy and sporting goods stores. Where the first wave had been cannon fodder, as had most of the second, the third wave was an organized combat force.

General Brownstone had gone up ahead to get a closer look. She jogged back toward him.

"General, have we entered the hotel yet?"

"No, Emperor," she said. "The human perimeter is collapsing and the building is on fire, but there is still resistance. Shouldn't be long now. The third wave is already setting up the containment ring — nothing is going to get out of that hotel alive."

Containment. That was the key. They'd kill Cooper Mitchell, then kill his killers and — God willing — forever wipe out his horrid disease.

Steve checked his phone: 4:19 A.M. The battle had taken only nine minutes. In warfare, apparently, things happened fast.

He pulled his coat tighter and watched the hotel burn.

REUNITED

Gunfire. Flames. Yelling and screaming, the sounds of panic, of fury, all barely audible over a high-pitched ringing.

Tim lifted his head. His body felt numb.

Cooper Mitchell struggled to his feet. The man looked terrified and shell-shocked. Clarence was still down, unconscious. His gas mask was gone. A long piece of metal jutted out of his shoulder blade, blood trickling from his CBRN suit.

The sight of that blood brought Tim out of it. He pushed himself to his knees, scrambled across the rubble to Otto's side. The shard hadn't penetrated that far. There wasn't time to do things properly, so he grabbed the shard and *yanked*.

Clarence twitched, moaned and rolled over.

Tim looked around for a bandage, a towel, anything remotely clean to press on the wound. Gunfire and the explosion had shredded his medical supplies, scattering them all across the burning lobby.

He helped Clarence sit up, waved Cooper over. Cooper stumbled toward them. Tim grabbed the man's hand and pressed it against Otto's wound.

"Keep pressure here," Tim said. "Press *hard*."

Clarence's lip curled up, his eyes scrunched tight in pain.

"My weapon," he said. "Someone find my weapon."

Tim heard a shout above the unending din, a single word: *grenade!*

Something exploded across the lobby, close to the front door. A Ranger fell back crying out in agony. Tim stood and started toward the wounded man, but Klimas sprinted through the doors and cut Tim off.

"Feely, *run*! Take the package to the stairwell, *move*!"

Tim reached for Cooper, then saw Otto's pistol on the floor. He snatched it up, shoved it into Otto's hands, then pulled Cooper toward the stairwell door at the rear of the lobby.

Tim looked back, saw Klimas lift Otto to his feet and push him toward the stairwell. The SEAL commander suddenly wheeled, fired at three men who ran through the entrance: *pop-pop*, slight turn, *pop-pop*, slight turn, *pop-pop*. The three men fell to the floor.

Another explosion hurled shards of metal, stone and wood across the lobby.

Cooper reached the stairwell door first. He pulled it open as Tim rushed through and stepped on the landing. Otto reached the door, pushed Cooper inside hard, then held the door open with his body. He aimed out into the lobby and started firing his pistol.

"*Klimas*," he screamed, "*come on*, get in here! Feely, take Mitchell upstairs!"

Tim again grabbed Cooper's arm.

"Come on," Tim said, then started up the steps.

And stopped cold.

One landing up stood Margaret Montoya.

Tim stared at her for a long second. She stared back. Both of them were too surprised to move.

Margaret reached for the gun strapped to her right thigh.

Save Cooper save Cooper save Cooper

Tim slid his body in front of Cooper, put his hands down and back, hemming him in.

Margaret raised her pistol, pointed it at Tim's face.

Tim wanted to close his eyes, but he couldn't — they stayed locked wide open. He wondered if his brain would be able to process the muzzle flash before the bullet ended his life.

Clarence stepped in front of him, his weapon aimed at his wife.

"Margaret! Put it down!"

Tim saw her face change, instantly morphing from a hateful, snarling-eyed visage to a soft expression of love and concern — like someone had flipped a switch.

"Clarence," she said, "Tim is lying to you. I'm not infected, *he* is. Kill him before he kills us."

The heavy stairwell door slammed open. Klimas came through, his weapon up and aimed at Margaret in a fraction of a second.

"Otto," he said. "You got this?"

"I do," Clarence said.

Clarence's aim didn't waver. Neither did Margaret's.

Klimas turned, opened the stairwell door a few inches and fired into the lobby. He yanked a grenade out of his webbing, pulled the pin, underhand-tossed it through the small gap, then slammed the metal door shut.

Tim heard the grenade explode, heard men and women screaming in agony.

An army of psychos and monsters were closing in from behind. An armed and infected Margaret Montoya blocked the only escape. If Clarence Otto didn't shoot his wife, Tim was going to die one way or the other.

SHARPSHOOTER

Cooper Mitchell was standing right there. *Right there*. Margaret had checked her suit, it was safe, *had* to be safe, the Antichrist was just a half-flight down and she couldn't die not now, *not now*, not when her people were coming.

Clarence stood in front of Tim, who stood in front of Cooper Mitchell. The look in Clarence's eyes: pained, yet committed to doing his job. He *wanted* to believe she wasn't infected.

"Margaret," he said. "Put it down."

Why hadn't she just fired right away? She'd frozen, surprised by Tim, shocked to see her target right in front of her. She'd missed her chance.

"Clarence, listen to me," she said. "Honey, Tim is one of *them*. Why do you think he told everyone *I* was inf—"

A *crack* sound echoed through the stairwell as something slammed into her hand. Her pistol clattered against the wall, then hit the concrete floor. She took a step back, looked at her hand . . . blood, spurting all over her CRBN suit . . . her index finger . . . *gone*.

She staggered, slumped down the wall.

But he didn't shoot, I was looking right at him . . .

Clarence ran up the stairs toward her. Down by the landing door, she saw Klimas, his rifle pointed at her.

A curl of smoke drifted up from the barrel.

HUSBAND AND WIFE

Clarence grabbed Margaret's pistol to secure the weapon, but there was no need — Klimas's single round had blown the trigger clean off, snapped the guard into two jagged metal pieces.

He grabbed his wife by the shoulders, righted her.

"Margaret! Are you okay?"

A stupid thing to say. Her finger was gone She was bleeding all over the landing.

He heard voices, both in his headset and from the people around him. He heard Klimas urging Tim and Cooper up the stairs, telling them to head to the eighth floor, heard feet hitting concrete.

Margaret looked stunned. Blood spurted from her finger stump. Clarence holstered his weapon, knelt before her and grabbed her right wrist.

"Hold on, baby, this is gonna hurt."

He squeezed down on the stump. Direct pressure. He had to stop the bleeding.

A man ran past behind him, then another.

Margaret looked at him. No sense of pain in her eyes, just a dull shock. Shock . . . and *hate*.

"Otto, get out of the way."

The voice of Commander Klimas.

Clarence turned quickly, keeping his body in front of his wife.

The SEAL commander had his weapon pointed slightly off to the right so it wasn't aimed directly at Clarence's chest.

"Otto, *get out of my way*."

Clarence held up his hands. "Please, don't do this."

She *couldn't* be infected. It just wasn't possible. She was the mother of his child.

Klimas stepped to his left, trying to find a shot. Clarence lunged right, cutting off any angle.

Clarence didn't even see the rifle butt come up before it slammed into his chin — not hard enough to do serious damage, but hard enough to knock him aside.

The rifle butt snapped back to Klimas's shoulder, the barrel aimed at Margaret's face.

Tim Feely screamed down from a half-flight up. "No! We need her alive. Trust me on that."

Clarence again put himself between Klimas and Margaret.

The SEAL's lip curled up in frustration. He lowered the barrel.

"You better be right, Tim," he said. "*Fuck*. Let's move."

Something big slammed into the stairwell door, hard enough to bend it inward.

Klimas turned, fired three shots through the metal door. He reached behind his back, then tossed two things onto the concrete landing next to Clarence.

"Look at her magazine," Klimas said. "If there's only one round gone, that's the bullet she used to kill Bogdana. Then the decision is yours. We're going to the eighth floor where there's a way out. We're not waiting for you."

Klimas sprinted up the steps.

Clarence looked at what the SEAL had dropped — two zip strips, one grenade.

He felt hands fumbling for his weapon.

He turned instantly and did something he had never thought himself capable of doing: he hit Margaret.

A short left to the jaw, snapping her head back. She let out a moan, sagged weakly.

Bullets tore through the dented metal door, kicking up puff-spots of concrete when they sparked off the cinder-block walls.

Clarence's left hand grabbed the zip strips and grenade, shoved them into his pocket even as his right drew his Glock. The door rattled once from someone hitting it, then bounced open.

He fired three times at the first movement. Bodies ducked away, leaving the door to automatically swing shut.

Her weapon . . . her magazine.

Clarence grabbed the ruined pistol and shoved it into his empty thigh holster. He reached behind Margaret's back, lifted her and tossed her over his shoulder even as his feet carried him up the concrete steps.

His legs drove him to the next landing. Behind him, he heard the first-floor stairwell door slammed open, this time from something bigger than just a man.

A *roar*, an inhuman sound that echoed through the enclosed stairwell.

Clarence bounded up the stairs, taking them two and three at a time despite Margaret's extra weight.

He heard footsteps behind him. Footsteps and a deep, giggling growl.

Careful to keep Margaret on his shoulder, Clarence shoved his pistol into his webbing belt, then pulled the grenade Klimas had given him. He squeezed the handle, lifted the grenade to his mouth, bit down on the pin and twisted his head to yank it free.

He tossed the grenade behind him, heard the handle flip away and bounce off the wall with a hollow, metallic *ting*.

Four seconds . . .

He kept driving upward, two steps at a time.

Two seconds . . .

He made it up a flight and a half before the *bang* rattled the stairwell, shaking the air and the concrete alike. Farther back, he heard a scream of pain, a scream just as inhuman as the roar had been.

Push, push, push . . . don't think about how your legs burn, and don't you dare think about Margaret . . .

Chest heaving, he reached the eighth floor. He heard yells from farther down the stairwell, but they weren't as close as before. He opened the door and carried Margaret into the hallway.

He turned the first corner he saw, getting out of sight of the stairwell door. Chest heaving, he set Margaret down. The right side of her jaw was already swelling. Blood ribbons coated her hand. She blinked slowly, tried to sit up. He gently pushed her back to the floor, needing only a tiny amount of pressure to do so.

"Margo, hold on. Just hold on."

He had to check her weapon, see if Klimas was right.

Margaret clutched weakly at his forearm. "Get . . . *off* . . . me." She looked at him with nothing but hate in her eyes.

This isn't my wife . . . this isn't Margaret . . .

Clarence drew her ruined pistol from his thigh holster, looked at it.

She couldn't be infected. *Couldn't be.*

He pushed the release and slid the magazine free. There wasn't time for it, but he couldn't help himself. He counted off the rounds. Eleven.

The weapon held twelve.

Just one round missing.

Margaret pushed at him, pushed *hard*. "Get off me! Give me the gun, honey, they're coming to get us! Save the baby!"

The baby.

Was she pregnant? Or was that another lie, created to manipulate him? She had played him for a fool.

He pocketed her magazine, then pulled out the zip strips.

She saw them and started to scream — not a scream of fear, but the guttural, throat-ripping sound of an enraged, trapped animal.

"Don't you tie me up you needle-dick motherfucker! Get your fucking hands off me!"

Clarence grabbed her arms, flipped her onto her stomach.

"I'll cut off your balls and feed them to you, you stupid nigger! Let me go, let me go!"

She squirmed, but she wasn't strong enough to fight him. He wrenched her wrists back. Her still-bleeding stump flicked blood across the hallway carpet.

With one hand, Clarence held her wrists together. With his other, he looped the zip strip around them, then yanked it tight.

"I hate you fucking insects we're going to kill you all kill you all!"

Clarence stood, lifted her and again threw her over his shoulder. His exhausted legs burned instantly. He ignored his body's complaints, thumbed the "talk" button.

"Klimas! I'm on the eighth floor, where the fuck are you?"

A WAY OUT

Clarence stumbled toward Room 829. He recognized the two SEALs crouched by the door: Bosh and Ramierez. Inside, he saw the big one, Roth, using a combat knife to saw through the drywall.

Farther in, Klimas was peeking through heavy curtains. Tim Feely and Cooper Mitchell sat in the middle of a king-size bed, trying to stay out of the way. Two more SEALs stood near Klimas. Their name patches read HARRISON and KATANSKI.

Clarence smelled smoke . . . the fire from the first floor, spreading. The room felt hot.

Klimas turned, saw Clarence and Margaret. His gun came up fast. Harrison and Katanski also brought up their rifles. Roth remained focused on the wall.

Margaret kicked and thrashed. "Please don't shoot me! I didn't do anything, *please*!"

Her hatred and anger had vanished. Now she sounded like a normal woman, a *terrified* woman. There had to be a way to save her, save the baby. Feely could do something, he could beat the infection. He just needed the right equipment and time to do the research, that was all.

"I've got her," Clarence said. "She's my responsibility."

Klimas took a step closer. "You tied her up. You checked the magazine, didn't you."

Clarence said nothing.

Klimas nodded. "She shot Bogdana. Put her *down*, Otto."

Clarence knew that Margaret had to die. His brain told him that, but his heart shouted a different message.

"No," he said. "You'll have to kill me first."

Feely slid off the bed, his hands out in front of him, palms up.

"Everyone just take it easy," he said. "Klimas, I told you, we need her."

Klimas didn't look away from his stare-down. "Why?"

"Because she's infected," Tim said. "She'll contract Cooper's hydras, the thing that kills the Converted."

Margaret stopped squirming.

Clarence forgot about the gun. He looked at Tim.

"You want to use my wife as a *weapon*?"

Tim started to talk, but coughed instead. Clarence felt a sting in his eyes. He smelled burning wood, melting carpet, odors filtering up from the fire below. Wisps of smoke curled near the ceiling.

Tim thumped a fist against his chest, coughed again, then continued. "Otto, if you're right and she's *not* infected, then she's got nothing to worry about." He looked at her, spoke sweetly: "Isn't that right, Margopolis?"

Clarence felt her shaking her head. "Our baby," she said, her words choked with deep sobs. "We don't know how it will affect the baby. Keep Cooper away from me, honey, keep him *away*."

Roth walked over, spoke to Klimas. "Commander, it's ready."

Klimas's eyes narrowed. He lowered his weapon.

"Otto, I'm getting Cooper and Tim out of here," he said. "If Margaret moves funny, I'm wasting her, and if you do anything to stop me, I'll waste *you*. Got it?"

Clarence nodded. "Fair enough."

Klimas tilted his head toward the man-size hole Roth had cut into the drywall. Through it, Clarence saw concrete.

"That's the exterior wall of the hotel," Klimas said. "It abuts another building that's only a foot away. We're blowing through both and entering that building. Then we're descending to a tea shop that's on the ground floor, at the corner of Pearson and Rush. I'm hoping the building is empty, and we can make it down without much of a fight. From there, we're going to figure out a way through the enemy lines."

"Enemy lines?" Clarence said. "They're just a mob."

"You'll see soon enough," Klimas said. "Everyone, into the hall."

Bosh and Ramierez were still at their posts, guarding the hallway in both directions. Smoke curled thickly at the ceiling; the place was going up fast.

Roth pulled the door shut. He held a small detonator in his hand.

"Fire in the hole," he said, then pushed the button.

It didn't sound like much of an explosion, more of a *whump* than a *bang*. Roth opened the door. A cloud of dust billowed out. Clarence looked in: the blast had punched clean through — he felt cold air pouring in, saw a brick wall beyond.

"First wall down," Roth said. "Now to blast our way into the other building. Sixty seconds."

He started placing small charges of C-4.

On his shoulder, Clarence felt Margaret start to shake. He turned, saw that Cooper Mitchell was standing right next to them.

He was holding his exposed wrist near Margaret's bloody hand. On that wrist, a red spot, a small patch of sagging skin: it looked like he'd just popped a huge blister, but Clarence saw no fluid. Tiny motes of floating white hung in the air for a moment, then dissipated into nothingness.

Cooper smiled wide. "Enjoy that, lady. You enjoy the *fuck* out of it."

He stepped away.

Clarence set Margaret down on her own feet. With her hands still zip-stripped behind her back, she leaned against the wall. She shook violently.

She stared at Cooper Mitchell, her eyes wide with terror.

HIT THE LIGHTS

Paulius lay on a tile floor, mostly hidden behind the low, brick wall of the dark tea shop's broken window.

Outside in the cold, windy night, the few remaining lights lit up hundreds of Converted running through the streets: yelling in victory, screaming in psychotic rage, sometimes shooting guns into the air. Most of the time they moved south, toward the Park Tower.

But sometimes, they seemed to get confused — they ran north on Rush, or west on Pearson, and when they did, their own kind shot them down.

Thirty meters along either of those roads, a line of cars, trucks and other debris ran from sidewalk to sidewalk, completely blocking any way through. Barrel fires burned in front of these bulwarks, blurring any sight of the forces that hid behind them.

Paulius had to figure out how to cross those lines.

The gothic Archdiocese of Chicago was directly to the north, across Pearson. Paulius saw troops and guns lurking in the church's broken stained-glass windows. He could lead his people into that building, search for an exit that would come out behind the Converted's street-blocking wall, but he had no idea how many enemy troops waited inside.

Kitty-corner to the tea shop — across the intersection of Pearson and Rush — was a ten-story brick building, but going for that would expose him to fire from the troops behind the bulwarks of *both* streets. Plus, there was no guarantee the place wasn't full of snipers just waiting for him to show his hand.

And due west, across Rush, a round skyscraper some forty stories tall. Same problems as the other buildings.

Every route seemed blocked, heavily defended.

There had to be a way.

He couldn't count on help from anyone else, because no one answered his calls. As far as he knew, all the Rangers were dead. He'd lost most of his own men: just six out of twenty left, including himself. But if he could get Cooper Mitchell to safety, his SEALs would not have died in vain.

The move from the Park Tower to the tea shop had bought a few minutes' reprieve, at best. The hotel was on fire, but if enemy troops were still in there, still searching, they'd soon find the hole Roth had blown through the wall. After that, Paulius had only minutes before the Converted swarmed in.

There was only one option: he had to punch an opening in one of the enemy lines. That opening wouldn't come cheap, and they had very little ammo left with which to make it.

He turned and crawled across the cold floor, his fatigues scraping against broken glass. He moved behind the shop's main counter to join the others: Feely, Cooper Mitchell, Bosh, Harrison, Katanski and Ramierez. Clarence and Margaret were tucked into an alcove near the bathrooms, out of sight of the windows. Margaret had a gag in her mouth, which Clarence had put there on Paulius's insistence.

If she made any noise, she died; Clarence and Margaret both knew that.

Feelygood was the only reason Paulius had let Margaret live. If they could turn that murdering bitch into a weapon against her own kind, that held a certain poetic justice.

Paulius waved his men close. Such brave soldiers, all that remained of SEAL Team Two. Clarence joined them, as did Tim and Cooper.

"We need to figure out a way past their lines," Paulius said. "We're outgunned. They've got excellent coverage on our positions. As soon as we show our heads, they'll start firing and it won't last long."

Ramierez tugged at his fatigues, drawing attention to them. "How about we lose these? Try to look like the enemy, get close enough to make something happen?"

"They're killing *anything* that comes close, including their own," Paulius said. He looked at the surrounding faces. "I need other ideas."

Bosh shrugged. "It sucks, but we're going to have to make a distraction. Shoot out the streetlights. We hit them up with grenades from here, then me and another guy head west on Pearson, try to draw their fire. Few minutes later, Commander, you and the others take the package north on Rush."

A suicide mission, but D-Day was perfectly willing to do it.

"Too many of them for that," Paulius said. He looked at Roth. "Any luck raising the *Coronado*, see if they have any ideas?"

Roth shook his head. "Negative, Commander. Short-range communication still works — not that there's anyone answering — but we lost all long-range communication in the assault. I'm trying to get through on the MBITR, but I need to find a line of sight to a satellite. That's hard to do from in here. I might be able to reach the *Coronado* from the roof of this building. If I can, we could request air support."

Tim raised a hand. "MBITR?"

"Satellite radio," Paulius said. "And our air support is gone — we saw both of the Apaches destroyed. We can't risk bringing in the *Coronado*'s Seahawks, not when the Converted might have more Stingers. That means the only way out of here is on foot, so we can get Mitchell to a place the Seahawks can land safely. We need something to blow a hole in those lines."

Ramierez shook his head. "Too bad we can't just drop some big-ass bombs on them. Not just on the blockade, but on all those fuckers packed in nice and tight around here. We'd kill a shitload of them."

A big-ass bomb . . . Paulius had forgotten about the mission's last element of air support.

"The B2 might still be up there," he said. "If we can contact it, maybe it can drop a JDAM on the north line, let us escape, then hammer all around the hotel."

Bosh laughed, a sound of frustration. He shook his head. "A JDAM to break us out? I've seen one of those take the top off a fucking mountain. The B2 crew would need pinpoint accuracy, Commander. If they're off-target to the south by even a few hundred feet, it'll kill us."

Bosh was right. A B2 strike was risky, damn near suicidal, but they were out of options and almost out of time.

"Roth, you're on," Paulius said. "You and Ram head up to the roof. Try to reach the *Coronado*, have them task the B2 to strike a hundred meters north of our location."

Roth let out a low whistle. "In bomb-speak, Commander, that's right on top of us."

"It is, and it's going to work. There might be enemy units on the roof of this building, so kill anything you see. Stay alive long enough to contact the *Coronado*."

"Wait," Clarence said.

Paulius glared at the man. He was the last person he wanted to hear from right now.

Clarence dug into his pocket. He pulled out a cell phone, held it up like a kid at show and tell.

"This gives me a direct line to DST director Murray Longworth. I'm pretty sure he's at the White House, sitting in the Situation Room with the Joint Chiefs."

Paulius stared at the bulky phone, then started laughing. The guy who refused to see reality had a direct line to the Joint Chiefs? Like this night needed to get any stranger.

"Well then, Agent Otto," Paulius said, "why don't you just go ahead and give the White House a call?"

Murray Longworth watched the world burn.

The Park Tower mission had ended in disaster. SEAL Team Two and the Ranger company, wiped out. Clarence, Margaret and Feely, undoubtedly dead.

And if all of those people were gone, then Cooper Mitchell was gone as well.

Vogel hadn't found any other survivors of the HAC trial. Mitchell had been the last hope of cultivating hydras.

The Situation Room's main monitor showed the next step in mankind's downward spiral: nuclear first-strike options against China. Porter wanted to launch. Albertson wasn't putting up much resistance. No hydras, nuclear war about to erupt — Murray realized it was all over.

The Converted had won.

He jumped a little when his cell phone buzzed. That was the one on his inside left pocket . . . the direct line to Clarence Otto.

He answered. "Otto?"

"Yes sir, Director," Otto said. "We've got Cooper Mitchell. He's alive."

Murray felt a slight pain in his chest.

"How the fuck did you get out of there? I saw Predator footage, they were all over you."

"Never mind that," Otto said. "We have Cooper and we can still get him out of the city. To do that, we need to call in an air strike from the B2. We need it right now. Can you make that happen?"

"You bet your ass I can. Hold on."

He lowered the phone.

"Porter! Put those nukes back in your pants for a minute, we've still got a chance."

ANTICIPATION

Cooper Mitchell knew he was going to die.

No way this would work. But it wasn't like he had a choice, and maybe he'd get to see some of those bastards die before he found out if there was an afterlife.

The SEALs all crouched down low behind the tea shop's counter, waiting for the boom.

"It's going to be a powerful explosion," Klimas said. "It'll probably knock us silly for a bit, but you have to get up fast and be ready to go."

Klimas was pretty badass. Cooper knew that all SEALs were badass, but this guy didn't seem fazed that his unit had been hacked to pieces and — probably — *eaten*.

"We go straight through their lines, and we stay together," Klimas said. "If you get separated, the rally point is First St. Paul's Lutheran Church, at LaSalle Boulevard and Goethe, seven blocks north. Everyone clear?"

Cooper saw the SEALs take cover behind anything solid that stood between them and the impending bomb.

Feely was trembling. Dude looked scared as hell. Cooper was scared, too, had been for days, but better a bomb or a bullet than a barbecue.

They ain't gonna eat me, *Sofia.*

Klimas looked at Cooper, and at Feely.

"You two boys stay with me," the SEAL said. "Visibility is going to be shit. Whatever it takes, *do not* fall behind. This is our one chance. Don't fuck it up."

Nine faces looked upward simultaneously, ears all responding to the same thing: a faint whistling sound, rapidly growing in intensity.

"Incoming," Klimas said. He tucked into a fetal position, laced his fingers behind his head and pressed his arms tightly against his ears.

Cooper did the same.

Tim Feely's world *shook*; it *roared*.

Glass and brick flew into the tea shop, smashing into shelves and tearing the walls to pieces. Big chunks of masonry pounded into the counter, cracking wood and splintering tile. Dust and smoke drove into his lungs. He coughed, screamed for help only to realize his voice sounded impossibly small and far-away.

He blinked, tried to see through the swirling haze.

A hand grabbed his collar.

"Get your ass up, Feely! *Move!*"

Klimas. His voice sounded distant, but it was a beacon.

Tim heard Klimas screaming at Cooper. Something collapsed from the ceiling and crashed into the floor. Tim stumbled toward the shattered window . . . they had to go north, they didn't have long.

"Move-move-move! Out the window!"

Tim stepped over the low sill and onto the sidewalk, out of the tea shop and into an apocalypse. The winter wind swirled up clouds of thick dust, cutting visibility to just a few feet. He heard things crashing, things falling, pieces of building crumbling and dropping to the street below.

Gunfire.

He stooped, tried to get low. His hands found a car. No, *part* of a car. He started to kneel down behind it when that iron-grip hand grabbed him again.

"Up," Klimas said. "Stay behind me."

Another SEAL fell in next to Klimas — Tim didn't know which one. They moved, he followed. They ran half crouched, rifles at their shoulders, turning left and right to fire while never breaking stride.

Tim saw a man on his right: Cooper Mitchell.

Something exploded off to the left, kicking up a fresh wave of dust and dirt. Tim shielded his face and kept moving.

People screaming.

Guns firing.

The *snap* of small explosions.

He looked forward, saw Klimas's back — but the other SEAL wasn't there anymore.

Klimas stopped at a red Prius that seemed to be embedded in some kind of cracked, fluid-looking masonry. He waved Tim forward.

"We're going over the top, let's move!"

Tim realized the car was part of a wall, a good six feet high, that stretched out both left and right. He threw himself at it, hands grabbing at anything he could grip. Broken glass and metal shards sliced into his skin but he didn't stop. Up and up he went until he reached the top.

He heard an automatic weapon firing, then the blast of a shotgun. He slipped and fell, tumbled down the hard wall's far side. Something whacked his left calf, knocking it cold and numb.

Clarence ran by, Margaret bouncing on his shoulder like a gagged rag doll.

"Keep going, Feely! *Move!*"

Clarence vanished into the swirling dust.

Tim's chest drew in panicked breaths of dirty, icy air. He felt a knife in his lungs, cutting and tearing. He was going to throw up.

Whatever it takes, do not fall behind.

Klimas. He'd promised to get Tim out of there. Tim righted himself, got his feet beneath him and started running, then slowed.

Cooper . . . none of it mattered without Cooper.

Tim turned back, saw Cooper land face-first on the rubble-strewn pavement.

And behind him, a stumbling man with half his face torn away, dust-caked blood sloughing down the white of his exposed temple and cheekbone, a big-toothed forever smile where his lips no longer were.

He held a red axe.

Cooper . . . none of it mattered without Cooper.

Tim ran toward them, or tried to, but his leg wouldn't respond, so he hopped instead.

On the ground, he spotted a head-size shard of concrete.

Tim bent, grabbed, lifted, hopped.

The man limped toward Cooper, one shredded foot dragging along for the ride. He raised the axe into the air, gurgled a wet battle cry, and arched his back to bring the blade down hard.

Tim got there first.

He didn't recognize the sound that came out of his own mouth. He'd never made a noise like that, not once in his entire existence.

With both arms, he shoved the jagged concrete forward, drove a rough point into the good side of the man's ruined face. The hard concrete *crunched* through tooth and bone, rocked the man's head back, dropped him like he'd been hit by a heavyweight hook.

The axe clattered to the slush-streaked pavement.

"Cooper! Get the fuck *up*!"

Cooper crawled forward on raw hands and torn knees, the jeans on his right thigh wet with dust-coated blood.

The half-faced man sat up. He reached for the axe.

Cooper . . . none of it mattered without Cooper.

Tim Feely stepped forward, the pain in his leg forgotten. He put one foot on the axe, raised the chunk of concrete into the air.

The man looked up — maybe he smiled, but now *both* sides of his mouth were destroyed, so who could tell?

Tim brought the concrete down like a misshaped hammer: the man's skull *collapsed*, folding in on itself in a sickening, liquid crunch.

The man didn't move.

Tim leaned down, drew a deep breath and screamed a long, unintelligible roar at his dead enemy. The intelligent part of his mind, the educated part, the *civilized* part, that part had checked out. Something primitive had taken its place.

A hand on his neck, pulling him.

"Feely, come on!"

Klimas. Klimas had come back for him.

The SEAL pulled Tim through the smoke, pushed him, did the same with Cooper, stopped and turned and fired, pushed and pulled them some more.

Tim stumbled forward. He didn't know how long, he just kept moving. His ears rang. He had no strength left. He couldn't breathe. He felt dizzy. He kept moving until someone grabbed him, shoved him to the left.

"In there," that someone said.

Tim shuffled through a door. So dark. The world spun, made it hard to walk. He was much closer to vomiting now. A strong hand on his arm. Someone dragging him along up a long flight of hard stairs.

Dizziness, nausea, weakness . . . right at the end, he realized those were the symptoms of blood loss.

Tim Feely fell to the floor, and blackness overtook him.

STYLISH OUTERWEAR

Dawn's light burned through the store's tall, second-story windows.

Paulius shivered from the cold. He sat still, waiting for a response from his missing men. There was none. He'd been trying for three hours.

He thumbed his "talk" button.

"Roth, Harrison, come in."

Paulius released the button and waited.

No answer.

"Roth, Harrison, come in."

Still nothing.

His hands felt numb, as did his toes. He pulled the long, fur coat he'd found tighter on his shoulders. They'd taken refuge in a clothing store — and, of course, it was a *women's* clothing store. He wore the coat like a cloak.

He was back far enough from the window that he couldn't be seen from the road, but close enough that he could look out. Four lanes of Oak Street running east and west, intersecting the three lanes of Rush that ran north-northwest to south-southeast. He had a wide, commanding view of the surrounding area.

Right after they'd cleared the barrier, Katanski had taken a shotgun blast to the throat. He was probably dead before his body hit the ground. Roth and Harrison were missing. Ramierez had made it, but he was badly wounded.

Only Bosh and Klimas were still in proper fighting shape. He'd sent Bosh out to the rendezvous point at LaSalle and Goethe. It was dangerous to send him out alone, but Paulius didn't have a choice — he had to stay with Cooper Mitchell.

Ramierez sat close by, his back against the wall. Cooper was asleep in front of a rack of shoes. Dr. Feelygood was also out, lying on a big pile of dresses. Paulius had cut away Feely's shredded, now-useless CBRN suit, then covered the man in a couple of fur coats.

Clarence and Margaret were on the far side of the store. Paulius didn't want either of them anywhere near the others.

"Roth, Harrison, come in," Paulius said. "Bosh, come in."

Nothing.

Ramierez lifted his head, a bloody bunch of gauze taped against the socket of his ruined left eye. He had a long velvet coat hung over his shoulders, another across his lap.

"Don't sweat it, Commander," he said. "Must be too much building interference to reach Bosh. I'm pretty sure Roth is an immortal, and we both know Harrison is made of iron."

Paulius forced a smile. Ramierez had lost an eye and taken a bullet in the belly, yet he was still trying to build up those around him. That was a SEAL for you. And just like a SEAL, Ramierez had his weapon in his hands — if the Converted came barging in, he was still ready to fight.

"We'll find them," Paulius said. If there was a time to lie, it was now. "How you holding up?"

"I'm just . . ." Ramierez leaned his head forward as a wave of pain washed over him. He stayed that way for a few seconds, then looked up. "I'm solid, Commander. But maybe I'll just take a little nap."

"Negative," Paulius said. "You stay awake, that's an order. Keep trying Roth and Harrison, got it?"

Ramierez managed a slow nod.

Paulius had done all he could for the wounded: stitches for Cooper and Feely, bandages for Otto, sure, but abdominal surgery for Ramierez? Out of Paulius' league.

He pulled off his headset and stuffed it into a pocket of his fatigues. He pulled the fur coat tighter, then walked toward Feely.

Paulius passed by Otto and Margaret. She was sitting on a chair, still bound, still gagged. Otto had covered her in coats, leaving only her head exposed. He had ditched his CBRN suit — the thing had been just as shredded as Feely's — but hadn't put on any extra clothing. The man preferred to shiver, apparently. Maybe it added to his self-indulgent misery.

Otto tilted his head toward Ramierez. "How is he?"

"Dying," Paulius said quietly. "Did you call Longworth?"

"Yeah," Otto said. "He knows we made it out."

"You ask him how many Stingers were in the reserve bases around here?"

Otto nodded. "The brass thinks the Converted could have over fifty of them in Chicago."

Fifty. *Dammit.* Sending in any helicopters for pickup would be suicide. Paulius would have to find a way to take everyone to a safer area and hope the Converted had concentrated their Stingers downtown. He'd look for a spot to the north, on the shore, make it easier for the Seahawks to approach. That was the best hope, and it still meant a hike of several miles for Feely and Cooper, both of whom had significant leg wounds, and for Ramierez, who couldn't move at all.

"That's just fantastic," Paulius said. "I don't suppose Murray can convince Admiral Porter to send a nice little armor division or two our way?"

Otto shook his head. "There aren't any armor divisions. At least not in the Midwest. What's left of our military is engaged in active combat, including all of our reserves. Testing kits are running low. The Converted are popping up in almost every unit, special forces included. Murray is even afraid to drop in reinforcements for us, because he can't be sure members of those units won't be compromised and try to kill Cooper themselves. It's real bad out there."

Paulius tried to control his temper. They had the package, they'd *done* it.

"It's real bad here, too," he said. "Doesn't he have *anything* for us?"

"He does. He's sent one of the last available Apaches to the *Coronado.* And he's stationed an AC-130U at Scott AFB down near Champaign, has it assigned just for us. The crew is sequestered to make sure no infected slip in. We've got those, plus one of the *Coronado*'s Seahawks for evac — the other Seahawk got reassigned to make room for the Apache. We give Murray one hour's notice, he can put those assets where we tell him."

Paulius worked through the options. The AC-130U was a ground-attack aircraft, armed with a 25-millimeter Gatling gun and a 105-millimeter howitzer cannon. It was an ideal weapon to use against ground forces, especially ones that packed in tight like the Converted tended to do. The plane could strike from high up — it still had to worry about Stinger fire, but not as much as the low-flying Apaches.

"At least that's something," Paulius said. "Just have to figure out where to go for pickup, and how to get there."

"Right," Otto said. "Nothing to it. Not like we're in the middle of enemy territory or anything."

Paulius nodded toward Margaret. "What about her? She magically cured yet?"

Otto hung his head.

Paulius looked at her. She met his stare, mumbled two syllables. The gag made her words unrecognizable, but the cadence reminded him of mush-mouthed Kenny from *South Park*. Her meaning was all too understandable: *fuck you*.

"Ma'am," Paulius said.

He walked to Feely. The little guy had taken a small-caliber round through the calf, probably a .38. The wound wasn't life-threatening, and Ramierez needed real help, which meant Tim's nap time was over.

Battle brought out a person's true nature. Paulius had gotten too far ahead, lost sight of the men he was supposed to protect. When he doubled back, he saw Tim fighting to protect the much-larger Cooper Mitchell. Tim Feely thought himself a coward, yet he'd killed a man in hand-to-hand combat, crushed the enemy's skull with a hunk of concrete.

That moment encapsulated the essence of bravery: cower and run from danger, or step up and face it, kill to protect your own. Maybe Tim Feely wasn't SEAL material, but he sure as hell had a warrior's soul.

Paulius gently shook the man's shoulder. "Doctor Feelygood. Wake up, brother."

Tim's eyes fluttered open. Like everyone else, his skin was caked with dust; it made him a dozen shades darker than his former, extrapale self. He stared out in confusion for a moment, then his eyes focused on Paulius. Tim sat up quickly.

"Easy," Paulius said. "We're safe for now."

Tim looked around, saw Otto sitting with Margaret, saw Ramierez against the wall.

"Where are we?"

"Barneys New York."

Tim paused, then nodded, as if that was the most normal thing he could have heard.

"Good, good," Tim said. "I was looking for a sale on Manolos. Size eight, if you please." He looked at the fur coats covering him, then at the one around Paulius's shoulders.

"Nice," Tim said. "Did you bring your pimp cane and my chalice?"

He was joking. That was a good sign. "How do you feel?"

Tim didn't answer. He lifted his leg, looked at the blood-spotted bandage on his calf. "Stitches?"

Paulius nodded. "Yep. Seven, I think."

"Blue Cross should cover that. Can I assume that your stitches are all nice and neat?"

"Probably not," Paulius said. "But they tell me scars are a mark of character."

"Gosh, lucky me. I'll have so much to talk about at my next book club meeting."

Paulius subtly pointed at Ramierez. "He's gut-shot, fading fast. Need you to fix him up."

Tim stood. He pulled on one of the fur coats and limped over to Ramierez.

Paulius watched. Tim pressed his fingers to the man's neck, then gently looked inside Ramierez's fatigues, which Paulius had left open.

Tim hobbled back, spoke quietly enough that Ramierez couldn't hear.

"I don't have anything to work with," Tim said. "Even if I did, I doubt I could save him. He's lost too much blood. As he is now, he's got maybe a few hours. Can we get a helicopter in here, get him back to the *Coronado*?"

"No, we can't take that chance. We're still too close to where the Converted have probably deployed their Stingers. We have to get farther north. Can we carry him?"

Tim pursed his lips, let out a long breath. "He wouldn't last a half mile. He's not the only one. I can barely move, hoss. Could we drive out?"

"Not without a tank. You saw the roads — too many cars blocking the way. We need something big, and I didn't see any semis out there."

Tim pulled at his lower lip as he thought.

Ramierez gave a halfhearted wave. "Commander, it's Bosh. He's got Roth. Coming in now."

Paulius's chest swelled with relief, but he tempered the emotion, pushed it down. Bosh could have made that call under duress.

"Otto, get up," he said. "Come with me." Paulius gripped Tim's shoulder, turned him toward Ramierez.

"Ram, you need something to do. Show this man how to use your M4."

Tim's eyes went wide? "Me? I'm no good with guns."

"Yes, you," Paulius said. "And you'll learn, right now. Go."

Tim moved to Ramierez just as Otto walked up, Glock in hand.

"With me," Paulius said, then walked to the top of the wide stairs.

One flight down, he saw Bosh quietly enter the store along with a big man wearing sweatpants, a red Chicago Bulls knit hat and a white-sleeved Chicago Bears letterman's jacket. The man might have passed for a civilian were it not for the SCAR-FN rifle in his trembling hands. *Roth.* The clothes looked cleaner than he did.

Bosh threw a quick salute, then turned back to guard the front doors.

Roth trudged up the stairs, each step an effort.

"Jesus H," Paulius said. "You look like a pile of spilt fuck."

Roth nodded. "At least I'm still ticking."

"And Harrison?"

Roth shook his head. "We tried to hide in an office building. We stumbled onto a bunch of them camping out. It got crazy, sir. One of those giant fucking things threw a file cabinet at him. He went down, they swarmed on him, I . . . I couldn't . . . I should have—"

"Forget it," Paulius said, perhaps a little too sharply. "Just forget it. He died doing his job."

Roth looked cashed out, mentally, physically and emotionally.

Paulius tugged the letterman jacket's faux leather sleeve.

"Thought you were a Bengals fan."

Roth patted the embroidered orange "C" on his left breast. "This thing kept me alive, sir. From now on, go Bears. Ramierez had the right idea — the bad guys were hunting us based on our uniforms. First store I found after I got away from that office was a fan shop. These clothes made it easier to blend in a little. From a distance, none of them gave me a second glance."

Paulius slapped the bigger man on the shoulder. "Grab some sack time. We might have to move quick."

Roth didn't need to be told twice. He nodded and walked to a rack of sweaters. He didn't even bother taking the sweaters down for padding, just crawled beneath them, lay on his back, and was out in seconds.

Margaret Montoya coughed, a lung-rattling sound that echoed through the cold store.

Clarence turned and walked toward her.

Paulius wondered what it was like to love a woman so much that you'd abandon reason and logic, let your heart blind you to what your eyes could plainly see. For the first time, he found himself feeling sorry for Clarence Otto.

Tim came at a fast hobble, his face lit up with excitement.

"Klimas, holy *shit*," he said. "Remember that firehouse we saw on the way in?"

Where I shot two brave men in cold blood?

"Yeah, I remember."

"I saw those cops," Tim said. "I'm not passing judgment, okay? Whatever had to be done had to be done, but I gathered they were guarding the firehouse. Were they?"

Feely seemed far too amped up. And in the fur coat, he did look a little like a pimp.

"Doc, what's your point?"

Tim tilted his head toward Margaret, did a bad job of trying not to make the motion obvious.

"Argaret-May is inected-fay with eydra-hays," he said. "She's *oughing*-kay. You get me?"

Paulius sighed. "I have no fucking idea what you're talking about."

"She's *infected*. If Cooper's story is accurate, she'll be dead in . . . wait, how long have we been here?"

"About five hours."

"Then she'll be dead in nineteen hours," Tim said. "But that's not what matters. What matters is the hydras are replicating inside of her right now."

He looked off. His lips moved like he was counting something, or speaking to himself in a language only he knew.

"I think I have a way to save Ramierez," he said. "A way that not only gets us north in a hurry, but lets us infect *hundreds* of those motherfuckers along the way. If any of them radiate out to other areas, it's very possible that the hydras will spread all over the Midwest. Klimas, if you can pull this off, we might even start a chain reaction that could kill them all."

Paulius stared down at the man. "If I can pull *what* off?"

Tim's eyes shone with a combination of intensity, hope and the dread of a nasty job that had to be done.

"The firehouse," he said. "And what's inside . . . the fire *truck*." He nodded toward Margaret. "We're going to put her in it, so to speak. Margaret Montoya gets to save the world one more time."

THE DEMOCRATIC PROCESS

A hand on his shoulder, shaking him lightly.

"Mister Mitchell, wake up."

Cooper opened his eyes. Tim Feely, standing over him.

Tim smiled. "How are you doing?"

Was he wearing a fur coat?

"Leg hurts," Cooper said. The understatement of the year. His right thigh throbbed, stung. "I cut it on something climbing over that poop-wall."

"*Poop*-wall? You mean that street barricade?"

Cooper nodded. "Yeah. That."

"Well, whatever caused it, the cut required fifteen stitches. You might have ligament damage as well, so walk carefully. Unfortunately, it was Klimas who did the sewing, as my deft digits are a bit dinged up."

Tim held up his hands. They were bandaged in a dozen places. Some of the white strips had spots of red.

Cooper remembered the half-face man with the axe. Tim could have kept running, but he'd come back.

He's not like you, Coop ol' dawg . . . Doc Feely doesn't leave anyone behind . . .

"Uh, what you did back there . . . thanks."

Tim's smile faded. "I don't want to think about that. Not ever again."

He pointed across the store to where Otto and Klimas stood along with two other men. Cooper recognized Bosh, and also that big SEAL — Roth, was it? — who for some reason was decked out in Bears gear. Ramierez sat by himself against a wall. Sleeping, maybe. And that infected lady, watching everything. She had a gag in her mouth and was practically buried in a pile of women's coats.

"Come join us," Tim said. "Time to talk about how we're getting you out of here."

• • •

Cooper listened to Klimas lay out the idea. Tim's idea, maybe, but Klimas was in charge so it was his no-bullshit voice that outlined what would happen next.

Whoever came up with it, the idea sounded insane.

Everyone looked at Clarence Otto, waited for his response.

The man stayed silent for a moment. His jaw muscles twitched. There was murder in his eyes.

Otto raised a hand, pointed a finger — right at Cooper.

"He's got the hydras, too," Otto said. "Why don't we use him?"

Oh, fuck *that*. This lovesick idiot wanted to save that diseased whore?

"Because I'm not one of *them*," Cooper said. "Your wife is. Deal with it."

He stared at Otto until the bigger man looked away.

Tim sniffed. "Margaret's already lost. We can't save her."

Otto stared at the floor. "She'll get those blisters, right? Isn't that enough? Between her and Cooper, isn't that enough?"

"It's not," Tim said. "Based on what we learned from Candice Walker, it will be another day, maybe two, before the pustules form on Margaret's skin — if they form at all, because she'll be dead by then. We just don't know. What we do know is she already has the hydras in her blood. I know this is hard, but you . . . we don't . . ."

Tim ran out of words. He looked at Klimas, maybe trying to get help. Cooper noticed that the SEAL had his pistol in his hand, down low against his thigh — subtle, but ready to go if Clarence got crazy.

"Using Cooper isn't an option," Klimas said. "We're not putting him at risk so he can pop his zits on the bad guys. The weapon we need is inside of Margaret. We need her blood. All of it."

Otto looked up. He was a man destroyed, a man gutted.

"Can't you all hear how insane this sounds? This is barbaric. You want to put my wife's blood into a *fire truck*? What the fuck are we, vampires?"

Tim pulled his fur coat tighter.

"Call it what you will," he said. "If we do this, then even if we *don't* get Cooper out alive, we can still start a plague that might kill them all."

"And you know that *how*?" Otto said. "You're going to butcher a woman who saved everyone in this room . . . to test out a *theory*?"

Klimas's hand flexed on the pistol. "That's exactly what we're going to do."

Otto looked from man to man, searching for support, finding none. His fists tightened until his hands shook.

Cooper almost felt bad for the dude. Almost. At least he didn't have to watch his wife transform into a monster.

Tears formed in Otto's eyes, spilled over, left thin trails of clean, wet brown through the dust that coated his skin.

"This isn't just about Margaret," he said. "She's pregnant. Just take *some* of her blood. A couple of pints — that won't kill her."

Pregnant? Cooper looked back at the woman tied to the chair. Didn't matter if she was. Why should she get to live when Jeff turned into a *thing*, and Sofia turned into dinner?

Cooper hadn't wanted to kill Sofia, he *hadn't*, but killing her had kept him alive. He could still taste her . . . still taste her charred skin . . . still taste the juice that had dribbled from her steaming flesh . . .

I had to do it had to do it I had no choice no choice at all.

Feely started to speak, then paused. He was trying to find the right words.

"She's lying," he said finally. "And even if she's not, if she actually *is* pregnant, then the baby is also one of them."

The last bit of fight slid out of Agent Otto, as clearly as if someone had pulled a hidden plug and let it drain away.

Klimas spoke again, softer this time.

"If you want to say your good-byes, Otto, you need to do it now."

Clarence sniffed back snot, hissed in a breath. More tears formed.

"Okay," he said. He nodded, slowly at first, then with exaggerated motion. "Okay, I . . . I see it. That's the way it has to be."

"Go for a walk," Klimas said. "You don't need to be here for this."

Otto's eyes squeezed tight. He pinched hard on the bridge of his nose.

"No," he said, his voice hollow and hoarse. "If she has to be set free, I'll do it."

The big SEAL wearing the ridiculous Chicago Bears jacket sniffed sharply, then turned and walked away. The other one, Bosh, just stared at the ground.

Klimas held his pistol in his right hand. With his left, he reached to his side and drew a wicked-looking Ka-Bar knife. He flipped it, held it by the seven-inch blade, and offered it handle-first to Otto.

"I'll honor your request," Klimas said. "But if you try anything, I'll put you down, and then she dies anyway."

Otto started crying all over again. His big shoulders shook as he reached out and took the knife.

BESIEGED

IMMUNIZED: 89%
NOT IMMUNIZED: 6%
UNKNOWN: 5%
FINISHED DOSES EN ROUTE: 10,134
DOSES IN PRODUCTION: 98,000
INFECTED: 6,000,000 (40,000,000)
CONVERTED: 5,125,000 (23,500,000)
DEATHS: 6,000,000+ (40,000,000)

It was all over but the crying, really. Thankfully, Murray wasn't much of a crier.

The tipping point had been reached. Twenty-three million Converted, worldwide. No army, no matter how well equipped or organized, could stop that many people. And Cheng's best guess was another forty million were infected — in the next three days, statisticians projected the total number of Converted to reach *sixty million*.

Industrial production of the inoculant had collapsed. So, too, had America's transportation network. It was now impossible to drive from New York City to the West Coast. Converted occupied the Rocky Mountains, making the range impassable. The last reliable form of transportation — airplanes — was in danger of falling; every remaining airport, both military and civilian, was under constant attack by hordes of monsters and screaming psychopaths.

Battles raged in the streets of D.C. The army manned a solid perimeter fourteen blocks square, with the White House dead-center. Admiral Porter's people estimated that thirty thousand Converted were pressing in on two thousand U.S. military defenders. And every now and then, one of those defenders would turn out to be Converted himself, slaughtering those around him in an effort to open up a hole in the lines.

Air support wouldn't last much longer. Fewer people to repair and rearm planes, fewer bases, and on three separate occasions — one F-22, one F-35, and one Apache — an aircraft had turned from defender to attacker. The burning hole in the West Wing came courtesy of the F-22 pilot's kamikaze effort.

At every level of the military, paranoia ran rampant. No one could say for sure if the man or woman next to them might be the enemy, the kind that didn't test positive.

Ronald Reagan Airport and Bolling AFB had fallen. There was no airport close enough that they could risk driving President Albertson to it, even with the five M1-Abrams tanks parked on the White House lawn. Three times the military had tried to bring in evac helicopters, and all three times the Converted had shot those aircraft down. The enemy had SAMs, and plenty of them.

The bottom line: no one was leaving the White House. Not even Albertson. Admiral Porter's best estimate was that loyal troops could defend the White House for another six days, seven at the most.

Murray had once dreamed of the Situation Room burning to the ground. Now it looked like that might actually happen, only with him still in it.

AFTERMATH

Emperor Steve Stanton, Minister of Science Doctor-General Jeremy Ellis, and Supreme Master of Logistics Robert McMasters stood on a tall pile of rubble, all shivering against the biting wind. They looked down at the ten-foot-deep crater that had once been bustling Michigan Avenue. Shattered vehicles, broken concrete, jutting metal and shredded bodies lay in and around it, all victims of the powerful detonation.

Those had been some *seriously* big bombs.

The once bright and gleaming Park Tower was a blackened finger pointing to the sky. Fire had consumed much of the building, gutting it, leaving hundreds of charred corpses inside like it was some oversized piñata of death.

A small army of hatchlings worked through the rubble, all with one specific task: find the body of Cooper Mitchell. Only then would Steve know he was truly safe.

"Doctor-General Ellis," Steve said. "Do you really think we'll recover Cooper's body?"

Ellis's eyes flicked to the pistol strapped to Steve's thigh. For some reason, the man always seemed to think he was moments from being shot.

"If Cooper is in there, he's probably too burned to be recognizable," Ellis said. "But we do have to try, Emperor. If I can get him to my labs, maybe I can find a cure."

If the good doctor-general didn't get infected himself and die in the process, of course.

Steve again stared into the crater. Unseen planes had dropped the bombs. One second everything had been fine, the next, all crazy explosions and total chaos. Steve wasn't sure how many of his people had died. Maybe the late General Brownstone should have spread them out a little bit more. Live and learn.

Poor General Brownstone. She'd been close to the hotel, directing the third wave when the bombs hit. At least someone had found her head.

That left Steve with no option but to make Ellis head of the army. Ellis didn't have the mind for the job, but he'd do until Steve found a soldier with command experience who had actually lived through the night. Steve had thought of giving McMasters the job, but he didn't trust the man — maybe McMasters was thinking of taking over.

Actually, when it came to the power structure, it was better to be safe than sorry. Steve made a mental note to kill McMasters later.

The bombs had been a brilliant stroke, he had to admit; they had wiped out most of his organized army. He was still the emperor, but now what he ruled was little more than a mob.

He had to start over. Start over somewhere else. He was lucky the humans hadn't used a nuke. That luck wouldn't last long.

"Master of Logistics, it's time we looked at moving on. I don't care for big cities anymore."

McMasters slipped a little on the concrete, regained his balance. "Yes, Emperor. General Brownstone's evacuation plan hasn't been affected. She organized caches of working vehicles. We could start clearing out a road, have the trucks and buses moving out in about four or five hours?"

Damn, but that was a big crater. Whatever had dropped the bomb that made it might still be up there, looking down, waiting for the next target.

"Make it so," Steve said. "But Doctor-General Ellis and I won't be with that group. General Brownstone had motorcycles as well, did she not?"

McMasters nodded. "She had a few caches of those as well. I know some are at the parking garage at Saint Joseph's Hospital, up north in the Boystown neighborhood."

Perfect. That location was five miles from where Steve stood, far enough to survive the worst effects of a large nuke if the humans decided to drop one on downtown Chicago.

"Start the exodus," he said. "I want hundreds of vehicles leaving at the same time, heading south, east and west."

Steve had wanted to rule from Chicago, but clearly that was not God's will. In a few hours, the Chosen Ones would radiate outward, drawing attention while he and a few others slipped away to the north, using motorcycles to navigate through the congested roads. He would find a place to hide for a while, and let things run their course.

Humanity couldn't last that much longer. And when they were gone, Emperor Steve Stanton would begin again.

A LAST KISS

His fingers flexed around the knife's handle. So light in his hand, so heavy on his soul.

This had to be done. Clarence knew that.

Roth and Bosh had found a ladder. They'd used pantyhose to strap Margaret to it, her back against the rungs, then tied each end of the ladder to a clothing rack. Her face was about two feet closer to the ground than her feet. Below her head, they'd put a scuffed, yellow plastic mop bucket.

Margaret saw him coming. She was still gagged. Her eyes flicked to the knife in his hand, then widened with both fear and anger. She chewed on the gag, made noises that were pleas, or curses, or probably both. Her body lurched against the restraints. The ladder and clothing racks rattled, but didn't budge.

What, had he thought that Margaret would go easy? Had he thought that at the last moment, she might accept this fate, look at him lovingly, forgive him for what must be done? Maybe in that Candyland vision, he'd remove her gag and she would whisper how she loved him, how she was sorry it had to be this way but she was so grateful he was taking away her pain.

That wasn't going to happen.

This would not be nice.

This would not be easy.

Margaret Montoya, or whatever had taken her over, didn't want to die. Just like any person, any animal, she wanted to *live*.

Clarence walked closer.

Her eyes narrowed. She screamed, a sound of desperate rage. The gag muffled some of it, but only some.

No. He couldn't do it. He just couldn't.

Clarence turned to leave, but stopped short — Klimas was standing just a few feet away. Had he been there the whole time? The SEAL nodded in man-to-man understanding. He extended his hand, palm up.

"Give me the knife," he said. "Take a walk. No shame in it — she's your wife."

Clarence looked at the extended hand. Then he looked at the knife. No, it had to be him.

"Was," he said. "*Was* my wife."

He turned again, faced her, forced his feet to move.

Margaret's body shook, this time from sobs. Tears filled her eyes, ran down her forehead to vanish in her dark hair. She drew a ragged breath in through her nose, paused, then screamed again.

Reality slurred for a moment. Everything shifted. He'd met her five years ago, fallen in love with her almost immediately. So brilliant, so hardworking, so utterly committed to doing whatever it took to get the job done. And what a job that had been.

She'd fallen for him almost as fast. For a while, things had been perfect. They had been so happy together. They thought they had all the time in the world.

They didn't. No one did. Ever.

No matter how much time you have, that time always runs out.

Clarence stepped forward.

Her screams grew more ragged as vocal cords gave way. She thrashed harder, so hard the whole ladder rattled, but the SEALS knew their business when it came to tying knots.

He reached out with the knife. The blade shook madly, so much so that it looked like a prop made out of rubber.

He was Abraham, ordered by God to sacrifice his own son. Only God wasn't here, and no one was going to appear in a cloud of holy light and tell him it had just been a test of his devotion.

Clarence started to talk, but his throat tightened and he choked on the words. He swallowed hard and tried again.

"Good-bye, my love."

He pressed the edge of the blade against her throat.

She screamed and screamed, she chewed madly on the gag, she jerked and kicked and fought for life.

Clarence closed his eyes.

He pushed up as hard as he could and slid the knife forward, felt the blade slice deep. The ladder rattled harder than ever. Still pressing up, he pulled the blade back, felt it bite into tendons and ligaments. Hers wasn't the first throat he'd cut. It wasn't like the movies — one slash didn't do it, you had to *saw* a bit to get at those arteries.

He pressed up even harder and slid forward again, then pulled back again. Hot wetness splashed onto his hand.

Her screams ceased.

Eyes still locked tight, he sawed forward one more time, back one more time.

The ladder stopped rattling.

He heard the sound of his wife's blood splattering into a plastic mop bucket.

From behind him, Klimas's command voice boomed.

"Feely! Get this blood ready to go!"

Clarence realized he was still holding the knife. He let it drop, heard it clatter, then covered his face with his hands.

He slowly sank to the floor.

All the time in the world . . .

All the time in the world . . .

MISSION OBJECTIVES

Paulius Klimas wasn't a religious man. His lack of faith, however, didn't stop him from a small prayer of thanks:

Thank God it's winter.

The Windy City was living up to its name. Snow, ash and dirt swirled, rose and fell as gusts curled off buildings and rolled down the streets. Paulius guessed the temperature was hovering in the single digits, but the windchill dropped it far below zero. The weather numbed him, made it hard to move, but he was thankful because it produced a much-desired side effect: the streets were mostly empty.

Even monsters and psychopaths hated the cold, it seemed.

He and D'Shawn Bosh moved quickly. Roth's sporting goods store had been stop number one. Bosh had gone for Cubs gear, while Paulius opted for a black, knee-length Bears coat and matching hat. They both wore gray Chicago Fire sweats over their fatigue pants.

Paulius also looked a little pregnant. He had a one-gallon milk jug of Margaret's blood strapped to his belly. Feely had said his body heat would keep it from freezing solid.

They were headed east on Oak. Dust from the JDAMs had billowed out even this far, some four and five blocks from impact, turning the standing snow from white to gray.

Though the bad guys clearly didn't like the cold, a few of them remained outside. Paulius saw several bundled-up people, heads covered in hats and faces wrapped in scarves. They all carried weapons of one kind or another: hunting rifles, pistols, knives, axes, even carbines. One fat guy lugged a chain saw. The dirt, the streets filled with ruined cars, an armed militia walking free — Chicago reminded Paulius of a subzero Mogadishu.

The monsters, however, didn't seem to mind the conditions. Three-legged hatchlings scurried everywhere. As for the huge, yellow behemoths with the wicked bone-blades sticking out of their arms, Paulius saw at least one on every block. It was all he and Bosh could do to keep walking, to try to pretend the creatures were nothing unusual.

Roth's experience held true: without uniforms, Paulius and Bosh drew little attention. They reached Michigan Avenue, looked out onto a park covered in gray snow. At the park's far edge lay U.S. Route 41, and beyond that, Lake Michigan.

"Damn," Bosh said. "We ain't getting out that way."

Paulius nodded. There were even more cars blocking the road than when he and his men had swum in the day before. He pulled out his binoculars, steel-cold fingers complaining at even that small motion. Through them, he saw the reason for the growing and already-impassable roadblock: two of the sickle-armed, muscle-bound creatures were rolling a burned-out Toyota pickup down the road. They pushed it near several other cars, then bent, lifted, and flipped the vehicle on its side as if it were nothing more than a toy.

He stowed the binoculars. "After we pick up the others, we'll have to use surface streets to drive north. Let's go."

They moved south on Michigan Avenue. On the far side of the street, a Converted woman was using a hacksaw to cut away at the arm of a frozen corpse. As Paulius and Bosh moved past, the woman didn't even look up.

The firehouse wasn't much farther.

THE ENEMY OF MY ENEMY

The president of Russia glared out from the Situation Room's large screen. President Albertson glared back. At least, that's what Murray *thought* Albertson was going for — in truth, it looked like he was trying hard not to soil himself.

Stepan Morozov's face sagged with prolonged anger and extreme exhaustion. He wore a suit coat, but no tie. His sweat-stained shirt was unbuttoned down to the sternum, showing graying chest hair.

"President Albertson, the time to act is *now*," Morozov said. "China is going to launch her missiles. Our intelligence confirms this. If Russia and America combine for a first strike, together we will *eliminate* China's nuclear capability."

Albertson opened his mouth to speak, then shut it. Murray saw beads of sweat break out on the man's forehead.

On the screen, Morozov's eyes narrowed. "Mister President? Did you hear me?"

"Yes," Albertson said quickly. "Yes, I heard you."

When Albertson didn't offer anything else, Morozov's face started to redden.

"The Chinese have already struck us," he said. "A million Russians are dead. The Chinese leadership says nothing — no apology, no explanation. We *must* assume that they are infected. If we strike while they are disorganized and silent, we might hit them *before* they can launch at all."

"And we might not," Albertson said. "They could launch in retaliation, get their missiles away before ours hit. I'll consider your proposal . . . I'll talk it over with my staff. Thank you for the call."

Murray couldn't believe what he was watching. The Russian president was asking the United States to join him in a large-scale nuclear attack on the world's most populous nation, and Albertson just wanted to get off the line. The man was overwhelmed, completely unprepared for something like this.

Morozov snarled. A string of spit ran from his top lip to his bottom, vibrating with each word.

"There is no time to *consider*," he said. The string of spit popped free, landed on his chin. "Maybe there is a reason *you* don't want to strike! Maybe *you* are infected, and you are already talking to the Chinese about first-striking *us*!"

Albertson shook his head. "I . . . we . . . of course we're not infected! We . . . we . . ."

Morozov shook his fist. "Then prove it! Strike now, before it is too late!"

"I . . ." Albertson said. "We . . ."

Murray stood up. "President Morozov, we are close to finishing a weapon that will wipe out the infected, all of them, *worldwide*."

In the Situation Room, faces pinched tight in anger or went blank in shock — two heads of state were deciding the fate of the world, and *Murray Longworth* was butting in?

On the screen, Morozov turned to look at Murray. The virtual conference technology made it feel like he was looking Murray dead in the eyes.

"You are Longworth?" he said. "The one who handles the . . . the . . . ah, yes, the *special threats*."

Murray was a little surprised to be recognized so quickly, but he plowed forward.

"Yes, President Morozov, I am the director of the Department of Special Threats. Our solution, sir, is *highly* contagious. It spreads from one infected to the next. Our team is in Chicago, testing this solution as we speak. If Russia's actions cause a nuclear strike on Chicago, then our solution will also be destroyed. And to be blunt, your weapons, our weapons — none of them can do a damn thing to save our citizens and our nations. If your people haven't told you that already, they are either ignorant of reality or they are telling you what they think you want to hear."

Morozov's face grew redder. His eyes widened.

"Who do you think you are talking—"

"*Shut up*," Murray said. He couldn't take this anymore, couldn't take the pressure and these people posturing while the world died around them.

He walked up to the screen as if Morozov was a real person and they were about to stand toe-to-toe. "If you launch, you doom the entire human race. We need more time."

Morozov stared out from the screen. His left cheek twitched.

"Our intelligence says your military has abandoned Chicago."

Murray nodded. "And what better place to run our test than in a city overrun with the infected? We need more time, Mister President. We can stop this thing *without* nuking the bejesus out of China."

Morozov turned to look offscreen. Murray saw him mouth the word *bejesus*, then shrug. Someone offscreen answered him. He nodded, turned back to stare at Longworth.

"I am told that you are a soldier?"

The question surprised Murray. "I was," he said. "I served in Vietnam."

Morozov spread his hands, palms up. "Once a soldier, always a soldier. I served my country in Afghanistan." His anger faded somewhat. "You have killed people, Mister Longworth? You have seen your friends die?"

What the hell does this have to do with anything?

"Yes to both," Murray said.

Morozov bit his lower lip. He nodded, turned slightly to look at Albertson. "You have twenty-four hours to prove this. Then, America *will* join our attack. As one of your former presidents once said so eloquently, you are either with us, or you are against us."

He made a gesture to someone off camera. The screen went blank.

Albertson's face glowed with a sheen of sweat. He put his sweaty hands on the table. He was trying hard to look like he was in control — trying, and failing miserably.

"Admiral Porter," he said. "If Murray's people fail, what do you think we should do?"

The admiral sagged in his chair. "I've been in this game for forty years. I never thought I'd say something like this, Mister President, but it's my recommendation that we join the Russians."

Albertson closed his eyes. "All right. I need some time to think. I need a few minutes of sleep, maybe."

He stood. As Murray and the others watched, the president of the United States of America walked out of the Situation Room to take a nap.

FROZEN FOOD

The bodies of the two policemen were gone. Probably hauled away, probably eaten — an ultimate dishonor that wouldn't have happened if Paulius hadn't killed them.

He wondered, briefly, if the cops were taking their revenge from the grave. He and Bosh couldn't find a way into the firehouse. The windows and doors weren't just boarded up, they were blocked by sheet metal that had been bolted in place from the inside. The public transit bus remained embedded in the firehouse door; the cops had even secured the area around it, blocking any way in. The bus's smashed-in front end meant no one was going through it without a blowtorch.

Paulius and Bosh knelt in the shadows of the firehouse's small backyard, out of sight from the main road. An eye-high wall — made of the same gray stone as the firehouse — lined the yard, providing a place to stay out of sight. It also gave some shelter from a constant wind that rattled a single, bare tree. Decent cover for now, but they had to find a way inside before they were seen.

The cold had finally got to Bosh. He couldn't stop shivering.

"What's next, Commander? Shoot through a door?"

Paulius's toes felt numb.

"Too much noise," he said. "If we can slip in unseen, we'll have more time. We don't know if the engine is damaged, or if it even runs. You said you saw the cops come out of the back of the bus?"

Bosh nodded. "We'd checked it minutes earlier, and it was empty. The cops must have seen the Rangers, then come out of the firehouse and into the bus to stay under cover while getting a better look."

"Could they have come *through* the bus?"

"Maybe," Bosh said. "I looked inside, but we were advancing so I just gave it a quick once-over."

"Let's check again."

Paulius moved to the corner of the firehouse, looked along the building's west wall out onto Chicago Avenue. Across the demolition derby of a street, a hospital: THE ANNE AND ROBERT H. LURIE CHILDREN'S HOSPITAL OF CHICAGO, said the big white letters above the glass building's front entrance.

He saw no movement. He advanced. Bosh followed, covering him. Paulius moved to the rear of the bus. He hand-signaled Bosh to stay put, then entered the open door halfway down the long bus's right side.

Inside, Paulius counted seventeen corpses. By the looks of them, they'd either died during warmer temperatures, or later thawed out long enough to start bloating before things returned to subzero. Some of the bodies had been gnawed on, meat torn away down to scratched bone.

Paulius realized why the Converted had taken the bodies of the two cops: they hadn't been frozen solid. Fresh meat.

He shuddered, got his head back in the game. The bus tilted up at a slight incline. He walked down the aisle toward the front, slowly, careful to make sure each corpse was just that — a corpse.

He heard a click in his headset.

"Commander," Bosh said, "three hostiles coming this way, from the west. Moving quick, maybe sixty seconds till they reach us."

Paulius had only seconds to search. There had to be a way in. The windshield? Spiderwebbed and smashed, but still intact — no one had come through there. The front-right entry door? Also smashed, so bent and twisted there was no way it would ever open again. No one had come through there, either.

If he'd been those cops, told to guard that facility, what would he have done? They'd taken the time to armor up the building, but they obviously left themselves a way in and out.

Paulius knelt down and looked under the dashboard. Right where the driver's feet would go, he saw a floor mat. He pulled it aside to reveal a hole large enough for a man to crawl through.

He hit the "talk" button twice, sending two clicks to Bosh.

The bus creaked slightly as Bosh entered and moved silently up the aisle. Paulius pointed to the hole.

Bosh handed his M4 to Paulius, then sat on the driver's seat and slid his feet into the hole. His Chicago-Cubs-jacket-covered gear made him have to wiggle a bit, but he popped through.

Paulius heard approaching voices.

"I heard something over here," a woman's voice said.

"Ah, the firehouse again?" said a man. "Fuck that, there's no way in."

Paulius handed Bosh's M4 through, then his own. He slid into the hole.

"I'm hungry," the woman said. "There's bodies in the bus."

Paulius was halfway in when his long Bears jacket snagged tight, pulling the sleeves up hard against his armpits.

"Those bodies are gross," the man said. "When we unthaw them, they're rotted and black."

"That's all that's left," the woman said. "Unless you know where there's some living meat that everyone missed?"

Paulius pulled, but couldn't see where he was hooked. He couldn't even turn all the way around to the hostiles if they walked into the bus.

"Come on," the woman said. "There's got to be something worth eating in there. Come on."

The voice couldn't be more than ten feet away.

Hands grabbed at his waist. He reached for the knife sheathed on his chest — it was gone, he'd given it to Otto. He raised a hand to strike downward, but saw Bosh's head wedged into the tight corner.

Bosh's shaking black hands fumbled at something. Paulius felt the coat snap free, then he was yanked down into a dark crawlspace. He landed on frozen ground.

Paulius reached a hand back up, quietly, and grabbed the edge of the floor mat. He silently pulled it over the hole.

He waited in the darkness. He wiggled his body enough to draw his sidearm. He heard footsteps inside the bus.

"This forearm looks kinda okay," the man said. "Kinda."

"Great," the woman said. "This is only temporary, Harry. I can't wait until we get out of here in a couple of hours. I bet cash money there's fresh meat down in Champaign."

A few more footsteps, then nothing. Paulius sat silent, listened to the Converted's fading conversation.

On his hands and knees, he scooted backward through the tight space, across the frozen ground until he felt concrete. He stood: he was inside the firehouse — a long, wide garage, gear hanging from the walls, electric heaters spaced around the floor, their coils glowing orange — and sitting there pretty as you please was the red, white, black and chrome bulk of Fire Engine 98, all thirty feet of her. Polished, clean and gleaming.

The boxy cab alone looked as big as an SUV; it would hold six people, easy, with plenty of window room to fire weapons out either side. The wide, wraparound windshield took up the top half of the vehicle's ten-foot-wide flat front.

A square, chrome grille sat below that windshield, lights and flashers on either side. The front bumper was a massive thing: red-trimmed white metal sticking out some two feet from the grille, perfect for smashing past abandoned cars. Below the right-side windows at the rear of the cab, inch-high gold letters spelled out CHICAGO FIRE DEPT. Up on the front right, gold lettering read ENGINE CO. And below that a big, white 98.

The boxy rear section of the vehicle was around fourteen feet long and ten feet high, with a bed full of neatly coiled hose. Long equipment boxes ran the length of the bed, a ladder strapped horizontally to each side. Anyone in the bed would be able to take cover behind those equipment boxes, rest weapons on the flat tops and be protected from most small-arms fire.

Separating the rear bed from the cab, a three-foot-thick section of chrome packed with hose connections and valves. And on top of that control section, the crown jewel, the thing that might let Tim Feely's plan actually work: a water cannon mounted on a swivel.

Bosh let out a low whistle.

"Ho-leee shit, Commander," he said. "I'd rather have a tank, but since we don't have one, this is pretty damn close."

Bosh opened the driver's door. He had to step up on a footrest to look inside. He reached in, grabbed something, then leaned back out and dangled that something in front of Paulius.

A key chain with a single key.

"Looks like they were considering bugging out," Bosh said. He pointed to the rear of the building. "There's a good fifty feet of space behind this baby, so we can build up a head of steam."

"How are we going to move that bus?"

"Don't think we have to," Bosh said. "It's just a shell. They took the engine out. Drive train, too. That's why we could crawl under it. They even kept it warm in here, maybe to make sure the fire truck would start right up. I think those cops were getting ready to ram their way out and take their chances."

Paulius nodded. If he'd left the cops alone, would they have driven to safety? He couldn't allow himself to worry about that now.

"I'll figure out how to get this blood into the water tank," Paulius said. "Have to make sure the water's warm enough, but Feely said the hydras should survive no problem."

He looked at Bosh. "You're qualified in heavy vehicles. You want to drive?"

Bosh smiled. "Hell yes, Commander. Navy SEALs was my second choice. As a kid, I always wanted to be a fireman."

BOOK IV

Road Trip

MEET THE PUBLIC

Ten tons of truck smashed into the firehouse door, denting the metal outward and knocking the gutted bus a good five feet back.

Paulius was standing outside the firehouse, rifle snug against his shoulder, waiting for the inevitable reaction from the locals. The big diesel engine gurgled as Bosh reversed, then revved when he floored it. The rolling door ripped outward as the truck again smashed into the bus, knocking it back at an angle. One more shot would create enough room for Engine 98 to pull out onto the street. Bosh reversed; the dented roll-up door slid off the truck, clattered limply on the concrete drive.

Paulius spotted two people rushing in from the west, a man and a woman, and another man coming from the east. From all up and down the street, people scurried out of buildings like angry ants defending a hive.

The people from the west were fifty yards away, shooting hunting rifles as they ran.

Paulius sighted in, breathed out and squeezed the trigger. The woman's head snapped back as her body fell forward — dead before she hit the ground. The man saw this, slowed. Paulius squeezed off another shot. The man spun right, left hand clutching at his shoulder.

The big diesel roared again. Engine 98 drove over the fallen roll-up door and smashed past the bus.

Paulius spun to the right, aimed and fired. The man coming from the east doubled over, fell face-first onto the snowy sidewalk.

Paulius sprinted for the fire truck, which was already turning left onto Chicago Avenue. He hopped up on the rear bumper, then scrambled into the hose-lined bed. He stayed low, picking targets as he went.

So many of them . . . coming so fast . . .

He didn't need to give Bosh instructions. The man had been given one clear objective: *get back to the others as fast as possible, don't stop for anything.*

Paulius dropped two more bad guys before Engine 98 turned north on Mies van der Rohe Way. He faced forward. The cab's roof topped out at his sternum, giving him excellent protection from the front while still providing a full range of fire.

He heard Bosh's voice in his headset: "Commander, you might want to hold tight. It's about to get violent."

Up ahead, Paulius saw a line of cars set up bumper-to-bumper, blocking the street. He ducked down, wedged himself between the back of the cabin and the water cannon's metal post. On the inside wall of the passenger-side tool box that ran the length of the bed, he saw a red fire axe held firmly in a bracket. If he ran out of ammo, it might come down to using that.

Bosh floored the gas. Engine 98 responded, picking up speed. The wide, flat, front metal bumper hit first, bashing a BMW to the left and a Ford truck to the right.

"Ho-leee *shit*," Bosh said. "You see that fucker fly?"

Paulius rose, looked for targets — there was no shortage, as Converted popped up on either side of the road, in building windows, just about everywhere he looked.

Aim, fire. Aim, fire.

The fire engine clipped the front of a UPS truck, spinning the delivery vehicle in a full three-sixty.

Aim, fire. Aim, fire.

The engine whined as Bosh shifted gears. He tried to weave through the obstacles as well as he could, but there were just too many cars. Engine 98 smashed into an old Buick, tearing the rear end clean off.

Aim, fire.

It was working. They were just a few blocks away from the clothing store.

Paulius thumbed his "talk" button, hoping the short-range comms would work this far out.

"Klimas to Roth. Klimas to Roth, over?"

Roth's voice came back almost immediately: "I read you, Commander."

"Pack 'em up, Roth. Extraction in three minutes!"

SCOTT SIGLER

Steve looks at Ellis, "kick me," at Brownstone, and then some bulls, "And then, get on with things."

Jeremy nodded and ripped to escape.

McMasters' Steve said into the phone, "I want that truck stopped. Said everyone. I want it destroyed."

BIG AND DANGEROUS

Steve Stanton's fingers squeezed tighter on the cell phone.

"A fire truck? McMasters, what the fuck are you talking about?"

"Spotters reported it just now," McMasters said. He was at a garage closer to downtown, preparing another group to flee the city. His voice sounded like he was about to hyperventilate. "The spotters said a guy in a Cubs hat was driving, but I think it's a soldier who survived the attack."

Robert McMasters was normally a smart man. He'd kept the city's power running, kept the water pumps working, made sure that Chicago didn't flood. He'd kept the city functioning mostly as it had before the awakening. But while he could handle problems that involved inanimate objects and mechanical systems, he clearly didn't do so well when the situation involved men with guns.

"Emperor, did you hear me? A *fire truck*! They're trying to get away!"

"Be quiet," Steve said. "I'm thinking."

He set the phone against his shoulder. He glanced around the municipal garage where Brownstone, God rest her soul, had gathered sixty vehicles. Doctor-General Jeremy Ellis stood there, looking afraid for his life as he always did. Jeremy was organizing thirty-one cars, eighteen trucks, three city buses, four motorcycles, and even three snowplows for the exodus. The snowplows' big, heavy scoops would let them rip right through the endless abandoned cars, allowing Steve's people to spread south, east and west.

A fire truck was also big, also heavy . . . heavy enough to smash through the thinner roadblocks. But if it was just a couple of soldiers, and they were clever enough to have lived this long, why wouldn't they just *walk* out instead of letting a city know where they were?

. . . because a fire engine was also big enough to carry passengers.

. . . and because Cooper Mitchell's body still hadn't been found.

Steve put the phone back to his ear. "Where is this fire engine?"

"Heading west on Walton," McMasters said.

Steve looked at Ellis. "Get me Jeff Brockman, and three more bulls. And guns, get me some guns."

Jeremy nodded and ran off to comply.

"McMasters," Steve said into the phone, "I want that truck stopped. Send everyone. I want it *destroyed*!"

THE MOTIVATIONAL SPEECH

Tim Feely had never fired a weapon in his life. Now his life might very well depend on the M4 rifle he held in his hands.

At least it was more efficient than a chunk of concrete.

He stood at the top of the wide stairs, watching Roth carry Ramierez down to the ground floor. Ramierez cradled a sleek, black shotgun, his weak fingers barely gripping the stock and the pump handle.

"Move him easy," Tim called. "Be as gentle as you can."

"Just hurry up," Roth said over his shoulder. "If you're still there when evac arrives, Doc, no one is coming up to get you."

Roth descended, but did so as gently as he could.

Cooper Mitchell limped over, Ramierez's Sig Sauer pistol in his hand.

"Your boy Clarence ain't coming," Cooper said. "He's moping about that infected woman of his." Cooper jerked suddenly, as if something had flown in front of his face, but there was nothing there.

He shook his head. "I don't want him to get eaten, but if he does, I do hope he's die-die-dielicious."

Cooper slowly hobbled down the stairs, leaning heavily on the rail.

Tim watched him go. That was one crazy motherfucker, right there. Hopefully he was sane enough to only shoot at the bad guys.

Tim jogged to Clarence. It was worth one more try.

The man sat on his butt, in the same spot where Margaret had been before they tied her to that ladder. His back rested against the wall, chin hung to his chest. His pistol was in its thigh holster. In his hands, he held the big knife he'd used to slice his wife's throat.

Did he want to die here? He acted like this was all his fault, when not a shred of it was.

"Otto, get your ass up. Come on, man, rescue is on the way!"

The big man didn't move.

He hadn't even cleaned the dust off his face. It made his skin almost the same color as his tight gray shirt.

Clarence *had* to come. Tim needed him there, needed his strength. Tim's plan had sounded great in theory, but now it was turning into reality, which meant he'd have to *go outside*, he'd have to face those killers. He had to find a way to get through to Clarence. Maybe a slap in the face? That always worked on TV.

Tim reached back and brought his hand forward as hard as he could.

Clarence reached up and caught Tim's wrist, stopping the palm an inch from his cheek. Strong fingers squeezed down. Tim hissed in pain.

"Ow," he said. "Okay, maybe that wasn't such a great idea."

Otto's cold eyes bore into him.

"You made me kill her," he said. His voice was little more than a growl, a hollow husk that befit the hollow man. "You got what you wanted, Feely. So get the fuck out of here and leave me be."

Clarence let go.

Tim stood, rubbed at his wrist.

"She's *gone*, Clarence. If you want to end it all, do that after we're finished, because your gun might make the difference. If we don't get Cooper out alive, then Margaret died for *nothing*."

Otto just stared, his face inscrutable. He made no motion to get up.

Tim remembered Margaret and Otto talking back on the *Carl Brashear*, remembered that word Margaret had used as a weapon.

"She wouldn't have quit," Tim said. "She was a *real* soldier."

Otto looked away, unable to meet Tim's gaze. That one had cut deep.

But he still didn't get up.

He reached into his pocket, pulled out a bulky cell phone and tossed it to Tim.

Tim caught it. "What am I supposed to do with this?"

"I called Murray a half hour ago," Clarence said. "Air support is on the way. If you have to abort the pickup location, hit 'redial,' let him know where you're going."

His shoulders slumped. His chin once again drooped to his chest.

Clarence wasn't coming. Tim had done all he could. He turned to head down the stairs, then paused and looked at the phone in his hand.

Just hit "redial" . . .

MAKE EVERY BULLET COUNT

A woman rushed toward Engine 98, a lit Molotov cocktail in her hand. Paulius dropped her with his M4's final round.

He drew his P226: fifteen rounds in this magazine, fifteen more in a second mag. After that, he'd have nothing left except harsh language.

Aim, fire . . . aim, fire . . .

He wanted to use the water cannon, splash these fuckers down with a face-full of Margaret Water, but Feely had told him to save it — it was critical to wait until the Converted were packed in as tight as possible.

Engine 98 was beginning to vibrate, just a little bit, a rhythmic pattern that increased or decreased in time with the vehicle's speed. Something wrong with a tire, maybe. The thing had smashed past dozens of vehicles so far. The fire truck had mass and that meant physics was on its side, but every hit took a toll.

Aim, fire . . . aim, fire . . .

Converted gave chase. Three men, a woman, a boy, two girls, three hatchlings and, coming in fast, one of the muscle-bound monsters. More hostiles were pouring out of buildings, either rushing toward the truck or stopping to fire. A few bullets punched into the truck's metal sides, but most of the rounds whizzed by. A trained army would have taken the truck apart. Fortunately, these assholes were anything but trained.

More Converted fired down from above, aiming from skyscraper windows. Their aim was just as bad; bullets smacked into the tops of the equipment boxes or punched into the coiled fire hose. Paulius hadn't been hit, but sooner or later one of them was bound to get lucky.

Aim, fire . . . aim, fire . . .

He stood and looked forward over the cab's roof. Up ahead, a bus lay on its side, blocking most of Walton Street — too much vehicle to drive through. Bosh angled the engine to the left. He had to slow down to go around the bus, and when he did the Converted closed in.

One of the men tried to climb up the rear. Bosh ran something over; when the rear wheels hit whatever it was, the back end bounced, flipping the man back out into the street where he hit face-first and skidded.

Two of the hatchlings leaped, scrambling up the truck's right side. Shoot them, or save the rounds?

Paulius jammed his pistol into its holster, then yanked the fire axe from its bracket. The first hatchling scurried over the stacked hoses. Paulius swung the axe like a baseball bat — the red blade sliced through the pyramid-shaped body, sending the top part flying over the truck's side. The thing collapsed, spilling purple goo across the hose.

The other hatchling leaped. Paulius didn't have time for a second swing. He brought the axe in front of him, rear point facing out. The hatchling couldn't change direction in mid-air: it impaled itself on the spike.

He shook the twitching thing from the axe, heard a gunshot from inside the cabin: Bosh shooting at someone who'd closed in and tried to yank open the driver's door.

Paulius felt something heavy land on the truck, dropping the bed down a few inches before the shocks lifted it back up. There, on the rear bumper, only his big head and gnarled hands visible, stood a yellow monster. Its hands reached into the bed, the long bone-knives jutting from the back of its arms. Muscles flexed as it started to crawl forward.

Paulius dropped the axe and once again drew his P226.

The creature looked up at him. Thick lips curled back from too-long, too-wide teeth. Yellow lids narrowed — even over the truck's engine, Paulius heard a deep growl.

He squeezed the trigger. The 9-millimeter round hit dead-center in the creature's forehead. A cloud of blood and brains puffed out the back of its skull. The muscle-monster fell back, crashed onto the pavement and tumbled forward.

Paulius realized the Converted had stopped firing while the monster tried to get in, because as soon as it fell away bullets started hitting all around him, punching into the equipment boxes, kicking up flakes of red paint. He dropped and crawled across the hoses toward the cabin, desperate for whatever cover he could find.

Bosh's voice in his ear: "Hold on, Commander! Turning right on Rush, and there's a *lot* more cars here!"

Paulius pressed his back against the cabin wall, and held on tight as the twenty-one-ton vehicle smashed past yet another obstacle.

THE CALM BEFORE THE STORM

Cooper Mitchell wasn't sure if he should hope. If he believed he might escape, would that jinx it? What if he wound up with a signpost rammed through his ass and out his mouth?

He hid behind a rack of pantsuits on the first floor of Barneys, not even fifteen feet from the front door. The SEALs had to get him out. They just *had* to; all this couldn't be for nothing.

The weird thing about a city with no traffic was the sense of stillness, the *quiet*. If he closed his eyes, he could have been in the woods of Michigan, save for the occasional roar of a bloodthirsty monster. That lack of sound let things carry through the streets — he heard distant gunshots, powerful crashes of metal hitting metal, and the growing-closer sound of a gurgling diesel engine.

Was that Klimas? Had he really pulled it off?

Tim came down the stairs, cell phone pressed to his ear.

"No, this isn't Otto," he said. "It's Tim Feely."

The little doctor came up next to Cooper. He leaned around the pantsuits to peek out the store's glass door. He leaned back suddenly, his face wrinkled in annoyance.

"I don't give a shit about *your* problems, Murray. This plan is ridiculous. Send someone to get us!" A pause. "No, Klimas isn't here." Tim looked around, saw Roth crouching just to the left of the front door, Ramierez lying on the floor beside him. "Hold on, Murray."

Tim duckwalked to Roth. The big man looked ridiculous in his letterman's jacket. Cooper hated the Bears.

Roth took the phone. "This is Petty Officer First Class Calvin Roth."

He listened for a second. "No sir, Director Longworth, Commander Klimas isn't available. Yes, we still need extraction at Lincoln Park, the south end." Roth looked out the window. Cooper followed his gaze, saw a dozen men and women rushing away down the street, toward the sound of that diesel engine.

Roth ducked back behind full cover. "Yes sir, we still need that air support.

We're going to be under enemy fire the entire way, sir." He paused, then nodded again. "Yes sir." He hung up, handed the phone to Tim.

"Well?" Tim said, taking the phone and pocketing it. "Is Murray sending the entire air force? I don't want to go out there. I *can't*."

Roth shrugged. "What air force? Washington is under attack. So is everything else. An AC-130 and an Apache are both en route. Those will have to be enough."

Feely shook his head. The man was about to freak out; Cooper didn't know what they'd do if Feely didn't get his shit together.

"*Two* lousy planes," Tim said. "No fucking way, Roth. Call him back! Tell him we need—"

Roth's hand shot out and grabbed Feely's shoulder. The sudden move silenced him.

"Doc," Roth said, "I need you to shut up now."

Roth turned slightly, made eye contact with Cooper. When he spoke, Cooper knew it was to him and Feely both.

"It's game-time," Roth said. "Stop worrying about shit you can't change. If you want to survive, focus on the job at hand. When the fire truck comes, we go out firing. We'll have a few seconds of surprise. The truck has to stop so we can get Ramierez inside. Cooper, how many rounds you have?"

Cooper lifted the Sig Sauer pistol in his hand. "Fifteen."

"Good man," Roth said. "Make them count. Doc, you remember what Ram told you?"

Feely nodded. "Single shots. Keep the stock tight to my shoulder, move the barrel where I move my eyes. Aim, then fire."

Roth nodded. "Excellent. And how many rounds do you have?"

"Ten," Feely said. "But I can't . . . I'm no good in a fight. Ramierez showed me how to shoot, but I *can't*."

Roth shook his head. "Too late for that bullshit, Doc. Commander Klimas told me what you did to save Cooper. You're a born warrior. That's what I need you to be for the next ten minutes, got it?"

A wide-eyed Feely nodded.

"Say it," Roth said. "Say, *I'm a warrior*."

"I'm . . ." Tim licked dry lips. "I'm a warrior."

"Good. Just keep saying that, Doc."

Cooper saw Feely mouthing the words, over and over.

The diesel's roar kicked up in volume, bounced off building walls — the thing had just turned a corner. Cooper saw it, saw the sun glinting off moving chrome, off red and white paint.

Roth nodded. "Here we go."

Cooper felt his heart hammering not just in his chest but in his head, his eyes, his entire body.

The diesel's roar grew louder.

Just seconds now . . .

WELCOMING COMMITTEE

Through the store's windows, Tim Feely watched the fire engine bear down on a charred, green Prius. A Converted stood behind the car, shooting a shotgun as fast as he could pump and pull the trigger. Tim didn't know dick about guns, but that wasn't going to do a damn thing. The man seemed to figure that out at the last second. He turned to run, but he'd waited too long — the truck smashed into the Prius, launching it three feet off the ground and spinning it like a cardboard coaster. The rear end hit the man and sent him flying, a rag doll that sailed through the air and hit the sidewalk in front of Barneys New York, splashing a spray of blood against the floor-to-ceiling windows.

The truck was so close that Tim could see Bosh's smiling face inside the cracked, blood-flecked, bullet-ridden windshield. The truck's grille had once been polished chrome: now it was twisted and bent, with a severed right arm dangling from the left side. The obnoxiously huge front bumper was scratched and dented, wet with blood, streaked with a dozen colors from its vehicular victims.

Bosh locked up the brakes. The wheels skidded through snow, kicking up sprays of dirty white. He swerved left as he entered the intersection, then curved sharply right. The truck slid to a stop, its left side just ten feet from store's revolving front door.

Roth handed his rifle to Ramierez, who held it along with his shotgun. Roth scooped Ramierez up.

"Feely, Cooper, let's *move*!"

Roth pushed through the rotating door. Cooper hobbled forward so fast he was in the next divider behind Roth.

Tim heard gunfire. His legs wouldn't move. He couldn't do it, he ꞌuldn't —

I am a warrior, I am a warrior.

The thought seemed to lift him and throw him at the still-spinning door.

He hit it on the run, shoulder smacking against the glass. He stumbled out into the windblown chaos.

He faced the engine's left side. So many bullet holes; how was the thing still running? Klimas stood in the truck's bed, aiming his pistol and firing, making each shot count. Beyond the fire engine, maybe a block down Oak, Tim saw a wave of people and monsters closing in.

Cooper turned right, started firing.

Roth opened the rear passenger door and set Ramierez inside. He grabbed his big SCAR-FN rifle, leaving the wounded SEAL with the black shotgun.

Tim stumbled forward, looked left, right, looked across the street — they were coming from *everywhere*. Hatchlings, people with blades and guns and clubs.

He was going to die.

A woman sprinted toward him, the butcher knife in her hand raised high. Tim pulled the M4's stock tight to his shoulder, just as Ramierez had told him to do.

He squeezed the trigger.

The recoil turned him a little: he hadn't expected that much.

The woman fell to the ground, her hands clutching at her stomach.

A screaming teenage boy with a shotgun. The shotgun roared. Nothing hit Tim. The boy pumped in another round, but before he could shoot again Tim aimed and fired. The bullet slammed into the boy's chest — he staggered back, dropped.

Klimas, screaming: "*Get in! Get in!*"

Cooper, running for the truck.

Roth, climbing into the back even as he fired short bursts down Oak at the onrushing horde.

A roar from Tim's right: he turned to see a nightmare — a huge *thing* t' had once been a woman. She wore the tattered remains of a blue-sequine ning dress. Yellow skin pockmarked with sores, too-wide neck, long, shards of bone sticking out the back of her wrists like a pair of chip swords.

He couldn't move. His body wouldn't react.

The monster roared again . . . her bone-blades reached ou

Clarence Otto walked out of the store's rotating door, hi

and steady, his pistol firing so fast, *pop-pop-pop-pop*. The woman-monster flinched, turned away. He fired three more times into her back. She dropped face-first onto the snow-covered street.

Clarence grabbed Tim's shoulder.

"Move, dummy," he said, and pushed him toward the truck.

Tim's paralysis broke. He ran for the rear driver's-side door.

A hatchling, crawling out from underneath the truck. Tim launched himself, raised both feet in the air and landed as hard as he could, smashing the pyramid body. Globs of purple guts splashed out against the trampled white snow.

Tim reached for the door.

"Feely, up here!" Klimas, yelling down at him. The SEAL pointed to the water cannon mounted behind the cab. "You're on that! *Move!*"

Hands grabbed Tim from behind and threw him over the bullet-ridden equipment boxes. He landed hard on top of canvas hoses. Tim scrambled to his hands and knees in time to see Clarence Otto hop onto the truck's rear bumper.

Klimas pounded on the cab's hood three times. The big diesel gurgled, and they started to roll.

TIME TO FLY

The SH-60 Seahawk pilot eased his helicopter off the *Coronado*'s deck. He was a good mile away from the shoreline, probably safe from any Stinger the Converted might launch, if the Converted could spot the Seahawk at all from that distance.

The 'Hawk headed north, over open water, following the Apache attack helicopter that had lifted off a few moments before. The two aircraft would fly well past the LZ, cut west over the shore, then fly south so they could approach the LZ from the north.

IFF picked up another friendly aircraft in the area: an AC-130 gunship.

That baby brought serious firepower. The SH-60 pilot hoped the survivors could make it to the extraction point — if any bad guys followed, the AC-130 would make a wonderful mess of them.

HELL'S ANGELS

Steve Stanton rode on the back of a Harley-Davidson motorcycle. He wore an American flag helmet, which he thought was pretty damn awesome.

In front of him, driving the bike, was the wide bulk of Jeff Brockman. Steve had duct-taped a map of Chicago to his back. Jeff didn't wear a helmet, because there probably wasn't a helmet in the world that would fit him. His bone-knives pointed straight ahead, parallel to the snow-covered road.

Two more motorcycles — another Harley and a crotch rocket — were driving on their right, and a BMW was on their left. A bull drove each of those bikes. Behind each bull, a man with a machine gun.

The biker gang (Steve couldn't help but think of it as a biker gang) rolled south on Lakeview Avenue. They drove fast where they could but had to slow frequently in order to maneuver around the cars that choked the road.

This time, Steve would take care of things personally. He'd find Cooper and shoot him dead. If Steve could get Cooper alone — and unarmed — he would have Jeff kill him slowly. Maybe use those bone-blades to skin Cooper alive.

Spotters reported that the fire engine — a frickin' *fire engine*, of all things — was heading north on State Parkway. The humans were smart. They wanted to get away from downtown. They must have guessed correctly that Steve had concentrated his remaining Stingers there. The humans wanted to get somewhere a helicopter could safely pick them up. Steve had sent more motorcycles to gather up the remaining Stingers and bring them north, but he didn't know where those helicopters would land.

Or did he? He looked at the map. The humans were driving north . . . they would want an open, flat place with no tall buildings. Steve's fingertip traced the roads.

There . . . Lincoln Park.

Just south of where he was now.

Considering the abandoned cars blocking the streets, it would take the fire engine about five minutes to reach that location.

Steve's biker gang could be there in four.

ON THE ROAD

Clarence Otto was soaking wet.

Tim Feely had yet to master the water cannon. He'd mishandled it twice, the errant, full-force blasts almost knocking Clarence off the truck to land at the feet of the pursuing horde. The big vehicle smashed its way north. The road had narrowed. Not as many tall buildings here, far more three-, four-, and five-story constructs. Snow-covered bare trees lined the sidewalks. It couldn't be far now . . . maybe four more long blocks to go.

Clarence returned fire as best he could. He had only three rounds left in his Glock. Subzero temperatures and wet clothes made his body shake so bad he could barely aim.

Margaret's blood is in that water . . .

He felt she was with him again. Not the husk he'd killed in the store, but the Margaret of five years ago. His wife. His *love*. They were fighting this nightmare together.

Roth was down: a bullet had shattered his right collarbone. He lay there on the ruined hoses, his body tossed left and right by the endless collisions — no one had time to help him.

Klimas had Roth's SCAR-FN rifle, was firing single shots to the right side.

Cooper Mitchell knelt on the hoses, taking careful aim to the left. He was *laughing*; he sounded just as insane as the crazies running after the fire truck.

"You want some?" he said, pulling the trigger. He looked at a new target. "Oh, you want some, too?"

Klimas had ordered Clarence to cover the rear. With the way Engine 98 swerved and slammed and smashed, anything beyond the ten-yard range was an impossible shot.

Constant obstacles kept the truck from outrunning the wave of pursuers. Bosh avoided what he could, but for the most part he just plowed through anything that was in the way.

The muscle-monsters were faster than the people, faster than the hatchlings. Four of them had pulled ahead of their fellow Converted and were only ten or fifteen feet behind the truck — if Bosh slowed down, even for a few seconds, yellow-skinned beasts would jump right into the back.

Clarence aimed carefully, trying to gauge the engine's continuous impacts. He fired at the lead muscle-monster. It twisted a little to the right, blood visible on its chest, but it kept coming. Clarence aimed lower, fired again: the creature clutched its belly. It slowed, unable to keep up. Clarence aimed at the next one, fired — his slide locked back. He was out of ammo.

He turned to face forward. Little Tim Feely aimed the water cannon to the right, shooting a long, spreading spray at the hatchlings, people and muscle-monsters that poured out of buildings, desperate to get at the still-accelerating fire truck.

Klimas dropped, blood pouring from his knee. He reached both hands to grab it; his SCAR-FN tumbled over the side to clatter against the snow-covered street.

Roth had yet to get up.

Cooper fired his Sig Sauer — his slide locked back. His weapon was also out.

A hatchling scrambled over the right side and shot toward Klimas. The SEAL saw it coming, managed to get his hands up in time. Tentacles wrapped around arms: Clarence saw what lay on the bottom of those pyramid bodies — thick teeth made to tear off huge chunks of flesh.

Clarence reached to his belt. He gripped the handle of the knife he'd used to kill his wife. Klimas pushed the hatchling against the inside of the equipment box. Clarence drew the blade and drove it into the plasticine body. The hatchling let out a high-pitched squeal. Clarence lifted the knife and flicked the creature over the side.

Klimas's knee was a bloody mess. He grimaced against the pain, but held out one bloody hand.

"Can I have my knife back?"

Clarence handed it over. He never wanted to touch the thing again.

He looked forward over the truck cabin's roof. Another wave of bad guys rushed down the middle of the tree-lined street, coming head-on.

Bosh floored it.

Engine 98's flat face hit people so hard the cabin rattled with each impact.

Bodies flew in all directions. The truck wobbled and bounced as killers of all kinds fell under the wheels, spraying blood onto the snowy street and even up onto the sidewalks.

And then, there were no more attackers in front. Bosh had driven through, broken free. Clarence looked out the back.

Hundreds of them — no, *thousands* — filled the street, a rushing mob straight out of a zombie flick. The closest ones weren't even fifteen feet away.

Tim was still aiming his spray off the right side. Clarence grabbed his shoulder. Tim yanked back on the cannon's valve-handle. The spray of water quickly faded and died, dripping down onto the bed's hoses. His face was a sheet of blood; a round had grazed his forehead.

Clarence pointed to the rear. "You wanted them concentrated."

Tim looked. He'd been wide-eyed the entire time, terrified of everything, but now his fear vanished.

Tim Feely snarled.

"Come get some," he said. He pointed the chromed cannon at the chasing horde and shoved the valve-handle all the way forward.

A concentrated blast shot out, hit a muscle-monster in the chest. Tim moved the stream side to side, knocking people down, kicking up a huge spray that soaked everyone around them.

And still the mob came on.

SLOW RIDE

Engine 98 slammed into something big, catching Tim unawares and smashing into the back of the pockmarked cabin. The blow stunned him. He blinked, tried to clear his vision. When he looked up, he saw Clarence manning the water cannon.

Clarence aimed high, creating a wide, spreading spray that rained down on the army of pursuers.

How many had been exposed? Five hundred? *More?*

Tim hurt so bad. Every bone, every muscle, if not from jarring impacts then from the endless shivering. His hands were so cold he couldn't move his fingers, which were curled up as if they still gripped the water cannon's handles.

Far behind, he saw some of the pursuers — soaking wet, chests heaving with big, deep breaths — giving up the chase. They would die within twenty-four hours, but not before, hopefully, exposing dozens of others.

We did it, Margo . . . we did it.

Tim looked around. Roth was moving again, struggling weakly to rise. Blood matted the right shoulder of his letterman's jacket. Just to the left, on the other side of the cannon's base, Klimas clutched at his bloody, ruined knee.

And in the middle of the bed, Cooper Mitchell, standing tall and flipping a double bird at the pursuers.

"How's that *taste*, motherfuckers?" Cooper grabbed his crotch and shook it. "Lick it up! Lick it *allllll* up!"

Engine 98 lurched. A grinding noise joined the diesel's gurgle. The truck started to slow.

Tim saw the street signs: State and Banks. They weren't far from Lincoln Park now. Two long blocks and they'd be on the green grass.

He heard a noise up above. There, two spots far off in the sky . . . helicopters?

Rescue. They had done it. They were going to *make* it.

Then he saw something else, something much closer . . . something hanging from a tree by its oversized, yellow-skinned arms.

Engine 98 drove directly underneath it.

The monster let go.

GOOD-BYE

Paulius didn't see it drop, but he saw it land in the middle of the truck bed, almost on top of Roth. In that frozen, awful moment, Paulius noticed the monster had almost a full head of curly red hair. He wondered if the person had been Irish.

A pale, sore-speckled arm stabbed down: a bone-blade slid through Roth's letterman's jacket, deep into his belly. The creature lifted the 250-pound man like he was nothing. Lifted, and *threw* — a screaming Roth sailed off the back of the truck to land hard on the pavement.

Paulius gripped his knife and reactively started to get up, but the agony of his ruined knee stopped him cold.

The wide-headed monster turned, locked eyes with Paulius. Rippling muscles drove its arm forward. Paulius flinched right — the tip of the bone-blade slashed the side of his neck before it punched through the cab's back wall.

A powerful blast of water caught the monster full in the chest and face, sent it tumbling over the equipment box. It smashed through the rear window of an Audi.

Fire Engine 98 pulled away.

Paulius reached up with his left hand, pressed it against the right side of his neck.

He felt blood pouring down.

Fifteen meters back, Roth managed to get to his knees before the horde descended upon him. A muscle-monster drove a bone-blade straight into his back. Paulius heard Roth's final scream, then the man vanished beneath a swinging flurry of knives, axes and lead pipes.

The water cannon's powerful stream slowed — what had been a steady, straight blast now curved down, the landing spot quickly growing closer as the pressure faded.

"Shit," Clarence said. "We're empty."

The truck suddenly started to wobble left and right, wobble *hard*.

Paulius heard another new noise. Over the grinding engine, over the sound of metal scraping pavement, and over the ravaged vehicle's broken rattle each time it hit a bump, he could just make out the *thumpa-thumpa* of rotor blades.

And also, something else . . .

The roar of motorcycles.

CHICAGO BULLS

Steve Stanton's biker gang rolled to a stop at the T-intersection of North Avenue and North State Parkway. The park — flat and green, dotted with snow-covered, leafless trees — lay behind them. The wind had finally died down. It was turning into a beautiful day.

There were five motorcycles now: the four he'd started with, plus one man who'd brought a Stinger missile from downtown.

One block south on North Parkway, a shattered fire engine shivered its way toward them. How was that thing even moving? The windshield had so many splintered holes it looked white rather than clear. Torn metal lined the bottom where a bumper had once been. No grille, just a squarish, black hole with an oddly bent dead man jammed into it.

The thing wobbled, left-right, left-right. Shredded tires flapped visibly.

Steve pointed at one of his bulls.

"You, go kill the driver."

The yellow-skinned beauty didn't ask questions, it just sprinted down the street on impossibly thick legs.

Steve looked at the others. He made a cutting motion at his throat.

"Kill the bikes," he said. "Get that Stinger ready. Let's finish this thing."

The bulls did as they were told.

When the last motorcycle's gurgle died away, Steve heard something else. He turned to look back.

Since his conversion, he hadn't felt fear. Not once. That emotion swept over him now — not even fifty meters away he saw a helicopter coming in just over the park's sparse trees. He thought back to that girl in his office, the one who said the helicopters she saw "looked mean." Now Steve understood what she meant.

"Well, shit," he said, then he felt strong hands wrap around his waist and roughly pull him to the right.

The Apache pilot made a judgment call. Those were monsters standing at the park's edge . . . genuine, straight-from-a-nightmare *monsters*. They were the bad guys. Ergo, anyone standing side by side with monsters was a bad guy as well.

Five men, five motorcycles, four monsters.

"Light 'em up," he told his gunner.

From inside the helicopter, the Apache's M230 chain gun sounded like a staccato, three-second roll on a toy snare drum.

Thirty-millimeter rounds tore into flesh, metal, grass and concrete, kicking up chunks of dirt, puffs of blood and flashing clouds of smoke. All targets dropped. The pilot saw a monster running right, carrying a small man in his arms. The pilot started to call out the target, but one of the fallen men rose to his knees, struggled to bring a long tube up on his shoulder.

"SAM," the pilot said.

Another three-second drum roll answered.

The man didn't *drop* so much as he *disintegrated*.

"SAM neutralized," the pilot said. "New target running right, get him."

"Tracking," the gunner said, but it was too late — the monster dove through the window of a gothic, white-stone apartment building.

The pilot looked down the road, to the approaching fire engine. Another monster there, rushing headlong toward the battered vehicle. The creature was too close to it: chain gun fire would also hit the truck.

The Apache pilot slowed to a stop and hovered, just thirty feet above the park.

"Wait for targets of opportunity," he said. "Be careful, we can't hit our people."

"Affirmative," the gunner said. "Should we elevate and hit that mob chasing them?"

"Negative," the pilot said. "Those assholes are already taken care of."

END OF THE LINE

Fire Engine 98 vibrated as if it was driving on an endless road of deep pot-holes. The motor finally died. The truck rumbled along on momentum alone.

Clarence heard the newly energized roar of the trailing mob — they saw their opportunity to finish the task.

He turned to look forward. Ahead, clouds of smoke floated up from shred-ded bodies and mangled motorcycles. A yellow-skinned behemoth rushed straight for them.

"Klimas, your knife!"

The SEAL offered it up handle-first. Clarence took it, saw that Klimas had a blood-covered hand pressed hard against the side of his neck.

"Tim! Help Klimas!"

Clarence felt the cabin shudder from impact, heard the *crunch* of break-ing glass, the deep-throated growl of a monster and the scream of a man.

He slid up and onto the cabin's roof, hands and legs spread wide to try to stay on the still-lurching vehicle. He slid forward across the slick, eight-foot-long, bullet-ridden surface.

Clarence looked up in time to see the engine bearing down on the mo-torcycles, the bodies and the sidewalk and park just beyond them. The truck ground over the obstacles, hitting so hard the cab bounced up, throwing him into the air. He came down hard, face *smacking* against the pockmarked metal. The knife flew from his hand.

The truck's front end plowed into the snow and dirt and grass . . . the knife skittered across the roof . . . Clarence pushed forward. The knife slid off the cabin's edge . . . Clarence reached out and down.

He caught it.

Half hanging over the roof, he looked into the cabin, saw a broad, yellow-ish back on top of concave spider-webbed glass, and the flailing, bloody hands of the man trapped beneath.

Fire Engine 98 finally rolled to a stop.

Clarence raised the Ka-Bar knife high. He plunged it down into the monster's neck.

The thing barked out a noise of confusion, surprise and pain, a single syllable that could have been a question mark. It reared up hard and fast, its head crunching into the cabin roof right below Clarence's waist, knocking Clarence up and forward and off — the frozen ground came up fast and smacked him in the face.

Cooper Mitchell had still been facing out the back of the truck and flipping off the horde when Engine 98 hit the motorcycles and the sidewalk curb. The truck had decelerated quite suddenly — Cooper had not. He'd flown across the truck's bed, stopping only when his head smashed into the water cannon's metal post.

Tim's hands pressed on Klimas's neck. To his right, Cooper rolled weakly, clutching the back of his head, face screwed up tight.

"Mitchell, *get up*," Tim said. "The helicopters are here!"

Tim heard the roar of a crowd; he looked back — the horde was rushing in, weapons held high, blades glinting in the morning sun. Not even fifty meters away and closing fast.

He took his hands off Klimas's neck, slid one arm under the man's legs, the other behind his back. There wasn't time to do things right. Tim pushed up as hard as he could, groaning with effort as he tried to lift the heavy man onto the equipment boxes and dump him over the edge.

THE GRIM REAPER

The horde closed in. They could see the red truck that they had chased across the city, now just fifty yards away. So close . . . *so close.* The humans had sprayed them with water. Such a strange thing to do, but the Chosen would dry out soon enough.

The Chosen knew the motorcycles had carried their emperor. As they ran, they shouted to each other, in shock, in sadness.

He's dead!

The emperor got shot!

No way he lived through that!

Few of them had met the emperor, but they all remembered the emperor's final order: kill Cooper Mitchell.

Forty yards . . .

They saw a small man push a bigger man over the edge of the truck. The bigger man fell hard to the ground below. The small man leaped over the side.

Thirty yards . . .

They saw another man stand up in the back of the truck, swaying, confused, his hands clutching the back of his head.

As a unit, they all recognized the man. They had all seen the pictures, and many of them had watched the video. It was him: *Cooper Mitchell, public enemy number one.*

The horde let out a unified roar. They had him now. They rushed down the street, so many of them that the humans didn't stand a chance.

Twenty yards . . .

The AC-130 was too high up for the engines to be heard. So far away, in fact, that the horde didn't even hear the plane's guns go off.

The street transformed into a flashing hell as 1,800 rounds per minute of 25-millimeter high-explosive fire tore into bodies, vehicles and pavement.

The horde started to scatter even before the first 105-millimeter howitzer round landed right on the dividing line of North State Parkway, pulverizing bodies, knocking cars on their sides and rattling the snow off of bare branches.

Confusion reigned. People took cover in buildings or sprinted back down the street, moved anywhere but toward the fire truck. They didn't know what was happening; they only knew they had to run and hide.

The emperor had ordered them to kill Cooper Mitchell, but he had given another order as well . . . the order to evacuate the city. The mob's will broke. The survivors fled, heading for their assigned vehicles, for the cars and trucks and buses and motorcycles that would take them north, to Milwaukee, take them east, to Michigan City and South Bend, take them south to Springfield, Champaign and beyond.

The exodus began.

MONSTER

Clarence knew he had to move, but his ice-cold body wouldn't react, wouldn't *obey*.

He heard something big land next to him, something that was still making a squealing noise.

He also heard Margaret's voice: *Get up, baby . . . get up . . .*

The fog cleared. Clarence reached out, use the shattered front of Engine 98 to help him rise.

In front of him, the muscle-monster did exactly the same thing.

Clarence stood just in front of the driver's seat, the monster just in front of the passenger seat. The knife still stuck out of the creature's neck. Jets of blood squirted out in red arcs that fell on the park's white snow.

The monster reared up to its full height: eight feet tall and very pissed off. Yellow hands flexed into fists. Arms vibrated with fury, making the blood-streaked bone-blades shake and shimmer.

Clarence wanted to turn and run, but his body wouldn't let him. It was all he could do to stay on his feet.

He was done for.

The creature brought its right fist back to its ear, aimed the bone-blade at Clarence's chest.

I'm sorry, Margaret . . . I'm not going to make it . . .

A clink of metal on broken glass. Just inches from the monster's left temple, the barrel of a Benelli shotgun slid across the bottom edge of the windshield housing.

The monster turned.

"FUUUUCK . . ." it had time to say, then the shotgun jumped and the monster's face disappeared in a spray of blood and yellowish flesh. The creature fell to its back, twitching.

Through the windshield, Clarence saw the ashen face of Ramierez.

"Hooyah, motherfucker," the SEAL said.

Clarence turned, letting the bullet-ridden truck carry his weight as he slid to the driver's door. He opened it.

Bosh was slumped down in the seat, covered in his own blood. He was still blinking, but not for long. The monster had torn his throat open. Clarence could see the front of Bosh's vertebrae.

Clarence shut the door. Out in the park, he saw a Seahawk helicopter coming in fast, nose tilted up for a landing.

"Everybody out!" he screamed as he stumbled around to the other side. "Move, move! Get to the chopper!"

He opened the passenger door to see that Ramierez had passed out again, shotgun still clutched in his hands.

Clarence lifted Ramierez out of the truck and started toward the helicopter. To his right, Tim stumbled along, supporting the limping weight of Commander Klimas.

Just one man missing, the only man who really mattered.

Clarence stopped only long enough to shout over his shoulder.

"Cooper! *Come on!*"

GAME OVER

Cooper Mitchell's head hurt, really, *really* bad.

He saw the horde scatter. Despite the pain, he felt elated. *He'd won*.

"Suck a bag of dicks, you fucking douchebags."

He looked up to the sky, saw a slow-moving plane — just a dot, really, but whatever it was, it had ended the fight. Too bad it hadn't arrived sooner; Roth might have made it.

Cooper had blood all over his hands. *His* blood, pouring out of a cut on the back of his head. He was probably going to throw up soon, thanks to the eye-narrowing throb going *boom-boom-boom* inside his skull.

He grabbed the water cannon's post, used it to pull himself to his knees. He put his right hand down to press up, felt something smooth and hard beneath it — the fire axe.

His pistol was empty. For that matter, he didn't even know where the thing was. He grabbed the axe handle, lifted it as he stood. His legs felt like rubber. He sat on the bullet-ridden metal box and slid his legs over the side. He dropped, almost fell when he landed.

His right hand held the axe handle. He pushed the top of the head against the ground, used the axe as a cane. There wasn't one spot on his body that didn't hurt.

The helicopter. Right there. He'd *made* it.

Cooper heard movement behind him. He turned sharply.

Not five feet away, slowing to a stop, was the Monster Formerly Known as Jeff, and hiding behind him, head not quite reaching Jeff's massive shoulders, was Steve Stanton.

Steve looked terrified. His eyes darted everywhere, but always flicked back to Cooper.

Only a part of Cooper noticed this, because he couldn't stop looking at Jeff — huge body, pale yellow skin gleaming from a sheen of sweat, mouth open, chest heaving slightly from exertion. *So goddamn big*. And those massive arms, the bone-blades jutting from the backs of his hands.

Jeff raised a hand to his head. His fingers flipped back imaginary hair.

"COOOOOOPEEEERRRRRR . . ."

"Hey, buddy," Cooper said. He didn't feel afraid this time, which made no sense at all — Jeff was a *thing*, a thing with fucking bone-swords for arms. And yet, Cooper had won. He couldn't die now . . . it simply was not possible.

Steve pointed a shaking finger at Cooper. "Jeff, kill him! *Skin* him!"

The Monster Formerly Known as Jeff blinked slowly. He took a step forward.

Cooper held up his left hand, palm out: *stop right there*.

"It's *me*, bro. It's Coop. Don't do this."

Jeff lifted a gnarled, yellow foot to take another step forward, then put it back down. His face was distorted, misshapen into a mask of evil, but Cooper could still read his lifelong friend — Jeff didn't want to attack.

Steve's screech tore at the air. "Kill him! *Kill that diseased motherfucker!*"

The monster's eyes flicked down to Cooper's feet, focused on something there. Cooper looked down as well — the red axe blade, resting against the ground.

Jeff looked up again. His eyes filled with the anguish of a heart torn in two directions. He didn't want to hurt Cooper, but he couldn't hold himself back much longer.

For just a moment, the monster wasn't a monster anymore. It was the boy Cooper had grown up with, the man he'd gone into business with. It was his lifelong friend, the person he loved more than anyone else in the world.

Jeff Brockman closed his eyes.

He let out a long, slow breath.

Cooper knew, instantly, that when Jeff opened those eyes again, he would give in to his nature; he would become the creature that Steve Stanton wanted him to be.

Cooper lifted the axe and stepped forward in the same motion. He swung it high and hard, brought it down with everything he had.

The red blade dug deep into Jeff's head with a dull *chonk*.

The Monster Formerly Known as Jeff opened its eyes. He met Cooper's gaze for two long seconds, then the eyelids sagged.

The massive body dropped straight down, like a yellow sack of boneless meat.

Jeff didn't move. The axe handle stuck up at a shallow angle.

Steve Stanton stared. The expression on his face said it all: the dude knew he was fucked.

He turned to run, but Cooper dove at his legs. Steve hit the frozen ground face-first. He screamed for help, but there was no one left *to* help.

Cooper rolled him to his back and straddled his stomach. He slid his knees over Steve's biceps, pinning the smaller man to the ground, a schoolyard bully about to inflict punishment on the class loser.

"This is all your fault," Cooper said. "I don't know how, or why, but I know it's your fault."

Steve stared up in pure terror, as if Cooper was ten times the monster Jeff had been.

And then Cooper remembered why.

"Oh, that's right," he said. "I make you assholes sick."

Cooper reached to the back of his head, rubbed both hands hard against his torn scalp. It hurt, but he didn't care. He brought his hands forward, held them palms out so Steve could see the blood.

"Your turn," Cooper said.

Steve bucked and thrashed, but he couldn't budge Cooper's weight.

Cooper Mitchell pressed his bloody hands down on Steve Stanton's screaming face. Cooper rubbed it around, rubbed it *hard*.

"That was for Sofia."

He drove his thumb into Steve's right cheek, three fingers into his left, and *squeezed*, forcing the man to open his mouth. Cooper shoved his bloody fingers inside, slid them across Steve's tongue, jammed the fingertips inside Steve's gums and slid them around real good.

"That was for Jeff."

To finish it off, Cooper hawked the biggest loogie of his life, then spit it into Steve's open mouth.

Steve froze. He stared up with the blank, disbelieving gaze of a man who has just received a death sentence. He moved his tongue around, trying to keep the loogie away from the back of his throat.

Cooper leaned close. "That was for *me*."

Cooper reared back and punched Steve Stanton in the stomach.

Steve let out a slight wheeze. He gasped like a beached fish, trying and failing to draw a breath.

He swallowed.

Cooper stood, reached down and patted Steve's cheek.

"And that? That one was for *you*, dickweed. Enjoy."

Cooper looked around — there was no one left. All the Converted had faded away into the city.

He was alone.

He had *won*.

He turned toward the helicopter. Clarence was already in it, beckoning madly.

Time to go.

Epilogue

Epilogue

HEROES

It was finally *over*. All of it. Over forever.

Clarence, Tim Feely and Commander Paulius Klimas stood in the Oval Office, waiting for the president to arrive. Klimas was on crutches. He wore a neat, fresh bandage around his neck.

Tim was using a cane. The cane's handle was a twisted coil of DNA — the same as Murray Longworth's. Clarence wondered if that meant something.

Clarence had asked both Tim and Paulius to be there for this. Ramierez was still in the hospital, but at least he was out of the ICU. He was going to live.

Clarence hadn't asked Cooper Mitchell to come, because Cooper hadn't known Margaret. Cooper had apparently moved to the Upper Peninsula, as far away from everyone and everything as he could get. That didn't stop him from fielding offers to turn his story into a movie, however. LA had been hit hard, but the film industry didn't miss a beat.

The Mitchell-Montoya plague, as the hydras were now known, had spread through the Midwest faster than anyone expected. Only two days after the Seahawk had carried the five survivors out of Lincoln Park, new batches made from Cooper's blood had been crop-dusted across Manhattan, Minneapolis, Philadelphia and Boston. Four days after, every major city had received multiple coatings.

Just one week after Margaret's death, most of the Converted lay dead, their bodies waiting to be collected, carted away and burned.

The hydras didn't seem to affect the yellow monsters, but that wasn't as big of a problem as Clarence had feared. The monsters couldn't blend in. When they were spotted it became an instant witch hunt. Special Forces handled the task if they were available, then cops, and if neither could get on the job, bands of armed citizens chased the creatures down.

Albertson had sent thousands of hydra doses to China, along with scientific advisors to help manage the massive effort of reaching the entire population. One Doctor Cheng, apparently, was part of that mission. Clarence hoped he enjoyed it.

America now focused her efforts on wiping out the Converted in Canada, Mexico and South America. Europe and Russia had already implemented their own hydra exposure campaigns, and were sending starter doses to Africa, Australia, India and all the corners of the earth.

For once, the human race unified in cause and spirit.

But it wasn't all smiles and roses. The final death toll staggered the imagination. Some estimates were as high as one *billion* dead, although more conservative guesses placed it at "only" eight hundred million. It was the worst disaster in mankind's history.

China had been hit the hardest, as far as body count went, but experts were saying the world might *never* know the full death toll in Africa. That continent had seen seven governments collapse, replaced by dictators who had swooped in to fill the power vacuum. The UN was at least a month away from having the ability to do anything about that.

As for America, the final death tally was estimated at over thirty million. No disaster in the nation's history even came close. By comparison, the influenza epidemic of the 1918 pandemic had killed some 675,000 Americans, and the Civil War around 700,000.

Nothing could have prepared the United States for that level of death, and yet the 284,000,000 survivors were working together to rebuild. Partisan politics didn't exist. Racism seemed to be something from the past. All that mattered was helping one another out, putting the pieces back together. Would this new Land of Brotherly Love last? Probably not. For now, however, it made the recovery process an amazing thing to behold.

The Oval Office door opened. President Albertson walked in. At his side was Murray Longworth, carrying two small, black lacquer boxes.

The president shook each man's hand.

"Gentlemen, the world owes you a debt of thanks," he said. "I can only imagine what you went through. And I can only empathize with the grief you must feel."

He looked at Clarence. "Agent Otto, I do wish you'd reconsider and let us share this moment with the nation. I think the people need to know who their heroes are."

Clarence shook his head. "I prefer my privacy, Mister President. Margaret would have wanted the same thing."

Albertson nodded. "Very well." He smiled at Klimas.

"Commander, fortunately you don't have the option of telling me *no thanks* when it comes to public recognition. I look forward to the Navy Cross and Medal of Honor presentation ceremony for you, Chief Ramierez and Lieutenant Walker. Thank you for what you have done. The world owes you a debt that can never be repaid."

He shook Klimas's hand.

Albertson turned to Feely.

"And as for you, Director Feely, I'm glad you will let us have a little pomp and circumstance for tomorrow's presentation of the Presidential Medal of Freedom."

"Love me some pomp," Tim said. "And I've earned all kinds of circumstance."

Clarence turned to him, surprised. "*Director* Feely?"

Tim nodded. He held up the cane. "As in, the Director of Special Threats."

Clarence turned to Murray.

Murray shrugged. "I retired. I'm getting too old for this shit."

Albertson frowned. "Mister Longworth, please."

"Sorry," Murray said.

Tim nudged Clarence.

"Can't wait for you to come back to work, Agent Otto, seeing as I'm your new boss and all. You can call me *Daddy*."

Albertson sighed. "Director Feely, please."

"Sorry," Tim said. "I'll be a good director from now on. Scout's honor."

The president turned, held out a hand to Murray. Murray gave him one of the black boxes.

Albertson faced Clarence.

"Agent Clarence Otto, for your service to the country, and to the world, I present you with the Presidential Medal of Freedom."

The president opened the box. Inside was a golden medal on a blue-and-white ribbon. Just a piece of metal and some cloth: meaningless. Maybe someday Clarence could appreciate it, but not now.

The president smiled. "Shall I put it on you?"

"No, thank you, Mister President. If Margaret can't wear hers, I won't wear mine."

"Very well," Albertson said. He closed the box and handed it to Clarence. Murray handed the president the second box. Albertson opened it.

"Clarence Otto, it is my greatest honor to bestow this award," Albertson said. "For immeasurable service to the nation, and to the world, and for quite literally saving civilization if not the entire human race, I present you with a posthumous Presidential Medal of Freedom for Doctor Margaret Montoya."

Clarence stared at it. It was the same as his, *exactly* the same, so why did this one seem so much more important?

He reached out a shaking hand and took the box. He closed it, held both boxes together. Lights gleamed on the black lacquer.

The president offered his hand. Clarence shook it.

"Your wife saved us all," Albertson said. "I will personally see to it that everyone, everywhere, understands what she did. The hatred she suffered from Detroit? That's gone, Agent Otto. Margaret Montoya will be remembered as the savior of the world. Her life — and her death — will be celebrated, forever."

Margaret Montoya. His wife. His best friend. The bravest person he had ever known.

She would never be forgotten.

She would be remembered as what she truly was.

A hero.

ACKNOWLEDGMENTS

A novel like this doesn't happen without tapping the expertise of people who know far more than I do about many things. The people listed below helped make this book as realistic as possible.

Also, I am terrible at taking notes about those who help me do what I do. If I left you off the list, my sincere apologies.

Military and Governmental Consultants

The public servants, active-duty personnel and veterans listed below provided governmental and military facts, and also guided me on how to best personify those who serve in the United States military. I thank them for their help, and also for their service: *Ted Arthur (Navy SPECWAR), Chris Grall (Army), J.P. Harvey (Air Force), Joel Palmer (FEMA), Scott Pond (Navy), Joseph Root (Navy), Josef W. Wimmer (TSA).*

The Scientific Secret Agents

I try to make the science of my novels as accurate as possible while still telling a fantastical story. These three gentlemen beat this tale up one side and down the other. I thank them for their efforts, and hope they continue to help me make my stories better: *Joseph A. Albietz III, M.D., Jeremy Ellis, Ph.D., and Tom Merritt, Ph.D.*

UUV Robotics and Underwater Salvage

In my research, I stumbled across Jin Tong's "Combined-bionic UUV" video on YouTube. The *Platypus* came to life in these pages thanks to his help. Chris "Cheffie" Otto spent many years working in the field of underwater construction and salvage. His experiences helped me bring Cooper and Jeff to life.

Siglerverse Continuity

My novels are interlinked and, as such, they require a great deal of internal fact-checking to make sure the stories fit the 800-year-long timeline. I thank John Vizcarra for his careful attention to Siglerverse detail.

That Toddlin' Town

Thanks to Shannon Fairlamb and author P.C. Haring, residents of Chicago, for checking on all the details of the Windy City.

My Partner

Since my novel *Contagious*, I have worked closely with my business partner, A Kovacs. Her guidance and organizational abilities were critical in getting this book made. She rocks. I couldn't do this without her, nor would I want to.

My Editor

This is the fifth book I have made with Julian Pavia as my editor. To have that kind of consistent editorial support is a rare blessing in the world of publishing. Shiv, thanks for a great run.

Fire Engines!

Thanks to Engine Co. 98 / Ambulance 11 for help with the details that made the final scenes truly rock.

Feel the Need for Feely?

Tim Feely is a character in the novel *Ancestor*. If you want to see what he went through on Black Manitou Island, pick up that book.